D0983606

Venture into the twenty-second century.

Meet Dr. Veronica Weslin: brilliant, sweet, innocent, and Catholic to the core. A tough childhood and the expectations of others define her more than she will admit to herself. This unpretentiously sexy, stunningly attractive twenty-nine-year-old virgin, known affectionately as the Angel of Adrenaline, is the daughter and granddaughter of doctors and a Nobel laureate for her work in pediatric research. She is at once extraordinary and ordinary. She lives the life for which she was destined...or so she would have herself believe.

Meet Capt. Jasmine Babasa: long, lovely, lean crime-stopping machine. A well-educated career FBI agent, her squeaky-clean, no-trace-left investigation skills are reserved for cases involving big money and high public profile. If only her heart and soul were so squeaky-clean. The FBI deploys her when the stakes are high, but will she discover that the only stakes that matter, the highest stakes of all, are out of this world?

Two women—so different and yet so much the same—both of them light years from fulfillment...

4.35172 light years to be exact.

ONE LIKE US

—the epic saga of two women, the men who love them, and the voices that beckon from another star. This is the story of their response to a God who calls us by name, and the forces at work to drown that call. It is a tale of desperation and hope, of proud shame and naked innocence: a prescription for wounded love.

Join the crew of Star Covenant.
Meet Elon, the great prophet and explorer.
Let him take you all the way—back to the beginning!

Take the plunge into the abyss of undiscovered bliss!

Eternal Demise

Although I knew solitude
It seemed I was never alone
Even in darkness you were there
I felt you in Mama's warmth
And heard you in Daddy's voice
I struggled to know you
To express you
I felt you in the wind and the rain
I was drawn into the storm
Buffeted, but still warmed in your presence
Indeed, I never fully knew solitude
Until I saw her

I was suddenly her severed limb
Her eyes were all lit up with you
Yet she appeared incomplete
Wonderfully incomplete
A quality wonderfully unbearable to me
Drawn into the storm together
You embrace us
As we dance upon the prow
Eyes fixed on distant shore
Awaiting shipwreck
The eternal demise
Of our solitude

Emmanuel James Voronin

ONE LIKE US

A Novel by

Jerome Linus German

FINAL MISSION PUBLISHING

Hudson, Wisconsin USA

www.onelikeus.com

For Patricia, my delight and inspiration,
who has supported me tirelessly.

Special thanks and blessings to my parents,
Clarence and Marcella,
whose marriage daily demonstrated
the immeasurable value
of purity of heart.

Copyright © 2006 by Jerome Linus German
All rights reserved

Paperback: ISBN 978-0-9789691-0-3
Hardcover: ISBN 978-0-9789691-1-0

www.onelikeus.com

Many thanks to family and friends who have supported my work and
given me invaluable feedback, especially my daughter Chris, without
whose fine editorial guidance this book would be but a shadow of what
it has become. Thanks to Jake for the computer model of Star
Covenant. Thanks for the feedback from all who have read and re-read
through my numerous re-writes, especially Fr. Tom, Nole, Nicole,
Amy, Gabe, Paula, Lester, Dave, John, Terry, and Linda.

ONE LIKE US

A tale of desperation and hope,
of proud shame and naked innocence:
a prescription for wounded love.

Chapter 1

No Regrets

"Access denied. You are not authorized to operate this vehicle," the computer announced, its voice rendered raspy by the forty-year-old loudspeaker. Seventeen-year-old Veronica Weslin blew a breath of exasperation at the black hair dangling in her face and initiated the retina scan a fifth time. "Access denied," her fifty-seven Caddy proclaimed again. She grabbed her big bag of books and headed off to school. With a little sprinting, she might actually make class on time. Her roommate and best friend, Melanie Lansing, had already boarded the school bus, and the head of the household, Mel's uncle, Dr. Jacob Lansing, had left for work hours earlier. As she trotted off with her load of books, Veronica began, for the first time, to regret her decision to go with real text books rather than electronic.

The heavy burden brought her thoughts back to her car. "A fifty-seven Caddy is a fine piece of machinery," Dr. Lansing had told her, "but 2057 was a long time ago; the car's more than twice your age, Veronica, I'm surprised they can still find parts for it." A gift from her grandpa, the car's sentimental worth far outweighed any practical value. Life would be so much simpler if she could just board a school bus with Melanie, but though they were the same age, Melanie was still a senior in high school, while Veronica had leapt ahead to college. *A two mile walk each way might do me some good,* she thought, *but I think I'll trade in these books!*

Eight hours later she watched as the minute hand crept up to 4:40 and thought *Yes!* as the buzzer signaled the end of the day's last lecture period. *Lord, you've given me the brains for this; please give me the stamina,* she prayed. She had entered college at the age of sixteen, starting with sophomore level work. In another summer and two intense semesters she would be ready for medical school.

Veronica escaped the mousy closeness of the lecture hall to be reborn into the lilac-laden spring air. She lugged her books to a cola-stained concrete bench, put her feet up and curled up sideways to place her back against the large, rounded arm rest and toward the warm April sun. That morning, songbirds had inspired her to wear a sleeveless, knee-length, canary-yellow cotton dress, and now she parted her long black locks so as to allow the evening sun to warm her bare upper arms. Pulling her skirt tight around her thighs for modesty sake, she plopped a book atop the cloth gathered over her knees and began to study. She planned to attend an evening lecture, and without transportation, decided that the apple in her book bag would tide her over.

As she munched on that apple she thought about the guest lecturer she would be seeing: Dr. Jacob Lansing. Though the handsome Dr. Lansing was the head of the household in which she lived, and she saw him nearly every evening, Veronica wanted to see the famous space traveler do his shtick in public. She smiled at her thoughts, admitting to herself that she really wasn't all that interested in astronomy.

A honking car horn interrupted her daydream. "Ronnie, you wanna go watch a track meet with me?" Melanie called from her uncle's car.

Veronica jumped up and went to greet her best friend. "Hi Mel. Thanks, but I planned on staying and listening to your Uncle Jake's lecture," she informed her.

Six years past, after the death of her parents, Melanie had become the ward of her father's famous brother. Melanie Lansing, a seventeen-year-old high school senior, was bright but not as gifted as her roommate. The two had met only two years earlier at a religious retreat and had become instant best friends. Veronica's parents had been reluctant to send a sixteen-year-old off to college, but they believed her to be in good hands.

"Come on, Ronnie, you can listen to Unc anytime. You have dinner with him almost every night!" Mel insisted.

Veronica could clearly see that Mel would be disappointed if she turned down her invitation. "Tell you what," she said. "I'll go with you if you promise to have me back here by 7:00."

"Done deal!" Melanie proclaimed. "You're really into this astronomy stuff, huh?" she said as they drove off.

"I guess so," Veronica answered.

"Then why don't you take some classes in it?"

"I don't know. Guess I'm getting everything I need to know from your uncle."

Two hours later, Melanie pulled up to the auditorium. "Sorry I cut it so close, Ronnie. I hope you can still find a good seat."

"It's okay, Mel; they're all good seats," Veronica insisted. "Thanks for taking me along to the meet, it was fun! See ya later."

Before driving away, Melanie glimpsed Veronica lugging her big bag of books into the lecture hall. "Why don't you leave your books in the car, Ronnie?" she called after her, but Veronica was already out of earshot, and the double-parked Melanie couldn't leave the car to catch up to her.

The lecture hall was filled to capacity, and Veronica stepped in just as the crowd stood to applaud the entry of the guest speaker. To her surprise an usher said, "We saved a seat for you right up front, Miss Weslin." Escorted to the front of the room, she took her seat just as the rest of the crowd sat down.

As he addressed the crowd, Dr. Lansing's smiling eyes and frequent glances told Veronica that he appreciated seeing someone from his own household in the front row.

About halfway through his presentation a dowdy, barefooted couple in straw hats strode up to the stage, stood in front of Dr. Lansing, and started shouting: "Our mother is angry! Lansing is a murderer! He has condemned our brothers and sisters to eternal wandering and wounded their dear mother Earth! He is destroying her! She is very angry and hurt and will soon lash out in her pain! She screams with earth quake and tsunami. 'Bring back my children!' she screams. 'Desecrate me no more!'"

Veronica approached the couple and stood directly in front of the man, who was doing most of the shouting. Her stature matched his, placing her face inches from his. He stopped shouting and growled, "Get out of my face, girl!"

"My friend, I'm very concerned about you. You seem very upset. Can we talk about this?" she asked.

"Get out of my face!" he screamed.

"You're going to get a sore throat," she said calmly in her soothing low-alto voice. "Please, let's go out and talk."

The woman with him yelled, "Show some respect, Weslin!" she grabbed Veronica's arm and said, "Don't you know who he is?!"

"I'm afraid I don't," she said. "How did you know my name?"

Police officers had made their way to the stage, and one of them grabbed the woman's hand and carefully wrenched her grasp from Veronica's arm. "Please return to your seat, Miss Weslin, we'll take care of these folks," the officer said to Veronica. They escorted the screaming, cursing couple from the building.

With the lecture finished, Veronica waited patiently while people pumped Dr. Lansing's hand and asked questions. She almost dozed and jumped a bit when he said, "Veronica, thanks for coming to my lecture."

"You're so welcome, Dr. Lansing!" she said, jumping up with her big bag of books.

"Why didn't you leave your books at home?" he asked.

"I have no transportation today. My wonderful, senile old car has forgotten who I am. Mel picked me up after class and we went to a track meet."

"Then why didn't you leave your books in my car after the meet?"

"That's a good question! Because I'm senile like my car, I guess."

"You must be starving and worn out from carrying these," he said, reaching for the books.

"It'll be good to get a ride home, that's for sure!" she said as she allowed him to take her books.

"Well, Mel has my car. She's at a youth council meeting. I can call a cab, or we can walk and enjoy this beautiful weather."

"I can't let you carry my books two miles!" she objected.

"*You* managed to do it this morning. I would enjoy carrying them for you," he insisted.

She smiled her grateful approval, and as they stepped into the evening air asked, "Who were those people, and what was with the bare feet, and where'd they get those outfits...and how did they know my name?"

"They knew your name?"

"Yes!"

"Wow! They're keeping closer tabs on my household than I would have suspected."

"Who are they?"

"That was Malcolm Fitch, the founder of Mole Nation, and his current insignificant other," Jake informed her.

"Oh...I've heard of them. They're some kind of environmentalist religion, right?"

"I guess that's an accurate assessment."

"Why did you say 'insignificant' other?" Veronica asked with a chuckle.

"Well...it just seems to me that Fitch is very much the center of his own universe. She is about the seventh woman he's been with since I've known of him."

"So why's he hollering at *you*? I heard on the news that the...I'm sorry, who is it that you work for again?" Veronica asked.

"The AGC: the Aerospace Governing Council," Jake reminded her.

"Yeah, aren't they getting this special environmental award?" Veronica asked.

"We get one nearly every year," Jake assured her.

"Then what's the deal?" she asked. "And what's that insanity about you being a murderer and condemning people to eternal wandering?"

"Mole Nation's philosophy is nowhere near the philosophical center of the environmental movement, and they are an embarrassment to serious environmentalists," Jake assured her. "Fitch's impromptu religion teaches that Earth is a god and our bodies *and* souls are manifestations of that god, so if we are laid to rest anywhere but on planet Earth our souls will wander the galaxy aimlessly in search of rest."

"And...?"

"And he perceives me, because I founded the Aerospace Governing Council, to be public enemy number one," Jake explained. "People are being interred on the moon and Mars, or torpedoed into the sun. Fitch sees the other planets as evil gods and the interment of Earthlings on them as an offense against *his* god."

"And you're to blame," Veronica observed.

"Apparently."

"You don't decide where people will be buried, do you?"

"Of course not. Fitch blames me because he sees me as a prime mover in space travel. His goal is to put a stop to all space travel."

"That's a pretty ambitious goal," Veronica noted.

"He's a very zealous man. I wonder what it is that drives him."

"How did the police and the ushers know my name?" Veronica wondered.

"The Moles are a consistent pain in the neck. They are constantly being locked up for misdemeanors like their little disruption of the peace tonight. The police have your name and picture on file because they believe that sooner or later the Moles will harass you for your association with me. They must have shared info with the ushers."

"The Moles will harass me just because I live in your house?"

"They don't believe in technology, Veronica. Their only weapon is annoyance, and they're working on perfecting it."

"I think they already have," she said, laughing.

"That reminds me," Jake said. "You were wondering about the clothes they were wearing..."

"Yeah, I'd have to hunt for weeks to find outfits *that* dreary. What's up with that?"

"I think its all about earth tones, natural fabrics, and an aversion to the style hype of mass-produced clothing," Jake said. "And speaking of earth tones, you should see them on Earth Day. They all come out and do their big parade wearing nothing but grass and leaves."

"Grass and leaves? Really? That actually sounds more attractive than what they were wearing tonight," Veronica opined.

"Well, in fairness to them, Veronica, not everyone's a power shopper like you and Mel," Jake teased.

"Power shopper?!" she said, with mock annoyance. Smiling, she added, "We have made an art of it, haven't we?"

"Maybe you should just do grass and leaves. You'd save a lot of time and money, and you could make an art of it. It'd be kind of like weaving baskets, wouldn't it? Kind of artsy-craftsy."

"No thanks. As you can tell," she said, taking a twirl to unfurl her canary-yellow skirt, "I like colors other than brown and olive drab."

After a little chat about the subject of his lecture, Jake said, "Tell me about your family, Veronica. I've met them but don't really know much about them."

"My dad is the greatest doctor. He can cure anything!" she said.

"Really?"

"Yup! Well...almost. He could cure everyone except my mom," she told him. "Dad doesn't like drugs. He believes God designed our bodies to heal themselves with rest, exercise, nutrition, posture; you know, all that natural kind of stuff."

"Natural's good," he assured her.

"Yes, but it took him a long time to admit that those things don't work when somebody's genes are all messed up the way Mom's were. When he finally did take her to a pharmaceutical doctor, she got temporary relief from the drugs, but it wasn't long before the side effects were just about as bad as the disease."

"You said your mom's genes *were* messed up?" Jake asked with eyebrows raised about her past tense usage.

"That's what I said," she verified, grinning at his perplexed look. "We had a nanny named Gertrude Moss, but it still seemed like I was a mom to Xavier, Fabian, and Marie. The boys came to *me* when they had troubles, not to Gerty. Dad's work kept him really busy, so he was gone a lot. Mom was always so sweet, a suffering saint. Even though she was in pain most of the time, she was patient and kind, never sulky or weepy. She was such an inspiration to me. Whenever I went to her with a problem, whether it was with the little ones, trouble at school, or anything, she would always pray with me. She lived on prayer. It was just a way of life. It became *my* way of life.

"When I was still real little, it just seemed to come to me that I had a choice. I could either be happy or sad; it was a choice. Life's hard, but life's not what makes us happy or sad. In the end it's up to us to decide which we want to be. Do you know what I mean, Dr. Lansing?"

"I sure do," he answered, amazed at the wisdom coming from her young mouth. Her vocal tone was so melodic, rich, and resonant that it seemed to emanate directly from her heart, and it took effort on Jake's part to listen to *what* she was saying, not just the music of her voice.

"I couldn't have been more than nine when that occurred to me," she continued, "and when it did, it was…well, it was so…"

"Liberating?" he offered.

"Exactly! I just decided to be happy. But it didn't take long for me to realize that it took a lot of prayer to stay that way. Whenever I felt sort of cheated out of my childhood—times when Mom was the sickest and Dad was super busy with work—I would gather the little ones around Mom's bed, and we'd pray. We'd always make her smile," she said.

"I'll bet you did!" Jake said, picturing the scene.

"Then, when I was thirteen, Mom got really sick. I thought she was going to die! Dad was out of town for the week and Mom's doctor had been in a really bad car accident. Gerty had Mom rushed to the hospital, then packed up the baby and headed there herself. She called a little while later and her voice was broken, like she'd been crying. I guess the people at the hospital didn't know what they were doing. Mom's doctor didn't keep very thorough charts and the disease and the medicine are so rare that the doctors on call were just kind of operating in a void. Gerty didn't tell me all that at the time, but I could tell that things weren't good. She told me to pray.

"I packed up the boys and headed to St. Monica's, the parish church that we attended. We went in front of the Blessed Sacrament, and I told the boys, 'God loves the prayers of children. He never says no to them.' Nobody had ever told me that, it just came to me. We prayed hard. I have never since seen two toddlers kneel so long! Eventually they zonked out in front of the tabernacle. I hadn't told

Gerty where we were going, and I was kind of in a trance when the church door popped open at eleven o'clock. I think my heart jumped right out of my chest! I turned around and there was Gerty. I thought maybe I was in for a scolding.

"But she practically skipped up the aisle with Marie in her arms. 'Your mom is doing great!' she told us with this huge grin that I'll never forget. Gerty was really a good, holy woman. I don't know how, but it was like she knew there was more going on with Mom than just temporary relief.

"Gerty had called Dad, but his plane didn't get him home till mid-morning. When he got there Mom had given Mrs. Moss the day off and was in the kitchen doing dishes. My happiest memory is of Dad and Mom in the kitchen that morning. It sticks in my mind like yesterday. The morning sun was chasing away the fog; the birds were chirping Handel's Messiah, and my parents couldn't stop kissing! Everything about them was just precious!"

Jake chuckled at the vivid image she'd painted. "You've rehearsed those lines," he said candidly.

"Yup. I've told this story more than once," she admitted with a giggle. "Mom was never sick again. Gerty died, but Dad never hired another nanny, and it seemed that for the first time in my life I *had* a life. I had time to play, time to just be a kid. But—I don't know—somehow it didn't seem to matter all that much. I was different. All the things I had longed for were suddenly not that important. Mom was healthy. Dad was happy. It's hard to explain. I had spent a lot of my childhood doing adult things, and all of sudden I could be a kid, but I just went back to doing what I had been doing: praying a lot, taking care of the little ones, and reading everything in sight."

"You're still reading everything in sight," Jake observed.

"Yeah, I guess," she laughed. "I started going to daily Mass, something Mom's illness wouldn't allow before. How weird is that? A thirteen-year-old going to Mass everyday with her mom and younger sibs. Mom didn't make me go, I just liked doing it. Some of the girls in school called me names because of it, but it didn't matter. It was like I was walking on air. Ever since then I feel like I'm about three inches off the ground!" she said, her face all lit up.

"What kind of names do they call a kid for attending Mass every day?" Dr. Lansing asked.

"They called me Little Angel Girl."

"Really? Could be worse," he assured her.

"I guess, but I didn't like it. I had just turned fourteen and while eating my birthday cake my dad had told me about how tradition had it that Mary was only fourteen when she gave birth to Jesus, so I figured fourteen was old enough to call myself a woman. So I told those girls, 'I'm not an angel, I'm a woman!'"

"What did they say to that?" Jake wondered. Veronica hesitated a bit. "That bad, huh?" he asked.

"They were always so vulgar," she said with a sigh. "They said, 'Woman? You don't even have tits yet!'"

"Ah...the size of the breast, the small mind's ultimate measure of womanhood," Jake noted. He stopped walking and turned toward her, and she reciprocated and stood looking into his eyes. Her books shifted in the bag, which started to slide from his grasp. She grabbed the bag to keep them from falling, which placed her face inches from his when he said, "I really enjoyed your story. It sounds like you have a beautiful family, which doesn't surprise me. You're a remarkable woman, Veronica!" She barely heard his words, for she was lost in his eyes, eyes she was sure were reciting poetry about her beauty and her womanhood.

"Thank you...Jacob," she said, surprising herself with the informality. She gently patted the bag of books as if to say, *There now, I guess they're not going to fall,* and turned away biting her lip. They had completed one leg of the walk home, and their change of direction took them out of the sun and under the trees. As she started to walk again Veronica crossed her bare arms against the evening chill. After setting down the book bag, Jake removed his sport coat and placed it over her shoulders. Veronica stopped biting her lip, smiled and said, "Thank you, Jacob." She would never again call him "Dr. Lansing."

Twelve years later...

Jacob Lansing smiled as he turned and recognized what he had bumped into in the dim attic light. *I don't remember what most of this junk is, but I never forget a friend!* he thought, looking at his old college computer. It triggered so many memories, in fact, that the veteran scientist found a comfortable spot on a box of musty *Geographics* and launched a mini life review.

Have I really done the right thing with my life? he wondered. The forty-nine-year-old tapped playfully on the keyboard. He hadn't touched that computer since earning his masters at age eighteen. Jake, the wiz kid, had submitted his doctoral thesis at age twenty-one and had begun lecturing at the university by age twenty-three, all while cultivating a career with the United States Air Force that would lead him to NASA.

What happened to that kid? he asked himself, trying to remember a time when there was more to his life than work. Then his deep loathing for nostalgia kicked in and said, *Man, you're gettin' old...and sappy! Is sentimentality the reward for an abbreviated childhood?* However, in a moment, still feeling sentimental, he let out a big sigh. *Man, you're good at burying feelings, something that old age isn't going to allow you to do so easily.* Realizing what he had just done, he laughed out loud thinking about all of the old people he'd known who carried on conversations with themselves, and thought, *You're well on your way, Mr. Split-personality!*

Gone were the carefree hours spent sitting at the computer he held, replaced long ago by a fascinating astronomy career, one that had taken him to the moon and to Mars to experience them first-hand. Those interplanetary jaunts had been the high points. More explorer than scientist, his fondest contemplation was the human side of our identity within the cosmos. *Are we alone?* he would wonder. *If there are others, what's our relationship to them?* As he reminisced, he wondered how these questions could be at once so cliché and yet so compelling. *How is it possible that so much science has turned up so little evidence of life in a universe so vast? Why would an infinite God create only a single intelligent species? Or does each intelligent species have its own universe?*

He completed his thoughts by asking himself out loud, "Have we not discovered our peers among the stars simply because we've stopped looking?"

Long ago, Jake had abandoned using his time to help in the search for extraterrestrial life. He had done so to make more time for the kind of science that pays the bills. Customers planning facilities on the moon had no interest in the possibilities of intelligent life in a remote corner of the galaxy. The commercialization of space had turned the search for extraterrestrials into spare-time work, something Jake's fabulous career had consumed into nonexistence.

Life's pace had slowed a bit now, allowing him to spend more time with family and friends and more time playing. The deprived child in him loved it, but the go-getter in him flexed his muscles, paced the floor, and longed for new adventures.

Absorbed by his interior debate, he had not heard the knocking at his front door, but now heard a voice from below.

"Uncle Jake? Where'd you disappear to?" his niece called.

Oh, it's Tuesday, Jake realized. Melanie came every Tuesday to cook for him and spend the evening. "I'm up here, Mel," he called. His niece hadn't been in his attic for years. Her eyes bugged as she surveyed the vast array of nonessentials, and she wrinkled her nose at the dusty smell. Jake lived an uncluttered life, but he dealt with clutter by parking it in the attic.

"Bet you'd be glad if I'd rid myself of this junk before I pass on so you don't have to deal with it," he joked.

"Don't talk about passing on, Uncle!" Melanie insisted.

He looked her squarely in the eye and said, "My dear child, I'm forty-nine years old; how long do I have to wait to talk about the inevitable?"

She just smiled an *Oh, you!* smile and started down the steps to go make dinner, but then turned and asked, "What have you got there?"

Her Uncle held up the dusty bundle and said, "It's my old college computer. I wrapped it in shrink-wrap and put it up here thirty-one years ago."

Mel grinned with authentic wonder and said, "Wow, an antique!" Jake followed her down carrying the computer.

After he took it outside to blow off the dust, he set it on an empty corner of his desk, removed the wrapping, and plugged it in. He didn't really expect anything to happen when he hit the power switch, but to his bewilderment, it turned on.

As the monitor lit up, he said, "That's impossible! There's no way this thing should work!" He sat and contemplated an image on the screen, a vivid reminder of a life he had not pursued.

Mel peeked out of the kitchen and exclaimed, "It works! It's a miracle!" and then, "Wow! Who's that?"

The background of the computer's desktop was a photo of a nineteen-year-old, swimsuit-clad beauty, framed by white sand and blue sky, sun bathing and smiling for the camera. Jake just gazed at the picture for a moment. "Sophie Miller," he said at last, wearing an expression that bore mixed feelings.

"What was she to you?"

"She was a woman who wanted to have my babies."

"Were you engaged?"

Her uncle smiled wryly. "She was engaged. I was scared."

"Where is she now?"

"Dead. Died in a car accident three years ago. She left behind quite a legacy, seven kids and five grandkids."

Mel stood beside her uncle with her arm around his waist, looking at the screen. She had always found it curious that the tall, handsome man, who had raised her since she was eleven, had never been snared into matrimony, and this evidence of a romantic side intrigued her.

"Any regrets?" she asked.

"Only that I wish I'd kept in touch more. But it was always awkward, being a former fiancé and all," he said.

"Why didn't you marry?" Melanie asked.

"I could not have had the career I've had *and* a family. One or both would have suffered," he assured her. "I don't regret my decision, but I've paid a fairly high price for that career. Through the years I haven't had much female companionship, at least, not like what I've enjoyed for the last few."

"You mean with friends like Dr. Weslin?"

At the sound of the name, Mel's uncle lit up. "Ah...Veronica," he sighed. "I guess I do have one regret, that I wasn't born twenty years later. All of the heavenly bodies in the galaxy could not compete..." he broke off, turned away and mumbled to himself, "I'm babbling like a fool!"

"Like a fool in love!" Mel muttered to herself.

Her uncle heard her, and gave her that "Dr. Lansing look" over the top of his reading glasses. "That's just silly," he insisted. "I'm old enough to be her father. You know, I think I enjoy the friendship you and I share more than any other."

"But I'm family," Mel protested.

"Doesn't matter," her uncle insisted, "there are few people on Earth with whom I can bare my soul the way I can with you. You're a great friend."

Mel gave him a loving squeeze and headed out to the kitchen to check on the food. Suddenly she heard a chuckle and a loud "Wow! There it is!" from her uncle, and she rushed in to see a funny little program up on the screen. "Day in and day out I used to watch this crazy thing with anticipation," he informed her.

"What is it, Uncle?"

"It's a little program that worked in the background to study little snippets of data collected by the Arecibo radio telescope, with hopes of finding a signal generated by intelligent life. It was all part of a program that got millions of people and their home computers involved. I ran tons of data sets through it. Many of them were interesting from an astronomical point of view, but none of them pointed to any hint of an artificial source."

Suddenly, as they were looking on, the program rendered a finished 3-D graph of the data it had been studying, the answer to calculations suspended in a thirty-year digital coma. Jake leaned forward and looked intently through his reading glasses. He just stared for the longest time before turning and looking at Mel, with his mouth agape, and looking back again.

"What is it, Uncle?"

Uncle Jake, now thoroughly Dr. Lansing, did not respond as he opened the source information file that accompanied the data. Mel couldn't stand the suspense.

"Uncle Jake, what is it?"

Finally Jake turned and said, "It's a miracle, that's what it is!" He scratched his noggin with scientific drama. "I don't know why I went up to the attic tonight. I didn't need anything from up there. Something just told me to go up, so I did, as if I've been meaning to do it for a long time and was finally getting around to it. And why did I bring this old thing down and turn it on when I didn't for a second believe that it would still work? And now this," he said pointing to the screen. "The data it was running contains evidence of an artificially produced waveform!"

Mel frowned quizzically. "Isn't there a large chance it's just interference from some source on earth?"

"Actually, no, and I've seen plenty of these graphs. See on the ends here," he said, pointing, "how the amplitude tapers up and then back down at the other end? That's the profile of an extraterrestrial signal. You see, this signal was picked up by the ancient Arecibo fixed dish radio telescope."

"Wait a minute. Isn't that the one we visited in Puerto Rico? The one that's been turned into a museum and theme park?" she asked.

"The same, and its demise thirty years ago pretty much marked the end of the search for extraterrestrials. But—back to the signal—if this was from Earth, its start and finish would be erratic. It would likely last much longer and not fade perfectly in and out. No, this narrow, communications-bandwidth signal came from outer space, and I have to figure out from where!"

Mel finished making dinner while her uncle transferred data to his new computer. "Come and get it, Unc," she called.

But Jake insisted, "Listen to this!" and played a twelve-second snippet of someone speaking a foreign language.

"I don't recognize the language," she noted.

"No one will!" he declared.

"Do you know where it's from?"

"Not yet. I will need to calculate the position of everything when this recording was taken—a lot of math. That's where this baby takes over," he said, patting his latest computer as he sat down to begin the work.

"Uncle! Dinner!" she insisted.

"Okay. It does smell good," he said.

After a hurried blessing, Dr. Lansing, usually a very slow eater, shoveled his dinner like a fourteen-year-old. Mel smiled and said, "Veronica's right: you are just a big kid!"

"Veronica said that?" he asked, his mouth half full.

"Uncle! Manners!"

"No, really, did she say that?"

"You should know; she said it to your face."

"Oh. Yeah, I guess she did."

"Unc, how could such a thing go undiscovered for thirty years? There are lots of other radio telescopes in the world, most of them way more sophisticated than Arecibo."

To her surprise he took the time to empty his mouth before answering. "And all of them busy working for hire," he said. "It is rather ironic that after space travel within our solar system became commonplace, our focus narrowed. Those telescopes are contracted to answer questions about our own sun and about planets that are suddenly accessible. There are none left randomly sweeping the sky as Arecibo did. Besides, though they are more sophisticated, the largest is barely a third the size of Arecibo." He gobbled half a dozen last bites and kissed the top of Melanie's head as he rose from the table.

The door bell rang, and Jake, rather annoyed by the interruption, said, "Now who could that be?" and hollered "Come in!" as he sat down to his computer. When the door opened, his annoyance turned instantly to a mix of embarrassment and joy, for in walked Dr. Veronica Weslin.

Jake jumped up and said, "Forgive my rude shouting, Veronica, I should have come to the door."

"Hi Jacob, it's quite alright," she assured him. "Hi Mel," she greeted her best friend. "Anyone up for a movie?" she asked, pulling a video chip from her pocket, "I rented *A Hard Nut to Crack.*"

"Hi Ronnie," Melanie greeted her. "Is that the true story about the Panama crisis and...what's his name?"

"Col. Cliff Lamans?" Veronica offered.

"Yeah. That's supposed to be a really good movie," Mel said.

"Speaking of good, it sure smells good in here," Veronica noted of the onion, garlic, basil, and oregano still hanging thick in the room.

"It was delicious as well," Jake complimented his niece.

"Uncle...how would you know?" Mel chided him. It was a huge concession on Melanie's part to forgive anyone for rushing through a meal she had prepared. She was a legend among friends and relatives for her memorable culinary adventures, but when confronted by a mirror, she often regretted her fondness for her own works of art.

Stepping up onto an ottoman, which served to level the difference between her five feet, five inches and Jake's six feet, four inches, Veronica gave him a peck on the cheek and a hug.

Jake's breath caught as he contemplated his friend upon her impromptu pedestal. She had always been for him a walking symbol of love at first sight, but on this night her radiance was blinding. Her thick jet-black mane, cut with just the right amount of curl ending all along its elbow length, was spellbinding in itself, and as she kissed his cheek, that hair brushed his face and gave him goose bumps. Smatterings of small freckles dotted her fair face in the most perfect proportion. Her eyes, robin's-egg-blue, large and deep, were framed by lush lashes and brows. From lips to hips and nose to toes, everything about her was perfectly formed. She had a very lively face. Every perfectly-placed, intricate little muscle brought delicate nuance to a thousand articulate expressions that said, *No poker face here; few secrets in this soul.* The old oversized sweatshirt and loose-fitting jeans that she graced seemed scanty camouflage for a perfect figure. With his beautiful friend still standing on the ottoman, her arm draped over his shoulder, Jake turned and motioned toward his computer.

"Thanks, Veronica, but I wonder if I might take a rain check on the movie. You see, I have the most wonderful surprise for you!" he declared.

"You have some new pictures of the cosmos to share?"

"No, my friend," he crooned, "I have something much more spectacular than that!"

"Well, let's have a look!" she insisted. Dr. Lansing pulled the graph up on the screen. Veronica looked closely. "Okay. What is it?" she asked, shrugging her shoulders.

"Just the greatest discovery of the millennium! You see, that is a graph of a radio wave from outer space, a radio wave that sounds like this," he said, and played the snippet.

Dr. Weslin's eyes grew wide. "That's…an alien talking?" she stammered.

"Well, we don't know that," he said. "Could be human. However, this we know: this radio message was not generated on planet Earth."

He told her all about the history of the search for extraterrestrial life via radio telescope data and about his involvement in the program. He looked past Veronica at Mel and said, "Mel and I were speaking earlier about what a miracle this is. Why did I put this computer into storage one minute before it revealed the discovery of a lifetime? Why did I take it out today?" He looked at Veronica, "And why did you come by today, unannounced?"

"I'm sorry, I didn't mean to barge…" she started to apologize, but stopped when he gently pressed two fingers to her lips.

"God wanted you here today…don't apologize," he said. "I am so happy that you are here to share this! But my mind is reeling to answer all of the *whys*."

With no further ado, he dived into something he *could* figure out. God would supply the *whys*, but right now Jacob Lansing needed to know the *where*.

"Are you hungry, Ronnie? Can I get you something to drink?" Melanie asked. "How 'bout you, Unc, thirsty?"

"I could use some water, thank you," Veronica said, but Jake was already lost to the cosmos.

Mel delivered Veronica's water, settled into the couch, and watched in silence for what seemed an eternity. Veronica and Jake managed to squeeze into his large office chair, a feat that amazed Melanie. Jake perched at the edge of the seat, glued to the monitor, while Veronica staked out the rest of the chair. Straining to see around him, she sat with one cheek against his shoulder. The intimacy her uncle and her best friend shared in that chair made Mel feel a little out of place sitting with them, and boredom with star charts and calculations soon set in. She startled Veronica, who was obviously not bored, when she broke the silence with, "Unc, I have to be going," quickly adding, "I didn't mean to give you the heebie-jeebies, Ronnie."

The startled Veronica, slumping back in her chair with her hand on her chest in mock heart-attack posture, only giggled and said, "Good night, Mel...and thanks for cooking for Jake. I'm thanking you for him because I don't think he knows we even exist right now."

Jake snorted a little and said, "I hear you. Thanks Mel." He faced her and said, "And thanks for being a good sport, honey. You're the best! But can you really live through the night without knowing where this signal came from?"

Melanie grinned and tousled his hair one last time. "I'll just have to give it a try," she said. "Good night, you two."

Melanie let herself out, and Jake settled back into his work, or at least, he tried. It was difficult, perhaps impossible, to concentrate with Veronica so close. She had never been quite so cuddly before and he wondered if everything was okay with her. However, the more he pondered her closeness, the less odd it seemed. *How can such a beautiful, perfectly poised woman have so little concept of personal boundaries?* he asked himself.

He recalled a little story he'd heard from an acquaintance. He had not let on that he knew the "Ronnie" of whom the young man spoke. The fellow had told of how overwhelming it had been to be in such close proximity with a woman who seemed as innocent as a four-year-old, as intelligent and mature as anyone he knew, and twice as sexy. "I thought my heart would jump out of my chest!" the young man had said, recalling the cold sweat her immediate presence had induced.

Jake chuckled out loud recalling the fond nickname, unknown to Veronica, that a small circle of friends had given her: The Angel of Adrenaline.

"Is there something funny in the source file?" she asked.

"It's hard to explain some of the things I find humor in," he answered, hoping to get off the hook. He had waited a lifetime to look at such data, but the beauty beside him had stolen his brain.

"Try me," she insisted, but after a moment of silence said, "Maybe you need rest, Jacob, you don't seem to be making much headway."

He turned to face her. Someone needed to tell her. It was no fair running around behind her back calling her The Angel of Adrenaline, no matter how respectfully it was said. Someone needed to let her know what her close proximity did to men. Looking into her eyes wasn't making the task any easier.

"I *am* tired, but I don't think I can sleep wondering about this data," he answered, avoiding the humor question *and* failing to address her proximity. *Coward! What are you afraid of?* he asked himself. The question was rhetorical, for he knew the answer. He was paralyzed with fear of hurting her feelings.

He recalled his own first encounter with Veronica. The memory sprang into his consciousness in a way that it never had before. *It was as though I was viewing woman for the first time,* he thought.

He was thirty-six when he first laid eyes on her. Like Veronica, he had been living a life of purity; however, unlike hers, his was not purity born of complete innocence. Like many men who walk the narrow road, he had gotten a taste of what lay in the ditches. That old college computer and the one to follow had been used for more than homework. *I'm just enjoying the beauty of the body, God's crowning creation,* he had tried to convince himself. He wasn't viewing hard porn, just pictures of pretty girls without their clothes. After all, weren't there a lot of nude images at the Vatican? With time he would slide far enough down the slippery slope of curiosity to be very thankful for the grace to stop.

Eventually Jake would come to appreciate the difference between the respectful portrayal of the body in art, and nude photos of real people: real people with names and families, real people with real needs and desires. He would come to realize that a photo allows one to engage a body with no opportunity to engage the soul—it is not so much what a photo shows as what it does not show that is the problem. "The body is the form of the soul," he would tell people, "but it is a living form, not the lifeless counterfeit rendered on paper or screen." Like zombies searching for their souls, the naked images Jake had seen would still attempt to haunt him.

However, though he had known lust, Jake wondered if it was possible for anyone to lust after Veronica. *Given her innocence and purity, it would be like lusting after the Blessed Mother,* he thought. *Still, if lust is impossible, desire certainly is not!*

The sun had set, and Veronica could see Jake's reflection in a picture window. He looked particularly dreamy to her in the ethereal image provided by the window glass. She knew that his rugged good looks coupled with cocker-spaniel eyes and thick, dark brown hair, now tastefully streaked with white, regularly caught the attention of many a healthy female. How had he managed to stay single? Watching for his reaction in the reflection, she placed her hand on the back of his neck, ran her fingers under his thick two-tone hair and said, "You amaze me!" Her touch brought the astronomer back to Earth, and he turned and looked into her eyes.

"Thank you," he said. "I typically don't care what anyone thinks of me, but I make an exception in your case." He returned to looking at his computer, but in a moment mustered the courage to turn back to her and say, "I...can't concentrate with your fingers in my hair, my dear."

Looking into her eyes, he realized how that first encounter with Veronica had changed his life forever. In her it seemed that love itself had taken flesh. Common parlance would have called it "love at first sight." He turned away from her with his mouth set to laugh at the notion, but his heart wouldn't follow through. *Why aren't you laughing?* He had known this woman now for thirteen years. Her presence had always been exciting to him, but what was with this pounding of the heart? He shuddered like a big dog ejecting rain from its fur.

"Are you okay?" she asked.

He turned and locked eyes with her. He *had* to tell her. "I...you...we..." he stuttered. With her fingers still in his hair, she pulled his lips to hers and put him out of his misery—the Angel of Adrenaline became the Angel of Mercy. At first Jake tried to escape, but shortly his flailing arms succumbed and found their way around her. When the kiss finally ended he looked into her eyes. "Now what?" he asked, perfectly clueless.

"No regrets, that's what!" she said, "I want to have your babies, and you so deserve to have posterity!"

Jake shook his head in objection. "I'm twice your age!"

"For a world famous scientist your math is pretty crummy. Two times twenty-nine is fifty-eight, not forty-nine. Besides, you're twice the man of any I've met!"

He threw up his hands in exasperation. "Woman, I was alive when they made coins smaller than a dollar!"

She giggled at his lame argument. "So?"

"So...you have at least fifteen good childbearing years ahead of you, Veronica. Why...we could have..."

"Eight! Or more!" she interjected with delight.

"Eight! Yes, eight!" he continued, "and by the time the youngest is eighteen I'll be..."

"Seventy-nine. I've done the math," she said, getting serious. "The only thing worse than losing you *then* would be not to have you *now*. Do you love me?" she demanded.

Dr. Lansing saw the trap, but oh, what a pleasant one! "You know that I do! You mean more to me than all the stars of the heavens...*and* all of the voices from outer space. If only I was twenty years younger..."

"Darling, you're not twenty years younger. I fell in love with a mature man. Don't try and change that to match your preconceived notions of romance."

There comes a time when a man must admit defeat, and Jake could see that his time had come. "So, it seems you know the script better than I. What happens next?"

Veronica fished herself out of the chair and jumped onto his lap. She gazed intently into his eyes and said with great authority, "You propose. I say yes. We get married, and I have your kids."

As though not wanting to break the meter, Jake shot back, "Okay, Veronica, my darling," and he dropped to one knee, nearly spilling her on the floor. With her resulting giggles coursing like champagne through his veins, he asked boldly, "Will you marry me?"

Veronica smirked. "Wow! You don't fool around once you know your lines," she said.

Jake got quiet. He just knelt there and looked at her quite seriously. She caressed his face with her hands.

"Sweetheart?"

Her man spoke softly now, "I really have no choice, my love."

Veronica frowned and pulled away a little, "Whadaya mean?" she asked.

"It's really very simple," Jake continued. "I can't imagine living without your friendship. That simply is not an option. When we're apart I count the hours until I will see you again. I've been kidding myself, denying my feelings. Now that you've exposed them I can never go back. Thank you! Thank you more than you will ever know!

"So...where were we? Oh yes, I believe there is a motion on the floor," he said.

Veronica smiled and kissed him half a dozen times, explaining, "I want to savor the moment." Then looking deeply into his longing eyes, she sighed, "I so move!" and after yet another kiss, "As soon as possible!"

Jake said, "Not so fast! Is there a second to the motion?"

A knock at the front door gave them a start. Veronica jumped to her feet and Jake yelled, "Come In."

"Sorry, forgot my purse," Melanie said as she went to the kitchen.

Jake and Veronica burst into laughter as Veronica implored her old college roommate, "Mel, will you second the motion?"

A frowning, grinning Melanie asked, "What motion? Have you two been drinking?"

Her response provoked more chuckles, and Veronica insisted, "Just say yes!"

"Okay. As long as I don't have to know what you clowns are up to—yes, I second the motion. Good night!" Melanie said, smiling and shaking her head as she exited.

The couple talked and laughed into the early morning hours. Jake had only dreamed of this kind of happiness. He felt a freedom he had never even imagined and wondered how such a heavy commitment could be so liberating.

When Veronica had gone, Jake lay awake thinking about marriage. Just hours earlier, marriage was nowhere to be found in his life plan, and now suddenly he was engaged. *How did this happen?* he wondered. *I have a theory about everything else...why not marriage?* Just as it entered his head that it was foolish to be committed to something he had given so little consideration, he fell asleep.

Meanwhile, back at home, Veronica slipped into her pink flannels and sat before her vanity brushing her long black locks. She put the brush down when finished, avoiding looking her reflection in the eye. As she rose to turn down the sheets she slowly ground to a halt. She was the absolute master of denial, and she knew it had to stop. Avoiding the mirror, she turned the other direction to snatch a framed 8x10 of Jacob from the top of her dresser, a picture that he didn't even know she had. She had blown it up from a photo in Melanie's family album, a process that suddenly seemed very school-girlish to her. She set the picture on her vanity and accidentally came eye to eye with her reflection. *Why did you do that to him?* she chastised her mirror image. *He was in the midst of relishing the discovery of his lifetime, and you threw yourself onto center stage! Why are you so impulsive?*

She had medical degrees coming out of her ears, diplomas enough to wallpaper her office, but couldn't get inside her own head. For ten years she had lived in denial, denying the nature of her love and attraction for this fabulous man. *Jacob's and my careers are vocations of love to the world,* she had told herself. After her denial-racked soul had demanded liberation, she had spent the next two years planning a grand exposé of her heart—so much for planning. What held her back?

Was it the same fear Jacob had expressed? Fear of spoiling a perfect friendship?

Why are you so impulsive? She demanded again of her two-dimensional self.

Her reflection looked her in the eye and said, *Am I? Maybe I'm just in a spiritual rut. Is there balance in my life? Maybe I practice self-denial to a fault! Is it impulsive to procrastinate until my entire being can no longer stand the strain, and I burst into self-fulfillment with an embarrassing gush? Could the friendship I'm so afraid of spoiling be called perfect even though I was dying inside?*

Veronica had a sudden moment of clarity and shared it with the shrink in the mirror. *It is one thing to sacrifice my personal desires, to pray with Jesus to the Father 'thy will be done;' it is quite another to deny my emotions and the stirring of the Spirit. Fasting is a good thing,* she decided, *starving myself is not!*

Her shrink agreed.

Veronica concluded that she had upstaged Jacob's discovery parade because it seemed certain to be one that would lead him away from her for a very long time; her starving heart had snatched the reins away from her martyr-bound mind.

She seldom brushed her hair before bedtime. She admitted to herself that she had just been keeping her hands busy while she contemplated how she would apologize to Jacob in the morning, but now her refreshingly honest reflection said, *You ain't apologizin' to nobody! Look at me, woman! Are you going to apologize for giving me to the man you love? I don't think so! You told Jacob 'No regrets'; take your own advice!*

She had to quit the conversation with herself; it was all getting just a little too psycho, and it was really hard to make sense of the pronouns. However, they had made good progress in their first session, she and her reflection. She smiled at herself now, a cute smile born of the freshness of her thoughts, a smile that reminded her of a seventeen-year-old Veronica she had once known, a pretty little college sophomore.

She remembered vividly her first long conversation with the man of her dreams, one sided though it had been. Jake had asked about her family, and she had immersed him in her entire life story, enjoying deeply how he drank in every word of it. She thought about the look in his eyes that night, eyes full of poetry about her beauty and womanhood. She had waited twelve long years for that poetry to get from his eyes to his mouth.

Veronica looked again at the therapist in the mirror. The cute smile was gone. *We have some unfinished business,* the shrink said with tears in her eyes.

Why the tears? Veronica asked her reflection. *I don't cry; I choose to be happy.* A tear fell on her hand, and she took the cue to reach for a tissue. When she looked back at the mirror, her shrink had shrunk. She saw now a nine-year-old Ronnie with tears in her eyes.

Her shrunken shrink said, *You never let me cry! I had so much pain and you never let me cry. What do I do with the pain? Does being happy mean I can't cry?*

No, honey, the twenty-nine-year-old Ronnie answered. *I'm sorry. You can cry. You can cry all we want.* She ended the long overdue conversation by promising little Ronnie that they would talk some more; they would make time for each other. Then with teary eyes and a smile on her face, she fell asleep.

In the morning Jake woke to his alarm clock. He could barely remember the last time he had slept until his alarm sounded. He rose with his head still full of dreams, funny dreams about marriage and not being ready for it. He nuked a cup of coffee left over from supper, and as the nasty sludge hit his lips he thought, *Is anybody ever ready?*

On his walk to morning Mass Jake's mind reeled with arguments for and against his new commitment. He toggled between considering himself to be the most blessed man in the world to the biggest old fool in the world.

On entering the church, as always, he knelt in prayer before a statue of the Immaculate Conception. The meticulously painted wooden sculpture, an ordination gift he had given to his dear friend, Fr. Ian Scofield, inspired fervent prayer in the scientist heart. Fr. Scofield, a teacher at Immaculate Conception University and frequent celebrant of morning Mass, had decided to grace the small church with the inspiring object, for all to enjoy. Fashioned after a famous painting by Murillo of the same subject, this work of captivatingly delicate beauty reminded Jake of his fiancée: so lovely, feminine, holy, and pure. During Mass he prayed for guidance, but mostly he prayed for Veronica. Indeed, he could hardly think of anything else.

Now that she's going to be my wife, I'll need to have that talk with my little Angel of Adrenaline, Jake thought. *After all, I can't have my wife putting young men into a cold sweat, can I?* On the other hand, he

asked himself, *Is she perhaps the only one who has it right?* He ran the
age old test question through his head: *Would the world be a better
place if everyone was like Veronica?* In his heart all of creation intoned
a resounding *yes*!

Jake smiled remembering the "ten-in-ten rule": if Veronica got
within ten inches of someone, within ten minutes he would be outside
of his comfort zone and would either be gone or baring his soul to her.
Actually, nickname notwithstanding, the gender of her victim mattered
not; everyone got the same treatment. She was transparent, and it
seemed everyone was transparent to her. Because of this, one did not
simply like or dislike Veronica; one either loved or hated her.

Attending Mass at Immaculate Conception church brought such
joy to Jake. Tucked into a corner of the university, two adjacent
modern dormitories dwarfed the little church. On that blissful morn it
pleased Jake a great deal to see his lifelong friend, Fr. Ian, at the altar.
Fr. Ian Scofield had no official affiliation with the parish, but enjoyed
helping the aging pastor. The pastor, a humble, shy, unengaging man,
preached to the world, but to no one in particular. One always felt like
a spectator at one of his Masses. In contrast, Fr. Scofield engaged one's
soul. Always the inveterate teacher, whether preaching or lecturing, it
seemed he addressed each soul directly.

After Mass, Jake waited on the church steps. Fr. Scofield greeted
him with, "Jake, you look tired this morning."

Jake smiled. "I had a busy night, my friend. I became engaged to
be married last night."

Fr. Scofield's eyes widened. "I didn't even know you were seeing
someone. How did that slip past me? Hmmm…Jacob Lansing
engaged…I should sooner expect to hear that intelligent life had been
discovered on another world!"

Dr. Lansing coughed like one caught off guard. "What did you
say?" he asked.

"I said that I'd sooner expect…"

But Jake finished the sentence for him and said, "I thought that's
what you said," and laughed a long and melodious laugh.

Fr. Scofield only shook his head at his old friend. "What's that all
about?" he asked, which only started the laughter back up.

Finally Jake said, "Actually, that did come sooner," and chuckled
some more.

Fr. Scofield simply decided to ignore his friend's seeming incoherence and said, "Congratulations my friend. A celebration is in order, and I shall buy. Is there any chance your fiancée might join us?"

"I don't know," he replied, with concern on his face. "She usually comes to Mass when she has your class, but we were up quite late. Perhaps she has overslept."

"Do I know your intended?"

"She attends your lectures, and I know that you've met, but I doubt you know all 200 students by name."

"You know I'm not great with names. I'm trying to picture the gals in your age group. I know there are several. Anyway, why don't you call her and have her join us, and I'll call Dr. Weslin and she can join us for a grand little breakfast foursome. I'm sure Veronica will be eager to meet your fiancée...or do they already know each other?"

"They do, but it's still a great idea," Jake answered. He quickly pulled out his phone and called Veronica on speed dial, hoping he could beat Father to the draw. When she answered, he stepped away from the priest and said, "Honey, Father's calling you to join us for breakfast...don't let on, okay?"

"Okay!" she said, and took Father's call. After a few words with her, Fr. Scofield hung up and said, "She'll meet us at Mick's in fifteen minutes."

"Good. My sweetie will be there shortly thereafter."

"What's her name?"

Jake thought quickly and said, "Patience, old friend. I know you've met her before and I want to test your memory."

"We're waiting for one more," Father told Mick as he seated them and offered to take their order.

"Yum...you can't come to Mick's and leave hungry," Veronica declared as her appetite succumbed to the rich potpourri of breakfast smells wafting from the kitchen. "What's the occasion?" she asked slyly.

Father answered, "Jake has an announcement to make, but we're waiting for one other person."

Veronica turned to Jake, "Is this about last night?"

Father looked at Veronica and asked, "You already know?"

"Only about the graph, not the origin," she said.

"What?" Fr. Scofield asked, looking ever so bewildered.

Jake laughed. "I knew you didn't follow a word I said in front of church."

"About what?"

"You said you would 'sooner expect for extraterrestrial life to be discovered than for Jacob Lansing to become engaged,' and I said…"

Father interrupted with, "Oh, *that's* what you were saying… What? Are you serious?"

Veronica jumped in with, "What? …You're engaged?"

Jake said, "Oops! Me and my big mouth."

Someone behind Jake said, "What? Jake's engaged?"

Fr. Scofield, expecting Jake's fiancée to arrive at any minute, saw this someone approaching the table from behind Dr. Lansing. "Jake…you're marrying your niece?" he joked as Melanie approached. Veronica had invited her to breakfast to celebrate Jake's discovery.

"You're engaged?!" Melanie repeated, staring at her uncle.

"Yes. Yes, I am engaged," Jake said with a twinkle in his eye.

Melanie's mind went into a tailspin. "When did this happen?"

Fr. Scofield jumped up, offered her the chair next to his, and said, "I'm sorry, Melanie, I don't mean to leave you out of the conversation, but I just have to know about this outer space thing that Jake is alluding to."

Veronica explained. "Last night Jacob played for us a voice recording from outer space."

A wary Fr. Scofield said, "You two are once again plucking my gullible strings, aren't you? It's frightening to see how this old tycoon gets an innocent girl like you to play straight man for him. Is your fiancée prepared for your shenanigans, Jake?"

"I think she knows him pretty well." Veronica responded.

"Speaking of her," Father said, "she should be here by now. I'm very eager to meet someone who's willing to put up with Jake as a husband."

Jake said, "Thanks a lot, Ian! Why don't I give her a call?" and dialed up Veronica's number.

"Dr. Weslin speaking," she answered.

"We're waiting for you. Father's getting antsy," Jake declared.

Fr. Scofield's eyes went wide as could be, wide enough for Veronica to see he was a bit overwhelmed. She found it hard to laugh about the little joke they had just played on their friend when she could see tears welling up in his eyes. Finally Father smiled, and then laughed, and then shook his head and really laughed, until the tears of joy became tears of laughter.

Melanie just sat wearing a smile and shaking her head. "I thought we were celebrating Jake's discovery," she said at last.

Jake fixed his eyes on the woman at his side and proclaimed, "We most certainly are!"

When the mirth had subsided, Jake said, "Fr. Ian Scofield, I've only seen tears in your eyes twice: when I was baby-sitting you and your parrot died, and when you were ordained. Are these sad or happy tears that we see today?"

Veronica put on a funny frown and gave Jake a little elbow in the arm. Father said, "It's okay Veronica. Jake doesn't mean to be insensitive. We guys don't know, so we ask." Then, as he wiped his tears, he turned to Jake and said, "These are tears of sadness, shed for the poor woman who has to put up with you!"

Jake's grin said, *I asked for that, didn't I!* Veronica gave the priest a high five, but immediately grasped her fiancé's hand, snuggled against his shoulder, and wrinkled her nose at him to say, *Just kidding!*

Father smiled at the love birds across the table from him, and reaching across to squeeze their joined hands, said, "Two people whom I love and admire are making a life together. You two are like family to me. Even battle-worn old priests are touched by deeply romantic moments, especially ones that touch their own lives. Congratulations! You make an absolutely wonderful couple." Then, turning to Melanie, added, "And congratulations to you, Mel. I trust that you and your aunt will get along just fine."

Mel put her hands to her face. "My aunt!" she exclaimed. "Oh my…that's strange!"

"By the way, Mel," Veronica said, "thanks for seconding the motion!" Melanie's face went blank for just a moment, then she closed her eyes, shook her head, and snickered as she reran the seen, filling in the blanks with the new info.

While they ate breakfast, Jake and Veronica answered their friends' questions about a romance that had never been a romance. Finally the conversation turned to outer space. After some explanation and much discussion, Dr. Lansing said, "Unfortunately, I can't tell you where the signal came from. I was preoccupied with some other important business last night and wasn't able to finish that quest."

Fr. said, "You're going to be a married man; get used to being busy."

"Don't worry. I will have the origin of this thing nailed down well before the wedding," Jake insisted.

Father looked at his watch. "Oh my! I'm supposed to be lecturing in a few minutes."

"And I'm supposed to be listening," Veronica added.

Jake said, "I leave you with your professor, my dear," and kissing her forehead as he rose, added, "I have work to do." He bade Father and Mel a good day and headed for home.

He sat for two hours at his computer while visions of Veronica paraded through his mind. He thought about their relationship and wondered if all relationships were as complex. He had known her for thirteen years, ever since she had entered college and roomed with his niece, a fact that made him feel somewhat like *her* uncle as well. He had always admired her beauty in a gentlemanly sort of way. After all, she was just a child when they first met, and he was an old man of thirty-six.

As he reflected now on all those years, he couldn't pinpoint exactly when his image of her had changed from that of a child to that of a peer. Her friendship had filled his needs on so many levels. As her confidant, his advice on life's decisions had at times been unavoidably parental in nature. For her part, she had loved him unconditionally, forgiving the many broken occasions when she had so looked forward to spending time with him, dates broken because his work had always come first. At the time, neither of them had thought of those occasions as dates, but looking back now he could see them for what they were, romantic encounters that wore a dozen different masks.

Now in full daydream, he turned away from his computer, and his eyes wandered about the room. There on the walls were pictures of Veronica everywhere he looked. They were all pictures of Veronica *and* Mel. He laughed at himself now realizing that he had used his niece, though he loved her dearly and treasured pictures of her as well, as somewhat of an excuse to hang huge pictures of Veronica. But he needed more than pictures at the moment. As he reached for the phone to call her, she gave a little rap on the front door and walked in.

He rose to greet her and she said, "Is it all right if I come to your house 'unannounced'?"

"The *uns* will just get better and better," he replied.

"What?" she smiled, knowing that some corny wit was imminent.

"Well," he explained, "in the future I'm looking forward to finding you uninhibited, unavoidable, unsurpassed, unpretentious, unforgettable... and..." he searched for a good finish, "undressed!"

"You be careful! You don't need to be thinking about that quite yet," she warned.

"Sorry, sweetheart...just trying to be funny."

She tousled his hair. "Mel's right. You are just a big kid. So...what have you figured out with the alien dudes?"

"I've figured out that my brain's a bowl of mush, and you're the spoon that's stirring it," he insisted.

"Well, can you get more done with me here or with me gone?"

Dr. Lansing looked a little puzzled. "Aren't you supposed to be at work?"

"I'll have a new career soon: homemaker. I have to prepare for it. I have marriage preparation classes to take, a wedding to plan, a honeymoon to plan, and a fiancé who needs me. I'm booked. Who has time for work?"

"Did you really quit your job, honey?" he asked.

"No, but I took two weeks off to spend time with you and to pray about our future life together," she told him in a more serious tone.

Turning serious himself, Jake said, "You know, speaking of your job, there is one thing that has always struck me."

"What's that, my love?"

"You're doing clinical research, an admirable endeavor and one for which you are well equipped intellectually, but there's so much more to you than intellect. You have a healing touch. In my humble estimation, you should be in the trenches working with the sick and dying where your incredible bedside manner becomes a medicine all its own. I guess I see you as more the missionary than the scientist."

Veronica sat speechless for a moment. There it was: everything she had ever felt was wrong for her about her job but had never been able to put into words. "You're amazing!" she exclaimed quietly. "And your love for me is amazing. You tell me things about myself that even I haven't been able to figure out."

"Not so, my love. I tell you things that you haven't been able to *admit*. In your heart you know very well you'd rather be at that hospital all day than a couple of hours in the evening."

Aside from time with family and friends, Veronica spent every spare moment in volunteer work at Children's Hospital, where she had interned as a pediatrician. She had made the mistake of going to school too long and piling up too many letters at the end of her signature. Her father, Dr. Ronald O. Weslin, and grandfather, Dr. Ronald A. Weslin, had both pointed out that she had the potential to save thousands of lives as a practicing physician, but millions of lives as a researcher. Never one to put herself first, she had conceded their argument and gone into research. However, her office walls were papered with pictures of children under her care, so many that her employer began to wonder if her mind was really on her research.

"I know that you went into research because you had been convinced it was where you could serve the greater good," Jake said, "but more is at stake than lives here, honey. You can save lives in that lab, but you can't touch souls. Aren't souls more important?"

"Souls *are* more important," she said, stepping into his open arms. She laid her head on his shoulder and closed her eyes. "In a few weeks we'll be one flesh, but it seems we're already one mind," she said.

"Okay then," Jake said, motioning to the computer, "you have made perfectly clear the reason why I cannot do these computations without you here; you possess half of my brain."

So she stayed and read, and Jake worked hard except for the occasional "Veronica break," as he called their little chats. By the time she brought him a sandwich for lunch, he had made several phone calls and web connections and was ready to make an announcement.

"If this is correct, it is absolutely astonishing!" he said. "This thing is in our back yard."

Veronica was enough of a student of astronomy to know that "our back yard" could still be a fair distance away. "Where is it, love?" she asked.

"Well, it's not really *our* back yard, but it is our neighbor's back yard. It's coming from the Alpha Centari system. It's just too good to be true! In terms of space travel, the current state of the art places us on the threshold of technology that will allow us to visit this place! I never thought I would live to see a discovery like this, and now I might actually have the opportunity to go there!"

Veronica sat stone-faced, in silence. It took Jake a minute to notice. "Oh, my dear!" he said, "I would never go on such a journey and leave you here."

"Can you raise a family on a starship, Jacob? If what you have discovered is real, if this is the culmination of a lifetime of work, I can't keep you from it. Marriage will have to wait," she said, biting her lip. *What is wrong with you, woman? Shut up!* her heart screamed at her, terrified by the words that old habit had just allowed to spill from her mouth. *Enough with the martyr complex!*

Jake got up and walked around the room in silence. After a bit, he looked back at his fiancée. Still biting her lip, she wore a look that was not difficult to read. "I would rather die than wait!" he said. "No discovery can hold a candle to discovering the rest of you!"

A teary-eyed Veronica ran to him. They held each other tenderly. Finally she looked up at him and said, "Our children will visit this place."

"Our children!" he echoed. "I like the sound of that!"

Chapter 2

When Does It End?

How Jacob Lansing became the most celebrated space travel figure of his time soon became abundantly clear to his darling Veronica. At first she had wondered if he would ever again amount to anything without being in her presence. However, as the end of her first week of vacation approached, she found herself engaged to a man deeply embroiled in his work, and realized how right Jake had been when he had told her that marriage and his career could have never shared the same stage. He did, however, work much better with her around for she never really left his thoughts completely.

At three o'clock on a Friday afternoon, Jake finished up a conference call. Veronica waited for the phone to hit the hook, then jumped onto his lap and put her face in his.

"You used to take 'Veronica breaks,'" she said and just sat there looking into his eyes. She had tied her hair, as best the cut would allow, into pigtails, making her look like the most elegant and irresistible sixteen-year-old he had ever seen.

When he did not answer immediately, she rubbed her nose on his, and the velvety black coils of hair that were too short to make the tails dangled in his face. He put his big hands on her cheeks and said, "Sorry love, but if you can wait just two more hours, I'm yours for the weekend. You see, many of the people I'm talking to work for the government in one capacity or another, and fortunately for us, they don't work weekends."

His offer pleased her a great deal. She jumped up and announced that she was going to the market to buy something to prepare for dinner, but as the phone began to ring for the next conference call, Jake insisted that he was taking her to a fancy restaurant, and that the reservations were already made.

A delighted Veronica headed for the door. "Where are you going?" he asked.

"You don't expect me to go looking like this," she said, motioning to her attire.

"I'll pick you up at six," he hollered, with his hand over the receiver.

When she had gone, he started his "conference call" with Mel. She had the plan. "Meet me at Mars Jewelers in a half," she said.

When Melanie reached the store, she found a clueless Jacob staring into a case of diamond rings, all huge and gaudy in her estimation.

"Uncle, you don't want to be looking in there. Ronnie likes simple, elegant styling."

Though he had heard it thousands of times before, Jake now smiled at the sound of his fiancée's nickname. A name used mostly for boys seemed so incredibly out of place for the epitome of femininity. Melanie led him to a different case, and he instantly picked out a ring. Mel approved. Though it had a fairly large rock, it was simple, elegant, and exquisite—like Veronica.

Jake said, "You don't suppose she'd rather have one of those gems from Mars, do you, considering that her fiancé's a space traveler and all?"

"That's a cute idea," Melanie answered, "but I'd save it for another occasion; weddings require diamond."

Back out on the street, Melanie's uncle thanked her profusely. She had never seen him so happy, so excited. They exchanged a peck on the cheek, and he headed home to dress for the evening.

Jake rang Veronica's doorbell and waited patiently on the steps. When no one came to the door, he rang it again. When no one answered, he tried the door, found it open, and went in. He hadn't spent much time in Veronica's home; their get-togethers usually included Melanie, and were always at his place. Her rooms were sparsely but tastefully decorated, with no hint of clutter, an apt reflection of her persona. As he was about to go search out his beloved, he noticed a huge picture of himself hanging above the fireplace. It almost made him blush.

"Veronica," he called. Momentarily a wet head peeked out of the bathroom.

"Jacob! You're an hour early!" she protested. Wrapped in a towel, she slipped into her bedroom to dress.

He came to her door, waited for the hair dryer to stop, and asked, "Mind if I read your diary?" He had seen it lying on the mantle in the living room. The bedroom door opened wide, and Veronica stepped out in her bathrobe.

At the sight of her, he pulled his collar away from his neck and said, "It's awfully hot up here," and started down the stairs.

Veronica called after him, "It's not a diary, honey, it's a journal, and you're welcome to read it. I have no secrets to keep from you."

As his future mate dressed, Jake immersed himself in her most intimate writings. If the picture above the mantle had almost made him blush, Veronica's journal finished the job. He paged back trying to find entries that did not mention him, but it was nearly impossible; she had been in love with him for a long time.

Finally she emerged from her bedroom in a simple but elegant blue dress. Jake wondered if this pure woman realized how much the simple garment showcased the perfection of her figure. When Veronica reached the bottom of the stairs, she found her man in the midst of emotional overload. In thirteen years of friendship, she had never seen him cry. Now, at the sight of her, a pair of bold tears found their way to his cheeks.

"Are those happy tears or sad tears?" she teased.

He smiled at her little dig. "A little of both," he said.

"Reeeally? How so?"

"Well, I'm happy to be marrying you..." he paused as he conjured up the script, "but sad that I will no longer be able to do just as I please, when I please."

"Oh, yeah, that's it: Jacob Lansing, playboy. Riiiight!" she laughed. "What would you be doing tonight if you weren't going out with me?"

"Watching the playoffs," he insisted.

She just laughed at him. "You would be relaxing instead of working?" she asked. "Not the Jacob Lansing I know." Jake just smiled at his defeat.

Veronica lifted the long raven locks from her neck as she turned her back to him and asked, "Can you help me? With this hair I need three hands." He zipped her dress up the rest of the way, but before she could lower her hair, he stooped and kissed the back of her neck. There was something irresistible about the delicate curly hairs that grew at her hair line, falling over innocent white skin that never saw the sun or enjoyed another man's gaze. But her nape was unused to such tender attention. She turned and faced him with a smile that bore the odd mix of deep delight and apprehension. They had been in love for a long time, so the intimacy seemed to be, on the one hand, long overdue, and on the other, too much too fast.

A couple of smooches later, he drove to the restaurant. Jake stopped his old, but freshly washed car curbside in front of Mick's.

Veronica turned to him with a puzzled and slightly disappointed look. "Aren't we a little overdressed for Mick's?" she asked.

Jake just smiled, opened her door, took her hand, and said, "Come!"

Veronica frowned jovially and asked, "What will your next command be, *sit*?!"

"You will see, my pet."

They were met at the door by Mick himself. Veronica had never seen Mick in coat and tails, and giggled at the sight of him. He laughed a little himself but quickly resumed the most formal expression he could muster. "Walk this way, please," he instructed. Mick's was somewhat of a home away from home and usually about as formal. Veronica had eaten there hundreds of times with Mel and Jake. Mick led them to an intimate little back room that she never knew existed. There, a lone table was set for two.

Jake pulled out a chair for Veronica and ordered, "Sit!" She looked around the small but tastefully decorated room.

"How do you like the VIP room?" he asked.

"I had no idea it was here," she replied. "Mel and I waited tables here in our sophomore year and...I don't recall...oh, wait a minute...this is Mick's office!"

"Not tonight!" Jake countered. "Tonight it's the most romantic spot on earth!"

Mick presented them with menus, and Veronica quickly spotted a couple of her favorite dishes that were not usually on his menu. In a moment, she realized why they were so familiar: they were entree's that were Melanie's specialties, ones for which she enjoyed fame among friends and relatives.

As Veronica perused the menu, a waitress asked, "What would you like to drink?"

Startled by the familiar voice, Veronica looked up and discovered an apron clad Melanie. After greeting her friend, she turned to Jake and asked, "When did you find time to set this all up?"

"Well, you've been leaving my house every night about 9:30. There's still a lot of night left after that."

As they enjoyed their meal, it thrilled Jake to see the rewards of all his planning: the pleasure in his lady's eyes. The sometimes serious Dr. Weslin was at her giddy best. Jake loved to hear her laugh, but alas, he had a serious task to undertake. As she was about to start on her desert, he fell to one knee and produced a small container from inside coat. Flipping it open, he said, "My pet needs a tag."

Veronica had not even thought about a ring. All that she had wanted was this very special man. Caught off guard and completely speechless, tears welled in her eyes as she offered a left hand with extended fingers. Jake had a little speech prepared for the occasion. "You are the queen of my heart, and though you are simply perfect just as you are, I would be honored if you would wear this one jewel as a token of my devotion," he said as he placed the rock on her finger.

Veronica had a head full of questions. When had he found time to shop for a ring? How did he select something that matched her tastes perfectly? The two reviewed the last week, and filled in the details for each other.

After a bit, conversation turned to the future. They quickly agreed on a wedding date; however, immediately after setting the date, they both wondered aloud if they could wait that long.

"I'm not getting any younger," offered Jake. Veronica reminded her man about the Church's six-month waiting period, to which he replied, "If I can get a dispensation, will you marry me sooner?"

"Are you going to pull some strings, you old puppeteer?"

"Whatever it takes," he assured her. "But right now, let's talk about what we're doing next week."

"Well, honey, you've been so busy that I kinda thought maybe I'd go back to work next week."

"Oh, no, no, no, you can't do that! I have the most wonderful week planned for you."

"You do?" she perked up.

"Apparently you haven't been eaves-dropping on my phone conversations. I have secured the services of two tracking radio telescopes to focus in on Alpha Centauri. We will be present at one of those sites when they turn this thing on!" His excitement was contagious.

"So, using tracking telescopes means we'll get more than a snippet of data, right?" she asked.

"Very good, my love. We could be the first to hear alien music! My calculations indicated that the snippet of data I analyzed came from the direction of Alpha Centauri, but to be certain of the source we must seek out a signal using triangulation."

"Which will verify direction *and* distance."

"Correct, my little collaborator, and I very much want you there with me when that happens!" he said.

Veronica leaned forward, and resting her chin on her thumbs, gazed into her man's deep dark eyes. *Why did I wait so long for all of this?* she asked herself. *Had I expected Mr. Astronomy to go domestic on his own?* In the coming weeks, her merciless glands would become an embarrassment to her careful, scientific brain. "Get working on that dispensation," she cooed. "Watching you work just..." she strangled the end of her sentence in a tight lipped smile and finished it in her head: *just drives me wild!* Though she had long been aware of her ability to turn heads, she was just coming to grips with the kind of power she could wield over a victim of her desire, and it was becoming a serious challenge to exact wisdom from her pounding heart. Jake could see the *wild* in her eyes; she could keep no secrets from him. No doubt, that is why he had taken to calling her "queen of my heart."

They spent the rest of the weekend happily preparing for the up-coming week. Veronica regretted that she would be missing Father's lectures, and when she expressed her regret to Jake, the man of action got on the phone to Fr. Scofield, or at least, to his answering machine.

"My dear friend, Veronica is taking a road trip with me next week to immerse herself in the world of the astronomer, and she has deep regrets about missing your lectures, so I wondered if you might be so kind as to have someone record them? I would be deeply indebted. Thanks! Oh, as long as I'm going in debt, could you please round up a dispensation so we don't have to wait another five and half months to wed? Thanks old pal."

Veronica gave him a funny look. "That's not the kind of thing you ask for in a voice mail," she said. "What if he has guests in the room when he gets his voice mail?" By the smile her question engendered on Jake's face, she could see that the prospect amused him and that she was wasting her time.

They were in the middle of a kiss when the phone rang. Veronica went to answer it, but Jake held her close. After four rings, the answering machine picked it up. "No problem, space ranger, recordings shall be made," Fr. Scofield said. "As for that other deal, I'm checking to see if I can't have your waiting period extended to two years!" then after a pause, "Actually, how's three months sound?"

Jake let an ecstatic Veronica grab the phone. "Three months would be fantastic!" she shouted into the receiver. She spoke with Father for a bit about both the trip and the wedding. He told her to go ahead and plan a wedding as close as ten weeks away, because he felt sure the bishop would grant the dispensation. When barely off the phone she began to wonder aloud how on Earth she could be ready in just ten weeks.

"You're talking silly," Jake insisted. "If Father was here he'd tell you that you're preparing for a marriage, not a wedding. If we keep it simple and keep our focus we can be ready in plenty of time."

She knew he was right, and besides, there was no way she was waiting any longer.

"Still, I'd better get busy. Even simple weddings require preparation," she said.

"Unfortunately, I doubt that I will be much help," he said.

"Honey, all you have to be able to do is shake your head yes or no when I ask a question," she told him. "I'll take care of the rest. With the wedding moved up, I'm not going back to work until after we're married."

"Wonderful!" Jake exclaimed.

The next week proved amazing for the two lovebirds. They were there when the telescope tracking began, and per Jake's prophecy, there was music, beautiful swinging music. He grabbed his bride-to-be and they danced. Not only was there music, but in the years since that first weak snippet of AM signal, alien technology had advanced to FM. "This calls for a celebration!" Jake informed his future bride.

Like all radio telescopes, the one they were visiting was far from any highly populated areas. It was out in the sticks where there's little chance of interference. Thus, the couple found themselves at one of the few night clubs within miles, a rustic steak shack carved into the woods. "Frank's Tamarac Wood Grill," Jake read the sign. "Sounds pretty authentic, doesn't it?"

"Complete with authentic cockroaches," Veronica ventured.

"Well the place is packed, so the cockroaches must be first rate," he assured her.

Authentic wood and tobacco smoke attacked their nostrils as they squeezed into a small, low-backed pinewood booth in the middle of a cluster of identical booths, most of which were overflowing with humanity. Veronica plugged her ears momentarily, sign language for *It's loud in here!*

"It's a good thing we don't know anybody here, because it'd be hard to keep a secret," Jake said.

"You've got *that* right," Veronica agreed. "I already know all the latest news, and we just sat down."

"FM radio! How about that!" Jake declared above the din.

"Isn't that something! FM from another star system!" Veronica joined in.

"I think we have to go there just to check out the hotels and spas," Jake declared.

Veronica laughed. "You're thinking with your hormones, man," she said. "You know, Fr. Ian tells me that he considers you to be one of the holiest men he knows, and...well, so do I. What I don't understand is how, with your hyper libido, you've managed to remain single and pure all these years."

"Hyper libido? Me?" he asked, pointing dramatically to himself, while thinking, *Is it that obvious that the sight of her grips my very soul?*

"I'm sorry. Do you prefer 'awe-struck appreciation of the opposite sex?'" she asked, leaning across the table, her face in her hands.

Jake just smiled. He'd been accused of worse things, and was intrigued by the opportunity to explain himself. He opened his mouth to speak, but hesitated as he gazed at her for inspiration. Finally, confident he could articulate his thoughts, he mirrored her posture and slowly and thoughtfully said, "Well, my love, I'm a guy: enthralled with feminine beauty, tempted by the sensual, with valves under pressure. But until recently, I did not know passion. Now my entire being is ready to embrace a single desire, the fulfillment of which is just a vow away. You and the Holy Spirit have lit this fire. No other has been able."

"Thank you, dear heart," she said, giggling at how serious her clown could be when he chose to be, but she had to ask: "Not even Sophie Miller?"

"So...you've been talking to Mel," he noted with mock annoyance. "No, not even Sophie. Had I felt then as I do now, those five grandkids would be mine."

Jake noticed that a rough-looking hombre in the next booth was inclining his ear toward them, but thought, *He's too drunk to remember anything by morning anyway.*

"Thanks for saving yourself for me, Jacob," Veronica beamed. "You know what a fuss-budget I am about clutter. One of the things I really like about you is that—mind, heart, and soul—you're so uncluttered. You're so focused. Every aspect of your life is purpose driven. You're a rare catch."

Jake laughed and said, "I may not be as uncluttered as you think, but I am rare. Forty-nine-year-old virgins are extremely rare."

The cowboy who'd been hanging an ear in their direction suddenly lurched forward to place himself at the center of the group in his own booth.

"Don't clutter my life with any fancy wedding presents, Jacob," Veronica told him. "The only gift I want is your virginity."

"That's all I want from you as well, my love," he said, as he put her hand to his lips.

Following raucous laughter at the next table, the eaves-dropper stood, sized up Veronica, swaggered up to Jake with his hand extended, and said, "Hi, I'm Pete." A scruffy man of medium height and build, Pete was thirty-five with fifty years of drinking experience. Accustomed to being recognized in public, Jake grasped the hand for a friendly shake. As they shook hands, Pete placed two fingers of his other hand on Jake's wrist, winked at Veronica, and said, "Just had ta come over 'n' see if a forty-nine-year-old virgin's got a fuggin pulse!"

"And?" Jake asked, tightening his grip.

"I don't feel no damn pulse!" the drunk insisted.

"How about now?" Jake asked tightening still more.

"Not a fuggin thing!" Pete shouted. All eyes were on them.

"Now?"

"Ouww! Son of a bitch, you *are* alive!" Pete squealed. While his friends chuckled, he grabbed a plate of Rocky Mountain oysters from their table and slid them in front of Jake, saying, "These might help git yer hormones goin' a little so ya kin at least find out if the dang thing still comes up or not!" He plopped down on the seat next to Veronica and turned to face her. When he opened his mouth to speak, the smoke and alcohol on his breath tore the mucus right off her eyeballs. She turned away as he driveled, "You poor, pretty little thing; you don't get no lovin'!" He put one paw on her shoulder and the other on her waist as he said, "Gosh, honey, I'd take care o' you right here in the booth!"

"Get your filthy hands off her!" Jake yelled as his long arm shot across the table. He grabbed Pete's shirt and yanked him to his feet.

"Anything you say, virgin boy," Pete hollered as he threw a punch. His reach was far short of Jake's grasp. The momentum of the missed punch and Jake's timely release propelled Pete forward and his body slapped the concrete floor like a dead fish. He lay moaning till his friends turned him over to find blood dripping from his nose and lips.

A refrigerator-sized Japanese man wearing an apron over his vest and tie emerged from the kitchen. "Are you okay, Dr. Lansing?" he asked.

"We're okay, Frank," Jake said.

"My deepest apologies, Dr. Weslin," Frank said, offering Veronica his hand. "May I offer you a private table in back?" She took his hand and they followed him to his own private quarters.

When they were seated and Frank had taken their orders, she asked Jake, "Why didn't you tell me that they know you here?"

"I usually have a lot of fun here," Jake explained. "I just like to surprise you. Nothing like this has ever happened here before." He thought it a good time to change the subject, and asked, "Darling, did you notice how at a point the radio telescope signal suddenly became much clearer?"

"Yeah, what happened there?"

"We had finished performing the triangulation, and decided to just beam an amplified signal in from the other telescope, which is on the moon. Reception is better on the moon. It's also a newer, more sophisticated telescope. Do you want to go there?"

"You're kidding aren't you?" she asked incredulously. "I mean, all I know about what's up there is what's on those tasteless casino ads hyping the pleasures of 'reduced-gravity intimacy,' and that it costs about half a year's salary to make the trip. You *are* kidding, aren't you?"

"I don't kid about such things," he assured her. "I've been to the moon dozens of times. How do you feel about honeymooning there?"

"Well...I...Wow! What if I get space-sick? Don't I have to train? I thought it was a big deal to go to the moon!" she stammered.

"It used to be, but with rotating gravity cabins and non-rocket shuttles the weightless moments are short and the acceleration force is very low. Almost anyone can do it. You're in wonderful shape. You'd be fine."

"*You* are still on contract with the AGC, but how would you get permission for *me* to go?" she wondered.

"The AGC is constantly looking to expand the horizons of space travel. Their reason for existing is to promote space travel, to demystify it a little to make it seem more accessible. To that end, they want to get professionals from all walks of life involved and comfortable with it in the hopes of generating more paying customers. Besides, I conceived the AGC and was a founding member. They let me do as I please."

"Then let's do it!" Veronica screeched. "Could I ask for a more perfect tour guide?" Jake took delight in her excitement. "There's something I need to know," she added. He waited for her final moon trip concern. "What was on that plate he slid in front of you? Was that supposed to be some sort of aphrodisiac?" she asked.

"Yeah," he answered, smiling at the sudden change of subject.

"What was it, oysters?"

"Yeah. Rocky Mountain oysters."

"What?" she asked, completely puzzled as to what sort of oysters might be found in the mountains.

"Do you want some?" Jake asked.

"I'm full, and neither of us needs any kind of aphrodisiac right now! I just wondered what they were," she said.

"Ask me again sometime when you don't have a full tummy," he advised.

The couple arrived home on Friday of the second week of their engagement. Having taken a late flight back, Veronica slept in Jake's guest bedroom. Exhausted from their trip, Jake had decided to forgo morning Mass, sleep in, and have a cozy breakfast with his guest. However, he was awakened by a familiar clatter on his front lawn.

I don't need to look out the window to know what that is, he thought. *Might as well get this over with.* As he passed the guestroom, he peeked in. His little night-person friend was still sound asleep. He gently closed her door and went to the front door. *Do I do this in my robe?* he wondered. *Eh...what the heck?* he decided, and opened the door.

In a snap, four microphones were in his face, and the questions started flying. "Dr. Lansing, can you verify that intelligent life has been discovered on another planet?"

He responded smoothly, "I can tell you that, in collaboration with my fellow AGC board members, I am preparing a statement that will soon be released detailing any recent discoveries. I will not issue any other statement before that or answer any other questions. Thank you for your interest in the mission of the AGC. Have a good day."

He ducked back into the house amidst a barrage of shouted questions, and quickly closing the door, found himself face to face with his bride-to-be. She looked comical in his old robe, which nearly dragged on the floor.

"You've had to do that before," she observed. "Were you always so cool and calm?"

"No, but I never used to have the support that I have now," he said, gesturing toward her.

"In a few weeks you're gonna know what real support is!" she said as she pushed him onto the couch and went to sit on his lap. Grabbing her waist, he intercepted her descent and redirected her landing to a place beside him. "I like sitting on your lap," she said, looking up at him, "It equals out our heights for kissing. I don't get a crick in my neck. I thought you liked it too."

"That's the trouble. I love it," he declared, "but it's very unwise to drop an A-bomb on a volcano." A momentarily nonplussed Veronica buried her face in her hands, shook her head, and amidst snickers exclaimed softly, "Oh! Jacob!"

He smiled and offered, "A little too..."

"Graphic?" she finished his question. "Yes! You! What am I to do with you?!"

"Do with me? Well...I do have some suggestions," he toyed, thoughtlessly dropping a bomb of his own.

She pulled her knees up and swung her body a full half turn, so that she knelt on the couch beside him, facing him. Though she had just been giggling, it was not mirth he saw in her eyes, and she seemed oblivious to the fact that her repositioning maneuver had pulled her borrowed old robe open, exposing her in a very brief, satin-n-lace, jade-green nightie. The sight of her stole Jake's breath. He closed his eyes but could still see her thighs. *Why isn't she wearing her flannels?!*

She delivered the knockout punch with a kiss, the like of which he had never known. Her kiss was not lusty, but was born of sacred desire, for her soul was given to love, and her passions, to new life. When at last she came up for air, she was noticeably trembling. A breathless Jake, his defenses melting away, called upon the Spirit to muster the fortitude to close her robe and tighten its sash. As she blinked a tear away, he nestled her cheek in his right hand, dabbed the tear with his thumb, and managed a compassionate grin. "My sweet love," he said, being very careful to avoid the least bit of condescension in his tone, "*now* who has the hyper libido?"

Veronica broke their gaze, spun herself around, and laid her head on his shoulder. She took his hand and sat in quiet contemplation for a moment before speaking. "You're right," she said. "This is getting dangerous. We need to put our gifts in a safe place." As she walked to the bedroom to get dressed, Jake could hear her saying to herself, "Nine more weeks, nine more weeks, nine…"

Back in the guest room, Veronica hung up Jake's old robe and made her way to the bathroom. As she did so, she passed in front of the vanity and caught sight of herself in its huge mirror. Just the evening before, she had stood in front of that same mirror and admired herself in her new green nightie, dreaming of the night when she would wear it for Jacob. She had purchased it for their honeymoon, but with school-girlish exuberance, had donned it amidst dreams of things to come. Now she nearly blushed at the sight of herself, wondering what had possessed her. Then something occurred to her. In her handbag, right there on the vanity, was her Omniscan, a tool a physician was rarely without. She fished in the bag, plucked out the instrument, and turned it on. Adjusting the parameters, she pressed it to her tummy. In a moment she had a reading. Sure enough, she was at the peak of ovulation. She had been ovulating for half of her life, but never before had she felt so…hollow, so…incomplete. She grinned wet-eyed at her seductive image in the mirror, shaking her head. *You're not a little girl anymore!* she scolded herself. *Never again underestimate the power of hormones!*

As she showered, she reflected on recent events. Until a couple of weeks ago, she had never sat on a man's lap. In fact, she had really never dated. There were many men in her circle of friends, but other than Jake, no man had ever sparked any serious interest. Now, suddenly, innocent little Veronica Weslin was the aggressor! Perhaps because she had given it little thought, it had never occurred to her that having a beautiful woman sitting in his lap might bring a man to arousal. Her innocence, a powerful attraction for Jacob, was now humbling naiveté for Veronica. She worried about the mornings events, hoping that Jacob would not be too disillusioned with her.

As she dressed, the smell of Jake's cooking captured her appetite.

"You never cease to amaze me!" she commented as she took the last bite of the omelet he had prepared. "That was exceptional!"

"Thanks. Not much to omelets, sweetie," he countered as he went to answer the doorbell.

"That's not the press again, is it?" she called after him, but he did not respond. Through the open door Veronica could see two men in black suits. One of them was showing Jake a badge. Jake invited them in, and gesturing toward Veronica said, "Gentlemen, this is my fiancée, Veronica Weslin."

The two men nodded politely and the lead man said, "Good morning, Dr. Weslin. I'm Alvin Dobbs, and this is Mr. Leonard Jones. We're with the FBI."

"Good morning. How did you know that I'm a doctor?" she demanded.

"It is important to know many things about the people we are assigned to protect," he explained.

"Protect? From whom?" she asked. Jake was much more at ease with the situation than Veronica, and invited everyone to take a seat.

With the speed of a New York taxi, and the nasal resonance of its angry horn, Agent Dobbs explained. "Jones and I have been assigned to your security. We've been monitoring all of your activity for the last two weeks, ever since your discovery, Dr. Lansing."

"How did you know about my discovery?" Jake asked, a little indignant.

"Your phone line is tapped, sir," Dobbs informed him.

"What? You tapped my line...so you could *protect* me?"

"Yes, sir, you see..."

"Who authorized such a thing!" Jake demanded. Veronica was now fully wide-eyed looking at her man. Other than the little steak house incident, she had never seen him so angry. *The big Teddy bear goes grizzly when you mess with his privacy,* she thought.

"*I* authorized it," Dobbs said.

"*You* don't have the authority!" Jake shouted.

"You're right, sir. But please believe that we did it for your protection."

"You should have sought my approval!" Jake insisted.

"That would have meant contacting you in one way or another, which, of course, always allows the possibility that the enemy will detect that communication and be one step ahead of us."

"Isn't coming to see us the worst secrecy breach of all?" Jake asked.

"Desperate times require desperate measures," Dobbs insisted. "We believe your lives may be in imminent danger. You have, of course, heard of Mole Nation."

"Heard of 'em? Ha! How blessed I would be if I had only 'heard' of those weirdoes," Jake assured him. "Anyone who's anyone in the astronomical field has had a run-in with them at some point."

"Well, we have good reason to believe that they are about to become much more than a nuisance," Dobbs said. "New leadership in their group is escalating the level of resistance they are willing to pursue."

"They haven't been bugging you all that much lately, have they, Jacob?" Veronica asked.

"Not like they once did," Jake acknowledged. "They've been putting a great deal of effort into their Earth Day parades, showing up by the thousands wearing nothing but leaves and grass. What other new tricks are they up to?"

"Leonard is the expert," Dobbs said.

In smooth southern drawl, Mr. Jones explained: "As you know, Mole Nation was started by Malcolm Fitch. Though it is now thought of as a religion, Fitch was anything but religious. He had a deeply held world political view that he pursued aggressively. His position can be summed up like this: The world is being destroyed by technology; technology is unnecessary to a simple agrarian society; and the world cannot return to simplicity as long as it does not control its population. Therefore, he proposed a forced one-child limit for every family on the planet until such time when the population was reduced to one half billion people, the population level he thought sustainable by a non-technologically advanced, agrarian society."

Mr. Dobbs, the fast talking, hyper New Yorker, noticed Jake nodding his recognition of Jones' string of facts. "Len, Dr. Lansing's well aware of their history," he told him.

"Jacob is, but I'm not," Veronica informed him.

"Very well," Dobbs said, nodding to the articulate, but slow-speaking Mr. Jones.

"Needless to say," Jones continued, "the membership Fitch attracted was small. Few people are ready to return to no running water and horse transportation. So he got out of politics and started a religion, one that supported his political agenda, of course.

"Oddly enough, his religion had way more appeal than his politics, and he added a significant number to the movement. Their outlook is, of course, diametrically opposed to that of the AGC, which sees more and better technology and the colonization of extraterrestrial bodies as the answer to population woes. Mole Nation despises the colonies on the moon and Mars, and is absolutely rabid about a trip to another solar system."

"If they're 'absolutely rabid,' why aren't they bugging me?" Jake asked.

"Because they're not small thinkers anymore, Dr. Lansing," Dobbs advised. "They have come to the conclusion that just being a pain in the neck will never get the job done."

"So, what do they think *will* get the job done?" Jake asked.

"Terrorism," Dobbs stated matter-of-factly.

"What?" Veronica asked, nervously.

"Terrorism," Jones repeated. "Malcolm Fitch was a deeply flawed egomaniac, but he *was* something of a scientist. After starting his religion, his egomania went into full bloom. The things he and his group stood for lost the continuity that his quasi-scientific, sociopolitical agenda once had. All technology came to be viewed as evil, and the aerospace industry represents the epitome of cutting-edge technology.

"However, Fitch was an advocate of non-violence. After all, we are all children of mother Earth, and he didn't want to hurt any of her children. This rendered the Moles fairly harmless. As long as he was alive they shunned technology, lived in gardening communes, and avoided motorized transportation. After Fitch passed on, his protégé, Ken Jensen, took the reigns. By Jensen's revised creed, a favor is done to any astronaut or potential space traveler by killing them before they have a chance to leave Earth, before they have a chance to place their soul in danger of eternal wandering. He and his henchmen are little more than ruthless thugs. They are talking in terms of unleashing a 'wave of terror to castrate the AGC.'"

"If you know that, can't you arrest them for conspiracy?" asked Jake.

"Until now their rhetoric has been private and general. That is to say, they haven't named a target or a specific act, so we can't really charge them with anything," Dobbs explained. "We have had an operative living among them, but we have not heard from him for nearly a week. His silence may indicate that they've purged their ranks. If their threats have turned to action, you may be in grave danger."

"So what are you suggesting?" asked Dr. Lansing.

"We want you two to disappear for a while," said Dobbs. "A long honeymoon in a distant place would be good."

"How about on the moon?" offered Jake.

"Getting off of the ground would be the trick," offered Jones, "but once you were there, it's a sure thing they wouldn't be bothering you. They won't endanger their souls with space travel."

Dobbs went on. "Part of the reason for tapping your phone line was to get in here and check things out to make sure that they weren't doing the same. With Fitch at the helm, their hatred for technology would have kept such things as phone tapping from happening. I don't think Jensen's doctrine is quite so pure. He is crazy but cunning. His downfall is that he desperately needs the adulation of the communes and seems willing to die a martyr to have his day in the sun. To that end, we're counting on him getting reckless.

"Getting back to your question, I think the best thing to do for tonight is to get you both into Dr. Weslin's house. We've rented a house across the street and will have armed surveillance guards on duty 24/7. The evening news will carry your little bathrobe interview, which I fear will draw the Moles to your door. We need to be one step ahead of them."

"When does it end?" Veronica needed to know.

"It ends when we indict and arrest their leaders," said Dobbs. "Protection is all that we can provide until then."

When the two men had gone, Jake and Veronica just stood looking at each other for a moment. Veronica was now very concerned about Jake. "The AGC should make no announcements," she proclaimed. "This discovery should be kept under wraps until a mission is planned and executed."

Jake shook his head. "I'm sorry, honey, but that's just not possible. You saw this morning how the story has already leaked. The AGC leaks like a sieve. We are a private agency with governmental liaisons, somewhat like the Federal Reserve Board, except that the Fed was started and defined by an act of Congress, whereas the AGC was born in the private sector and became so highly successful that the public sector has a vested interest in keeping it healthy."

"Tighten up security," she suggested.

"What security? We have no government mandate. We accomplish what we accomplish through donations from, and the cooperation of, the private sector. There is practically no secrecy protocol in place anywhere within the organization. The whole idea of the council's creation was to make space travel a household term. Disseminating information is what we are all about."

"I see," she said, feeling somewhat deflated.

"I'm packing my clothes," Jake said. "Let's get out of here." As he climbed the stairs, she called his name. "Yes, love?" he answered.

"Honey...I want you to be safe, but...who will keep *us* safe?" she asked, recalling the morning's temptations.

He descended the stairs and seated himself on the second from the bottom. "I'll talk to Dobbs," he said. "Maybe I can stay across the street with them, and Mel can move in with you." Then he frowned and added, "But not being there to protect you also makes me uneasy."

"Maybe we can get Mel to stay. You can protect us both, and she can protect us from us—two's company; three's a crowd," Veronica offered. Jake smiled his approval.

The next morning, Veronica watched out her picture window as her flowers did a little dance in the soft rain. She loved the smell of rain and went to the front door to get a dose. When she opened the door, Dobbs and Jones were coming up the walk. "It's them, Jacob," she called to him.

Stopping at her doorstep, Mr. Dobbs spoke. "I'm sorry to bother you again, Dr. Weslin, but if we may come in for just a moment..." With the door closed behind them, he said, "As you may recall, yesterday I told you about one of our agents who had infiltrated the Moles, and that we had not heard from him for over a week. Well, he's been found. Dead! Murdered! I thought it would be good for you to know how real and present the danger is. We have a task force working to connect his murder to the Moles and are hoping to uncover enough evidence for an indictment. How successful we will be depends on how well they covered their tracks. Murder is a new thing for them. Maybe they left plenty of clues."

"Thank you, gentlemen," Jake said. "Are there any further changes we need to make in our lives?"

"I would lay very low for the next two weeks. Stay away from the AGC offices. Let others make announcements. With your natural charisma and fame, Dr. Lansing, you are a veritable poster boy for space travel. We believe that makes you their prime target. We are contacting all of the AGC board members to warn them to avoid video-recorded announcements and personal appearances. We want to keep the Moles debating their next target until we get something on them. Ideally, I'd move the two of you to somewhere out in the sticks, say...Idaho, or Oklahoma, or the Dakotas. Like similar whacko cults of the past, Mole Nation has no appreciable following in remote rural areas. For recruiting purposes, every commune is within a short distance from a major metropolitan center, and because they have traditionally opposed motorized travel, you would likely be quite safe out in the sticks."

"What about my friends at AGC headquarters?" asked Dr. Lansing.

"We are doing all we can to secure AGC headquarters, including scrutinizing the phone system and web connections. You will be safest communicating with them by cell phone or the web," said Dobbs.

"Thanks again gentlemen," Jake said. "We will inform you if we decide to make a move."

"If you'd allow me, I'd really prefer to plan that move for you," said Dobbs. "We have several locations picked out and can help with the arrangements."

"Jacob, let's do it," Veronica said. "We can have a tiny wedding in a country setting. Running away together sounds romantic in a scary, weird sort of way."

Jake agreed. "Do any of these out-of-the-way places happen to be near a ski resort?" he joked.

Chapter 3

Gravity

The old moose held his pose, stately antlers thrust toward the ceiling. Veronica grinned, imagining the creature posing for the hunter, envisioning his own immortalization. He and his furry companions on the wall, clustered around a stone fireplace that crackled and breathed a little smoke, completed the rustic ambiance one comes to expect with a ski chalet.

A waitress in ski gear, still red-cheeked from an early morning run, delivered a couple of steamy cups of cocoa. As Veronica pursed her lips and blew the surface of the molten liquid, she thought about how fast life can change. She had gone from planning a wedding with a hundred and seventy-five guests, to one with about a dozen. She had her dress, and reservations were made at the club where they would dine and dance. She had nothing left to do but enjoy her last seven weeks as a single woman.

Her future groom sat across the table from her going on and on about space travel and the technology that would allow them to travel to the "FM planet," as he called it, but Veronica wasn't hearing a word of it. She was admiring his strong jaw and watching how his dimples appeared and disappeared with different expressions. She thought about how much of a sixteen-year-old schoolgirl she still was at heart; how that man in his middle thirties had fascinated her then just as he did now.

"So, what do you think about that?" he asked suddenly. Her loving but blank look prompted him to observe, "You weren't listening, were you?"

"I'm sorry, darling," Veronica apologized. "I was really just enjoying looking at you; your face fascinates me."

"You are so forgiven. What I was saying is how this trip to the FM planet will require married couples, or at least, eligible single folk. No astronaut's spouse is likely to want his or her better half to leave for anywhere from twelve years to forever. The spacecraft will need to be equipped with a nursery," he explained.

"This trip to the moon that we're making wouldn't be your idea of priming me for a longer voyage, would it?" she asked with mock indignation.

Jake smiled, sipped his cocoa, and said, "I'm just sharing my work with you, dear, relating a conversation that is currently taking place among AGC board members."

"This stuff is too sweet, and I need to wake up," she said, getting up without further explanation.

Jake watched her walk toward the bar and made a huge effort to look beyond her sexy walk and natural poise. As he contemplated his bride-to-be, he fell into full daydream, rerunning in his mind a conversation written on his heart, a conversation between a thirty-seven-year-old scientist and a seventeen-year-old college sophomore. *She was so articulate,* he recalled, *and so comfortable speaking to a man twenty years her senior. There's this timelessness about her. She doesn't fit into any herd, generation, or era. That night was the beginning of something that can never be undone.*

He had known few people who lived life so immersed in thanksgiving. The seventeen-year-old Veronica had told him about how, ever since her mother's miraculous cure, she felt as though she was walking on air. Now as he watched her sashay toward him, he pictured that three inches of air under her feet and thought, *Perhaps that explains why she moves so divinely!*

The twenty-nine-year-old Veronica took a seat and just sat there sipping her drink, watching him reminisce. "Hey handsome, what's chasing through that ever-busy brain?" she asked at last.

"You! What do you have there?" he asked, sniffing at her drink.

"Baileys and coffee. I'm not a morning person, remember. I need a little jump start to keep up with you."

"Okay…I understand the caffeine, but what's the alcohol doing for you?" he asked, smiling.

"There's alcohol in here?"

"Honey…you got it at the bar, didn't you?" Jacob asked, with eyebrows raised. He shook his head and sat there grinning at her, and she just took it all with a smile. For all of her intelligence and wisdom, she lacked street smarts and readily admitted it. "Just don't do too many of those," Jake advised, "You'll be skiing uphill!"

They skied the afternoon away. Veronica marveled as she watched her fiancé out ski folks half his age, including herself. As vigorously as he went at it, she hoped he would have energy for the dance floor she had glimpsed earlier in the day.

Back at the chalet, on their way to dress for dinner, he stopped with her at her room for a moment to get a drink of water. Veronica excused herself to use the bathroom. As he quenched his thirst, he took the liberty to browse through her wardrobe, pulling out the first thing that caught his attention. When Veronica came out, she found her man with a hot-pink dress in his hands and an intense sparkle in his eye. "Will you please wear this to…" he began, but was interrupted when she snatched the garment from his hands, clutched it close to herself and turned full away from him.

"Snoop!" she scolded, looking over her shoulder.

"I'm sorry, love," he apologized, "I didn't mean to ruin your surprise. I'll go dress while you put it on." Before Veronica could respond, Jake was out the door. In an hour, wearing a nicely tailored sport coat, he rapped on her door. When she opened for him, she could not help but see his face fall.

"I'm sorry, snoopy," she said, "but that other dress was not a surprise for tonight; it was for the honeymoon!"

"I'm the one who should be sorry, love," he said with true contrition, "but we do have plenty of time before the honeymoon. You can pick out another. I *really* want to see you in that *tonight!*"

"Which is exactly why I won't be wearing it *tonight!*" she insisted.

After dinner, between twirls, she talked of wedding plans to her loved one on the dance floor, but Jake wasn't hearing a word, only the sound of her voice. He was lost in her blue eyes and mesmerized by her black hair and how, with each twirl, it played hide-and-seek with the nape of her neck. She had brushed her hair to one side of her head, revealing a perfectly exquisite right ear. She was wearing the blue dress she had worn the night he gave her a diamond. Though modest compared to the little hot-pink number that had excited the snoop's imagination, she moved so divinely that he was lost in the sight of her, and its color brought him back to drink of the love in her blue eyes, eyes which pierced his heart and soul.

"Honey? Aren't you going to answer my question?" she asked, ever so politely.

"I'm sorry," he said. "I'm not much of a multitasker, and it seems that watching you dance is all my brain can process at one time."

"You are so forgiven," she said, and then, gesturing to her dress, said, "If I drive you to distraction in this old thing, you can see why I didn't grant your wish with the pink one!" He grinned sheepishly and nodded his understanding.

Later, as he sat on his bed removing his shoes, Jake reflected on the evening. He had never felt so overcome with desire, so driven by a single purpose. He smiled as he thought about how Veronica had been so sweet and yet so strong. He remembered a time not too long ago when he had been the strong one and she had battled with her own runaway passion. *The Spirit moves as he pleases*, he thought, *that we may be humbled.* The beauty of their threesome relationship with their Creator unfolded more to him each day. In a world that placed no value on self-control, and therefore, on virginity, they were oddballs and the butt of cruel jokes. It didn't matter. God willing, they would achieve their goal of pure, consecrated love, cruel jokes or no cruel jokes.

The next five weeks proved wonderful, but difficult. On the Saturday before *the* Saturday, they sat silently together before the Blessed Sacrament. For an hour they shared the company of their Savior, listening with their hearts. As they left, they clutched each other on the front steps of the church as a snowy winter gust enveloped them. "Gosh it's cold!" Veronica whimpered as Jake threw his arm around her and walked her to the car.

He started the engine, and as he waited for the car to warm, turned to her and said, "I think we should spend this last week in prayer, separated from each other."

After a moment of silence, she sighed an answer. "Maybe. Each week I get a little more excited about the wedding, which just seems to make the waiting that much harder. I've never had this much fun in my life, Jacob, but I feel like I've been pretty self-indulgent."

"Which was long overdue!" Jake insisted.

"I suppose. But I sure miss the kids at Children's Hospital," she said, picturing them as she gazed through the windshield at the snowfall.

"Your absence from their lives couldn't be helped, dear heart. But you could spend this next week praying for them, and for our marriage," he suggested.

She slid over and cuddled up to him. "Okay, but when you meet me at the altar, I'll be starved for love, baby. Starved!" she told him, sealing her prediction with an appetizing kiss.

"And I'll have a big helping all prepared!" he assured her, "Complete with dessert!"

So it was decided: Veronica spent the week at the local convent, enjoying the company of six wonderful sisters, while Jake spent the week at the lodge, with daily trips made to the adoration chapel.

In the blink of an eye, it seemed, Veronica found herself at the altar in her wedding dress. Their miniscule wedding was held in the adoration chapel, which gave the gathering a cozy feel.

Her mom and dad, Judy and Dr. Ronald Weslin, were there, along with her twin brothers, Xavier and Fabian, and her baby sister (now seventeen), Marie. Marie had agreed to be her flower girl a dozen years past, and Veronica wasn't letting her off of the hook. Jake had chosen Air Force Captain Michael Benson, his long time friend and fellow space traveler, as his best man. Veronica could not escape noticing how stunning this gentleman looked in his uniform as he walked up the isle with her maid of honor, her dear friend (and soon to be niece) Melanie at his side. Finishing out the guest list were their mutual friends Antonio and Juanita Escobar, twin brother and sister, and Antonio's fiancée, Jeanine Martin. These three had often been Veronica's classmates through the years. All three were astronauts and were well acquainted with Dr. Jacob Lansing.

Captain Benson read the first two scriptures, and Fr. Scofield read the Gospel and began his homily.

"There is little left for me to say," he started. "The fine scriptures chosen by this wonderful couple, along with their exemplary lives, have already preached a homily to this humble priest's heart." He reflected a bit more on the readings and then added, "The gospel chosen for this occasion reminded me of something I had recently read, written by a certain Emmanuel Voronin. I will read for you a portion of his booklet entitled *Two's Company; Three's Liturgy.*" He paused a moment to locate his page, and read:

"'When choosing a marriage partner, it often seems we are attracted to people very different than ourselves; as the saying goes, opposites attract. Have you ever wondered why? It seems to me that, through God's design, we simply are not destined to marry someone who has the same faults that we have. We get a whole new batch when we marry: a whole new set of nasty habits! My bride's perfection was seriously compromised when she and I became one flesh, but with Jesus' help, she struggles to see beyond my weaknesses and imperfections, to see me with His eyes. Having assimilated each other's faults through marriage, we are less likely to hold in contempt others who display the same defects. As each of our spiritual boundaries widens, and our spiritual family grows, if we are Christ-like, we assimilate more and more faults, and our love and tolerance grows, not love and tolerance for sin, but love and tolerance for sinners. Scripture teaches that Christ *bore our sins in his body*. Although I believed this teaching to be true, it did not become concrete for me until I saw it in this light. Now at last I see the beauty of Christ's metaphor, how completely we are *his bride*.'"

Fr. Scofield invited the couple to join hands before the altar. A sweet moment lingered as the two slowly and clearly recited the vows they had memorized. They knelt, and time stood still as they prepared their hearts for the Eucharist, melding into oneness with the Gift.

Though Jacob and Veronica had been skiing and hanging around the lodge for weeks, it seems everything takes on a new dimension after marriage, so they skied for another week while preparing for the moon jaunt. Veronica was nervously excited about the trip, a nervousness that tended to make her talk incessantly. Jake just smiled, listened, and calmed her fears. On the morning of their departure, she opened the bathroom door on her shaving husband to show him her new winter dress.

"That's lovely, honey. Are you planning on wearing it today?" he asked.

"That's why I put it on."

"You might just get more attention from male passengers and crew than you'd like," he warned out the side of his mouth as he dragged the razor across his face.

"What are you talking about?" she asked, with just a hint of annoyance, "You like it when I wear dresses, and this dress is anything *but* seductive!"

He wiped the remaining shaving cream from his face, turned to face her and grinned. "Thanks for putting it on for me, honey; it is modest, but can you say the same of your underwear?"

"What?" she demanded, with a look that said, *don't toy with me!* but soon her face relaxed as his game became clear. "Weightlessness!" she exclaimed.

"Um hum," he responded with a smirk.

"Well, why didn't you just say so, you big tease!" she said, poking him in the ribs while he chuckled at his own game.

A couple hours later they were disembarking the shuttle and climbing weightless into the foyer of the planetary cruiser.

"How long does this weightlessness last?" Veronica asked as she placed her fingers over her mouth.

"Are you okay?" Jake inquired.

"I don't know if it's the weightlessness or the smell of someone else's vomit that's getting to me," she said as she clutched one of the railings that allowed them to pull themselves through the space.

"See the series of rings on the wall over there," he said. "That is actually a circular ladder. In a moment we'll be instructed to pull ourselves through this weightlessness to the opening in the center of that wall. On the other side of that opening the cabin is rotating and there is a similar circular ladder. As we make our way to the outside of the hull on that ladder, the centrifugal force will increase with each step down until it equals Earth gravity."

Within a few minutes they were in the gravity cabin comfortably seated. Veronica giggled at the sight of people seated sideways on the walls and thought it would be even funnier to see them stuck to the ceiling, but the cargo bin down the center of the cabin prevented that view. In less than eight hours they were at the moon. The flight was not very relaxing.

"It seems that all we did was accelerate and decelerate," she noted.

"That sums it up pretty well," her husband agreed.

Within the hour they were checking into their hotel. "Gravity or non-gravity," the desk clerk asked.

"What?" a bewildered Veronica responded.

Jake had decided to let her discover things on her own. The clerk went on to explain that they had rooms with rotating beds that replicated Earth's gravity for those who slept better that way, or who were concerned about retaining muscle tone.

Jake answered for her. "Gravity, please."

As they headed for their room she asked, "What about that 'reduced-gravity intimacy' the ads are always talking about?"

Jake smiled a broad, appreciative smile. "Gravity beds are a perk. Low gravity is readily available," he said.

"Is there a separate bed for that?" she asked.

"The couch pulls out."

"They're never very comfortable," she insisted.

"At this gravity level, the table top is comfortable," he assured her.

Jake laughed at his bride as she hopped and skipped like a little girl, enjoying the reduced gravity as they walked along.

That night they found the casino dance floor, which proved to be a unique experience. "This is like learning all over again!" Veronica noted, regarding their struggling steps. "It would probably be easier if we had no experience!" The only thing that seemed to work at all was slow dancing.

"Want to get in the hub?" Jake asked.

For the next fast tune they climbed into a large rotating funnel that boosted the gravity up to Earth's level. "Wow, I don't know which is weirder, next-to-no gravity or a curved dance floor!" Veronica shouted above the music. She wore the hot-pink little dress Jake had begged her to wear just a few weeks earlier. It had a single strap over the left shoulder, and a neckline that dove fairly low on the right. The skirt's hemline slanted in the same direction as the neckline, starting at four inches above the left knee and dropping to about six below the right. It was flared for dancing, and had a bold kick pleat placed strategically over the right thigh. Over the top of the pink dress she wore a garment of delicate white sheer. This nearly invisible outer dress, adorned from the bust up with small, lace doves-in-flight, covered her arms, shoulders, and the back of her neck, culminating in a thumb's width choker collar with a single mother-of-pearl button-and-loop closure over her lovely throat. Below the collar, the front of this outer dress was an open V, as wide as her neck at the top, terminating at her waist. Though not terribly revealing, the styling was so alluring that Veronica had been uncomfortable with the idea of wearing it in public, but it was a slow Tuesday evening and Jake had pointed out that the few honeymooning men who were on the dance floor had serious beauties of their own to entertain.

As he watched his bride dance, the sacredness of the ritual caught hold of him. Suddenly she was not wearing a dress, but a vestment, a sacred vestment donned for a sacred ritual, a liturgy of the domestic church. Like her negligees, this dress had taken on a certain sacramentality, a pledge of humility and love.

Jake recalled a time when he had gone for a walk with Fr. Scofield and a seminarian. After a young woman wearing a sheer negligee over a flesh-colored halter top and biker shorts had crossed their path, the seminarian had remarked that he was embarrassed for someone who would "go out in public in such sinful clothing." After a moment's reflection, to the young man's puzzlement, Fr. Scofield had said, "That was not sinful clothing. Objects are never sinful, though our use of them may be. In the proper context, wearing such garments may be an act of humility and love, symbolic of offering to spouse the gift of one's total self. Out of context, it is an act of pride, an act filled with disregard for genuine self-worth."

Jake could not daydream for long watching his humble wife. Her genuine self-worth transfixed him. Before marriage, his discovery of this pink dress, like his accidental preview of her in her green nightie, had been for him a great temptation. Ironically, both garments were now an invitation from the Almighty. He thought about her vulnerability and the awesome power he had over her, and the sight of her rendered those thoughts poetic and prophetic: *The difference between the sacred and the desecrated is invisible, but so profound!* he thought. *Commitment to love is the thin line between the pious and the profane, between the blessed and the bane, indeed, between life and death.*

With all of that swimming in his head, Jake twirled his bride and generated some kick pleat action, which pleased him a great deal. Her thick black hair played peek-a-boo with her lace bedecked right shoulder, while from between the lace doves, her bosom beckoned him to the promised land. He had waited many years to cross the Jordan, to explore the sacred hills and valleys that lie beyond. Now his crossing had brought new challenges. Like most of the rest of the world, would he come to take milk and honey for granted? Would he wallow in the nectar without appreciation for the flower? Indulge in the gift, without a thought to the Giver? Would he discover what all lovers eventually discover? That the only discipline tougher than abstinence is that of true appreciation?

Once again, Veronica spoke to him between twirls, and once again he heard not a word she was saying, only the sound of her voice. She could not help but notice that his expression bore the evidence of deep pleasure mixed with deep contemplation. She also knew that, though his eyes seldom seemed to leave hers, he somehow drank in her entire being and swam in its essence. She thought about the awesome power she had over him, finally realizing what Jake had already known, that she truly was the queen of his heart.

She stopped dancing for a moment, and in reference to her last remark asked, "What do you think about that?" knowing full well he would have little idea what she had been saying. Caught again! His mind reeled in his eyes, but his merciful queen pressed herself against him and said, "It's okay, sweetheart. Talk is overrated!"

Back at the room, the bride unbuttoned a single mother-of-pearl button, lifted her arms, and began to pull the sheer outer garment over her head. She reached a point where she seemed stuck, and peering through the lace doves, asked, "Will you give me a hand, love?" In

typical Jake fashion, he smiled and began to applaud. Veronica made a
face at his antics, and after managing to remove the garment without
his help, threw it at him. It fell on him and draped over his head and
shoulders. He just stood there smiling at her through the lace, then
gathered the whole thing together and held it to his face. "What are you
doing?" she asked after a moment.

"It smells so lovely!" he exclaimed.

"Uhg! How can it? I've been sweating in it all night!" she
objected.

"Exactly! It's the prettiest smell there is: You!"

She just grinned at him as he reverently folded the garment while
asking, "Do you want some wine?"

"Please!" she answered, throwing herself down on the low-gravity
bed. He poured the wine, turned on some music, and came to her side.
She was lost in thought as she gazed at the moonscape through a floor-
to-ceiling circular window. Jake lifted her black mane, kissed the back
of her neck, and began to open the long row of buttons that ran from
her nape all the way to the hem of her skirt. The buttons reminded him
of rosary beads, and on them he contemplated the mysteries of the
liturgy he was initiating. With buttons undone, he pulled the lone strap
from her left shoulder and began to rub her shoulders and back.

"You're awfully quiet," he observed. "What deep thoughts are
running through that pretty head?"

She moaned with pleasure and relief wrought from his massage
and said, "I was just enjoying you enjoying me. But I was also praying
for Fr. Ian, thinking he might be lonely these last couple of months
with us gone. Though he's faithfully mailed the recordings of his
lectures, I really miss his presence. He's such a dear holy man. I miss
drilling him with questions after a lecture. When most of the rest of the
students would leave, Antonio, Juanita, Jean, Mel, and I—you know,
the crew—we would sometimes keep him for another hour. He's such
a fascinating man, so full of the knowledge of God."

"So what made you think of Ian right this moment?" he asked with
surprise in his voice.

She rolled onto her back to face her man, traced his eyebrow with
her finger and caressed his cheek. "Probably the fact that he told me to
trust my feelings and follow my heart," she said.

"You talked to him about *us*?"

"Yes, but Father didn't know who the mystery man was. I only
told him that my brain and my heart were at war with each other

concerning a man with whom I had fallen in love. He said something like this…" She lowered her voice, pursed her lips to mimic their friend, and said, "'We are all called to fecundity: called to bear fruit. Do not forget that mankind's original fruit-bearing mission is literal: the call to Matrimony. Keep your mind open, pray hard, and follow your heart.'"

Her impersonation provoked a belly laugh from Jake. "You sound just like him!" he chuckled. "I must remember to thank him. Sounds like you two had quite a talk."

"Oh, that was just the headline. He went on and on talking about how, in old English, the word Matrimony literally meant motherhood, and about how John Paul the Great suggested that woman is the archetype of humanity in that she is the embodiment of receptivity to God. Father said that he knew I was open to God in a spiritual sense, but that God might also be calling me to be open in a physical sense."

"In a physical sense? How so?" Jake wondered. "And if woman is the 'archetype of humanity,' what's left for men?"

"Oh, I'm so glad you asked!" she whispered. "I am open to God in the physical sense in that I am open to you, his gift. Though God is infinitely receptive to our love, he is first of all both Giver *and* Gift. God the Father is creator and initiator, the Son is gift, and the Holy Spirit is power, power to accept, reflect, and share the gift. In John Paul's parlance, though we all are created in the image of God and are meant to be gift to one another, men are initiators, the embodiment of gift."

"Initiators, huh? Well, I think that you, by your very existence, are the one who starts everything."

"Precisely! My receptivity turns you on, just as our receptivity turns God on," she said.

"Turns God on?" he asked, raising his eyebrows.

"Do you prefer *excites God's love?*" she asked.

"No, I'm fine with turns on; you just surprised me a little," he said.

"I like to surprise you!" she whisper shouted. She loosened his tie as she added, "Actually, God makes love to us continuously, but too often we're oblivious to his gaze, deaf to his love song, and numb to his touch. We don't need to turn him on; we just need to tune in. Do you remember what I said a minute ago when you asked what was running through my head?"

"Well…you said you were just enjoying me enjoying you."

"That's really what my prayer life consists of, honey," she said, tracing his lips with her finger. "God doesn't see my sins when he looks at me. All he sees is his reflection, however dim. He just enjoys me enjoying his eyes on me."

"And there you have it," Jake proclaimed dramatically, "my first theology lesson in the middle of making love!"

"Your body is always a theology lesson to me, love," she insisted, "and trust me; we're nowhere near the middle yet!"

"Well, if I am the embodiment of gift, this gift has your name on it and needs to be delivered!" he informed her.

"Ummm, I like gifts. I'd hang mistletoe if I had some," she said.

"Ho, ho, ho!" he intoned.

Veronica wrinkled her nose. "You've been dancing real hard, Saint Nick," she said as she sat up next to him. "I like *your* scent too, but right now it's a little too much of a good thing, like maybe you've been sleepin' with the reindeer! I'll be Santa's little helper." She picked the big man up, slung his lunar-lightened frame over her shoulder, and ho-ho-hoing with glee, hauled him to the shower.

The next day they traveled to the little lunar town of New Arecibo where radio telescope scientists researching the Alpha Centauri System had discovered many radio stations in different languages, and were enjoying a wide variety of alien music. Jake could not contain his excitement. He had been out of the loop for a week and a half and the new information was like a new toy to a child.

"Is this new information generating a lot of activity at the AGC?" he needed to know.

"Dr. Lansing, I'm sorry to be the one to tell you this, but there's trouble on Earth," the head researcher said. "A warrant has been issued for Kenneth Bell and his thugs, but the authorities have been unable to locate them. With killers at large, it's like there's a huge cloud hovering above the whole Freqmod discovery."

"Freqmod?" Jake asked.

"Well, you were calling it the FM planet..." she tipped her hand in a small flourish that said, *C'mon, you can figure it out.*

"Ah," Jake caught on," Frequency modulation...Freqmod."

"We've been calling the planet that for a while," she told him.

He laughed. "Thanks, Francesca. You folks are doing a great job up here!"

Jake tried to remain upbeat, but Veronica could see the cloud following him. She led him to the chapel at the casino. As they knelt, she prayed, "Lord, help our friends at AGC, and help Jacob to let it go for just a few more days. Please Lord." Jake smiled and hung his head. She was right; this was their honeymoon. There would be plenty of time for worrying later.

The next day the two took a tour of the moon in a rover. Veronica admired the stark, lifeless beauty and thought that, for many scientific reasons, the moon was an interesting place to visit, but she needed to know, "Why would anyone choose to live here?"

Jake didn't have his usual quick answer, but the rover driver did. "I live here because of my arthritis," he said. "The wear and tear on joints is next to nothing. It's also a good place to live if you have varicose veins or a bad back. Just one problem: if you live here for very long because of those problems, you're probably avoiding the gravity beds so you can sleep at night, and you're probably avoiding the exercise hubs and opting for light exercise at moon gravity, and...well...it's unlikely you'll ever be able to return to Earth, which wouldn't be a problem except that this is one darned expensive place to retire."

Veronica turned to Jake and said, "Sorry I asked, honey. Just pretend you didn't hear that."

But Jake just smiled and shrugged. "Just one more opportunity for the AGC," he said.

They spent their last four days in the lunar town of Oasis, an entire city built under huge, blue fabric, air-filled domes. As they walked through lush gardens, enjoying the well-filtered daylight, they were startled by sudden bursts of light from above. "Fireworks on the moon?" Veronica asked, amazed by the silent explosions.

"Well, I guess you could call it that," Jake said with a chuckle. "Domes like these used to be way too expensive to maintain because of the constant repairs necessitated by meteorite damage, not to mention the safety concerns. The explosions you're seeing are those of meteors being taken out by automatic tracking lasers. We're getting quite a shower. This was the proving ground for the safety equipment on the planetary cruisers. It's great technology!" Just as he finished speaking, a softball-sized piece of debris crashed through the dome and slammed into the ground just twenty feet from them.

Veronica doubled over, coughing from the dust cloud the impact had created. Jake swept her into his arms and ran. Safe inside a hard-surfaced building, as her coughing subsided, she raised her eyebrows and wheezed, "Great technology? I hope they work better than that on the cruisers!"

"I said great, not perfect. The cruisers have backup shielding," he informed her, "but I've neither seen nor heard of an incomplete interception here in all of the years since these guns were installed."

"Maybe God's trying to tell us something," she replied, with a you-know-what-I'm-talking-about roll of the eyes.

"I think you're right," he said.

"You do?"

"Yes. He's trying to tell us to fix the lasers!"

Twenty-four hours later they were in the shuttle resting on the tarmac of terra firma. The gravity of the Mole situation was about to hit them like the gravity of their home planet. Before deplaning, Jake was already on the phone with Agent Dobbs.

"There will be two agents waiting for you at the bottom of the stairs as you deplane," Dobbs said. "They will escort you to waiting transportation." That waiting transportation turned out to be a limo parked right out on the tarmac, with Mr. Dobbs on board.

"Was I elected president while I was gone?" Jake asked as he and Veronica climbed into the big vehicle.

"The AGC does not want to take any chances," Dobbs explained. "Two days ago a Mole couple paid the police a visit. They had seen the news clip about our murdered agent. They had known Hank as a fellow Mole and had heard Bell comment that 'if he was an FBI agent, he got what he deserved.' This couple wanted to distance themselves from anything criminal, and they started naming names.

"We now know that Bell has placed the reins of the organization into the hands of his most trusted followers, Plato and Venus Sweeney. We've picked up the Sweeneys for questioning, but so far they seem clean regarding the death of our operative. In fact we believe more and more that Bell operated alone in Hank's murder, and given the group's aversion to technology, it is likely that most of the membership has not even heard about his death, or that he was with the FBI. Unfortunately the Sweeney's are either complicit or do not believe Bell had anything to do with Hank's death, and they will not help to locate him. Our current plan is to release them and to let them lead us to him."

"Where does that leave us?" Veronica asked.

"It leaves you with us as shadows," replied Dobbs.

"Looks like the honeymoon's over," she sighed.

Life for the newlyweds somewhat returned to normal. Veronica returned part time to her research job and finally got back to attending Father's theology lectures, all accompanied by two FBI agents. Jake spent his days at the AGC trying to put together a voyage to Freqmod, as it was now commonly called, and was also accompanied by agents everywhere he went.

The AGC headquarters had always had a security system requiring ID badges to get into the testing areas, a measure now applied to the museum and conference sections as well. The guards at the entrance were well acquainted with the faces of the suspected terrorists.

Though Dr. Lansing had given a mission to Freqmod a lot of thought, the mere scale of the endeavor finally hit him. In a short while he came to the same conclusion his colleagues had in his absence: There was just no way a mission of this proportion could be handled in the usual manner. Finding sponsorship in the private sector would not suffice.

"My dear friends, I have heard your discussion, and I concur completely. I think this mission will require the involvement of NASA and the military to ever get off of the ground," Jake proclaimed at one of the sessions. "All of its existence the AGC has acted as a clearing house, a bulletin board, and a support mechanism. Now we are considering taking on the role of primary promoters for a mission of gigantic proportion. The military will have interest in this mission, but they will have no delusions about any immediate payback. The private sector will also be interested and will contribute if it is allowed as a tax shelter, or if they can be reasonably assured of monetary return, but we will need multiple sponsors.

"NASA wants to lead this endeavor, but we all know how their budget looks. The government's lack of commitment to the space program is the reason I conceived the AGC. Some will argue that this mission should be an international endeavor. The AGC is currently the most multinational organization in the world. Unencumbered by politics we are able to morph rapidly and become whatever it is that we need to be to accomplish our goals. It is this prowess, this spontaneity that has eclipsed other government-based multinational space efforts. I believe that the work we do with the private sector should indeed take a multinational approach. However, trying to brokerage a deal between governments of nations is not something I want to be involved in— been there, done that, and don't want to do it again. I doubt I would live long enough to see them come to enough agreement for a mission to proceed. It's difficult enough to get corporations to focus on common goals. If we involve NASA, I believe that we will automatically be involving the military, so we might as well be prepared to deal with them in a way that will encourage the kind of mission we want to foster. What is our motto?"

"The first one with a plan wins!" they all responded.

The chairwoman of the AGC, Melissa Banks, capped his remarks. "I concur one hundred percent, Jake. Other than chanting our motto in unison, it's hard enough to get the people around this table to agree on anything. I'm not about to go to the U.N. to plan a space voyage."

Accordingly, the AGC planned a series of conventions, taking the opportunity to do all the things they do best, and more. They soon realized that the *more* would require more people on staff. In its new role of project management, the AGC itself would first need to go through growing pains. Jake proposed what he coined the *self-fulfilling strategy*. Through this strategy, the AGC would expand in part by hiring the personnel who would actually be making the voyage: young, bright individuals who would serve the AGC well to assure their place on a starship.

As the project advanced, Jake's proposal proved difficult to implement. The military/NASA connection brought many challenges. The military would not budget for this little excursion unless all personnel were sworn into duty for the duration of the voyage—this would be a military mission. It seemed to make sense, in a way. A voyage of this length would require a serious protocol for keeping order and settling disputes. Military discipline would be the obvious first choice for a mission with so much at stake. In addition to demanding that all of the crew be inducted, the top brass were insisting that key command positions be filled by experienced military officers. This stance made the idea of hand-picking persons, and hiring them first as AGC employees, a seeming impossibility.

But the AGC had its ace in the hole: Dr. Jacob Lansing. The well-connected Dr. Lansing would pull some strings. Through the years, he had spent time in the Oval Office with four of the commanders in chief, including the sitting one, and was on a first name basis with the Secretary of Defense. He already had a person in mind for the position of starship captain, and decided to start there. He submitted the name to the council and got their unanimous approval. Next stop: the Secretary of Defense. Jake knew he was about to make an unusual request. He would seek to have a colonel in the U.S. Air Force assigned as full time liaison to the AGC while still actively employed by the military.

Mr. Dobbs shook his head. "So much for keeping a low profile," he muttered to Jones when he learned that Jake was about to visit the Oval Office. "This is gonna be all over the news, and our lives will be plunged into paparazzi hell!" he declared. "There aren't enough of us to pull off this gig!"

With Kenneth Bell still at large, Mr. Dobbs was under a lot of pressure. Not only was Bell at large, but the Sweeneys, who were supposed to lead him to Bell, had slipped through his net. They weren't in any of the communes, so wherever the three of them were, they probably had access to media reports.

Activity had become so intense at the AGC that Veronica had quit her research job to act as Jake's personal assistant, going to every meeting he attended and some that he didn't. Before long the council members started asking her opinion, especially in the area of health. Finally one of them proclaimed, while gesturing toward Veronica, "You know, this just is not right!"

"I'm sorry?" Jake replied.

"It is not right," continued the councilman, "that this wonderfully talented woman comes here and *donates* her time. I nominate Mrs. Lansing to the council."

The loosely run council rarely invoked Robert's rules of order. They cast a unanimous vote in Veronica's favor before someone bothered to say, "I hope you don't mind, Mrs. Lansing."

"I'm thrilled and honored!" she responded. "And please, call me Veronica."

"In that case," continued the same councilman, "I move that Veronica be hired as an AGC full time employee to fill the vacancy left by Dr. Klein." As seconds to the motion boomed from around the table, the chairwoman reminded them that a final hiring decision could not be made until the hiring committee had made a recommendation.

A councilwoman stood and said, "Madame Chairwoman, the hiring committee is all present. I call for a committee vote. All in favor of hiring Dr. Lansing signify by saying 'aye'." A unanimous committee vote ensued, followed by a unanimous council vote.

The Chair just smiled and shook her head. "Congratulations, dear," she said, "and welcome to the anything-goes operation we call the AGC!"

That evening, Veronica quizzed her husband about the AGC. "Now that I'm on the council, I feel obligated to learn a little more about the AGC. The director of the AGC is Waylon Sommerville. What is his relationship with the council? Who has what powers?"

"It's time you learn. Which AGC do you want to learn about first?" Jake asked.

"Huh?"

"Well," he went on, "There's the Aerospace Governing Council Inc., the nonprofit corporation, and there's AGC Corp., the privately-held, for-profit corporation. Waylon is the director of AGC Corp., which is to space travel what the National Weather Service is to air travel, to space travel what Federal air traffic controllers are to air travel, and the list goes on. One sure way to secure a niche in business is to bring order to chaos. When NASA became grossly underfunded and could no longer lead the space community, we stepped in and took up the torch—took it up on every imaginable front."

"The first one with a plan wins!" she said, proclaiming the motto she had learned a few hours earlier.

"Precisely! Imagine flying airplanes without a weather service. There was no weather service for outer space," he explained.

"Weather, honey?" Veronica was confused.

"Of sorts, dear. You can't take a ship, like the one we rode to the moon, and fly it through a meteor shower; people will die. Someone has to keep track of the meteors, or at least provide a venue for the information. The AGC stepped up to the plate. Space vehicles were being launched from all over the globe, and many of these launches were not being reported to NASA. Even when they were, NASA did not have the resources to oversee the activity. The situation was growing more dangerous each day. Once again, the AGC stepped up to the plate. There is scarcely a facet of the space industry that is not monitored, specified, tested, or coordinated in some way by the AGC."

"Okay," Veronica began to understand, "so the director runs the everyday business. Does that mean that the council is like the board of directors?"

"No dear, AGC Corp. is a privately held corporation with its own board of directors that makes the business decisions. The council that you sit on is actually just an advisory council of industry professionals. They make decisions involving industry standards, space protocol, and a host of other issues involving the space industry."

Veronica began to think that she would never catch on. "So...these people the committee is talking about hiring...where will they work? What will they do?"

"Okay," Jake answered, "I see where I've confused you. To date, the only AGC Inc. employees, other than the council members—whose compensation barely covers traveling expenses—are the secretaries, technical writers, archivist, and customer service folks. The people we would hire would be a mission team. They would work for AGC Inc., who, with input from this team, would define the mission. Key persons from the team and from the committee would work with NASA and the military to reach agreement on a mission statement. With an approved mission statement, the various team functions would be divided up appropriately, and funding sought."

"Okay. Where will funding for the initial hiring of the team come from?" Veronica asked.

"Inc. has money from private donors. Corp. will make an initial large donation. We will have enough to get us through the first eight months or so." Jake explained.

Then changing the subject, he said, "But the effort needs a new, fresh poster person. You would be perfect for the job. You're beautiful, young, brilliant, and with a little coaching, articulate." Veronica's drooping jaw informed him that she could not believe what she was hearing. "Don't worry, dear heart, I wouldn't even think of putting you in that position until Bell and his thugs are under control."

"Jacob...honey, why do you think I would do well as a poster person for space travel? I've gone to the moon once; that's not exactly a large résumé."

"You're married to one of the most famous space personalities of all time, and you're much better looking than he. Seriously, my love, you have charisma, that intangible ingredient that makes everything work. You show up at a committee meeting a few times to take notes for me, and suddenly you're on the committee. What do you think that's all about? It's about charisma. You are easy to love. People meet you and they love you; they want to please you. You're a natural walking billboard for any cause you take up."

"That's sweet, honey, but I don't know if I want it."

"I understand, dear. But consider what happened at the committee meeting today. If you hang around me long enough and visibly enough the task will be in your lap, whether you want it or not. You're a magnet; there's just no denying it."

Mrs. Lansing lay awake pondering the day. The more she thought about her situation, the more she realized that Jake may be right. "Honey, are you awake?" she whispered.

"Huh?" he grunted.

"Who's Dr. Klein? The guy that I'm replacing. What was his job, and where'd he go?"

"Oh...you missed our previous meeting," he yawned and switched on a lamp. "Shawn Klein was the director of all things medical at AGC Corp."

"Wait a minute," Veronica interrupted him. "isn't Shawn Klein..."

"Yes. He's the newly appointed Surgeon General of the United States. We had just moved him from Corp to Inc. when he got, what he considered, 'a better offer.'"

"So," stammered Veronica, "I'm the first person hired onto 'the mission team?'"

"I see it's finally sinking in." Jake replied. He playfully lifted his little wife up on top of himself and declared. "There are serious consequences for waking your husband up at 1:00 A.M.!"

"Then get serious!" she demanded.

"Okay...you want serious?" he asked. Caressing her gently, he closed his eyes and slowly and reverently prayed, "Bless us, oh Lord, and these thy gifts, which we are about to receive..."

Veronica regained her composure in time to join him in, "from thy bounty, through Christ our Lord. Amen!"

Chapter 4

Still No Regrets

After a serious night's sleep Veronica awakened with thoughts of the AGC chasing through her head. She tried to flush her brain with morning prayers, but the questions remained. The twosome took in morning Mass with agents in tow. Back at the AGC, they were finally agent free in Jake's office, and their conversation turned to Veronica's new position.

"Wait a minute; I'm on the team?" she asked. "Isn't the team supposed to be composed of people going to Freqmod?"

"Remember, I didn't make the motion to hire you," countered Jake.

"I thought we were staying here to raise a family? What happened to that?" she needed to know.

"Nothing happened to that, my love. If you don't want to go to Freqmod, we won't go," he said, staring out the window into space. "The committee will still want you on the team. Making the trip is not an absolute requirement for helping to put this thing together."

"Do you want to go, Jacob? Do you want to go with me at your side?"

"I can't ask that of you, dear. I *won't* ask that of you. I promised to be your husband and the father of your children. A starship is not the ideal place for that. I want to be the ideal husband."

"Thank you, darling," she said, and gave him a hug from behind. "How dangerous do you think it is?"

Jake pondered the question as he stared out his office window. Though the morning sky was cloudless, a pervasive haze hugged the AGC air fields, blurring any distinct forms on the horizon beyond. "Extremely!" his contemplation yielded. "It's extremely dangerous. We might hit undetected space debris. Traveling over a half billion miles per hour is no walk in the park. We might make the journey just fine but be killed in a political skirmish on Freqmod, or die of some disease for which we have no immunity. Who knows? We have far more questions than we have answers. This mission is about as sure a deal as the first moon shot or Leif Erickson's voyage. As you may recall, in neither instance did they take along the wife and kids."

"You know," she said, "when the excitement wears off a little I ask myself: Why is it important that we go there at all? Is it for curiosity sake? Is there a certain amount of vanity involved?" Jake was a little taken aback by her questions.

"We go there because Christ came here," he suggested, turning to face her. "He only died once for all flesh. We must bring him to others."

"So...you don't think he would also sacrifice himself for another race? Another world?"

"When he died in Israel, the Americas *were* another world. Why didn't he live and die here also? There were people here. It took fifteen hundred years for missionaries to get here. He died once for all flesh, and for all time. It is our mission to spread the good news, even to other worlds."

"But everyone on this world, regardless of what continent they occupy, is a descendant of Adam and Eve," Veronica insisted. "Christ became one of us in order to redeem us. Wouldn't he need to become a little green guy with a huge brain and big bug eyes in order to redeem little green guys with big brains and bug eyes?"

"He's God, honey. He *chose* to become one of us, but he could have redeemed us with a wink and a nod. My *us* is just bigger than your *us*," Jake explained.

"Huh?" she asked.

"He came to heal *us*. My *us* includes all flesh on all worlds," he reiterated, and intoning the universal taunt melody, began to chant softly, "My us is bigger than your us. My us is bigger than..."

Veronica made a huge effort not to be amused, but had to smile in spite of herself. Now she was the speechless one gazing out his office window at the hazy horizon, and he gave her the hug from behind. "I don't mean to insinuate that this belief changes a thing," he said. "Missionaries don't drag their kids along. We're going to have a family, and it's too late in life to wait. God understands that."

"Honey, if the trip is so dangerous, how can you let other married couples go? You said that it was extremely..."

"Yeah, I know what I said," he interrupted.

"Well?" Veronica pressed, "Are we different? Why wouldn't the same logic apply to us?" Jake did not answer right away. She sensed that for once he didn't have a pat answer.

"I'm sorry, honey," he said. "The fact is, I've been working you a bit, softening you up to the idea of making the trip. But as you've gotten softer, the notion of putting you and our posterity into harms way has somewhat taken the wind out of my sails. Other couples will need to make their own decisions after weighing the risks and benefits. As for me, I've spent an awful lot of time looking at the cosmos, and not enough at terra firma. I'd really rather explore planet Earth with you. Besides, someone needs to baby-sit the AGC. It might as well be me."

Veronica really wanted the dust completely settled on the entire issue, once and for all. "Let's suppose you wanted to go," she conjectured, "could a forty-nine-year-old pass the physical requirements testing?"

"That's a good question," he answered, "which brings up another thing I've been meaning to talk to you about. Our old Screamin' Eagles aerobatics team has been asked if we'd care to ride along with the current team when they do their show for the AGC's twenty-fifth anniversary celebration."

"Wow! That would be great! You want to do it, don't you?"

"Of course. Problem is, even if we're just along for the ride, they don't want us passing out or dying from the G forces, and considering our ages, we would all have to train and test out for it. I'm excited because they will be flying Ranger 250Ks, a plane that was conceptualized by the AGC."

"What's so special about the Ranger?"

"It's the first real fighter plane to be built in over thirty years. It is both agile and fast *in* the envelope, and has good range and maneuverability *outside* the envelope."

"Wait a minute," Veronica said, "a fighter that goes into space?"

"Yeah! Isn't that cool! These things have a manned range that takes them to the moon, hence the name 250K. They have dual cockpits so they can be used by a team of two for space repair work."

"That's awesome, dear. Will they take you into space when you go up?" Veronica asked.

"I hope so. It's not like I've never been in outer space before, but it's always fun."

"Do you think they would take me up for a ride?"

"Well…If you train and pass the G force test, I'm betting they'd have a really hard time saying no to you."

"You know, honey," Veronica said, her tone turning serious, "I took both semesters of Aerospace Health, and they said that the G test itself can be fairly dangerous, and that the danger level rises with age because the veins and arteries are less robust."

"We can train together. If you don't think I'm robust enough, I won't go through the testing," he assured. She giggled at her thoughts. "What's so funny?" he asked.

"Oh, I was just picturing the look on Mr. Dobb's face when he finds out you're going up with the Screamin' Eagles!"

The next morning, before dawn, the telephone rang and Jake read 5:45 on his alarm clock. "Jake, sorry to call you so early," AGC's Waylon Sommerville apologized, "but there's something you need to see. Go to your computer and log onto the Martyr 1 site."

Jake managed a sleepy, "Okay, buddy," and slipped into his bathrobe. By the time he had the site open, a nightie-clad Veronica was looking over his shoulder. She was no stranger to the web site. Martyr 1 was an experimental craft, a modified planetary cruiser operating at near light speed with two chimpanzee passengers aboard. Captured on video was footage of a piece of debris tearing through the hull of the craft. The chimps, Alphonse and Loretta, screamed in horrific pain as their cabin depressurized.

"Turn it off, Jacob!" Veronica said, looking away. She wandered to the couch, sat, and curled up in an effort to warm herself against the chill of the house and the event she had just witnessed.

Jake looked up some statistics on the site, then came to join her on the couch. "They used up all six of the shield bursts within a fifteen-minute period," he said. "We had begun to think that they would go on and on until they ran out of food." He paused and sighed his exasperation. "This was a horrible death, but quicker than starvation."

"Is that what we'll say after watching a star cruiser crew explode before our eyes?!" she asked. Jake got up and walked to the bedroom. He came back and draped Veronica's bathrobe around her. She looked up with appreciative eyes and glimpsed the concern in his.

"It's all math," he said simply. "We could perhaps decrease the number of nose cones, replacing the weight with fuel. That would give us more shield bursts, but would it be enough? The cones are there to deal with dust. You can't be wasting electromagnetic shields on dust."

"Sounds like you need to construct a mathematical model of the journey, based on the limited data you have, and compute the odds to find the best solution," she advised. His smile and nodding head said in reply, *What would I do without you?*

Other than church involvement the only non-AGC activity left in Veronica's life was Fr. Scofield's class, and she was so glad to be back with all the gang.

Father Scofield visited at the podium with a student as the room began to settle. The large wood and stone lecture hall, with windows perched high in its three-story walls, had the acoustics of a carpeted gothic cathedral. With the din of visiting students subsiding, Veronica smiled as Father's resonant voice did its familiar dance about the room.

"I'm breaking with tradition today, students," he began. "No lecture. Instead, I want to challenge you and see how you apply what we have learned.

"Intelligent life has been discovered on a planet just 4.3 light years away. By the sound of the voices we hear on their radio signals, they are almost certainly humanoid. So...are they a fallen race, or are they sinless?"

Antonio, always ready for a lively debate, answered, "Fallen."

"Why do you say fallen, my friend?"

"Well, if I lived in a garden where all of my needs were met; if I walked with God and had the love of family; if I suffered no illness, war, or crime; if I slept in perfect comfort outdoors; in short, if my life was perfect, would I wake up one day and say, 'I think I'll invent the radio today?' I don't think so. Necessity and laziness are the parents of invention, and neither of these flaws would be present without the fall."

"Okay. Very good. Anyone else?"

"What if they were perfectly happy," offered Melanie, "but God wanted them to contact us as...well, say...a missionary activity?"

"Very interesting thought," Father said. "Anyone else?"

"Radio technology," offered an engineering student, "is built upon five millennia of prior art. If God told them to build a radio, they'd have to develop metallurgy, glass making, batteries, and...well...the list is almost endless. It's a very unlikely scenario."

"Very good," Father said. "I happen to agree with the fallen world theory on this one, as the technology-in-the-garden scenario seems highly unlikely. But just for discussion sake, what if they were *not* a fallen race? What could we expect to find? What kind of civilization grows up in Eden?"

"Well, that brings up one big question for me," said a student known simply as Doofus. "How could it be paradise if there's, well, no running water?"

"So, Mr. Hoffman, you think they'll stink the place up," Father surmised.

"Well…yeah! I mean…well, why not?" asked Doofus.

"What if their poop doesn't stink?" offered Veronica.

"What?" screeched Doofus. "How could that be?"

"Well," Veronica went on, "if they're not a fallen race, their bodies aren't deteriorating. Nothing in their environment is dying, so there's no need for bacteria to bring about decomposition. Maybe their fecal matter would be a sweet smelling ash."

"Hey, like my niece," a girl named Joan offered, "her poop hardly stank at all while she was being breast fed. Then I went to change her one day and didn't know they had started her on solid food. Man, I thought the poor kid had died!"

"Or," Veronica jumped back in, "maybe their food is so perfect it's completely absorbed by the body without any waste products."

"Well," Doofus added, "that would explain the fig leaves! Can't you just hear 'em after the fall? 'Whoa! Is that you or is that me? Better put a lid on it or the Big Guy's gonna know what we've been up to for sure! Whoa!'"

After class, Fr. Scofield and Veronica (and two agents) took a walk over to Mick's. One agent went ahead and one followed. Both were just far enough away for a wee bit of private conversation. Veronica said, "I wonder what your captive audience thinks of your lectures." She smirked thinking about what a possibly uncomfortable situation it might be for the agents assigned to them.

"I don't know, but I'm sure glad they're guarding you!" Father said. "And I'm wondering what they think of this doctor with all her fancy medical terms."

"Huh?"

"Terms like *poop*."

She giggled and changed the subject, "Father, I have a question. On a world like Freqmod, if theirs is a fallen race, would God live among them and die for their sins just as he did ours?"

"Well…I really haven't completely thought this scenario through," he said, "but Holy Mother Church teaches that Christ died once, for all time, and for all flesh. While we can be fairly certain that the church fathers had not considered intelligent life on other planets when elucidating this dogma, one could argue that Freqmod is more accessible to us today than say...Hawaii was to the apostles."

With mock annoyance she asked, "Have you been talking to Jacob about this?"

"Nope. Did he say the same thing?"

She just smiled. "But what if there's intelligent life in a distant Galaxy?" she pressed.

"I don't know. You're more the scientist than I, Dr. Lansing. My understanding is that technology advances exponentially: the deeper the prior art foundation, the more rapid the changes. Two hundred years ago horse transportation was common. Two hundred years from now the unimaginable will be reality. And two millennia from now? Wow! It took nearly two millennia for the Good News to get from Israel to Hawaii, so...other galaxies? Maybe."

"Hmm," she pondered.

"Hmm? Hmm what?" Fr. Scofield pried.

"Well, in a way I feel as if I've missed my calling," she said. "I really feel called to do missionary work, and I'm trying to decide if this trip qualifies as such."

"It certainly does in my mind," he replied. "I'd be on that ship in a heartbeat if I was invited, but I'm not qualified."

"What do you mean?" Veronica asked.

"Well, Jake tells me that the crew will experience this trip as a twenty-six month voyage because of relativity, but the actual time lapse will be nearly sixty-four months—a twelve-year round trip—so it's not as if a new batch of priests can be sent in a timely fashion. The request, by radio, would take over four years to get here, and the priests, if available, would take six years to get there. Better to send an apostle on the first ship."

"I'm sorry?" she said, looking confused.

"A bishop, dear. They need to send a bishop," Fr. Scofield informed her. "He can ordain priests as required."

"Oh. You wouldn't just send a lone bishop. Even the apostles went out two by two," Veronica noted.

"Well, I'm still not *one*," Father pointed out. The two had a nice breakfast together and caught up on recent events. "I'll see you tomorrow," she called as they parted. Father took on a blank look. "The wedding?" she offered.

"Oh yeah," he said, "Antonio and Jeanine!"

"Do I need to call you in the morning?" she teased.

Antonio and Jeanine wed the next day huddled with family and friends in Immaculate Conception church while rain pummeled the stained glass. Though the skies were dark, all was sweetness and light within the sanctuary. Veronica thought she had never seen a more beautiful couple, and whispered to Jake, "Aren't they just darling? I can't wait to see their kids!" Then, placing her hand on her tummy, she slipped into a little daydream.

The next morning, the Lansings slept in. They had decided to go to the eleven o'clock Sunday Mass. Still snuggled in each other's arms at half past nine, they heard a knock at the door. Mr. Dobbs started apologizing just as soon as a bathrobe-clad Jake opened the door. "I know we're an hour early, Dr. Lansing, please forgive us."

Jake smiled. "Alvin, Sunday's your day off. To what do we owe the pleasure?"

"I'm sorry Jacob, but there will be no pleasure in this," Dobbs insisted. Looking at Veronica he said, "You may want to sit down, Mrs. Lansing. A horrible thing happened last night. Juanita Escobar was murdered on her way home from the wedding dance."

When Veronica's ensuing hysteria had finally lapsed into sobbing, Jake asked, "Bell?"

"We don't have a coroner's report yet," Dobbs said, "but at first glance it sure looks like his work."

When the couple had dressed, the two agents begrudgingly accompanied them to church. Dobbs didn't want them to go *anywhere*. They all sat in the choir loft and Veronica sobbed softly through the entire Mass. When they were all back to the house, Mr. Dobbs said, "Apparently Bell has enough respect for Fitch's creed that he refuses to use a gun. Both victims have died of multiple knife wounds. Please help us to get the word out to the aerospace community to have no one go anywhere alone. Juanita Escobar might still be with us had she not been out alone."

The next morning, Jake awoke to the sound of his wife gagging in the bathroom. He poked his head in and said, "You all right?"

"One of my best friends was just murdered! I'm tense as the Wicked Witch of the West at a water park, and you want to know if I'm all right!" she barked. She threw up in the stool. Jake waited outside until he heard a flush, then came in and rubbed her back while she hunched over the stool. She became faint, and as he caught her in his arms she started to weep bitterly. When the sobbing subsided, she began to apologize profusely, which, of course, brought more tears.

"What's wrong with me?" she sobbed. "Why'd I talk to you that way?"

When Jake had convinced her that, in extreme circumstances, even the best people say things they regret, the conversation turned to the day's tasks.

"I'm scheduled to take the old 'slingshot' test at 1:30 this afternoon," he said. "I've arranged for Melanie to come over and stay with you."

"You have?" she sniffled.

"Yes. She's bringing lunch…and another agent, of course."

"You're so sweet. I don't deserve you!" she insisted, and quickly added, "You be very careful!"

That afternoon, when Jake stepped out of the house, Mr. Dobbs came out of the rented house across the street. "Where are you headed, Doc?" he asked, when near enough not to be overheard.

"Over to Corp."

"I'm right behind you," Dobbs said, and climbed into a car with Jones at the wheel. All went well until Jake cut them off by squeezing through an intersection on the last bit of a yellow light.

"Damn it!" mumbled Dobbs. "Run the damn light!" But it was too late. Jones nosed a little into the intersection, but could not squeeze through the heavy traffic. "Throw 'er in L!" Dobbs hollered. Jones obediently shifted to levitronic drive. The car rose twenty feet off the pavement and charged into the busy intersection, only to be struck by another levitronic vehicle. Their Nexus LX twirled like a boomerang, lost altitude, and plopped down atop the van of a passing semi. Dobbs was beyond hollering. "What did you do?" he asked, quietly.

"It appears we're out of flight time, sir."

"Which means you need to push the little red button on the steering wheel before taking off, or we have no ACA (Automated Collision Avoidance)," Dobbs noted.

"Yeah," Jones said, hanging his head.

"That would explain the blinking red light on the instrument panel that says *Danger*," Dobbs said, rubbing it in. It was the little things that got under Alvin Dobbs' skin. It was amazing how calm he could be while riding in a wrecked car atop a semi headed in the wrong direction. The semi came to a stop and Dobbs called another agent to come and pick them up. "You'll need to fly in here to get us off of this thing. Don't pull a Jones. I don't need two wrecks on the budget."

Dobbs hung up quickly to take another call. It was Lieutenant Eggars with the police.

"The Sweeneys are in my office," Eggars said. "They witnessed Escobar's murder and were sickened by it. It seems that terrorism was a good idea till they saw what it looked like. They're afraid of Bell and are seeking protection, but most importantly, they believe that Bell is committed to taking out Jacob *today!*"

Dobbs and Jones climbed out of the wreck and waited atop the semi van. "Do you suppose there's an easy way to climb off of this thing?" Dobbs asked.

"I don't know, but I'm not in any hurry," Jones replied, nodding in the direction of the truck driver who was staring up at them. In a few minutes they were picked up by another agent, but air traffic wasn't flowing much faster than ground traffic. When they finally arrived at Corp, police officers were standing outside discussing the situation.

"What's happening?" Dobbs demanded.

"Dr. Lansing's not here." They told him.

"What? What?! His car's right there!" He screamed. He stormed inside. "Frank," he said to the front door guard, "Dr. Lansing's not here?"

"His card's not scanned in right now, Mr. Dobbs," Frank said.

"Were you out here at lunch hour?" Dobbs asked.

"No, the new guy was."

"What new guy? What's his name?"

"I dunno. He scanned in his card and the door opened for him. Said he was on for lunch hour. Let's look here," Frank said, and opened the computer log. "That's funny, this says Arturo was here. Art wasn't here."

Dobbs was beside himself. "Did the new guy look like this?" he asked, showing Frank a picture of Bell.

"Kinda, except he had a mustache," Frank said.

Dobbs pushed by him and ran to the front desk. "What test room was Dr. Lansing scheduled for?"

The secretary stared at her screen for a moment. "Room 33B," she said.

Dobbs hollered, "Show us Frank! NOW! RUN!"

Frank went running with Dobbs and Jones in tow. As they approached 33B, Dobbs motioned them to quiet down. He looked through the small, mesh-reinforced glass window in the door and saw someone hurrying his direction. He motioned the others against the wall. The door flew open. Bell spilled into the hallway and was greeted by the words "Halt! FBI!" He turned toward them, and seeing two revolvers trained on him, hurled his knife at them and leapt over a banister, plunging thirty feet to a concrete floor below. Jones hunted for the nearest stairwell that would take him down to Bell's limp body. Dobbs and Frank rushed into 33B. The centrifuge technician lay face down on the floor, a bad gash in the back of his head.

"Jacob?" yelled Dobbs, but no one answered. The centrifuge was turning. He looked at the control panel and found the emergency off button and pressed it. Waiting for the centrifuge to slow down, Dobbs had a minute to look at the control board. Whoever was strapped in still had a slow, weak pulse and slow, shallow breathing. Minutes later they pulled Dr. Lansing from the slingshot and placed him on a stretcher.

When the phone rang at the Lansing house, no one wanted to answer it. Finally Mel picked up. It was Dobbs. "You and Mrs. Lansing need to get to the hospital," he told Melanie.

As they came in the emergency entrance, a gurney with a body fully draped rolled by. Veronica caught her breath with her hand over her mouth, and held Melanie close to her. Mr. Dobbs saw them and came over.

"Mrs. Lansing...ma'am, that's Bell's body that just went by. Your husband is in the emergency room."

"How is he? What happened?" she managed to say.

"He's unconscious. That's all we know for now. Apparently Bell overpowered the centrifuge operator and turned up the speed of the unit, taking your husband up to the equivalent of ten G's. The force caused him to lose consciousness. We don't know how long he was at that force level before we arrived."

Ten minutes later the doctors were out of the emergency room. "I'm Dr. Morton," one of them said. "Dr. Lansing's heart beat and breathing are approaching normal resting rates. We will be keeping a careful eye on him. A brain scan indicates some activity. We're unsure just how long he was at the higher G level. The reduced blood flow to the head could have serious ramifications for a full recovery. I'm sorry. All we can do now is keep him fed and warm and pray that he will heal."

The two women went in, kissed him, and sat with him until evening. Mel went to get food and brought something back for Veronica.

"It pains me to see him all hooked up with tubes and wires. He's always been so strong, and now he's utterly helpless," Veronica lamented.

Mel went home about nine, but Veronica stayed the night, and the next night. After several days of refusing to leave his side, the doctor pleaded with her. "Mrs. Lansing, your devotion to your husband is heart-warming, but you're a doctor; you know that this kind of healing can take months. You really need to take care of yourself. Some rest in your own bed would be good. We will take good care of Jacob."

She took his advice. Her own bed did feel good, though horribly empty. Twenty days passed, then thirty. Dignitaries came and went, as did visitors from all walks of life. Thousands of get well cards kept her busy during the day.

On a Tuesday morning, day thirty-six, she sat with her chair facing the window, enjoying the sunshine on her face. Jake made a small motion with his hand, and she heard the faint rustling sound it made. She turned his way, and his eyes were open. She was instantly stroking his hair, and kissing his face, and talking the sweetest love talk to him. At last he spoke a belabored "Veronica."

"Yes, my love, I'm here for you. I love you so much! We're going to have a baby, Jacob. You're going to be a daddy! You have to hurry up and get all better!" She had pushed the nurses' alarm if for no other reason than to share her joy. They rushed in to find a conscious patient, began to test all of his vitals, and informed the doctor of the change in his condition. Veronica did not go home that night. She slept in the chair with her face near Jake's, watching him as he slept.

In the morning a cheery nurse looked in on the two. Veronica was still asleep. The cheery fingers that went to check a pulse fell on a cold wrist, and their owner caught her breath and jumped back in horror. Veronica awakened to see the look on the poor woman's face and knew instantly what had happened. The long wait was over, but Daddy wasn't coming home. She took one long last look at her husband's remains. Jake had received the last rights. He was squared away with his maker. Veronica did not doubt that the man who had lived a life of love would now be one with that Love.

Later, after Mel and Fr. Scofield had been contacted and the word was spreading, she knelt before the Blessed Sacrament, but she felt not the usual solace and doubted that the questions that haunted her would classify as prayers. *Why did Jacob wake up and talk to me? What was that, a cruel joke? What part of my prayers didn't you get?* She shuddered a bit, stunned by her own raw emotion. She didn't claim the words running through her head; they were just there. Still, her heart labored under what seemed to be a ton of broken innocence.

She wondered about her faith; was it real? Jesus' words ran through her head: *Blessed are those who have not seen and yet believe.* She had seen. Her mother had been cured of an incurable disease. *What would my faith be without the signs?* she asked herself. She thought about the many faithless people she encountered in everyday life and wondered now if she had been judgmental toward them. Had she been proud? Proud of the gift? Was Jacob's death a wakeup call to a holier-than-thou?

She shuddered at the thought. *Don't try to make yourself the center of everything!* she thought. *Pride. Presumption. Self-centeredness. You're compiling quite a list. Maybe you should give yourself a break and just be what you know how to be: God's little girl who thanks him for everything, even this. After all, Jacob is in heaven! Do you believe?*

There is a point when one's world is turned upside down and life seems absurd. These are the times when souls try to reinvent themselves, wither, or allow themselves to be grafted to a stronger tree. Veronica felt plenty withered. It seemed that half of her was missing. It was a time to numb the pain by filling up her life with the necessary activities, like planning a funeral. As a couple they had frequented the wonderful little church of the Immaculate Conception. *That will be the place*, she thought, and went to speak with Fr. Scofield.

"Veronica, Jacob was one of those people often called 'larger than life.' There are four presidents who will want to attend his funeral, and numerous other politicians, papal nuncios, and heads of state. In short, a torrential outpouring of condolence is headed your direction. If you like, I will confer with the funeral director on how you might best accommodate such a gathering."

Veronica agreed, but as she walked away she turned and smiled for perhaps the first time since Jake's death. "I know what Jacob would like," she said. "His favorite church in the entire world was the Shrine of the Immaculate Conception in Washington D.C. Let's have his funeral there!"

Veronica's smile warmed Father's soul, and tears filled his eyes. She went to him and embraced him. "I'm sorry," she said, "I've been so attached to my own pain that I haven't noticed anyone else's!"

Jake's funeral was a spectacular event, attended by thousands, and covered by all the major media. Six bishops concelebrated. As at other times, Veronica sensed that the Jake she knew and loved was just the poetic prelude to the epic that comprised the whole man. That humble man had affected the world broadly and to great depth.

Back at home a couple days later, she awoke hungry. The aroma of onion, bell pepper, cheese, and egg, all perking in a puddle of butter, drifted from her kitchen. Bright, smiling, and humming a tune, Melanie greeted her from the stove: "I hope you're not feeling too queasy this morning, Auntie, I've made a pile of food."

Veronica smiled. She had rested well for the first time in days. "Odd," she said, "I'm not feeling queasy. In fact, I was fine yesterday too. I just didn't think about it with the traveling and all. You know, it's probably time to go see a doctor and have this pregnancy checked out."

"Ronnie, *you* are a doctor."

"It's not good to practice medicine on yourself, Mel. I don't even know where my Omniscan is. I haven't seen it since before the wedding." Still at the stove, Melanie heard Veronica sniffling behind her.

"What is it, sweetie?" she said, turning and rubbing her shoulders.

"Oh…talking about doctors just made me think of Juanita. She would have been my first choice."

"Today might be a good day to go," Melanie proposed, as cheerily as she could. "I'll go with you if you like."

"That would be great, honey. Thanks."

"Say, I know where your Omniscan is, Ronnie. It's in the hall closet upstairs. I saw it there when I was helping you get your luggage down for the trip."

Melanie retrieved the instrument for her aunt, who immediately plopped it onto her full tummy and attempted to turn it on. "Humph. Dead batteries!" she lamented.

"How about the antique stethoscope that's decorating your wall in the living room?" Melanie asked. She fetched the antique and laughed at her aunt's grimace as the instrument's cold metal bell made contact with her bare tummy. Veronica handed the listening end of it to Melanie.

"I'm not the doctor," Melanie objected.

"It doesn't work very well to listen to things inside of your own body," Veronica insisted.

Melanie began listening. "I hear *your* heartbeat...and your breakfast!" she laughed, then listened intently as she moved the scope from place to place.

After a while, Veronica couldn't stand the suspense. "Mel, I think you're wasting your time. I don't even think you're supposed to be able to hear anything with one of these at this stage of gestation."

Mel handed her the ear pieces. "Here, you listen," she insisted. But Veronica, now a bit nervous, insisted they go see a doctor.

They visited the clinic of a classmate, a Dr. Jeffrey Weaver. "Good morning, Veronica. My condolences on the loss of your husband," he said.

"Thanks, Jeff. I need you to help me take care of the gift Jacob has left with me."

"I'm delighted to hear that you think of your pregnancy that way," he said with a smile. "How many periods have you missed now?"

"I'm a week past my third missed period."

"How has the pregnancy been going?"

"I've had a fair amount of morning sickness up until the last three days," she said.

"She ate like a body builder this morning without so much as a belch!" Mel reported. Veronica gave her a little pat on the arm, and a smile.

But Dr. Weaver didn't smile. He said, "Let's take a look." He placed his Omniscan on her tummy and began to run the diagnostics. After a minute of looking at the scope's screen he asked, "When you say you've missed three periods, are we talking normal twenty-eight day periods, which would put you at about...eleven weeks?"

"That should be right," Veronica answered. She sensed his apprehension. "Jeff, what's wrong?"

"We should be detecting a heartbeat, brain activity, and lots of other things," he declared softly. "I'm ordering up a blood test."

"Jeff, do you think...?" it hurt too much to finish.

"We need to know what's going on in there," he said. "You're a doctor, Veronica; you know that it's the developing baby's control of the whole mother/child hormonal system that causes the morning sickness. I'm sorry, dear. You've had so much to suffer. I don't want to guess. Let's just see what the blood test shows us."

As Veronica and Melanie drove home, the silence in the car was deafening. Finally Veronica broke it with, "Mel...don't leave me alone tonight! Please?" and she started to cry. Melanie assured her that she would be there for her. Veronica knew that the Omniscan was hardly ever wrong. Was ordering the blood test Dr. Weaver's way of breaking the news slowly and gently?

Shortly after settling in at home, the phone rang. Veronica just sat and watched it ring. Finally Melanie picked up. It was Dr. Weaver. Melanie handed the phone to Veronica, who sat frozen faced as Jeff affirmed what she had not wanted to believe. She listened numbly as he told her that, if her body did not slough off the remains of the deceased child in a timely fashion, she would need to undergo a procedure to cleanse her womb—all things that Veronica already knew, yet each word hit her like a slow, dull bullet. There would be no dying child to baptize or to hold. Though death is never pretty, death without a corpse seemed unusually cruel.

She thanked the doctor for his call, and for his kindness and well wishes, and hanging up the phone, stared at the large picture of Jacob hanging above the mantel. Her desolation was now complete! And yet, as the Evil One taunted her heart, she beat him back with questions *of* the heart. *If I had to do it all over*, she asked herself, *would I do it again?* She pulled Jake's picture down from the wall and placed her forehead against his.

"In a heartbeat!" she declared through sobs, "In a heartbeat!"

Chapter 5

Jake's Friends

Lavender's healing bouquet owned the air and hijacked Veronica's cares as she sank into a steamy tub. The hot water soothed the knot in her neck, which she grasped with both hands and attempted to untie. The telephone rang, but she did not feel like talking to anyone, and the voice-mail message went to speaker.

"Mrs. Lansing, this is Waylon," the voice said.

Waylon? she thought, *Waylon never calls me.* Waylon Summerville, the director of AGC Corp, was her employee, but they had barely gotten to know each other. "Speakerphone," she commanded the device. "Waylon, this is Veronica. Sorry I didn't pick up right away, but you caught me in the tub."

"Oh, so sorry to disturb you, Mrs. Lansing…"

"Quite all right, Mr. Sommerville, and please, call me Veronica. What's on your mind, my friend?"

"Actually, Veronica, I'm here with Captain Tessa Oakley. She's on loan this week from the Air Force and has been going over some things with a team of my colleagues, so if you don't mind a double invasion of privacy, I'll put you on speaker."

"Speaker it is," she answered.

"Good morning, Dr. Lansing," Captain Oakley greeted her.

"Good morning, Captain. Now that the formalities are out of the way, may I call you Tessa?"

"Of course, Doctor, I mean, Veronica."

"Veronica, Tessa and I are old friends," Waylon informed her. "I invited her here because I have a very high regard for her fine technical mind and vast experience."

"You sound black, Tessa," Veronica noted.

"Black as coal," Tessa confirmed, bewildered as to what the point might be. "You sound white," she shot back.

Veronica chuckled at her spunk. "When you meet me, you'll be wondering where I'm hiding the seven dwarves," she said, sliding lower into her bath.

"The Freqmod mission needs more women and more genetic diversity, Tess," Waylon explained. "Veronica has read my mind. I would very much like for you to become part of the mission team and will not attempt to hide the fact that I'm trying to lure you in."

"Is it working, Tess?" Veronica asked.

"I'm very intrigued, Ma'am," Tessa answered.

"Good! Are you fertile, Tess?"

"I beg your pardon?" Tessa asked, raising her eyebrows.

Waylon started laughing. "This is a side of you I've not seen, Veronica. I'll have to catch you in the tub more often!" Then turning to Tessa he explained: "Because this mission will take people such a great distance from Earth, procreation may become a vital long-term survival necessity, so this crew will be comprised of an equal number of men and women, and fertility is a requirement."

"I see," Tessa said, smiling at Veronica's shock-value humor.

"About why I called, Veronica," Waylon said. "Tessa and my colleagues have been busy for some time following up on your husband's work, digging through his notes and computations. In his notes Jake mentions a suggestion that came from you. He acted on your suggestion and completed a risk analysis to find the best balance between electromagnetic shields and nose cone layers. Did he talk to you about this?"

"The risk analysis *was* my suggestion, but he didn't inform me of any findings," she told him.

"By the way," Waylon said, "Jake's notes also say that you suggested naming the star ship Star Covenant. I've been bouncing the name off of a few folks around here, and so far everyone loves it."

"Great!" Veronica responded. "It's easier to rally around something that has a name."

"You're right," Waylon agreed. "Anyway, Jake completed this shield vs. nose cone analysis just minutes before he headed in for the slingshot test, so he had no opportunities to share it with anyone. Tessa and my team have been checking his calculations, and he was right on. What I have to tell you is not good news, Veronica. Calculating the best possible balance between the two safety measures, Jake projected that Star Covenant has a seventeen percent chance of arriving at Freqmod safely."

"Wow, that good, huh?" the wet, relaxed Veronica commented dryly. "So, if we send six ships and crews, statistically, one of them will arrive safely."

"I guess that's one way to look at it," Tessa laughed. "Do you suppose anyone's going to sign up for that? Do you know a bunch of people with a martyr complex just dying to give it all?"

Veronica, worn with grief and relaxed enough to accidentally drown in her bath, suddenly came to attention. "What did you just say, Tess?" she asked.

"I asked if you know a bunch of people with a martyr complex who would…"

"That's it, Tess! That's it!" Veronica proclaimed gleefully as she splashed to an upright position.

"What? Veronica, a seventeen percent chance of success would require kamikazes, not martyrs!" Waylon insisted.

"No, no…Martyr *ships*, Waylon, *unmanned* Martyr ships! Send a half dozen or so out in front of Covenant to clear the path. Wouldn't that reduce the risk to an acceptable level?" she asked, excited about her insight.

Tessa thought out loud: "With no passengers or payload, all power could be devoted to shields and drive…"

Waylon thought for a moment. "My gosh…Veronica, that just might work!" he proclaimed at last.

"It really might!" Tessa agreed. "Veronica, you're a genius!"

"I'll get the team working on this right away!" Waylon declared. "You just sit back and enjoy your bath, boss lady. You've already earned your keep for the day!"

"Alvin! Alvin! Alvin! What is with the martyr complex?" Jasmine Babasa asked Mr. Dobbs from across the table.

"What do you mean?" Dobbs asked.

"You know darn well what I'm talking about!" she insisted. The six-foot-two, amber-blond Capt. Jasmine Babasa, also known as Jazz or Bubba, leaned forward on her elbows. "Why'd you tell Spinelli that you were the one who authorized the Lansing phone taps? You don't need to take a bullet for me, Alvin. I can look out for myself. What's with the misguided loyalty?"

"If you wouldn't have given me permission, I'd have done it anyway," Dobbs insisted. "You know that. So why should you take the blame?"

"Because that's what managers do!" Jasmine insisted. A formidable FBI captain, Jasmine Babasa tried to run a tight ship, but

Dobbs was her bad egg, always floating to the top where he was noticed for all the wrong reasons. Not so oddly, he was also her most effective agent. "Look, Alvin, you know how I operate. I let you do your thing. You break some rules here and there, try to keep a low profile and you get stuff done. There was a time when getting stuff done was what mattered in the agency. It's not that way anymore. Spinelli threw this last offense of yours on top of a heap of screw-ups he's been collecting. On this case alone, besides unauthorized wire-tapping, you paid exorbitant prices for information, you let the Sweeneys slip through your net, you used up all of your air license hours and smashed a levitronic vehicle in the process, and you left the scene of an accident…"

"I left the scene of an accident to save a man's life!"

"I know, Alvin."

"And what's with givin' a man a flippin' flyin' vehicle that's only licensed for a lousy twenty hours of air time per month? We're undermanned, under-equipped, and…"

"I know, Alvin. I know. You're preaching to the choir."

Mr. Dobbs noticed that Jasmine was still wearing her I.D. pin from GGT, her 'place of employment.' *Gundersen, Gundersen, and Tradewell Legal and Financial Services* the gaudy gold and black plastic pin said. Unbeknownst to the folks at GGT, the F.B.I. had assigned Babasa to seek employment there so that, undercover, she could protect Jacob Lansing's interest from any subterfuge the liberalized Mole Nation might attempt.

"And speaking of wire tapping," Dobbs said, "didn't you tap the hell out of GGT? Hell, you tapped into all of their computers and set up perimeter monitors. You probably know more about Jacob Lansing's finances than Jacob Lansing ever did! You did all kinds of illegal crap over there."

"I didn't get caught, Alvin. No one turned in a complaint. I shouldn't need to tell you that that's the nature of the game!"

"You took me out to lunch to fire me, didn't you, Bubba?" Dobbs asked, searching Jasmine's face. It was a good face to search, one he had enjoyed searching for years. She had an infectious smile and luscious lips. Her well proportioned nose had a cute little bump, and small but deep, piercing brown eyes rested on high, prominent cheek bones. But Mr. Dobb's eyes had searched more than Jasmine Babasa's lovely face. Indeed, with difficulty would any healthy male ignore the rest of her. Her ample breasts were enthroned high on a relatively short torso, which terminated in wide but trim hips, all supported by slender, perfect legs that went on forever.

"That's what I've always liked about you, my man. You have that ESP thing going," Jasmine said. Her smile faded and she sat quietly looking at her hands.

Dobbs broke the silence. "It's all right, Bubba," he said.

"No, Alvin, it's not!" she insisted. "I told Spinelli that *I* authorized the wire taps and that you weren't driving the car that got smashed, but he didn't want to hear it. He says that if I don't fire you, he'll fire me and then he'll fire you. Maybe I should call his bluff."

"Spinelli doesn't bluff, Jazz," Dobbs asserted. "I've watched him work his way up the ladder. I was always pulling off too much goofy crap to make my own way up the ladder. If one of us has to go, let it be me. I'm eligible for pension. Don't know why I'm still hangin' around. Too dumb to retire, I guess."

"We need good men like you. I hate this!" Jasmine sighed.

"You don't need trouble like me," he said.

"What will you do?" she asked.

"In retirement? I don't know. I'll stick around, I like it here. Probably keep my apartment. Maybe I'll do some freelance investigation. We can stay in touch."

"I'd like that. We've been working together for nine years. Where does the time go?"

Dobbs laughed. "Jazz, I'll never forget the first day you sashayed into the department. You turned a lot of heads. All of a sudden everybody needed a partner!" He recalled that first sight of her, dressed in her perennial miniskirt. Her long slender thighs were her calling card. Supporting a wide hip frame, they always had an inviting amount of open air between them, a gap that had narrowed as she filled out and became the mature woman of thirty-two who sat before him. *What am I doing thinking about my partner's thighs!* he chastised himself, and then thought, *Wait a minute, she's not my partner anymore! Or my boss!*

"But partner, you were the lucky man!" Jasmine reminisced. "I wish it would've stayed that way. I mean, I was proud to be your boss, but it wasn't near as much fun as being your partner. You taught me everything I know."

"Thanks kid. So what's going on with the AGC/Mole Nation case now? Does everyone consider this thing all done? Are they pulling you out of GGT?"

"The official answer, my man, is that you no longer work for the FBI, so I can't tell you."

"And the unofficial answer?"

"I'm hanging around a week or two to tie up any loose ends. After all this time I don't think Josh Gundersen suspects that I'm anything other than a legal secretary, which I can't understand, because I'm one stinking poor secretary!"

"I have one regret in all of this, Jasmine," Dobbs said quietly.

"What's that?"

"I regret that, being your partner and subordinate, I was never able to...ask you out," Dobbs muttered. *Where'd that come from?* he asked himself. Jasmine was speechless. She just sat and looked into his eyes for a moment, then at her hands. "I'm sorry, Jazz..." Dobbs began.

"No, no, no, Alvin...gosh...don't apologize! That's sweet man! Look, um...I've never really thought about whether I'm romantically attracted to you, maybe because of the work situation, I don't know, but I love you like a brother, man! Gosh we had fun, didn't we?"

"We sure did, partner! So what do you think about me now, now that the work situation is gone?" *I can't believe I'm doing this!*

"Are you asking me out, Alvin? I...I just fired you!"

"So?"

"Look. Hey...my beds barely cooled off from the last fool, I'm..."

"Jazz, I just wanna spend time with you—I mean, like an old-fashioned date, just a man and a woman enjoying each other's company—no pressure. I won't even try to kiss you! Promise!"

"Alvin, that sounds really nice. Let's put it on the calendar."

"You know, Jazz, there's another thing about being fired that I like."

"What could that be?"

"You've called me Alvin more times in the last nine minutes than in the previous nine years!"

"Listen, jerk, if you're trying to get me to cry, you're getting awfully close," she declared, breaking into a warm smile.

At Chubb's Sports Grill, Jasmine tucked her miniskirt under her thigh and wrapped her ankles around the single post of her bar stool. As usual, she had commenced her Saturday evening on Chubb's bowling lanes, gracefully launching her sixteen-pounder with deadly accuracy. She liked bowling in a tight miniskirt; it added an "extra challenge." A band named Misplaced Aggression was pounding out a raucous rhythm and Jasmine had already turned down two invitations to dance.

To her right sat her long-time friend and high school classmate, Martha: Martha the mouth. Martha's tightly-attired full figure jiggled rhythmically to laughter generated by their vulgar conversation. If she wasn't cursing, she was laughing. To Jasmine's left sat Martha's younger cousin, Zelda, a tawny, scrawny mass of sinew and sass whose every gram of body fat appeared to have migrated to her little beer belly. Martha and Zelda were busy cackling at each other's worn out stories.

"The funniest thing ever," Martha announced, "was what we did to that little sweetie-two-shoes down on the beach. You remember that?"

"I'll never forget the look on the little wench's face," Zelda answered, "and our little lesson put an end to her stupid moralizing in the school hallways!"

"There she was, just minding her own business, walking down the beach in her proper little swimsuit, watching the birdies fly, and all of a sudden—bam!—she's butt naked!" Martha hooted. The two laughed until it seemed they would fall off of their stools. Jasmine just sat silently sipping her drink. She had heard the story before and hadn't thought it funny then. They weren't even getting a courtesy laugh this time. "Hey Jazz, what's with the long face?" Martha asked at last.

"Sorry, Mouth, just not in the mood," Jasmine answered. "Besides, what did that poor little gal do that was so hideous that you would strip a fifteen-year-old stark naked and leave her on a public beach? What the hell kind of trashy people do something like that and still laugh about it fifteen years later?"

"Whoa! Is this still because of your breakup with Doug?" Martha asked, ignoring the chastisement. "You know what your problem is, don't you, Jazz? I keep telling you: You gotta quit trying to make it permanent. They're men, Jazz. If God meant for 'em to stay in one spot he'd've made 'em with roots. They can be a lot of fun, but ya can't let 'em get under your skin."

"I see. Treat them like sex machines so I can be happy like you, huh Mouth? Would the world be a better place if we were all like you?"

"Hell no! Ha! Ya see, that's the beauty of it. I'm getting way more than my fair share of everything, especially fun! What do I give a damn about leaving the world a better place? I won't be here, so what's the damn difference?"

What am I doing here? Jasmine wondered. *I've outgrown this life, this place, and these people. In fact, I outgrew them years ago. Am I too numb to move on, or too scared?* She chugalugged the remaining two thirds of her Long Island iced tea, stood, and hitched her purse strap over her shoulder.

"You're not going home already!" Zelda insisted.

"I'm afraid so, girls. I won't spoil your fun anymore."

The cool night air was sobering, but not nearly enough. She wedged a heel in a sidewalk crack and nose-dived onto the hood of a car that had just been parked. The man in the car quickly came to her rescue.

"You okay?" he asked, gently grasping her shoulders to help her up.

"Yeah, I'm okay. These heels can be tricky," Jasmine said as she turned to face the stranger. She was pleasantly surprised to behold an army man in dress uniform. His face, though fairly expressionless, reminded her of Alvin's. *Kinda like Dobbs without the droll smile,* she thought. Though not overly handsome he looked quite magical in his uniform and was a lot taller than Dobbs. "Sorry about landing on your car," Jasmine apologized as she straightened out her attire. The stranger stooped and retrieved her severed heel and offered it to her. "Thanks," Jasmine said reaching out to take it, "but I don't think it's repairable."

He withdrew it and dropped into his pocket saying, "Then I'll keep it as a souvenir of the night the prettiest lady in town crashed on my hood."

"You're very kind," she said, stooping to pull off the shoe that still had a heel. He grasped her opposite shoulder to help her maintain balance. When fully upright and heelless, she realized that he was actually taller than she. "Do they teach you all this chivalry stuff in the Army?" she asked.

"They train us to be savages on the battlefield and gentlemen in town," he said. He was close enough now to pick up the scent of her Long Island tea. "Look, pretty lady, you're not going to drive, are you?"

"No sir, I'm not; my car is," she declared. "My new wheels do all the work, iced tea or no iced tea."

"Are you sure? I'd be glad to see you home."

"Quite sure, my knight in shining armor. Ya just can't beat technology. But if you would be so kind as to walk me to my magic carpet, I would greatly appreciate it."

"Which way?" he asked.

"North, my good man," she answered. He offered her his arm and they began to walk, but she soon became so unsteady that he put his arm around her waist and she reciprocated. Finally at her car, she turned and kissed his cheek. "It says something about my pathetic life when the most fun all evening is the walk to the car," she proclaimed.

Unsure whether or not her comment was a compliment, Mr. Army simply asked, "Are you sure you'll be all right? I can give you a ride. I can help you retrieve the car tomorrow."

"No, no. Look, I'll be fine. These new LXs are unbeatable," she said, sliding into the driver's seat. "See here: it scans my retina, I hit the *home* button, and I wake up in front of my apartment. Pretty cool, huh?" In the aftermath of the Lansing case, her department had opted to purchase unlimited air time for all of their levitronic vehicles.

"Well, good night then," he said, stooping with his face close to hers through the side window.

"Good night," she said, turning and planting a kiss on his lips. "And thanks for being a gentleman."

She hit the home button, but the car didn't make a move because of Army Man's close proximity. A computer generated voice said, "Please step away from the vehicle." The soldier stepped back, and the car rose swiftly to an altitude of thirty feet, turned, and sped off to the south. As she rode home, she thought about Martha's question: What difference does it make if we leave the world a better place? *Maybe Martha's right,* she thought. *If this is it, if this is all there is, who gives a damn!*

Fr. Scofield paced thoughtfully before a full house, collecting his thoughts and praying for wisdom while the students settled in. "It has been said," he began loudly, stopping to give them a bit more time to settle. When the last shoe had shuffled and the last note book plopped, he resumed softly: "It has been said by saints and philosophers that each one of us is born with a God-sized hole in our hearts. It has been said that if God did not exist, we'd have to create him. Man is a religious being. That being said, if you want sure proof that the God of the Judeo-Christian ethos is the true God, just take a jaunt through history and see what kind of gods humankind invents—suffice it to say, they are not gods of love."

Veronica smiled within, wondering, *Are this man's lectures sermons, or are his sermons lectures?* She decided his lectures really were fifty-minute sermons that included more footnotes than the average Sunday homily. The university graciously allowed alumni to sit in on classes in which they were already accredited, and the schedule allowed Veronica to take in Father's lecture and still get to work on time.

"In the early half of the last century," he went on, "there was a mass exodus from traditional religion and its strong ethos of self-discipline. But we are religious beings; the rejection of one ethos is an invitation to a replacement. A rejection of religious convention that demands self-discipline always paves the way for self-indulgent invention, resulting in religions that demand that we discipline others. Pride, of course, is the all-necessary and constant ingredient in this process. Mole Nation is, perhaps, the best example I can sight today of such a religion." He tried not to look at Veronica. He didn't need his eyes watering up and his throat tightening up in the middle of a lecture. "Of course," he went on, "I would be remiss if I did not note that the tendency to discipline others rather than ourselves is rabid throughout our race, regardless of our religious persuasion or lack thereof.

"In this lecture series we have already covered every major dogma and the associated apologetics. What I've chosen to introduce today is an understanding of the cyclical nature of culture and how it affects, and has affected, the belief systems of peoples throughout the centuries. In keeping with my introductory comments, it will become apparent that these cycles are largely the result of our sins of pride.

"Throughout my life," he continued, "I have heard people say 'What are we coming to?!' It seems that every generation, at some point in their journey, believes that the whole world is going to hell. This dark outlook is partly because our ungrateful nature pushes us to always see the glass as half empty rather than half full, and also because the slothfulness of that same nature dislikes change. But I think we take this pessimistic outlook primarily because we so desperately want to control our own destinies. Our pride wants to put us in control of all things, while our innermost being immediately recognizes the impossibility of fulfilling that desire, and—ta-da—we have instant cynicism.

"So, is the world getting progressively worse? I think not. Actually, religious and secular cultures both go in cycles. At various points in history we can see those cycles, and with a little training we can begin to observe them in our own recent experience and to even see similar cycles within our own spirituality."

He began an outline on the writing board, and as he leaned against the board in contemplation, Veronica wondered how he ever got through a Sunday homily without writing.

"Let's start with the first cycle," Father continued. "There are distinct points within history where it seems that all is well: the nation is at peace; the free practice of religion is flourishing; prosperity abounds; poverty is alleviated; there are no major class struggles; religious vocations are bountiful; education of the masses is gaining ground; and then, just as it would seem that we are tasting what the reign of God was meant to be, it all comes crashing down. Why do you think that happens?" he asked the class as he wrote on the board:

Phase I – Faith, Peace, and Prosperity.

As several hands went up, he added, "I'd prefer one or two word answers over soliloquies." The hands went back down, which made him smile.

Doofus had an offering. "Spoiled brats," he said dryly.

"Explain, Mr. Hoffman."

"Well, we don't get to peace and prosperity accidentally. There's always a price paid, but the next generation has nothing invested."

"I see," Fr. Scofield said as he wrote on the board:

Phase II – Complacency, Entitlement, and Greed.

"Excellent. Next phase?"

Melanie raised her hand and said, "Rejection."

"Explain please, Miss Lansing."

"Well, if we feel entitled to what we have and we don't attribute it to someone else's efforts or God's generosity, the fallen tendency to see others critically and ourselves favorably soon sets in. We reject the rules and establish our own, seeing our generation as enlightened."

"Excellently put, Melanie. Let's see...how to summarize..." and he started to write:

Phase III...

Melanie offered, "Rejection, Perceived Enlightenment, Revolution."

"Okay, Melanie, we'll try that," Father said as he wrote it down.

When he turned around, Doofus had his hand in the air. "Chaos," he said simply.

Father said, "You know, I like that. But I think, on that note, we need to revisit phase one." He rewrote it like this:

Phase I – Order: Faith, Peace, and Prosperity.

Then he wrote:

Phase IV – Chaos: Hedonism, Power Struggles, and Desolation.

Veronica asked, "Father, seeing as you have *Peace* in phase I, why not simply put *War*, rather than *Power Struggles*, in Phase IV?"

"Mrs. Lansing, I'm glad you asked. Is war really the opposite of peace? I prefer it this way simply because it is too easy for everyone to think of war as something that victimizes us, rather than something we cause. Do you see where I'm going? How do I put this?" he thought out loud.

"Well, do you mean like the way we group the word *war* in sentences like 'war, famine, and plagues,' as if war was just one more act of God of which we can wash our hands?" she offered.

"Exactly!" Father responded. "You see, war is not the opposite of peace, anxiety is. Peace is born of love and trust; anxiety is born of fear and mistrust. The lust for power springs from anxiety, the lack of personal peace. How about phase V, class?"

"Reform," offered a student named Alex.

"So, you think we've bottomed out and the cycle's on the rebound, eh? Could be. Is there any other possibility?" Father asked the class. When no one responded, he continued, "In many instances, Alex, your suggestion may in fact be the next phase. However, consider this as a common phase V of some ages, for example, the twentieth century," and he wrote on the board:

Phase V – Dark Order: Fear, Oppression, Mind Control.

"I think it is important not to forget about this phase. Satan would love to trap us at the far left of the pendulum's swing, and in fact, there's a certain part of our nature that doesn't want to have to make decisions. The cage, gilded or plain, has a certain attraction. Whether we are enslaved to our own invention or to someone else's, there is a simplicity diametrically opposed to Christian simplicity, a brute simplicity: eat, drink, sleep, partake of life's pleasures as much as possible, and work when you're told to work. Dark order might stand to seriously compete with Christianity, but its creators and promoters have heretofore supplied no plausible vehicle for conquering greed. While it could be said that many who aspire to follow Christ also fall prey to greed, other followers soar to sainthood, to the highest realms of selflessness. But dark order has no saints."

He then wrote on the board:

Phase VI – Renewal: Rediscovery, Obedience, and Self-Discipline.

"Somewhat the same idea you had, Alex, but I like *renewal* better than *reform*. The word reform suggests that we have something that's somewhat good and we're going to straighten it up a little to make it better. However, when we get done butchering what God has given us, it is often beyond recognition and we need to let God make it new again as opposed to trying to fix it ourselves.

"Now, what do you think class? Are there cycles similar to these in our own spiritual lives?" Father saw a lot of nodding heads among his listeners. "Certainly have been in mine," he admitted.

"For your penance, I want you to come to class tomorrow prepared to discuss examples of this phenomenon in history. I'm hoping all of you don't pick the most obvious ones, as *I* also want to learn something new from this exercise. Remember, these are cultural cycles; there are both secular and religious cultures to consider. In some ages these overlap more than in others, though they are never completely separate in any instance. Also, it would be naïve to expect these phases to be completely consecutive. In fact, I think it is safe to say that none of them are ever fully dormant or totally dominant. Think about our culture today, and think about whether or not you have seen these cycles in your own spiritual lives."

That afternoon, Veronica knocked on her professor's door. "Come in, my dear Mrs. Lansing," he invited. "To what do I owe the pleasure?"

"I'm hoping you have a few minutes to hear my confession, Father," she said. They stepped into his study and he closed the door. He offered her a chair facing his. Both were next to a huge picture window facing a beautiful tree-lined avenue out front. She peered out at the drizzle and fog as he placed a stole around his shoulders. Father prayed the opening blessing, inviting her confession.

"Thank you Father," she said, "my last confession was...um..."

After an awkward moment he said, "It's okay, dear. It was probably with me just a few weeks ago." She nodded in teary-eyed agreement.

"Sorry to be so stuffy and stiff," she said, "I just don't feel like myself anymore."

"I wouldn't expect otherwise," he observed. "You've been to hell and back...but Jesus has his arms extended as always."

"How can he?" she asked through tears. "I yelled at him! I doubted him! What does he see in me?!"

Fr. Scofield choked back emotion to answer: "He sees his repentant daughter, so small and weak, so dependent; and yet, he sees his own reflection and the likeness of his own mother, so pure and holy. My friend, everything you have felt over the loss of your spouse, I have also felt over the loss of my friend, perhaps at a different level and in a different way, but I also have had to fight feelings of anger toward our Creator. I felt that kind of anger for the first time in my life at the age of five when my parrot died."

She perked up and said, "Jacob talked about that."

"Jake was a good and holy man then already, an inspiration to me. Can you not still feel his eyes on you, admiring your holy beauty?" he asked.

Surprised by what seemed a cruel question, Veronica cried, "Well, yes...yes I can, but...I can't go to him!"

"Just as when I was five and he took my hand and talked to me about Gang Plank..."

"Who?" She asked through sniffles.

"My parrot. As I could then, I can feel his hand on my shoulder now. I have offered many prayers for the repose of his soul, but I have also offered many prayers through his intercession, for I feel certain that he is with the Lord! So, in a sense, you *can* go to him," he said.

When Father had given her absolution and removed his stole, he asked a now lighter-hearted Veronica what her plans were over the next few days.

"Wait. Before I answer that—'Gang Plank?'" she asked.

"You know: every nasty pirate has his parrot. Jake had suggested the name, and my favorite baby-sitter was my main hero at the time."

Veronica smiled, and then laughed a silly, through-the-nose laugh just picturing the whole thing. When her laughter subsided, Father asked, "Well?"

"Oh...my plans?" she said. "I don't know. Why do you ask?"

"Well, I've been ordered to go to Rome and I don't want to abandon you at a time like this without making provision for your pastoral care."

"Go to Rome? Why?"

"I have no idea, Veronica...just following orders. Maybe it has something to do with Jacobs's trip over there last month."

"What do you mean?" she asked.

"Jake was busy putting together his crew list. He was the absolute master of pulling strings, you know. If he wanted missionaries along on the voyage, a trip to the Vatican makes perfect sense."

"He asked me to go along," Veronica told him, "but I glanced at his itinerary and it looked like a very tightly booked business trip. I was still exhausted from the moon trip. I didn't take to outer space quite as well as Jacob, so I told him that I'd rather go another time and make it a pilgrimage."

"Well, would you and Mel care to accompany me? We'll make it a pilgrimage."

"Wow! When are you leaving?"

"Day after tomorrow."

"Well, I know you're a single man, Father, but even you must know that forty-eight hours is hardly enough time for a pair of women to prepare for a trip to Europe. Besides, Melanie and I are scheduled to go to the reading of Jacobs's will tomorrow at his lawyer's office. Any chance you can wait for a couple more days?"

"Sorry. No can do. When's the reading?"

"9:00 A.M."

"I don't fly out till 8:00 the next evening. You have plenty of time. Pack light and shop when you get there."

"Shop in Rome?" she asked, getting dreamy eyed. "You know, for a priest, you sure know how to grab a girl's attention! Question is, are there tickets available, and can I afford to go?" Father gave her a funny look.

"You're joking, aren't you?" he asked. "I'll check on tickets, and if they're available I'll pick up two more, assuming Melanie can make the trip."

"Didn't you hear me, dear flying padre? I don't know if I have the money to pay you back right away. Jacob took care of all of our financial dealings, and I haven't worked in months."

"Trust me; you can afford it," he declared. She pressed him about what he knew, but he insisted that she would know everything she needed to know after her morning meeting. With her still hemming and hawing, he realized that he needed to set the hook. "His Holiness will be very pleased to meet you, I'm sure," he announced. She turned her head in disbelief and gave him a sideways stare.

"Are you serious?" she pleaded for honesty.

"You have to come along to find out."

The next morning, as the hum of their engine faded away in the parking lot of Gundersen, Gundersen, and Tradewell Legal and Financial Services, Veronica looked over at Mel, and with a tired smile, let out a sigh that said *I'll sure be glad when this is all over*.

"Good morning, and welcome to GGT," the receptionist chirped.

A tall, slender woman standing next to her said, "Hi, I'm Jasmine Babasa. Mr. Gundersen is expecting you. Right this way, please."

They were immediately exchanging amenities with the elder Gundersen as they made themselves comfortable in his office. Josh Gundersen was a jovial, rotund man in his early fifties. His warmth and unpretentious charm put them at ease with the whole process, and he produced a simple two-page will from a file.

"As the two of you are believed to be Jacob's only living heirs, and as this is a very simple will, this reading should be fairly quick and painless," he said. Melanie and Veronica grinned at each other. On the way over they had been discussing dividing up Jake's possessions by drawing a chalk line through the junk in the attic or arm wrestling for his old car.

Mr. Gunderson continued. "Shortly before his death I received this note from Jacob signed in his own hand:

> Dear Mr. Gunderson,
>
> Josh, as you are well aware, I have recently wed. I regret that, because of security considerations, we were forced to keep the wedding guest list so small, and further, that I have not been by your office to introduce you to the love of my life. I think the two of you will get along famously. In the event that I meet with an early demise, it would be my hope that she would continue to use your fine service, which has allowed me to forgo daily financial minutia and focus on the things I do best.
>
> Please reword my will so as to contain the following: To my dear niece Melanie Lansing, daughter of my brother and as much daughter to me as niece, who has graced my home since her eleventh birthday, I leave my house, my car, my furniture, with exception for the bedroom suite I shared with my dear wife, and all personal effects in the attic and house, knowing that she will gift my beloved Veronica with those things she deems appropriate. I also leave to Melanie forty percent of my remaining estate.

To my dear wife, Veronica, love of my life and my soul's desire, I leave the aforementioned goods, and sixty percent of the remaining estate.

Sincerely,
Jacob Lansing

"Ladies, this clause was added to the will, but Jacob had been too busy to come by here and sign it. Nevertheless, as this document is written in his hand and dated and signed by him, it is legally binding. Yet, I must ask: Is there any objection to this proceeding so far?"

"All I want is what Jacob wanted," Veronica said. Melanie nodded agreement.

"Very well," Mr. Gundersen said. He read the rest of the will, a few paragraphs of legal mumbo jumbo that made Veronica yawn.

When he had finished, Mel asked, "So...what *is* the rest of my uncle's estate?"

Mr. Gundersen looked surprised. "I can see by the look on your face that you really don't know, do you?"

"Wouldn't ask if I knew, Josh," she said.

"Okay. Well...where to start? You *are* familiar with the AGC of course, and have been to the headquarters there," he said.

"Yes, of course," they both answered.

"It's yours!" he said.

"Whadaya mean?" asked Veronica.

"The Aerospace Governing Council Inc. is a nonprofit corporation. It owns nothing other than a few copyrights. All assets and most of the really important copyrights are owned by AGC Corp., a for-profit corporation. Jacob Lansing *was* AGC Corp., the sole owner. Now you two are. Congratulations!"

The two sat with their mouths hanging open.

"So...what exactly, I mean, how big...? I mean, Jacob lived in a two-bedroom house and drove a beat-up old car..." Veronica stammered.

"Let me give you a quick rundown without boring you with exact figures. We have been doing Jacob's taxes for many years. The AGC has billions of dollars worth of taxable assets, including satellite corporations operating under their own corporate identities. Gross income is in the billions with a twenty-three percent net profit. Your combined net worth is nearly one quarter trillion dollars."

Veronica and Melanie were entirely speechless.

"Did you enjoy your trip to the moon, Mrs. Lansing?" Josh asked.

"Please, call me Veronica. The trip was fine." Her facial expression and tone of voice told Josh that she thought he had asked an odd question.

"I ask because you own that service, from the shuttles at each end, to the planetary cruisers themselves."

Veronica and Melanie were completely overwhelmed.

"You also own one of the three lines that serve the Martian community," he went on. "How did you like the accommodations on the moon?" Veronica had figured out that these were purely rhetorical questions and answered with only a smile and a sigh. "Didn't you think it odd that the casino hotel has a chapel, complete with a tabernacle with the Blessed Sacrament present?"

She couldn't let this one go. "Yes, I did find that surprising."

"Yeah, that's something only a Catholic owner would do!" he said excitedly.

"We own that too?" Melanie asked.

"Actually, *we* do." Josh said, motioning to himself, Veronica, and Melanie. Jacob owned forty percent, and I sixty." He extended his hand for a shake and said, "I look forward to our partnership."

Veronica shook his hand and laughed a somewhat hysterical laugh with tears in her eyes. It seemed of late that everything she did involved tears, but for good or for bad, finding out that you're a multi-billionaire is bound to have some emotional impact. "If we own it, why do we run those tacky 'reduced-gravity intimacy' commercials?" she wanted to know.

"We own the facility, but we lease it to an operating company. The ads are theirs. Part of the lease agreement included the upkeep of the chapel and keeping a priest on staff. Unfortunately, the agreement did not cover the nature of their advertising campaigns. Of course, it's not that reduced-gravity intimacy is a bad thing, but the commercials are a bit too flagrant for prime-time TV."

"Well then," Melanie chuckled. "I guess we *can* afford to go to Rome with Fr. Scofield."

"Rome?" Mr. Gundersen asked. He fished in his desk drawer, found a short list of hotels, and handed it to Melanie.

"These are hotels in Rome that you recommend?" she asked.

"These are hotels in Rome that you own," he answered.

"Mr. Gundersen," Veronica stammered.

"Please, call me Josh," he interrupted.

"Josh, we're just overwhelmed. I mean…can we go to Rome right now? Fr. Scofield invited us to make a pilgrimage with him, but…we own big companies. Don't we have to be here to run them?"

Josh grinned and said, "Jacob's been gone for two weeks, and was in a coma for five weeks before that. Have you been running these companies?" He came over and put his hand on her shoulder. "Your companies are in very good hands, my dear. Jacob Lansing was, above all else, an impeccable judge of character. *You* are living proof of that.

"Besides, a large portion of AGC's income is now effortless, just a matter of making sure the checks keep coming. You see, most of the world admires Jacob for his contribution to space travel, as do I. However, being a money man, I admire him even more for his business savvy. He had the vision to see that the money was not to be made in space travel, it was to be made in hype: toys, video games, logos, clothing, stickers, books, advertising, and movies. Jake was a relentless copywriter. Any time his organization was doing the conceptualizing for a new space entity, he laid claim to the copyrights to any names, logos, or signature shapes and such. That's where the fortunes are made.

"Here is a list of names and phone numbers of the various persons in charge of your business entities. It would be good, at your leisure, to call these individuals and get to know them and slowly become involved. Right now, you have an opportunity to make a pilgrimage to Rome with a holy priest who really knows his way around. What better place for the two of you to grieve the loss of your husband and uncle and to plant yourselves firmly in the bosom of your Creator?"

"Just one more thing before we go," Veronica said. "Jacob lived like, well…a bit of a miser. Why?"

Josh actually bristled a little at the word miser. "My dear lady, Jacob Lansing lived like anything *but* a miser! Perhaps more like a saintly hermit. Last year alone, Jacob gave more than twenty billion dollars to charity, all donations handled through this agency. I can tell you where every cent of it went. Jacob was not a philanthropist; scarcely a soul knows of his great charity. Nothing was ever given in his name. We have gone through considerable legal gymnastics to keep recipients and the media from knowing the source of contributions.

"After removing what little profit went for his personal upkeep and amusement, Jacob invested the remainder primarily in space travel. He believed with all his heart that space travel is the will of God; that the colonization of other globes is, in part, an answer to what he considered the greatest moral evil of our time: contraception.

"He used to go on and on about how contraception was ruining the family, the most basic unit of church and society. There are not too many woes known to modern man that he did not attribute to this act that he referred to, in the words of Paul VI, as 'intrinsically wrong.' 'When Christians embrace an evil as good,' he would say, 'they have no choice but to attempt to sacramentalize it to save their sanity.'"

Josh could not help but notice the look on his secretary's face. She had been called into the meeting simply to take notes, but the business part of the meeting was over and Josh could tell that something was bothering her. "Jasmine, you look perplexed. Do you have a question?" She had not expected to be noticed, and now blushed at the attention she'd drawn to herself in the midst of a serious legal proceeding.

"Well, I...uh...no...well, yes, actually. I mean...it's just what you said about contraception," she stammered. "I mean...really...'The greatest moral evil of our time'? How could Dr. Lansing think that wanting to make love to your husband more often was worse than, say...ethnic cleansing, or...child molestation?"

"Did you hear what you just did?" Josh responded. "You equated the desire for something with the means of obtaining it."

"What?" she asked, missing his point.

"You said, 'How could Dr. Lansing think that wanting to make love to your husband more often was worse than...ethnic cleansing.' You equated preventing conception with the desire for more intimacy."

Jasmine looked a bit flustered. "I hope I'm not embarrassing you," Josh said, apologetically. "You see, I really like this kind of conversation. We can learn so much from each other. And you needn't let these stuffy old billionaire Lansing gals intimidate you!" Veronica and Melanie acted out mock indignation, and Melanie threw her purse at Josh. He caught it and said, "I like this new customer; she throws money!"

"There's not much in there!" Melanie insisted.

Jasmine smiled at their foolery, and Josh continued. "What I was getting at is that we can never equate the morality of the desire for something with the morality of a means of obtaining it. If we do, all crimes are moral, for there is no end to human desire." He did a little lawyer strut and thought for a moment about how he might make his point. "You see," he said, "I have a desire to eat deserts but I may be eating too many of them. It is not necessarily evil to seek pleasure for its own sake, unless in doing so one frustrates the primary purpose of the act that brings the pleasure. Providing nutrition is the primary function of eating, but to eat too much junk food is to frustrate health by misusing a God-given gift. It is gluttonous." He seated himself on the edge of his desk as though resting his case.

"So…what exactly are you saying? That sex without a chance of pregnancy is…junk sex?" Jasmine asked.

"Hmmm, I've never heard that term…it's not one of the three kinds that are familiar to me," Josh answered.

"Huh? Three kinds?" she asked with one eyebrow raised.

"Yes, three: excellent, unbelievable, and out of this world!" he quipped. Then turning serious, asked, "But, why *do* we call sweets *junk* food?"

"Because they're low on nutrition," she answered.

"Ah, but they're great in the areas of flavor, texture, and temperature," he pointed out, his eyes glazing over a bit as he pictured an ice cream sundae. "So…you tell me; is something that is good in many ways still to be considered junk because it lacks a critical dimension?"

Man, this guy is lawyer through and through, Jasmine thought, rather amazed by his instant articulation. "I just don't get how birth control can be the 'greatest moral evil of our time'!" she repeated her mantra, ignoring his question.

"Jacob saw the destructive force that it has been for families," Josh told her. "He saw that choosing to use contraceptives places self-gratification ahead of all other considerations, and self-gratification is certainly not the backbone of a healthy home."

"But making love is more than self-gratification," Jasmine insisted. "Are you saying that it can't be an act of love to bring pleasure to someone else?"

"To passionately gift one's mate with erotic pleasure is to perform an act of charity that is fundamental of our nature. It is to love as God loves, giving the gift of self," Josh assured her.

Wow! Lawyer and theologian. Weird! Jasmine thought. "So…if a husband wants pleasure without getting his wife pregnant, can't giving it to him still be an act of love?" she asked.

"Here we go again, connecting the morality of the desire with the morality of the means," Josh sighed. "She has a desire to give him pleasure. That is very good. He has a desire for that pleasure. In and of itself, that is neither bad nor good, but if he is willing to pursue that pleasure while frustrating one of the primary purposes of the act, that is bad."

He put his finger to the side of his nose and thought for a moment. "I love to eat, but I love having a trim figure as well. So I eat and eat and eat till I can eat no more, and then I go and throw up so I don't get fat."

"You do?" she asked, staring at his middle. Josh chuckled while holding his substantial belly. As his laughter subsided, a smiling Jasmine said, "Your point is that it's wrong to frustrate the natural purpose of something just for the sake of pleasure, but we don't eat for the purpose of getting fat, so, in your example, forcing yourself to throw up isn't frustrating a natural purpose."

"Hmm...true. But it does frustrate the proper assimilation of nutrients."

"That's true," she agreed.

"So what if I don't care about my weight and just keep throwing up so I can eat some more, disregarding any health considerations?" he asked.

"That's disgusting!" Jasmine declared.

"Isn't it disgusting to frustrate a primary purpose of sex so that we can gorge ourselves on sensual pleasure?" he asked.

She shrugged her shoulders and said, "I don't know. I mean...it's not like it's unhealthy."

Thinking that the conversation had become just a little too personal for mixed company, Melanie diverted it by asking Josh, "Did Uncle Jake ever show you his collection of quotes? He collected statements about contraception made by the leaders of the Reformation. Luther was really out-spoken. He scolded poor people who claimed they couldn't afford children, while condemning some of the rich who avoided marriage just because they didn't want to waste their wealth on raising kids."

Noting Veronica's and Josh's nods of agreement, Jasmine just lost it. "Hold it!" she said, with her right hand in halt position. "Aren't you guys all Catholic?" They nodded their yes. "You're the ones with all the single priests and nuns," she continued, "and here you are agreeing with Luther for saying it's sinful not to marry. I'm lost. Where are you going with this?"

"It's about motive and relationship with God, Jasmine," Veronica told her. "Luther condemned those who chose the single life for the sole purpose of pursuing more wealth. Indeed, history even shows instances of individuals who have chosen *religious* life for the wrong reasons, especially in Luther's day."

"I've seen Jacob's quote collection," Josh added. "Luther was very concerned about God's plan for our lives, and because the children whom God longs to give us already exist in His mind's eye, Luther practically equated contraception with murder. Jacob did a lot of research on the subject.

"Do you remember his famous Rose Bowl Parade shout-down with Fitch?" he asked.

"I was there," Melanie answered.

"That's right. You were right beside him," Josh recalled.

"I was very young, but I remember it like it was yesterday. The Moles sabotaged the moon-cruiser float we were riding. Fitch started bellowing at us with a bullhorn, but Unc just answered him calmly."

"What you were probably too young to remember or appreciate is that your uncle insisted on *encouraging* that conversation. He motioned for the police to stop trying to pull Fitch from the float and flagged an invitation to a camera crew to aim a shotgun mike in his direction, and amazingly, everybody complied. You see, Melanie, your widowed Grandma Lansing owned LPI, the production company responsible for delivering the parade coverage to the network. In a nutshell, Jacob had power over that production that others didn't realize.

"There he was, with a stalled Rose Bowl Parade, on National TV, having this debate with Fitch. Fitch was shouting his usual stuff about Christians destroying the planet, but Jacob yelled back, 'I think that you must be a Christian too.' When Fitch asked him what the heck he was talking about, Jacob simply started quoting statistics that showed the birth rate among many Christian sects in the U.S. to be well below replacement level, to which Fitch responded, 'Then it's the damn Catholics!' Your uncle shot back, 'Ah, now we're getting somewhere!'

"And then on national TV," Josh continued, "Jacob went on to point out that, shortly after the Christian churches embraced contraception in the 1930's, all hell broke loose. Divorce was allowed by those churches. Divorce levels skyrocketed, and broken homes gave rise to every form of emotional self-identity problem known to modern psychology."

"Wait a minute, correlation doesn't prove causation," Jasmine insisted. "You can't make the claim that the only thing that contributed to the rise in divorce was the increased use of contraceptives."

"You can assert the assumption if you have some kind of a control group," Veronica informed her.

"Who would that be?" Jasmine asked.

"That would be all of those couples who continued to use natural family planning down through the years," Veronica told her. "You see, the divorce rate among them is practically non-existent, lower than it was for the nation before 1930."

Jasmine grinned cynically and said, "Where's a woman going to go when she's barefoot and pregnant!"

"So…people who don't use contraceptives are ignorant hillbillies who spawn uncontrollably?" Veronica asked indignantly.

"Well…I…" Jasmine stammered.

"My mother has a masters degree, and my grandmother was an Assemblywoman!" Veronica informed her.

"I'm sorry. I didn't mean to…" Jasmine apologized, her voice trailing off.

"The old cliché is simply not supported by demographics," Veronica informed her, and turning to Josh, said, "It's fascinating to me that, in 1930, even some people in the secular press predicted the rise in divorce and the resultant ruin of the family."

"Yes! Isn't it amazing that the Washington Post agreed with the Pope!" Josh added. "How often does that happen! And their dire predictions came true. Fitch was no ignoramus. He was well aware that history had fulfilled these predictions. He was left speechless. Apparently, even to Fitch, the middle of a Rose Bowl parade just didn't seem like the right place to attempt to convince America not to worry because the family unit is obsolete anyway. There was enough of a lull in the conversation that the production company pushed the police to get the float moving or out of the way.

"There were, of course, many things Jacob *didn't* get to say on TV, like the way the killing of innocent unborn human beings had become a backup to contraception, and therefore had enjoyed the same 'sacramental' status contraception enjoyed, no matter how disgusting late term procedures were."

Jasmine suddenly bolted from her chair and excused herself. Veronica watched with concern as she left the room.

"Uncle Jake pointed out to me," Melanie added, "that the arguments to rationalize same sex marriage were based on the contraceptive mentality. Its proponents had argued that 'Procreation is no longer the primary object of the sex act, even for modern

Christians.' Unc would also point out that the very same argument was used to support the sickening notion of adult/child marriages, and to support the disgusting practice of marrying animals. Remember the 'Marry your pet' campaign the Moles were so proud to be part of? I guess things get pretty boring out at the old agricultural commune."

"Mole Nation had many reasons for hating Jacob," Josh said, "but the primary one was his great resistance to their 'One child, one Earth, world-wide' campaign. An interesting cultural by-product of the phenomenon known as Jacob Lansing is that space exploration has come to be thought of, by some Catholics, as somewhat our own thing. We're serious about bringing population and Christ to other worlds. Some competing religions have had in their culture a tinge of the Amish notion that too much technology is bad. However, except for those technologies that attempt to supplant or frustrate God's gift of life, technology has been embraced by all of the modern Pontiffs as a gift from God, a gift that must not to be used to replace the Savior, as is so often the temptation, but one to be harnessed for his greater glory.

"Veronica, Jake often told others that he had refrained from marriage because he could not do justice to both marriage and his career. But he never spoke to me of his career. He always called his work his 'vocation.' Promoting a culture of life was his passion, and he thought of his marriage to you as the 'crown jewel' of that vocation."

Veronica smiled at Josh's recollection of her man, though she was somewhat distracted. She had been watching Jasmine out of the corner of her eye. After filing the notes from the meeting, the tall Ms Babasa had gone out the front door and was sitting on a bench enjoying the morning sunshine.

Veronica and Melanie thanked Josh profusely for everything, and Veronica asked, "Mel, what are your plans?"

"I was just planning to go home, Ronnie," she answered.

"Good," Josh jumped in, "no plans! How 'bout I take you both to lunch. It would be a great honor."

"I would enjoy that," Melanie answered.

"Thanks, Josh," Veronica said, "but I'm a little concerned that a certain someone might feel like she's just been beat up by three Catholics. I'd like to see if I can get a little one-on-one time with her."

"Well, I'm hungry, Josh," Melanie said. "Ronnie can call us on her cell when she's ready to head home."

As Josh and Melanie headed for his car, Veronica strolled over by Jasmine. "Mind if I sit with you, Jasmine?"

"I would be honored, Mrs. Lansing."

"Please, call me Ronnie."

"Okay, if you call me Jazz," she said, forcing a smile.

"Look, Jazz, I hope you didn't feel like you had three Catholics ganging up on you in there."

"It's okay Mrs., I mean, Ronnie. You guys were just saying what you believe. I admire that. I guess what I admire the most is that you have some sort of framework around what you believe. It isn't just a collection of slogans. Everything you say fits together to make a whole. That makes it hard to argue against. In my job I pride myself on logical deduction, and I got a little embarrassed during that discussion for not having much of a central theme."

"Actually, I thought you did, and it's a good one," Veronica countered.

"Really?"

"Yeah. Your theme was that sexual intimacy is more than just for procreation, that pleasure is a gift from God as well. Yet, I thought that both of you were missing a central point."

"Why didn't you bring it up?"

"I wanted to, but couldn't get a word in edgewise with our lawyer friend in full swing."

"He's something, isn't he!" Jasmine said, smiling.

"He's very good at what he does," Veronica agreed. "But to me, the conversation was bouncing back and forth between two points, procreation and pleasure, and completely missing an all important element: unity. There's something about two bodies and souls intertwining and the spiritual connection to the Creator that it offers that, well...complements but...transcends the physical pleasure," Veronica explained.

"Wow! If that's what making love is supposed to be, I've never made love. You make it sound so beautiful."

"Thanks. Say, I have no plans for the afternoon. If you're up for more conversation, I'd love to take a walk."

"So would I, but not here. I get claustrophobic walking in this part of town. The beach is just a short drive from here."

"Sounds great!"

They jumped into Jasmine's Nexus. "I drive a Nexus too," Veronica said.

"Does yours do this?" Jasmine asked, watching Veronica's face.

"What?" Veronica asked, but before the word had completely rolled off her lips, her eyes went wide as the vehicle rose quickly to thirty feet above the parking lot. "Wow! This must be a brand new LX. Are these things safe?"

"I don't know. It's a first year model, which is a little disconcerting, but so far, so good." She pressed one of the destination presets, and the car whooshed off in the direction of the beach.

"Aren't you worried about cancer?" Veronica asked, remembering newscasts about health concerns with levitronic drive.

"Do I look worried?" Jasmine replied with a jaded grin.

The vehicle piloted itself slowly toward the sea. Though new and expensive, levitronic travel was already extremely popular, and the air was thick with vehicles around lunch time. "I hope I'm not prying too much," Veronica said softly, "but you seemed a little distraught when you left the room before."

Jasmine just stared forward for a moment. "I usually don't tell people this," she said at last, "but I have a real strong feeling that you already know. Our conversation had turned to the subject of abortion… I've had an abortion. It isn't legal here so I went to Japan. I have relatives there who helped to set it up for me. I was eighteen, stupid, and confused. It's not something I like to talk about."

As the Nexus swerved through a grove of trees in a park, Veronica prayed for the right words. "Have you ever talked to God about it?" she asked after a bit. "He loves us more than we can imagine."

"Really?" Jasmine asked, cynically.

"Really! Scripture says that he desires intimacy with us. He wants to be our spouse," Veronica proclaimed joyfully.

"Our spouse?"

"Yeah, St. Paul talks about it all the time, and Isaiah says, '…your Maker is your husband.' Isn't that cool!"

"Ha! Trust me, honey; no self-respecting god wants to be *my* husband!" Jasmine declared as the Nexus gently plopped into the beach sand at the end of the ocean-front parking area.

"Why? Because you're a sinner? We're all sinners, Jazz."

"Sinner? You?" Jasmine jeered as she got out of the car. "Listen, you great big sinner, you don't even know the meaning of the word. Don't tell me there's a god out there who wants to get cozy with a slut like me!"

She slammed the car door and sprinted, as best her heels would allow, toward the beach. Her stride got shorter and her pace slower as the distance increased. Finally she stopped, took off her heels, and turned around to look back at the passenger still seated in her car. *What an ass I am!* she thought as she started back, *but she's just a little too perky!* As she approached the car Jasmine could not help but notice Veronica's tears. *Oh, God, she's crying!* she thought. *Hope she doesn't need a hug. Hugging chicks is not my thing!*

"Look, Ronnie...I didn't mean to hurt you," she said, throwing her shoes in the back seat.

Veronica stared off at the sea. "Your attitude just opened an old wound," she said, as she opened her door, adding, "and...I just recently rediscovered tears." She blew her nose and started toward the beach with Jasmine as she explained. "Something happened here many years ago. I was taking a walk right over there when a couple of girls from school came up from behind me, pushed me down, and ripped my bathing suit right off me. There I was, hundreds of yards from the bath house and stark naked without a soul I knew in sight. I was bleeding, all scratched up from their finger nails, with sand from the beach stuck in the scratches. They knew me from school and didn't like me because...well...for the same reason you just got upset. They took my suit with them and ran off giggling and calling me horrible names."

"God, girl, what did you do?" Jasmine asked, thinking to herself, *Martha and Zelda, you disgusting witches!*

"I hid out in that U-shaped cropping of rocks over there until my dad came looking for me. When I saw him I shouted to him and started crying all over again. He came running and really got shook up when he saw the blood and scratches all over me."

"He saw you naked?" Jasmine asked.

"I was trying to warn him but I think I was crying so hard that he didn't understand a word I was saying," Veronica explained. "Anyway, he's a doctor. He sees people naked all the time."

"Yeah, but not his daughter!" Jasmine said.

"Hey...I'm his little girl!" Veronica insisted.

"I guess," Jasmine said with a distant look. "What'd he do then?"

"He took off his shirt and wrapped it around me. He just held me for a long time while I cried, then took little peeks under the shirt around my shoulders and back to see how bad the scratches were."

"I wish they still made men like that," Jasmine said, wistfully.

"My Jacob was a man like that!"

"Yeah, Ronnie, he was. He really was. Josh Gundersen is a good man too. Just two problems: all the good men are from your dad's generation, and they all have gold rings on their left hands. I've never been in a relationship that's lasted more than a couple years—no gold rings for me. Jeez, listen to me babbling about myself!"

They strolled along the beach for a while in silence. Seagulls circled about them against a backdrop of popcorn clouds that were in no particular hurry to cross the blue-blue sky. Veronica was struck by the similarity between the day and that day on the beach long ago. The memory was bittersweet: sweet because of her father's tender love and attention. She thanked God for the love foundation that made her who she was, and wondered about her companion's foundation.

"Maybe you've just gotten off to some bad starts, Jazz. I mean, like…maybe you didn't start in the right place."

"The right place?"

"Yeah. I mean, no relationship can stand on its own. Everybody needs God at the center." Thinking back to their discussion at GGT, she added, "That's what's so beautiful about natural family planning. Life and love need to be spontaneous."

"Am I going to get another rant about contraception?" Jasmine asked with an impatient sideways glance.

"Not if you don't want it," Veronica told her flatly.

After a moment's silence, Jasmine said, "Okay…dang it, girl! You got me curious as to where you were going with your little speech. 'Spontaneous,' huh? Isn't that why people *use* contraception, so they can be spontaneous?"

"Have you ever watched cats mate, Jazz?"

Jasmine's befuddled look said, *Where's this going?*

"How about cattle?" Veronica asked when she got no reply.

Following a belabored sigh, Jasmine said, "Yes! What's your point?"

"Were you struck by how much they loved each other?" Veronica asked.

Jasmine's blank stare said, *Of course not! Make your point, girl!*

"Love is always a decision, Jazz. Animals don't make decisions, they just respond to instinct—spontaneously! They don't love. Contraception wasn't invented to prevent pregnancy."

Jasmine sighed the tired, confused sigh of one unable to connect the dots. "Okay. Why *was* it invented?"

"There already was a way to prevent pregnancy," Veronica informed her. "It's called abstinence. Contraception was invented so that humans can be spontaneous—like animals—without weighing any consequences. It allows us to respond to urges without having to make any decisions, just like our furry friends, except that they actually reproduce as a result."

Jasmine's expression had lost some of its cynical gloss but had gained some distance. Her lips were parted narrowly, waiting for a question to settle into the starting gate. Veronica didn't wait:

"Contraception takes God out of the equation, Jazz. *Human* spontaneity must involve our whole being, soul and body. The decision to either abstain from or proceed with intimacy must be a decision to love, not just the response to a bodily urge. To be a decision to love, it must include the source of love, our Creator. For love-making to include the Creator, we must make a gift of our total, uncompromised selves, just the way he created us—open to creation."

"So...why would an *it* give a rip about any of that?" Jasmine asked sharply.

"What?" Veronica asked, lost as to what she meant.

"I said, why would an *it*...oh...never mind!" Jasmine was quiet for a moment, and then said, "I'm sorry I'm so snotty. So...if I may ask, did you and Jacob use natural family planning?"

"Well, sort of—in reverse, you might say. We wanted to have lots of babies, so we abstained for a week during the infertile part of my cycle."

"Abstained during the infer...? What? Why?!"

"To spend time in prayer and to make sure that we would never take each other for granted."

"Really? So...you've never tried abstaining when you're fertile."

"Sure have, from age thirteen to age twenty-nine!" Veronica noted. Jasmine rolled her eyes. "But no, not when I was married," Veronica continued. "However, I have many friends that do. In discerning His will, most of them have learned to 'Let go and let God.' In answer to their prayers, he might strengthen a couple's resolve to abstain, or—if his answer is new life, and they are really open to him— he might quickly bring them to the point where they are hardly able to keep their hands off each other."

Jasmine put an arm around her new friend's shoulder. "That's just lovely, honey," she said, her voice all sing-songy, "but it seems that I can hardly keep my hands off of *any* man, and it's gonna be real hard for me to get cozy with a god who keeps sending me losers."

"Well...are you starting in the right place? I mean, with prayer?" Veronica asked.

"Humph. I don't think there's much in my life that's started in the right place, kid. My parents divorced when I was sixteen, and things weren't pretty before then."

"I'm sorry, Jazz."

"Yeah. So am I."

"What happened?"

"Well, let's just say that my dad was a broadminded man."

"Yeah?"

"Yeah. He had 'em on his mind all the time! He was always gawking at broads, and Mom was always mad at him."

"Um, Jazz...*broads*? The last time I heard that term was in an old mafia movie."

"Yeah. My pop watched 'em all the time and used the term all the time, along with other sweet terms like *dame* and *bitch*. He was quite the piece of work. The first time I came downstairs in a miniskirt Mom came unglued, but Dad just gawked and whistled this long wolf whistle and said something like 'You're gonna make some young man very happy!' I was fourteen. After that, I no longer felt like his little girl when he looked at me; I was just another broad.

"Eventually the fighting came to be nearly constant, and I stayed out of the house just so I didn't have to listen to it. I started sleeping around. The first great love-of-my-life demanded that I abort his baby or he'd stop seeing me. Like an idiot, I complied. Of course, we broke up a few months later. By the time I met my second big love, I was drinking and doing drugs. So was he. We were quite the pathetic pair. Our addictions got so bad that we hardly ever made love; just got naked and laid there drugged out of our minds. That ended when he died of an overdose." Jasmine stopped to wipe a tear. "Sometimes I think he was the lucky one."

"Jazz, don't say that!"

Jasmine threw her arm around the doctor's shoulder and started walking again, pulling Veronica along. "You really *are* an Angel!" she said.

"What?" Veronica asked, stopping.

"I said, you really are an..."

"Okay...who told you about the Angel of Adrenaline thing?!"

"Gosh, Ronnie, I don't know. It's not like it's a big secret, you know."

Veronica just rolled her eyes. "Go on," she coaxed, starting to walk again.

"Jeez, girl, you're really into my sordid story, aren't you!" Jasmine kidded. "Maybe I should write a book about my pathetic exploits. And as long as I'm spilling my guts, I should tell you that there were at least a dozen one-night-stands between each of these serious lover boys I'm telling you about." She looked at Veronica to catch her reaction, expecting her to be shocked or annoyed, but all she saw in her companion's eyes was concern. *What makes this girl tick?* she wondered.

"I made it through college," Jasmine continued, "got off the drugs and booze and landed my first job. While drying out I stayed away from men, except for an occasional one-nighter. My next great love was a janitor at the apartment. He was hanging outside my third floor apartment washing windows. I forgot he was there and came out of my bathroom naked. I caught his eye and froze and just stood there for the longest time with him looking at me." She faced Veronica wearing a deliberately annoying smirk that said *I'm naughty!* and proclaimed, "I like to be looked at!"

"So do I," Veronica chimed in. "Everyone craves affirmation."

Don't patronize me! Jasmine's glare said as she continued her story: "Anyway, I soon found out that Mr. Clean could do more than windows. But eventually he got bored with me and moved on to windows with a better view.

"Maybe that's my problem, Ronnie. Maybe I'm just boring."

"I'm not bored," Veronica informed her.

"Um, Ronnie…you're a chick, so…what does it matter?"

"God's not bored with you."

"You're sure of that."

"Absolutely, Jazz! He invested a lot of love in making you, and he's fascinated with his own work. He thinks you're beautiful and loves you more than you can imagine."

"It's getting harder and harder for me to imagine anything good!" Jasmine declared, cynically. "If God loves me so much, why doesn't he give some of that love to some nice man to pass on to me? Anyway, Doug didn't seem to get any of it. Doug: the guy I thought was different than all the rest."

"He was your last boyfriend?"

"Yeah. He was such a charmer when we first met; made me feel so special. I thought, *This is gonna be the one!* but it wasn't long before something just didn't feel right. Then a few weeks ago we were in bed and really going at it, but he was hesitating for some reason. All of sudden he got up and left the room saying he'd be back in a few minutes. I waited and waited. He walked right past the bathroom, so I thought maybe he'd gotten hungry, but I didn't hear the fridge door or anything. He already had me all worked up and the waiting was killing me.

"Finally I couldn't stand it any more and I went looking for him. You know where I found the fool?" she asked, turning toward Veronica. "He was at his computer viewing porn! Wretched, sickening, disgusting, hard porn! It turns out that it's the only thing that will get the freak up anymore. I'm back there dying for love, and the sick bastard's looking at dirty pictures instead of me. So don't tell me I'm beautiful and wonderful and sexy and all that happy crap!"

She shoved Veronica to the ground, crouched over her, pulled an automatic weapon from her purse and hollered, "FBI! Drop your weapon and move into the open!"

A frightened, skinny little man moved out from a rock formation and asked, "Do I really have to drop my camera, Bubba?"

"Skink!" Jasmine shouted. "Skink, you damn fool! You almost got yourself shot!"

"Bubba, I'm just trying to make a living," Skink said.

"Give me the camera, buddy," Jasmine instructed him. "*The Voyeur* doesn't need to show the world any more pictures of a grieving Mrs. Lansing." *Oh crap!* she thought. "Mrs. Lansing...Ronnie, are you okay, honey?" Veronica was back on her feet, spitting repeatedly to get the sand out of her mouth. "Oh, sweetie, I'm so sorry. Just trying to keep you safe!" Jasmine said as she helped Veronica brush off the sand.

"You tried to save my life, Jazz...or...is that your real name?"

"Yeah, it's my real name, and this is Skink. Ronnie, Skink. Skink, Ronnie."

"Glad to know you," Veronica said, walking over to the photographer. She stood real close to him and started to ask personal questions, and Jasmine just lost it.

"You can't save Skink, Angel! Bottom feeders aren't redeemable, are they Skink?"

"Everybody's redeemable," Veronica insisted.

"Ya hear that, Skink? You can be saved! Now get your sorry ass outa here and *save* me from having to put a bullet in it just for spite. After I dump the pictures, I'll put your funny little camera in the mail and send it C.O.D."

"Good day, Mrs. Lansing," Skink said as he retreated to his car.

"Why'd you treat him that way?" Veronica asked Jasmine.

"What way?"

"Like he's trash."

He is trash, honey, Jasmine thought, and then thought, *If he's trash, what am I?* "I'm sorry, Ronnie, it's just that..." she began.

"Don't tell *me*; tell him!" Veronica insisted.

"Tell him?"

"Yes! Tell him you're sorry. Sins are trash; sinners aren't!" Veronica insisted with eyes fiery enough to goad her companion.

"Whoa! Okay...okay!" Jasmine muttered. She closed her eyes and shook her head thinking, *Oh, God, I can't believe I'm doing this!* then turned and yelled, "Skink! Skink...wait up!" as she trotted after him.

Veronica went to the placid blue sea and was vainly attempting to skip stones when Jasmine caught up to her.

"You throw like a girl," Jasmine noted with a snicker.

Veronica smiled. "F.B.I., huh?" she said with admiration as she launched another stone. "Wow! Exciting career, keeping people safe and all that! Thanks for all that you've done for us!" Veronica's nice flat stone went ka-plip as it hit the water all wrong and sank instantly.

"Yeah, well, if I was really any good, your husband would still be alive," Jasmine said, getting uncharacteristically emotional.

"We don't know that!" Veronica insisted. "If God wanted to take Jacob now, there's no way that you or Dobbs or anyone else could have prevented it."

"Wow, honey, your faith is unbelievable! How can you be that resigned just a couple weeks after he's gone?"

"Oh, don't think it hasn't been a struggle. But peace comes from God, not circumstances, Jazz. Anyway, it's really sad how your last relationship ended. Maybe it could still work. All things are possible with God. Doug could be cured of this, you know. He could get help. You could help him."

"He could get help if he wanted to. I don't think I made him feel any better about himself. It's just too strange, Ronnie. I don't think I could set foot in his apartment again. There's something spooky going on there. You talk about love being a threesome: a man, a woman, and God. Well, I think Doug had a threesome going, but it was a man, a woman, and...something else." Jasmine trembled trying to express the ugliness. "I used to think all of that demon stuff was a bunch of mumbo-jumbo, but when I think back about his place now, it just creeps me out! There was something in the air, something chilling, something…"

Veronica said nothing, but Jasmine could not help but notice the ocean of concern in the little woman's bottomless blue eyes. "Thanks for listening, Ronnie," she said after a bit. "I just met you and somehow it seems like you're the only friend I've ever had. I don't know if I can ever completely forgive Doug. The bastard made me get an operation before I moved in with him. As you so aptly pointed out, I'm lower than an animal now! I'm an *it*! I'm nothin' but a friggin *it*!"

"Jazz you're not an *it*!" Veronica insisted. "There's much more to womanhood than fertility! And you're certainly not an animal! Anyway, I'm sorry if you thought that's what I was trying to say."

Jasmine's subdued silence seemed to say, *I know. It's okay.*

"Why'd you do it, Jasmine? Why didn't *he* get an operation if it was so important to him?"

"Because he's a psycho coward! Gave me a line of bull about childhood trauma and how he was absolutely psycho about being cut. Said he couldn't bear the notion of being a dad for fear that he would turn out to be cruel like *his* dad."

"And…you thought this guy was the one and you didn't want to chance losing him?"

"Pretty stupid, huh? Can you say 'self-image problems'?" Jasmine asked, more than a little embarrassed.

"Jazz, we're all born with a self-image problem. It's our heritage. It's never resolved until we can see Jesus in ourselves."

"You know, Ronnie," Jasmine said turning toward her new friend, "I've never been into hugging chicks, but I could so use a hug from you."

The two embraced for a moment, and Jasmine lovingly flicked some more sand out of Veronica's long black hair. A full nine inches taller than her charge, the FBI agent had a good view of the curly locks. The odd twosome strolled along the water's edge.

"This is gonna sound really corny, Ronnie," Jasmine said, breaking the silence, "but I somehow feel that, well…like all of this was supposed to happen today; that…you hold the key to…untwisting my twisted existence."

"That doesn't sound so corny. God put all of us here for each other."

"You seem to have put a lot of thought into this whole sexuality thing. Isn't that kind of odd for a…holy person?" Jasmine asked.

"Oh, not at all!" Veronica insisted. "The body and sexuality are sacred! Several modern popes have written extensively about erotic love."

"Seriously? Well, I still don't get the whole contraception thing. I had a friend back in college who used to say that the Church lost all credibility a century and a half ago when it said that natural family planning was okay, but contraception wasn't. She insisted that, since both prevent conception, there's no difference."

"Hmmm." Veronica thought for moment. "Are things really that simple?" she asked.

"Whadaya mean?"

"Let's say there are two men. One's love for his wife keeps him from committing adultery, but the fear of contracting disease keeps the other one from straying. Are the two men on an equal spiritual plane? Is one motivation as commendable as the other, just because they achieve the same result?"

"Well...no...wow! I think I see where you're going," Jasmine answered.

"Love is a virtue..." Veronica began.

"And...fear certainly is not," Jasmine finished. Then, taking the stance of a first base umpire making a safe call, she brought the concept home, saying, "I've got one. There are two men: One's love for his wife allows her beauty and love to arouse him, and he makes love to her. The other has no idea what love is, and looks at porn to get it up before he does it to his wife. They both have intercourse with their wives..."

"But one's way is beautiful..." Veronica interjected.

"And the other's disgusting!" Jasmine finished.

"Bingo!" Veronica affirmed, giving her a high five. "Achieving the same end does not necessarily put the actions on an equal plane. If a nun lives her life in service to others, she's not sinning by denying her natural call to procreation. However, the woman who avoids marriage so she can selfishly build a greater fortune is denying her God-given call to espousal and fecundity, and she sins against charity. Still, her sin could not be classified as a sexual sin."

"Fecundi-what? You gotta slow down, girl, I'm no theologian!"

"Sorry, Jazz. Fecundity is such a beautiful word, but I'm afraid not a very popular one."

"Apparently. This college grad's never heard it before," Jasmine assured her. "What's it mean?"

"It's the quality of being fecund."

"And sadly, you think you're funny," Jasmine said, rolling her eyes.

They shared a snicker and Veronica continued. "We are fecund when we allow God to be creative through us—spiritually, mentally, and physically. To be truly fecund is to be like God. Anyway, my point was simply that, if one stays single and childless for selfish reasons, she's committing a sin of selfishness, but it's not a sexual sin."

"Okay...I got that. And...?"

"Well, if a couple abuses natural family planning, using it to exclude pregnancy for totally selfish reasons, they too commit a sin of selfishness..."

"But not a sexual sin," Jasmine finished. "Got it! It's not some perversion like...oh, like trying to make love through a piece of latex!"

"Very good!" Veronica exclaimed, impressed by her companion's deduction. "Still, though they don't pervert the act itself, they frustrate their natural call to procreation."

"Okay. So...it's a sin for married people to be childless on purpose?"

"Sin is always a choice, Jazz. The *choice* to remain childless can be a sinful choice if it's not made for a very serious reason."

"And...as serious reasons go, a second home in an exotic place doesn't quite cut it."

"Right!"

"Okay...well, condoms aside, what about the methods that are not so obviously disgusting? What about sterile *its* like me? Or, for that matter, what about taking a drug that makes you a temporary *it*. If I ever do find the right man, will I be sinning every time we make love?"

"No. Sterilization is a tragedy, but what's done is done—and you are not an *it*!" Veronica proclaimed dramatically.

"Sorry. That's just how I feel."

"It is a sin to *choose* sterilization, Jazz, but it is not a sin to *be* sterile. However, I don't think I need to tell you that there's a lot of emotional aftermath that goes with the decision. You can't lie to your own body, a body designed for love *and* life. God always forgives; nature never forgives."

Jasmine gazed out across the water. "I feel so...I don't know...incomplete."

"I'm not a spiritual advisor or anything, Jazz, but I *am* a woman. I crave fulfillment. Motherhood can be devastating. It's fraught with worries and frustrations, and yet I crave it. The loss of my husband ripped my heart out, and yet I crave marriage. It's like there's all these opportunities for grace calling me."

Slowly, with keen interest, Jasmine asked, "What do you mean?"

"Well...when we live according to God's plan, marriage is an opportunity for grace. It's a sacrament and marital intimacy is a sacramental act, which, when offered to God, becomes a really sweet prayer. When couples allow themselves to be vulnerable to God—allow him to gift them with life, or seek his help in practicing self-restraint—he rewards them with unbelievable spiritual favors."

"Like...?"

"Oh...like seeing one's spouse through His eyes, or for that matter, seeing everyone and everything through His eyes," Veronica explained. "He teaches us the art of spiritual lovemaking and gifts us with the humility to see his plan for our lives.

"I have a priest friend who's an author and professor, and he says that war is not the opposite of peace, anxiety is. Holy couples are almost never anxious; they're resigned to God's will. They have a peace of soul that comes from trusting their Creator.

"You see, love is always a decision. Contraception and sterilization are de-humanizing. They remove decision, destroying opportunities for spontaneous self-giving *or* self-denial. They take trust in God out of the equation, destroying opportunities to be receptive to grace, and removing opportunities for self-mastery. One's life comes to be overshadowed by these huge, spontaneity-killing decisions."

"You still sound like a theologian."

"Sorry."

"It's okay. I think I kept up with you!" Jasmine said, showing more than a little satisfaction in having done so. "Seems to me that natural family planning is a misnomer; it should be called *super*natural family planning."

"Hey! I like that!" Veronica said as they walked along. They strolled in silence for a few minutes. When Veronica glanced up at her quiet companion, there were tears running down the tall girls cheeks.

"What do you think happened to Doug and I, Ronnie? How did such a seemingly sweet man turn into such an animal? What did I do wrong?"

Veronica sighed thoughtfully and said, "You willingly became his possession."

Jasmine stopped walking to wipe her tears with a tissue that Ronnie offered. A dramatic look of resolve came over her face, and she proclaimed, "Never again!"

They were at the water's edge, and Jasmine searched the ground for a flat stone. She launched it, and as the stone ceased skipping and hydroplaned smoothly out of sight, said with an air of hope, "I've heard that sterilization can be reversed."

"Now you're talking sense, woman!" Veronica said with a huge grin, "And I can help with that. But...don't misunderstand me, Jazz. People who have been sterilized and have repented can still give their lives to God—there are still lots of opportunities for grace. Reconstructive surgery is a wonderful option, but it's not necessary for forgiveness. We're all sinners in one way or another, all called to lead lives of repentance. Also, some people are naturally infertile, and there's certainly no sin in that. In fact, the pain of infertility can be turned into a sacrifice and offered back to God."

Jasmine smiled her understanding back at Veronica, but then cast her eyes down in contemplation as they started to walk again. Veronica broke the silence. "I'm concerned about you, Jazz. This will all be just a blur tomorrow if you don't pray about it. Only God can turn your life around; you're powerless to do it on your own. Conversations like this one are quickly forgotten if they're not followed by conversions." After a moment's silence, she added, "You have to become a new person."

Jasmine stopped walking and turned toward her new friend. Mouth agape, she stared hard into Veronica's big blues, deeply into her soul.

"A new person..." she repeated at last. "I...I want that. Yes, I want that!" she declared from the heart. "I really do!"

"Great! Have you been baptized?" Veronica asked, as they started to walk again.

"Believe it or not, my parents were Catholic, and I was baptized. The family quit attending church right before I was to make my first Confession and Communion, and they never went back."

"Can I take you back, Jazz? Back to God? I would love to help."

Jasmine chuckled a little, surprising Veronica. Her laugh was cute but sad.

"What?" Veronica asked.

"Oh...I was just thinking about how I've let just about every man I've ever known have his way with me. Maybe it's time I let Jesus have his way with me."

Veronica grinned. "Can I set you up?" she asked.

"Huh?"

"For a date."

Jasmine returned her grin. "I suppose you have his number."

"He has mine; calls every day."

"I wouldn't be surprised!" Jasmine said, beaming with respect for her new friend. Then, getting serious, added, "Veronica…you know, there's a large part of me that's just dying to become someone like you!"

"You'll have to."

"Have to what?"

"Die. The Gospel says that becoming like Christ is all about dying to yourself, putting to death the old selfish you and taking on the image of Jesus."

"Wow! That's a wild concept! You know, I've heard that before, but it never made sense till now," she said, turning to look at Veronica. "It makes sense now because…well…I look at you, and I see Jesus! That is, I see the kind of person he would have to be if he is what they say he is. Oh, here we go…I'm making you cry again! Come 'ere, you," she said, and gave Veronica another hug.

They walked in silence back to the Nexus, Veronica deep in prayer, Jasmine deep in thought.

"I'm scared, Ronnie," Jasmine said, her hand on the car door.

"Of what, Jazz?"

"Of being alone. Of demons. I put on this big front, this big FBI-woman-of-the-street facade, and inside I'm cowering in a corner! I've come to my rope's end! You said that you're leaving for Rome tomorrow. Well…I wish you weren't going. I must sound like a big baby, but I'm scared…and lonely. You talked about praying. I don't even know how to pray! I don't have the faintest clue where to begin!"

"I can teach you to pray. But…well…why don't you come along?"

"What?"

"Come to Rome with us. You've been assigned to protect us. You ought to be able to make the case to your boss that it's necessary to make this trip for our safety."

"You know, that's brilliant! That just might work! You don't think your priest friend will mind?"

"Fr. Scofield? He'll be delighted. He loves showing people around Rome, the more, the merrier."

"Great! Yes! I want to do it! Wow! We need to get busy!"

Jasmine unlocked her apartment door and stepped into the emptiness. She had smiled more in the last two hours than in the previous two months, but now she was alone. It was odd suddenly having a meaningful relationship with another woman, especially one that made her smile.

Her thoughts fell to her protective but bitter mother, who had died of an unintentionally lethal combination of liquor and sedatives six years past. Jasmine tried to picture the poor woman smiling, but the happy times were too distant, the memories too faded.

She telephoned Spinelli to square the trip to Rome, and then plopped onto her bed feeling as if she'd been rung out. Realizing that sleep was nowhere near, she opted for a well needed shower.

Refreshed, awake, and naked, she stepped out of the bathroom and caught sight of herself in the full length hall mirror. She moved closer and studied her cosmetic-free face. *What happened to you, girl?* she thought. The lines on her face and her puffy, baggy eyes seemed to scream *Who are you, old woman?*

"Who am I?" she asked herself out loud. For years, futilely seeking self-identity, she had thought of herself as somebody's girl, and now pent-up rage made her shudder with self-disgust as her heart admitted that, deep inside, she still longed to be somebody's girl. As she had most recently been Doug's girl, it occurred to her that his picture was still in a nearby trash can where she had chucked it weeks earlier. Still warmed by Veronica's all-things-are-possible-with-God attitude, a part of her wondered if she could ever love Doug again. She remembered Veronica's words: "Doug could be cured of this, you know. He could get help. You could help him." Forgiving others suddenly seemed attractive, even freeing.

She pushed aside crumpled wrappers to grab the picture, but as she pulled the image from the trash, it seemed that its paper eyes were lusting for her, leering as if she was just another lurid piece of web meat. "You sick bastard!" she screeched, launching the picture like a Frisbee. It crashed into the living room wall, taking out two other pictures. In rage she marched over to it and cursed as she stomped on it—not a good idea with bare feet.

The color of blood brought her to her senses, and she began to weep. Barely able to see through the tears, she crept out of the jumble of twisted frames and broken glass, but turned, and with an unbroken stream of obscenities, got the last word in with the paper Doug.

An hour later, wounds dressed and tears dried, she went to survey the mess. With the side of her shoe, she flipped the bloodied likeness of Doug face down as her heart screamed *Men!*, but her anger dissipated as she viewed a picture she had uncovered, one knocked from the wall when paper Doug went flying. It was a photo, snapped at an FBI get-together, of her and her partner, Dobbs. She carefully rescued the print from the broken shards. "Alvin, you funny, simple, sweet little man," she whispered. "You make it impossible to stay angry at *all* men!"

Veronica and Melanie, still a little stunned by the disclosure of their tremendous wealth, rode tired and quiet to the airport with Fr. Scofield and Jasmine the next evening.

"I trust that the last couple days have been eventful for you, Ladies," he said. "Are you looking forward to this trip?" Seated in the front, Veronica looked back at Melanie, and Jasmine gave her a big smile. Veronica and Melanie had not discussed how much of the previous day's education they would be sharing with mutual friends. Father sensed their apprehension and addressed it.

"If you're concerned about what you can and cannot say in front of me concerning your fortune, rest assured that there's not much I don't already know. I was Jake's confessor and spiritual advisor."

"Then you know about this?" Veronica said, showing him the list of hotels they owned in Rome.

"I have that list," he said. "We're staying in the third one from the top. They all offer rooms free for priests, but I usually pick that one because it's closest to the Vatican. I hope the new owners don't intend to change the free-rooms-for-priests policy."

As they flew across the Atlantic, Veronica contemplated Fr. Scofield's last lecture, wondering where her spirituality was in that cycle of change. It seemed she had hit rock bottom and was barely on her way back up. She prayed that, through this pilgrimage, the Spirit would rescue her from the valley of death.

Still thinking about that lecture, she leaned over Mel and asked Father, "So, where do you think we're at in those cultural cycles, Father?" When met with a blank look, she added, "The ones you talked about in your last lecture."

"Oh. Well…by 'we' do you mean our country, our church, our planet, or the four of us?"

"Our country."

"Well, as I mentioned in my closing comments, these phases never run completely consecutively. The beginning of the twenty-first century saw the gradual decline of the neo-paganism that began in the end of the twentieth century. In fact, the first half of the twenty-first century is more notable for irreligion than odd religion. Mole Nation is one of the last desperate fizzles of the neo-pagan trend.

"The Catholic Church, along with other Christian churches, was engaged in serious renewal in the first half of that century. That renewal was driven primarily by the laity, and I would dare to label the 40's through the 80's as a virtual Catholic renaissance. For the last twenty years, we have witnessed a growing phase two and are now seeing a budding phase three. Given our current level of technology, the prospect of entering a new age of enlightenment is a particularly scary one. I am excited about the Freqmod mission, because giving the world a new frontier may be exactly what is needed to divert attention away from the pampered egos of the next enlightenment."

Emblazoned by the rising sun, the Alps pierced the stratus in stark defiance of all things bland and announced the imminent appearance on the horizon of the antithesis of bland, the eternal city. As she admired the glistening peaks, Veronica thought about how funny life can be. They hadn't really taken the time in Josh's office to go down their entire list of assets. Ten years past, she made this trip as a relatively penniless college student. Now, for all she knew, she might own the airline. She mentioned this to Mel.

"If you knew it was ours, would you upgrade yourself to first class?" Melanie asked.

Veronica frowned. "Would that make us snobs? I don't know. Besides, it's not like we can't afford to be up there if we want to be, regardless of whose airplane this is."

Mel blew a sigh through tight lips and puffed-out cheeks and said, "It's gonna take a while to get used to being this rich. I'm not sure I like it."

Veronica nodded her agreement. She looked at Jasmine in the seat to her right. *My little sister in the faith,* she thought, gently touching the arm of her sleeping friend. Jasmine had been zonked out for most of the trip, and Veronica had not ceased praying for her.

In a few short hours they were settled into *their* hotel. The further this excursion progressed, the more Veronica appreciated its potential to fill her present needs. The eternal city seemed a little cleaner than the last time she'd been there, but just as busy. Still, as before, a sort of odd peace permeated the bustle. "Like bees on pilgrimage," Fr. Scofield would say.

"Tomorrow morning you ladies must go shopping," Father announced. "I will take you to a store where you can get everything you will need."

"And what *is* everything we will need?" asked Melanie.

"You will need black dresses, shoes, and hats or veils."

"Is it Halloween here?" she joked.

Fr. Scofield shook his head and said dryly, "I'm traveling with comedians. Tomorrow afternoon you must wear the only attire deemed appropriate for a private audience with His Holiness."

"Will there be no end to the surprises?" Veronica squealed. "We better get some sleep or the Pope will think we *are* witches!"

In the morning the ladies picked out fine black outfits while Father shopped in the religious goods store next door. He returned, carrying a small bag, just as the women had settled on the outfits they wanted and were fully dressed in them. "I thought maybe you'd like these," he said, gifting them each with a miraculous medal pin.

"They're beautiful, Father!" Mel gushed, while Jasmine quizzed Veronica about the nature of the gift.

"Are these your other clothes?" Father asked as he picked up a merchandise bag.

"Yes. Why?" Veronica asked.

"Because you're leaving wearing what you have on." He pulled something from his wallet and showed it to the lady behind the counter. She put on her reading glasses, took a close look at it, and showed it to another lady, apparently the owner. The woman smiled wide-eyed as Father explained something to her in Italian while pointing to his lady friends. She handed back the card and rambled on in Italian as the four travelers found their way out of the store, finishing up with "Arrivederci!"

As they stepped into the street, Veronica said, "Father, we haven't paid yet, unless you did. What were you showing to the owner?"

"I wasn't showing the owner anything," he answered. "I was showing the manager something that Jake gave to me. The owners are going to the Vatican with me in their new clothes."

It seemed so unfair. They owned stuff they didn't know about, but Fr. Scofield did, and he had a get-stuff-free card that they hadn't known about. As Veronica contemplated the irony of the situation, she got the giggles. *No sense getting upset about it*, she thought. Apparently Mel read her thoughts, and the two grasped hands and skipped down the street giggling as if they'd lost their minds. Father thought they looked like a pair of crazy dancing nuns, and he and Jasmine just grinned at each other and shook their heads. He took them to lunch at a little pizzeria, but before being seated Melanie insisted on knowing whether or not they "owned the place."

"Yes," Fr. Scofield answered, "but just this one."

"So how many religious articles stores do we own?" Veronica asked.

"Four," he informed her. "Jacob wanted everyone to be able to afford religious articles, so these four operate at zero profit here amongst all the others." Shock had taken its toll. The ladies were getting harder and harder to impress.

Why did it take me so long to come back to Rome? Veronica thought as she passed through the door into St. Peter's, for it truly seemed as if she had just come home. They had a few hours to kill before their scheduled meeting. They knelt for a while to pray before one of the many altars in that greatest of basilicas. Interred beneath this one, in a glass reliquary, lay the incorrupt body of His Holiness, St. Pope John XXIII. It would be just one of several incorrupt bodies to come to their attention during their pilgrimage. As Veronica prayed and viewed the flawlessly incorrupt remains of the Holy Father—whose corpse, though dead for nearly a century and a half, had the appearance of one who had just lain down for an afternoon nap—she thought about Fr. Scofield's class and the discussion they'd had concerning the Garden of Eden. She couldn't help but think that Eden has been here all along.

Jasmine found the incorruptibles completely overwhelming. "Why isn't this all over the news?" she asked naively. "Isn't this a big deal?"

"Think about the news, Jazz," Veronica told her. "Think about guys like Skink. Who do you think has his grip on the media? Do you think it's God's territory?"

"I guess not," Jasmine answered. "I guess to get the real news you have to dig deep, huh?"

"Like FBI work, Jazz," Veronica teased.

At four o'clock sharp, the foursome entered the presence of the successor of Peter, Pope Pious the XIV. Following Fr. Scofield's lead, the ladies knelt and kissed the Holy Father's ring as they were introduced. Tears welled up in the Pontiff's eyes, and to Veronica's surprise, he gave each of them a big hug. He expressed his great joy in meeting them, his wonder and respect for the work of their late husband and uncle, and the sorrow he felt at Jacob's passing.

Then wiping his grief away, he smiled and said, "But today we are here for a joyous occasion. Our friend Jacob Lansing has done us a great service in pointing out that the newly discovered world is in need of the Savior, and that it is not enough merely to send missionaries. No, the journey is too long, too serious. We must send apostles!" Veronica knew what was coming; she wondered if Fr. Scofield did. "Tomorrow," continued His Holiness, "if he consents, a wonderful son of Mary, who stands in the place of Christ at his holy altar, shall become an apostle to the new world. Fr. Scofield, will you accept the position of Archbishop of Freqmod?"

Fr. Scofield somehow managed a stammering, "Yes, Your Holiness." Meanwhile, Veronica studied Father's face, and thought, *Nope, he never saw it comin'!*

As if a private audience was not enough, they dined that night with the pope. They were introduced to Fr. David Hadrian, a South African whom had been selected for consecration and the mission to Freqmod.

Just after they were seated, the Pope reached into the layers of his clothing and produced an envelope. He handed it to Veronica and said, "Veronica...you don't mind if I call you Veronica do you? I so like that name." She smiled and wiggled her head in the tidiest little I-don't-mind fashion, displaying her usual childlike elegance. "As you are probably aware," the Holy Father continued, "your name comes from the Latin *vero-icona*, or true image. Jacob told me that you were indeed a true image of the Immaculate. Speaking of Jacob, I think he would want you to have this letter. I hope you don't mind that I have kept a copy for our archives; you know how we are here about history!" Veronica pulled the letter out of its envelope, immediately recognizing Jake's beautiful longhand. In it Jake told the Holy Father all about his fiancée and asked a special blessing on their upcoming marriage. Once again, Veronica was in tears, but then, so was the Pope.

His Holiness went on to explain that the consecration ceremony the next day would be small. He pointed out that sending a known bishop would create a lot of attention and controversy. "We want to put our best foot forward in this new world," he explained. "Christ should come to these people whole, not schizophrenic. No doubt, crewmembers that are not Catholic will express their faith traditions to these faraway brethren. Let us make sure that ours is the most solid, the least-divided Christ they will encounter.

"Fr. Scofield and Fr. Hadrian, you were chosen, first of all, for your holiness, but not solely for that." He smiled. "I don't want you two to start thinking that you're the holiest men on the planet!" he said and laughed with childlike delight. "Please keep in mind that, though *we* have chosen you for this mission, our choice in no way guarantees that the AGC will concur. Working in our favor is the fact that, before his passing, Dr. Lansing placed your names on a list of recommended crewmembers, but we have no guarantee that the AGC will heed Jacob's advice, especially now that he hails us from above. This part of the mission now rests in Mrs. Lansing's capable hands."

Capable hands? thought Veronica. *When did that start?*

His Holiness went on addressing the priests. "You were chosen for a variety of reasons. Both of you are multilingual and learn new languages with ease, and you both are extensively educated, Fr. Hadrian in the sciences and Fr. Scofield in theology, philosophy, and psychology. If objections are made to sending two Catholic priests on the mission, it will serve our purposes well, Veronica, to point out that each of these fine gentlemen has a triple Ph.D. behind their names, in addition to being skilled linguist: credentials not so easily trumped. Also, it would be best if the world sees you as priests. Sending two bishops elevates controversy to a whole new level. For this reason, we will refrain from publicly addressing you by your proper title until the star journey is nearly complete.

"You gentlemen will be traveling with your shipmates for two years before reaching Freqmod. In this short time you are to choose, from among the Catholic men on the crew, two or more whom you would consider suitable candidates for the priesthood. Their holiness and suitability shall be considered without regard to their marital status. The celibate priesthood shall remain the norm, but we must flex with this opportunity. This selection process must begin early on, as there will be relatively little time for training priests in the early days of evangelizing a planet.

"This crew will be comprised of an equal number of men and women. The balance between the sexes is not accidental. If this mission becomes crippled in such a way that return to Earth with the vessel is impossible, procreation may become an important part of long term survival. If some calamity prevents return to Earth, you are released from your promises of celibacy at your own discretion.

"Finally, I want to communicate a point so poignantly made to me by my blessed friend, Jacob Lansing. It is not by accident that we sit upon this threshold. God has placed a task before us. It is not our task, but his. We are weak instruments, but instruments nonetheless, and perhaps most importantly, the instruments he has chosen."

$$\approx$$

The following day, in the Holy Father's private chapel, two humble priests were consecrated into the ranks of the apostles. As Pious XIV lowered the miter on Ian Scofield's head, Jasmine thought, *What a sneak-preview of the Divine Ian is, but so extremely off-limits!* and then asked God, *Where is the man who will treat me with the love and dignity Fr. Ian has for me?* She had only known the man for three days, but what a glorious three days! Later, she knelt and kissed Bishop Scofield's ring, doing so with such love that she could not utter the words of congratulations she had prepared, for her heart was stuck in her throat. *I'm turning into a sentimental sap,* she thought. *Where's the tough F.B.I. woman now?* The last week, with all of its surreal spiritual excitement, somehow seemed like the only real part of her life. The rest loomed like a bad memory, a desperate invention to fill the emptiness.

The next morning Jasmine awoke with visions of the prior evening parading through her mind. *You dined with the Pope and two bishops,* she thought. *If holiness can be absorbed, you should be dripping with it!* At breakfast, Veronica and Melanie stated their intention to act on Fr. Scofield's pre-trip enticement to "shop in Rome."

"I'm over-packed as is," Jasmine said, declining their invitation. "I'm hoping the dear bishop will allow me to be his student," she said.

"Nothing would please me more!" he responded, "but you must not call me bishop, remember?"

"Oh, yeah. Sorry, Your Excellency," she said, winking at him.

After seeing the two shoppers off Fr. Scofield asked Jasmine, "Where do you want to go first?"

"To Confession," she said, plaintively.

"And where do you want your first Reconciliation to take place?"

"In St. Peter's."

"Excellent choice!" he proclaimed. Within half an hour they were in the Basilica.

"Father, are you there?" Jasmine asked through the privacy mesh.

"Yes, my daughter, I'm here," he answered.

"Father, I'm in love with you!" she proclaimed, and then chided herself with, *Dang it, woman, what is wrong with you?!*

"Jasmine, I am a messenger of love serving a world starving for love. For this reason, many women have felt that they are in love with me, but I am a promised man."

"I know, Father, I know. I'm sorry. Still, it seemed I had to say it. Doing so…filled some need in my soul," she thought out loud, trying desperately to understand her own feelings and impetuous behavior.

"Jasmine, like other women before you, you see in me a pale image of the God your soul is seeking. You have experienced a healthy love-at-first-sight. I say healthy, because the love you feel is love for the God you see dimly reflected in me. You had a need to tell me because your soul is dying to express that love, love that is the basis for all real and lasting relationships. Never be ashamed of such love, unless of course you allow run-away passion to pervert the desire it expresses. Woman was created to complete man, and man to complete woman. You and I complete each other, not in the physical sense of marital intimacy, but on a spiritual level. In a way, whether celibate or married, by our very nature we are completed in the opposite sex. In you and in all women I see a preview of the Divine, and in my acts of love I am completed by his presence within you. We are the Church, the bride of Christ. Our true completeness can only be found in him. No counterfeit will do."

Jasmine recalled Veronica's words on the beach. "Your Maker is your husband," she had said, quoting Isaiah. What had seemed extremely corny that day beside the sea suddenly loomed within reach.

"Father, I've spent most of my life chasing counterfeits," she said, segueing into her sordid life story. With Fr. Scofield's direction she bared her soul to her Savior, who turned the sordid to sorrow and her sorrow to joy. Two and a half hours later she emerged from the ancient wooden stall and knelt before one of the many tabernacles in St. Peter's. She had prepared for her first Confession at the age of seven but had never confessed. *There is no way that it could have been for me then what it was now,* she thought. Her new freedom was exhilarating.

While Fr. Scofield heard two more confessions, she thought about the penance he had imposed. "With your permission, I will give you a penance designed to help you heal," he had said. "With the Holy Spirit as our guide, we will explore what it means to be angry." When at last he emerged from the confessional, she went to him.

"Is it wrong to hug a priest?" she asked.

"Is it wrong to hug a brother?" he countered.

"No, dear brother, it's not," she said embracing him.

When she had released him, he gazed thoughtfully at her, and after a moment, said, "You're not quite done yet, Jasmine."

"Oh, I know it, Father! I have a long ways to go!"

"No, I mean for today," he told her. "You must do your penance. Let's take a walk." He phoned their traveling companions to set up a rendezvous.

Fr. Scofield switched to tour guide mode as he and Jasmine headed toward the Castel Sant'Angelo. They met Veronica and Melanie at the Ponte Sant'Angelo, the Bridge of the Angels, and the foursome descended an ancient stone stairway to the edge of the Tiber's murky water. Father took Veronica and Melanie aside to instruct them, and leaving them, continued on with Jasmine until they were out of earshot. "Now you can finish," he told her.

"Finish what, Father?" she asked, glancing back at her girlfriends and wondering what was up.

"You must deal with your anger, Jasmine."

"The Lord took away my anger."

"No. He took away your sin. But you must deal with your anger. Anger is not a sin; it is an emotion, one you need to express to save your sanity. Who are you angry at, Jasmine?"

"No one," she claimed, but her eyes betrayed her.

"No one has made you angry?" he pressed. "Are you sure?"

Jasmine had been feeling so free. She didn't want to go where Fr. Scofield was leading her, but it was already too late. After two and half hours of baring her soul in the confessional, the memories were raw, lurking just beneath the surface. Her thoughts had already turned to the man who had insisted that she abort her child, and to her relatives who had arranged that abortion. What kind of a family helps you kill your own child?! The bitterness ran deep. She had not spoken to them since. She thought about her fighting parents and about their divorce. Would she have gotten pregnant if they had been there for her? Staring at the murky green waters of the Tiber, she cringed remembering her dad's drunken, lecherous behavior. How could she not blame him for her mom's untimely death?! She blinked back tears.

"Tell them how you feel, Jasmine!" he entreated her, gently.

"Stop, Father! Please!"

"Tell them how angry you are! Scream at them! Tell them what you think!"

Jasmine could feel the anger rising, like fire in her very flesh. She began to tremble. Her broken heart accused a parade of demons: all of the men who had used her, who had pretended to love her! Their parade was joined by coworkers who ogled her like a piece of meat, followed by the parade's grand marshal, the man who loved dirty pictures more than her—the same man who demanded that she mutilate herself to qualify for his love! *Do you call that love, Jasmine?* her heart screamed. *Doesn't that make you angry?!*

"Give voice to it, Jasmine!" Fr. Scofield encouraged.

Jasmine's anger became so intense that she began to convulse. She leaned limply against the great stone wall that lines the Tiber, then falling to one knee, picked up a broken fragment of that wall. Groaning, she hurled the rock into the Tiber's green water and began to verbally vomit her outrage. Father cheered her on with "Come on, tell them what you *really* think!" She shrieked on and on until she lost both voice and strength, and collapsing in tears, sank to her hands and knees on the moist, green stained rock.

Father signaled for Veronica and Melanie to bring their comforting embrace. A sea of tears later, he released the two ladies to finish their shopping, while he and Jasmine slowly meandered back toward the Vatican, their conversation quietly exploring the mysteries of forgiveness and healing, blending them with the mystery and beauty of Rome.

"I hope that you appreciate how necessary that was," Fr. Scofield told her. "In fact, you need to know that even this is only a beginning. You may need to give voice to your anger many more times. You must let God heal all of you. If anger leads to hurt and hate, it is sinful, but short of that, you have every right—and a great need—to vent. If you need a target when you vent, my ears are available."

"I don't want to do that to you, Father!" she objected.

He grinned and said, "Good! So when you do it, make it count! Do it up good!"

"Okay," she said, smiling her deep appreciation.

At dinner that night Veronica and Melanie talked about their day. They were both looking quite divine in the new dresses they had purchased. Father redirected all of the fashion chatter with a simple, "I think Jasmine has something to tell you."

"You're invited to a celebration tomorrow!" Jasmine announced, and they guessed the occasion immediately. Indeed, her joy could not be masked.

"More shopping!" Melanie gushed. "In the morning we get to help you pick out a first Holy Communion dress!"

The next day, Jasmine approached the altar in a sleeveless, knee-length, white satin dress, and a long-sleeved lace jacket. As she walked up the aisle, the similarity between first Holy Communion attire and wedding attire struck her for the first time. Isaiah's words rang through her heart and head: *Your Maker is your husband.*

Come to me, my love, she prayed. *Come and make me whole!*

Chapter 6

Poster Girl

It's good to be home, but... Veronica thought, as she contemplated the huge pile of mail before her. Most of it was letters of condolence from well-wishers. She sorted aside the tearjerkers from the business letters. She would need to go through them, but not at the moment. First, she would get her voice mails. *Thirty-six of them,* she sighed. *I don't know if I have the strength.* She didn't get past the first one.

"This is Mike Benson," the message said. "I trust that your Rome trip has lifted your spirits." Veronica smiled picturing the tall, handsome Capt. Benson who had been the best man at her wedding. It had been such a comfort seeing him at Jake's funeral. "I have great news," the message continued. "Thanks to Jake's efforts I've been appointed as military liaison to the Freqmod mission team. I am really looking forward to working with you, and hoping we can do lunch some day soon to catch up on things."

The next day, as he sat in his uniform across the table from her at lunch, she had the same impression as when he had marched up the aisle with Mel. *What an extraordinarily handsome man,* she thought, and then, *What is it with me and older men?* But Captain Benson was not all that much older. At forty-two he was the youngest of the original Screamin' Eagles team. In fact, he was the only one who would be able to actually fly his own plane in the upcoming AGC twenty-fifth anniversary celebration.

"Actually, Veronica," he said, "I told you in my voicemail that I had been appointed as liaison to the mission. What I didn't tell you is that I've also been offered the position of mission commander, and I'd like you to be the first to know that I've decided to accept."

"Wow! That's quite a commitment, Mike! Congratulations!"

"Thank you. I have more good news. I spoke with Tessa Oakley last night, and she said she's accepting the position of mission Engineering Chief."

"Really? Waylon will be excited to hear that. He thinks she's the best. I haven't met her yet other than in the bath tub," Veronica informed him.

"What?"

She laughed at the look on his face. "Waylon and Tessa called and ended up on speaker phone while I was in the tub. It was kind of bizarre."

Smiling at her lame, shock-value humor, he said, "You poor thing. Did Jake have to bequeath his sense of humor too?"

Veronica giggled a little and then was suddenly distant. She gazed out the window of the little café, watching a young mother and her two toddlers in the playground across the street. For the first time in ages, she nervously bit her bottom lip.

Mike placed his hand on hers and said, "I'm sorry, I shouldn't…"

"It's okay," Veronica said. "I loved him for a long time. You just pointed out that he's a bigger part of me than I realized. That's not a bad thing, just a little painful right now." Turning her hand over to grasp his, she said, "So…tell me about the Screamin' Eagles."

"We fly."

"Oh, really?" she said, rolling her eyes.

"Yup. Do you want to fly too?"

"What?"

"Do you want to be in the copilot seat when I go up?" he asked.

"Absolutely!" she chirped. The pleasure in his smile made her wonder the same thing she had always wondered about Jacob: *How has this guy managed to stay single?*

"Well, I guess I should really have given you all of the facts first," he said. "These are multi-billion-dollar aircraft, so operation of them is obviously restricted to only the most experienced pilots and copilots. One of the things about these planes, however, is that the controls are unbelievably intuitive. A child could fly one."

"Sounds just right for me!" she admitted.

"The Air Force will allow you in the copilot seat only if you take lessons and are able to actually land the craft. You will need to spend two hundred and fifty hours in the simulator before even getting into the cockpit of the actual plane."

"Wow," she said, "how will I ever find time for that?"

"Well, in your recent absence I have had several conversations with the AGC concerning this opportunity. They think that the coming twenty-fifth anniversary celebration is extremely important to the Freqmod mission. They envision a media hubbub—about the beautiful widow of the illustrious Jacob Lansing flying the most expensive fighter plane ever built—as one more layer of frosting on the old space-is-accessible-to-the-masses cake they've been baking for the past quarter century."

"I see," said Veronica. "Poster girl."

"Yes, poster girl," agreed the colonel. "Do you object?"

"You know, there was a time when I might have. It was Jacob who changed my view. He said that sometimes Christian people are inclined to see physical beauty as a sort of curse; however, while the gift, like any gift, can certainly be a cross, it is anything but a curse. It was Jacob who first proposed to me the whole 'poster girl' notion. When he was done with me, I felt I had a deep obligation to leverage my beauty to further the kingdom of God."

"Well, give me some hints," the colonel said, "what do I need to do to keep you thinking that way?"

"Spend time with me," she suggested, gazing into his eyes.

That afternoon Veronica found herself on Fr. Scofield's doorstep. "Good afternoon, Veronica," he greeted her, "please come in. What can I do for you today?"

"You know, Your Excellency, you've often addressed me as your 'dear Mrs. Lansing.' If anything, I expected that you'd get a little more formal as a bishop."

The new bishop just laughed. "If His Holiness can call you Veronica, so can I," he said, adding, "if that's okay with you…" She just smiled. "What brings you here on this fine sunny day?" he asked.

She looked at the floor as they seated themselves in his study, still a little short of words. "Well…here I am, a widow for barely a month now, and I find myself flirting with a man like I'm some fifteen-year-old schoolgirl!" she scolded herself.

"And…flirting with a man is wrong because…?" the bishop inquired. The look she gave him told him she didn't have an answer. "Look, Veronica, *Jake* died, not you. It is very important that you go through a period of mourning, but that mourning is not for Jake's sake. He's in the bosom of the Father cheering 'Go get 'im Ronnie, he's a looker!' It's impossible for you to hurt his feelings. And don't put any stock in the notion of 'dishonoring his memory.' That's all a bunch of rubbish! No, the mourning period is for you and for whomever you have an attraction. Right now you have a Jake-shaped hole in your heart. That hole must be given time to heal before it takes the shape of the next love in your life. Trying to fill the void too fast can be disastrous for everyone. The church imposes a six month waiting period for engaged couples. This time, there will be no dispensations," he proclaimed with a smile.

His proclamation made her smile too. "You old string-puller, you," she teased.

"I learned from the best!" he said, pointing to a wedding picture of her and Jake on his desk.

As she prepared to depart, he added, "Just one suggestion, if I may. You heard the Holy Father's directions to me. Bishop Hadrian and I are to find two or more holy men and ordain them as priests before reaching Freqmod, or shortly thereafter. So…you may want to ask yourself whether or not it's a good idea to be married to a priest."

Veronica took on a frown as if something had just been stolen from her. "Am I that transparent?!" she asked. "I come to you talking about a man, and you know who he is before I even tell you. That's just embarrassing!"

"I'm sorry, Veronica, did his name not come up in our conversation?" he asked with a grin, knowing full well that it had not.

Her frown turned to a laugh. "No, I'm sorry. What's wrong with me! Why would I ever think I could, or would need to, keep a secret from you? I guess I can't be nursing a privacy fetish if I've chosen a spiritual director who can read my very soul!"

"Ronnie's new friend, Jasmine, will have a serious case of envy when she finds out about these," Antonio Escobar told his bride as he placed a gravishifter into a strongbox with another eighteen of them. They had just finished a training session with the mission team and Antonio was responsible for securing the weapons.

"What do you mean?" Jean asked.

"FBI agents only dream about playing with toys like these," Antonio informed her. "I hope you had fun with them this week, because you'll probably never see one again."

"What? We're not done training yet," Jean objected, as she admired the weapon in her hand.

"As of this morning, international law bans the manufacture, sale, distribution, and possession of gravishifters," Antonio informed her. "The law takes effect in thirty days. Give it up," he said, extending an open hand. Jean reluctantly relinquished the amazing weapon.

"That law doesn't make them illegal on Freqmod," she said. "How are we supposed to protect ourselves against little green men?"

"Actually, the AGC hasn't made a ruling yet, but we're in the military, which makes these off-limits to us immediately. If the AGC decides they want these on the star voyage, I doubt they'll be willing to put up the kind of fight required to make that decision stick. This would not be a good time to get hung up on something so controversial."

"So…how do we fight the little…"

"Green men?" he finished for her. "With *regular* guns like they'll have. Based on their level of radio technology, we know they don't have anything like a gravishifter. The classic argument will be that, should these fall into the wrong hands, it could seriously disrupt the normal political/cultural development of their world."

"I suppose so," she said, pensively. As Antonio closed the strongbox she came from behind him and placed her hands in his front pockets. The bride had quickly discovered the groom's most ticklish area: the front of his hip bones. The tickling began.

"Jean! Stop!" he yelped. He pushed away from the strongbox and whirled around. His legs tangled with those of his bride and the two went crashing to the floor, laughing as they fell. Antonio sat up and looked at his bride, who was still sprawled on her back, giggling. She turned to her tummy and fanned her long lashes at him. He surveyed her every move, counting his blessings. *How can anyone look that good in camo khaki?* he wondered. His five-foot, brown-eyed, brunette spit-fire from Louisiana was half French, one quarter Choctaw, one quarter trouble, and one hundred percent woman.

"How'd I get so lucky as to marry a ticklish man?" the little tormentor asked. Her voice was high pitched, yet throaty and a little raspy, like that of a small child who'd done too much screaming.

She crawled over to him, straddled his legs, and locked eyeballs with him. "I'm looking forward to two years of captive husband on a starship!" she informed him. "But I can't wait until then for the fun to begin. There's a nice little surprise for you in your locker."

"What'd you get me?"

"Go see," she answered.

"What's the occasion?" Antonio asked as he went to the next room to fetch the gift. Jean didn't answer him. She was busy opening the strongbox. She quickly and quietly removed a gravishifter, closed the box, and placed the weapon in her purse.

Antonio came back into the room with a small gift-wrapped package. "What's the occasion?" he asked again.

"You married me! I'll be celebrating that forever!" she answered.

"Thank you, sweetheart," he said, giving her a quick kiss. "Do you want me to open it now?"

"Um…you should probably wait till we're home. Let's get going so you'll have time to enjoy it."

"Okay, let's go," he said, grabbing her hand and trotting toward the door.

"Tony, don't you have to do something with these?" Jean asked, motioning to the strongbox full of gravs.

"Oh, yeah! Wow! Thanks, honey," he said, as he moved the strongbox into the vault.

I suppose I should see what my phone's blinking about, Jasmine thought. The little red light called her to a life she would just as soon forget. She and her new friends had returned from Rome the night before, and she had no intention of going to the office. She needed a day to rest and reflect.

"I want you back," Doug's voice said plaintively in the first message. She quickly hit *delete*.

"How the hell are we supposed to bowl a decent game without our own personal spy on the team," Martha the Mouth screeched from the little box. "I expect to see your skinny ass down here Saturday night. We're running way behind!"

"So much for expectations," Jasmine said as she hit *delete*.

The third message, and the last one she would listen to, was from her boss. "This is Spinelli. Come see me!" the terse message ordered. Within the hour she entered the tyrant's office. He was uncharacteristically quiet as she seated herself. He pulled a copy of *The Naked Truth* from a desk drawer and plopped it in front of her.

"Skink doesn't work for *The Voyeur* anymore. He works for *The Naked Truth*. Read it and weep!"

In horror, Jasmine picked up the paper. A picture of her and Veronica hugging on the beach filled the entire cover page. The headline read, "Angel of Adrenaline Saves F.B.I. Wretch." The blood went from her face.

"Your entire conversation can be found on the inside," Spinelli said, in a tone somewhat more merciful. "And if that's not bad enough, check this out," he said typing in a web address given in the article.

The web site opened to the same cover photo, and Spinelli clicked on a video icon.

"Don't tell me that there's a god out there who wants to get cozy with a slut like me," Jasmine's words and image opened the segment. She slid down in her chair, her face another shade lighter. Spinelli dragged the position indicator a couple inches and the video resumed with, "The bastard made me get an operation before I moved in with him. As you so aptly pointed out, I'm no better than an animal now! I'm an *it!* I'm nothin' but a friggin *it!*"

Jasmine stood and bolted for the hall bathroom. There was no time to close the door. Spinelli could hear her heaving her guts out. Babasa, the tough F.B.I. agent, was vulnerable after all.

A quarter hour later she was cleaned up and back in front of Spinelli. "Bubba, I'm sorry you had to go through this. I really am. At first I was really riled. You're not one to break protocol and get business and personal things all balled up, but you're human. We all need people like the Angel once in a while. But I don't have to tell you that this is bad. It's embarrassing for you, for me, and for the agency.

"Skink had just gotten this upgrade in jobs, there's no way you could've known what you were dealing with. *The Voyeur's* just a *Naked Truth* wannabe. His new employer's been around for almost a hundred years and has nearly unlimited resources. There was a whole team following you that day. Skink was wearing several button cameras. In short, they have equipment *The Voyeur* only dreams of having. Skink's little hand held was just a decoy. The other unfortunate thing is that, unlike *The Voyeur*, these people hardly ever fabricate a story. They have a reputation for uncovering certifiable muck.

"Anyway, I don't want to blow this out of proportion. It's not like the damn Mexico scandal last year. It's just another embarrassment. The director called me this morning."

"The director?! What'd he say?"

"He said, 'I told you to keep the Lansing/Mole thing low profile! This isn't low profile!' He also said that it looks like we're so sloppy with covert operations that Skink was able to follow a known agent around and pick up stories—like candy tossed from a stinkin' parade float! It's like the FBI is their vehicle to get at the celebs, and they got away with it. That's what's so damned embarrassing."

"Where does all this leave us?" she asked.

"It leaves us with an impossible mission. The director wants us to get that web site shut down and to get *The Naked Truth* to print a retraction and apology, and—get this—to not do anything illegal in the process!"

"What planet is he from?"

"The way I see it we have two choices, neither of them pretty," Spinelli said. "We can play by the director's rules, in which case we will fail and pay the consequences, or we can break the rules, succeed, and pray like crazy we don't get caught."

"What *are* the consequences?" Jasmine asked.

"Scapegoating," Spinelli answered.

"Like with Dobbs?" she asked.

Spinelli shifted uneasily in his chair. "Look, I know you two were close. This is a tough business. The reason I'm having this talk with you is because I don't want to have to do that kind of crap anymore."

"You wouldn't have had to do it in the first place if you had any…"

"Look, Bubba…this isn't getting us anywhere. I'm trying to be more up front than I've ever been before. Give me a little slack, okay?"

Jasmine sighed hard, swallowed a big hunk of pride, and said "Okay, Chief. You said we had two choices, the directors way and the not-so-legal way. There is a third way," she offered.

"Yeah?"

"Yeah. We could 'pray like crazy' and *then* try to do it without breaking the rules."

"Pray? I was just using an expression, Bubba. Jeez, the Angel really did get to you! Good luck with that! But whatever you do, I don't want to know about it. Got it?"

"Got it."

On her way back from a haircut, Veronica's thoughts distracted her so badly that she wished her old car had autopilot. She thought about what Fr. Scofield had said: Would she want to be married to a priest? Her budding relationship with Mike could lead to that. In thinking about it something suddenly occurred to her. "They expect me to go on this mission!" she said out loud to herself. "What are they thinking? I can't run a huge corporation from another planet!" Then she felt really dumb, and asked herself, "What was I doing flirting with Mike? He'll be gone for thirteen years! And what am I doing talking out loud to myself? Man! I'm even talking out loud to myself about talking out loud to myself!" She was still yapping with herself as she parked in her driveway. Melanie was sitting on the front step. "Hop in, favorite niece," Veronica yelled from the car. "We're getting late. Sorry I took so long."

As they headed toward AGC headquarters, Melanie asked, "Were you singing as you pulled up the drive?"

"No…why?"

"Cause your mouth was movin' like crazy."

"Oh. No, I was just carrying on a conversation with myself. Did you realize that the AGC is expecting me to make the trip to Freqmod?" she asked. Melanie turned to look at her, and Veronica could see the gears turning in her eyes.

"Gee. I guess nobody's come right out and said it, but it has kind of been implied, hasn't it."

"Well, what do you think about that?"

Mel didn't need to think. "Well, let's see, thirteen years without my best friend in the whole world? Goober! Whadya expect me to think?"

"Thank you, Mel. That's sweet," she said, and thought about how her life had become one huge, never-ending emotional roller coaster. "But aside from that?" she pressed. Now Mel looked scared.

"Are you serious, Ronnie? Is this mission something you really want to do?"

"Please, just answer my question, Mel. Is it a good thing for me to do?"

"Okay," Mel mused, "you want me to pretend I'm not your best friend and I'm not a walking estrogen-inebriated emotion factory and to look at the situation objectively."

"You own a huge corporation, Mel, you need to get used to operating that way."

"No, we own a huge corporation and you want to run off and die on some distant star and leave me with this thing in my lap!" she insisted. "Have you given one minute of thought," she went on, "about to whom we'll bequeath this…this…behemoth?"

The question caught the widow Lansing off guard. She had controlling interest in a multi-billion-dollar corporation but had no last will and testament. "That's easy Mel. I'll just draw up a little will and leave it all to you."

"You haven't thought about this at all, have you? You have parents and siblings. Aren't you giving anything to them? How about your favorite charities? I'm a billionaire. Why would you leave it to me?"

"Well...have *you* thought about it, Mel?"

"No. I'm sorry. Owning all this stuff is stressful. I don't like it."

"You know," Veronica thought out loud, "your Uncle Jake sure handled it well. We need to discover his secret. He took many trips around the solar system, was gone for weeks at a time, and everything kept running. You never saw him upset about anything. That's pretty amazing."

"Yeah, well I'm not my uncle and neither are you!" Mel declared, somewhat hurtfully.

"So what are you saying, Mel?" Veronica pressed. "That we shouldn't finish this conversation? That we should go on pretending we have no problems to solve?"

Melanie started to cry. "I don't want to fight with you, Ronnie," she said through sobs. "I hate this!"

Veronica drove into a little park along the road and stopped the car. She touched a weeping Melanie on the shoulder, got out of the car, and walked to the bank of a small stream. She seated herself on the bank, without regard for the trendy dress she had donned for the AGC meeting, and started to throw pebbles into the stream. In a few minutes Mel came and knelt behind her and rubbed her shoulders a bit. Resting her chin on Veronica's head, she said through sniffles, "Things will never be the same again, will they, Ronnie?"

Veronica reached up and touched her friend's face. "No, Mel, they won't," she said.

"You go get cleaned up, Tony," Jean told her husband as she pulled up to their front door. "I need to make a quick trip to the market. Don't open that gift before I get back because it won't be any fun without me in it," she advised. Antonio smiled. His wife was the personification of surprise package.

Fifteen minutes later, Jean sat in her car looking at a circle of eight scruffy earth-tone cottages with thatched roofs. "Mole Nation Central," she muttered to herself, "also known as slime ball city!" She removed the gravishifter from her purse, checked the safety, and tucked it into her jeans.

Chickens and ducks scurried out of her path as she walked to the center of a hundred-foot diameter garden space encircled by the buildings.

"Mole Nation!" she shouted, and kept repeating her greeting until she saw faces in windows. "Hey, cowards! Where the hell are you? You like to murder women? Come and get me! Quit wasting my time and get your sorry butts out here! I'm an astronaut. Come and save my soul from wandering the universe! You don't want mamma E to lose her temper, do ya? I'm talking to you, cowards!"

A young, clean-shaven Mole wearing a rough cotton garment came out of one of the buildings and stood looking at her. He was in his late twenties, tall and muscular, with sun streaked auburn hair and a California tan. *Poor sap must be a new recruit,* Jean thought. *These cowards gotta send the new kid out to do their dirty work!* "Come and get me, little coward man!" she taunted. He walked about half the distance toward her and stopped.

"You're an astronaut? Give me a break," he said, laughing.

"I'm Dr. Jeanine Martin-Escobar, Marine Corp. Captain. I'm an astronaut, Chief Surgeon on the Freqmod mission team, and you, sir, are a cowardly, self-obsessed slime ball! You slime balls murdered my sister-in-law! Come and finish the job if you're man enough!" she taunted, looking about to be sure no one was sneaking up behind her.

"Go home, half-pint; we don't want any trouble," the man said, walking away from her.

"Then you shouldn't have started it!" Jean insisted, pulling the grav from her jeans.

Mr. Mole heard the weapon power up and turned to look. "Ooh, realistic noises and everything!" he jeered. "If you came here to scare us, you might have considered finding a more believable looking prop!" he said, laughing over his shoulder.

Jean checked her backside again. Four other men and two women had come out and were circling around her at a distance. The Mole in front of her took advantage of her momentary distraction and rushed toward her. She fired into the ground in front of him, and the earth exploded beneath his feet, propelling him four feet into the air.

She took a few steps toward him and said, "Is that realistic enough?" She looked around and the other six cowards were hightailing it to the cottages. "You don't look so well," she said to the debris covered Mole. "Let me help you up!" she shot the ground beneath him, propelling him into the air again.

As she came toward him again, he begged, "Please, no!"

"You still don't look so well," she said. "Maybe you could use something to eat." Aiming the gravishifter at an apple tree, she pulled the trigger and dispatched it. The big tree fell on the adjacent cottage, its jutting trunk shredded like the work of a rabid beaversaurus. The man stood and bolted toward the house. "You still hungry?" she asked, aiming the weapon at a goat that had entered the space. She cranked up the gravs power level and blasted the ground beneath the nanny. The exploding earth sent it sailing to the roof top where it landed safely in the limbs of the felled tree. At the sound of his bleating friend, the fleeing Mole stopped and looked up, and then stared hatefully back at Jean.

"So...I finally figured out what it is that matters to a slime ball!" she noted. "How about some meat for supper, slimy?" she asked, leveling the grav at the poor, confused nanny goat. A hand came from over Jean's shoulder and grabbed the grav. She fired one last time, blasting the cottage's chimney. The goat climbed out of the limbs and onto the thatch just in time to be swept from the roof by an avalanche of bricks. Mole Man positioned himself to break the critter's fall, taking a few lumps from falling bricks in the process. He quickly carried his darling into the cottage.

In the struggle, Jean lost her grip on the grav. As it fell to the ground she began to punch her assailant, connecting several times before realizing who he was. She froze and began to tremble when their eyes met, her mouth hanging open and her heart pounding. Then she went to him and buried her face in his embrace. She clutched the front of his shirt with both hands, and twisted it while she cried, "They murdered her, Tony. They murdered my sister-in-law!"

"I know, honey. I know," he said, putting his arms around her. A U.S. marshal stooped and picked up the missing grav.

Through tears she screamed, "I loved her so much, Tony! I never had a sister. They killed my only sister! I just want to kill them all!"

"It's okay, Jean! It's okay!" he said.

"No! It's not okay! They stole our honeymoon!" she managed between sobs. "Our honeymoon was a funeral! You call Juanita's name in your sleep! You cry in your sleep, and I hold you, but you won't stop crying. Sometimes I wake you up, but then I see this horrible empty look in your eyes! I hate what they did to you, Tony! I hate what they did to us! I hate it!"

"I'll be okay, Jean. I'll be okay. You have to forgive so you can be okay too," Antonio told her. Jean started sobbing so hard that she couldn't remain standing and he took her in his arms and carried her to the car. When he had her seated in the vehicle, he turned to speak with the U.S. marshals who had accompanied him.

"It's a good thing we stopped at the AGC to pick up the gravs when we did," one of the marshals said. "She's in a pretty rough state. There's no telling how this might have ended. As far as what went on here tonight, Captain Escobar, I didn't see a thing. This never happened."

The other marshal nodded his head in agreement, "Never saw a thing," he said. "Take care of her, son. We're pulling for you and the rest of the Freqmod team. Hang in there!"

"Thank you!" Antonio said. "Thank you so much!"

Antonio trembled as he drove home. A sea of adrenaline searched for an outlet. Jean sat beside him, one foot up on the seat and her forehead on her knee. Sobs of grief mingled now with tears of relief. She was beaten but triumphant. She had taught the Moles a lesson and had not gone to jail for it. Antonio placed his hand on her sandaled foot and gently rubbed her toes. He was proud of his wonderful, unpredictable wife, but wondered what the evening's events might cost him.

Col. Benson had been, with Antonio's permission, socializing the Marine captain's name for the position of chief of security, fourth in command for the star journey. His dual master's degrees, one in criminal justice and the other, oddly enough, in botany, filled a critical need on the mission team. However, he now wondered what to do. If he reported Jean's behavior, would she be disqualified? If he did not, and it became known to the AGC, would *he* be disqualified?

He went from rubbing Jean's toes to tickling them. She grasped his hand, brought it to her lips, kissed it, and gave him a teary, fiery-eyed smile. Antonio smiled back. *She's all that I'm really committed to,* he thought, *and she's all that really matters!*

The day after their heart-to-heart spat and chat, Veronica and Melanie visited Josh Gundersen, who had already drawn up simple wills that made them each mutual beneficiaries of the other's passing.

"We can always get to the finer points later," Josh told them, "but this gives you some protection against chaos for the immediate future."

Just as they were finishing up, Jasmine came into the room to let Josh know that the governor and first lady were in the lobby. "Well, I better not keep them waiting," he said, bidding them all a good day.

When Josh had gone Veronica gave Jasmine a hug and asked, "How are you doing, Jazz? You look a little under the weather."

Jasmine motioned the two into her office. "Have you seen this?" she asked, producing the copy of *The Naked Truth* from a desk drawer.

"Oh no! Veronica said as she viewed the cover. "Oh no!" she said again as she paged through the article. "I'm so sorry, Jasmine!"

"Well, look, they invaded your privacy too," Jasmine said, trying to be matter-of-fact.

"Can they do this?" Melanie asked.

"They did it. They just recorded an event and published it."

"They were stalking us. Can't they be charged with stalking?"

"You'd have to charge every reporter who's ever lived, Ronnie. The director expects us to get a retraction and apology out of them without breaking any rules. I don't see how that's possible."

"What kind of rules would you usually consider breaking?" Melanie asked.

"We'd need to show them that we have something on them, something damaging," Jasmine answered.

"You mean...like blackmail?" Veronica asked, a little shocked.

"Yeah, Angel, like blackmail. But don't worry, the only thing we have on them is some sordid video footage of the owner/editor's extramarital exploits, and that train has already left the station."

"What do you mean?" Melanie asked.

"I mean, Mr. James Pierce got divorced last year. What would we threaten him with? Showing this video to his eight-year-old daughter? Or his mother? He would know that even the FBI's not *that* low."

"Pierce? What's his daughter's name?" Veronica asked.

"Kimmie. Why?"

Veronica's jaw dropped. "I take care of an eight-year-old Kimmie Pierce for four hours a week," she said. "It's part of my volunteer work at Children's. She has an incurable disease. In order to leave the hospital, she needs to be accompanied by a physician at all times. Spending time with me allows her to get out and do some fun things."

As Veronica spoke, Jasmine connected her computer to her F.B.I. file. After a minute she announced, "She's his daughter!"

"Wow!" Veronica exclaimed quietly. "I'm scheduled to spend a couple hours with her this afternoon. Maybe it's a good take-your-daughter-to-work day."

"I can't let you go alone. Who knows what these creeps are capable of?" Jasmine wondered. "When are you scheduled to pick up Kimmie?"

"In forty-five minutes."

"Hmm...just enough time," Jasmine estimated. As they strode into the parking lot, she said, "I see you two are still keeping a low profile." Veronica didn't catch on, but Melanie started to snicker.

"She's referring to our mode of transportation, Ronnie. I guess there aren't many billionaires out there driving an '82 Nexus. Is that what you're getting at, Jazz?"

"You guys are funny," Jasmine said, grinning.

"The styling hasn't changed much, how did you know it was so old?" Veronica asked.

"Are you kidding? I saw you *drive* into your parking space. Nexus has been making side-shifters for a quarter of a century. How the heck do you guys find a parking space?"

"We just have to drive around until we find two adjacent spaces." Veronica explained.

"Well, that only rules out three quarters of the spaces in town!" Jasmine said, laughing. "And...don't you get parking tickets for using up two spaces?"

"We're grandfathered in," Melanie informed her.

"Niiiice," Jasmine said, rolling her eyes. "Let's take my car. Kimmie will love it."

"That leaves *you* with the limo, Mel. Sorry," Veronica said in mock apology. "See you later."

The receptionist at *The Naked Truth* was panic-stricken as Jasmine, Veronica, and Kimmie stormed in and breezed right past her without saying a word. Kimmie remained in the hallway with Jasmine while Veronica barged into Jim Pierce' office. Skink was with Mr. Pierce and the two were considerably disconcerted by her sudden presence.

"Mrs. Lansing!" Pierce said, as he stood up behind his desk. "To what do we owe the pleasure?"

Veronica came around the desk and stood very close to him. Her eyes came to mid-chest level on the huge man. *How can anyone so large be so small,* she asked herself.

"Oh, no," Pierce laughed, "I'm afraid the Angel-of-Adrenaline routine's not gonna work on me!" he proclaimed.

"It outa work on you just as well as it did on me!" Skink clucked.

"I'm not the only angel around," Veronica said flatly.

"Oh, my gosh! You brought reinforcements?!" Skink hissed. "Did you bring along the FBI's now famous *it* to shame us into submission?"

"Shut up, Skink!" Veronica ordered. The two men looked at each other with impious grins, like two delinquents shamed by a teacher.

"Kimmie, come see your daddy," Veronica said. Jasmine came through the door carrying the little girl. Kimmie's genetic disorder had left her small and frail for an eight-year-old, and she could easily be carried in the arms of a well-muscled woman like Jasmine. Jim Pierce's mouth was hanging open. He brushed past Veronica, fell to one knee, and held his arms out to Kimmie, who evaded his embrace and slid by him to get to Veronica.

Speechless for a moment, Pierce finally said, "What's going on, Mrs. Lansing?"

"Nothing's going on, Jim, and please, call me Veronica."

"Okay, Veronica, what's my daughter doing here with you?"

"The same thing she does every week at this time, Jim. She leaves the hospital with her volunteer care giver. You signed the papers. Didn't you know that the acclaimed Dr. Veronica Weslin, Nobel Laureate and inventor of a breakthrough pediatric nutricuetical delivery system—the volunteer care-giver whose name was on the release form you signed—was the same Dr. Weslin who had married the illustrious Jacob Lansing? Aren't you a journalist, Jim? How did such a headline escape you? Was the news not close enough to the bottom? Close enough to your feeding grounds?"

"I apologized to you," Jasmine said to Skink. "Why did you try to ruin my life?"

"You're always so high and mighty," Skink sneered, "I just thought it was time you got a taste of…"

"Shut up, Skink!" Pierce shouted.

"But…"

"I said shut up!"

"Daddy, don't shout!" Kimmie said. "You scare me!"

"I'm sorry, Kimmie," he said, putting out his hands, but she drew back.

"We're headed for the zoo, Jim; would you like to join us?" Veronica asked.

A stunned, beaten Jim Pierce just stood and looked at her for a moment. "Yes. Yes I would. Skink, shut down the video site of the beach conversation," he commanded.

"But…"

"Shut up and shut it down!" Pierce shouted. Skink left to do as he was told.

"Daddy, let's go now," Kimmie begged, frightened once again by his shouting.

Forty-five minutes later, Veronica was holding Kimmie so she didn't have to look through the chain link fencing of the zoo. The child giggled at two bunnies chasing each other about in the grass. Mr. Pierce was lost in thought gazing at a pair of swans. The pure white creatures stood with their necks entwined, lost in each other's company. Somehow the image of them directed his thoughts to the beautiful woman just inches from his side. *What kind of a woman has her privacy invaded by a tabloid and then goes to the zoo with the owner of the damn scandal sheet!* he wondered. *What kind of woman?* Thirty-eight years of selfish living churned in his soul like so much half digested chili looking for an exit. His own thoughts mocked him. *And you thought you were immune to the Angel! Now what?*

With Kimmie safely back in her hospital room, the three adults stepped, lobby bound, into the hospital's elevator. Pierce broke the silence. "I want you to know that I will personally write a retraction to the story we did. The retraction will state that the entire thing was a fabrication, a theatrical production."

"We're not asking you to lie, Jim," Veronica informed him.

"I've never had a problem with it before," he admitted. "This time it will be for a good cause. If my attorney was here he'd tell me I'm nuts, that I'm opening myself up for a lawsuit. But I trust that angels don't sue."

A week later Jasmine was seated across from Spinelli. "How'd you accomplish it, Bubba?" Spinelli asked, throwing the next printing of *The Naked Truth* in front of her.

"Uh, you said you didn't want to know," Jasmine reminded him.

"Only if you did something…inappropriate. But, if you didn't, I'd love to know how you got it done."

"*I* didn't, Chief. Mrs. Lansing went and spoke with them. They couldn't outdo the Angel."

"Maybe I should hire the Angel," he said whimsically.

"You will need to hire *someone*," Jasmine informed him.

"Whadaya mean?"

"I'm leaving the agency, Spinelli," she said.

"Don't do that to me!" Spinelli moaned.

"Always thinking of others, aren't you, Chief."

"What will you do?" he asked.

"What I've *been* doing, working for GGT. I'll be with all of my favorite people in the world!" she said exuberantly.

After a morning of debriefing, she went to lunch with Veronica to celebrate her new freedom. "I'm so excited for you, Jazz!" Veronica gushed. "What was Josh's reaction when he found out that you had been living a double life all this time?"

"He's excited to see how well I can do when he has my undivided attention. I've only been working mornings for him, but I'll be going to full days next week. I only worked there a couple of months and I spent half of my time spying. The agency wanted to make sure that the Moles had not infiltrated GGT to try and destroy Jacob and the AGC financially. Gathering data was unbelievably easy. GGT is one of the least secure places on Earth. Hard to believe when you consider the massive fortunes that have been managed from there. I'll bet that I know more about your money than you do!"

"Well…that's not all that impressive!" Veronica assured her, giggling about her own lack of knowledge.

"I'll be doing more than secretarial work now that Josh knows my full background. I'll be initiating security measures! My only regret is that I had to give up the LX; no more flying for me." Slowly the smile left her face and she became very quiet.

"What's wrong, Jazz?" Veronica asked.

"I was just thinking about you leaving for Freqmod. Except for Dobbs you're the first real friend I've ever had, Ronnie. I don't know if I can make sense of life without you. Do you have to go?"

"Maybe the AGC should hire you for the mission," Veronica suggested.

"As what? Your personal bodyguard?" Jasmine joked.

Before Veronica could respond, a waitress came to the table with a tall iced drink. She set it before Jasmine and informed her that it was "from the military gentleman at the bar." Jasmine turned to see the Army man who had pulled her off of his hood a couple weeks back. She returned his smile and began to relate the story to Veronica.

Lifting the drink up to her nose, she took a whiff and cringed. "I don't think I can drink this," she said to Veronica with a wrinkled nose. "I remember all too well the last time I had one of these!"

While she spoke, Veronica studied the face of and exchanged smiles with that Army officer. Suddenly her jaw dropped and she turned back to Jasmine. "Do you know who that is?" she asked.

"I don't know his name."

"That's the 'Hard Nut!'" Veronica exclaimed.

"Huh?"

"You know that movie, *A Hard Nut to Crack*? It's a suspense thriller about what happened to Col. Cliff Lamans in the Panama crisis. The officer who just bought you a drink is the real Col. Clifford J. Lamans! I've seen his picture in the papers. I'm sure it's him!"

"Wow! So...he not only saves the country from nuclear terrorists, he pulls drunken women off of car hoods. Doesn't sound like such a bad guy. Maybe he's the answer to my prayers."

"Well, it looks like time for me to make my exit," Veronica observed with music in her voice. "But,,,you have to get back to work don't you?"

"I only work mornings. I don't start full time till next week, and I can walk home from here, or the colonel can give me a ride. I expect he'll be a perfect gentleman like he was the other night." She thanked Veronica for joining her, and when her friend had gone, turned her attention to the man at the bar and lit up the brightest smile she could conjure. The colonel took the invitation, and after a polite "May I?" seated himself in the booth across from her.

"My friend says that you're the famous 'Hard Nut.' Is that true?"

"The one and only," he answered. "Col. Clifford J. Lamans at your service."

"I'm Jasmine," she said, extending a hand, "Jasmine Babasa."

He took her hand, kissed it, and said, "Jasmine Babasa hangs out with a pretty high class crowd! How long have you known Mrs. Lansing?"

"Not long. Only a few weeks actually."

"Listen, doll, I was going to play dumb, which comes naturally for me, but I won't do that to you. I won't pretend that I didn't read the article in *The Naked Truth* or the retraction that followed. That had to be tough."

"Which did you believe, the article or the retraction?" she asked.

"You're very direct. I like that. I believed the article. Sleazy gossip magazines can't afford actresses of that caliber, and that was either the finest acting I've ever seen or the real thing. Besides, it would be hard to find two actresses who were perfect look-alikes for two of the most beautiful women in the world."

"Well, thank you, sir. What brings you to town, Colonel?"

"Freqmod. I'm here with Capt. Benson scoping things out."

"Are you interested in being part of the mission?" she asked.

"I'm interested in checking it out to see if I'm interested," he said. "Mike Benson has already made the commitment. The Army will not order anyone to be part of a mission like this. It's purely voluntary. I'm honored to be chosen as a candidate, I just haven't thrown my hat in the ring yet." Jasmine giggled. "What's so funny?" he asked.

"Oh…Veronica asked me today if I want to be on the mission team. I just laughed and asked her 'as what, your bodyguard?' I just don't see how I would ever be qualified for a thing like that."

"Are you kidding? FBI experience, marshal arts expert, a Masters in criminal justice, a minor in political science, trilingual, and computer savvy? Sounds like pretty good qualifications to me!"

"How do you know all that about me?"

"Umm…that would be courtesy of *The Naked Truth,* assuming it's all true."

Jasmine snickered at the irony. "Why print lies when the truth will make millions?"

Col. Lamans nodded toward the drink he had supplied. "You're not going to drink that, are you?" She smiled, looked at the drink, looked back at him, and shook her head as they shared a laugh. "You're not up for hood diving tonight, eh?" he asked through the laughter.

After chatting for an hour, he walked her home in the bright afternoon sunshine. *I've never dated a man with manners this good,* she thought, but then asked herself, *Is this a date? I don't think I'm ready for dating!* He walked with her up to her room, and when she had unlocked her door, Jasmine said, "I've really enjoyed visiting with you. Perhaps we can get together again some time."

"You're a wonderful woman, Jasmine. I would like that very much," the colonel answered.

Invite him in! a voice inside shouted. *No way, I'm not ready for that!* another voice countered. She just stood there in the open doorway with an odd expression on her face while the argument raged inside her.

"Are you okay?" he asked after a bit.

"Oh…I don't know…"

"You can't decide whether or not to ask me in, right?"

Jasmine let her shoulders slump and her hands drop to her sides like a wet dish towel. "How did I ever accomplish anything in the FBI," she wondered out loud as she turned and walked into her apartment. "Am I that darn transparent?"

"It's okay. I'm sure you weren't always so. You've been through some tough times," he said, following her in. "If you're uncomfortable with me being here, I'll go," he added, closing the door behind him.

For the first time in five weeks, scared and exhilarated, she was alone with a man behind closed doors. She seated herself on the couch but he remained standing at the door, waiting to be invited to take a seat. *What great manners!* she thought. "Please have a seat," she said after a bit. He took a seat at the other end of the couch.

"I like your apartment," he said. "It's very cozy." She studied his face. There was something sort of robotic about him. She felt none of the "love at first sight" she felt for Fr. Ian. This man did not stir her soul, and yet, a part of her wanted him. She fought to stop the images, to stop undressing him in her mind. Was he undressing her in his mind? That thought enticed her more than any other. She wanted to be undressed. She wanted a man to take off her clothes, look at her, and be amazed! To look at her and experience love at first sight! But this was not the man. Something was wrong.

She stood suddenly. She had not responded to his compliments about the apartment. She had just sat there staring at him. It was all very awkward and embarrassing. "I…think you have to go now," she stammered.

"Of course. Whatever you wish," he said, standing. He walked to the door, put his hand on the knob and said, "Perhaps you can join me for dinner?"

"Um…not tonight. I will need to look at my calendar," she answered.

He handed her a business card. "Give me a call," he said simply, and bid her a good day. When he had left, she locked the door behind him and just stood there listening to the sound of his footsteps as he descended the stairs. Finally it occurred to her what it was about him that was bugging her. *There's just something…Dougish about him,* she thought. *He's all charm and no soul, nothing behind the eyes.* She felt betrayed by her body. *Why does a certain part of me want to crawl into bed with this guy? He's not even all that good-looking. What's wrong with me?* So many questions. Perhaps Fr. Scofield would have the answers.

A quick phone call verified that he was home, and the afternoon sun lifted her spirits as she walked to his place. After exchanging amenities she took a seat facing him next to the huge windows in his study.

"To what do I owe the honor of your presence, Jasmine?"

"I...I met a man. He walked me home. He was in my apartment for a little bit. I didn't find him all that attractive or lovable, and yet...in my mind I kept having images of making love to him...images of him undressing me. I'm a terrible sinner, Father!"

"Jasmine...these...images. Did you concentrate on them? Did you take them beyond what flashed into your mind?"

"No!"

"Then what is it about them that makes you think you're a terrible sinner?"

"If I was a holy person, I wouldn't be thinking like that!"

"Wait a minute. You weren't *thinking*. You said these images just popped into your head...that you didn't dwell on them or further them or attempt any enjoyment of them. Is that accurate?"

"I guess. Yes, Father."

"Then you did not sin. Look. Suppose that I'm a reformed alcoholic and used to beat my wife and kids when I drank; and suppose I'm at a party and others are drinking, and the smell of all that alcohol gets to me. I want to have a drink. I can taste it. I can remember how all the tension will just drain from my body after just a drink or two. All of the sensory images come back to me, but I don't dwell on them. I move away from the drinkers to remove the temptation. Eventually I leave the party on account of it. Was it a sin for me to have those desires?"

"No. You couldn't help but have them...being a former addict and all," she answered. As she finished the sentence her eyes opened wide. "I'm an addict!" she said. "I'm an addict. That's what you're trying to say, isn't it? That's why I've always ended up with losers. I'm a sucker for the first warm body that comes along." The words had no more than left her mouth when she chastised herself, thinking, *If they're losers, what are you, toots?*

"It's very dangerous to your spiritual life, Jasmine, to equate temptation with sin," Fr. Scofield explained. "It is through temptation that Satan loses the battle. Every temptation is an opportunity to chose, and every choice is an opportunity for victory. Addiction is a sign of election."

"A sign of…what?" Jasmine asked, confused.

"Addiction is a sign of election," Fr. Scofield repeated, "a sign that God has chosen you for great things. You see, the only way to truly overcome addiction is to stay constantly connected with God. When we bring ourselves into his presence, he rewards us with his ability to love, turning our lives from self-centered to other-centered. Thus, addiction is an opportunity for spiritual greatness."

As he spoke, Jasmine noticed something new on the wall behind him. It was a picture of a crucifix, a very unusual crucifix that captured her gaze and would not let her go. Father turned to see what had stolen her attention.

"He's not wearing a whatchamacallit," she declared.

"A loin cloth?"

"Yeah."

"The Romans crucified people naked. Total public humiliation was part of the punishment," Fr. Scofield instructed. "Christ's nudity on the cross bears great significance. The book of Genesis tells us that, before the fall, Adam and Eve were naked without shame. The new Adam, Jesus, was stripped naked before the world, but there was no shame in his naked, sacred, sinless body."

Gazing intently at the image, Jasmine said, "I guess I never thought of him as…" Her words trailed off.

"As whole?" Father offered.

"Yes. When I receive him in Communion, do I receive…I mean…"

"You receive *all* of him, Jasmine: body, soul, and divinity! He is the bridegroom, awaiting us in the honeymoon suite. We are to strip ourselves of all worldly cares, of all attachments to material things, and stand naked before him. We are recreated through his gift of self, reclaiming our innocence."

Though stunned by what he said, Jasmine smiled at him. Between Veronica and Fr. Scofield, she was becoming accustomed to getting a sermon every time she asked a question. "I've never seen such a thing. Where did you get it?" she asked.

"I bought it in Rome. It's a photo of a crucifix carved by Michelangelo for the Santo Spirito convent in Florence."

"Convent? This was hanging where nuns could see it?"

Father pointed to the picture hanging beside the one in question, a picture of the Immaculate Conception. "Whenever I am tempted by lust," he said, "which is nearly every day, I pray before a picture of the Blessed Virgin. She is a very special expression of Divine love. My devotion to her sacred beauty, her sacred womanhood, and the grace it brings, has helped me to overcome lust more than any other prayer."

"I'm sure the graces you receive from the sacrament of celibacy are also very helpful," Jasmine ventured.

"Um, there is no sacrament of celibacy, Jasmine," he informed her.

"Huh? Don't you get that when you become a priest or a nun?"

"I received the sacrament of Holy Orders, which gave me the powers of the priesthood, but there's no sacrament of celibacy."

"Why not?" Jasmine asked.

"Christ did not institute one," Fr. Scofield informed her.

"But, you said that Jesus said, 'Some men are born eunuchs and some choose to be for the kingdom of God,' or something like that. Why wouldn't that be like instituting a sacrament?"

"Well, the scriptural basis and historical development of the sacraments is a long story, but consider this: Jesus also told the Sadducees that, in the next life, men and women are neither given nor taken in marriage. In other words, marriage is for this life. In the next life we will be eternally espoused to the Trinity.

"Therefore, celibacy is a celebration of glory, a participation in the next life. In a way it is the ultimate act of faith. Men and women forgo the earthly fulfillment of their sexuality to more fully embrace their eternal espousal to Christ. We embrace a *heavenly* fulfillment, laying claim to glory while still pilgrims, and for this, the world views us as the ultimate fools."

"I view you as the holiest man I've ever known!" Jasmine told him. "But what do you do when you're…" she blushed searching for the right word.

"Horny?" he asked.

"Gosh, Father, the word sounds so…odd coming from your lips!"

"I didn't mean to offend you, Jasmine, but I have to fight the same things that others fight. I have a healthy libido and a deep love and appreciation for women. In the presence of a beautiful woman, I'm…well, a bit giddy—I'm a guy. I have to fight an inclination to touch and hold and be intimate with a woman. It's what my body is designed to do."

"Isn't that terribly hard?" she asked.

"Hard? Yes. Terribly? It is impossible without the power of the Spirit," Fr. Scofield assured her. "In this way, my weakness is my strength. I would not be the priest or the person that I am without this craving, for it drives me to communion with my God."

"Wow!" Jasmine responded, lost for any other words.

"It seems daunting, doesn't it?"

"Terribly!" she agreed.

"It may take a while, Jasmine," he told her, "but if you continue to allow Christ to pick you back up when you fall, you will come to be strengthened by his continual presence, and you will be filled with joy, as I am. Then, if your Creator sends a man to you, you will know the joy of a passionate threesome with God!"

He thought for a moment and added, "When that happens, you will find that abstaining from intimacy in such a relationship can be 'terribly hard' as well, but your desire will fuel your prayers for each other, and in Christ's hands, your weakness will become your greatest strength."

He rose from his chair, pulled the picture of the crucifix from the wall, and presented it to her. "I want you to have this. When you are tempted by lust, pray to Jesus while contemplating his image, his humanity. It will be for you what it was for the sisters of Santo Spirito, a great weapon against lust."

Jasmine took the picture from him, contemplated it for a moment, and pressed it to her heart. "Thank you, Father! I...I love you! I will cherish this forever!" she said, getting up to leave.

"I love you too, little sister. You are very welcome. May I give you a lift? Sixteen blocks is a long way to walk carrying a picture."

She smiled down at him. "*Little* sister, huh?"

"Okay, so you're six inches taller than me," Father said with a grin, "but three inches of that is heels!"

Back at her apartment, Jasmine set the picture up on her desk, leaning it against the wall. She contemplated it for a moment, and remembered Fr. Scofield's definition of truth: "Truth is the knowledge that we are created for love."

You are the real Naked Truth, she prayed to her Savior. *Fill me with the knowledge of your love!* The longer she gazed, the less shocking the picture became, and she knew intuitively that the day would come when the image would no longer shock her, and she would know that her heart had been healed.

Back home, Fr. Scofield went to his closet, fetched an identical picture, and hung it in the same spot. He stood back and pondered how he had chosen to use the image. Some would question his methods, he knew, but Jasmine seemed a proper candidate for spiritual shock-therapy.

Though Melanie had given up her apartment and moved in with Veronica, they were seeing less and less of each other. Veronica was taking flying lessons and spending so many hours in simulators that her life began to seem like a virtual reality. "I feel like a video game junkie," she told Melanie one evening.

"You know," Melanie said, "I wandered away from the AGC meeting the other day, the one you missed, and I watched you run that thing for a while. You're really good!"

"Thanks, Mel. It just seems to come naturally to me."

Mel smiled. "Sure it does," she said a little sarcastically. "I wonder where you ever got an idea like that."

"Okay, so Michael keeps saying it over and over," Veronica admitted.

"Oh, so it's *Michael* now. Last week it was *Col. Benson.*"

"Well, Mel, it's not unusual for people who work together to be on a first-name basis."

"Veronica, honey, wake up and smell the testosterone! I've seen the way he looks at you. He's single, Catholic, and gorgeous, and that gleam in his eye is enough for the two of you to populate a dozen worlds!"

"Mel, what are you saying?"

"Ronnie, how many times do you think I have to watch you fall in love before I've got it down pat? Sometimes I think I know you better than *you* know you. You're already in love with Captain Benson; you just haven't figured it out yet, which is not surprising considering how long it took you…" She stopped short, not wanting to bring up Uncle Jake and start another sob-fest. Veronica stared at her, waiting for a finish. Mel did not disappoint. "When that starship departs, you'll be a fool if you're not on it with him!"

"Thanks for planning my life, Mel!" she said curtly, upset about being analyzed.

Melanie closed her eyes and sighed with self-disgust. "I'm sorry, Ronnie," she said at last. "Maybe I'm just trying to undo the guilt trip I laid on you a few weeks back about deserting your best friend and leaving her behind to struggle with owning a big corporation. I don't want to get in the way of what's best for you. My love for you just keeps kinda turning me inside out."

"Thanks, Mel. He is a catch, isn't he?"

"Ya think?! Uncle Jake picked him to lead this voyage. That's quite an endorsement. Ronnie, in a few short months you *will* get on that shuttle, and we will never see each other again. I want to be remembered as the friend who gave you great, unselfish advice."

"Hey! I'll be back!" Veronica countered.

"No. No you won't. Think about it. The trip is dangerous. You'll be married, maybe to a priest. The church will be growing like crazy, and you'll be having babies. You'll be lucky to find the time to send me a radio message, much less set aside thirteen years to come back and pay a little visit."

Veronica knew that Melanie was right. It did seem that it would not be long before her relationship with Col. Benson would be one neither she nor he would want to culminate in any way other than marriage. Was it a good idea to marry a priest? She thought about that Jake-shaped hole in her heart. It would never heal completely, not in one lifetime. However, it seemed to her that maybe Mike was already filling it as well as any man could.

The months flew by. As the big AGC anniversary shindig approached, Veronica appeared repeatedly on all of the nation's magazine covers. She made flight suits seem very sexy as she and Mike posed next to a Ranger 250K. They were the stuff of tabloids and romance novels.

Veronica, Jasmine, Mel, Col. Benson, and Fr. Scofield were invited to Antonio and Jeanine's for Thanksgiving dinner. Bored with football Melanie picked up a Christmas sale catalog lying on the coffee table and started to page through it. Just inside the front cover, a pair of dolls in flight suits stood next to a miniature Ranger 250K. "Smattel has done it again!" she proclaimed. "Anyone want a Mike and Ronnie doll for Christmas?"

Veronica just had to have a look at the anatomically disproportionate renderings of their bodies. "If my chest was inflated like that," she proclaimed, "I could just *float* into outer space!"

However, though Veronica and Mike had spent hundreds of hours together, the couple was not a couple; they were only friends. Mike had never even attempted a kiss, and Veronica didn't feel driven to make the first move the way she had with Jake. *Maybe it's just as well,* she thought. *Maybe Bishop Scofield's been prepping him for ordination.*

Springtime made its triumphant return, and the two would be spending less and less time together. Her training nearly complete, Veronica was a licensed pilot and had successfully landed the Ranger hundreds of times in simulation. In a few weeks, buoyed by adrenaline, she would gain an instant appreciation for the difference between simulation and the real thing, and she would be ready for the big Oshkosh anniversary shindig. Jake had been so right. The forthcoming celebration, with his widow as "poster girl," had drawn plenty of positive attention to space travel without drawing much scrutiny to the specifics of the mission at hand.

The Ranger pilot smiled from ear to ear as she drove to the AGC for a meeting. Twenty-eight hours ago she had successfully landed a real Ranger 250K, and the exhilaration was far from worn off. She received endless hand shakes and hugs of congratulations as the committee settled into their places. As typical, the meeting would be done in two stages: First the committee would meet, and then the mission team would be brought in. Completion and commissioning of the star cruiser was projected for a mere six months away, but the crew was still scant. Col Benson had been invited to the committee meeting to give an update of all recruiting and training activities.

"Ladies and gentlemen," the colonel began, "in an hour we will be joined by one of the most talented and dedicated groups of people I have ever known, the Freqmod mission team. Most of you are well acquainted with the formidable task we are attempting, but as I see a couple of new faces, I will cover the mission from basic on up.

"Travel to Mars is statistically safer than driving your automobile. A large part of that safety factor is due to our ability to predict space weather within our solar system. However, that will not be the case with our trip to Freqmod. Our sensing and shielding technology continues to improve, but it will not be sufficient to give us the reliability factor to which we are accustomed in interplanetary travel. Interstellar travel is a baby, one that is about to take its first steps into the dangerous world outside the nursery.

"Early on, the team had to make a choice between a sluggish journey with a huge ship, and a quicker journey with a leaner ship. Our planetary cruisers employ essentially the same technology for dealing with space debris as what is used on the moon to deal with meteors. The debris is simply detected and eliminated. However, this technology becomes less and less effective as the speed of the craft increases. To be anywhere near fool proof, speeds would be reduced so as to make this mission a forty-year journey each way. A second generation would need to be bred, raised, and trained en route. Not many couples showed interest in signing up for that.

"A lean, fast approach has gotten the most attention. Slowly accelerating to over a half billion miles per hour gets us there in sixty-four months, but thanks to relativity, the crew experiences it as a little over two years. This approach greatly increases the fuel requirements, while obviously decreasing the personnel support requirements. There remains, of course, the issue of safety.

"Quasidyne Systems, the designer and builder of the craft, has devised a nose cone solution that at first glance might appear to be a little child's solution, but computer modeling shows it to be effective. They have simply designed an extremely long and pointed nose cone. At the planned speeds, an average amount of space dust will incur a predictable rate of wear, and modeling indicates the cone will deflect debris slightly smaller than a marble without catastrophic damage. The full nose is actually a series of sixty four of these cones.

"Based on the computer simulations we've run, the craft will survive a single collision with a golf-ball-sized piece of debris, depending on the hardness of that debris. It is expected, from what we know of the dusty space between here and Freqmod, that the craft will burn up its first eight cones on the flight out and another eight on the flight back, but if it hits one piece of debris a little too large, fifty people may go to their death.

"The nose cones serve a secondary purpose. They are part of the shielding package that will protect the crew from the peripheral waves of the gravitronic engines. The six huge engines are buttressed away from the fuselage in a hex array at the front end of the ship. It is believed that, at least at lower speeds, space debris will tend to be sucked into the engines rather than striking the fuselage. This makes such debris a two-edged sword, because the crew cannot make the trip without engines; however, as we have six engines and can successfully make the trip with only three, it does increase our survival odds.

"On viewing drawings of the cruiser last week I remarked that it looked like a pregnant Mars cruiser with a long snout. The designers did not think my remark very flattering, even though it is an apt description. It is the rapid adaptation of existing cruiser designs that has allowed us to aggressively pursue this mission.

"Of course, you are all aware that no human has ever traveled anywhere near as fast as is planned for this trip. Until four years ago our chimpanzee friends, Alphonse and Loretta, in a ship called Martyr 1, were traveling at ninety-eight percent of light speed. Electromagnetic shielding is inefficient at near-light speed, requiring a tremendous burst of energy, and is insufficient protection against large objects. Martyr 1 had enough fuel to provide six such burst. They had traveled two and a half light years before the hull of their shield-spent ship was finally pierced by a piece of debris.

"Their ship provides for us yet another template on which to build for this mission, thanks to my co-pilot's marvelous insight. Thank you, Veronica," he said with a wink, pausing to instigate a brief burst of applause. "Star Covenant will be preceded in flight by Martyr ships. These duplicates of Martyr 1 will travel unmanned ahead of Covenant, hopefully deflecting debris out of the big ship's path. While it is conceivable that a single meteor shower could take out all seven martyrs at once, they will still add a considerable margin of safety.

"In summary, if the Martyrs, shields, and nose cones do their job, there is always the possibility that all three of the shuttle craft could malfunction when they get to Freqmod, and the crew would live out their days orbiting the planet. Given the data available, we compute an eighty-nine percent chance of reaching Freqmod safely and a seventy-one percent probability for a safe round trip: better odds than the flip of a coin but worse than Russian roulette. The obvious gut response is to add more Martyrs, but the challenge of control and communication with ships so distant from the mother ship is daunting, and a poorly managed lead ship could quickly become a dangerous piece of space debris.

"Needless to say, these projections have put somewhat of a crimp on recruiting. Scientist types have their egos to feed. It's one thing to discover something; it's quite another to go without the accolades that accompany having done so. This mission is attracting only those who have something to give, only those with a missionary's heart. Thirty of Earth's finest are signed up. The Army has offered a man for the second in command position, Col. Cliff Lamans of 'Hard Nut' fame. He is held in high regard for his combat duty, but also holds a Ph.D. in anthropology. Both his field combat and academic skills could serve us well, and his high public profile is a public relations dream come true. His résumé is in with the papers you received at the beginning of the meeting."

When Col. Benson had finished, they were joined by the mission team, a strapping bunch of young men and women who were eager for adventure and ready to die for what they consider God's work. Most of them were Jake's picks, and he had done a marvelous job.

"In your opinion, crew, how can we best go about attracting the remaining eighteen people needed to fill out this roster?" asked Chairwoman Banks.

"There are a couple of obvious means that come to mind," offered Antonio Escobar. "Delay the launch, or reduce the requirements."

"Delaying the launch may be fatal to the project," the chairwoman told him, "and that may be unavoidable; only time will tell, but please expound on your suggestion to 'reduce the requirements.'"

"Well Ma'am, when we first went about setting up the personnel requirements, we were looking for quadruple redundancy in all twelve fields of expertise. While I still think that to be a wise plan, we could consider triple redundancy with onboard training of the fourth individual. Adopting this approach would mean that, right now, we are only six individuals short of triple redundancy."

"What does the rest of the team think about that?" Mrs. Banks wanted to know.

Veronica spoke up. "Madam Chairwoman, I believe that God either has his hand on this mission, or he doesn't. I don't mean to say we should purposely choose to make stupid decisions to test him, I just think that the quality of the people we choose, that is, quality in terms of their basic humanity, is at least as important as the skills they possess."

"Okay. How exactly would you apply that to our situation, Doctor?"

"Well, in many areas we're requiring Ph.D. or Masters level education where we can perhaps get by with a BS, giving more consideration to personal attributes and experience."

"Thank you, Veronica. What do the rest of you think about that?"

After a few minutes of discussion, the committee decided to proceed in accord with the crew's recommendations. Later that day, Veronica fished out her late husband's original list. Many more of those persons were now eligible. As soon as individuals were hired they were immersed in training. The sessions were so intense that

Veronica remarked to Melanie, "I think they'll all be Ph.D.'s before we're done!"

Later that week, Veronica stopped by GGT. As Jasmine tidied her desk to end the day, Veronica stepped into her office.

"Hi Ronnie! I thought of you often today," Jasmine said, placing some things in a drawer. "In fact, with your launch date looming, my new friends never leave my thoughts. I pray for you all day. Makes me wonder if I'm accomplishing anything around here."

Veronica came around the desk, put her hands on Jasmine's shoulders and whispered, "Jazz, do you want to come along?"

"Along? To where?"

"Freqmod!"

"Ronnie, don't kid about such things!" Jasmine insisted.

"I would never do that to you."

"I'm sorry. You're right; you wouldn't!" Jasmine said, turning and looking up into Veronica's deep blues. "Hey…so…what are you saying? That it's a real possibility?"

"That's what I'm saying. We have a dire need to fill a couple positions. The requirements have been reduced to the point that your credentials are actually pretty attractive. Also, the owners of AGC Corp. would put in a good word for you. So, do you want to come along?"

"More than anything, Ronnie!" Jasmine exclaimed, standing to hug her friend.

Veronica smiled, and nearly short of breath from the vigorous hug, teased, "I thought you didn't like hugging 'chicks.'"

"You're not a chick, Ronnie, you're an angel!"

Melanie, much to her own surprise had taken to being a corporate leader. She would occasionally reflect on her sharp retort to her aunt— "I'm not my uncle and neither are you!"—and laugh, for, in the ensuing year, she had found herself to be quite like her uncle. Her employees loved her. She had talent, common sense, and believed in people. She had lost weight and toned up by working out.

It had been years since she'd been pursued by any serious suitors, but the new Melanie had a new problem: she had the added chore of trying to weed out suitors who might just be after her cash. However, there was a marvelous, humble fellow with an eye for her. He had originally been on her uncle's crew list, but would now not participate in the mission because he was caring for aging parents in ill health. He had been invited to remain on the mission preparation team even though he wouldn't be making the voyage.

Veronica saw what was happening and took the opportunity to use Mel's own words on her: "'Honey, wake up and smell the testosterone! I've seen the way he looks at you. He's single, Catholic, and gorgeous, and that gleam in his eye is enough for the two of you to populate a dozen worlds!'" adding, "I don't want to miss the wedding, so get to work."

At the last meeting before the big AGC anniversary celebration, as usual, Melanie and Veronica sat side by side. The co-owners of Corp. had made it obvious that, as far as they were concerned, this mission was the culmination of Jacob Lansing's life work, and they would support it to the bitter end. Their attitude had given the proceedings an air that shouted, *We will make this voyage, so let's do it as best we can!*

On this occasion, Veronica took the opportunity to stand up and make a simple point. "I have been, for better or worse, AGC's poster girl for the last year and a half. Tomorrow is my big day in the sun flying with our Col. Benson, but four months from now I will climb aboard Star Covenant and possibly never be seen again. Your new poster girl is seated beside me—the co-owner of AGC Corp., my best friend for seventeen years, Jacob Lansing's niece, and I'm proud to say, mine as well—; Melanie Lansing is the future of AGC." Veronica remained standing and began to clap, instigating a standing ovation for the new poster girl.

Melanie stood and motioned for everyone to be quiet and sit. No longer the teary-eyed, self-conscious Mel that Veronica had known for years, a self-confident Melanie Lansing smiled and said, "My dear friend, Dr. Veronica Therese Weslin-Lansing, has, more than any person on this earth, helped me to find myself. Her life has always pointed to Christ, the one in whom all of us are able to find ourselves. I am happy for the people of Freqmod, for they are gaining a true princess. That happiness will need to suffice to stave off the bitterness of saying goodbye to my best friend." She made no attempt to hold back tears that needed to be shed. "Veronica has given me a new challenge. I accept! Get me that flight suit, baby, and I'll see you on the field!" The two hugged. Black hair mingled with blond, and tears mingled on cheeks. Cameras flashed and the room exploded into applause. The occasion became a photo op, the first of many to take place over the next four months.

The gatherings for the air show at Oshkosh are always large, but that year's was endless. The promised showing of the Screamin' Eagles accompanied by the Lansing women had made the celebration a sell out. Huge video screens had been erected so the masses could see more than a couple ant-like figures in the distance. Veronica and Melanie loomed thirty feet tall before the world as they climbed aboard the Ranger for photos. Melanie had begun to take lessons and was chosen to spend a few minutes explaining the many wonderful attributes of the Ranger aircraft. At the end of her little show-and-tell, she added, "Of course, I'm just a beginner. Ronnie can actually fly this thing!" The throng burst into uproarious applause as the team and their special copilots climbed aboard the five craft.

Cameras had been set up in the plane Veronica occupied, one showing the view in front of the craft and another showing her face. She also had a microphone in front of her broadcasting her every scream and comment. Listening to Veronica's shrieks and seeing the flesh on her G-force-deformed face sag as though it would soon run off, Melanie and Jasmine giggled till their tummies hurt.

Jasmine had arrived late for the festivities. She had been delayed at a criminal trial, called to testify on behalf of the state in a case she and Dobbs had worked the prior year. Consequently, her parking spot at Oshkosh was about halfway across the state. When the festivities ended, she began the long trek back to her rental car. Someone asked, "Need a lift?" and she turned to see Col. Lamans in the back of a mile of limo. Lamans was receiving the VIP treatment for his cameo "Hard Nut" appearance with a sky diving team.

"I *do* need a lift, Cliff; I think I parked in North Dakota!" she answered, making her way to the black Lincoln. At the end of the long ride, as she unlocked the door of her rental car, Lamans noticed her camera still setting beside him. He rolled down his window and began to pick it up to show her, but stopped and thought, *Fool! You almost wasted an opportunity!*

Jasmine glanced back, and noticing his window down, yelled, "Thanks again, Hard Nut!" He rewarded her with a smile. Though not fond of him, she thought she'd better stay friendly, as he would to be her superior officer for several years to come.

A few hours later, as she closed and locked her apartment door, she heard her shower calling and began to tear off clothes to answer the call. A day in the hot sun and the closeness in the airplane had left her craving refreshment. Naked by the time she reached the bathroom door, she grabbed a glass from the sink, filled it with the first water out of the shower head, and jumped into the cold stream to drink it. By the time she had downed the glassful, the shower was beginning to warm, and she began to sing.

Life is good, she thought as the blow dryer tossed her waves of sun-streaked amber blond. She briefly admired the extra length it had gained since she'd quit the FBI and let it grow. She stepped naked into her living room and stooped to pick up her clothing. When she stood back up, arms came around her from behind. She screamed but the arms held her tight, and a hand went over her mouth.

"Don't scream, baby! Please don't scream!" a voice ordered quietly. "I'm sorry I sneaked in, but I just had to see you, Jazz!" He removed his hand from her mouth and released his grip. She pulled away from him violently and grabbed a table cloth to cover herself, sending a dry floral arrangement crashing to the floor. "Relax, Jazz, I'm not going to hurt you. It's not like I've never seen you naked before!"

"Doug! How the hell did you get in here?"

"Relax, baby, relax! I used to live with this FBI chick who showed me all the secrets to getting through closed doors. I'm well trained."

"Get out of here, Doug! Now! Before I call the cops!"

"You can't just dump me like this, Jasmine. I never stop thinking about you!"

"You sorry sack of lies! Now that the door's open, I can see what you never stop thinking about!" she said, in reference to the glow of her computer monitor on the spare bedroom wall. "You've been in there getting yourself all worked up so you can do something. What am I, hamburger? You're just looking for something to rub yourself on, but it won't be me!"

"You're wrong, Jazz. I really do love you."

"You poor man, you don't even know the meaning of the word. I have nothing to give you, Doug, nothing but pity. You have to leave now!"

"Just give me a little, Jazz, it's not so hard. You've done it hundreds of times before!"

"Give you what?"

"Sex, dammit, give me a little sex!"

"There's no such *thing*, Doug!"

"What the hell are you talking about?"

"Sex is not a thing, Doug! You don't go to the deli and say, 'I'll take two quarts, hot and spicy, please!' It's not a thing, and I'm not a dispenser! I'm a person!"

"Where you gettin' all this high-minded crap? Sex is sex! What's the big deal? It's a friggin instinct, for cryin' out loud! Animals do it!"

"Good! Go do it with one of them! I'm a human being, and I want to be treated like one!"

"Don't insult me like that!"

"Insult you?! You're on the porn elevator to hell, Doug! Where do you think it ends? Doing it with animals is on the bottom floor. You might as well get out there and get it over with!"

"I don't have to take this shit, bitch!" Doug growled.

Jasmine picked up the telephone, hit the emergency button, and tossed the phone behind the couch.

"You shouldn't have done that, Jazz. Why are you doing this to me? No one will be coming. I unplugged the phone. What kind of FBI agent are you?

"You were wrong, you know…about the bottom floor, I mean," he said, referring to Jasmine's porn-elevator-to-hell comment. He stooped to pick up a broken shard from the vase of the flower arrangement that had met its demise. "Doing it with the dead is the bottom floor, Jazz! Is that the floor you want me to get out on?" He pointed the shard at her and offered, "I'll put the broken glass down if you lay down for me."

Jasmine let out an agonizing scream. Doug knew he could not possibly prevail in hand to hand fighting, so he began to slash at her. Evading the impromptu weapon, she tripped on the corner of her tablecloth sarong, fell over the arm of the couch, and landed on her back on the floor, naked and screaming as she fell. He pounced on the opportunity and held the shard to her throat. "Now just relax and everything's gonna be alright," he whispered.

A pounding at the door startled Doug. With his attention diverted, Jasmine punched him in the ribs and screamed while she pulled away from him. One decisive kick flung the front door wide, and Cliff Lamans quickly put himself between Doug and his prey. Knowing he was no match for the two of them, Doug scrambled for the door. When he was gone, Veronica wrapped herself in the table cloth and retreated to her bedroom while Lamans blocked the door with a chair. He came to the open door of the bedroom where Jasmine sat weeping on the bed.

She looked up at him and mouthed a silent "Thank you!" He came and sat on the bed beside her and put his arm around her.

"No one's going to hurt you now, Jazz. He's gone," he said. "It's a good thing I came by to return your camera." They sat until Jasmine ran out of tears. Her eyes went wide when Lamans left her side and turned down the sheets on the bed. "You should crawl in here and get some rest," he suggested. She did as he said. After he tucked her in she began to cry again. "What can I do for you?" he asked.

"I'm afraid of being alone, Cliff." He lay down on top of the covers and pulled himself to her. It was early evening. She was mentally, emotionally, and physically exhausted, and feeling safe with the colonel at hand, soon fell asleep.

She awoke two hours later with Lamans still at her side. However, he was no longer on top of the covers. She sat up quickly and looked about. His clothes were on a chair. She opened her mouth intending to scream, but nothing came out. Her heart had begun to pound in a familiar and delightful way. She lay back down beside him. It seemed like forever since she had been touched by a man. The warmth of his body thrilled her. He brought his lips close to hers, and she took the bait. Like food to the starving she gulped every advance. Twenty years of special operations experience kicked in for the colonel and he worked with military precision: target identified; mission accomplished. A few minutes later he lay puffing at her side. The pace was dizzying. A disoriented Jasmine reached for him, her soul yearning for completion, but he was gone. She heard the toilet flush. In a minute the conqueror stood by the bedside, dressed, with hat in hand.

"You need to rest now, Jasmine. I'm glad I was here to help you," he said. "I need to be going now." She just lay there, stunned, unable to speak. She heard her front door close behind him. Numbly, she pulled an automatic pistol from a drawer beside the bed, blocked the broken door as best she could, and dressed with her pistol at her side. Lamans had left without offering to fix the door, without offering to call the police, without regard to her feelings. His good manners mocked her now, for it seemed that she had been politely raped. Just when she thought she was out of tears, she began to weep again. She went to her desk and looked at the naked man on the cross. Looking at him only increased her pain, that is, until she started to pray. She prayed for forgiveness and she prayed for help.

Unable to cry anymore, she began to put her life back together. She pulled her couch away from the wall, picked up her phone and plugged it in. Before she could dial the police, the phone rang.

"Hello," she answered, her voice disclosing her pain.

"Jazz? Are you okay?"

"Dobbs? Alvin? Is that you?" she asked, starting to cry all over again.

"I'm in the neighborhood, Jazz. I'll be right there!"

When he arrived she had called the police and was pacing the floor, fully dressed with gun in hand. Dobbs got the embrace of his lifetime. Giving her a full hug was awkward, for the combo of his scant stature and her high heels placed his face at cleavage level, and the poor man could only take so much. "Why did you call?" she asked.

"I don't know," he said. "I was just in the neighborhood and was missing you, so thought I'd see if you could use a little company." When the police arrived ten minutes later Dobbs still had one arm around the waist of a woman unwilling to be released

"You shouldn't stay here tonight, Ms Babasa," the police officer said after hearing of the day's events. "Your door is broken and you're being stalked. You need to go someplace secure where you won't be alone until we pick this psycho up."

"Where do you want to go, Jazz?" Dobbs asked.

"I need to see Fr. Ian," she said. She directed him to the bishop's house and they parked right in front of the big picture windows of his study. It had just turned dark and they could see the holy man seated in his big leather chair reading some classic. "Alvin, I'm such a pain in the butt! I don't know how long this will take. Do you need to be somewhere?"

"I'm retired, Jazz. I'll pretend it's a stake-out, just like old times."

"You're the best, my man!" she said, brushing his cheek with the back of her fingers.

As Jasmine seated herself facing the bishop in front of the big windows, something hanging on the wall immediately grabbed her attention. Fr. Scofield didn't need to turn around to know what. "Did you buy a whole case of them?" she asked, looking at the picture of a naked Christ hanging on the cross.

Father just smiled and said, "You can't escape him, Jasmine; don't even try."

Under the seal of confession she described the night's events, the sorrow in her heart for the sins she had committed, and the fierce anger and hatred she felt toward both her assailant and her self-serving rescuer. When he was certain that she had sufficiently vented, the man of Love offered his humble counsel.

"Jasmine, a most important thing has happened to you today. You fell flat on your face and got right back up and took Jesus by the hand. That kind of courage only comes from the Holy Spirit. I am proud of you!"

"Father, I just committed...fornication, and you're...proud of me?"

"Yes! It is one thing to sin. It is quite another to wallow in your sin. A soul espoused to Christ will never wallow in sin. She will pick herself back up and embrace humility so she may become strong in Him. Humility is strength; never forget that!

"Sin is a symptom, Jasmine. While it is glorious to feel that lifting of the burden that comes with a heartfelt confession, Jesus, the Eternal Healer, is much more interested in healing the disease than in relieving the symptoms."

"If being easy is my symptom, what's my disease?" she asked.

"There are a thousand symptoms, but only one disease: like our first parents, we all want to be God. Many of us pray 'Thy will be done,' but with stubborn mistrust of our Savior we continue trying to control our own destinies. The saints among us are those who have figured out that their true self-worth can only be found in doing His will."

"Father, if I ever do find the right man..." Jasmine's voice trailed off, unable to express her heart.

"Yes?" Father invited her to finish.

"Well...even while I had sex with this man, images from...a thousand past encounters swarmed my mind. What if that happens when I'm married? How do I overcome what I am?"

"What is it that you think you *are*, Jasmine?" he asked. She opened her mouth to answer, but nothing came out. "What *are* you, Jasmine?" he pressed.

"A slut!" she proclaimed tearfully.

"That's the Devil talking! You are a child of God!" Fr. Scofield proclaimed with quiet drama. "Any other label is an offense against your Father, the King! Do you dare to insult the princess?"

Jasmine stared back at him in shock, her mouth agape. "I'm sorry, Father," she said with tears streaming down her cheeks, "but I don't know what to do! If I ever marry, what will I do about those images?"

"Give them to God, Jasmine!"

"What?!"

"Pray for those men you see. Acknowledge their humanity, body *and* soul. See Christ's body in theirs. He is the one you were seeking when you found them. See Jesus in them and offer Him back to the Father; it'll drive the Devil nuts!"

"But...I feel so...dirty, Father, so guilty."

"Jasmine, before you gave your life to Jesus, you denied your guilt; you tried to drown it in booze and numb it with drugs. You tried to rid yourself of the gift of conscience. Now, letting go of your guilt scares you because you don't want to go back to being what you were. The Devil wants to trap you right there, in a circle of doubt. If you let him have his way, your fear will paralyze your progress while your guilt gives you a sense of false righteousness. You'll snuggle safely in the arms of guilt, and the longer you stay there, the longer you resist perfect forgiveness, the more your guilt will become your god. Give it up, Jasmine! Give it back to God! Worship the Giver, not the gift!

"Jesus, well aware of our tendency to succumb to a dizzying cycle of sin and guilt, said, 'No one, after putting his hand to the plow and looking back, is fit for the kingdom of God.' Jasmine, letting the Father's forgiveness transform your self-image is the only thing that can make you fit for the kingdom. You must stop looking back. You must see in yourself the image of Christ."

He stood and paced a bit with his head bowed in contemplation, and then asked, "When you look in a mirror, Jasmine, what do you see?"

"Hmm...a woman who doesn't get enough rest. A woman who needs to paint her face so she doesn't scare people," she mused through tears.

"Let's change that," Father said. "For your penance, I want you to get plenty of rest and spend some time looking at yourself."

"What? Like...in a mirror?"

"Yes."

"Isn't that vanity?"

"Did you make yourself?" he asked. She just sat and looked at him. "How can it be vanity," he continued, "to revere the sight of your body if it's not the work of your own hands? The piece of furniture with the big mirror is called a vanity because we come before it with makeup and jewelry and try to improve on God's creation—that's vanity!

"With your permission, I will call Veronica and Melanie and ask them to let you move in with them. You shouldn't be alone. There's a maniac at large. You need to be somewhere safe, a quiet place where you can heal spiritually and emotionally. I will have Veronica call Josh Gundersen for you in the morning to let him know that you are indisposed. I want you to sleep in. After your morning shower, before you apply your makeup, will be a good time to perform your penance. Having put out of mind all earthly possessions and worries, I want you to take yourself before a mirror wearing only what you were wearing when you came into this world."

"Naked?" Jasmine asked, a little shocked.

"Yes, unless, of course, you were fully dressed when you were born. Look at your reflection and pray for the gift to see yourself through Christ's eyes. See the beauty! See the love! See his reflection! See his glory! Spend time offering each and every part of your body to your heavenly spouse as a beautiful prayer. Remember that your body is the expression of your soul, and your soul is the image of Infinite Love. We are the body of Christ. In our flesh he is glorified!"

Jasmine sat gazing blankly at him, attempting to digest his words, and looking a bit uneasy. "*Each* part of my body?" she asked.

"Each and *every* part! You will need to spend time in contemplation; this is no two-minute exercise. Let me give you some examples: God created your soul to love; your heart is the physical expression of that gift. Your head is the physical expression of the gifts of intellect and free will. Your sexual organs are very sacred, for they are avenues of creation and are therefore an expression of the Creator himself. There is no part of your body that is not a beautiful expression of your soul, and therefore an expression of the Creator in whose image we are created."

With Jasmine still looking apprehensive, Fr. Scofield thought for a moment and said, "Tell me, Jasmine, do you think we will wear clothing in heaven?"

She was momentarily lost for words. "We will wear robes, won't we? Isn't that what the bible says?" she asked at last.

"Real or figurative robes?" Father asked. "Scripture says that our robes will be white, washed in the blood of the Lamb. Does that sound literal to you? I mean, real clothes don't get white when you wash them in blood. To paraphrase the Book of Job, we are *clothed* with skin and flesh, and knit with bone and sinew. If our bodies are the expressions of our souls, which are the image of God, wouldn't it be offensive to cover them, to place a barrier between him and us?"

"So, what are you saying? That our bodies are the robes that the bible talks about? The robes...washed in the blood of the lamb?" she asked.

"Christ came to save Jasmine—*all* of her," Father answered. "He came to save your soul *and* body. His sacrifice washed away sin *and* death. White is the symbolic color of purity; *all* of you is made pure in the blood of the Lamb."

Jasmine silently returned his gaze. It was not unusual for conversation with Fr. Scofield to take her outside of her comfort zone, but this one had *started* outside of her comfort zone.

"We wear clothing out of necessity, Jasmine, but it was not so in the beginning; Adam and Eve were 'naked without shame.' In my humble opinion, when we come face to face with The Eternal Lover, I think that clothing will be an abomination, much like a condom is to real lovers in this life."

Jasmine found her voice: "You mean, everybody will be hugging Jesus and each other, and we'll all be naked—naked men hugging naked men, and naked women hugging naked women?!"

"You find that offensive?"

"Don't you?! I mean...doesn't the bible call that an abomination?"

"Touching? No. St. John called himself 'the disciple whom Jesus loved.' In his narrative of the last supper, while reclining at table with Jesus, he lays his head on the Savior's chest, an act which prompts modern pundits to speculate about the nature of the relationship that they shared. Our fallen nature wants to paint all intimate contact the color of lust, but sexual acts between members of the same sex are disgusting to God primarily because there is no way that they can be fruitful—no way that they can be open to the Creator. In that regard, they are an abomination for the same reason that contraception is an abomination. However, there will be neither marriage nor procreation in heaven, and we will be cleansed of all shame."

Despite his efforts to de-secularize Jasmine's perception of the body, Fr. Scofield sensed her continued apprehension about going before a mirror. "You're uncomfortable with your penance, aren't you?" he asked.

"It just seems so...self-centered," she said, shrugging her shoulders.

"Of course it does, because intuitively you know that true fulfillment is found in serving others, not in concentrating on yourself," he told her. "However, though your life is a gift of inestimable beauty and value, before you can truly be gift to others you must reclaim your body; you must reclaim your sexuality for Jesus! You must come to realize how unique and beautiful you are to him. When you do, you will be dying to share him with others."

There's that word dying again! Jasmine thought.

Father picked up the telephone and said, "Let me see if I can get Veronica on the line."

"Seeing the Angel always helps me heal," Jasmine said with a smile that anticipated the comforting presence of her friend.

When Fr. Scofield was off the phone, he said, "The Lansing girls are very excited about their new roommate!"

He paused thoughtfully and said, "Jasmine, I know that it is with respect for her purity that you refer to Veronica as 'the Angel,' but I want to caution you: angels have no bodies. There are good and bad angels, just as there are good and bad humans. We believe that the most exalted creature in heaven is human—the Queen of Heaven is a woman, not an angel.

"Veronica is pure woman. It borders on insult to call her Angel. There is grave spiritual danger in associating holiness with being bodiless. Our bodies are the expressions of our souls, which are made in the image of God. Veronica's holiness embraces her sexuality. We are sexual beings; we cannot hide from ourselves or from a Creator who seeks intimacy with us. It is with that in mind that I have assigned to you a penance to foster self-appreciation.

"On the other hand, I don't want you playing doctor," Fr. Scofield warned.

"Huh?" Jasmine asked, totally lost as to what he meant.

"Down through the centuries," he explained, "mirrors have oft been prohibited in monastic life because of their potential to initiate autoerotic sins."

"Autoero...I don't do that stuff," Jasmine informed him.

"I know you don't; I'm your confessor. However, there's an old adage: One man's cure is another man's poison. This spiritual exercise may not be appropriate for some, so you need to avoid zealously sharing any success it may bring you. Not being a confessor, you have no way of knowing which souls may suffer from sexual self-abuse."

Jasmine contemplated his point for a bit, then changing the subject said, "Father, there's something I don't understand. I dated Doug for more than a year. He was never violent. What would bring him to threaten me?"

Fr. Scofield searched a moment for the right words. "Jasmine, we are designed for a love triangle. Sexual intimacy was intended to include God. Jesus told us that whenever two or more are gathered in his name, he is there with us: unity in trinity. God's inclusion in intimacy marks the line between love and lust. The viewing of porn crosses still another line. It falls into the arena of the autoerotic, the next stop down on the slimy slope of human degradation. In intimate relations, it is spiritually unnatural to exclude God, but it is physically and psychologically unnatural to exclude a person of the opposite sex. Slaves to porn fool their psyches with pictures of the real thing. Such a gross distortion of the desire for unity in trinity is an open invitation to the powers of darkness to complete the threesome. Doug simply succumbed to that darkness.

"Jasmine, you must do everything in your power now to keep that darkness from your doorstep. Prayer is the answer, and the most efficacious prayer in the world is the Mass. Immerse yourself in the Eternal Trinity. Daily Eucharist will bind you to Christ more than anything you can imagine. Your life must become a perpetual thanksgiving!"

"Eucharist...I know that means Communion, but...well, why are there two words for the same thing? It's kind of confusing," Jasmine noted.

"The English word Eucharist comes from a Greek word which means thanksgiving," Fr. Scofield told her. "When we eat the body, blood, soul, and divinity of Christ, we *share* in his life—Communion. He gives himself to us, and in *thanksgiving* we offer him and ourselves to the Father—Eucharist. You need to become whole, so you can give God your whole self."

When she had gone, Fr. Scofield reflected on the penance he had chosen to impose. It was a creative approach, or a least, one he had never before tried, and he was not totally without second thoughts. He would be praying for her.

Jasmine closed the car door, and Dobbs viewed her face in the dim glow of the street lamps. "Your face is nearly glowing in the dark, Jazz," he said. "What'd he say to you?"

"He heard my confession, gave me absolution, and told me to go to Ronnie's house and sit naked in front of a mirror," she informed him, but then thought, *Oops! So much for not playing doctor!* Dobbs just sat there and looked at her. Giddy after her confession, she giggled at the dumbfounded look on his face, and gave him a peck on the cheek. "I couldn't ask for a better brother," she said. "Could you please take me to Ronnie's house?"

Dobbs just looked at her for a moment, his sad eyes diminishing his droll smile, "Always a brother, never a lover," he muttered as he started the car. She returned his melancholy smile and squeezed his arm.

After her morning shower, Jasmine blew her hair dry while avoiding the bathroom mirror. It was 9:49 AM. She couldn't remember the last time she'd slept until 9:30 before crawling out of bed and into the shower.

Veronica heard the hairdryer, and when its whoosh had subsided, knocked on the bedroom door offering breakfast. As the bathrobe clad Jasmine broke her fast, Veronica said, "I'm scheduled to spend a few hours at AGC and then head to the hospital for volunteer work. Do you want to spend the day with me?"

"I would love to, Ronnie! That is, as soon as I'm done with my prayers."

Melanie arrived back from a morning errand and stepped into the kitchen. "Wow," she said, looking at Jasmine.

It took Jasmine a moment under Melanie's gaze to figure out what had incited the *wow*. "So, what do you think of your warrior without her war paint?" she asked, adding, "Give it to me straight!"

"Your eyes look smaller, so your face looks a little longer, which actually complements the rest of your physique better," Mel opined.

Jasmine looked at Veronica with a well-what-do-you-have-to-say-about-it expression. "Honey, I think you look spellbinding," Veronica said. "Mel's right. Your eyes do look smaller, but…well, it's your eyes that we see now, not the paint, and looking into them just warms the soul!"

Back in her bedroom, Jasmine sat at the foot of the bed, positioned in front of the vanity, and let her robe fall from her shoulders. *Be brave girl!* she thought, as she stood boldly before the huge mirror. At first glance she saw what she expected every man to see: an impressive bust line, sleek waist, and curvy, trim hips supported by towering, silky thighs. *Is that what defines you?* she asked herself. *Is that what Fr. Ian wants you to see?*

She felt a chill and pulled her robe up around her shoulders, covering more and more of herself the longer she looked. "I feel so dirty," she had told Fr. Scofield. He had addressed that feeling, saying, "the longer you resist perfect forgiveness, the more your guilt will become your god."

Jasmine gazed at the mirror, into the reflection of her eyes, and asked herself pointedly, *Who is your God?* In reference to those same eyes, Veronica had told her, just moments before, that, "Looking into them just warms the soul." Jasmine had spent plenty of time looking *at* those eyes every morning as she painted her face, but no time looking *into* them. Now she caught a glimpse of a Jasmine from another time, perhaps a seven-year-old Jasmine, a glimpse into a soul from a time before her innocence was scattered to the wind. And she saw something else, or was it some*one* else? Yes! It was that same eternal someone she saw when she looked into Ronnie's or Father's eyes. She was seeing the Giver through the gift!

Looking beyond her eyes now, she cast off the robe, stood before the mirror, and watched the Giver blossom in his gift. She saw herself for the first time, and she was so beautiful! It was her first taste of what it felt to be whole, and it felt amazing! What she saw was not the kind of beauty defined by glamour and trend, but transcendent beauty, the kind you can only see with the eyes of Christ.

She thought about Fr. Scofield's words, about falling and picking herself back up. *If I fall again,* she thought, *it will be from a much higher precipice; it will be much more painful. Lord, save me from falling!*

Jasmine enjoyed her day with Veronica, especially the time spent at Children's Hospital. After leaving the facility, as they nestled into Veronica's comfy old car, she turned to her friend and said, "Ronnie...I want to have that operation! I want my fertility back!"

Veronica's pained smile forewarned her listener. "Jazz, that's wonderful! But...I'm afraid it's too close to launch date. There's a moratorium on elective surgery for crew members until after the first leg of the voyage is complete," she said, grasping her passenger's hand. "Having the surgery now will disqualify you from the mission. I'm sorry!"

Jasmine squeezed her friend's hand. "It's okay, Ronnie. It's okay," she said, forcing a smile. "I won't be ready for a permanent relationship before then anyway." She let out a long sigh and added, "Still…I just feel kind of…incomplete." She noticed that Veronica appeared to have something on the tip of her tongue. "What is it?" she asked.

"Oh…um, I was just thinking about all the people I know who are naturally infertile. Maybe you could offer your pain up for them. They have far less options."

"That's a beautiful thought, Ronnie," Jasmine said. "It's sad that there are women out there crying for the gifts I've thrown away."

On the way home they stopped at Jasmine's apartment to pick up some things. Remembering that she had stupidly taught Doug how to get through locked doors, Jasmine decided to take no chances. She pulled an automatic weapon from her purse before unlocking the door. Veronica cringed at the sight of the gun. Once inside, Jasmine went through the apartment, pistol in hand, checking for intruders. She retrieved the messages from her blinking phone.

"Jazz, I'm so sorry! God! I'm so sorry!" the first message said. She hit *save* to archive Doug's message for evidence.

"Ms Babasa," the next message said, "this is Officer Becker calling to let you know that your assailant is behind bars. He was picked up without incident last night and is being held in the County Law Enforcement Center pending filing of charges." Jasmine breathed a huge sigh of relief and put her gun back into her purse.

She played the last message. "Jasmine, this is Cliff. I hope you slept well and are recovered from your little episode last night. I hope to see you again soon. Don't hesitate to call if you need anything."

Jasmine hit *delete* so hard that Veronica wondered how her finger survived. "What's the matter, Jazz?" she asked out of concern.

"I don't like the famous Cliff Lamans," Jasmine answered. She could see the concern on Veronica's face, so she added. "He may have saved my life, I know. I should be more thankful. It's just that he's so…cold!"

Like the other members of the mission crew, Jasmine would be divesting herself of nearly every earthly possession. Each crewman would only be allowed a few precious pounds of personal possessions, an allotment that could easily be eaten up by wardrobe. Things like family pictures would all need to be converted to digital files. She grabbed something from her desk.

"Oh my!" Veronica exclaimed, never before having seen the Santo Spirito crucifix. "Let me guess: a gift from Fr. Ian," she said smiling.

"Of course," Jasmine answered. "I can't take it with me, and I've already taken a digital photo of it, so I need to gift someone with it."

"Can we deliver it now?" Veronica asked.

"I'm not sure, but let's give it a try," Jasmine answered, adding, "But I can't take it like this." She grabbed a pair of pliers from a drawer and after a couple of minutes, to Veronica's bewilderment, had the print removed from its beautiful frame and rolled and taped into a compact tube.

Under Jasmine's direction, Veronica drove to their destination. Her eyes went wide when directed to park in front of the law enforcement center. "Will you come in with me?" Jasmine asked.

"Of course," Veronica said, finally realizing what was about to take place.

"I can't believe you came!" Doug said through the mike in front of the little window.

"Doug I want you to know that you are forgiven," Jasmine told her assailant. "In fact, I brought you a gift to remind you of me. In a few months I will be gone, possibly never to return. You need to know that, whatever happens, you and I can never again have a romantic relationship. But you can be cured, Doug. I will be praying for you."

As she finished speaking an officer delivered the rolled up print. Doug unrolled it and viewed it, but was unsure what to make of it. He finally looked up at Jasmine and managed a belabored "Thank you!" Looking into his eyes, it seemed to Jasmine that some of the darkness had already lifted.

"Doug…look…I'm a sinner. I'm afraid I wasn't much good for you when we were together. I should have told you to go to hell when you asked me to get that operation. I've hated you for it ever since. Even when we were together and doing it every day, I hated you for it. I never told you so, because I never realized it until you tried to rape me. But I don't hate you anymore. Please don't give up on yourself. If it's okay with you, I will find someone who can help you. Would you be open to that?"

Doug nodded a trembling yes. Tears fell on the image of Christ, now partially rolled up in his hands. He forced a smile and turned and left the window. Veronica put her arm around a teary Jasmine and walked her to the car.

They drove a while before Veronica broke the silence with, "I'm so proud of you, Jazz! That was really brave!"

"Thanks Ronnie," she said after a bit. "I could have killed him with my bare hands, you know. I'm a marshal arts expert. I could have knocked that ridiculous piece of glass out of his hand and flattened him so fast he wouldn't have known what hit him, but thanks to Jesus and Fr. Ian, all I felt was pity. That day by the river in Rome, I flushed a sea of festering anger. I think I left the Tiber a little murkier and a little greener.

"None of this would be possible if it wasn't for you," Jasmine added, smiling at her friend. "I shudder to think where I would be if you hadn't asked me to take a walk that day. Life has gotten so wild and wonderful!"

Veronica smiled at the words. "Wild and wonderful," she echoed. "I guess that pretty much describes life with God at the wheel!"

Veronica had been selected as fifth in command for the star journey, serving as chief medical officer. "Keeping a crew of fifty healthy inside a tin can for twenty-four months may prove to be a daunting task," she told Mel at lunch one day.

"I think I would get a bit claustrophobic," Mel commented.

"No one can do a stint like this without getting cabin fever," Veronica assured her.

"I'd probably be a basket case," Mel convinced herself.

"Does this mean you won't be coming on the next bus?"

"What?" Mel asked, giving her a funny look.

"The next bus," Veronica repeated. "Five and a half years from now we will arrive at Freqmod. Our first order of business will be to transmit a radio message indicating that we are safe on the planet's surface. That message will take over four years to be received on Earth. In that lapse of ten years, technology will have come a long way here on Earth. *Your* bus will likely be a luxury cruiser compared to ours and will probably make the journey in much less time. In eleven years or less of life-perception time, we could be having coffee together on Freqmod laughing about old times." Veronica could tell by the look on Mel's face that such a notion had never crossed her mind.

"What about AGC Corp.?" She asked somewhat rhetorically.

"No problem. Here's the plan: Sell everything and create a single business entity solely devoted to interstellar travel. Find a wonderful holy man or woman to run the new entity. Build Star Covenant II, and come see me and the hubby and kids."

"You know, that actually sounds pretty good," Mel admitted, "but what about *my* husband and kids?"

"You'll have to make that call Mel, but it should be much safer to travel by then."

Mel thought for a moment and said, "Well, no matter what, it's still two years of 'Are we there yet?'"

Chapter 7

Freqmod

The thick, intoxicating balm of lilacs in bloom filled Elon's senses. Though glad for the lilacs, it was not their perfume that made Lilac Valley his favorite part of the Garden. Their year-round plumes had come to be but a reminder of what really drew him there: children. Nowhere else in the Garden were there to be found more children than in this beautiful valley. The families of the valley were the people who most often walked with God, who listened most intently to his voice, and who passed on to their children, with the most fervor, the stories of those who had gone into glory, into the actual bosom of the Almighty.

As Elon took his morning walk, he enjoyed the familiar sight of couples making love. He observed with great joy the pleasure their caresses afforded them. The tender beauty of the act astounded him, and he recalled, as he oft did, the legend of Tohmor and Valletta, who were said to have gone into glory while offering their intimacy as prayer to their Creator. *What a way to go!* Elon thought.

As he walked along he prayed for the pleasure of the lovers, for their fertility, and for their hearts to be filled with joyful praise for the Almighty. Perhaps one day the Lord would see fit to provide a mate for Elon. The holy man had expressed this desire in fervent prayer as he walked with God every evening, but as always, he prayed that the Almighty's will would be done, not his own. Besides, he was only 113 years old. God would provide when the time was right.

After the morning intimacy, when all of the children had awakened, came the part of the day most precious to Elon. He loved music, and music in Lilac Valley was music as God had intended it. Valley dwellers did not build huts to store the work of their own hands. Elon had heard drums, bells, and tambourines, and he did not care for them. They were, he thought, the symbols of vanity, ear candy for their makers, not for The Maker. What he loved most about the music in the valley was the pure and glorious sound of children's voices.

As the fathers and mothers finished their morning intimacy, and the infants were all nursed, the older children started with the morning chant. Starting soft and low, they were soon joined by fathers and the virgin men, who added a low bass chant. Then the mothers and virgins produced a melody like unto that of angels. Well, almost, that is; at times Elon was certain he heard the angels as well. When all Gardeners had joined the angels in singing their morning praises, the dumb creatures could not help but join in the rejoicing. Elephants trumpeted a counterpoint, not the haphazard trumpeting of earthly elephants, but the on-key, on-time trumpeting of Garden elephants. The birds added perfect trills and glissandos, and Gorillas beat their chests in time. Even flapping insect wings carried the symphonic strain.

And then there was the dancing. The poetry of bodily movement begged the question: Did God not create us to dance? Sometimes it seemed that the dancing would never stop, and indeed, why should it? Every beast danced in its own way. Elon was an especially talented dancer. In his dancing, soul and body were inseparable. Virgins would watch him and pray with all their hearts that God would grant him for a mate.

When the music had subsided, the men would go to involving the beasts in pruning and landscaping the Garden. The elephants could be seen rearranging rocks, and each creature in turn doing its service under the loving direction of its masters.

Then women would imagine what sort of loveliness they might add to the Garden. What if this flower could be shaped like so and be that color? What if this tree could be taller and have leaves like so? Whatever they imagined and laid their hands upon in prayer, the Creator would inspire them to achieve through their loving care.

After fruit had been gathered for the morning meal, and all had eaten, came the time when the children would play, and Elon was their favorite playmate. If a child had a choice between riding lions and tigers and riding on Elon's back, one might expect that Elon would stand no chance of gaining a rider, but the beasts' speed and fuzzy fur were no match for the love these children found with Elon. They would listen to his stories of the glories of the Creator and pray with him for the grace to know and walk with the Father as Elon did.

Later on, Elon's walk took him to the seashore. Across the strait he could see the land called Ogeeremma, but he did not know that name, for Gardeners knew nothing of those in Exile. Gardeners never left the Garden. And though Earthmen had given Elon's planet the name of Freqmod, Gardeners had no name for their globe. Being unaware of any other worlds, they had no need to differentiate their own. Their universe consisted of Garden and Exile.

On the seashore, Elon knelt in the sand and called upon the Almighty to shower those in Exile with His love and mercy. This shore was the saddest place in the Garden for Elon. Here men and women of the Garden wasted their lives in idle pleasure. Here were couples who had been given the gift of passion—the gift of a mate—but squandered their gifts on idle pursuits. Here were the shacks and huts that protected the work of their hands from the morning dew and from the blessed rain. Here there were but few children, and they were children whose hearts, though guilty of no sin, burned not with desire for their God. In fact, their hearts burned not for anything. Elon contemplated the words of a friend, who said, in reference to the beach people, "It seems that the poison of Exile affects them from across the water!"

Elon watched for a moment in prayer as the others wasted their day. A group of them sat in the sand looking up at the top of the adjoining bluffs. High on a sheer cliff loomed the silhouette of a man and a woman. Elon knew what would happen next. He watched as the two jumped off, doing silly twist and flips as they fell. They hit the hard ground at the bottom of the cliff, and their bodies flattened in an ugly mess, and just as soon, they were whole again and laughing and walking back to their companions As he watched, Elon remembered the story of Eddilk. It was said that Eddilk had performed this trick too many times without returning to the tree of life, and had remained lifeless. His body was said to lie in a cave along these bluffs, but Elon had never found it.

As he turned to leave the shore, he heard someone shout his name and glanced back to see his mother and father coming in his direction, standing upon the backs of dolphins. He laughed at their simple joy. It had been a long time since he had played with the dolphins. His mother and father jumped off into the shallow water of the strait, and the dolphins, still eager to play, beckoned Elon to join them.

"Hi Mother, hi Father," Elon called, and then to the dolphins, "I'm sorry guys, maybe tomorrow."

"Where are you headed, Son, that you have no time to play?" his mother asked.

"I'm headed up to the north wood, up on the hillside to pray with some friends."

"Such a holy man!" she said admiringly, and hugged and kissed him.

After their embrace Elon held his mother's hands and admired her beauty at arm's length. As he did so, he couldn't help but wonder what had gone wrong in the Walnut Forest where his family lived. When he would walk through the Lilac Valley, mothers would beckon him to themselves that he might bless their wombs, and he would kneel before them, place his hands upon their waists, and offer prayers in veneration of that tabernacle wherein the Creator would soon place an immortal soul, for God would rarely refuse this one whom they had come to revere as a prophet.

However, this custom had all but died away in the Walnut Forest. Only a few of the prophets, Elon's friends and prayer companions, on the rare occasion when they were requested to do so, still performed this time-honored homage to the Creator. *They might as well start wearing clothing,* Elon thought, concerning his fellow Forest dwellers.

As a child he had seen clothing once. It had been more than a century ago, but he remembered it well. Pirates from an Exile nation had landed their wooden ship on the Garden's shore, and the angel of the Lord had destroyed them. Elon had looked upon their remains with disgust. *The vanity of man,* he had thought, *to cover God's most beautiful creation with the work of their own hands!* To him, wearing clothing was even more vain than wearing jewelry, and tattoos were the most vainglorious of all.

With his father over visiting the bluff jumpers, Elon asked his mother, "Will you and Father come and join us in prayer?"

"Thanks for asking, Son," she replied, "but we're busy this afternoon."

"More dolphin riding?"

"No, just visiting some friends."

"I should not be surprised to see you jumping off of the bluffs!" Elon teased. His mother blushed noticeably.

"Mother?" he pried.

"It is not a sin to play, Elon! I have raised seven sons. Can I not have a little time for myself?"

Elon's father called to his wife, "Amla, we should be going."

"Mother," Elon resumed, "your youngest son is fifty-five. How much time do you need? What is your plan for attaining glory?"

"Why are you so eager to be rid of *me*?" she asked. "Your grandparents and great grandparents are still here!"

"It is not right!" insisted Elon. "We were not created for the Garden; we were created for the bosom of the Creator!"

"So…is it so bad to stay here a little while?" she asked with a childlike demeanor that she thought would tug at his heartstrings.

"If my father desired intimacy," Elon proposed, "would you make him wait for years?" His mother was surprised and offended by the question.

"Why, no! What do you mean by asking *that*?"

"Simply this, Mother: Your Creator loves you more than any of us ever will. He is waiting to draw you into his heart, to make you the object of infinite affection and to thrill you with delights beyond your wildest dreams, but you have no plan for joining him." Elon's father came over and took her by the hand.

"Sorry, Son, got to go," he said.

As his parents walked away, with his mother occasionally looking back, Elon shook his head and mumbled to himself, "They probably need to get over to the tree of life so they're ready for more bluff jumping!"

His walk then took him past the bluffs and high into the wooded hills. The air was a little cooler up there and a nice breeze coming in off of the strait mingled the smell of the sea with that of the fir trees. There, in a sun dappled opening, his friends sat or knelt on a mossy green forest carpet. Because they were already in prayer he was greeted only with a smile and a bow by those whose eyes were open. Elon joined them in silent prayer. He preferred to pray standing up. It allowed him to move about, to "walk with God," but after a few minutes of prayer, he fell to his knees and raised his arms to heaven.

The others began to whisper, "Elon has a vision." For a long time the vision transfixed him. Finally he closed his eyes, bowed his head, and prayed aloud.

"Glorious Creator, thank you for sending the One who is like us to lead us into glory. May we sacrifice our lives for you as this One has. Father we pray today for all those in Exile, and we pray that all within the Garden will take a holy interest in their brothers and sisters in Exile. Give us the courage, Father, to visit them, to be your loving hands to them. We petition you, as always, through the intercession of the One like us, who dwells within your bosom."

When Elon had finished praying, he noticed many faces turned toward him in disbelief. "What is it, my friends?" he asked.

"We cannot go into the world of the Exiled!" one of them insisted while the others wagged their heads in support.

"Why not?" Elon demanded.

"Because their evil will poison us!" another said.

"Do you not have free will? What is it that they have that you want?" Elon asked.

"Why, nothing!" came the answer.

"You have spoken well, nothing indeed, for our Father provides us with overflowing abundance! Do we have need of gold trinkets? Or buildings? How about machines? Is there any pleasure we lack?" As their heads wagged no to his questions, he continued, "What is the poison that you fear?" Alas, they could not answer him. "You cannot name the poison you fear in Exile, and yet, the Garden is already poisoned. Why have so many wombs dried up?" he asked.

A woman near him opened her mouth to speak, but refrained.

"Aniram, queen of my heart, what is it?" he asked.

She looked into his eyes for a moment, searching for the right words. "King of my heart, I fear your innocence shields you from the truth. The wombs of our women have not dried up."

"What do you mean?" Elon asked. "So few give birth."

"They have discovered," she went on, "the signs their bodies give when they are fertile."

It took a moment for what she meant to sink into Elon's brain before he asked, "What are you saying? That...they don't *want* children? Why would someone, anyone, not want children?!" Then it occurred to him, and he answered his own question. "So that they have more time for idle pursuits!" Indeed, there was no other reason possible for a Gardener, for they enjoyed total health of body and mind, and all of their needs were perfectly met. Furthermore, while practicing self-denial may be virtuous for a fallen race, where is the merit in denying passions that are well-ordered?

"Elon, why are so many, like all of us here, not given mates?" one of them asked. "Is the Creator angry at us?"

Elon thought for a moment. "If by 'us,'" he said, "you mean those of us without mates, the answer is a definite no, but if you mean to ask if he is angry at the Garden, I believe the answer is yes. I fear that his heart is wounded on our account. We have been chosen to lead others to glory, both Gardeners and Exiles. All are destined for the Father's eternal love. Yet, few from the Garden have entered that fullness in these last centuries. We were not created for the Garden, we were created for Glory. Have any of you found it here?"

As he finished speaking, his words seemed incomplete to him. Perhaps there was a more profound reason that they had not been given mates. After all, no mated Gardeners were among this little troop, among these men and women so dedicated to prayer. Mated Gardeners were very busy. In the Lilac Valley mated people offered their every action as prayer, but their actions were all for family and community. Who would first serve the poor in Exile, if not the virgins? Was their virginity ordained by God? Was this little band already partially glorified? Mated to their Maker? His thoughts were too raw to share with the group. He would ponder this more. Perhaps the One would enlighten him.

That night Elon did not go back to the Walnut Forest. Instead, he climbed through the hills, ascending to the very crest of Mt. Ekim. Even in the Garden, mountain peaks were cooler than the valleys, and the cold breeze would work to his advantage. It would keep him awake and alert for his vigil. That night he kept watch with the sinless One, praising, thanking, and imploring the Father. All night long the One instructed him in the wisdom of the Creator, and exposing everything to wisdom's blinding light, showed him the folly of humankind.

When his vision had faded, as the morning sun chased the dew, it occurred to him that the One, born of Exiles and in all things, save sin, an Exile, always appeared fully clothed. Elon had long considered clothing an offense to God. Perhaps, his contemplation suggested, the immense beauty of the One is reserved only for the Creator. What a glorious compliment to a creature *that* would be, and what a divinely romantic thought!

After a full night of prayer, his vision was clear. He would visit the land of the Exiles. He would follow the example of the One and fashion garments for himself. Perhaps an Exile could tell him the reason for clothing.

No Gardener had ever left the Garden and returned, but to Elon's knowledge, no *sinless* Gardener had ever left. He would be the first. He fashioned clothing from grass and leaves, copying the roofing methods of the hut makers. *Even vanity can serve God*, he thought. With the water at low tide, he would be able to wade the sea and hoped his new clothing would hold together.

As he crossed the narrow strait, he could see on the other shore a familiar silhouette, that of an old prophet who frequently came to the sea to pray. As Elon waded through the sea, he caught the old man's attention. The eyes of the prophet grew wide at the sight of a Gardener coming into Exile.

As Elon came upon the shore of Ogeeremma, he received an unspoken answer to a question in his mind. An early winter zephyr beat down upon him nearly pushing him back into the sea, and to the small degree that Gardeners are allowed to feel discomfort, his cold wet garments stung his flesh. *Reason number one for clothing*, he thought. An occasional snowflake dotted the gray sky. He had seen snow before. He had played in it on the highest peaks in the Garden. Though he had seen it from across the strait covering the ground of the exiled world, it had not occurred to him before now that the temperatures that accompany it cause grave problems for poorly dressed Exiles.

As Elon approached the prophet of the exiled, he was struck by his appearance. He had never before witnessed the effects of advanced aging. Noting the old man's flowing white hair and evidence of a lifetime of laughter and sorrow in the lines of his face, he thought that the aging process had rendered him with a sort of ghastly beauty. The old prophet held something, the like of which Elon had never seen. It resembled a pile of flat, square leaves that had markings on each side.

The old man prostrated himself before his guest and addressed him. "Hail, unblemished son of Ekim and Ateer. What brings Your Grace to your servant in Exile?"

Elon stooped and helped him up, and brushing the sand from the old man's garments, said, "I am Elon, son of Elokin and Amla of the Walnut Forest. I have come to serve the children of Iddra. Tell me what I might do to ease the misery of those in Exile, for I tire of trying to help those in the Garden. What is your name?"

"I am Oilenroc, humble servant of the One," he answered.

Elon could not believe his ears. "You are a disciple of the One?" he asked excitedly.

Though appearing confused, Oilenroc answered, "I and others are disciples of the One who, though born in Exile, is an Exile in all things save sin."

Elon danced for joy, and the old man was amused by his animated visitor. When his feet had spent his newfound joy, Elon took interest in the object that Oilenroc held so tenderly. "What is it you hold in your hands, Oilenroc?"

"It is a book of scriptures, sinless one." He could tell by the look on Elon's face that his words meant nothing to the Gardener, so he opened the book and showed a page to him. "These markings represent words. When I look upon them, I am able to know the thoughts and prayers of those who have made the markings."

"Who has made these markings?" Elon asked with keen interest.

"Those who have gone before us, prophets of ages past," Oilenroc answered.

"You are able to know the thoughts and prayers of prophets from of old?"

"That is correct, holy one. Are there no books in the Garden?"

"Gardeners have excellent memories, and we live for a very long time," Elon pointed out, "so we have felt no great need to create such things."

Oilenroc changed the subject. "Holy one, you have confused me. You spoke of 'tiring of trying to help those in the Garden.' I do not understand. What help do Gardeners need?"

Elon smiled at the question but quickly became serious, and urging his new friend to seat himself on an ominous-looking piece of driftwood, began to tell him about life in the Garden.

"I have foreseen that holy Exiles are reserving for themselves the highest places in Glory. Though Gardeners have not broken the Lord's command about the tree, they have forsaken his will in other ways. Let me explain:

"For fourteen generations after Ekim, no one partook of the fruit of the forbidden tree, and many among them went into glory. Then a man of great eloquence, Retsel by name, spoke to the people about the dangers of the forbidden fruit. He spoke of how he himself had almost succumbed to its lure, and that, for the sake of all, a tall wall should be built around it to remove the great temptation lest someone fall into sin and offend the Almighty. And so it was done.

"Gradually the ensuing generations failed to teach their children about the dangers of the tree, and unfortunately, they gradually spoke less and less about the glories of the Almighty as well. He to whom we owe our very existence was praised with well-rehearsed verse: praised by mouths, but not by hearts.

"Then for fourteen generations, added to the task of caring for the Garden, was the task of guarding the wall around the tree. Eventually not even the guards knew exactly what it was they were guarding, for no one had bothered to teach them. Gardeners had found no use for these things you call books. It seems that such things proceed from necessity, and all had been well up to that time. So all teaching was done by word of mouth, and the necessity of such teaching became less and less obvious.

"During that time, Gardeners grew shallow. They busied themselves with the making of shiny trinkets and jewelry, and hanging these things upon their bodies, flattered themselves by believing they had rendered God's creation more beautiful. They also began to make for themselves instruments of music and devices for games. Forgotten, it seemed, was the Lord's command to be fruitful, multiply, and fill the land, for they had discovered the ability to refuse even the gift of life, seldom giving the gift of self to mate or to God, for it is the same burning of the heart that prompts the desire for each. And their activities became more and more frivolous. No longer was their dancing a means by which to worship or invite love, but had become instead a ritual to break the boredom they had created for themselves.

"Then it was at last that Iddra and Lerrol, great among the trinket makers, were deceived by the Exaggerator to scale the unguarded wall and eat from the forbidden tree, so that they might become like God. They were easily deceived, for in truth, they had little idea what God was like, though he maintained their lives and supplied their every need. After partaking of the fruit, a great dark cloud surrounded the two, and all within the Garden took notice that some evil was among them. Iddra and Lerrol fashioned clothing for themselves from leaves and hid themselves, but the Lord sought them out and exiled them to the land beyond the sea.

"All within the Garden were shocked that such a thing should happen, and they once again took up the training of their young ones concerning the wiles of the Exaggerator and the dangers of the tree. But more importantly, they began again to teach of the glories of the Lord and the danger of disobeying his simple command. And they built around the wall a second wall of even greater height, and placed between the walls great beasts, commanding them to sound an alarm with their bellowing and trumpeting should any person come between the two walls. Those who lived near these great walls of the forbidden tree, especially those in the Valley of the Lilacs, began to implore the Lord for the sake of Iddra and Lerrol, who had gone into Exile, so that the Lord would have mercy on them and free them from the bondage of the Exaggerator.

"For fourteen generations a great teaching and devotion concerning the Creator grew up in the valley, and with it, a great love for the Lord. The people abandoned frivolity and forgot the work of their hands, and many holy persons were assumed into glory, and the praises of the Lord never ceased from morning till night. Husbands gave themselves to wives, and wives to husbands, and the Lord blessed them abundantly for their faithfulness, for beautiful children abounded among them, and with voices that rivaled the angels, they praised God.

"But the Exaggerator never rests, and he confounded the minds of those in the Garden whose hearts burned not for their Creator.

"Meanwhile, in the land of Exile, Iddra and Lerrol, fully aware of the evil they had committed, offered sacrifice to the Lord, burning up the best from the land as a sign to the Creator that they understood that he was the source of consolation for their every need. And the land was filled with everything that would support their needs, but only through the wearing out of their hands and the bending of their backs. And as they saw that their bodies were deteriorating and that the elements were against them, they prayed for children to love and cherish, children who might in turn care for them as they aged.

"The Lord was pleased with their request, and a great nation issued forth from them, a nation of artisans. They began to build great cities. But the children of Iddra and Lerrol were born in the image of their parents. Their hearts were fickle, their wits dull, and their passions unbridled, so that, in a few generations, certain tribes among them knew not their Creator. However, feeling the need within their hearts to acknowledge something greater than themselves, they began to worship the work of their own hands and to do great evil before the Lord.

"Though the Gardeners had abandoned their former ways, some close to the sea began to look across the strait and to see the great cities of the Exiles. They listened to the lies of the Exaggerator, who told them that those who were exiled actually *were* more like God, for they built great cities and created things that Gardeners cannot create, and after all, is God not first of all the Creator? Therefore these men must be the more like God. Thus, these Gardeners were deceived in their hearts, but because they had not great needs as did the Exiles, and as their passions were not disordered, they simply returned to their vanity, making the instruments of frivolity, and their dance honored not their Creator, and they sought not his face."

Oilenroc, both amused and amazed by his animated teacher, asked, "If you have not books, how did you come by this great wisdom?"

Elon answered, "All through the night I remained in prayer, a student of the One, who teaches to all the wisdom of the Lord."

Oilenroc could not contain his joy at finding a sinless one so grafted to the heart and ways of the One. "My lord Elon, prophet of the

Most High and humble student of the One, I implore you to speak to
our gathering. Teach us and lead us in prayer."

"I will certainly do as you request," Elon agreed, "but first, dear
sir, teach me more about the world of the Exiles."

Elon seated himself and Oilenroc began.

"You might think, my lord, that being mortal would encourage
Exiles to remain focused on being ready for the next life, and to some
degree, it does. Indeed, we get progressive reminders of our impending
demise."

"Reminders? Like what?" Elon asked.

"Like these," Oilenroc answered, lifting his glasses off of his nose.

"What are they?" Elon asked.

"They're called glasses. They allow us to see when our eyes began
to fail."

"Oh my!" Elon said, reacting to the thought of loosing a gift as
precious as sight.

"However, although we are bombarded with such reminders,"
Oilenroc continued, "disordered passion and dull wits rule the day for
many. The One has told you that the highest realms of glory have been
reserved for Exiles. I fear that the lowest realms of the abyss are
reserved for us as well. Our world is characterized by extreme vanity,
greed, poverty, fear, oppression, and addiction. Lives are wasted
grasping at pleasures and powers that never satisfy and last but a short
time. Health is a constant battle. Sickness and death are everywhere.
The gift of life is spurned, and the beauty of sex reduced to a toy, an
addiction. Adultery, fornication, prostitution, and abortion are
widespread. In Exile you will find great saints, but you will also find
great evil. Demonic possession is common."

Elon had to interrupt Oilenroc to inquire about the meaning of
demonic possession. The explanation left him visibly unsettled. "How
can one willingly give his entire will over to the Exaggerator?" he
pondered aloud.

Oilenroc's simple answer unsettled him all the more. "The Evil
One has great power in the realms of Exile. He pits husband against
wife, child against parent, brother against brother, sister against sister,
and nation against nation. He causes divisions between believers and
inspires false gods among unbelievers. But I have foreseen the fall of
his kingdom!"

"Kingdom?" asked Elon. "I only know of one kingdom, the
Kingdom of Heaven."

His response surprised Oilenroc. "I see," he said. "We use the word more freely. A kingdom is simply the realm ruled by a king," he explained.

"Ruled?" Elon puzzled. "A king is a father. A king is a friend, a lover who showers his lovers with gifts. His love is all that we need and we owe him our rapt attention. What is *ruled*?"

Oilenroc began to see that his new friend had no concept of government. "God is the King of Heaven, the *ruler* of heaven. He has the power to rule," he proclaimed feebly, unimpressed with his own explanation.

Elon's expression waxed and waned between confusion and understanding. "So to rule means to love," he deduced.

"Hmmm...not exactly," Oilenroc sighed in frustration. After a moment, his face brightened and he declared, "A king has power. God has the power to forgive. He has the power to grant us favors. He has the power to give us gifts. If we are evil, he has the power to shield us from seeing his face."

A look of understanding came over Elon's face, but then he frowned. "And...the Exaggerator is the king of...what?" he asked.

"Of darkness, my lord," Oilenroc responded. "By the power of his lies he plots to lure souls into his kingdom of darkness, shielded from the vision of God, where he may taunt them forever."

Elon's vigorous countenance paled. "Forever? Eternity without...the Lord?" he pressed, gazing into Oilenroc's eyes.

"Yes, my lord...eternity."

The poor Gardener sat in shock. Why had the One not revealed to him this great horror? Had this truth been withheld from him that his pain might be greater? That he might know greater depths of remorse for not responding to the Spirit sooner? How could he have been so blind? Had he assumed that all Exiles entered Glory upon death?

He thought about Oilenroc's use of the word *power*. Curious word, power. Curious concept. He had never before thought of God as powerful, but now, in the midst of his great remorse, the One revealed the power of God. His face brightened and he assured Oilenroc, "You have indeed foreseen the fall of the Exaggerator's kingdom!"

Oilenroc resumed his teaching about the world of Exiles. "The land you have entered is the kingdom of Ogeeremma. We have an elected parliament and a kindly king named Einniv. Though he is a holy man, a student of the One, many evil forces are at work against him. There are many who do not believe in the existence of the One and fail to recognize the wisdom in the prophecies of the disciples. They await the coming of the 'Unifier,' a great warrior king who they believe will unite the Garden and the world of Exile."

"And what do you think of this teaching?" Elon asked.

"When the One teaches me about the Unifier, I shall immediately begin to look for his coming," the old man answered.

Oilenroc then took his guest to meet with the prophets. As they approached the building the sound of music fell upon the sensitive ears of Elon, and by the time they had entered the hall he could hardly contain himself, for his feet so wanted to render worship. However, as he danced a few steps in the vestibule, Oilenroc indicated, with a gesture and an expression, that dancing during worship was not their custom and would not be appreciated.

Elon's ears were tortured by Exile voices that only threatened to be on key, but their sincerity warmed his heart. A chorus of swan horns rattled the windows, while a pair of chapel horns, like French horns the size of Sousaphones, massaged the heart and soul. Elon had never heard brass and was quite taken with the sound of it. In fact, he liked all of the musical instruments he heard. He had always disliked the sound of instruments made by the trinket makers of the Garden, but now he wondered if it was the sound they made or the music they played that had been so distasteful. Noting the amazing exuberance of the stout Exile woman who led the singing, the difference finally came home to him: passion. The trinket makers lacked passion, but there was no lack of it in this room.

When there was a break in the singing, Oilenroc took his guest to the front of the gathering. All fell silent at the sight of this beautiful man, with hair and beard down to his waist, dressed in a garment of leaves and grass. With bronze skin, auburn hair, and deep blue-green eyes, Elon instantly had the attention of every Prophetess in the building, while the Prophets wondered, *What sort of man is this?*

Oilenroc addressed them. "Tonight is the dawn of a new age. The man before you is Elon, prophet of the One. He has come today from across the strait to bring to us the joy of the Garden. He is a sinless son of Ekim and Ateer, the first to journey to the land of Exile."

"If he is sinless," a man spoke up, "why does he wear the garments of our fallen parents, Iddra and Lerrol?" His question evoked much murmuring among the Prophets.

As Oilenroc attempted to quiet them without avail, Elon stood upon a chair and raised his hands in the air. "Shall I remove my clothing? Is that your wish?" he asked.

The murmuring continued. "If you were sinless, you would not need clothing for warmth," one shouted.

Elon yanked a large section of grass from his garment, revealing a perfectly muscled right arm and shoulder. He took the section, stepped down, and broke it over the back of the chair. "Does wet, frozen clothing provide warmth?" he asked.

More murmuring ensued, until a prophetess came forward. Her face was dark and weathered for her age of forty-eight, and though her hair had already turned snow white, it served well as a backdrop for blue eyes that shined with a youthful glow. With a motherly, loving smile on her face, she touched Elon's robe and felt its frozen shards. Then she touched his shoulder and arm, which were amazingly warm to the touch. Placing a hand on each shoulder, she looked deeply into his piercing eyes. For a long moment, all of the assembly gazed on in perfect silence. Finally the prophetess bowed deeply before Elon, and turning and facing the crowd with a broad smile accented by tears of joy, she gestured with the sweep of an arm to the prophet, inviting others to do homage. The entire assembly followed suit, bowing deeply before him, and the murmuring ceased.

"Speak, my lord," came Oilenroc's gentle command.

Elon began to relate to them those things he had told to Oilenroc, that is, the wisdom obtained at the feet of the One. He pledged to bring help to them from the Garden, and a great excitement arose among them. As a sign of his commitment to them, he allowed them to cut his hair and beard to a length similar to theirs, but he refused the beautiful robe offered to him by the prophetess, because he considered that his leaves were, at least, the work of God's creation. She seemed to understand and to accept graciously his refusal of the garment.

As the meeting ended, Elon noticed the white haired prophetess leaving the building.

"To whom do I owe being reconciled with this crowd," he asked Oilenroc, while gesturing toward the lady.

"Ah, her name is Airrellav; she is a prophet of the One," he said, with great love in his voice.

"Why did she not speak?"

"She is mute, my friend. She has had no voice since birth."

"And yet," Elon responded, "she is a prophet among her people? What a wonder of the Lord that is!"

Oilenroc added, "Not only is she a prophet, but she is a great servant. She cares for orphans and homeless children with whatever means are at her disposal."

Elon's first experience with mechanized transportation proved to be a rude one. Oilenroc's monstrous jalopy, a grand, art deco styled, pregnant roadster, was so consumed by rust as to nearly obliterate its original color. Oilenroc loved to drive, and Elon smiled at the simple joy in the old man's smile as he chauffeured the Gardener back to the strait. As they went, Elon had much fodder for prayer and contemplation. He had taken his first glimpse at the necessity of technology for Exiles. It would take a while to process all that he had seen and heard.

They arrived at the beach after the sun had set, and Oilenroc insisted, "My Lord Elon, I cannot send you out into the sea in the dark with this tempest at your back! Stay the night with us. I will take you to a fine house in the city."

"I will stay," Elon declared, "but I will stay with *you*, however humble the dwelling."

On the way to Oilenroc's home, they noticed a child snuggled into the tall grass of a thicket at the road's edge. Oilenroc went to offer the little one a roof for the night, but she sprang up and ran away in fear. The thought of a child spending the night without parents or shelter from the gripping cold tore at Elon's heart as nothing ever had.

He spent the night in Oilenroc's humble little house near the graveyard, and in their twilight conversation the cement of their new friendship grew deep and unbreakable. After a meal, the origin of which Elon feared to inquire, and long after Oilenroc had fallen asleep on his cot, Elon stared out the window at the orange night star rising above the graveyard. In the midnight gloom an unpleasant image filled his mind: the image of those pirates, so long ago, rotting on the shore of the Garden. He looked upon his newfound friend as he slept. Someday Oilenroc would lie rotting in that cold ground in the sleep of death. The horrible thought hardened Elon's resolve to save souls. He finally fell asleep praying for the little girl who had escaped their kindness.

Chapter 8

Star Covenant

A ladybug meandered down the lovely arm and across the hand of the wonderful old statue, took flight, and landed on Veronica's forearm. Like a little gift from heaven she allowed it to wander about until it stopped to rest on her folded hands. She opened her hands and blew the little creature, like a kiss, back toward the image of Our Mother. Halfway expecting the statue to open its hands to receive the gift, Veronica looked intently upon the likeness of the Immaculate Conception. It embodied, she thought, the perfect combination of joyous excitement and perfect peace, a combination that doesn't come often in this life. She thought about how little we are, not unlike the ladybug in the whole scheme of things. It came home to her that size and distance have little consequence in the Creator's plan. Surely little Veronica Lansing was about the same size as the Queen of the Universe. Faith overcame sin. Faith could surely conquer space.

She had come to having these little conversations with the Blessed Mother on more and more regular occasions as the launch date neared. In just thirty days they would test their craft with a quick trip to Mars and back. Unfortunately, they would not be able to achieve anywhere near the speed planned for the actual star voyage, so a number of unknowns would remain.

On the other side of town in his office at AGC headquarters, Col. Cliff Lamans contemplated the coming saga. He had been chosen for the voyage and had almost immediately accepted. It had seemed like an intriguing adventure. The idea of broadening his image as a national hero appealed to him a great deal. On his return to Earth, thanks to relativity, he would be a relatively young man; all of his rivals would be retired. The world would be his on a silver platter.

Lamans was a late comer to the mission compared to the other officers. As second in command it was critical that he understand the mission; however, as he read the mission charter he asked himself aloud, "Who wrote this, the Pope?" The charter seemed overly philosophical to him. "I thought this was a science mission?" he said to no one. Talking to himself was a bad habit he had acquired in Panama. Month upon month of solitary confinement had taken its toll. The memories of that tragic year haunted him continually.

His Special Ops team had parachuted in to gain control of nuclear warheads terrorists had set up along the canal. However, his entire band had been taken captive by the terrorists when they had no more than touched foot on the ground. If someone wanted to raise the hair on the back of Col. Lamans' neck, they needed to say just two words: military intelligence.

As he looked over the Freqmod mission charter and reflected upon aspects of the mission that seemed vulnerable because of apparent knowledge gaps, he began to do exactly what he was chosen to do, to think about the mission in a way that only a soldier could think. "It's one thing to rot in a prison in Panama, but quite another to do it on a God-forsaken planet four light years away," he said to himself.

It had been years since the man had let down his guard. He had been very close with his Special Ops team. They had seen a lot of action together both on and off the battlefield. Early on, his captors had singled him out as the man in charge—he just had that aura about him—and they had reserved for him a special torture.

A former medical student, one of the terrorists had skills advanced enough to amputate limbs without killing a man. Thus it was that all of Lamans' companions lost their limbs, little by little. Each time, Lamans was told they would be spared if he would give up information. Each time, the terrorists joked that the lost flesh of his friends would end up, or had ended up, in the colonel's food. Each time, they told their victims that, if they begged him enough, Lamans might give up enough information to allow them to retain a remaining body part—and beg they did!

There came a point when the torturers became convinced that Lamans really had no valuable information to give, and the whole thing became a game: the crack-the-hard-nut game. When they were finally rescued, four limbless men were carried out in baskets, and one walked. He had retained enough of his sanity to ask himself out loud, for years to come, if his limbless friends weren't the lucky ones.

Yet, there was no hint of any psychological damage recorded in the Army's records: no hint that the man was anything other than rock solid. Indeed, he had seen action since the Panama incident and had performed admirably, and successful combat action was the Army's ultimate yardstick.

As the Hard Nut contemplated the pending mission, the faces and bodies of the female crew members paraded through his mind. To be sure, there were some beauties, but would he be up to the competition?

Though he strived always to be discrete and to keep up appearances, he was no stranger to casual intimacy. He had made love to beauties all over the world. With pride he mentally reviewed his off-field conquests.

He was maturing now, and while permanent companionship no longer seemed a trap, Lamans had no interest in producing offspring. *As a father, I'd probably be as lame as my old man,* he thought. He thought about Veronica, the most beautiful woman on the crew. "The Angel's out of your league, buddy," he said to himself, "and she wants to have lots and lots of babies!" The words having barely escaped his lips, he wondered how soundproof the AGC's walls were and blushed at his verbal indiscretion.

His thoughts drifted to Jasmine Babasa. *Jasmine!* He thought, *the perfect woman: young, healthy, beautiful, sensuous, vulnerable, and... sterile!* He doubted his ability to compete for women against the mostly younger male crew. It would be best to begin the voyage with a bird in the hand. It was time to further the good start he had made.

Melanie caught the phone on the fifth ring. Her hands were gooey with cake dough so she commanded "Speakerphone," and answered with, "Lansing residence, Mel speaking."

"Hello, Miss Lansing, Commander Lamans here. I was hoping I might speak with Jasmine. I understand that she is staying with you."

"Sorry, Commander, she's unable to come to the phone. I can put you into her voice mail."

"That would be fine, thank you," he said. When he heard the beep, he said, "Jasmine, this is Cliff. I hope you're doing well. I'd really like to take you to dinner some evening soon. I so enjoy your company. Please give me a call at..."

Mel called to Jasmine, "Lover boy left another message. Should I hit *delete*?"

"Yes, please," Jasmine called from the bathroom. It was her only day that week with no training sessions at AGC, and she was about to leave for Children's Hospital. She had been volunteering with Veronica and was now permanently hooked. Her bedroom walls were covered with pictures of the kids, and she could tell you anything you wanted to know about any of them.

"My you look wonderful today," Melanie bubbled at the sight of Jasmine in her fresh white cotton dress. The miniskirt queen had died and the new no-cosmetic Jasmine looked very sweet in her knee-length cotton collection.

"Thanks, Mel, so do you!"

"Do you know what I'm making?"

"Hmm…cake?"

"Yup. Do you know why?"

"No clue," Jasmine said, dipping her finger into the batter. "Umm, chocolate," she said, "My favorite."

"Exactly! What's the date today, Jazz?"

"It's…oh my gosh, it's my birthday! I forgot all about it! I'm thirty-three today."

"The age of perfection," Melanie declared.

"What does that mean?"

"That you've been getting better and better every year, but from here on out you start to deteriorate."

"Well, I happen to believe that, from here on out, I will get more beautiful every day," Jasmine assured her.

"Really?"

"Yes, ma'am. It's happened with other people, and I can prove it to you," she insisted as she left the room.

"It *has* happened," Melanie yelled after her, "but can you afford all of that plastic surgery?"

Jasmine picked up her Bible from the coffee table and pulled out her bookmark. She showed it to Melanie and asked, "Have you ever seen anyone more beautiful than that?"

Melanie studied the picture for a second, smiled, and said, "No Jazz, I haven't. You win! How old was she in that photo?"

"Eighty-two," Jasmine answered, placing the photo of St. Teresa of Calcutta back between the pages of her Bible.

Veronica arrived at the AGC a few minutes early for her meeting. The meeting had been called only the day before, and she had not yet seen an agenda. She stopped by Col. Benson's office to get the low-down.

"Just wanted to get everybody together to tie up any loose ends," Mike told her. "Before last week, Cliff hadn't seen the mission charter, or known that one existed. That's my fault, and I want to make sure there aren't any other gaps in communication. We also need to plan time to take the entire crew up to the Covenant to check it out and perform any diagnostics or hands-on training that they may deem necessary before launch."

All six top ranking officers attended the meeting. Col. Benson became Capt. Benson, with Col. Lamans, now Commander Lamans, as his right-hand man. The sassy, beautiful, sweet-n-sour Air Force Capt. Tessa Oakley filled the third position: Chief Engineer. Her formidable career included the engineering, designing, and test piloting of air and space craft. As Chief Security Officer, Antonio Escobar held the fourth position. He would also oversee all onboard gardening. Veronica held the fifth position as Chief Medical Officer, with the sixth position filled by Fr./Dr. Scofield, chaplain under the captain and mental health director reporting to Dr. Lansing. Each of these individuals, as well as everyone else on the crew, had various extraneous duties to suit their many and varied talents.

"Welcome. Take a look around the table," the captain began. "I hope you like the faces you see, because you'll be seeing them a lot! In the eyes of this old military man, this mission will be unprecedented for more reasons than the obvious. No nuclear sub crew has ever had to face staying under for two straight years, and our tin can will not be much different than theirs. If our tenuous technology allows our survival, our greatest challenge will be cabin fever.

"Last month I ordered Fr. Scofield to do a psychological profile on everyone assigned to this mission. That task is completed for everyone except four of the people sitting at this table and one last minute replacement recruit. Father and I had one done by Dr. Talbot over at the Air Force Academy. I am ordering the rest of you to do the same. Please get it done sometime this week. Dr. Talbot will make the time and is eminently qualified. I do not expect that the findings of this procedure will affect the roster for this voyage. On the other hand I don't want any surprises. If a problem arises, prior knowledge may help Father, Dr. Lansing, and I to know how to deal with it. For those of you who don't know, our new recruit is Jasmine Babasa, a former FBI captain with an admirable record. Dr. Lansing, I know that she has become a close personal friend of yours. She will need all the help that you can give to get her up to speed these remaining weeks."

They went on to discuss the time for inspecting the star cruiser, and the captain adjourned the meeting.

That night Fr. Scofield, Capt. Benson, and Veronica joined one another in the VIP room at Mick's.

"I have some concerns," the captain said. "I have a very specific reason for ordering a profile done by a third party. I believe, Father, that you are too close to Antonio, and I think he has issues surrounding the death of his twin, issues that need resolution. I am a twin myself, as you are aware. It took ages for me to come to grips with the death of my brother."

"I think you've made a wise decision, Captain," Fr. Scofield said. "I have been Antonio's confessor for years, but haven't seen him in the box for quite some time. He may have found another confessor, or he may be trying to go it alone. Sometimes the hurt is just too deep to open the wound and let it get some air."

"You know," Veronica added, "he's just not the happy-go-lucky guy he was. Although a grieving period is normal and healthy, he may need help getting past it, and now would certainly be a good time to start." She noticed that the captain looked a little distant.

"Do you know," he said, "that when I would call my brother, he would often pick up the phone before it rang?" The look in his eyes told Veronica that the pain lingered, and she took his hand and squeezed it lovingly.

"Jasmine Babasa is my close friend and Fr. Scofield is her confessor," Veronica noted. "I think that perhaps we have become too close to her to be objective, and that she should also be evaluated by Dr. Talbot."

"I agree, Doctor. Thank you for your candor," the captain said. "Could you please follow up with her to be sure it gets done?"

"Certainly. And what about our illustrious Commander Lamans? There's a deep one. I sense plenty of armor," she observed.

"We will need to deal with that armor," Father asserted.

"It is crucial that we complete this before the impending induction ceremony," Captain Benson declared. "Once the crew members take on official military status, we launch into a whole new level of bureaucracy."

After the meeting Veronica went to help tuck in the kids at Children's and found Jasmine on a couch surrounded by munchkins, all enthralled with the children's bible story she was reading. Two nuns, Missionaries of Charity, were seated on the rug in front of the couch, helping to answer whatever questions the children might have. Veronica smiled at how at home Jasmine seemed in that setting.

Back at the house, they shared a bedtime snack of birthday cake and ice cream. As Jasmine opened some little gifts, Veronica remembered the scene with the sisters and teased, "You know, what you need to make your outfit complete is blue lines around the hem."

Jasmine looked at her, smiled radiantly, and said, "I know."

There was standing room only in the University lecture hall. The guest lecturer, a well known and loved theologian, was an officer on the Freqmod mission team, and this was the last time anyone would hear him for a long time, if ever again. Among those seated were alumni who would be making the voyage, and a certain Jasmine Babasa who had sneaked in with her friends. The launch date, like the autumn air, nipped at their heels. This first lecture of the new semester would cover basic subject matter, but one could hear Fr. Scofield talk on the same subject a hundred times and still glean something new.

"All things of importance have everything to do with relationships," he began, "and the most important relationship of all is our relationship to God.

"God, like his first creation, the angels, is a spirit being composed of intellect and will. Intellect is an essential good. It is never, in and of itself, evil. Oh yes, we can pervert it, just as we can make perverted use of our bodies, but that does not change the essential nature. God's intellect is infinite and is infinitely good. He is the creator of all other intellects.

"All of creation finds form within the intellect of God, held in existence by an act of his will. This does not mean that God is the universe or that the universe is God; they are separate realities. However, the universe would cease to exist if God ceased to will its existence—ceased to hold it in his thoughts. Our free will, in as much as it is the ultimate gift from God—that thing which separates us from dumb creatures—is an essential good, but with a single choice, it can become the source of great evil. Ultimately, good vs. evil comes down to choices. God's will is infinitely good, and all of his choices are profoundly good.

"Humans are creatures composed of intellect, will, and matter. As we have discussed, intellect is an essential good. Matter is also an essential good. Therefore, our bodies are essentially good. You, no doubt, have seen bodies you may have judged to be otherwise, but personal tastes aside, our bodies are essentially good, a gift from God intended to bring *us* joy, and *him* glory. Like our intellects, our bodies would cease to exist if God did not perpetually will their existence.

"Though God's infinite intellect conceives all things and they are held in existence by his will, and though he is everywhere, there is a certain place where his presence is totally shielded from those persons within. It is important to remember here that God is infinitely good. He is incapable of evil. He is incapable of unkindness. He is infinitely condescending.

"I notice some frowns, which is a good thing; it tells me that you're awake! I said that God 'is infinitely condescending' and you're trying to figure out what that means. Condescension on the part of one human towards another is a bad thing, but condescension on the part of God—that is, lowering himself to our level, for example, by becoming a human being—is a very good thing.

"But, I digress. I was speaking of a place wherein persons are shielded from God's presence. The place I speak of is called hell. Hell is afforded as a great kindness to errant souls. No one is there who has not chosen to be there.

"So I ask you: How can hell be a kindness?"

A stocky, pizza-faced sophomore in a number 33 jersey timidly raised his hand.

"Yes, young man."

"If we haven't responded to God's grace, don't trust him, don't trust in his love, and want to have everything our own way, we'll be uncomfortable in his presence. It would actually be more painful for us to be in his presence than to be cut off from him," he said.

"Wow! Did you hear that?" Father asked. "This is going to be a good year, class. I'm really beginning to be sorry that I'll be missing it."

A hand shot up in the back of the room.

"A question?" Father asked.

A fifty-something lady with a serious frown asked, "What about fire? I've always been told there would be fire in hell, that it would burn the flesh of the damned when their bodies are resurrected."

"Well," Father hesitated, "I didn't really plan to go there right now, but I also don't want to leave you hanging." He thought for a moment. "I cannot recall an instance in which fire is used symbolically in scripture, where it does not symbolize the Almighty. Just off hand, I can think of the burning bush, the fire on Mount Sinai, the pillar of fire in the dessert…and the fiery tongues at Pentecost: all flames that lead to God. Jesus speaks of hell in terms of Gehenna, a valley that was the location of Jerusalem's dump grounds. Ancient Jerusalem was a sizeable city, large enough that the trash fires never went out. I submit that the fire in hell is the same as the fire in heaven. It is the burning love of God. Though the damned may be kindly shielded from the beatific vision, they can never forget the love of God that burns for them, the love they rejected. However, unlike the souls in heaven who are consumed by the fire of God's love—eternally deified—the souls in hell will never be consumed, and the fire of God's love will never be quenched. That awareness of the love they rejected will torment them forever."

"What about the burning of their very flesh," she pressed, "wouldn't that be torture?"

"Fire in all of these examples is used metaphorically, not literally," he informed her.

"That's not what I was taught!" she retorted.

Wanting to move on, Father answered her question with questions: "Okay. Are there self-inflicted spiritual torments and disappointments so great that stepping into flames might seem a welcome distraction? Would it be a cruelty to provide such a distraction?"

As she attempted to digest what she had been given, he went on: "Where do we, the living, fit into the scheme of things? If God's presence is shielded from those in hell, and fully manifest to those in heaven, where are we?"

Number 33 raised his hand again. "Yes, sir," Father acknowledged him.

"We're in exile," the fullback told him.

"Exile!" Father responded. "Interesting! Explain please."

"Well, it seems to me that we're kind of in between heaven and hell. We're not ready to be exposed directly to God, but we also haven't decided to reject him. It's kinda like, when Adam and Eve were created, they were right in the heart of God. He communicated his will to them perfectly, and they didn't choose to do anything nasty because they really didn't even realize they had choices. Their wills hadn't been perverted yet, and..." he coasted to a stop as if he'd run out of gas.

"Ah! They had what has been called original justice, an innocent, unspoiled state. That's excellent, my friend. Go on, I know you have more to say," Father prodded him

"Well, I'm thinking that after they sinned they realized they had lots of choices, choices that they didn't even know existed before. Maybe God had regulated everything for them—their appetites for food, drink, and sexual pleasure—kinda like the way we don't need to make decisions about our heartbeat and breathing. Maybe, in the beginning, there just were no decisions to make."

"Wonderful!" Fr. Scofield declared. He paraphrased and recapped what the young man had said, and then asked, "So…what about us? After we confess our sins and are reconciled, or baptized, and our souls are full of divine grace, how is it that often times we still fall so easily? Is the power of God's grace real?" No one raised a hand. Father looked earnestly at the young man in the football jersey. "It's okay…what's your name, son?"

"Cory, Father."

"The others have had their chance, Cory, you can go again. I know you have something to say; I can see it on your face," he said with a grin.

Growing ever more self-conscious, and yet more confident, the young man spoke again: "Well, Adam didn't have a lot of choices to make. I mean, it was Eden, not Vegas or Sunset Strip. He didn't know he had choices until God told him about the tree of knowledge thing, allowing him to choose between fruit and no fruit—between death and life.

"But we know from birth that we have choices. God's not regulating our passions for us, so we're out of control from the moment we pop out of the womb! And then we develop habits—some of them nasty—and addictions. The power of God's grace is real. Through the Sacraments he gives us the power to choose good, but it's up to us to use that power and dedicate ourselves to that choice."

He smiled and added, "My dad says that habitual sin is like a comfortable old shoe. God wants us to grow, to move outside of our comfort zone—to walk in his shoes. But if we're used to living loose, we find his shoes a little too tight. We get so comfy with our favorite sins that we start to think maybe they're not really sins after all. So…we allow our passions to be enslaved, while our intellects are distracted by everything under the sun."

"Like football?" Father kidded.

"Ha…yeah…like football!" Cory chuckled.

"My son, it doesn't seem that too much is distracting you! I don't know that I've ever heard a finer explanation from anyone, myself included. I sense that perhaps your dad has something to do with that. You just keep on doing whatever it is you're doing, and you'll be taking my place up here someday. Thank you so much for contributing."

The fullback raised his hand. "Father, where does conscience fit in?" he asked.

"Well, I'm glad you asked, Cory. Dictionary definitions will point to conscience as our awareness of rules for moral choices—mores derived from church, secular, and parental sources—and certainly that's a part of the developed conscience. Adam and Eve were created in God's image, but scripture tells us that they begot children 'in their own image.' They passed on their fallen nature. But remember what else scripture tells us that God said about our parents after the fall: 'Now man is truly like us, knowing good from evil.' If our first parents passed on to us their fallen nature, they also passed on this inherent consciousness of good and evil. This innate sense of right and wrong is the beginning of conscience. We are not born with an evil nature, just with runaway passions—sort of a soul/body disconnect."

Fr. Scofield paused a moment, searching for a way to drive home his point. "Several years after a certain tribe of headhunters had been converted to Christianity," he said, "they were asked how it was possible that they had not known that cannibalism was wrong. They indicated that they had known it was wrong, but that they hadn't known why. You see, the Seducer will always be busy drawing attention to our appetites, hoping to drown that still voice in our hearts that cries continuously for us to make good and just decisions."

Fr. Scofield glanced at the wall clock and paused for a moment to collect his closing thoughts. "Is exile a blessing or a curse?" he asked.

The dozen or so responses that he received were equally split between blessing and curse. "Mr. Hoffman, you said 'blessing.' Why?" Father asked him.

"That's simple, Father; God owes us nothing. We are the offspring of fallen parents. God doesn't owe our race a second chance, and yet, he died to give us one."

"Well put, my friend. One last question: What are some things that help to keep our thoughts on God so that we might make holy decisions in line with his will?"

Discussion ensued listing every form of prayer, the reading of scripture, and nearly any other spiritual practice that would keep God in our thoughts.

"Anything else?" Father asked. Jasmine raised her hand.

"Suffering: physical, mental, emotional, and spiritual. It can all be offered as a sacrifice to stay centered on God," she said.

"Very good, Jasmine. Veronica, you also had your hand up?"

"Pleasure, Father," she said. "Satan hates it when we use pleasure to stay fixed on God, because he thinks pleasure's his territory."

"Did you hear that class? Isn't that interesting! Is pain an essential good or an essential bad?"

"Bad," several students blurted simultaneously.

"Wouldn't that leave pleasure as an essential good? But Dr. Lansing thinks that the Devil sees pleasure as *his* territory. That would make pleasure a painful dichotomy for a demon, wouldn't it? Of course, they have a similar situation with pain, which *is* their territory, so to speak. They enjoy our pain until we make a sacrifice of it to God—an act that's gotta drive 'em absolutely nuts! Hmmm...I would pursue this subject further, but I think I'll leave it for the new professor. Dr. Emmanuel Voronin is replacing me in this capacity, and he will do a wonderful job of covering this subject."

After class Veronica and Jasmine rode with Father out to the AGC. "So you didn't want me quoting a bunch of Dr. Voronin's work and stealing his thunder, eh?" Veronica asked. "That's really cool that he's teaching here. I'm going to stay on Earth so I can go to his lectures, okay?"

"No, it's not okay. I need a captive audience for *my* lectures!" he insisted.

≈

Dr. Talbot, an Eastern Indian woman in her early seventies, looked very dignified seated behind the acre of mahogany desk that separated her from Fr. Scofield and Veronica. Veronica thought she had never seen white hair quite so long and daydreamed momentarily picturing herself with a long white mane.

"If you two were any more stable, we could put you at the poles to keep the Earth from wobbling," Dr. Talbot proclaimed in reference to their psychological profiles. "Same goes for Captain Benson. And this Oakley woman is something else. Don't worry about anything being bottled up in her; it all diffuses every time she opens her mouth! But I have some concerns about the other three.

"Escobar's a sweet man with a very stable background, but he needs to get this grief thing behind him. It's subtly showing up in a few areas. It may only take a session or two. In fact, all it may take is a good confession, Father. He's mad at God. He needs to give it up and move on.

"Babasa is in the throes of casting off dependency. She has a lot going for her and seems to be building a firm foundation, something she lacked as a youth. In a perfect world, she's not someone I would choose for such a mission. I'm just not sure she's ready for it."

"How about Commander Lamans?" Veronica asked.

"Ah...Lamans! The computer nearly spit his tests back out! As you both know, this psychology stuff is not an exact science, but these tests are designed so as to recognize, at least to some degree, when a person is trying to cover something up. I can't report to you any problems that the man may have; I can only report that it seems he deliberately tried to appear different than what he actually is. His problem may be as simple as an inferiority complex, but there's just no way of getting into his head based on these test results."

"What do you suggest, Doctor?" Father asked.

"Is it too late to replace him?" Dr. Talbot asked.

"Probably. The politics would run awfully deep," he assured her.

"Then I think you should order him back in here and I'll try and pry the can open. Even if he's not willing to make an effort to work on himself, anything I can pry out may help you later on."

"And Babasa?" Veronica asked.

"I would be wary of putting her into any sort of command position in the near future. As a rank and file crew member, however, I think she will perform wonderfully if nurtured and mentored."

"Good morning, Commander," Veronica greeted her crewmate as Lamans seated himself across the aisle from her and Jasmine on the shuttle. They were on their way to inspect Star Covenant. "Are you ready for all this flying?" she asked. "It's a lot of flying for an Army guy."

"Good morning, Dr. Lansing, Ensign Babasa. You know, neither motion nor height has ever bothered me. I've done a lot of parachuting. Besides, aside from a short flight to get on board Covenant, this mission will just be a lot of sitting in a tin can, and as Captain Benson said, 'When it comes to sittin' in a can, Lamans is the king'; been there; done that!"

"You're talking about Panama?"

"Yeah...Panama." His eyes became distant and he stared off for a moment collecting himself. "You know...they fed me, and I was warm enough, dry enough, and clean enough. They never tortured me physically, but they sure tried to get inside my head. If you'll forgive me for saying so, one big difference between that can in Panama and this one, is that there were no beautiful women with me in that one."

Veronica smiled at his attempt at sweetness, even though it was an obvious come-on. "I think there are many nice people on the team who will make this mission considerably better than your Panama stay," she predicted.

"Believe me, Doctor, it couldn't possibly be worse! I am actually looking forward to the trip. Did you know that we'll have on board the largest library ever compiled? It's amazing what they can store in a little tiny space these days. If you're a movie fan, I guess we'll have one of just about everything that's ever been filmed. Music fan? We have all that too."

"We're going to need it," Veronica assured him. "You know, I made a list of things I wanted to check out on Covenant today, and it's lying on the dashboard of my car. Excuse me, please," she said, hurrying off. They were among the first crew members aboard, and no one was sitting near them. Without saying a word, Lamans crossed the aisle and seated himself next to Jasmine.

What happened to Mr. Manners? she thought.

Lamans leaned close to her and asked, "Jasmine, have you gotten any of those numerous voice mails I've left for you?"

"No, I haven't," she answered.

"Someone must be screening your calls to keep you safe from unsavory elements," he joked, attempting to hide his perturbation. "I have just been calling to say that I was so glad I was able to help you the other night and that I really enjoyed your company afterwards. I would like to get together sometime soon."

Who gives a damn what you enjoyed? Jasmine thought, but bit her tongue. It seemed to her that all of Lamans' insightful charm in their first meeting had been the insights of reconnoitering, the charms of a spy. Now that the initial conquest had been made, he had all the charms of an occupation force. She lowered her voice and said, "I was in deep distress the other night, Commander. You took advantage of me! You did not call the police! You did not fix the door! You politely raped me and left me weeping!"

"I did not rape you!" he screamed in a whisper.

"You might just as well have!" she whisper-screamed back. "You used me! I'm not a thing to be used and discarded!"

"Nor am I! And I'm not discarding you! I'm trying to further our relationship! I bonded deeply with you the other night. I am committed to us."

"There is no *us*, Commander!"

"What is the harm in enjoying me, Jasmine? I would never hurt you. I think you're beautiful! I think you're the perfect woman!"

"What does that mean?"

"You're young, beautiful, intelligent, charming..."

"And neutered!" she finished for him.

"I considered that as well," he said candidly. "I admit that I'm not really looking to start a family."

"Get away from me!" she said, no longer whispering.

Lamans glanced around to see if they had drawn any attention. "Fine," he said, "but it's unfortunate you won't be making the star voyage."

"What do you mean?" Jasmine demanded.

He brought his voice very low. "We all went through the same battery of tests, Jasmine. Fertility is one of the requirements for this mission. Someone's covering for you. I don't know how they're getting away with it; your infertility was blabbed all over the front pages. I bonded with you the other night." Jasmine began to get nauseous from the repetition of this mantra. "My rank may allow me the leverage to keep your medical condition from becoming an issue. Your inclusion in this crew may be justifiable if you have an ongoing relationship with another crew member, especially one of high rank. But if you have no such relationship..." he trailed off, raising his eyebrows.

"I see. You're saying that I need to give you sexual favors or you'll get me kicked off the mission." Jasmine had ceased whispering and the cabin was beginning to fill up.

Lamans glanced around uneasily, wanting to speak, but afraid to do so. Veronica returned from her car and the commander recovered enough of his manners to move so she could take her seat.

The tour of the cruiser proved challenging because of the extremely low gravity. For simplicity sake, like the Martian cruisers before it, the vessel had no rotating cabins. A gravity effect was achieved through acceleration, deceleration, and gravitronic force field (artificial gravity). Acceleration would be maintained at one G for forty weeks, the time required to reach top speed. The craft would remain at top speed for thirty-two weeks and would complete the voyage by decelerating for a reciprocal forty weeks. During the weeks at top speed, the gravitronic floors would provide a mere one tenth G. Though floors could be built that were capable of sustaining much higher levels of force, the infant technology yielded waves that were fairly "dirty." The harmonic distortion caused bodily fatigue when humans were subjected to higher force levels, and no one knew the effects of lengthy exposure. At the end of thirty-two weeks of top speed and artificial gravity, reversible furnishings would be slid down fixed poles, and the ceiling would become the floor when the deceleration process began.

Struggling and giggling at one tenth G, the crew ran through all of their simulations. Everything on the ship checked out perfectly.

"Did they issue you guys one of these?" Veronica asked the two priests, pulling something from her purse. She unsheathed a slender titanium dagger, special starship issue.

"Yeah," Fr. Hadrian answered, "I guess we're in the military so we have to be armed. You never know when somebody will come through that door when you're two billion miles from nowhere."

The captain interrupted their joking. "You have one special surprise left," he told Veronica and the two priests. Having momentarily forgotten about this portion of the tour, he had already given the helmsman the nod to shut down the gravitrons. Now completely weightless, he led the way to the front of the ship. "After the multiple nose cones comes our real protection: the Blessed Sacrament!" he proclaimed.

He opened the portal and they floated their way into the chapel.

"There's real wood in here!" Fr. Hadrian exclaimed, "The walls! The altar! Wow!"

"You're the one who told me, 'You cannot have a chapel without real wood to represent the cross and Jesus, the New Tree of Life,'" the captain reminded him.

"Yes...but I never dreamed it would happen. Thank you! The wood makes the room so warm and inviting, so special."

"It's going to be a long trip," Captain Benson assured him. "We'll all be spending a lot of time here; it should be special."

"And speaking of special, I really love this!" Veronica said as she viewed a huge oil painting of the Immaculate Conception on the wall to the left of the altar.

"That was a special gift," Fr. Scofield explained.

"From whom?" Veronica wondered.

"Jake commissioned it for this vessel right before his death. He wanted it to be a special surprise for me. Of course, he wasn't around to make sure it stayed a surprise for me, but I managed to keep it from you."

"Thank you!" she said, and went to give him a hug, but thanks to weightlessness, they ended up banging their heads together.

As the two rubbed their noggins and giggled, Fr. Hadrian gently reminded them that they were in the presence of the Blessed Sacrament, to which Fr. Scofield whispered reverently, "I'll bet *he's* giggling too!" but then he remembered something and added, "Actually Father, I'm so glad you reminded me! I feel terrible; I've had the host in a pix in my pocket all this time."

He reverently placed the host in the new tabernacle. "There. Now the ship is finished!" he quietly exclaimed with a deep bow, and after a few minutes of fervent prayer, whispered, "If you would be so kind now, Fr. Hadrian, please show us how to genuflect in weightless space."

Just then Chief Engineer Oakley swam through the portal. "Where's a good Baptist supposed to pray on this ship?" she asked quietly but sharply.

"I would be glad to worship, pray, and sing with you anytime, Tessa!" Veronica said, struggling through weightlessness to put a hand on her shoulder.

"I know you would, dear," she said, putting an arm around Veronica while brandishing a smile that indicated she had just been kidding around. "Lord knows prayer may be all that holds this big high-tech tin can together!" she added.

On the day before the big induction ceremony, at a meeting of the commanding officers, Captain Benson tried to bring business to a close. "Does anyone have anything else?" he asked.

Commander Lamans shifted in his seat, opened his mouth, closed it again, and finally grunted, "Well...I..."

"It's not like you to hold back, Cliff," the captain laughed, "Spit it out, man!"

"I'm sorry. You're right; I usually don't have any trouble being candid, but this is a sensitive subject and I don't want to be perceived as insensitive. You see, this mission is different from any other military mission, at least, any within my own experience: different because of the unique strategic importance that has been placed on procreation. I am an eligible bachelor. I heartily concur with the importance the mission charter places on fertility, and my unmarried state is a default state, not the purposeful result of a conscious decision. There is the distinct possibility that, for reasons unforeseen, my options for matrimonial bliss may be reduced to the twenty-two unmarried women who will be aboard this craft. If this reduced playing field becomes reality I would want all twenty-two of those women to fully meet the criteria laid out by the AGC, for example, in the area of fertility. There is a hum on the street, generated by a *Naked Truth* article, that has somewhat reached the level of scandal involving the relative fertility of Jasmine Babasa. I am concerned on two counts: the impact that this is having on public relations, and on the personal side, the reduced number of eligible fertile women. Bluntly put, I want all the options that were promised when I signed up. I think that goes for the rest of the men on the crew as well," he said, glancing at the men around the table.

"Unfortunately, Commander," Veronica said, "You were unable to attend our emergency meeting concerning this subject, but you should have gotten the memo. Extensive testing of Jasmine's condition shows her to be the perfect candidate for reconstructive surgery. This surgery has a ninety-eight percent success rate in women with her relative state of health. I have imposed a moratorium on elective surgery until after the first leg of this voyage is complete. Jasmine approached me on her own to request reconstructive surgery. That was before she was officially a crew member, but after we had started the process of evaluating her for this mission, and unfortunately, after the moratorium was in force. With all of this in mind, this group decided to wave the requirement."

"I see. Very well then," was all the response Lamans could muster.

Chapter 9

Family Tree

As Elon stepped back upon the shores of the Garden, the warm breeze only reminded him of his newfound friends in their wintry land.

He went to the Plateau, a wide area of smooth stone that lay above the Valley of Lilacs and below the bluffs. To the south it paved the way to the Walnut Forest and to rolling hills that announced the splendid mountains beyond. On this plateau Retsel had addressed Gardeners about the need to build a wall around the tree of the forbidden fruit. The hard stone surface carried one's voice far and wide.

When Elon arrived, children were playing games with sticks and balls, enjoying the wide-open area as they were accustomed. "Elon, what happened to your hair?" they shouted as they swarmed around him. He told them that they would know in a moment. With the help of a pair of rhinos, he moved a three-foot tall boulder to the center of the Plateau, and standing upon it, addressed anyone who would listen.

"Fellow Gardeners," he began, "please gather to hear what I have to tell you concerning our sisters and brothers in Exile." When a few of the virgin men and women from the Valley gathered before him, he asked them to go out and return with more people, as he had an urgent message for all. However, though these messengers made a genuine effort, few people came to hear the prophet. Gardeners were, after all, people without government, organized religion, or utility companies. They had no need for mass communication or meetings: truly paradise.

Elon began to address the small gathering comprised mostly of children and virgins. They were receptive to his words though, it seemed, a little frightened by them. With impassioned speech, he implored his listeners to reach out to their brothers and sisters in Exile, to help save them from sin and early death.

There was a skeptic in the crowd, a man who lived in the far hills and had come to the area to partake of the tree of life. Unfamiliar with the prophet, he asked boldly, "How do we know that you have been to the world of the Exiles? And, if you have, should we not fear the poison that may have infected your thoughts?"

At this, the others rebuked the questioner and urged Elon to speak, but Elon recognized the difficulty of his task. *How shall I reach these people*? he wondered.

Finally he simply asked, "Who among you will help me?" A few of them offered prayer support, but no one stepped forward to offer themselves in service to the Exiles.

Then, noticing that none of his evening-prayer companions were among his listeners, Elon went up into the hills and remained there in prayer until the time had come for their evening gathering. His friends were surprised to find him there, for his daily walk usually brought him in later than the others. They were also surprised by the length of his hair and beard, now barely touching his shoulders.

Elon wept as he told them of the miseries of the Exiles and of their great confusion, and yet, of the great love they had shown him when he had come into their confidence. He told them of the little girl who had fled from them in fear. "Fear is what the world of Exile is all about," he told them. "Fear is both their weapon of self-preservation, and the weapon they wield to control one another." After much more explanation, he made his plea. "I have promised my friends in Exile that I will bring helpers to preach of the love of the Father, and to alleviate their misery. Will you please join me?"

His plea met with deafening silence. Finally Aniram came to him. With his hands, Elon parted the long golden locks that enshrined her perfect body and pressed her innocent flesh to his in a loving embrace. He had always loved this beautiful virgin and had often implored the Lord to grant her to be his mate.

"Give me time, my king. I will pray about it," she said. "If my heart tells me that it is God's will, I will join you." The others indicated likewise.

Evening found Elon on the seashore, staring in the direction of Ogeeremma. The rising tide would make his crossing difficult, but he knew he must go. Two old friends showed up to ease his journey. With his feet on their backs, the dolphins carried him to the shore of Ogeeremma. The sight of Elon arriving by dolphin greatly amused Oilenroc.

The two bowed to each other, and Elon began to apologize. "I am sorry, my friend, that I come alone. I found myself without the eloquence to convince anyone to join me on a mission to your shores. The others are so filled with the fear of things unfamiliar to them."

"Fear runs deep in the family tree," Oilenroc observed, "but do not be disheartened, my friend, for the Lord is trying you."

His words sank deep into Elon's soul. *Why, of course! That's it!* Elon thought. Nothing in the Garden had ever cost anyone anything. The only trial that had been laid before them was that of the forbidden fruit, and they had essentially thwarted the Creator's plan by removing the temptation from their daily lives. The Lord was indeed trying him, and in turn, his friends and all those who dwelt in the Garden.

"My very existence must become for them a great trial," he announced. "They will wag their heads when they see me coming and will pretend not to hear my words, for my words will wound their hardening hearts!"

"Now you're talking!" coached Oilenroc.

A mischievous glimmer appeared in the eye of Elon, so out of place in a sinless eye that it made his new friend laugh and ask, "What mischief crosses your mind, my lord?"

"Mischief?" Elon asked, not understanding the concept.

Oilenroc saw no need to clarify. "What are your thoughts, sinless one?"

Elon lovingly rested his hands on the old man's shoulders, gazed into his eyes, and in hushed tone said, "Last night at the meeting of the prophets, I saw someone speak into a device. When they did so, their voice became like thunder! With such a device I could disturb many within the Garden. Can it be done?"

The quest amused Oilenroc. "I don't know much about these things," he said, "but I know someone who can help us."

The old man drove his grand, rusty roadster through the heart of Aseeremma. Elon was mesmerized by downtown neon, curious about the industrial park, and generally overwhelmed by things he had only glimpsed from the other side of the strait. Finally, in a quiet old residential district, they arrived at the home that was their destination, parking in front of the garage. Even before he got out of Oilenroc's car, Elon heard music—loud music! He started to open the car door, but quickly closed it again. He had never heard music so loud and was bewildered as to the source, for he could see no musicians in sight.

"Do you want to stay in the car, my lord?" Oilenroc asked him.

Elon shook his head. "I will join you!" he declared bravely.

When they had gotten out of the car, Elon looked all about for musicians, even though it seemed to him that the music was coming from within the house. But how could it be so loud? Oilenroc motioned him over to a small door beside the garage door. Elon was about to be christened into the world of garage bands.

Oilenroc opened the door, and placing his arm around the prophet, pulled him inside. The sound assaulted the virgin senses of Elon, who cringed in shock and amazement. Creating the thunder were three short-haired young men, two playing stringed instruments, with the third on the swan horn. A fourth one, black-skinned with black kinky hair puffed and hanging like a great weeping willow, sat among percussion devices that he tortured with sticks. The four were accompanying a singer, a petite girl who sang into one of the thunder devices about which Elon had inquired. To Elon it seemed all wrong that such a sweet voice should be so ear-shattering.

When the thunder ceased Oilenroc praised them for their vivacious music and introduced them all to Elon, who responded stiffly because he was still in shock. The boys had heard of him, for their father was among the prophets. The girl came forward, knelt, and bowed so low before him that her short hair touched the floor.

Elon helped her up and asked, "What is your name, young one?"

"I am Sunil, an abandoned child saved from the streets by Oilenroc and Airrellav. It was they who found for me this home and my brothers!" she said as she gathered two of the shorthaired young men standing on either side of her into a threesome hug. "What can we do for you?" she asked.

Elon looked at the boxes that bellowed the tremendous sound, and picking one up said simply, "I need one of these."

That night Elon dined in the home of these newfound friends. Their father, a prophet named Leinad, took a keen interest in Elon's plight, and offered to lend a hand. An electrical engineer, Leinad immediately set about making a converter that would allow one of the amplifiers to be powered by a car battery.

When he had assembled and tested everything, Leinad expressed just one concern. "What I have assembled is a lot of technology for a novice to haul across the strait and set up by himself. I wish we could go along to help."

"I wish that you could as well, but I do not know if the angel of the Lord will allow it, and I cannot risk your lives," Elon said.

"Then we'll just have to give you a crash course," Leinad declared.

They spent the next day setting up and tearing down the system until Elon could do it by himself and trouble shoot it when they had deliberately caused a problem.

"You learn very quickly, Elon!" Sunil declared. "You'll have no trouble!" She gave him lessons on how to hold the mike and how to project his voice into it so as not to distort. At first, his natural humility encumbered him and made Sunil giggle at him more than once, but eventually she talked him through it. "We will be able to hear you from over here!" she teased him.

"Pray for me," he begged, as he and Oilenroc prepared to leave. He kissed her on the forehead and climbed into Oilenroc's car.

Looking at the rusty monster, Sunil smiled and shook her head. "I'll pray that this thing gets you there!" she said.

A telephone call had summoned one of Oilenroc's friends to the shore with a row boat. Oilenroc helped to load the gear and prayed a blessing over his friend. As Elon rowed away, the old man knelt to pray. There he would remain while Elon pursued his mission.

Having mastered the oars and crossed the strait, Elon pulled the boat ashore and loaded himself with gear. *It is a good thing that Gardeners are strong*, he thought. But as he carried his burden, two apes came to his assistance, so he had only to carry the mike and cords.

As they neared the Plateau many thoughts whirled in his head, and imagining what a sight this little troop must be to onlookers, he asked himself, *How did it come to this?* But he entertained no second thoughts, for a certain impishness in his nature liked the idea of shocking his fellow Gardeners.

Meanwhile, back in Ogeeremma, four boys, a girl, and their father joined Oilenroc on the beach. "We want to hear him," Sunil said simply as the band knelt to pray beside the old prophet.

He took her hand, kissed it, and said, "God loves the prayers of children. Though you are becoming a beautiful woman, always remain a child in your heart and God will grant your fondest desires."

"But, I only desire God," she objected.

"See what I mean!" the prophet declared.

Arriving at the plateau, Elon hooked everything up just as he had been taught. Then, with friends in solemn prayer on each side of the strait, he tapped the mike and said, "Testing, one, two." From the other side of the channel, Sunil heard him and just lost it. She fell into the sand holding her tummy in laughter. With a grin on his face, Oilenroc quieted the troop and brought them back into prayer.

Elon began to speak. "My fellow Gardeners…" He looked about and saw that he had indeed gotten their attention. "I am here today to tell you that the highest places in Glory have been reserved for Exiles." It was the most provocative thing he could think of to say. "A great sin has entered the Garden!" he announced. His innate intelligence was figuring out this speaking thing. Pauses give them a little time to chew; give them little bits, then give them time to chew. "An evil greater than the eating of the fruit!" he announced, still trying to be provocative. "Let me say it again," he continued, repeating the remarks about Exiles and glory and sin in the Garden.

"Repetition is the mother of study," Oilenroc had instructed him, adding, "They may be Gardeners with great intelligence, but resistance to the Spirit of the Lord has dulled their wits along with their hearts."

Now it seemed that everyone in the Garden was descending upon the Plateau, and Elon bellowed into the mike, "DO YOU HEAR ME?"

Looking about, he saw that the Plateau had become a sea of humanity. He knelt atop the rock and prayed aloud into the mike for the gift of humility, that the Lord might guide his words.

"I am Elon, son of Elokin and Amla, of the Walnut Forest," he began. "All of my life I have tried to do the will of the Father, and all of my life I have failed! Many of you hail me as a prophet, but if I am a prophet I am a sinful one, for I have been stubborn in heeding the law that the Lord has instilled in my heart. For all of my life I have felt his urgings to serve those in Exile, and while I did indeed pray for them, I did not go to them to serve them as I should have.

"But I have now made my first trip to them. Yes, my brothers and sisters, I have been to the world of Exile. I have found the Exiles to be much like us, in need of God's love and care, in need of family. Are not we all from the same tree? Are not they our brothers and sisters?"

As he spoke he saw his mother and father and brothers among those in the crowd, alongside their friends, the bluff jumpers. "Who among you is not guilty of saying no to your hearts?" he continued. "Who among you is on a sure road to glory? It has been centuries since Gardeners have gone into Glory. How long must the Almighty pine for our love?"

"We cannot enter Exile! Their sins will poison us!" a woman shouted.

"We have children of our own to look after, and the Creator has placed us in charge of the Garden. Who will do these things if we leave?" demanded a man.

Elon's brother, Enor, stepped forward and spoke angrily. "Why is it always this way with you? Why do you always stir up trouble? You make Mother cry! You make Father wag his head! Are we not good enough for you? Are you so holy that we should take abuse from you?"

Elon remained undaunted. Looking his brother in the eye he spoke through the mike. "Do you see how you are? My own brother screams at me in rage. Is this the demeanor of perfect innocence? Will you continue to insist that you are sinless?"

"It is this loud evil junk that you have brought back from Exile that makes us this way!" Enor insisted, pointing to the amplifier. "You have brought evil into our midst!"

"No, my brother," Elon retorted, "it is our cooperation with the Exaggerator that makes us this way!"

Another man shouted, "We are not subject to sin! We have not disobeyed the Lord's command. We have not eaten from the forbidden tree. The Exaggerator is banished from our midst and the tree is fortified. We cannot sin!"

"Oh, but you already have!" insisted Elon. "Tell me," he continued, "who tempted the Tempter?" The question baffled them. "Are we not told that the Temper, the great Exaggerator, was once an angel of light? Why did he fall? Who tempted *him*? Cannot we also be our own undoing? Have we not free will? I tell you that the Exaggerator has not been banished; he simply has better things to do because you are already doing his will!" With the mike turned off, he said to himself, "Fear owns this garden." A great debate ensued among his listeners.

An angry Enor came forward. "Brother, do not sin!" Elon warned him. Enor had picked up the car battery that powered the amplifier, and now dashed its sixty pounds down upon the amp, smashing it to pieces. The battery spilled its contents upon the remains of the amplifier, the acid hissed and smoked, and the smell of sulfur filled the air.

"Do you hear it hissing like the Serpent, brother?" Enor shouted at him. "Do you smell its rotten stench? Will you dare to tell me that it's not from the Evil One?"

Some of the bystanders felt badly for what Enor had done, but most of them kept their distance from Elon. A few of the trinket makers came forward to investigate the technology. "Great!" Elon mumbled to himself, "Just what we need: loud music in the Garden!"

However, seventeen people came forward to answer Elon's call for help, eight men and nine women. Most of them were Elon's evening prayer partners. All of them were virgins. They came meekly and were apologetic for the others. Elon urged them not to judge harshly. "Mated people have a larger chunk of paradise to lose," he advised them.

Aniram came forward and spoke for the group. "Beloved, it is our desire to serve with you the souls in Exile. We see the passion and love in your eyes for our brothers and sisters, and we want to help. We will do whatever you deem necessary."

"Time is a gift from God," Elon began to instruct them, "a gift that is not appreciated by Gardeners. We must no longer waste this precious gift. With every passing minute, hunger and illness take another life in Exile. I also fear that, with every wasted moment, souls are lost to the Evil One. I must warn you, my friends, being a missionary will be very hard work; however, work offered up to the Almighty for the love of souls becomes a precious prayer that will not be forgotten. Tomorrow, we will become the servants of Exiles, so tonight we must prepare ourselves in prayer."

As the group began to make their way back up to their prayer spot, Elon turned and noticed his father standing just a few feet from him, close enough to have heard the instructions given to the seventeen. For an awkward moment they just looked into each others eyes. Then his father seated himself on the rock, and looking at the ground, spoke softly.

"You have uncovered shame within my heart. I feel...naked," he stammered, struggling in vain to find a word to express the new way he felt. "Suddenly I seem gross to myself," he added.

Elon placed his hands on his father's shoulders. "Look at me, Father. Everything that I am I owe to you. Rise up to be who you know you must be. Your body is a reflection of your soul, and you feel shame in that soul. But do not put on clothing unless you are doing so to join me in Exile."

"I cannot abandon your mother. I must stay and pray with her. She is not yet ready."

"I understand. I have been praying for both of you. God is answering my prayers. He always does," Elon assured him.

That evening's prayers, with the seventeen who had come forward, brought many questions, most of which Elon answered with a simple "You will soon see."

When the vigil ended and all had gone for the night except Aniram, she came to Elon, pressed herself against him, and kissed his lips. He had embraced and kissed her like this hundreds of times before, but something was different now. Aniram's flesh had taken on a chill with the night air, and there was something different about her kiss, a certain...hunger.

With the prayer vigil completed, Elon put out with the row boat to visit Ogeeremma. Each day grew shorter with the approach of winter, and darkness was upon him. He did not find Oilenroc in prayer on the beach, but a short distance away he heard the whine of a car's starter and saw headlights pierce the dusk. As Oilenroc looked up from his shifter and eased out the clutch, Elon stood suddenly in his path. The ambush nearly gave the old man a heart attack.

"Son of the One! Are you trying to get killed?!" he wheezed.

Elon smiled at the suggestion, but apologized to his friend for startling him. "I have seventeen who want to serve Exiles," he told him, "eight men and nine women."

"Praise the Lord! Get in. We can talk as we go to return Leinad's equipment. He needs his car battery back," he informed Elon as he drove to where the boat was beached. When Oilenroc turned to look at his friend, the old man could see the stress on Elon's face. "You didn't bring the equipment?" he asked. Elon fished the microphone and cord out from under his leafy robe.

"This is all that is left," he said. "I'm afraid that they destroyed the rest."

Oilenroc was astonished. "Violence in the Garden?" he asked. "Is no place sacred? Perhaps we should be missionaries to them!"

Elon thought for a moment and declared, "You already are! Is not the one who has needs also a missionary to the one who has bounty? Is not the decision to love at great cost more valuable than the decision to love without cost? Great sacrifice requires great love."

Slowly a twist of puzzlement in Oilenroc's brow smoothed into understanding. "The Evil One can have no lasting triumph!" he declared with a grin.

"Well put, my friend!" Elon answered. "The spiritual and material poverty of Exiles is the Gardener's ticket to Glory, but I fear that time is running out. My brother's violent outburst is a warning signal. I received a second signal tonight as I embraced a friend. Something was very different. Gardeners must allow their hearts to be softened, or I fear that the Lord will cease to regulate their passions."

Oilenroc heaved a deep sigh. "When that happens, Elon, the Garden will be no better than Exile."

"No better? I fear that it will be much worse!" Elon ventured. "At least Exiles are accustomed to making decisions."

They returned the mike and cord to the ever-gracious Leinad, who not only forgave the loss of his equipment, but insisted on donating money for clothing. Oilenroc drove to a thrift store in the neighborhood, and with Sunil's help, found suitable clothing for the seventeen.

The next morning Elon returned to the Garden to find his friends praying on the Shore. He brought out the brown paper bags of clothes and showed the men how to dress themselves. After a few laughs they were clothed and in the boat. "I will return for you soon," he assured the ladies. However, upon his return they were still all naked.

"What do we do with these?" Aniram asked, holding up a bra.

Elon took the garment from her. "I saw one of these on a statue in a store window," he said, attempting fit it over his leafy cloak. When he had accomplished the task, the ladies enjoyed a good giggle.

"What is it good for?" Aniram asked.

"I don't know," he said, placing it back into the bag. "Just put on the other clothes." Elon had seen enough different fashions that he was able to help them figure out the various closure methods, and soon the ladies were all in lovely dresses.

"Must we wear these?" they said, pointing to the coats.

"You may want them when we get to Ogeeremma, so put them in the boat," Elon instructed them. They also put the bags of socks and shoes back in the boat. Wearing shoes designed more for style than comfort was too much to ask of women who'd been barefoot all of their lives.

"We have something else to take," they told Elon. They had gathered fruit from the Garden while he had made the crossing with the men, and they now placed it in an empty bag that had contained dresses. As they approached the other shore the bag of fruit, setting on Aniram's lap, suddenly became much lighter. When she looked inside, it was empty.

"Elon, the fruit has vanished!" she informed him.

He simply smiled and said, "If missionary work was easy, it would be of no value."

When they arrived in Ogeeremma they were indeed a sight to see: nine flawlessly beautiful women in short, out-of-style dresses, strutting barefoot through the sand and snow without coats.

"Aren't you cold?" Oilenroc asked.

"The elements have no effect on us, sir," they pointed out.

Oilenroc's concern turned to another matter. "We must be very careful not to leave the holy women alone!" he warned Elon.

"Why?" Elon asked innocently.

"They are extremely beautiful," noted Oilenroc, "and they are unaccustomed to the wiles of Exile men. I fear that they will be raped or murdered!"

After having rape explained to him, Elon smiled and said, "Fear not, my friend, for they are Gardeners. They cannot be killed so long as they continue to eat from the tree of life. As for rape, I believe you will find that the women of the Garden are stronger than the men of Exile."

The troop of eighteen followed Oilenroc and his friend Airrellav, who had come especially to meet the holy women. The two took them through the poorest streets of Aseeremma, Ogeeremma's capital city and only seaport. Under railroad bridges and underpasses they saw children in groups, children who slept in cardboard boxes and begged, foraged through garbage, or stole to make a living. The Gardeners' hearts ached at the sight of the poor creatures. For decades unending these holy virgins had longed for mates, that they might give children back to their Creator, and here were children without parents, children with no hope left in their eyes. However, those despairing eyes opened wide at the sight of these beautiful strangers.

Airrellav had furnished the troop with food to fill their pockets so they could offer it to these little beggars as they went. Soon there were Gardeners everywhere speaking with older children who feasted on morsels, while the younger children did their munching cuddled in the laps of these new friends. Everywhere they went the words, "Will you come again tomorrow?" could be heard from tiny lips as their new friends left them.

Finally their walk took them to the craggy hollow of the graveyard. Oilenroc said to the group, "I wanted you to see the power the Exaggerator has in the world of Exile." As they entered the graveyard, those who were immune to death still felt its horrible essence creep up the backs of their necks. Toward the back of the graveyard, a possessed man thrashed about in the bushes. Nearly naked, his beaten body reeked horribly, and he frothed at the mouth like a rabid dog.

Elon proceeded with what he had learned from the One. "In the name of the Word, the Holy Son of God, come out of him!"

The possessed man rushed toward them a few feet and growled, "The Word I know, Garden Variety, but who are you?! Talk is cheap! Power requires sacrifice: HUMAN SACRIFICE!!!" he roared, and began to laugh an evil, hideous, bone-chilling laugh.

As they left the graveyard Elon's friends began to ask, "What did the demon mean by 'human sacrifice'?"

"The first thing to remember always about demons," Elon responded, "is that they are liars, or worse, great exaggerators. They will always give you just enough truth to support their lie, to fool you into offending your Creator." As they walked back to the shore he assured them, "I will consult the Lord through the intercession of the One. We must all implore the Lord that we may know what to do about this evil."

Oilenroc had obtained for them a second boat so that all were able to return to Paradise in a single trip. As they rowed away from Ogeeremma, their eyes were filled with tears at the thought of the children whom they had left in the streets. It was not enough to give them food and leave them to the elements. As they neared the shore of the Garden, Aniram cried out, "I want to go back! I want to be with the children!" and all joined in with her request. That night the streets of Aseeremma gained eighteen beautiful beggars.

Chapter 10

White with Blue Stripes

"This is the end of the road!" Veronica warned Jasmine and Jean as she smoothed the skirt of her new Star Corps uniform. "After the induction ceremony tomorrow, you'll need to get seriously ill to get out of this mission."

"You three look really hot!" Mel gushed as her three friends crowded in front of her old vanity.

"I just realized something," Jasmine said, smoothing her own skirt. "Won't these be a bad idea when we're weightless?"

"There are only a few hours of weightlessness in the whole voyage," Veronica answered. "There's no way that *this* Star Corps woman was going to wear pants all the time just to cover those few hours. There are also slacks in your wardrobe, so try them on."

"Gosh, Ronnie, I don't know if I like the idea of wearing a uniform all the time," Jean said. "I don't think I look all that great in white with blue stripe accents."

"So? The important thing is what does Tony think?" Melanie advised.

"I think the colors are absolutely wonderful!" Jasmine said. "I could wear them for the rest of my life!"

"Well, you both can have it your way," Veronica told them. "Apparently you didn't read your email, Jean. We're only required to be in uniform for special occasions. There will be certain hours of certain shifts when photo images are being sent to Earth. Other than that, the only required times will be liftoff and landing."

"So we can wear what we want, when we want?" Jean asked.

"Within reason. It *is* the military. I doubt that Mike will let you parade around on duty in a bikini," Veronica said, "but the usual need for an officer's uniform to instantly flag rank is hardly necessary when we're a small crew that's been training together for months. However, when you're wearing civvies, you'll be required to wear a rank badge, like this," she said, producing one from her bag.

Jean reached in her own bag and pulled out a badge. "Oooh, Chief Surgeon!" she said, while holding it up to her shoulder. "These rank names don't seem to follow any existing scheme. How can you tell whose has rank?"

"There are nine levels of command, represented by the pyramid made of horizontal lines on your badge," Veronica explained. "Your name is etched across one of those lines. If it's the top line, you're the captain."

"And if it's the bottom line, you're a slug, like me!" Jasmine said, giggling at her own badge.

"Listen, sister, your badge says *Chief Investigator*," Melanie noted. "That's pretty impressive!"

"Sure it is," Jasmine said, laughing. "It's etched on the bottom line, and I'm the only investigator on the crew!"

"That's not true," Jean insisted. "Tony's an investigator."

"I'm sorry. Of course he is," Jasmine corrected herself. "In fact, he's the officer I report to. But guessing by the badge, he plans on letting *me* do the investigating."

"What will the two of you investigate in a tin can full of PhDs?" Veronica wondered, amused by the discussion. "I think all your investigating will be done on the garden decks, but you'll be investigating grime, not crime."

"Isn't it customary to party hardy the night before you sign your life away to Uncle Sam?" Jean asked.

"Yes, if you're nineteen," Jasmine retorted.

"I *feel* like nineteen. Does that count?" Jean joked. They were all sorting emotions as the launch day loomed, bouncing between giddiness and apprehension, and Jean was definitely giddy.

"You may feel nineteen, but you look nine," Melanie said dryly. "In fact," she went on, beginning to giggle about the comic appearance of a five-foot, eighty-five pound Jean standing beside a six-foot-two, thorough-bred Jasmine, "you look like Jasmine decided to take along her Star Corps doll!"

"Very funny," Jean said, patting Melanie on the cheek as she went to the door. "I'm going to go show Tony. He won't think I look nine."

"Good, you go show Tony," Jasmine encouraged. "Maybe the two of you can supply a real doll about half-way through the journey."

"Maybe," Jean said, smiling as she opened the bedroom door. She stepped into the living room where Antonio greeted her with a wolf whistle.

"Well, that's a good start!" Jasmine noted.

"I don't know about you guys," Melanie whispered with little girl excitement, "but I gotta see how Tony looks in *his* uniform."

The three stepped quietly into the living room just in time to catch the couple sharing a deep kiss. When Antonio finally came up for air, he did so to a giggling, applauding audience.

"You three need something to do!" he said.

"And you two need a room!" Melanie insisted, nodding toward the bedroom where Antonio had changed.

"They're relentless!" he said, shaking his head. "She does look hot though, doesn't she?" he added, looking at his bride.

"If you're into dolls!" Veronica kidded. Jasmine took the cue, and placing her hands on little Jean's waist, hoisted her up to Antonio's level for another kiss.

"Now that's service," he declared. "Do that again!" But Jean slapped Jasmine's hands and turned around to tickle her.

The deathly ticklish Babasa draped her basketball-star grasp atop Jean's noggin, held her at bay, and shouted, "Halt! FBI! Put your fingers down and step away from the chick!" while Jean groped madly in her direction.

"Okay, dolls," Antonio said. "What do you say we slip back into our civvies and go out and party on *your* last night of freedom?"

"Oh, that's right, you and Dr. Jean already *are* government issue," Veronica observed.

"Yup. We're just changing uniforms," Antonio confirmed, "from one Corps to another."

After a few phone calls most of the crew began to gather at Mick's. It was not a large facility, and when Mick recognized a few faces and realized what was happening, he began to turn away non-crew customers telling them that "everything is reserved." Veronica and friends had just gotten past Mick when two such customers came to the door.

"What the hell are you talking about," the big one said, "half the friggin tables are empty. Whadaya got, a wedding? At Mick's?"

Then the loud-mouth noticed a tall woman waiting to be seated. She stared intently, thinking she should know her. Finally the light came on and she yelled, "Jazz? Jazz is that you?"

"Are these people with your party?" Mick asked Jasmine, eager to escort the foul-mouthed person to the door.

"No, they're not," Jasmine answered.

"Jazz, where the hell have you been?" Martha the Mouth demanded. "We go to your damned apartment and somebody else is living there! You don't call! We thought maybe you were dead! We'd have gone to the FBI, but you *are* the friggin FBI! Where the hell'd you disappear to?"

"I'm sorry, Martha, Zelda. I should have called. I was just in the middle of some big life changes and…well…I guess I didn't want to deal with your attitude," Jasmine informed them.

"Attitude? Us? What the hell are you talking about? And who are these people?"

"These are my friends, Martha."

"And what the hell are we?" Zelda demanded.

Jasmine hesitated for a moment, wanting to be resolute without being unkind. "You're a vivid reminder of what I used to be," she said at last.

"Up yours, bitch!" Martha shouted back at her. "Up yours!" Mick immediately went to escort them from the building. Regarding Jasmine's unpainted face, Martha yelled over her shoulder, "This must be the friggin goody-goody league, little miss plain-face! You can kiss my fat…" Her obscenities faded as the door swung shut.

Veronica gave her friend a sideways hug, pressing her head against the tall girl's shoulder. "See what I told you," Jasmine said. "You were my first *real* friend."

"Not entirely true, Jazz, and I hope I did the right thing," Veronica said.

"What do you mean?" Jasmine asked.

"Look," Veronica said, grasping Jasmine's elbows and turning her around. At a corner table for two sat a little man with a droll smile.

"Dobbs!" Jasmine whispered. She smiled at Veronica and headed for the little table. Her friend rose to greet her.

"You weren't going to leave without saying goodbye, were you, boss?" he asked, extending his arms for an embrace.

"Of course not, partner," she said, stooping to accept the hug. "After our induction ceremony, we'll still be here for a couple weeks of final indoctrination. Gosh it's good to see you! I'm sorry I've been so busy, Alvin. Maybe this could be the date we've been promising each other."

Dobbs seemed a little preoccupied. "Jazz...tomorrow's kind of your decision day, isn't it?" he asked, as the two of them took seats at the small table.

"If you mean that I can't back out after I'm inducted, that's right. This is my last night of freedom."

"Good. Then don't go, Jazz. I beg of you!" he got down on one knee and pulled a ring from his pocket. "Marry me, Jazz. Please stay and marry me!"

A speechless Jasmine finally recovered the mental resources to send a signal to her drooping jaw: "Alvin. No...Alvin. I'm sorry, buddy. I'm so sorry. I love you my friend; I really do love you, but no. I don't think marriage is my thing."

"That's because you've been burnt so many times, my love. I won't burn you! I swear I'll never hurt you! I'd take a bullet for you!"

Jasmine began to cry. "I know you would, Alvin!" Her tears were for Dobbs, not for herself. She stood, grasped his hands and pulled him up off of his knee. She touched the ring but folded it into his grasp and placed her hands around his. "Thank you, my friend," she said. "You're a beautiful man, Alvin. You deserve someone to share your life, and I'm sure there's someone out there for you, but I can't be that someone. I'm committed to this voyage for many reasons. I'm in the middle of learning what life is really all about. You need to find someone who's already figured that out."

"I've found the woman I want!" he insisted quietly.

"I'm sorry. I'm so sorry, my friend!" she whispered back. They just stood looking at each other for an awkward moment. Then, wiping her tears and putting on a smile, she tried to cheer her companion. "Do you want to meet the crew?" she asked, feeling as the words left her mouth that perhaps it bordered on insult to try and change the subject so quickly.

"No, honey. No, thanks. I think I've made a big enough fool of myself here," he said, noting several pairs of eyes on him.

"There's nothing foolish about love, Alvin!" she proclaimed quietly. "I'm so proud of you for coming in here and doing this tonight!"

He pushed the ring into her hand, folded her fingers over it, and clasped her closed hand with both of his as she had done to him. "I bought this for you, Jazz," he said. "Take it as a going away gift. I don't want you to ever forget me!"

"I will never forget you, Alvin! I don't deserve a friend like you!"

"Yes you do!" he insisted. "Yes you do!" However, realizing it was over, he took her face in his hands, slid his fingers back under her hair, tiptoed up, and pulled her lips down to his for an innocent kiss. "Goodbye, my love," he whispered, then turned and headed for the door.

When he had gone, Jasmine sat back down at the table for two, clutching the diamond. She would have enjoyed a long conversation with her old friend, but it was not to be. Veronica cringed. *Way to go, Ronnie! That went well!* she thought as she watched Jasmine cry from across the room. She would comfort her friend, but not yet; some tears cannot easily be shared.

The next afternoon at 1500 hours sharp, fifty of Earth's finest, decked out in their new whites and blues, marched into the AGC's largest auditorium. They filed in two by two to the uproarious greeting of family, friends, politicians, and a media mob. Those who were not married were paired with the opposite sex by height. Jasmine winced when placed next to Lamans and was glad the officers would separate from the crew for the ceremony. Tessa Oakley, never afraid to reveal her feelings, beamed from ear to ear when coupled with Fr. Hadrian, whom she had been admiring mostly from afar.

The existing military officers, Benson, Lamans, Oakley, and Escobar, all preached short little welcomes extolling the virtues of the newly formed Star Corps, and to the delight of the crew, the much hyped induction ceremony lasted less than an hour. Veronica and Melanie each received a dozen roses and posed for a gazillion photos.

The next morning, as Veronica ate her breakfast, the sun caught one of the cut-glass vases containing those roses, and the resulting rainbow on the fridge made her think, *We don't need two dozen of these sitting here.* She picked up her roses and said to Melanie, "Do you want to help me deliver these?"

Melanie read her thoughts and said, "Sure."

Half an hour later Veronica smiled as she read Jake's headstone. The inconspicuous, level-with-the-ground marker seemed especially appropriate for the simple man whose passing it marked. She set the vase on the stone and prayed silently. *Lord, how many times can one heart break? Is it not enough that I lost him once? Now I won't even be able to visit him here!* This was her fourth visit since his death, and would be her last. Though it oft seemed that a large part of her was in the ground with him, this was not a wet-tissue day. *Am I all cried out?* she wondered, *or am I denying my feelings? Lord, you know me better than I know me. Don't let me bury my feelings with my man!*

It's all up to you, dear, a voice said to her heart. *Jacob will always be with you. You know that.*

She surprised herself. Despite her pain, she still felt called to marriage and motherhood. In prayer she had been telling Jacob all about it, and now actually felt joyful and lighthearted. Jacob was praying. He would continue to pray for her, and Jesus would continue to carry most of the burden. Life is beautiful! Her joy would please both Jacob and Jesus.

"How about John the Baptist, Cecilia, Steven, Felicita, Paul, Joan of Arc, and Peter, in that order?" Jasmine asked, in reference to names she was researching for the Martyr ships. The ships were scheduled to be commissioned the next week.

"Wow, you've really been studying!" Veronica complimented her friend. "Sounds like a good line-up to me. Hopefully they'll all be around for the return trip."

"Researching the martyrs is a pretty humbling experience," Jasmine noted. "Did you know that they threw Cecilia into boiling water for a while before they beheaded her? I hope that I have that kind of faith and courage when the time comes."

"Are you expecting to be martyred?" Veronica wondered.

"I'm expecting God to deal with me as he sees fit. I've been praying that he will make me his instrument. We're missionaries on our way to a strange frontier that may prove as dark and cruel as any the faith has ever tamed. If the Father decides to glorify me with martyrdom, I pray that I'm up to the task," Jasmine explained.

Veronica marveled at the neophyte's articulation. "Jazz, you've come so far so fast. I'm so proud of you!"

"Yeah, well...fancy talk is cheap," the ex-FBI agent said matter-of-factly. Veronica just smiled at her friend's humility.

Two weeks later, the crew of Star Covenant huddled around every available monitor on the ship to watch the fading image of planet Earth. The aft camera reached the extent of its telescopic range, and the image of their home planet slowly dwindled to an indiscernible single-pixel dot.

A myriad of mixed emotions raced through Veronica's heart as the captain's voice came over the intercom. "Ladies and gentlemen, I am happy to announce that Engineering and Navigation have given me the thumbs up: all systems go. The Martyr ships are all tracking our acceleration nicely. Prepare to go to full thrust."

With everyone seated at their official stations, the ship slowly built to full acceleration, reaching a G force equivalent to Earth's gravity, and the Captain announced, "Congratulations, team, we are on our way! Despite the excitement, we need to acclimate into three alert crews to operate this vessel properly, so all you folks on third shift need to hit the hay. That's an order. Goodnight. Second shift comes on in three hours. Any of you that can should get a little shuteye."

Tessa was third shift, but was not about to go to bed. "I have fifty people relying on this machinery, Captain," she said. "I won't rest until I'm convinced this thing is running perfectly."

"It's a machine, Tess. It'll never be running perfectly," the captain philosophized. "Don't push yourself too hard."

Six hours later, she was still on the bridge verifying every bit of data that her subordinates were already managing. Veronica came up behind the chief, cupped her hands, and spoke into them to create the drone of a cheap intercom. "All micro-managers and control freaks report to their beds immediately," she said mechanically. Tessa turned and gave her a tired smile. "You've been up for twenty-two hours, Tess," Veronica noted. "As health officer, I'm ordering you to bed unless you can show the captain data that indicates we're in serious trouble."

"I'll call it quits if he does," Tessa answered, nodding toward the captain.

"Don't worry, he's right behind you," she assured Tessa, adding in a hush, "Anyway, he's just in charge. We can live without him more easily than we can without you, so get some rest."

Following orders, Chief Oakley sat in prayer on the bed in her tiny room. *You just watched everyone and everything that ever mattered to you dwindle to a single pixel on a screen,* her heart said to her. She hovered for a moment contemplating sinking into remorse, but was far too self-disciplined to allow that to happen. She had been a good soldier, a good daughter, a good aunt, and a good friend: all the things she had ever wanted to be. Now, suddenly, she was a bona fide space explorer in charge of keeping a big boat aimed at a distant star. In the process, she had allowed herself to be poked and prodded and tested and retested.

"I'm fertile!" she had shouted gleefully after Veronica had delivered her test results. Something about the word had tickled her funny bone, causing her to laugh and say, "This sassy soldier is a good place to grow babies!"

"You're thirty-six, dear," Veronica had said. "It's getting toward the close of planting season, but with your excellent health, you have ten to fourteen good fertile years left."

But what had been hilarious to Tessa on terra firma now seemed almost cruel as they pierced the abyss. All of that poking and prodding had awakened something in her soul.

As chemistry would have it, she was romantically attracted nearly exclusively to black men, and there were only six on the crew. Two were married, and three were eligible bachelors, one Episcopalian and the other two Catholic, but the last one—the black man who lit her Bunsen burner and shook her flask—was a Catholic priest!

Nestling into her pillow she prayed, *Lord, you have an interesting sense of humor. We're such a bunch of oddballs!* She was moved by desires that hadn't been stirred in a long while, but the mission team was a tub of fish who'd put off marriage for a career, not the most romance driven group of folks ever assembled. She wondered if the others were feeling what she was feeling, and finished her prayers with, *I trust that you have a loving plan, Lord.*

Seven months later...

"Good evening and good morning," Tessa said to officers from all three shifts who were assembled around the table. "The Captain and I thought it important to get everyone together and up to speed with the performance of our craft so far.

"We have achieved three-quarter light speed, and are far outside of our comfort zone in terms of what we know about the space we are entering. Our lead ship, John the Baptist, has already expended over half of its shielding capability. The closer we get to light speed, the less effective those shields will be. If what we have encountered to date is a sampling of what we can expect, we just barely have the resources to make a round trip. Long story short, we all need to pray for clean space. Questions?" she asked, looking from face to face.

Before anyone could respond, the helmsman entered the room. "Yes, Mr. Stokes," Tessa said.

"Chief, Captain, I thought you should know: John burned up all of his shield power, and we've lost all contact. The ship is assumed destroyed. Cecilia is at seventy-eight percent shield."

The room grew very quiet. "Thank you, Jim," the Captain said at last, and addressing the others added, "You heard the chief. Pray hard! There's nothing else we can do."

"Actually, Captain, there is one other course," Chief Oakley countered. "We could abort mission. Statistically speaking, the odds are already against making a safe *round* trip to Freqmod. Of course, aborting mission and attempting to turn this train around brings with it a whole separate set of challenges."

"Okay," the captain said, sizing up those around the table. "I'm letting you folks speak for your subordinates. What should we do?"

Veronica thought about what her subordinates might say, and about the resolute Ensign Babasa. "God has just given us a little fortitude test," she said. "I say we forge on!"

When no one else offered an opinion, the captain adjourned and stood, saying, "Stay tuned, ladies and gentlemen, the fun has just begun!"

Chapter 11

Glory

Aniram attempted to catch the snowball Elon had lobbed in her direction, but it burst in her hands and sprayed her naked body with refreshing crystals. *Oh! It's wonderful to be naked again!* she thought, grinning at her assailant. Once a month the Gardeners returned to their homeland, but this special trip marked the first anniversary of their efforts in Ogeeremma. The seventeen were enjoying the opportunity to shed their clothing, but Elon was unwilling to part with his. On his first night in Ogeeremma, he had refused the splendid robe offered him by the prophetess, Airrellav, but now, as an anniversary gift, she had woven for him a beautiful garment from the finest grasses and weeds. Elon was so taken with her act of kindness that he was foregoing the opportunity to be naked once again. Renewed by a trip to the tree of life and refreshed by the snows of Mt. Ekim's peaks, the troop was ready for their prayer vigil.

Much had changed since that first frigid night spent with the street children of Ogeeremma. The prophets of Aseeremma had been stunned to learn that the Gardeners were so dedicated that they were sleeping in the bushes and alleys. Soon a few old buildings had been donated, and in no time, turned into orphanages.

At first all eighteen Gardeners had stayed in the same place with the children, but when they took in their first prostitute to shield her from the wrath of her pimp and win her heart for God, Oilenroc had made it very clear that there would be dire public relations issues with their coed housing arrangement. "There is a lot of murmuring around town," he told them. "Exiles cannot even imagine that your love for one another is pure." So there came to be one orphanage for boys, and another for girls.

In the ensuing months they had taken in various troubled adults, some of them drug addicts and alcoholics, and brought them to the faith. Also, some of the prophets had joined their ranks, so that each orphanage had enough people to set up a school and to do gardening on a plot of land they had been given.

With so much to celebrate on the night of their anniversary, they would not take up their customary vigil in the wooded hills, but would approach Ekim's highest peak and pray on the very spot where the One had exposed Elon to the wisdom of the King.

"Dear holy One of God," Elon began, "like us in all things but sin. As you stand before the Almighty, we beg of you to present our requests to him. Hear our prayer for Gardeners, that they will abandon fear and be moved to pity for their brothers and sisters in exile."

Thus they prayed until the night turned black as a hole in tar. Then into that blackness, a light appeared among them, shining on Elon. Aniram searched the sky to see if a heavenly body was shedding light through some crevice in the mountain's skyline, but the more she searched, the more she realized that the glow was coming from beneath Elon's clothing: His very flesh was glowing! The light became ever brighter as Elon was caught in ecstasy, until they could no longer stand to look directly at him. Then the brilliance waned, and his friends stared as he faded completely from sight.

The small, distant sun of their binary star system, Alpha Centauri B, escaped the clouds, and its orange light flooded the snowy ground where the prophet had knelt.

"Elon has gone into glory," Aniram proclaimed, tears streaming down her face. The face she wore bore an odd mix of joy and agony. All Gardeners had always had mates; therefore, no virgin had ever before entered glory. To one who loved him so much, the unexpected had the impact of a sudden death.

Likewise, the little troop was filled with joy and wonder at the power of God but saddened that their friend and leader was gone.

"We must take up Elon's work," Aniram told them between sobs. "Perhaps God has taken him from us so that each of us might grow to become the kind of leader he was." Under Aniram's direction her companions formed eight twosomes to go out and preach to the Garden, while she remained on the mountain to pray and ease her pain.

They preached with great fire and zeal, telling of their work among the Exiles and informing their listeners that Ogeeremma was but one of many countries that needed their help. They witnessed to them of Elon's going into glory, of how he had shown like the sun and was now in the bosom of the Father.

The Spirit filled their hearts and minds and descended upon their listeners, who received their message with joy and wonder. Even a repentant Enor (Elon's angry, amplifier-smashing brother) bowed before them and with great contrition offered his services.

Thus a sort of religious devotion blossomed in the Garden, with organized prayer vigils. The morning and evening praises returned to their former glory. Mission trips were organized to the fallen world, but the Gardeners soon realized that they lacked many of the skills required to relieve the burdens of a fallen race. Therefore, Gardeners studied to become teachers. With the ability to read and write, they would no longer be restricted only to preaching and gardening.

Veronica awoke from a nightmare. In her dream the whole fuselage of the ship had suddenly jolted with a disturbing noise. She sat up, contemplating how real the dream had seemed. In a moment the communicator on her jammies buzzed, tickling her collarbone annoyingly.

"Lansing, here," she answered.

"Ronnie, this is Mike. You'd better come to the bridge. No need to suit up; this will be short," the captain said.

She carefully made her way to the ladder. It seemed she would never adjust to weighing a mere ten pounds. With the voyage nearly half over, they would soon be switching from constant velocity to deceleration, and all of the rooms at the top of the ladder would be at the bottom, and the furnishings would all be backward—what fun!

It had been an interesting year. Captain Benson was indeed studying for the priesthood and was apparently leaning toward celibacy, which meant there were only a half dozen men currently seeking Veronica's hand in marriage. Politely fending them off had become a full time job. She was determined to marry and have children, but none of them seemed quite right. Then again, echoing Lamans' concerns, perhaps these were the only twenty men that would ever be available. For this reason, a voice in the back of her head kept shouting, *Better get one while the gettin's good!*

It had also occurred to her that there was another good reason for the captain to stay unattached. It allowed him to make unaffected decisions about relationships. From the time the ship had left port, there had been a lot of aligning going on. Nobody wanted to be on a different shift from the person plucking his or her heart strings. One begged to share garden duty with his beloved, while another pleaded to be moved to a different shift to avoid someone's unappreciated flirting. The captain had to somehow stay above it all. It was the smallest town he had ever lived in, and it had a host of small town problems.

"I believe you all heard the noise," the captain said to them when all the officers had filed in. "Chief Oakley has some news for us." Tessa was the officer on duty.

Yikes! It wasn't a dream! Veronica lamented.

"I have good news and bad news," Tessa said with dry military professionalism. "As you know, two weeks ago we lost Cecilia, and our current lead ship, Steven, is at sixty-percent shield, facts that already made a return trip to Earth unlikely. Now Star Covenant itself has been hit by an object. Apparently this piece of debris had sufficient transverse speed to strike from the side, bypassing the Martyrs. The navigation crew is checking feverishly, as you can see, to assure that the ship remains in proper aspect and on course. The good news is that we're all still breathing. The bad news is that our sensors indicate we have a serious hole in the first forty-two nose cone layers. Hit another object of the same size, in the same location, and we're history. We have some hull repair ability, but this damage is pretty major. Bottom line: as chief engineering officer of this mission, unless we find our destination planet to be entirely uninhabitable, I very strongly recommend against attempting to return to Earth with this vessel, regardless of how many Martyr ships remain."

When Tessa had finished speaking, she noticed that Fr. Hadrian had entered the room. She went to him, embraced him, and began to cry. She had left a lot of family on Earth and seriously intended to return there one day. This collision had wounded her about as much as anything could. Fr. Hadrian and Chief Oakley shared the same shift and had become very close. He was quiet and reserved; she was loud and brash. He was from South Africa; she from North Carolina. It would seem that the only thing they had in common was their dark black skin, yet they got along famously.

As Veronica watched the two embrace, she remembered the Holy Father's words to the priests: "If this mission becomes crippled in such a way that return to Earth with the vessel is impossible…you are released from your promises of celibacy at your own discretion." She wondered if the sassy but beautiful Baptist engineer and the quiet, prayerful Catholic bishop were destined for marriage, and then it occurred to her that there were now more eligible bachelors at *her* disposal as well. Maybe Captain Mike would consider marriage…and how about Ian? The thought of it threw her into mental, spiritual, and emotional overload.

"Doctor?" The captain said quietly, waving a hand mockingly in front of her eyes. "You okay, Ronnie?" he asked.

"Oh…I'm sorry. This whole thing has put me into a daze."

"Being awakened in the middle of the night doesn't help, I'm sure. May I escort you to your room?"

"Sure."

As she left the bridge with the captain, she noticed Commander Lamans, sitting alone and staring into space. She wondered if he was okay but didn't really want to engage him in conversation while in her robe and jammies, considering how glaringly obvious it had become that he had the hots for her.

Oblivious to his surroundings, the commander's mind reeled. Things were happening that were beyond his control. He hated that. His dreams of glory—among his more rapidly aged colleagues, upon his triumphant return to Earth—were obliterated. Dr. Talbot had managed to pry the man open just enough to know that the sum total of Lamans' self-worth lay in his perception of his accomplishments and his position within the power structure. That power structure was his home, the U.S. Army, and that home had just become an outhouse.

Talbot had died suddenly after that session, her notes from it never found. They were perhaps with her personal effects, but with the mission upon them there had been no time to deal with her estate executors, no time for the legal red tape of doctor/patient confidentiality, and no time to seek the opinion of another therapist.

Now, shaken by their collision, Lamans analyzed himself. His life was a lonely story. He was an army brat whose family had moved frequently. His parents were unchurched as children, but had found Christ later in life. Not wanting to offend anyone, they had attended whatever Christian church was nearest to them after each move. Lamans had been baptized Methodist, and had taken his first Communion as a Lutheran. Though Confirmed Catholic, he had not been to Mass since his Confirmation day.

His mother's death, shortly after his ninth birthday, left a deep scar in his soul. She had been the stabilizing force in his life. His father, an emotionless, high-ranking army officer, had traveled extensively for work, leaving little Cliff with a string of professional nannies, some nice, some not. The boy simply had not been able to rely on them to supply his emotional needs.

As he contemplated his life now, Lamans could watch it happen. When things had become too painful, he had stepped outside of himself. The young lad he watched on the screen in his mind wasn't him, it was some poor chap whose mom had died, an unfortunate kid who had to suck it up and get on with life. His father had shown little grief at her death. Cliff had received no endearing hugs to ease the pain. They both suffered in silence, alone.

Alone! It was the story of his life. Thirteen years after his mother's death, Lamans was part of a Special Ops team. The Army had teamed up with the Navy. His team was on a secret mission that would take them under the polar cap in a nuclear sub, a full eight weeks in the big sardine can without surfacing. It was there, in the first week of the voyage, that he had learned of his father's death. Secret missions are not cancelled because of family tragedies. Special Ops teams and Navy brass are unlikely sources of tender, endearing sympathy. He would go it alone. He always had.

His life had been about survival. Though he was a famous survivor, he had to ask himself, *What's so great about survival? It's characterized by fear, by crafty preparation for the next great threat!* Still, as the word chased through his mind it sounded somewhat…noble. He thought that perhaps instincts are the only real virtues; after all, aren't instincts from God? But to hell with fear! If he was to survive, he would do so with style and grace, and that would require power. He had always been taught that survival is our strongest instinct. His developing theology now made it the principal virtue.

And what was the second strongest instinct, closely tied to the first? Why, it was procreation! He had laughed at the philosophical tone of the mission charter, but now the charter's eloquent words about propagation loomed in splendor. Children were humankind's first retirement investment. There would be no way to collect those glorious pension checks he had earned! So there it was: His flirting with the pretty doctor was a virtue, a response to his survival instinct. God is good! Cliff Lamans would rise to the top of the heap. Veronica had married a powerful man before; she would marry one again. He would father the multitude she craved!

But how would he endear himself to her? Suddenly it became crystal clear. He needed to recreate himself to fill her needs. His psyche remained just objective enough for him to admit that he really had no experience in considering the needs of others. His life had been such a drag that he'd had a full-time job surviving. But somehow he now knew precisely what he must do. His plan could not miss.

Meanwhile, Veronica and Captain Benson reached her room, and Veronica invited him in.

"Mike, I just need to know something," she said, peeking through the open door into the hallway to make sure there was no one within earshot. "All that time we spent together on Earth...well, I enjoyed it immensely. I always wondered if maybe you and I would become...a couple. Now, all of a sudden, I need to know: Have you ever thought of us that way? Are you embracing celibacy? I need to know what the future of our relationship is."

Mike searched a moment for the right words. "Ronnie, if ever I was to take a wife, you would be my first choice. If you were not available, you would be the...benchmark by which all others would be measured. But I don't think marriage is right for me now. I don't think it's what this mission needs right now. I am deeply honored that you would think of me that way, and when such time comes that I feel God is calling me to that vocation, I will not waste a minute seeking your hand."

As she lay awake in bed she wondered what had driven her to put Mike on the spot. Was it the anxiety of the moment? She prayed quietly, inviting the Spirit to fill her emptiness. She had always been so happy, so fulfilled. What was this strange feeling of desperation? She had lived most of her adult life as a single woman, but one deeply connected to a man. Jacob had always been just a kiss away. She missed her little friends at Children's hospital. She craved fulfillment. She asked God's forgiveness for all the times she may have judged harshly the desperate among us, and fell asleep feeling a little desperate.

As each shift came on, their commanding officers informed them of the condition of the ship. At the breakfast table, Veronica informed Jasmine of the catastrophe. Ensign Babasa just smiled with resignation. "Life with God at the wheel is wild and wonderful," she said. "I can hardly wait to see what he has in store for us! I envision lots of babies, lots of little souls in our future." Veronica recalled her own feelings of desperation the night before and felt humbled in the presence of this one still new to the faith.

≈

Antonio Escobar sang as he made his rounds through the garden, cheered by the bright day-lighting lamps the plants required. The security chief had no security issues, which suited him just fine.

As he studied his planting medium PH test scan results, he was reminded of high school biology class. His lab partner had always been his twin sister, Juanita. He smiled remembering the fun they had and the trouble they got into. And for Antonio, no school-day reminiscing was ever complete without remembering psychology class. When the teacher had tried to convince the class there was no such thing as ESP, Antonio and Juanita had given each other a look that screamed a sarcastic, "Yeah...riiiight!"

Antonio's reminiscing about psychology class brought to mind the psychological testing he had undergone with Dr. Talbot. It seemed so long ago now. Her words had been so simple: "You can spend another four sessions with me, while I tug and pry at your soul, or you can just go visit Fr. Scofield and make a good confession. He can help you better than I." She had been so right. He said a little prayer for the repose of her soul as he went about his chores, for she had died suddenly just four days after his last visit.

As he studied a panel of gauges, he noticed a short burst of light in the already solarized room, and then noticed the reflection of a person in the lens of one of the gauges. When he turned around he couldn't believe what met his eyes.

He had seen the Mole's Earth Day marches on TV news, with them all decked out in their grass and leaves, but the only time he had ever encountered one in the flesh was the night of Jean's little shooting spree, and all he had seen then was one of the poor saps carrying his battered, beloved goat to safety.

Now one of them was in his face, one of the sons of bitches who had killed his twin, standing there all proud in his grass and leaves. In fact, this was the same one: the goat rescuing coward that had threatened his wife. He had the same sun streaked auburn hair, the muscular frame, and the California tan. He had to be stalking Jean! But how could the sucker have gotten on board? How had he stayed hidden for nearly a year? How had he managed to stay clean-shaven? What did he eat? The fact that none of it made sense did not inhibit Antonio's soaring adrenaline.

He had been healing. Jean was happy to report that he no longer called Juanita's name in his sleep. But now suddenly, in an instant, his wounds were torn wide open.

"How the hell did you get in here?!" he demanded. Trembling with anger, he unsheathed his dagger and moved toward the man. The intruder just stood and looked at him. "Answer me, dammit! Whadaya want? Sabotage? I'll give you sabotage!"

The man in grass extended his hand in greeting, but mistaking his intention, Antonio gripped his dagger and lunged. To Chief Escobar's amazement the intruder made no attempt at avoidance, and the dagger plunged deeply into his chest, right through his heart! Antonio stepped back, shocked at his own action. The knife rested in its new home, buried to the handle, but the man stood fully erect.

The intruder looked at Antonio for a moment and then removed his bio-clothing to get a better view of the knife. Standing stark naked in a pile of grass and leaves, he extracted the knife from his own chest and offered it back to Antonio. Reluctantly, a stunned Chief Escobar took the knife from his victim. There was no blood on it and no wound where it had been.

"My name is Elon. I am from the Garden. It appears that you are a gardener too, yes?"

Antonio sheathed his dagger and grabbed his communicator. "Captain…I…I need you on garden deck four, sir," he stammered.

"I'm in the middle of dinner with Dr. Lansing. Can it wait, Tony?"

"No! I don't think so, Mike. I think you need to see this."

"Should I bring the good doctor along?"

"No! Let her finish her meal."

"What is this place I am in?" Elon asked.

"You can do your talking with the captain, buddy."

The captain poked his head through the portal in the floor. "What's the emergency, Tony?"

"Turn around, sir."

"Oh my!" he said, as he finished climbing the ladder. "Where'd *he* come from?"

"Well, sir, *that* would be the question of the day," Antonio said, informing the captain about everything that had just taken place.

"Tony…you stabbed him with your dagger? Was he threatening you?" Antonio just looked at the floor. The captain came and stood before Elon.

"So, your name is Elon?" he asked.

"That's right, sir."

"And you're from where?"

"From the Garden, Captain."

"The Garden?"

"Yes, sir. You know, on the other side of the strait."

"No, Elon, I don't know."

"I'm sorry. I thought everyone in Ogeeremma knew where the Garden was."

"Ogeeremma? What is Ogeeremma?" the captain asked.

Elon laughed and said, "You make a joke! The Garden's on one side of the strait, and Ogeeremma's on the other; everyone knows that!"

"Hmmm. What's the name of the world you live on?" the captain asked.

"I don't understand the question. Is there more than one world?"

"Does everyone on your world wear hay?" Antonio asked.

"Oh, no!" Elon said, laughing with childlike joy. "Only *I* wear grass and leaves. Everyone in the Garden is naked, and everyone in Exile wears clothes, somewhat like yours."

"Exile? What is exile?" the Captain asked.

"All those places that are not the Garden: Ogeeremma, Addanac, Revotfell, Eknarf, and many others. Anywhere that is not Garden is Exile."

"How did you board our ship?" Antonio asked.

"Am I on a ship?"

"Yes."

"Well, I don't know how or why I am here. I was praying with my friends on top of Mt. Ekim, and I was deep in conversation with the One, contemplating the ways of the Almighty, and then suddenly I found myself here on your…ship."

"Why did Antonio's knife not kill you?" the captain asked.

"Gardeners can't be killed."

"And that's why you made no attempt to avoid being stabbed," the captain surmised.

"Yes, sir."

"Antonio, find some clothing for this gentleman." Antonio left, and the captain continued to question Elon. Shortly, a pretty head popped up through the portal.

"Mike. Are you here?" Veronica called.

"You might not want to turn around," he answered.

Too late. Veronica could not believe what she saw…and could not take her eyes off of him. "Wow!" she whispered. It was completely unlike her to stare at a naked stranger. It seemed the sight of him had stolen her brain. "Where'd *he* come from?" she managed, at last.

Except for Elon, all of the Gardener missionaries to Ogeeremma had taken to wearing regular clothing. Elon's grass and leaves had come to be revered by many as a sign of his unique prophetic position within the renewal. However, they had convinced him to shave his beard and cut his hair to match the styles worn in Ogeeremma. With his naturally bronze skin, perfectly muscular frame, and auburn, sun-streaked hair swept back on each side of his head, he looked like a beach boy from heaven. Those delights notwithstanding, it was his eyes that held Veronica's gaze.

The captain, who only hours before had stated his disinterest in matrimony, suddenly seemed oddly protective. He took a step to block Veronica's view and said, "I'll fill you in a little later, Doctor."

Antonio returned with clothing. "Do you know how to put these on?" he asked.

"Yes, I have friends who wear these."

"Tony, I'm taking him up to see Father," the captain said.

"Will you be safe alone with him, Mike?" Antonio asked.

"If you're done here you may join us, but…how will you keep me safe anyway? Sink that titanium blade into him again? Good luck with that!"

They found Fr. Scofield in the lounge watching an old movie. "Television. Like Ogeeremma's, but with color." Elon noted. Father rose from his chair at the sight of a new crewmember. Still adjusting to the insanely low gravity, he tripped over the next chair and fell to the floor, a very soft landing, of course. Elon helped the wide-eyed priest back to his feet.

"Where did *you* come from?" Father asked.

"I'm from the Garden," Elon informed him, and it started all over. The four seated themselves for a discussion that brought Father up to speed.

"How is it that you speak English if you're not from Earth?" Father asked him.

"What is English?" Elon asked.

"English is the language we're speaking. There are many languages on Earth. Are there not many languages on your world?"

"Oh, yes." A look of understanding came over Elon's face. "But Gardeners do not speak languages."

"What do you mean? You're speaking English right now," the captain insisted.

"No. You're *hearing* English. Gardeners have no language. We speak with our hearts and hear with our hearts. Words just make the activity sound pretty."

"So, what are you saying? That you hear what we're thinking when we're not talking?" Father asked.

"Oh, no. If you don't say it, I don't hear it."

"Why not?" Antonio asked.

"Because you do not want me to. Speaking is a communication from the heart. If you do not will to communicate, I do not hear it."

"I don't believe it!" Antonio declared.

"You believe that you can stick a knife in my chest without hurting me, but you don't believe what I am telling you now?" Elon gently chided him. Then he remembered something he had seen in Ogeeremma. "Do you have a disk recorder?"

The captain unclipped his communicator from his lapel. "No, but I have this. It automatically holds in memory all conversations from the last twenty-four hours. Why do you ask?"

"Play it. You will see," Elon insisted.

"Communicator, replay conversation from fifteen minutes ago," the captain instructed the tiny device as he plugged it in to the A/V system. The conversation played back just as they remembered it, with one huge exception: Elon was not speaking English! They were all dumbfounded and sat looking at each other wide-eyed and speechless for a minute.

"Is it possible for you to speak in English so that it will record?" Father asked him.

"Someday it will be," Elon told him. "Gardeners learn much more quickly than Exiles, but I have not heard enough of the language yet."

"Antonio, your lovely wife learned shorthand to help with note taking in medical school. Do you think her skills are still sharp enough to help us out?"

"I think so," Antonio answered. "It's been a while, so we might have to speak slowly."

They summoned Dr. Escobar, and all other officers who were not busy or sleeping. Veronica could not leave her post. A heap of testing needed to be performed before beginning deceleration, testing necessitated by the resulting return of a normal gravity level.

Elon was asked to give an account of himself. For the next two hours he held his audience spellbound. Just when Captain Benson realized that Elon could talk for days, and was looking for an opportunity to end their session, his com began to buzz. "Captain, this is Ensign Stokes. Do you have a minute, sir?"

"Hold on for a second, Jim," he said, and turned to those gathered. "Elon, thank you so much for telling us about yourself. Just one thing: Do you have a last name?"

"I am Elon, son of Elokin and Amla, of the Walnut Forest. That is all the name I have."

"Very well. I think some of us need to get back to work. Father, please take Elon on a little tour. Keep him out of secure areas, show him his room (the brig), and...why don't you take him up to see the chapel. Tony, I want you and Jean to go with them, you for security reasons, and Jean, please keep recording. Thank you."

"What is it, Jim?" the captain asked the helmsman over the com.

"Sir, we just lost Steven and Felicita," Mr. Stokes informed him.

"Wow!" the captain exclaimed in a whisper.

"One second Felicita had full shields, and the next she was gone!" the usually stoic Stokes lamented. "We only lose ships on my shift, Captain. Maybe I should retire."

It was hard to keep Mike down for long. "That's funny, Jim," he laughed, "but no such luck, my friend!"

Chapter 12

The One

"Why is everything so light here?" Elon asked, fascinated with the low gravity. Antonio gave him a quick little scientific explanation but could clearly see by the look on Elon's face that the Gardener lacked any frame of reference by which to make sense of it. Their little tour took them to the chapel. As Elon stepped off the ladder and turned around, the huge painting of Our Lady caught his eye. He bowed and fell to one knee, extending his open right hand toward the painting in an act of fervent prayer. As he prayed, the realization came to him that it was just an image, not a vision.

"You know who that is?" Father asked.

"It is the One, the One who is like us in all things but sin. I am her son, a prophet of the Most High by merit of her intercession."

Father was now fully flabbergasted.

"Is this," asked Elon, pointing to the tabernacle, "is this the sanctuary of the Word made flesh?"

"How do you know of the Eucharist?" Father asked.

"The One has taught me. As I prayed on the mountain before I came to your ship, she revealed great mysteries to me. She is the mother of the Word made flesh, who is the Savior of all Exiles. She is the queen of my heart! So, you are from the far away land in which the Word became one of us!"

"Yes, Elon. Yes we are," Father asserted.

"He lived among you? Amazing! Does he have an English name?"

"Yes. His name is Jesus. Jesus the Christ."

"Jesus! Jesus!" Elon said, falling to his knees. "Here you are before us in this simple bread, the food which angels envy." And then to the bishop he said, "Must I be an Exile to receive him?"

The bizarre situation sent the speechless Fr. Scofield on a mind trip back to the catechism. "You cannot receive unless you have been baptized," he said at last, doubting himself as he spoke.

"What is Baptism?"

"It is a gift from God, a sacrament, as we call it, by which we are born again of water and the Holy Spirit. Through Baptism Exiles partake in a new spiritual life and attain the dignity of adoption as children of God and heirs of his kingdom," Father said, wanting to be textbook correct.

"So…Baptism removes the flaw left by the fall of your ancient parents," Elon noted.

"Exactly," Father said.

"But, I am not from a fallen race," Elon insisted. "May I please partake of this Bread of Life?"

The good bishop wanted to be correct, and yet so wanted to please this holy man. While he contemplated the situation, Elon took notice of something on the man's belt, something very familiar to him. With lightning speed he reached and drew the bishop's dagger from its sheath. Jean jumped back in shock, and Antonio drew his own dagger—perhaps multiple stabs would do the job.

Elon placed his left hand against the wood paneled wall, and with his right hand, thrust the dagger through his left and just stood there with his hand impaled to the wall and a smile on his face. Just as quickly, he removed the dagger and showed his undamaged hand to the bishop.

"Can Exiles do *that*?" he asked, and immediately renailed himself to the wall. Then, falling to his knees with his impaled hand outstretched above him, he raised his other hand in like fashion and pleaded, "Please, Father. Please."

A now visibly shaken Fr. Scofield fished the tabernacle key from his pocket. In a moment, with shaking hands, he had obtained a host and held it before Elon. But then he stepped back and hesitated a bit. "You need to know that this is more than a communion. It is commitment to a sacrificial life!" he declared.

A knowing look came over Elon's face, as though the meaning of a long-standing mystery had just been revealed to him. He remembered the words of the possessed man in the graveyard by Aseeremma. "Human sacrifice!" he murmured to himself, with a smile that indicated that the great Exaggerator was about to lose another battle. With quiet resolve he proclaimed, "So be it!"

A look of great joy and peace came over him as he prepared to swallow the host, but as he swallowed, his countenance turned to one of intense agony, and he quickly turned his head to see blood streaming from his left hand.

Fr. Scofield removed the dagger and helped a now joyful but pain-stricken Elon to his feet. Finally, standing eye to eye, the bishop asked the strange guest, "Do you know what you have done?" Elon's only response was a knowing smile.

Veronica sat at a screen reviewing crew records of every kind, from exercise records to blood pressure charts. She was ready to declare the crew fit for the long deceleration.

When Elon entered with the bishop, she stood to greet His Excellency, but noticed Elon's hand wrapped in a bloody towel.

"Elon, I'd like you to meet Veronica Lansing, the ship's doctor," the bishop said.

Elon grasped his chest with his good hand and grimaced as if something had just pierced his heart. Seeing this, Antonio wondered about residual damage from the stabbing incident on the garden deck.

"Queen of my heart," Elon addressed her, and bowing reverently continued, "I should think that all that would be required for my queen to heal a man would be for him to look upon her!"

She thought his remarks to be a little too fresh for a new acquaintance. "So, we meet again," she said to him, and then to Father, "Do we know yet where this fresh one came from?"

"He's fresh from the Garden!" Father answered.

Veronica was too much the physician to take time to give his veiled answer more than a funny, frowny smile, and went right to work on the wound.

"How did you do this?" she asked.

"He did it to himself with my dagger," Father answered.

"Why?"

"To demonstrate a point. It's a long story that, thanks to Dr. Escobar, you'll be able to read about in the morning paper."

Veronica sighed a big *okay, whatever* kind of sigh. As she dressed Elon's wound, she felt his continuous gaze. "What do men do all day where you come from," she asked, "sit around and stare at women?"

"No, not *all* day, my queen," he answered without blinking.

His response gave her the giggles. *What the heck am I dealing with here?* she wondered.

"So, are you Elon the Great, interstellar comedienne extrordinair, traveling from ship to ship doing your stand-up routine?" she kidded.

"I don't think so, my queen," he said with such childlike innocence that it almost made her feel guilty for joking.

"I am *not* your queen!" she insisted.

"I am sorry, my...um...that is, I am very sorry, Veronica, um...Dr. Lansing," he stammered.

As the bishop led him from the infirmary, Elon kept turning and looking back. The doctor and he had something in common: they could not take their eyes off of each other.

After work Veronica read Jean's record of the dialogue and events of the day. She thought that Elon's story was fascinating stuff, science fiction with a holy twist. The brig was only one floor away from her room. She would try her bedside manner on her new patient. She found Antonio along the way and asked about their prisoner.

"Ronnie, I just came from a meeting with the captain and the commander. We don't know what to do with this guy. He somehow boarded a ship traveling over a half billion miles per hour. How can we expect to contain him? We've decided to tag team baby-sit him."

"Who has him now?" she asked.

"Father has him. Elon wanted to go back to the chapel," Antonio explained.

"So when do *I* get him?" she wanted to know.

"Well, we had a long discussion about that, and the captain and the commander are definitely not in agreement on the subject," he informed her. "The commander doesn't think Elon should be allowed anywhere near the female crew members by himself, but the captain sees no harm. Frankly, I don't know how we would stop him from doing anything he wants to do anyway."

"So...same question," she pressed.

"You've got dibs."

"Great! But I understand where the commander's coming from. So...I'll take Elon to the lounge or cafeteria, someplace where we won't be alone. It only makes sense until we know him a little better."

Veronica found Elon and Father in the chapel and then headed to the lounge with Elon. On the way they met Jasmine, who was on her way to evening garden duty.

"Jasmine, this is Elon," Veronica said.

Jasmine gave Elon her hand, and he gently kissed it, saying, "Queen of my heart, you make me complete." Veronica watched as her friend seemed to slip into a trance. In a moment the ensign was down on her knees looking up at their intruder.

"May I have your blessing?" she asked. Elon placed his hands on her head and prayed silently. When he had finished his prayer, Elon removed his hands, but Jasmine remained in ecstasy, her gazed fixed on heaven.

"Jazz?" Veronica called to her. "Jazz, honey, we need to get you out of the walkway here." Jasmine was not responding.

"She is in conversation with the Father," Elon said simply, as though extremely familiar with the state. He stooped and scooped the ensign into his arms. "Shall I place her somewhere else?" he asked. Under Veronica's direction, he placed her on an infirmary bed and stood back looking at her. "She's so beautiful!" he said after a moment.

Dr. Escobar was on duty. "How long will she be this way?" Jean asked pointedly.

"I don't know," Elon said, "but do not be concerned. She has special gifts. I sensed that she could hear my silent prayer, and knew that she would be drawn into ecstasy." He took her hand in his and stroked her hair for a minute. "She may be this way for many hours. She is on fire!" he said. Veronica said a little prayer and kissed her friend on the forehead as she pulled a blanket over her, then she and Elon headed for the lounge.

Before Veronica knew it, the two of them had been talking for three hours. Thrilled about the possibilities for missionary work in Exile, she said, "I wish Jasmine had been awake to hear this!"

An on duty Commander Lamans stopped by on one of his breaks. "Good evening, Dr. Lansing, Elon. How are my favorite doctor and my favorite intruder doing this evening?"

"Good evening, Commander," Veronica answered, "we're doing just fine, thank you. Elon certainly has fascinating tales to tell."

"Mind if I join you?"

"Please."

"Thank you, Veronica. Is it okay if I call you Veronica? I've been accused of being a little too stiff-shirted for this mission."

"Veronica is fine, sir."

"Well now, *that* doesn't work. You're Veronica and I'm *sir*?"

"Okay, Cliff," she said, laughing at herself.

"I wish we knew for sure if the world we're headed for is Elon's home," the commander said. "As he just appeared out of nowhere, we really have no way of knowing."

Elon did not respond to anything Lamans said. Veronica noticed that he appeared to be straining to understand. "Elon, is there any way we can know for sure that the world we're traveling to is your home?" she asked him.

"I'll ask," he answered simply.

"Ask who?" the commander wanted to know.

Elon did not respond. "Who do you need to ask, Elon?" Veronica reiterated.

"I will ask Our Mother. She will know."

"Our mother? What?" Lamans was confused.

"Mary, the mother of Jesus," Veronica explained.

"How would he know about her?"

"There's only one heaven, Cliff," she pointed out.

"Okay. Well...I guess so. You know," he said, changing the focus to himself, "I've been thinking about that heaven a lot lately, wondering if I don't need to clean up my slate a little. My parents were indiscriminate Christians, so I've been to just about every sort of church there is, but it's been a long time since I've been in any of them. Veronica, I'd really like for you to teach me more about the faith. Do you think you could find time for that?"

"I guess so, Cliff, but Fr. Scofield knows more about the faith now than I'll know in two lifetimes."

"Well, maybe between the two of you, you can straighten me out. Gotta go. I'm on duty. Goodnight."

After the commander had gone, Veronica needed to know something. "Elon, why is it that you can't seem to understand anything the commander says?"

"My English isn't very good," he said.

As Antonio escorted Elon to his quarters, Veronica went to check on Jasmine. She touched her friend's hair and Jasmine's eyes opened. "Veronica!" she said with a smile. "Ronnie, Elon is a great prophet! In his presence, the boundary between heaven and earth becomes blurred. It is impossible to describe what I felt!"

Staring dreamily into nothing, Veronica said, "It may be impossible to describe, but it's not hard to appreciate! His presence is..." She smiled, unable to finish. It was hard to describe!

The next day, Veronica went early in her shift to visit Elon, who was helping Antonio on garden deck three. As Veronica approached him, he bowed deeply and said, "Queen of...I mean, Veronica, I am honored to see you."

"It would seem that 'queen of my heart' is a common greeting where you come from," she noted.

"It is," he admitted, "but only among the prophets of the One. Before Our Queen introduced us to the whole idea of the kingdom of heaven, we only thought of God as our Father and Lover. There are no kings or queens in the Garden, so we did not know of these things. There is a special bond among those in the Garden who are prophets of the Queen and sons and daughters of the King, and it is with great love that we profess our humble service to one another."

"It's not that way in our culture," she instructed him. "On Earth, when a man calls a woman 'queen of my heart' it is because she has a special place above all others in his heart." The words had barely rolled off her tongue when she thought, *There must be no jealousy in his 'Garden': truly paradise!*

"I did not know," he said apologetically. "From now on, queen of my heart, I shall use this title only for the woman who has a special place in my heart, a place above all others. Thank you for teaching me." She giggled a little wondering if he realized what he had just said.

"Why do you laugh, my queen?" he asked.

Oh my! He realized it! He meant it! she thought, feeling both elation and panic. "I laugh because you say funny things, Elon, but just keep saying them; I like to laugh!"

Commander Lamans was on duty, but his mind was on Veronica, repeatedly rerunning his conversation with her concerning the faith. At last he decided that he would simply surprise her. He took her advice and met with Fr. Scofield, who was delighted with his interest. As he was already confirmed Catholic, he was quickly reinstated to full communion. A few days later, he stood beside her at morning Mass. At the kiss of peace, she gave him a little sisterly welcome hug, and he took the opportunity to whisper, "Father already has me back in full communion," which earned him a second hug. Jasmine, standing on the opposite side of Veronica, watched with concern. She had outgrown her animosity toward Lamans, but was concerned about Veronica. She had sensed a certain desperation in her sister and prayed that she was not being drawn into Lamans' web.

Encouraged by his progress, Lamans sought to increase his opportunities, and working on a different shift than the doctor was a definite disadvantage. At his next meeting with the captain he said, "Mike, I think we may be missing an opportunity." They met daily as the captain came off of duty and Lamans came on.

"How so, Cliff?" the captain asked.

"Well, I have this degree in anthropology, and all indications, right down to DNA, are that Elon is as human as you and I," Lamans told him. "In fact, his genes appear to yield a perfect combination of the better qualities of every race that exists on Earth. The society which produced him is apparently so integrated that race differences no longer exist. He is the greatest anthropological find in all of human history, and our schedules are making studying him a near impossibility for me. We need to pull from his head everything we possibly can about our destination. Ideally we should all be speaking Ogeeremman before we reach the planet surface. I think Elon could help to make that happen."

"Wow, Commander, I'm a little embarrassed that I hadn't thought of that myself. How much time do you think you can spare for study and still perform your other duties?"

"As you know, Mike, I have the loosest schedule of anyone on the ship. I'm sure I can free up two hours during my shift, but actually, I was hoping just to be able to get together with him after work."

"Let me take a look at the schedules and see what I can do."

"I'd be glad to look at them with you."

"Can't right now, Cliff, I have a previous engagement. I'll look at it tomorrow."

What ensued became Lamans' worst nightmare. The captain simply instructed Elon to be available to the commander for two hours before shift change (late afternoon for Elon, early morning for the commander). This arrangement still left Lamans on a different shift than Veronica and allowed her to spend every evening with Elon. In fact, Elon began helping her in the infirmary for the other six hours of her shift. The arrangement delighted the captain, because it allowed the doctor to be more thorough and kept their intruder from wandering.

That fast-learning intruder also became an asset on the garden decks. Besides their regular duties, all crew members had garden duty, and if one was unable to find Elon and had already checked the chapel, the place to look was the garden. There his helping hands further endeared him to a crew that already thought of him as one of their own. Like Veronica, they were charmed by his love, joy, and childlike enthusiasm.

The captain arranged for the two priests and Jasmine, the ships most able linguists, to join the commander and Elon in their two hour sessions. They soon developed a thorough Ogeeremman study course and a basic course in Revotfellian, and in preparation for their missionary work, began to translate portions of the Bible. By order of the captain, everyone was to use Ogeeremman in all casual conversations for the remainder of the voyage, and all were to familiarize themselves with Revotfellian as well. Fr. Hadrian had figured out how to receive Freqmod television, and the captain encouraged the crew to watch these countries' television programs to become familiar with their culture.

Elon, however, was enjoying Earth movies. Veronica and Jasmine came across him watching something called *Sand Babes*. He watched intently as the camera followed a dozen gorgeous women in very stringy string bikinis as they walked along a beach. Veronica wondered how such a trite flick had made it into the catalogue and was taken aback at the sight of Elon watching such a thing.

"Does this remind you of the Garden, Elon?" she asked.

"Hi, Veronica. Hi, Jasmine. In some ways it does."

"And in other ways it doesn't?" Jasmine asked.

"I thought I understood why Earth people wore clothing, but now I'm confused," he told them. "You and the other crew members always dress with most of your bodies covered."

"We don't have much choice; it's usually not exactly warm in here," Veronica said with a grin. "But modesty *is* very much a part of most Earth religions."

"Before I visited Exile, I thought that clothing was evil, the result of vanity. But you wear clothing so that you do not tempt others to sin. Still, when I look at these women in the movie," Elon said, "with these tiny flaps of cloth barely covering their sacred parts, my mind just wants to complete the scene, to view the whole picture as God intended. It seems like the cloth just calls extra attention to their sacred parts. Wouldn't that make it even more tempting to Exiles than complete nudity?"

"You're right, Elon. I think it does," Veronica said.

"So...Earth people sometimes use clothing to avert sin, and at other times, to invite it," he deduced.

"That sums it up pretty well," Jasmine asserted.

"But sometimes married people use clothing to invite love," Veronica instructed him.

"I see," Elon said thoughtfully. "Clothing can be very good, almost sacred, but it can also be bad, depending on how it's used."

"You're a very wise man, Elon," Veronica told him. "For exiles, almost everything has the potential to be used for good or for evil."

Elon turned the movie off, saying, "I don't like how watching this makes me feel."

"How does it make you feel?" Veronica asked with keen interest.

"Disconnected. I can see them, but they're just a picture. They can't see me. They can't appreciate my loving gaze. It's just a waste of time." Veronica smiled at his honesty, thankful that she could spend time with him without sitting through a bunch of B-grade movies.

She lay awake that night as she did on many nights, but on this night her thoughts weren't wandering and her prayers weren't eclectic. She could focus on nothing but Elon. "They can't appreciate my loving gaze," he had said of the images in the movie. *I can!* her heart shouted. *In his loving gaze I feel like I've died and gone to heaven!* She was spending eight or more hours a day with him and missing him every moment they were apart.

Tired of wasting her time in bed, she made a midnight trip to the chapel and knelt before the Blessed Sacrament. She thought about that Jake-shaped hole in her heart that Fr. Scofield had said would take time to heal, and about the God-shaped void that wounded our hearts from birth, a void begging to be filled. With deep trust in God, she had been filling all of the voids with prayer, the Eucharist, and works of charity. Her heart was healing, but now something strange and wonderful and scary was taking place. It seemed that the claim being staked out by just one man had the potential to swallow the void left by every man she had ever known. The void she felt in Elon's absence was of the same shape as the void left by God: the shape of perfection. Was it right to be so completely fulfilled by a human being?

$$\approx$$

Every day Elon took a holy hour during the fifth hour of his shift. He liked that hour because the chapel was always empty, leaving him completely alone with the Blessed Sacrament. One day, as often happened, an off duty Jean stopped by to chat with Veronica.

"Hey early bird," Veronica greeted her, "you're up two and a half hours before your shift, girl. Trouble sleeping?"

"Tony woke me with his snoring, and I couldn't get back to sleep. Where's your helper?" she asked.

"Elon? He's at chapel. Goes every day at this hour. As you know, he's been assisting with most of the kinesiological studies, and he's usually done by early afternoon. He likes to go to chapel at this time because everyone from last shift is in bed, and the next shift is not out and about yet, except you, so he gets the chapel all to himself." .

"Well, as long as I'm up, I'll watch your station if you'd like to go say a few prayers with him," Jean offered.

The chapel took up one entire floor, the only completely open floor on the ship. The tabernacle area could be enclosed with folding doors, allowing the rest of the space to become a dance hall, exercise room, or full-crew meeting room. The ladder entered the level fully opposite the altar.

Veronica crept quietly down the ladder until she had Elon in view. She was surprised to see that he was not in the enclosed tabernacle area, but had opened the folding doors and stood in the center of the space. Still more surprising was the fact that he was in his bathrobe. Elon stood quietly before the Lord with his head bowed for a moment and then cast off his robe and began to dance.

As she watched him pray with his entire being, a myriad of questions and feelings raced through Veronica's mind and heart. Was it sinful to watch a man who was not your husband dance naked, even if he was dancing for the Lord? It did not feel sinful. Was that because of his purity? His dancing was not erotic, at least, not purposely so; it was just plain beautiful. It displayed the perfect design of the human form, making of it an offering to the Creator. At any rate, Veronica could not take her eyes off of him.

She thought about her first words to him that day in the infirmary. "What do men do all day where you come from, sit around and stare at women?" she had asked. The memory made her smile at herself. She also remembered what had happened when he was brought to the infirmary, how he had clutched his heart in agony, causing Antonio to look at the floor regretfully.

While Elon danced he began to sing. The words were strange to Veronica. Why could she not understand him? Then it occurred to her that Elon was communicating, not to humans, but directly to the Father. For the first time she was hearing the language of the Garden. She remembered what he had told her: "We speak with our hearts and hear with our hearts. Words just make the activity sound pretty." Pretty indeed; she had never heard anything more beautiful! The melody he sang sounded so familiar to her that she began to search her memory, realizing at last that it was similar to a song she had learned in youth group at church. Now the words to that song, based on a scene from Samuel 2, danced through her mind.

David danced before the ark
To the shame of his queen
Exposed himself to all the slave girls
In the apron of a priest

Before the Lord did David dance
With wild abandon leapt
Bare your hearts now let them prance
For too long have they slept

Cast off you cloaks of greed and lust
Throw off your pride and shame
Humble hearts dance for the Lord
And they proclaim
Yes they proclaim his name
The name that fills us to the core
Proclaim the name
The one we'll serve forevermore
Dance without shame
Though they will hate you for the Lord
Proclaim the name
Of One so easy to adore

Jesus hung upon the cross
Naked without shame
Inviting slaves to become priests
Whose lives proclaim his name

David danced before the ark
In the apron of a priest
To serve the Lord was his delight
And so he would not cease

His queen went childless to the grave
For having scorned the Name
So may all our hearts give birth
And never be the same
Never be the same
Let them proclaim the Name
Just let them dance

The songs appropriateness for the occasion was so uncanny that a warm sensation rushed through her senses, and she felt the Spirit's presence in a powerful way.

Upon her return, Jean asked, "Well, was he pleased to see you?"

"I didn't talk to him."

"What?"

"I didn't want to disturb him. He seemed really deep in prayer."

"That's sweet. My man is very prayerful too. It's hard to disturb him even when I need to," Jean told her.

Veronica smiled, "You say 'my man' 'too' as if Elon is *my* man."

"You know, Ronnie, Mel told me to look after you, that you always fall in love while entertaining a large dose of denial." Veronica blushed. "Don't be embarrassed," Jean insisted, "lots of beautiful people use denial as a defense mechanism. Men are always falling in love with you, so you have to be careful with reciprocating, or you'll wind up with some weirdo like…well, I shouldn't say."

Veronica crossed the room and approached her five-foot tall friend. She inclined her head until her forehead pressed against Jean's and said, "Thanks for being so honest with me." Then, looking up at her schedule on the screen, said, "You know, we're really in good shape here in the infirmary, thanks to your hard work and Elon's help. Instead of our usual little meeting, let's do breakfast together at shift change."

In another two hours Elon had finished his daily stint with Lamans, and the three were joined by Jasmine for breakfast.

"How's it going with the commander?" Veronica asked Elon.

"He's asking many questions for which I do not have answers. I think that I have already told him everything important that I know."

"What did you talk about today?" Jean asked.

"He's been watching Revotfellian TV and wanted to know why the Revotfellians are so ugly."

"Are they?" Veronica asked.

"Haven't you seen their television programs?" Jean asked. "Don't expect to see any beauty pageants!"

"And did you know the answer, Elon?" Veronica asked.

"Actually, I think that's the only question today for which I did have an answer," he said. "In Revotfell they lost all the knowledge of their forefathers, on either side of the strait, and with it all knowledge of the True God. They practiced idolatry and human sacrifice for many centuries. One third to one half of all children born were offered in sacrifice, always the most beautiful children."

Jasmine moaned picturing the horrible scenario, which prompted Elon to throw an arm around her shoulder and give her a supporting squeeze.

"So the gene pool has lost some diversity," Jean speculated.

"If you say so, Doctor," he shrugged, not at all grasping the concept of a gene pool.

That evening Veronica left Elon playing chess with the captain, and went to visit Fr. Scofield. "Do you have time to counsel an old widow?" she asked him.

"I always have time for a prophetess," he replied.

"Thanks, Father. A prophetess?"

"Your life is a sublime template by which other lives may be lived. Prophesy is so much more than words."

"Thank you, dear man," she said, and then emptied her heart to him about the chapel visit and the deep love that gripped her heart and soul. "Can an Exile marry an innocent Gardener?" she asked.

"Of course. You are both human. In fact, you are both Catholic. At my request Elon subjected himself to conditional Baptism, perhaps not out of necessity, but more out of formality. I haven't really sorted out all of the theological dynamics of this situation yet, but I figured Baptism couldn't hurt. After all, Christ himself submitted to it as an act of humility. However, there is one thing you must consider: Elon is immortal. Theoretically, he could live in the Garden forever. You are an Exile; you cannot enter the Garden. Are you comfortable with asking Elon to remain in Exile with you, separating him from family and the tree of life?"

"I...don't know," she answered. The thought had not occurred to her.

Her visit with Fr. Scofield brought more questions than answers, and she lay awake once again. It seemed that marrying Veronica always demanded a huge sacrifice. Marriage would not have allowed Jake to travel to another star, and now it would keep Elon out of Paradise. Was it too much to ask of him? If she could, by some strange grace, enter the Garden with him and eat of the fruit of the tree of life, would she become like the complacent Gardeners whom Elon described? Would her craving for the glory of God be so placated by His blinding reflection in Elon that she would tarry for century after century, procrastinating her ultimate fulfillment?

At last she smiled at herself and laughed at her fears. *You're no longer feeling desperate,* she informed her heart. *The Spirit is guiding you. Must you invent new fears for yourself? Is that not the work of some other spirit?* She fell asleep giving her heart and her new love back to God in prayer.

Chapter 13

Changes

Ten minutes into her shift and halfway through a yawn—in need of the cup of coffee she had spilled all over Elon at breakfast—Veronica answered her buzzing communicator.

"Is Mike with you?" the commander asked.

"No, Commander, I thought he was meeting with you."

"He's fifteen minutes late. It's not like him to forget. I buzzed his quarters and no one answers," Lamans informed her.

"I and Elon had breakfast with him. He was headed for his quarters to do a little reading before your meeting. That was about half an hour ago. Have Tony find him," she suggested.

"Good idea, Veronica. Thanks."

From the bridge, Antonio immediately did a ship-wide page. When there was no answer he proceeded to the captain's quarters.

"Ronnie, get up here on the double!" he yelled into his communicator.

When she got there, the captain was on his back and Antonio was administering CPR. From her medical bag, Veronica produced a device called a Resusciman. She turned it on, positioned it over Mike's heart while waiting for a beep to indicate the correct location, and pressed a button that triggered the firing of four probes deep into his chest. The unit scanned the captain's heart while applying test stimulation and was soon achieving a perfect heart rhythm. While Antonio continued to administer mouth to mouth, she pulled an Omniscan from the same bag and began to perform a series of standard tests. After a few minutes of testing, as Antonio went to administer another breath of air, she placed her hand on his cheek. "He's gone, Tony," she said, "we won't be able to resuscitate him." She removed the Resusciman, and they sat in horror staring at their lost friend and at each other.

"He was sitting in his chair, slumped over the table when I found him," Antonio said at last.

While Antonio informed the commander and began investigating the captain's quarters, Veronica accompanied Elon and another crew member as they took the body to the infirmary. In half an hour Antonio joined them there. Elon had seen death in Ogeeremma, but he had never lost someone whom he had come to love. Chief Escobar found him and Veronica in tears.

"What caused his death, Ronnie?" he asked.

"It's the strangest thing, Tony. My scan indicates clearly that it was a brain aneurysm, but my records show absolutely no area of prior weakness in his tissues in that area. I spent hundreds of hours combing every fiber of every body on this ship before giving my approval. How could I have missed something like this?"

"I don't know," Antonio responded, quietly staring at the body bag.

"What did *you* find?" Veronica asked.

"Nothing yet. Any reason to believe that his death was the result of foul play?" he asked.

"Only that, to my knowledge, Mike was perfectly healthy and now he's dead, but I don't know how anyone could *cause* this kind of death." She reached to the table beside her. "You'll want this," she said, handing him the captain's communicator.

All of the officers were notified, and Fr. Scofield came to anoint the body. There would be no embalming. The funeral would take place immediately with those mourners available; such were the exigencies of star travel.

Three days passed. The crew slowly adjusted to calling Lamans *captain* instead of *commander*. Antonio informed the new captain that he and Jasmine had completed their investigation.

"Well, let's hear it, Tony," Lamans said.

"I'm sorry, sir, but in instances such as this, the protocol is clear: Evidence will be revealed only in the presence of all senior officers."

"Then get on with it, my friend."

Later, Antonio and Jasmine looked grim at the head of the little conference room table. "I really don't have much to report," he said. "There's this." He played a snippet of audio. "It was taken from the captain's communicator record. At the beginning, we hear pages being turned. Mike reads aloud to himself, and then we hear a clunk, which I believe was his head hitting the table. He was found slumped over the book he had been reading, and text on the open page contains the phrase we hear him mumble on the recording. But listen again closely. There is a sound right before the thud. I keep thinking I've heard that sound before, but I just can't think what it would be." He played the audio again with that particular part highly amplified. The sound in question was a sort of electrical humming noise.

"Antonio, when Elon first appeared in the Garden did his entry make any sound?" Lamans asked.

"Not that I can recall, sir, just a bright flash of light."

"Do you still have the audio from that day?"

"Yes, sir, I archived all of it, standard protocol when anything unusual takes place."

"I want it scrutinized for this sound," the captain said.

"Yes, sir."

"You got anything else, Chief?"

"Ensign Babasa did the fingerprinting."

"I found many fingerprints in the captain's quarters," Jasmine explained. "Mostly his own, two of Veronica's, one of Fr. Scofield's, one of Elon's, and five of yours, sir. We all know that, because of space constraints, it's not unusual for officers to hold meetings in their private quarters. Had we found prints of a crew member who is not part of the command structure they might raise some suspicion."

"What are you talking about, woman? Elon's below a crew member; he's an intruder! Why would he not be suspect?"

"Well, sir," Antonio explained, "Elon is nearly always accompanied by an officer."

"You said it, Tony, *nearly* always! Where was he when the captain died?"

Veronica responded. "As you know, sir, he left his meeting with you to have breakfast with us. After breakfast, I left him at his quarters. I had just spilled hot coffee on the poor man and he needed to change his clothes."

"When did you see him again?" Lamans asked.

"After the captain was discovered."

"Where?"

"In the captain's quarters."

"He came to the captain's quarters? How did he know you were there?"

"I...I don't know," Veronica stammered.

Jasmine spoke up. "Captain, Elon has perceptions that are beyond those of...well, of a fallen race. He can..."

"Jeez, Jazz, don't give me that fallen race versus gardener garbage!" Lamans said tartly. He turned to Antonio with a look of serious resolve. "Chief Escobar," he said, "I order you to place Elon under arrest. I want him placed in restraints in his quarters." He stopped speaking for a moment and surveyed their faces. "Dr. Lansing,

I know this situation is difficult for you," he went on, "but I must do what I think is right for the safety of this crew. I have a feeling that Elon will easily remove himself from restraints. If that happens, we will at least know what we're up against. I don't know what we'll do about it, but we'll cross that bridge when we come to it.

"Ensign Babasa, my apologies for being so gruff. I agree with you actually. That is, I agree that Elon has great powers of perception. He has them, and they scare the hell out of me! I just haven't bought into the whole fallen-race-versus-gardener story yet."

$$\approx$$

Captain Lamans knew he was in trouble with Veronica. Maybe it was time to rock her world. He was accustomed to spending two hours with Elon before his shift began. It would be a good time to go see the Doctor instead.

"Good morning, Dr. Lansing, how are you this morning?"

"I'm fine, Captain, but rather busy. I'm a bit spoiled by all of the help our intruder was providing."

"Speaking of that chap, I got the most disturbing news about him last night," Lamans informed her. "A few days ago Mr. Hawkins from environmental made a quick chapel visit on his coffee break. Turns out that our friend Elon was there dancing naked. Can you imagine! The thought of someone cheapening the Eucharist by stripping and dancing offends me to the core!"

"I've never heard of such a thing!" Veronica declared. Her transparent innocence did not lend itself well to acting, and she feared that her performance was unconvincing.

"I wonder what else those animals do on his planet!" Lamans rambled on, thinking he was making points. "Imagine if a pure woman like you had walked in on him. Imagine!"

"That would be just awful!" she feigned.

"Well, that won't be happening anymore. At least, I hope not. There's no telling what powers the man may possess. So far we've managed to keep him in restraints overnight."

"Cliff, we don't really have any compelling reason to believe that Captain Benson's death was the result of foul play. Is it really necessary to keep Elon in restraints?"

"He's an intruder, Veronica. He should have been in restraints from day one. I shudder when I think that Captain Benson's kindness may have been the cause of his own death."

That night, as Veronica knocked on her confessor's door, she wondered when the kind man would tire of her tears.

"The captain has him chained up like an animal!" she lamented. "I just can't bear to see him that way!"

"The time grows short, Veronica. Soon we will be to Ogeeremma, and the captain will have more to worry about than Elon. Be patient and pray."

Captain Lamans called a meeting of all the commanding officers and all the lead officers in each discipline, a group of fourteen in all.

"This meeting will be the first of a series of information sharing sessions as we near our destination," he said. "You are all aware that we have taken on an extra passenger, not by choice, but he is here nonetheless. Elon has proven an invaluable asset to us in learning the language of two principal countries of our destination planet. Unfortunately our Captain Benson has died unexpectedly, and I have been unable to rule out foul play on the part of our guest, simply because we do not know all of his capabilities or intentions. Why is he here? He appeared out of nowhere on a ship doing nearly light speed. What else is he capable of doing? No one can say.

"As you know, I am an anthropologist, and my training may prompt me to take a somewhat different approach to life's questions than others take. I try always to see things in their scientific perspective first. I think that Fr. Scofield operates in the same manner. Correct me if I'm wrong, Father, but you will not attempt an exorcism without first having the subject undergo a psychological examination, will you?"

"That is correct, sir," Father answered.

"So it is that I expect no less professionalism regarding all of our duties aboard this vessel," Lamans insisted. "Our friend Elon is a remarkable individual and very likeable, but what do we really know about him?"

He flashed up on a screen a picture of a full sized icon of an airplane, an icon made from vegetation.

"No doubt, if you've studied anthropology 101, you have seen this picture, yes?" he asked.

Antonio offered, "It's an icon of a fighter plane. It was made by south sea islanders during one of the world wars. They were found worshiping it."

"Very good, Chief Escobar. Those natives knew about as much about aircraft as we know about Elon. It is our innate tendency to worship the mysterious, things which possess powers we do not understand. We do so for a variety of good reasons.

"You see, religion is really very self-serving. If there is something that we don't understand, there is a chance that it may be greater than us and have power over us, in which case we had better show some respect. Has the notion crossed your minds that perhaps Elon was beamed aboard this ship via extremely advanced technology, rather than by a miracle? No doubt, that suggestion conjures up silly images of archaic sci-fi origin, but think of how our own technology has advanced exponentially in the last century and then add about 4,000 years to that. Father, you are on a mission to save souls, and I applaud that, but you are also an officer on this ship, and as far as the AGC is concerned, this is primarily a scientific mission. I need for everyone to keep an open mind. You see, I believe that Elon knows our language, not because he has the gift of tongues, but because his people have been listening to our radio waves for hundreds of years."

"Then how is it," Fr. Hadrian wondered, "that they are just first using very rudimentary FM radio?"

"Elon is telling you the truth. Those radio messages are coming from a society that is exiled from the main society. It is a fractured, barbaric society compared to Elon's 'Garden.' Let me explain. I believe that Elon is a member of a society which produced incredible technology a very long time ago. I believe they have the same genetic makeup as us because we are not native to Earth; we were taken there 7,000 years ago by a space flight similar to this one. Our Genesis story came from them! The story was handed down from generation to generation before it was finally written down. I believe that the Ark of Noah *was* that spaceship, a ship that, through years of retelling, came to be known as something a simple agrarian society could understand, a sea vessel. If you have been following my orders, you have been watching Freqmod TV and have noticed by now that they appear to have all of the same animal species as Earth. Once again, the story of Noah comes to mind. It would seem to be the only plausible scientific explanation."

"Captain, if Elon knows our language from listening to Earth broadcasts, and he is not speaking in tongues, how do you explain the fact that, when recorded, his voice sounds like gibberish?" Veronica demanded.

"Frankly, Doctor, I have no explanation. But why does the answer need to be spiritually based? It is apparent that Elon is incredibly intelligent. I believe your testing found his I.Q. to be substantial. Have they perhaps developed powers of telepathy that would explain this phenomenon? I do not claim to have all of the answers, but I am attempting to elucidate theory that will lead to the best path for retrieving the rest of the answers."

"But, sir, if your theories are true, why is Elon totally unaware of technical things?" she pressed.

"Very simple, Veronica. You have younger brothers, right?" She nodded her head. "Are they into video games?"

"Yes."

"Could they make a video game? We're talking about a society so advanced that almost no one has to work. They have a force field protecting their borders, your angel with a revolving sword. They control the weather so they can sleep outside. They require no housing and no clothing. Their food grows with little or no effort on their part and refreshes them so thoroughly that they incur no illness and do not age." He turned to Veronica. "Perhaps this effect is diminishing with Elon. I notice that his hand has not yet healed. Pay close attention to his health; we do not want to lose him."

Returning to the subject, he said, "All of these marvels could be controlled by an industrial complex that is out of sight and out of mind. The technology is so advanced that machines repair machines and design new and better machines. A tiny fraction of the population actually works, but like the machinery, they are out of sight."

"Wouldn't the working people be jealous of those who don't have to work?" Jean wondered.

"No, Dr. Escobar. You see, there's power in knowing truth. They are in control of their own destiny *and* that of others. They know things their fellow garden dwellers will never know and see things they will never see. It is a system that works well for all."

"So...why do you think they would send someone like Elon into our midst rather than someone who knows something?" Tessa asked.

"Well, Commander, Elon is the perfect spy. If detected, what secrets can he divulge? We have no technology they want, so why would they send a technician? If he tells you that God placed him here, he is probably telling you what he believes. Why would they tell him otherwise? They simply want to give a false impression of what the Garden is all about. If we believe that Elon is a sinless holy man from paradise, we're not likely to mess with an angel with a revolving sword at their borders. These are a very civilized people. They really don't want our dead carcasses strewn about the perimeter of their living space, but they also do not want us trying to figure out how to take down their shields. If they've been listening to our radio broadcast for two centuries, they have our religious beliefs figured out. In short, there are many reasons for sending an Elon. So once again, I warn: Enjoy his charisma if you will, but keep your eyes, ears, and mind open and be true to this scientific mission. Thank you. That is all."

Before anyone left, Veronica objected, "Captain, I'm really confused. You suggested earlier that Elon knew our language because he's been listening to our radio broadcasts, but now you have classified him with a group of people that live a life of paradise shielded from technological things…which is he?"

Veronica had never before seen Lamans totally without words. His normal poker face was replaced by one that twitched as though he was withholding anger, or denying it because he refused to make the girl of his dreams the object of it. Finally his face relaxed and he looked very pleased with what was developing in his mind. "You know, Veronica, your question frames perfectly my reason for calling this meeting," he said at last. "We are a science team, and communicating like this generates a great deal of creative synergy. You have uncovered a hole in my theory, a small hole, but a hole none-the-less. Perhaps I have greatly underestimated Elon. If he is telepathic, as I suggested earlier, does telepathy perhaps transcend language? It is a subject about which we know very little."

Lamans dismissed the crew, and as everyone was leaving, Jean marched over to him and got in his face. "Sir, Elon did not kill Captain Benson and he is not a spy, and you are about as wrong as you can be!" she declared. Lamans smiled and looked at Tony for approval to disregard his feisty little wife, but Tony did not smile back.

"Opinion noted, Chief Surgeon Escobar. Please return to your post," Lamans said. The fiery-eyed Jean left with her husband, and only Veronica and Tessa remained.

"Commander? Doctor?" the captain invited. "Do you want to chew on me too?"

"Sir, what about charity to others? How do you explain that away?" Veronica asked.

"I do not mean to explain anything away, Veronica; I only hope to open up possibilities. But since you ask, charitable works can be self-serving. Consider the old saying 'What goes around comes around.' If I don't want to be kicked, I shouldn't kick. If I don't want sand in my eyes, I shouldn't throw sand. If I want to be fed when I'm hungry, I should feed others when they are hungry. It's just simple self-interest."

"If religion is all about self-interest, why are some people not religious?" Tessa asked.

"Ah…because they believe, Commander Oakley, that with time everything can be understood, all miracles explained and harnessed. They believe they can live the do-unto-others protocol without giving credit to some higher, mystical, unproven power."

"Why is it unscientific to believe in God? There is plenty of evidence to demonstrate his existence!" she insisted.

"Did I say that I do not believe? But I must ask: Why does power always have to be a person? The only thing we can measure, but cannot see, is power: gravity, magnetism, electromagnetic radiation, and a host of others things yet undiscovered. But we are about to change all of that. Let's save our worship for God, not for his creatures. They are to serve *us!*"

As the two ladies left the meeting room, Veronica could see that Tessa was nearly exploding. When they had put enough distance between themselves and the captain, she blew.

"What kind of idiots does he take us for?" she demanded. "Next thing you know he'll be tellin' us that hangin' on a cross with nails through your hands and feet and a crown of thorns on your head is an example of 'simple self interest!' I've never heard so much nonsense come out of one mouth in all my life!"

Veronica tried to calm her down, but Tessa just wasn't ready.

"Listen, Ronnie," she said, "it's bad enough I gotta put up with him hittin' on me like I'm the love of his life. I'm not putting up with him insulting my Savior!" Veronica was a little stunned. She'd never suspected that she was perhaps just one of many being romanced by the illustrious Captain Lamans.

Fr. Scofield peered quietly through the open door of the brig. Elon knelt in prayer, his hands raised, his eyes closed. Just as Father decided that he would not disturb his friend's prayer time, Elon turned toward him.

"Father! Please, come in!" he insisted.

"How are you doing today, Elon?"

Struggling with his restraints, Elon rose from his knees and hugged the priest. "Every day I am plunged more deeply into the mysteries," he said. "The One has shown me that, to understand Jesus, I must fully understand what it means to be an Exile. Meanwhile the Spirit is prompting me to offer up my sufferings for the salvation of those in Exile, and that the Father may heal Gardeners of their complacency. It brings me great joy to make this sacrifice, but it causes me pain to see Veronica hurt by my sufferings."

Fr. Scofield smiled the smile of one warmed in the presence of great love. "You see in Veronica's suffering but a small example of the great suffering that the One, Mary the mother of Jesus, has had to suffer. Unite your suffering with her suffering and that of her Son, and your life, joined to Christ's, becomes part of the only sacrifice that is pleasing to the Father."

"Father, everything has become so different for me," Elon told him. "I used to walk with God every day in prayer. Now he no longer speaks directly to me, and neither does the One. Like the woman I love, I have truly become an Exile. More and more I experience the Creator through my love for Veronica and her love for me. In our love the Father renews us. It is as though our hearts have become inseparable; I become more the Exile, and she becomes more the Gardener. It is overwhelming."

"Is God preparing you for the sacrament, Elon? If so, you must not refuse him," Father instructed.

Dr. Lansing didn't realize how angry she was until she stood staring at her coffee cup, an island in the dark sea she had created by slamming the thing down on her desk. *I suppose anthropologists have to come up with some sort of a fanciful story to justify their existence,* she thought. *Science, schmience! Cliff wouldn't know a sound theory if it slapped him in the face!* As she wiped up her mess, Captain Lamans entered the lab.

"Still readjusting to full gravity?" he asked, noting her coffee mess.

"After nearly five months? Nah…still adjusting to being a klutz!" she joked, hiding her anger so as to avoid any heart-to-heart with a man who increasingly made her nauseous.

"Veronica, I stopped by to…well, that is, I know I haven't made any points with you lately. I'm trying to do what's right and I'm finding out just how lonely and unpopular that can make a guy. Last night, as I contemplated the situation we have with Elon, I had to admit to myself that there is a part of me, a fairly large part of me, that would really rather do what pleases you than to do what I think is best for this mission. There has been a gut wrenching battle going on within my soul. Maybe I'm just a big coward. Maybe I just don't want to die sitting at the table in my quarters the way Mike did. I just wish we had more to go on. I've had to make some tough decisions."

"Cliff, I spent eight hours a day with Elon for many weeks. I am well trained in the sciences, and I agree that there is not enough data to indicate whether or not Elon could have taken part in Mike's death. However, there is data in here," she said, placing her hand over her heart. "At the risk of sounding sexist, I am a woman, and every ounce of my womanly intuition says that it is impossible for Elon to commit such an act. I could sense the love he had for the captain whenever they were together. That which you fear is just not possible."

"I respect your feelings, Veronica, as I respect you deeply. I will continue to give this whole matter more thought. On a different note, I'm wondering if you would join me for dinner tonight."

Veronica swallowed hard. Dining with Lumans rated just below cleaning bed pans on her list of preferred activities, but if warming up to him would ease Elon's suffering, she could put up with it. "My last duty is to check on our prisoner and make sure that he is healthy and comfortable. I would be glad to join you after that...say at...oh, 1800 hours?"

"Shall I pick you up at your quarters?"

"Actually, I will be coming to the mess from the chapel. I'll meet you there."

Veronica unlocked the brig door and went in. Elon was sitting on the floor, his head bowed in prayer. Before his arrest, she had never been in his quarters. She was impressed by the lovely smell that was everywhere. It smelled, well...like Elon.

"Have you had enough to eat today? Did Tony come by and uncuff you so you could shower and change?"

"Yes, queen of my heart, he did."

Veronica read for him the scriptures of the day, and gave him communion. He took her hands in his, and the two sat silently in prayer for a long moment. He looked up into her eyes, and she removed her hand from his to wipe a tear from his cheek. In doing so, she noticed blood on her hand.

"Oh, my dear man, I can't believe your hand has not yet healed!" Then a great look of wonder came over her. The blood on her hand had come from the palm of his right hand, not his left—both hands were bleeding!

Elon changed the subject. "Ronnie, do you remember the second time you ever saw me?"

"Are you kidding?" she answered, as she continued to inspect his hands. "You were my first emergency treatment aboard this vessel. When our eyes met, you were clutching your heart as if you were about to die."

"I was! I mean, I could barely feel Chief Escobar's knife enter my heart, but your eyes pierced me through with a passion I had never known. I had always been told that when the appointed time came I would have no doubt about whom God had selected as my mate; however, I did not think it possible that she would be an Exile." Veronica's eyes went wide and her mouth agape as Elon went on. "Since then, I have borne my great passion for you as a sacrifice for souls, while I prayed to know God's will, but the Almighty has decided to deal with me as an Exile. My prayers are met with silence. The answer comes only to my heart. He has left me to come to my own conclusions."

Veronica placed her fingers over his lips, lest what was about to escape might be the conclusion she did not want to hear. "I too was pierced through the heart when my eyes met yours," she said. "It happened already on the garden level where you first appeared. I have never experienced such a thing at the first sight of a man. In fact, I felt absolutely no shame in looking upon your nakedness, something that I am just now beginning to understand."

Elon smiled a knowing smile. "I love you Veronica. Will you please be my wife?"

Struggling to keep from sobbing, Veronica said, "But I will never be able to go into the Garden with you!"

He pulled her close and spoke with his lips touching hers. "My love, you will *be* my garden!"

Chapter 14

Extra G's

"I'm sorry, honey," Veronica told her new fiancé, "but I had better not be late for my dinner meeting with the captain. I don't want him to suspect anything."

"What do you mean? Do you think that he will not approve of our marriage?"

"Elon, *he* wants to marry me!"

"He does? How do you know?"

"I'm a woman, honey; I know. We can talk about this later. I love you so much!"

"Good evening, Veronica," the captain greeted her. "I trust that our detainee is doing well."

"Actually, Cliff, I'm very concerned about him," she replied. "He thrives on affection and companionship, and he seems so depressed."

"Well, I've been giving this a lot of thought," Lamans assured her. "In fact, starting tomorrow, I have assigned one of the ship's gardeners, Mr. Schmidt, to full time duty with Elon. Elon will be restricted to the garden decks for four hours a day helping Schmidt, and after that the two will be cuffed together wherever they go. Captain Benson had given strict orders to keep Elon off the bridge and other secure areas, but the bridge is where I spend most of my time. In the coming weeks this arrangement will allow me to pick his brain as needed."

"Cliff, that's wonderful! He will be so happy to be back into the garden! Thank you!"

"You're really fond of this fellow, aren't you, my dear?"

"Yeah. He's like a brother to me. In fact, he reminds me of my brothers. Man, do I miss those guys! Elon kinda fills the gap."

"You're too sweet, Veronica. I've seen the way he looks at you. I don't think your brothers look at you that way!"

"That used to concern me, but I think there is a whole different set of rules where Elon's from. On Earth we have cultures that consider it impolite *not* to belch after a meal. My understanding is that, in the Garden, it's impolite *not* to stare at a woman."

The captain chuckled and declared, "I was born on the wrong planet!" His mirth was interrupted by the arrival of Chief Oakley, who was in her bath robe. "Tess, what are you doing up in the middle of the night?" he asked.

"I couldn't sleep, Captain, so I went to the bridge to see how things were going and got there just in time to see the passing of another Martyr. Paul is gone," she said.

"We're down to two Martyrs? Good Lord! Are we gonna make it, woman?"

"There's no way we can make a return trip to Earth, Captain, a fact which has allowed me to divert tons of extra fuel to the shields, enough extra to allowing widening the shield sensor field so we don't get side-struck like we did before. Let's just hope that Freqmod is more than a nice place to visit!"

Jean stepped out of the tiny shower. Through a crack in the bathroom door she could see her husband kneeling in prayer by the bed, so she looked up at the view screen to see what image he might have chosen for contemplation. There she saw a classic painting of the Sermon on the Mount, but Antonio wasn't looking at it. His gaze was fixed on a chair near the bed. She came out of the bathroom wrapped in a towel. He concluded his prayers and stood to embrace her.

"What are you and Jesus talking about these days?" she asked.

"Oh, it just occurred to me how much you and God have in common," he answered.

"Really? Like what?"

"Well…every time I look at the chair by the bed I'm reminded of how you love to get up on it and dance for me," Antonio told her.

"So…you think dancing and stripping for you makes me like God," she said, attempting to summarize what he was saying.

"Umm hmm. With each little revelation you make, I rediscover my love and fascination for you," he told her. "It's a beautiful thing. God is…um…the eternal dancer. He reveals himself and is thrilled with our discovery and appreciation."

"The 'eternal dancer,' huh?"

"Yeah. So…heaven is a never ending cycle of revelation, discovery, and appreciation. You can never reveal all of yourself to me, because God keeps forming you, and there is no limit to the beauty he can give you, and therefore, no limit to the beauty that I can see in you.

You're a little piece of heaven here and now, a channel to God. Of course, in heaven he will never run out of things to reveal about himself."

Jean slid her hands under Antonio's already unbuttoned shirt and caressed his back while she kissed his chest. "Are you ready for a little revelation and discovery?" she invited, tiptoeing up for a kiss.

"Honey, whoa! You're ovulating!" he whispered, cupping her lovely face in his hands as he kissed her. "You better be careful! We decided to wait until we were out of this boat to have babies, remember? You said you didn't want to endanger a child's life."

"Then you shouldn't be talking about dancing and stripping!" she insisted. "And why do you have to be so hot?"

"Hey, that sounds like a husband selection protocol issue," Antonio replied, beaming from her praise. "You'll have to answer that one yourself. Besides, if you think *I'm* hot," he said, "you're not exactly turning me off standing here wrapped in a towel! And why on Earth do you have to smell so delicious?"

"Umm, Tony, we're not 'on Earth,'" she noted.

"Okay, so your fragrance is out of this world! Or…is it out of *that* world?" he toyed.

"Don't hurt yourself," she said, smiling and rolling her eyes.

They pulled on their jammies and snuggled into bed. Antonio was on his back with Jean's arm across his chest and her head on his shoulder. Her fine, straight brown hair spilled across his neck and face. Right before he fell to sleep, he brushed her hair from his face and whispered, "I don't think I can fall to sleep with you touching me."

He dreamed of his wedding night. He was dancing with his twin sister, Juanita. In his dream she teased him as she had that night: "You and I have always done everything together," she had said. "Half the time we finish each other's sentences." Then in reference to the impending honeymoon, she had asked, "Are you sure you'll be able to do this without me?" Antonio laughed out loud in his sleep, waking Jean. A few minutes later, when he laughed again, she touched his face.

"Whaa…oh…hi," he said, waking. He grabbed her hand, kissed it, and asked, "Is something wrong?" As he awaited her answer, he heard her favorite dance music playing ever so softly. It was a joyful jazz tune that celebrated the poetry of the body's motion with every beat. She switched on a lamp, and he noticed that the jammies she had put on before going to bed were hanging on the wardrobe door. She crawled on top of him and kissed his lips. "Jean, I thought we weren't..." She stopped his objection with another kiss.

"If we're going to die out here, Tony, won't God be pleased if we bring along another beautiful little soul?" she asked. "Why wait?"

≈

Jasmine stepped into the chapel confessional. She took a seat facing Fr. Scofield, who was a little surprised by her presence. She sensed his surprise and said, "I know I was to Confession this morning, Father, but I forgot to ask you something."

"Okay, Jasmine, what's on your heart?"

"Father, how does one go about becoming a Missionary of Charity?"

His delight with her question was written all over his face, and Jasmine, a little giddy about the whole idea, giggled quietly at his apparent joy. "Well, dear lady," he said, "I have in my possession a digital copy of every rule of order for every religious community that has ever existed. In short, I have all the information required *and* the authority to approve the establishment of religious orders, and as you can tell, I am delighted with your inquiry.

"However, I am a little surprised. I have been, for the last two years, providing spiritual counsel to a woman who wanted to be ready for matrimony when God sent the right man her way. This wouldn't by any chance be a means of escape for you, would it?"

"Escape? From what, Father?"

"From your past."

"Forgive me for saying so, Father, but you are my confessor and spiritual director; surely you know my soul better than that!"

"I'm sorry, my dear. You're right; I do, but as your bishop I am under obligation to ask such things."

"My dear Bishop Scofield, you prepared me perfectly for marriage. How were you to know that the man whom the Father would send to be my spouse would be his very own Son? What man can compete with him?"

"You can have both, you know. You can espouse Jesus directly *and* through another. Some will argue that is an even greater sacrifice to love him by proxy: to love perfection through imperfection."

"Perhaps, but...well...I'm already too spoiled for that!"

≈

Ironically, the newly engaged Dr. Lansing was seeing less and less of her fiancé and more and more of the captain. Often times she could think of no graceful way to get out of having dinner with Lamans, so she tried to throw Fr. Scofield into the mix as often as possible. She just couldn't think of enough good excuses.

As the weeks flew by and the voyage progressed, however, she didn't need much for excuses. She had a full slate and began working long days. They would soon reach their destination, and she was busy tracking everyone's vital signs and monitoring their exercise in preparation for any necessary rapid deceleration. She had taken to retiring as early as possible so she could rise in the middle of the night and spend time alone with Elon.

Fr. Scofield knew about their midnight rendezvous schedule and invited himself to the party one night with a gentle rap on Elon's door.

"Father!" Veronica exclaimed quietly as she opened the door. Elon sat on his bed in his robe, wearing shackles, as the captain had ordered.

"I'm sorry to come unannounced," Fr. Scofield apologized, "but I've been thinking about your upcoming wedding. Once we're on the planet's surface there's no telling what might happen. Perhaps you should wed before we arrive there."

"Father, you said you'd *never* give me another dispensation."

"I've changed my mind. You two belong together, but I can see that this wedding will need to be done in secret."

"*All* of my weddings are done in secret," Veronica mused.

"I haven't spoken to Tony about this matter yet, and I'm not so sure that he'll like the idea," Father said.

"Does he need to?" asked Veronica.

"If you want to get married in the chapel, he does. He has the keys to Elon's restraints. Also, to keep things proper, you should have witnesses for the ceremony."

The next day, at Veronica's request, Antonio and Jean went to meet with her in the chapel. "Before you tell us why you wanted to meet with us, we have something to tell you," Jean said.

Intuitive Veronica immediately grabbed the back of Jean's dress and pulled the front of the garment tight against the little woman's tummy. "Congratulations, you two!" she chirped, placing her healing hands on Jean's bulbous little middle. "Oh, this is so exciting!"

"Thank you," they both said, beaming.

"We're so happy!" Jean said. "We wanted you, Elon, and Jasmine to be the first to know."

"Now, what's on *your* mind?" Antonio asked. When she had explained her predicament and Fr. Scofield's suggestion, he said, "Let me get this straight. You want me to release Elon from his restraints so that you two can marry in secret in the middle of the night?"

"That sums it up pretty well," she answered, "except that I also want you and Jean to be there as witnesses."

"Well, let me see," Antonio pondered aloud, "Tessa Oakley is commander of this mission. She is able to give any command as long as it is not in direct defiance of the captain's orders, or contrary to the spirit of the mission. The captain said to keep Elon under restraints except for the four hours that he is confined to the garden. So...if Elon is handcuffed to an officer, like you, Veronica, that should fulfill the captain's orders, provided you can get Commander Oakley's blessing."

"Don't worry about Tessa, I'm heading to see her now!" she assured him.

"Just one thing, Ronnie," Antonio said, "We are rapidly approaching our destination, and the navigators have informed me that they may need to slam on the brakes. We may need to go to as high as three G's to keep from overshooting our target. You have little time to accomplish this wedding."

"Why don't you just do it during the day?" Jean asked. "Tell Lamans to take a hike! He can't tell you who to marry!"

"Actually, honey, we're in the military and a gazillion miles from Earth," Antonio told her. "He can pretty much do as he pleases and get away with it as long as there's not..." he leaned close and whispered, "a rebellion."

"I'll give him one!" Jean said boldly.

"Honey, just cool it!" Antonio said in a hush, gesturing with his hands for her to lower her voice. "Lamans can't undue a marriage once it's been done," he said. "He would make a lot of enemies within the command structure trying to do so. He's too politically savvy for that. Marrying in secret is the least messy route."

Two nights later, at Elon and Veronica's usual meeting time, the small ensemble huddled in the chapel. Veronica wore a white evening gown that she was sure Elon had never seen. Antonio wondered if it was the first wedding with a bride and groom handcuffed together. He winked at Jasmine, wondering if she was the first flower girl nine inches taller than the bride, and squeezed his wife, who proudly displayed her pregnancy via her first public appearance in maternity clothing. Scriptures were read and vows spoken between yawns. The bride and groom knelt and received communion.

Just as Fr. Scofield removed his keys from the tabernacle door, the ship's alarm system sounded. "All personnel report to their stations and prepare for rapid deceleration," the intercom bellowed. The bride and groom hovered for a moment, lost in each others eyes.

Antonio brought Elon to the brig, and Veronica helped him into a pressure suit and strapped him in for deceleration. As a commanding officer, she needed to get into uniform and head for the bridge.

"Rapid deceleration in fifteen minutes," the helmsman announced.

"Wow! Aren't you a little overdressed for rapid decel!" a voice from behind said as Veronica stepped into her quarters. It was the captain.

"Aw, this old thing? I've found that it makes for comfy jammies. I have Elon all suited and strapped in. See you on the bridge, Cliff." She wrestled into her uniform wondering if Lamans had bought her story.

After a grueling hour of deceleration, a fifteen-minute break was announced. Veronica rushed to the brig to check on Elon, and then to the infirmary to assist with any health issues that may have resulted. She helped Jean to contact every crew member, and then gave the captain the *all clear* for round two.

"Deceleration in five minutes," the helmsman announced.

"This should be a short one," the captain added.

Seventeen minutes later the gravity dropped to near zero, and the captain came on the intercom. "Break out the champagne, ladies and gentlemen! We have entered the Alpha Centauri system!" A volley of cheers resounded throughout the vessel. After a few minutes, Lamans said, "When you're done with the champagne, secure all objects. We will be in planetary orbit in approximately sixty-seven minutes."

Veronica's communicator buzzed. "Ronnie, the captain wants Elon on the bridge," Antonio informed her. "You have the key to his restraints. Do you have time to take him there?"

"Sure," she responded, closing the brig door and locking it. She uncuffed Elon and helped him out of the pressure suit. "Oh, no!" she said realizing that he was still in Antonio's dress uniform which had been borrowed for the wedding. "Good thing Lamans didn't see *you*! Let's get you changed."

She unbuttoned his shirt, exposing his exquisite chest. Putting her hands on his hips, she took advantage of the scant gravity to pick him up and kiss his chest over his heart. Then, swinging one arm under his knees, she held him as one would expect a groom to hold his bride as he carried her across the threshold. She tried to act as masculine as possible as she carried him to his bed and gently laid him down. Though she was having fun, it was a little disappointing that Elon seemed to have no appreciation of the humor suggested by the role reversal. *Maybe the bride carries the groom over the threshold on Freqmod—who knows?* she thought.

"I long to give myself to you," he said sweetly.

"I am yours. Soon you will know me completely, but I fear not today!" she lamented.

As Veronica came to the bridge, the captain remarked, "You look absolutely radiant this morning, my dear. How do you do that on four hours of sleep?"

"Must be the idea of escaping this prison," she answered.

"Elon, does this look familiar to you?" the captain asked, referring to a live picture of Freqmod up on the huge helm display.

"No, Captain. What is it?"

"It is your world, Elon. I'm hoping that you will be able to recommend a good place to land our shuttles." Noticing that Elon was handcuffed to Veronica, the captain asked, "By the way, Doctor, how did he become *your* charge?"

Antonio explained: "I had concerns about the effects of rapid decel on our garden decks, sir. Dr. Lansing had concerns about Elon, as he is not well trained in the use of a pressure suit."

"Very well. Please secure him in a chair. Elon, what happens to airplanes that attempt to fly over the Garden?"

"They disintegrate," Elon informed him.

"What about satellites?"

"There is only one. The Revotfellians put it up last year. It is able to go over the Garden and not be destroyed."

"Excellent!" the captain declared with relief in his voice. Veronica wondered what Lamans had been asking Elon in all of those sessions if he had not yet covered this very basic information.

"Commander, Joan's not responding to communication, and has ceased deceleration," Mr. Stokes advised Tessa. "She's headed strait for the planet, ma'am."

All watched in amazement as the image of the nearing planet gained clarity on the huge screen. "There she goes!" Stokes announced as Joan left a trail of fire in the pre-dawn sky over Aseeremma.

The early-rising Oilenroc knelt in his favorite prayer spot on the beach, praising God as he awaited the glory of daybreak. Joan interrupted his prayer as her burning mass tumbled through the atmosphere, culminating in a thunderous explosion above the Garden. *Shooting stars don't explode!* Oilenroc thought. *Lord...what sort of sign is this?*

"Captain, I am happy to report that Peter has entered a perfect geocentric orbit above Aseeremma," Tessa announced.

"Sir, we are ready to enter orbit," the helmsman said.

"Advise the crew, and proceed," the captain ordered.

"How about now, Elon? Anything look familiar to you?" Lamans asked, referring again to the image on the huge screen. Elon gazed intently at the image. "Where is the Garden Elon? Where is Ogeeremma? Here there is an extremely narrow sea," the captain said, pointing to the image with an interactive pointer. "On one side we see city lights: Ogeeremma? On the other, no lights: the Garden?"

"Oh yes. Yes! This is like the picture taken from the airplane!" Elon exclaimed at last. "Yes, that is the strait, and Ogeeremma, and the Garden, just as you said."

The captain, quite pleased with his own deduction, grinned from ear to ear and announced, "Short night or not, I'm not staying in this tin can another hour! After two years of salads and protein packs, and that government-issue, non-alcoholic, sad excuse for champagne we just had, I'm up for seeking out something real! Commander, surface scan report."

"Everything looks A-OK, sir," Tessa reported. "It is just before sunrise in Ogeeremma. Temperature is 20° C. The atmosphere appears to be just like Earth's, including industrial pollution. We should be right at home. There are no signs of war or other social unrest."

"Elon, where should we set down with our shuttles?" the captain asked.

Elon studied the image. "The biggest bunch of lights by the strait is Aseeremma, the capital city. The city is not built up along the strait where it is too shallow for ships, so there is just a long expanse of public beach. The only other thing out there is an old graveyard nestled into a rocky hollow. Between the graveyard and the sea would be a good place."

"Commander, I will travel to the surface with Team 1," the captain announced. "Assemble Team 2 and prepare to launch shuttle on my command. You mentioned earlier that you had detected Doppler type radar. They may have already detected our presence in orbit. At any rate, there's a good chance they will detect the shuttles, as Aseeremma has an airport. Have your craft armed to vaporize anything that they throw at you, but I don't want to harm them in any way."

"Yes, sir," Tessa acknowledged.

"On successful touchdown, contact me before ordering Tony and Team 3 to embark. We're all dying to get off this thing, but I don't want that death to be literal."

Team 1 flew their craft to the landing site without incident. The spot proved a good choice except for surface dust stirred by the auxiliary landing thrusters. This dust cloud would have remained unnoticed were it not for Elon's friends who were out for their morning walk with the orphans. As usual, their morning preaching and teaching had attracted a small crowd, most of them prophets of the One, who were open to their message. Among them were Oilenroc and Airrellav.

Aniram had become enough of an Ogeeremman to know that the strange craft which hovered behind the graveyard was not one of theirs. The small crowd made its way toward the craft, stopping just short of the graveyard that lay between. In a minute, the feet of the craft settled into the soft coastal sand, and the dust cloud subsided.

As the shuttle craft door opened, an eerie morning mist hovered yet in the craggy hollows of the graveyard, and catching the red rays of the morning sun, it gave Team 1 a surreal first glimpse of their new world. A quick scan had detected no weapons or other threats within the immediate area, and no alarming microbial signatures. The helmsman and team leader would remain in the craft to monitor defense systems and the progress of the other shuttle craft. The team leader would monitor, from the shuttle, the progress of the environmental team, which immediately set about testing the soil, air, and sea water. The captain headed up the engagement team, whose mission was to establish friendly relations with the occupants of Ogeeremma. The team consisted of himself, Dr. Lansing, Ensign Babasa, Fr. Scofield, Elon, and Mr. Schmidt, the gardener in charge of Elon.

The company of the seventeen made their way through the cemetery. Behind them, in the shadows and bushes, lurked the possessed man whose demon had resisted Elon's command. The man had become so defiled that he appeared animated solely by the power of evil. On the far end of the graveyard, eye met eye and Aniram recognized the now beardless Elon. She ran to him, threw her arms around him, and kissed his lips.

"Where have you been, king of my heart? We thought you had gone into glory, and now here you are among strangers. Why have they taken you prisoner?"

Before he could answer, the demon of the possessed man had also recognized him. Stepping out of the morning mist he shouted, "Garden Variety!" and hurled a stone as he shouted, "Are you back for more?" The stone struck Elon in the face and a small stream of blood began to trickle down his cheek. Suddenly panic stricken, the possessed man shrieked, "He bleeds!" and began to flee.

Elon felt the hand of the archbishop on his shoulder, heard him reciting an apostolic blessing, and felt the power of the Spirit come upon him. He raised his hand in the direction of the fleeing man and shouted, "Unclean spirit, in the name of Jesus the Christ, son of Eve and Son of the Living God, I command you to come out of the man!"

The poor creature twisted and contorted as the demon took his leave. All were amazed. None had ever witnessed such a thing, including the captain. Power of any kind always grabbed his attention. While he did not believe in demonic possession, if Elon was able to instantly heal what Lamans considered to be insanity, the anthropologist was still interested in the power that enabled it. Never one to miss an opportunity, he stepped forward and addressed the gathering.

"We have come to free you from such bondage. Take us to your king, that we may help your whole nation!"

Oilenroc came forward, and bowing low before the captain, said, "My lord, I am a personal friend of the king, and I can take you to him, but before I do, I must inquire: why is it that you have the great prophet Elon in chains?"

Lamans' poker-face demeanor complemented his slick knack for reinventing reality. "When your lord Elon first came upon our vessel, we knew not from where he had come, and he wore the garments of our enemy. Now, of course, we are certain of his holy mission," and he commanded, "Unbind the great prophet at once!"

Seeing Elon freed, Oilenroc declared, "My lord, I will be glad to take you to the king!"

A few minutes later, as they approached the vehicle that would take them to the king, the captain stepped away from the others to confer with Tessa on his communicator. "Commander, where are you and Team 2?"

"We're about a kilometer directly above you, Captain."

"Great! We're just about to climb into something that looks like a stretched-out 1930s roadster on steroids, with a raggedy old guy who's a friend of Elon's. We're going to see the king. The old guy says that he and the king are close personal friends—go figure. Anyway, I want you to go to hover and follow us in at a hundred meters up or so, high enough for safety, but not so high that they won't get a good eyeful. Hold off Team 3 until this visit is done."

"Yes sir. We're on it."

"And, Tess...I don't want to start anything, but I also don't want to die. I leave all to your incomparable discretion."

"Thank you, sir. We'll keep our eyes peeled."

The seven of them piled into Oilenroc's jalopy. The captain's eyes bulged when Veronica made more room by jumping onto Elon's lap. Lamans looked away when their eyes met, but his jealousy did not escape her.

As Oilenroc drove them into the city, the Earthlings became enchanted by the grand art deco motif that crowned life in Aseeremma. In autos, architecture, clothing, and everything else, style and beauty were first priorities for those who could afford to choose the best.

King Einniv III slammed his fist down on the table. "The Gardeners are the best thing that's happened to Ogeeremma in ages," he said to a room filled with leading members of Parliament. "They are the first to break the vicious cycle: Our people get hooked on drugs; their families disintegrate; children are left in the streets; they sell drugs to stay alive; they become prostitutes, or are sold, like livestock, to wealthy Revotfellians. It is a system that will last forever as long as we keep supplying victims.

"The Gardeners are reclaiming the victims, saving lives and mending hearts, but now we have people trying to pass legislation to keep them out, claiming that they're breaking the law by not filling out the proper paperwork, and that they're ignoring the courts. It's all hogwash. I don't think the children of this nation should continue to eat out of trash cans and sleep in alleyways just because our laws stink! If Parliament won't lighten up on this, I will make a proclamation. Are you ready to deal with that?!"

The king was a big, robust man with red cheeks, huge shoulders, a bit of a tummy, and fists the size of two-quart jars. His heart was sensitive but brave, and he lived life passionately. On this day, his burly, curly red beard seemed to bristle even more with his anger. For too long Ogeeremma's legalistic attitudes had strangled progress. He wanted to be a part of it no more. By Ogeeremman law, if a king made a proclamation, the proclamation stood unless the king received a two-thirds majority vote of no confidence from the general populace: To get rid of the proclamation, they had to rid themselves of the king. In such a case, if no heir to the throne was of legal age, the majority leader of Parliament was to take the throne until an heir came of age— a vote of no confidence was permanent. Only three such proclamations had ever been made, and no king had ever been voted out. The threat of proclamation was the king's trump card. Parliament would find a soft approach to placate the judiciary.

"Your Highness," the majority leader said after an awkward silence, "we will see what we can do to streamline the system. Rest assured that our friends from across the strait will not be hampered in their labors."

"I cannot believe that those of you in this room are so naïve as to believe that no one in Parliament or the judiciary profits from all of this street trade," the king went on. "I have failed the people of Ogeeremma. I have been too lax with law enforcement. It is an error I shall correct."

Several people in the room shifted uneasily in their seats, which came as no surprise to the king. He had become familiar with the evil alliances, but had decided that he would no longer live in fear. He knew that this decision could very well bring him to an untimely death, a price he was now willing to pay. Vast fortunes were made on vice within the kingdom. It was a social condition Einniv had inherited from his father, Aniretac VII. The old alliances were all intact and did not rely on Einniv in any way other than for him to look the other way. In the five years of his rule, there had been no wars, no uprisings, and no demonstrations, but it was an unholy peace, a peace with many casualties.

Einniv, through the recent influence of his childhood friend, Oilenroc, had become a disciple of the One and no longer saw things with the jaded view that was his inheritance. However, Ogeeremma remained a jaded kingdom. For centuries they had followed the old ways, worshiping the One True God, offering the best of what he had given them back to him and singing his praises throughout the day. In fact, the kingdom was known throughout all of Exile for its wonderful songs and music. Then the great prophets had come predicting that one day a Great One would come among them to wipe from their hearts their evil inclinations and to save them from the ravages of death. It was commonly thought that this Great One would come from among the Gardeners, and now those from the Garden who visited Ogeeremma had to constantly deny that adulation of Ogeeremmans that would place them upon a pedestal.

But there are always those who do not want to have a better world, those who believe that their own wealth and health is God's blessing on them for being better and more deserving than their fellows. Adherents to this mindset had organized a religion, calling themselves The Heirs. They ignored the writings of the great prophets of old. They did not believe in works of charity. They believed that if one lived by the ancient laws of worship and stewardship, God would provide abundance and health. Therefore, if God had not provided abundance or health to people and one was to share his abundance with them or nurse them to health, one would be robbing them of an opportunity to align their lives with the ancient teachings, thus robbing them of an opportunity to gain God's favor. In fact, according to this perversion, helping someone in need could actually bring the helper into God's disfavor.

In stark contrast to the Heirs, those who followed the prophets of old had come to be known simply as the Prophets. They awaited the coming of the Great One predicted in the scriptures. The Great One would come from a far away land, and would bring unity of heart to all believers in the true God. By the power of God he would free humankind of its slavery to the basest of passions. It was among the Prophets that the cult of the One had sprung up: the One who is like us in all things but sin, the One who would point the way to the Great One of God.

But there was a third major religion whose malignant growth had come with modern times and mass communication. It was a religion that borrowed from everyone and stood for nothing. Like The Heirs, followers of this new faith believed that wealth and health are deserved and should not be shared, and like the Prophets, they believed that a Great One would come. However, these people, who called themselves Unifists, did not look for a Great One who would heal them of their lust, but one who would unite the planet into a great kingdom. Under this Chosen One's rule, God would return the entire planet to its garden state. Only those who followed the ancient law, and whose worship was ordained by God through the signs of health and wealth, would survive the Unification. They alone would gain immortality in the plenty of the Garden.

This philosophy allowed the Unifists to sell illicit drugs, but not to use them, for to place sinful choices before one's fellows was to offer them yet another opportunity to conform to God's ancient law, thus to qualify themselves for the great unification. Unifists could act as pimps, so long as they did not partake of the prostitutes themselves. They were forbidden to steal, but free to buy stolen goods.

Rejecting the prophets, they had rejected 1,200 years of spiritual reflection on the law, allowing the text to be stretched to suit their perversions. On the subject of slavery, they had stretched it beyond recognition.

In ancient times, slaves were often acquired as prisoners of war. Winning a war was seen as a sign from God, and imposing ten years of enslavement seemed just retribution against those who had chosen to war against God's people. The ancient law had allowed the selling of slaves, but not the buying, and believers could not enslave a person for more than ten years. For 1,200 years prophets and apologist alike had proffered an understanding of the law that tended toward abolition.

However, the Unifists had no theology. All they had was the law: the cold, callous, merciless law. All they knew or cared to know about slavery was that, though they could not buy or own them (owning slaves was forbidden by Ogceremman law), they could sell them. The ancient law did not regulate the acquisition of slaves other than through purchase. Thus, the Unifist reading of the law allowed them to gather homeless children from the streets of Aseeremma and sell them into slavery. After all, these children were penniless—obviously their worship was unacceptable. They were clearly not destined for the immortality of the Unification.

In short, every time someone else sinned, even if that someone else was invited into sin by a Unifist, it was God's way of showing that the Unifists were indeed blessed and chosen for immortality.

The king had watched the growth of this mongrel religion with great dismay. It was the Unifists around the table who squirmed in their seats. He knew that some were not even true to their own sick creed, as many were victims of their own sex and drug trade. They lived a lie: Wealth, not the ancient laws, had become their *only* measuring stick. Though all of these manifestations of their religious machinations were against Ogeeremman civil law, there were many Unifists in high places, making prosecution difficult. They would not think twice about having a zealous king murdered. While it was against God's ancient law to kill, it was righteous to *hire* a killer; after all, hit men need opportunities for self-improvement.

As the king's meeting came to a close, a messenger entered the room. "Your Majesty, I beg your pardon for my intrusion, but I was told by the captain of the guard to inform you that an audience is sought with you by visitors from...outer space!"

Laughter broke out all around the table. Everyone laughed but the king, whose expression seemed to indicate that he was expecting such a visit. The messenger motioned them to the window and pointed to the shuttle hovering overhead. Amid the gasps of the onlookers, he then pointed to the group of men and women below in the street. "Why, they look no different than us!" came the comments. The king recognized his old friends Oilenroc and Airrellav among the visitors and sent word to have all of them brought to him immediately.

They were quickly escorted to a parlor to meet with the king and all of the legislators who were in the previous meeting. An awkward moment ensued as they first entered the room; visitors from outer space were not an everyday occurrence. Finally the king spoke.

"Welcome to Ogeeremma. I am King Einniv and these gentlemen are members of our parliament."

"Thank you, your majesty. I am Captain Cliff Lamans of the star cruiser Star Covenant, from the planet Earth. This is our Chief Medical Officer, Dr. Veronica Lansing; Mental Health Officer and Principal Chaplain, Fr. Ian Scofield; Security Agent, Jasmine Babasa; and Lead Gardener, Mr. Will Schmidt. Of course, I am told that you know our hosts, Oilenroc and Airrellav, but I am unsure if you have met the illustrious Mr. Elon."

The king's mouth dropped open. "I have heard of Elon," he said. "He is the stuff of legends, but the legends say that he had gone into glory! I certainly want to welcome all of you to our world. But, of course, we have many questions. I must know, Captain, how is it that you all speak perfect Ogeeremman?"

"Elon came onto our vessel shortly before we had traveled half of the way here, almost three years ago for you, a little over a year ago by our time. It was Elon, assisted by your television and radio broadcasts, who taught us your language."

"I don't understand…are years longer on your world?" the king asked.

"Time slows down for those traveling at nearly the speed of light," Lamans instructed.

The king's eyes grew wide. He looked about with a drop-jawed smile of delight and wonder before asking, "How did Elon board a ship that was traveling so fast?"

"Ah…I suggest that you ask Elon about that when you have plenty of time to listen," Lamans advised.

The captain went on to explain about the discovery of Freqmod's radio waves, about Jacob Lansing's work building the foundation for the voyage, and all of those things leading up to the adventure. He read for them the mission statement, which outlined all of the scientific, humanitarian, and spiritual reasons for embarking on such a voyage, and emphasized the peaceful intentions of all those on Earth. "In short," he concluded, "our goal is to learn from each other, for the betterment of both worlds."

The king rose and said, "I'm not sure that we have much to teach, but I am very interested in the things that we can learn from you. Many of our prophets, like my good friend Oilenroc, have prophesied about the salvation wrought by the Word of God made flesh, once and for all, for the entire universe. It is said that his gifts will come to us through the church he established in a far away land. Could that far away land be your world?"

Elon rose to answer. "Yes, your Highness. These sons and daughters of Adam and Eve, by virtue of Baptism into the faith they hold and keep, dispense that grace which can defeat the Exaggerator!" Bishop Scofield beamed at the performance of his catechism student.

The king asked, in a most humble voice, "How may we go about receiving this…'grace'?"

Bishop Scofield was filled with joy at the opportunity before him. "Your Highness, first allow us to visit your sick, your possessed," he told him. "Let the people see the power that God has to heal their flesh, that they might desire spiritual healing as well. Then, at the proper time, when the Spirit has stirred hearts, we will teach with the Word, and those who wish to make of their lives a sacrifice may be baptized."

"A…sacrifice?" the king asked, bewildered as to the meaning.

"You will understand," Elon assured him.

The meeting disintegrated into a number of side conversations, allowing everyone to get acquainted, and closed with Einniv pledging his protection for the visitors. Captain Lamans explained that an environmental team was already deployed, for they needed to know the health risks associated with their new home, and that, with the king's permission, he would deploy a humanitarian team, led by Ensign Babasa, to assess the country's needs. The king immediately approved the deployment of the humanitarian team and sent guards to accompany them wherever they would go. Supplying them with armed guards also allowed the king to keep track of them, an understandable move. The captain offered the king and his colleagues a tour of the shuttle craft, which had since set down in a square near the palace. Their hosts were fascinated with the vessel.

"You call it a shuttle…apparently this vessel only carries you to a much larger ship," speculated Senga Namreg, parliament's minority leader.

"That is correct, sir," answered the captain. "Our star cruiser is a huge ship with an onboard garden large enough to support fifty people indefinitely. It is a totally self-contained city."

Lamans took the king up into the cockpit area to show the controls and the weapons system to him, explaining that a DNA scan was required to activate the weapons or to fly the craft.

"Are there also weapons on the star cruiser?" the king asked.

"Enough to blow up your entire planet!" the captain lied, hoping to give the king a healthy fear of offending his guests.

"If your mission is peaceful, why do you need so many weapons?"

"I keep a gun by my bed. I've never used it, and hope that I will never need to, but I still will keep it by my bed," the captain informed him.

Einniv did not look impressed. "I don't keep a gun by my bed," he said. "The Lord is my protection. If I am killed, it will be his will."

Chapter 15

Pentecost

"Elon talks nonstop about his beloved orphans," Jean said to Jasmine and the rest of the humanitarian team. She turned and looked up at Jasmine, who was standing right behind her. "If memory serves me, they were located somewhere near the sea."

Jasmine pulled a slender pair of binoculars from her pocket and focused them beyond the graveyard. "Jean! I see children!" she said, lowering the binocs down to her friend.

While the captain, Chief Oakley, and Mr. Schmidt led a tour of the shuttle, Elon, Veronica, and Bishop Scofield, accompanied by Oilenroc and Airrellav, toured the orphanages. They smiled from ear to ear when, on their arrival, they found Jazz and Jean engulfed in tikes. Many hugs, kisses, and congratulations were shared as Elon introduced his mate to the seventeen. Aniram's joy over his happiness did not totally hide her own disappointment. Sensing her pain, and remembering the tender kiss she had given Elon by the graveyard, Veronica took her aside.

"You and Elon are very close, aren't you?" she asked.

"Elon and I have been best friends for as long as I can remember," Aniram informed her. "He is older than I. As a child I used to ride upon his shoulders and pick fruit and feed it to him." Her eyes glowed with the memories. "He would go all about the Garden with me on his back, visiting all of his friends. He taught me to love and trust the Father and the One. As I grew to womanhood, I prayed that God would grant us the gift of passion and Elon would become my mate, but it was not to be. I guess he shall remain forever my big brother."

Veronica smiled, warmed in the glow of Aniram's transparent innocence. "So how many years have you known him?" she asked.

"Oh...ever since I was an infant. I am seventy-eight."

Suddenly Veronica felt very silly. In all of their conversations she had never once asked Elon his age. "How old was he when you were born?"

"Let's see...forty? Yeah, forty, because he is 118 now."

Veronica just smiled to herself and shook her head. *You and older men!* she thought.

"How old are you, Veronica?" Aniram asked, taking her hand.

"Thirty-two."

"Oh! You're so young!" she exclaimed. "I feel as though you are my little sister."

"I would be honored to be your little sister," Veronica assured her.

Aniram turned and looked at Elon, who was now smothered in children. There had come to be so few children in the Garden, and the lack of them had been the most difficult thing about his year on the starship. He had always drawn children to himself like little bears to honey.

Aniram giggled at the sight of them and squeezed her "sister's" hand. "Soon I will be an aunt!" she proclaimed.

"Oh, honey, I hope so. But first I have to get him alone somewhere!" Veronica lamented.

The children, especially the little girls, began to take notice of Veronica and were pulling at her hands and crawling up onto her lap. They succeeded in pulling her into a game that Elon had started; however, just as her turn came, the cooks sent them outdoors to play so that the older children could ready the dining room for lunch.

The small children dutifully trudged outside, but before Elon could follow them out, Veronica grabbed him from behind and pushed the door shut. "I am a bride who will remain childless if we are never to be alone!" she insisted. "Are there beds in this facility?" Outside, the children suddenly realized that Veronica was not with them, and she could hear them saying, "Where is she? It's her turn." Upon hearing them, she sighed, "I guess now is not the time."

"Tonight it will truly be 'your turn!'" he promised.

They spent the afternoon playing and praying and catching up with Elon's friends on the activities of the three years since he had left them. From that brief time together Veronica already felt as though she had known these people her entire life, especially Aniram, who instantly had become the big sister she never had.

By the edge of the playground, Elon noticed a beautiful woman accompanied by four young men. She looked familiar to him, but he was unsure why. Finally their eyes met and she came running to him, threw her arms around his neck, and kissed his cheek.

"I didn't recognize you at first without your beard and grass and leaves," she laughed, "but then I saw your eyes."

Elon never forgot a pair of eyes or a voice, especially not a voice this lovely. "Sunil! Look at you!" he said. "Where is the little girl I knew?" he asked, for she was no longer the pert little fifteen-year-old who had tutored him in the proper use of a microphone. "Will you sing for us?" Elon asked.

Her smile displayed her pleasure at being asked, and she and her brothers began to sing a song she had written about Elon. The last verse spoke specifically about his going into glory. Their angelic five part harmony was no longer the stuff of garage bands.

"It's obvious that I will need to add verses now that you have returned," Sunil noted when they were done.

"I am very honored, Ṣunil, but I would rather that you sing the Creator's praises than mine."

"It is your *life* that sings the Creator's praises, Elon. To praise a holy life is to praise God."

"But my life's journey is not complete," he objected. "I am still a pilgrim, and you must be careful not to tempt my pride."

"But...you're sinless," Sunil pointed out.

"No, I am not," he insisted. "My praise is imperfect, and my response to the Spirit is too often procrastinated. The One is the only creature whose praise was flawless, whose response was perfect. Yet, while still a pilgrim she steadfastly refused to be the object of praise. You may sing my praises when glory seals my fate."

Their little exchange was interrupted when the palace guards, who had accompanied them throughout the day, informed Elon and Veronica that the king would be very pleased if they would join him for dinner, and that they would need to leave now if they wanted to freshen up and make it on time.

Jasmine was glad that she had not been invited. God willing, her guard would allow her to spend the night in the orphanage. She sent off the bride and groom with a prayer. They said goodbye, promising to return soon, and walked away slowly until the last tugging urchin was removed from their legs. Jasmine turned to see Jean in the midst of the orphans, some of whom were taller than she. "You better be careful, little Jean, or somebody will adopt you!" she kidded.

Jean just laughed and said, "Hopefully, it'll be Tony!"

The palace guards escorted Elon and Veronica to guest rooms the king had ordered prepared for them. Because their marriage was unannounced, they were given separate rooms. The king, marvelous host that he was, had taken the liberty to have his tailor eye up his guests before they left for their tours that afternoon. The talented tailor had found for each of them perfectly fitting dinner attire to suit the times and the occasion. Veronica looked at the extravagant dress laid out for her on the bed and imagined Elon's eyes upon seeing her. She also wondered what they had found for him. She finally figured out the strange bathroom hardware and stepped into a steaming shower, a welcome break from those rationed, pitiful excuses for showers that were on Covenant.

She smoothed the sides of the black satin dress and stepped into the hallway. Elon was already waiting in his tux. "Were you able to figure out the shower, honey?" she asked.

"The king came and showed me how."

"Einniv himself came in to help you?"

"Well, it seems that I am somewhat a hero to him. He said that Ogeeremma is forever indebted to me."

"You're a hero to me too, honey, and you look absolutely fabulous in a tux! Do you like my dress?"

"I guess," he said, but then saw the disappointment in her eyes. "You make the dress look very nice, my love. It's just that, well…you know, I really don't like clothing."

"I'll see what I can do about that," she cooed.

The guards escorted them to a huge dining hall filled with dignitaries. The captain was already there and appeared to be the life of the party. This was a side of him they'd not seen before: Lamans, the schmoozer. His ability to recreate himself to fit the occasion was nothing less than astounding. The man who faced life alone and talked out loud to himself was now surrounded by diplomats, governors, mayors, and legislators, all trying to ingratiate themselves with this one who seemed to know something about everything. He was loud, but gracious, and just bawdy enough to still be considered a gentleman.

At the sight of Veronica in a stunning black satin dress, the captain excused himself from his fan club and came to grovel before her. Taking her hand he bowed low and kissed it. "If I should die tonight," he slathered, "my life will not be loss, for I have lived to see you in this dress!"

"Thank you, Captain," she managed.

Einniv stepped in from behind the captain, and mimicking the Earth etiquette Lamans had displayed, kissed her hand as well. "Doctor, I pray that you find the attire to your liking," he said.

"Oh, yes, Your Highness, it is exquisite! How thoughtful of you to have all of this prepared for us. We are in your debt."

"I would be in *your* debt if you would allow me to call you by your first name, Veronica. It is such a beautiful name."

"I would be delighted, Your Highness."

"Now, that won't do! Please...call me Einniv." Then, wearing an artificial frown, he shook his finger at those around him and said, "But don't any of you guys try it!"

The king ate dinner seated at a round table with the five interplanetary guests, the majority and minority leaders of parliament, and the mayor of Aseeremma. He also ordered food to be taken to Covenant's working crews, who were ecstatic over meat and seafood after two years of eating out of a flying garden.

When the lengthy dinner party had at last begun to fizzle, and when the bride and groom saw that the captain had once again made himself the center of attention, they bade the king a good night and went (escorted by their personal guards) to the rooms the monarch had provided.

On the way, the joy within them grew as they recalled that their rooms were adjoining. The only thing separating them was a balcony rail. As soon as she had closed her door, Veronica headed immediately to the balcony door, and climbing over the railing, went to the balcony entrance of Elon's room. Elon opened the door, swept her off of her feet, and carried her to the bed.

"This is the way it's supposed to be, right?" he asked. She gave him a puzzled look, but then realized that he was referring to her foolery on the cruiser, when, aided by seriously reduced gravity, she had carried him about in a similar manner.

"The way you had reacted, I didn't think you appreciated my attempt at humor," she answered.

"How was I to know if this was not just one more thing that really was backward in your culture?" he asked, as he gently placed her on the bed.

The patio door had been left open, and the wonderful smell of the night air filled the room. Their rooms were on the backside of the palace with balconies that opened to the fragrant royal garden. They were just in time for Veronica's first experience with a dual star system. Alpha Centauri B was just rising above the garden. It was smaller, orange, and much farther away than Alpha Centauri A, but its light was brighter than Earth's moon. It bathed the room and the lovers with an orange glow that lit up their loving eyes.

"Alpha Centauri B," she said matter-of-factly, pointing to the star. "It's very beautiful."

"It is called the *oola lana*, in Ogeeremman," he told her, "which means *the love light*. For me, its beauty lies in its ability to shed light on you. You are *my* love light."

As they completed the tender task of removing each other's clothing, the bride sensed a certain hesitance in her sweet man.

"What is it, my love?" she asked.

"Love making is for outdoors, close to nature, close to God," he insisted.

His playful mate sprang from the bed, grabbed the cushions from the suite's couch, and placing them on the balcony, lay down on them and motioned for her husband to join her. Though they were on third floor and a long way from the vegetation, outdoors is outdoors.

As they embraced in the fresh air, there came a knocking at her door. When there was no response, someone called her name. Veronica wondered if she had locked her door. The knocking resumed, and with no response, resumed yet again. In a moment, the door opened and a man entered. When he had switched on the light, they could see that it was the captain. As some of the light fell onto the balcony, they swiftly rolled into the shadows. The captain called Veronica's name twice more while briefly snooping about the room. Two palace guards remained at the door, appearing as though they were not sure what to make of his behavior or of the fact that Veronica was not in the room. "I thought you were guarding her?" she heard the captain complain.

In a bit, he was knocking on Elon's door.

"What will we do?" Elon whispered.

"I bolted your door. The guards will not allow him to break it down," she assured him. When there was no response, Lamans tried the door. "Who does he think he is?" Veronica asked.

"He thinks he's your man. He must be told that you are mine."

"I'm afraid of what his reaction will be," she said.

Elon and Veronica woke to a glorious sunny morning in Ogeeremma. Though intimate encounter had claimed much of the night, they felt miraculously well rested. Interestingly, most of the exiled world was on a seven-day week with a two-day weekend. This morning fell on the second day of a weekend, and Archbishop Scofield had declared it to be Sunday.

Elon rose from his bed, stooped and kissed his beautiful wife's closed eyes, and intoxicated with the freedom of their love, strode stark naked out onto the balcony. There he stretched and yawned in the brisk morning air. His bride could scarcely believe her eyes when she finally opened them.

"Hey, nature boy, this isn't the Garden! Get those beautiful buns in here!" she called.

Elon said, "I'm sorry," with a sheepish grin on his face, and quickly came inside.

"Don't apologize to *me*," Veronica giggled, "I'm not the one who has a problem with this, but I'm sure others in Aseeremma might!"

Within the hour they had gathered with the rest of the crew in an area encircled by the three shuttles, next to the sea. They were joined by the staff and children of the orphanages. Bishop Scofield arrived, escorted by the king, who wanted to see what Sunday Mass was all about. This particular Sunday Mass was to be a bit extraordinary. With Bishops Scofield and Hadrian concelebrating outdoors, it would be the first Mass said on the planet, and a sort of Pentecost for the crew. During the prayers of the faithful, Bishop Scofield called upon the Spirit to descend upon all and strengthen them for the work of the day. Upon his words a brisk wind tousled skirts, scarves, vestments, and neckties before dying down again.

After Mass, all enjoyed a breakfast catered on the beach. As they sat on beach blankets enjoying the feast, Jean remarked, "This is delicious. This king is going to spoil us."

"He's very generous," Jasmine agreed.

"And a bit unorthodox," Antonio added.

"A bit?" Veronica asked, nodding her head toward the activity that was out of Antonio's field of vision.

The king had just declared, "It's getting hot out here," and was in the process of removing his royal red suit. When he had stripped to a pair of swim trunks, he pointed toward four chests filled with swimming attire. "My tailor tells me that there should be a suit in there to fit each of you," he declared, and shouting, "Man overboard!" charged into the sea.

The captain stood and declared to the crew, "When in Rome..." and quickly went to pick out a swimsuit for himself. In a few minutes the entire crew, bishops and all, had taken to the water. Elon laughed as the mountain of a man they called their king became a human diving board for the ladies. He would crouch low in the water, so they could place their feet in his hands, and then hurl them over his back. Veronica laughed at herself as she got in line for this entertainment, and looking over her shoulder, saw that her husband was equally amused. When Einniv flung her 104 pound frame, it seemed for a moment that she would end up on the other side of the strait!

Refreshed from their brunch and their swim, and back into their clothing, the king addressed them all. "God has given me a great deal for which to be thankful. But indeed, there are many within Ogeeremma who are not so fortunate. I have gained, in this last week, all of you wonderful friends from another world, but I cannot keep you for myself." His expression now became troubled. "There is much sin and sadness in my kingdom. Our wonderful friends, the Gardeners, have come to help alleviate the damage the Exaggerator has done. But now," and his countenance brightened, "now I am told that salvation has come to our world; that the power to defeat the Exaggerator lies within the sacraments you bring. I want to partake, and I want my kingdom to partake, but we must be readied. Bishop Scofield tells me that, through your prayers, the Spirit will ready our hearts. I felt the Spirit warm my heart as I prayed through the night, and our Heavenly Father renewed my body in the sea as I prayed for each precious soul I cast over my shoulder. But now, dear bishops, dear believers, I am but a poor child, lucid and ready for training. Show me the way."

The captain wondered how these priests had become bishops. *How long must he to suffer this continual annoyance of being the last to know?* he wondered—a position so offensive to one who considered himself to be street-smart.

The entire crew, except for the captain and those on shuttle guard duty, set about following Einniv, Oilenroc, and Airrellav on a tour of the city. "I could take you to see all of our beautiful buildings," Einniv said to the assembled column, "to all of those monuments to human ingenuity of which we may rightly be proud. But I am not feeling proud at this moment. Instead, I will give you a challenge. I will take you to see our dark side. You will know of our great spiritual need. I pray that the Spirit will enkindle an appropriate and proportionate response." Then he said to the royal guards, "You may leave us."

"Sire?" the captain of the guard addressed him with raised eyebrows.

"The Spirit will be our protection on this holy mission, Captain. If you wish to join us, remove your coats and weapons and come as servants," the king insisted.

The group set out immediately for the city's worst ghettos. Huddled between the industrial parks and the rail yards, the disenfranchised lived gray lives in stacked hovels. Their existence begged for redemption.

As the troop walked, the Gardeners in their midst began to sing songs of praise. As with every utterance of a Gardener, all within earshot who listened with their hearts were able to hear in their own language. Their singing proved to be a wonderful introduction as these pilgrims entered the divided city with its Addanacian, Revotfellian, and Eknarfian towns, wherein little to no Ogeeremman was spoken.

In a small square, Elon jumped up onto the concrete base of a flag pole and addressed the crowd that was gathering, for word had gotten out that the king of Ogeeremma was wandering about the city unguarded, and everyone wanted to see if it was true.

"My dear people," Elon addressed them. "Perhaps you have come to see your king who has humbled himself to come into your midst, but we have come today to announce another king—a king far greater than Einniv—who has come into your midst: a King of Kings who will give sight to the blind, hearing to the deaf, and healing to all flesh. Bring us your sick, bring us your dying, that the glory of the new king may be revealed."

Soon the sidewalks were jammed with people in wheel chairs and people on crutches. Blind people were led into the sunshine, and people with every type of illness imaginable were brought into the street. Then, one by one, Elon and the bishops laid hands on them and prayed, and all who were within their party prayed, and those brought forth who had even the slightest faith were healed completely and marched about praising God.

In this manner they made their way through the ghettos and back toward the shuttle craft, until a great throng had assembled behind them. They paraded through a suburb where middle class people played on lawns and in parks, enjoying the beautiful sunny day. Many of these also followed the king and his entourage. Suspecting that this little parade had something to do with the space travelers, they hoped to learn more about them.

The large crowd gathered in the area encircled by the shuttle craft, and those on guard duty became very busy trying to keep kids from climbing on the crafts. Elon, the bishops, the king, and the captain entered Shuttle 1 and emerged from a portal in the top of the craft. They stood upon the shuttle like a stage from which to address the people. The king held up his hands to silence the crowd, and then spoke through a microphone which the captain offered him.

"Today is a new beginning for Ogeeremma and for our world. We have among us men and women from another world and from the Garden, men and women filled with the Holy Spirit of God. Today, I walked with them about the city, watching them heal the sick and cast out demons in the name of their king, Jesus, the King of Heaven. They are on fire. Open your hearts to them." He went to hand the mike to Bishop Scofield, but it was intercepted by the captain.

Lamans seized the opportunity to charm the crowd. He promised them a better world, better because of the improved technology that Earth men would bring to them. His was the wrong message for the wrong crowd at the wrong time. He had not gone with them on the walk through the ghettos. He was oblivious to the Spirit. He could not charm his way into this league. No one was impressed. No one cheered or applauded. He had difficulty hiding his exasperation as he handed the mike to Bishop Scofield.

The holy apostle began to preach. He nearly glowed with the Spirit. He spoke of the oneness of the two worlds, identical in flesh and in spirit, with one and the same Creator. On this occasion, that oneness was amplified by that charism of the Garden which Elon always enjoyed, the charism of tongues. All who listened with their hearts heard the bishop in their own language.

He explained that all on Earth are Exiles; therefore, the Father had chosen to bring salvation there first. He spoke of the holy prophets of Ogeeremma and of the Garden, telling how they had desired to heal the broken, but lacked the power to bring the Savior to all who would hear. He spoke of Elon's miraculous journey to their spacecraft, and how, though sinless himself, the great prophet had adopted the salvation of Christ that he might bring others to glory.

As he went to hand the mike to Elon, he was struck by the profuse bleeding of the Gardener's hands. He shut the mike off for a moment and asked, "Are you alright, my friend? You are bleeding much worse than usual."

"Father, I have never felt finer!" Elon responded joyfully. The bishop wiped his friend's bloody hands with a clean kerchief before handing him the mike.

Elon praised Bishops Scofield and Hadrian for their love, devotion, and leadership. He praised the "most beautiful Dr. Veronica Lansing" for her love and guidance, and gave great thanks to the friends he had made among the prophets of Ogeeremma and the crew of Star Covenant.

Then he began to extol the Savior. He explained how his life was now filled with the incredible joy of doing the will of the Father. He held the crowd in a hush as he witnessed to his own faith journey, from his reluctance to enter Exile or address his peers, to the Spirit giving him the courage to address large assemblies; from his failure to praise God adequately for the Garden's pleasures, to praising him for the opportunity to suffer for the love of others. He told of their walk through the city, of the many wondrous cures that had been obtained in the name of the Savior, and how those who were cured had followed them to this place. Then he handed the microphone to Bishop Hadrian.

Bishop David Hadrian was not a man of many words, but he was a man of deep prayer. He led all now in a prayer from the heart, a joyous prayer of thanksgiving to the Holy Spirit, and a fervent plea for The Spirit to continue fueling the faith of this new church. Tessa Oakley beamed as she gave Veronica a squeeze. "Isn't this wonderful!" she asked, and then, looking back at the bishop, "Isn't *he* wonderful!" Veronica, overwhelmed by the occasion, could only nod in teary agreement and return her companion's hug. Then, as the sun slid low over the city, Bishop Hadrian invited the multitude to come to the water to be baptized.

The two bishops waded into the sea and began to baptize those who came to them. As the numbers were so great, they soon instructed Elon, Veronica, Antonio, Jean, and Jasmine to take up the task as well, and asked the Prophets to make a list of names and addresses of those baptized. About four thousand were baptized as the sun set over the city, and the Prophets led them back to their homes singing songs of praise as they marched along.

Despite the miraculous work of the Spirit, few Unifists came to the waters of Baptism. Christ had come to the poor and marginalized in Aseeremma, but the wealthy Unifists had not heard his voice. They were not in the ghettos where the healings occurred, and did not understand the words to the hymns the Gardeners sang from the heart. To them it was all gibberish.

They believed that salvation would come from the Garden. A great prophet and king would come forth and conquer all of the exiled nations with an army of naked, invincible warriors, and reestablish the admission of all to the Garden and the tree of life. They believed that the bodies of their dead would rise and become whole again. They believed that, when the tree of the knowledge of good and evil was destroyed, all of the effects of sin would be gone, banished along with the Exaggerator, and that the chosen would enjoy life in the Garden forever.

They had hoped Elon would be the prophet and king they awaited, the great invincible general. But the Elon they had hoped for did not exist. Who was this bleeding fool who stood before them admitting his every weakness? Who would follow *him* into battle? Indeed, he spent his time in the ghettos, the hospitals, and the orphanages. He would never build an army. The Unifists were not interested in healing their own hearts, hearts which required no healing. They needed a champion who would destroy the tree of the knowledge of good and evil, forever banishing the Evil One, the one who deters others from obeying the ancient law. When the law became universally obeyed, their world would be restored and they would eat again from the tree of life.

Chapter 16

The Chosen One

Revol Refficul paced the floor as his peers waited for his words. As he paced, he wondered what idiot had decided that all Unifist councils should be conducted in the nude, and then suddenly remembered that *he* was the idiot! A hairy, heavy-framed man in his mid fifties, his belly shook as he paced, making him feel as though he had set himself up for mockery. However, the Grand Enabler must set the tone and follow the rules, even if he made them thirty years ago when he was in his prime, a proud specimen of masculinity.

He had called this meeting as a follow-up to the events of the previous evening, when thousands of Ogeeremmans had embraced the Christian faith.

"We were wrong," he began. "It appears that we were very wrong about Elon. He is indeed a leader, but he cannot be *our* leader. His is a creed of brotherhood through charity. Ish! Is he a woman? Is his work not the work of cowardice? We all know that the Evil One's dominion came to us through the tree of the knowledge of good and evil. When that tree is destroyed, the Exaggerator will be powerless. It is no good to pretend that anything else will do."

"But if we reject Elon, then who?" Lap Slyved, the Vice Enabler demanded. "The scriptures indicate that the Unifier will come from the Garden. None of us has access to the tree! Elon was the first to come from the Garden into the world of Exile. Does that mean nothing? Did God so direct him that we may laugh at him? And who gave him the power to board a speeding starship? Who has that power but God?"

"Are you so easily deceived?!" the Grand Enabler growled. "We do not know where Elon has been for the past three years. I don't know where he was or how he got in league with Earth men, but as the scripture says, we must judge a tree by its fruit, and his fruit is womanly weakness. Do you think that he will lead you into battle? He spends his days changing diapers and wiping noses! Is that your idea of a general? You sicken me with this idle chatter!"

The words having barely escaped his mouth, Refficul could not help but notice that this dispute between the highest officers of their cult was destructive to the faith of the common Unifist. He could see the confusion and disillusionment in their eyes. The tall, gaunt Mr.

Slyved was his right hand man. Refficul could not afford to alienate him. He drew a deep breath and addressed his friend loudly enough for all to hear.

"I'm sorry, Lap. I spoke too harshly. I know that you have the good of the cause at heart. If we would unite the world, we must first be united. The scriptures are clear; the time for the Unifier has come, but he will come with great knowledge and power. He will understand his mission, and lead with strength."

"Grand One," Slyved began again, "at the risk of incurring your wrath, I must ask: Is it weak to love children? I have seen you with your own. You are a strong man, but you are tender with your children, I dare say as tender as Elon with his orphans," Slyved insisted.

"Exactly my point, my friend; they are not *his* orphans! In fact, most of them are not orphans at all; they are abandoned children! If Elon and his friends care for these children, what will be the catalyst for Ogeeremma's wayward parents to return to their duties? When there were homeless children living in the streets, the people of Ogeeremma could see that parents were not living good lives. What do they see now? They see that all is well! That we can all drop the torch and someone else will pick it up! What does anyone learn from that? Elon's focus is on life after death in some fantasy place he calls heaven. Isn't it hypocrisy for him to say that life on this world is not an end to be pursued for its own sake, while everything he does to improve the lives of others would seem to indicate that he believes otherwise? If our focus is to be on the next world, why worry about alleviating suffering in this one? Why is it such a big deal? We'll all be gone soon anyway!"

Refficul's last point caught Slyved off guard, and he had no response. Finally he said simply, "We must study these things further, my lord."

≈

Captain Lamans sat on a stone bench in the royal garden and lifted a tall brandy water to his lips. "You're drinking before dinner!" he said aloud to himself. "What is this, vacation?" He rose and strode about momentarily until his gaze fell upon the third floor balconies. "My room has no balcony, but theirs have *adjoining* balconies. That's where she goes at night! Dammit!"

This realization did not do his already somber mood any good. He had not expected some sort of Pentecost to occur the evening before, and was still trying to sort the whole thing out. He had been invited to an ordination. Schmidt was to be ordained at 8:00 that evening. How could everyone assume that was fine with him? It was a Monday, a work day, and his science officer and morale officer were out playing bishop: setting up parish boundaries, compiling lists of the baptized, and looking for buildings that might be converted to churches. And as if that wasn't enough, they thought they should be able to ordain another officer and render him worthless as well. Did he dare order them not to do so? They were 4.3 light years from Earth. How much power could he wield over these people?

Commander Oakley had declared the ship unworthy of a return trip. Earth would not send another ship until they had received the radio message declaring that this crew was safe on the planet. That message would take more than four years to reach Earth, and the AGC would want to make improvements to the star cruiser design to avoid the problems Covenant had encountered. Why, it would be a minimum of twelve years before another vessel would arrive, should Earth decide to send one. By then Lamans would be nearly sixty years old, past his prime. *Would I really consider returning to Earth, even if I had the opportunity?* he asked himself.

Reality was closing in on him. Power is imaginary if you don't wield it, but who cares about having power over a ragtag bunch of geeky scientists, engineers, doctors, and priests? Was that real power? That womanly, pie-in-the-sky mission charter was not working in his favor. He was a dedicated soldier, one who had never abandoned a mission, but this pseudo-scientific mission was no mission for a soldier! In fact, there were only four real military personnel on the whole crew, and he was the only real soldier, the only one who had seen action.

He strolled to the back of the palace garden, the quietest and most remote part bordering the river. As his mind sought a moment of peace in the flowing water, the corner of his eye caught an old man in tattered robes seated beneath a weeping willow. Oilenroc was contemplating the Gospels. This whole new world of scripture was a bottomless reservoir to the old prophet's eyes. He drank them in voraciously. The captain, not wanting to seem callous by interrupting, pretended not to notice him and broke the holy man's concentration by skipping a stone on the water.

"Captain Lamans, you skip stones very well!" the old prophet complimented.

"Oh...Oilenroc. Please...forgive my disturbance."

"Quite all right, Captain. Isn't this a wonderful place?"

"Indeed it is...a good place to filter through one's thoughts and feelings."

"Filter? Perhaps. To me, contemplation is more like a settling pond; some ideas sink and some float. You see, rotten things tend to float, to rise to the top before they eventually sink, a good thing to remember when sorting ideas, especially new ones."

Lamans surveyed the old prophet's face. He wondered what people found prophetic about such meandering utterances; still, probing the old man might be of some use.

"What do you make of these Unifists, Oilenroc? They do not seem much taken with our faith."

"For sure they are not. Everything the Word teaches," he said, holding up the Christian Testament, "is diametrically opposed to their point of view. Christ came to redeem the weak, the poor, the oppressed..." he drifted back into the reopened book.

"And the Unifists?"

"They belie their name! They hope to achieve unity in the future while living an every-man-to-himself creed now. They believe that a single act, the destruction of the tree of the knowledge of good and evil, will banish the Exaggerator and place God on their side, making of them an invincible army that will bring the entire globe under one rule, one huge glorious garden. They can twist the Ogeeremman scriptures to yield such a scenario, but from what I have read so far, no amount of wringing will squeeze it from the Christian text."

The captain put his fingers to his chin thoughtfully, and offered, "It seems their vision for the future is based solely on power: Destroy one tree; gain God's favor. Eat from another; become invincible. Offer their enemies life or death, and do it all with God's blessing."

"I think that sums it up quite accurately, Captain Lamans. We must be cautious of them, for their interpretation of scripture morphs to match their needs." Oilenroc had spoken to the captain without looking up from the scriptures, and when he did look up, the man was nowhere to be seen.

Lamans had grown weary of being followed by a palace guard everywhere he went. The royal garden was completely enclosed. Two tall walls ran down into the river. The only way out other than through the palace was to scale a wall or swim the river. He had slipped away from Oilenroc by ducking behind a little knoll and making his way down along the bank, eventually coming across a fishing party. He hailed them from the shore.

"Gentlemen, would you consider giving me a lift to the other side? I want to visit the market before sundown, and I don't want to go into that traffic. It would be just perfect if you could give me a lift."

"It is forbidden to land a boat on the palace property," insisted the driver of the boat.

"I am a personal friend of the king, which is why I am in his garden. I assure you that he will be grateful for whatever kindness you show to me."

"Okay, if we can be quick about it!"

They nuzzled the boat against the bank and Lamans jumped in. The driver of the boat wore a pendant about his neck. It depicted a large tree, the roots of which grew out of a fallen tree. *Surely that must be the Unifists' symbol*, Lamans thought.

"Tell me about your faith," he said simply.

"What faith?"

"You are a Unifist, are you not? I want to learn about your beliefs."

"And what will you do with this knowledge?"

"Perhaps I will join your cause."

The man looked at him with great mistrust. "These are strange times," he said. "For all we know, you may want to infiltrate our ranks to do us damage. Already some of our members have gone over to that new religion from Earth, and unless my ears deceive me, your accent is that of an Earth man. The ancient law prevents us from killing you, but there are plenty of thugs in Aseeremma who will do it for a loaf of bread. Now get the hell out of my boat!"

Fortunately for Lamans, they had made it to the other side of the river before insisting that he get out. He shopped around the market until he found a casual ivory linen suit and hat similar to those worn by the men in the boat, and a novelty shop provided him with a realistic mustache. A cabby pointed out the location of Unifist Hall. In an entrance side window, Lamans found a tiny schedule of the regular meetings. There was nothing scheduled all week.

"Can I help you?" a thin little man asked as he placed a key in the front door.

"I was unsure of the meeting time and was looking to see if it was posted."

"It's in half an hour. Four thirty's a little early for some of the working guys, but so it goes. Bar opens right now if you're thirsty."

Lamans followed him in and ordered a brandy water.

"I don't recall seeing your face around here before," the bartender noted.

"I'm from out west. Not a lot of Unifists out there. Came to town to go to the beach and see the spaceships, but there are so many guards down there now that it's hard to get close."

"Isn't that something!" the bartender declared. "Visitors from outer space! It would actually be kinda cool if only they'd left their damned religion at home!" Leaning over the bar to get closer to the captain he said, "Did ya hear? They don't want to sacrifice animals, they want to sacrifice themselves. What the hell's that all about? The one guy's hands bleed all the time, and four thousand idiots signed up for this deal. Go figure. Now we know why those idiots live in slums; they'll fall for anything!"

"What's even weirder," Lamans added, "is that the guy with the bleeding hands is a Gardener. Did you know that?"

"Oh yeah, Elon, the great prophet. The Grand Enabler had him pegged as the real deal, but not anymore. Now he thinks he's just a big sissy."

As the Unifists filed in, when asked, the captain identified himself as Iddra Namreg, a rancher.

"You related to the minority leader?" one asked.

"Oh, no, I'm just a little old rancher," he insisted.

"Well, that other Namreg's a hell of a good man. He's one of ours, you know. Helps us keep that sissy king in line."

"Will he be here tonight?" Lamans asked.

"Doesn't show up often. They keep him awfully busy up there."

After everyone had stripped naked, the meeting began. Discussions resumed on unsettled points from the previous meeting. When Lamans could take it no more, he put up his hand and said, "Now wait a minute. What is it that we're accomplishing here? Are we presuming to sit at this meeting and pick the Chosen One? Don't you think it more likely that he will come to us? That we will know who he is when we see him?"

"Who the hell are you?" Revol Refficul demanded to know.

Lamans jumped up on a table, flung his fake mustache aside, and stomped his feet into a defensive stance. "I'm Captain Cliff Lamans of the starship Covenant. Maybe *I'm* your Chosen One!"

"Get someone in here to kill this arrogant hyena!" ordered Refficul.

"Yeah, you do that! And when this sensor in my chest tells my crew I'm dead, that starship will flatten a ten mile radius around this spot. Is that what you want? Look at yourselves! *You're* the army of God? You're a bunch of fat, drunken business men who think you can decide who the Chosen One is! What if it *is* me? You want power? *I'll* show you power!"

"What are you gonna do, bleed on us? Like Elon? We can give you some help with that!" Rev Refficul cackled. "Or are you gonna change diapers? Ha! We've seen Earth-man power!"

"Oh, no...no you haven't. You haven't seen anything! I can show you power! Do you want a little demonstration?" With that he activated his communicator.

"Mr. Stokes."

"Yes, Captain."

"Code 6 1 6, Stokes."

"Yes, sir."

"Engage!"

"Engaged, sir."

The Captain stared at the clock on his communicator.

"What the hell was that all about, Lamans?" Refficul demanded. "We come to a meeting honorably naked, and you come with a handful of junk so you can be tricky."

"In forty-eight seconds everything within a hundred feet of me will be killed," the captain informed him.

"You too?"

"Oh, no, not me. The computer uses my implant beacon as a targeting point and kills everything around it. Thirty-nine seconds."

Refficul just stood and stared at him for a bit. "You're bluffing!" he declared.

"Maybe. Thirty seconds."

"Well...would you consider calling this thing off, or should we all run like hell?"

"For your sakes, one or the other needs to happen. Nineteen seconds. I'm not too crazy about doing this because I'm not so sure the building will withstand the demonstration."

"Then call the damn thing off!"

"Mr. Stokes."

"Yes, Captain."

"Abort code 6 1 6."

"Yes, sir."

"Stand by for a 6 2 6."

"Yes, sir."

Refficul had to take the bait: "Okay, Captain, what's a 6 2 6?"

"It's the same as a 6 1 6, but without the one minute wait."

"Then how about a 6 3 6? What's that?"

"Well, if you're trying to figure out how bad it gets, a 6 6 6 blows up the whole damned planet."

The captain jumped down from the table. Revol Refficul shuffled around the room for a bit looking at the floor.

"Your scriptures don't say that the Chosen One will come from the Garden," Lamans instructed, "they say he will come from a far away land. Even the farthest extents of the Garden aren't very far away."

A Unifist came from the coat room with a long dagger and slashed the air in the captain's direction. "If you are sinless, I can run this blade through you and you won't die," he said.

"Where do you get this stuff?" Lamans laughed. "The scripture does not say sinless, it says 'One who has eaten of the Tree of Life.' If I am able to enter the Garden and eat from the tree, what will you say then?"

"The angel of the Lord will not allow you to enter," one of them declared.

"Unless I *am* the Chosen One!" Lamans insisted. "I will prove myself within three days."

"We'll be waiting," Refficul said with a smirk.

"No, you will go with me, my friend," Lamans insisted.

While Lamans sparred with the Unifists, the rest of his crew prepared for Schmidt's ordination Mass. It was to be held in the Temple of the Prophets, that hall in which Elon had first addressed the Ogeeremmans nearly four years past. It had now been renamed the Church of the Immaculate Conception. A quick trip with a shuttle had recovered the painting from the Covenant's chapel, and it now graced the wall of the old building, just left of the new altar which had been hand made by Sunil's father, Leinad. The king's tailor had produced the finest vestments. The ordination would be a royal affair, attended by the king and all of his recently baptized friends.

Archbishop Scofield was disappointed but not surprised that the captain had not yet arrived for the ordination. When the clock struck

8:00, he told Bishop Hadrian, "If the captain was coming, he would surely be on time; tardiness is not one of his flaws."

In a few minutes the archbishop was making opening comments from the altar. "Tonight, we call upon the Spirit to consecrate one who will serve others as another Christ. 'The harvest is plenty, but the laborers are few.' Nevertheless, the labor must begin. We must begin the organization of this new fellowship and see to the training of souls. It is important that we train Ogeeremmans to teach their brothers and sisters. It is crucial that changed hearts reach out in witness if change is to hold momentum. We must not frustrate the Spirit."

After the Mass, Bishop Scofield and Fr. Schmidt said goodnight to the last of the well wishers and stepped into the sultry night air. Antonio, Jean, and Jasmine had stepped out just ahead of them and were about to make their way back to the shuttle, but the bishop's eyes met Jasmine's, and she ran to him and knelt before him.

She looked up at him and he caressed her chin with his fingers. "What is the question that's filling your eyes, Sister?" he asked.

"Excellency...and you too, Fr. Schmidt, I want to receive your blessing and the Sacrament of the Sick."

"Are you ill, Sister?" the bishop asked.

"No Father, but I am damaged. Tomorrow Ronnie and Jean will perform surgery on me to restore my fertility. I want to embrace my groom arrayed with all of the beautiful gifts he has given me!" She turned the bishop's loving hand over and kissed his ring, but the poor man could pray no blessing, for he was choking with emotion.

As he sipped his morning tea King Einniv looked past his Tuesday morning meeting calendar and stared into the gentle rain falling in his garden. "Tell me that I don't see Refficul and Slyved on my calendar!" he said to no one. He downed the rest of his cup and headed for his meeting room. Shortly, the two were brought in and seated.

Refficul spoke first. "Your Highness, thank you for seeing us today. We shall be brief."

"Please," Einniv encouraged the commitment.

"Sire, it is our understanding that you have embraced the religion of the Earth men."

"What if I have?"

"The scriptures say nothing, Your Highness, of salvation coming from outer space," Slyved insisted.

"The scriptures do in fact say that the Savior would be born in a far-away land," Einniv pointed out. "Is not another world a far-away land? Furthermore, the Unifists argue that the Savior will come from the Garden, yet there is nothing in scripture that specifically says just that."

Refficul looked at his colleague and wondered if he too was mulling the same question in his mind: *Are the king and Lamans in league with each other?*

"Excellent King, the scriptures are all about life," Refficul insisted. "The most startling thing about this Earth religion is that it is all about death. These people just want to help each other through the misery that Exile has brought upon us, and then die. How is that to be considered salvation? Salvation consists of being returned to the Garden and eating again from the tree of life. The real savior will unify our countries by destroying the tree of the knowledge of good and evil, thus banning forever the Exaggerator. When he has demonstrated our oneness and all are assembled under a single banner, God will forgive the transgression of our parents and restore admission to the Garden."

The good king laughed a sad laugh. "Our ancient parents' transgression pales in comparison to our own! It is one thing to stop the fighting, but how will you stop the hatred? Will God restore paradise to hearts that hate?"

"There is hatred because people vie for limited goods to fill their needs," Slyved declared. "Fulfill the needs of everyone beyond all desire, and the hatred will cease. Hatred requires the Exaggerator, and he will be banished forever!"

"Hate requires nothing! You hate because your hearts are black, devoid of the love of God! Filling your needs has nothing to do with placating your lust!" The king hung his head and shook it. "Can you not see the absolute irony of your stance? You live by a libertarian code that says you must enable people to be tempted in order to provide opportunity for them to choose good, while you maintain that the temptation offered by the existence of the tree of the knowledge of good and evil is a bad thing!" He got up and paced for a bit, and then stood before them in an attempt to reach into their hearts. Abandoning his anger, he stooped and spoke softly and slowly. "Look at the Gardeners in our midst. Have they come here to fill their needs? Were not all of their needs met in the Garden? I tell you, my friends, they have come here to fill their hearts!"

The king's last point bounced right off of them. Slyved said, "Your Highness, I might ask your question in reverse: How can you promote allowing the existence of the tree, while maintaining that placing evil choices before others is sinful?"

The king sighed, and offered a parting thought. "God placed a choice before our ancient parents. Their sinful choice placed many bad choices before us all. I am not God. I cannot judge the ability of my sisters and brothers to resist the Evil One; therefore, I shall be cautious in placing temptation before them, but I shall honor God's right to do so."

Once outside the palace, Slyved sighed and said, "What a waste of time that was!"

"Do you think so? Are we not now more informed and more resolute?" Refficul asked. "The king is even more of a woman than I thought him to be! These Gardeners do our cause damage. The king has blocked legislation designed to keep them out. We must not allow him to thwart the Chosen One."

"So, what are you saying? That perhaps Lamans *is* the Chosen One? But can he do what he must do if Einniv remains on the throne?"

"Lap...we must be careful! We have a fairly large contingent within our fellowship that will not entertain disloyalty to the king. We must be very cautious."

"Maybe our fellowship just needs to get to know the king a little better," Slyved told him.

"What do you mean?"

"Have you seen the Garden women that come to the palace? Have you seen them all lining up in their bathing suits so that Einniv can throw them over his shoulder into the sea?" Slyved asked.

"I have. So?"

"Come on, Rev, wake up! Have you ever looked into the Garden through a telescope? All they do all day long is make love. Doesn't matter where or when or whose watching. Do you really think that Einniv's fun ends with swimming? I can guarantee you that those beautiful babes are lining up for more than just a diving board!"

"You can guarantee it, can you? You have proof, do you? You're not just breaking another one of the ancient commandments, like the one that says not to give false witness?" Refficul drilled him.

"Okay. Maybe I'm out of line," Slyved admitted.

"You have brought up a very interesting point though, Lap. Anytime I've ever looked through a scope there are people doing it, like you say, anywhere, anytime, in front of a crowd; it doesn't matter."

"They're not bound by the ancient law, Rev. A Gardener can make love to any woman he chooses. I have heard that all of the Gardeners who run the orphanages are single, yet they all lived in the same building until Oilenroc split them up. What do you suppose was going on there? It's impossible for a kid to starve in the Garden. Everybody does everybody and they all take care of the kids. They have no need for the law. A Gardener can't murder a Gardener. Nobody has anything of value to steal. Their lives are free from all of that."

"So...they do it anywhere, anytime, with any*one*? Wow! When the tree is destroyed and the planet unified, like them, we'll no longer be subject to the ancient law! How did I not realize that before! Our fellowship needs to understand this, Lap, ole buddy. Such information should go a long way toward improving moral!" Refficul declared, wearing a big grin.

They scheduled a meeting with Lamans, who had become very adept at losing his palace guard. He met with only Refficul and Slyved in the open public square near the market.

"So Einniv did not see things your way? I'm not surprised," Lamans told them. "He's very fond of the Gardeners. He really has the heart of a child."

"Ha! The heart? Perhaps. The mind? Definitely!" Refficul insisted.

Slyved just shook his head and bit his tongue. *Einniv is fond of Gardeners, all right,* he thought, *the female kind!*

Lamans played the apologist: "Einniv holds a position that, in his mind, makes him responsible for alleviating the suffering of others. As captain of a star cruiser, I can relate to that. He is a good-hearted man, but I would agree, a simpleminded one. We can work around him. He will not hinder our progress. In fact, in the end, when all are gathered under a single banner, he is sure to appreciate the peaceful world that will result from our efforts.

"Do you now see," he went on, "that your naked army cannot come out of the Garden? Gardeners are not warriors; they are lovers! They have no weapons. Why, they've never even seen anything die! They are like children, sweet and innocent. They have no need to conquer anyone. They feel the need for unity, which is why they are over here doing good things; they are Unifists at heart. But rank-and-file Gardeners are already too far misled by Elon and his troop of do-gooders. Elon and company must be stopped and contained. They have been away from the tree of life for a long time; they are becoming vulnerable. No, my friends, the naked army will not rise from within the Garden. We must be that army, but it is Elon and his friends who are our ticket to the tree."

"But Elon enjoys the protection of the king," Slyved pointed out. "You will not be able to force him to do anything!"

"Then I shall have a word with the king," Lamans insisted.

"It is useless, for he also has decided to make of his life a sacrifice!" Refficul sneered.

Lamans turned to look across the river at the palace. "So he has," he granted, "but it is up to us to convince him of the proper cause for which to offer that sacrifice." As he strode away from his companions to catch a taxi back to the palace, Lamans hummed a tune to himself. It was a tune he had learned at the last meeting, the tune to the Unifist hymn "All Shall Rise to Feast on the Tree."

That evening the Covenant's officers dined once again with the king, who had a special treat prepared for his guests. They were all invited to the roof of the palace to view the Garden through his telescope. Elon declined, saying that he had seen plenty of the Garden, and that he had been invited to play games with the children at the orphanage. Veronica, on the other hand, was eager to learn about her husband's homeland and was disappointed that he had not stayed to answer her questions.

The King accompanied them to the tallest tower and sighted in the telescope. The palace was situated upon high enough ground to give an exceptional view, and the king sighted in on Lilac Valley, breathtaking with all of its flowers, wildlife, and beautiful families.

Much to Veronica's dismay, after Lamans had viewed the Garden through the scope, he engaged her in conversation, and she became the last to view. The other guests followed the king back down to get a drink. Even Bishop Scofield, who usually tried to keep Veronica company to shield her from the captain, had abandoned her to pursue his conversation with the king.

Without realizing that only the captain and she remained, Veronica viewed at length and rambled on and on about the beauty of the Garden. "I must bring Elon up here and have him tell me what everything is!" she said.

"Can you see the orphanage with that scope?" Lamans asked.

Veronica searched the horizon and at last said, "Oh yes! And there's Elon! They're playing some sort of ballgame."

"Elon has found his home," the captain remarked. "How about you, my dear? Have you found your home?"

Veronica quit looking through the telescope, and finally realized that she was alone with the captain. "Right now my home is in service to my country," she insisted.

"Right now your country is light years away. I want to offer you a home, Veronica."

She looked away.

He went on, "I have looked in two worlds, and today I have searched Eden. In all of creation there is no greater beauty than you, Veronica! Be my wife, and I will be the happiest man alive!"

"I can't, Captain!" she insisted.

He took her hand, went down on one knee, and begged, "Why not, my love?"

"Because she is married," the bishop's voice boomed from the stairwell.

"What? When? I gave no permission! This is a military mission! How was she married without my permission?"

"I knew that you would not grant permission, and I could plainly see that their love was blessed by the Spirit, so I married them in secret."

"Then the damned marriage is not valid!"

"It is valid!" the bishop retorted.

The captain got into the bishop's face and growled, "You'll regret this, Scofield! Dammit! I'm telling you, heads will roll!"

Lamans stormed off of the rooftop. When they were sure that he was out of earshot, the bishop said, "I have seldom seen such rage in a man's eyes. I suggest that you and Elon spend the night aboard the shuttle. The captain is an ambitious man, and ambition often equals danger. I am concerned about his influence on the king, so I will visit the king tonight. You and Elon should stay close to Tess and Tony. The captain knows that they command the respect of their subordinates. For now you will be safe in their company."

The bishop saw her to the palace door, where she was ever so glad to see Oilenroc pull up to the curb.

"Goodbye, Excellency, and thank you!" she said as she sought a ride. "Oilenroc, can you give me a ride to the orphanage?"

"I would love to, dear lady. You look alarmed, Veronica. Is something wrong?"

As Oilenroc's monstrous, six-wheeled machine rattled and banged away from the curb, she began to explain recent circumstances and concerns, to which he only responded, "Oh my!"

She fell into contemplation of their mission. It all seemed somewhat like Oilenroc's old car; that is, as if it was powered by God, because nothing else seemed to be holding it together. She was reminded of Jesus' words to Pilate: "You would have no authority over me, unless it had been given you from above." Surely God would use the captain. There must be a reason he had placed him in command of this mission. She said a prayer for him.

Elon was chest deep in boys when they arrived. It was time-out during a game of hoop ball, which could be thought of essentially as tackle basketball, and Veronica could plainly see that Elon had spent some time on the ground. When he saw his wife and friend, Elon excused himself from the huddle and went to greet them.

"Did you enjoy your view of the Garden, my love?" he asked.

"I would have enjoyed it more if you had been there to answer my questions."

"I'm sorry. I'm sure the king will let us look again."

She took Elon aside and explained the situation that had developed with Lamans, and then tried to contact Antonio. "Chief Escobar," she called into her com. Channel selection was voice activated, but she knew that Lamans usually had his set to *all active* so he could keep tabs on all activity.

"Yes, Doctor," came Antonio's voice.

"Tony, where are you?"

"I'm with Jean in Shuttle 2."

"We're on our way."

Though it was only a short walk, Oilenroc drove them to the beach. As they walked from the car to the shuttle, Veronica realized that, for the first time in several days, they were unguarded. She wondered if that was a good thing or a bad thing. Once inside she gave Jean a long hug, the kind girlfriends give each other when they're really scared. She explained to them what had taken place at the palace, finishing her story with "I'm scared!"

"We knew this subject would come up sooner or later," Antonio pointed out. "What do you want *me* to do?"

"I'm scared of him, Tony. You didn't see the look on his face. I'm afraid he'll kill me or Elon."

Antonio leaned back in his chair. "No doubt, he heard you call me, so he knows where you are now. What do you propose I tell him if he calls?"

Veronica paused. "Tell him that I wasn't feeling well when I called you, that Jean scanned me and diagnosed my headache and nausea to be the result of emotional trauma, and that after a massage and some tea I'm sleeping soundly in a back bunk. And tell him that the two of you are staying the night to keep an eye on me."

"I don't know if he'll buy it, but it's a good line," Antonio admitted. He went back to his work, checking all points on his security checklist. Suddenly his eyes bugged out at the log on his screen. "Ronnie, take a look at this!" he insisted.

"What is it?"

"It's a record of security related activity having to do with the starship. Lamans attempted to initiate the self-destruct sequence!"

"He did what?" Veronica and Jean screeched in unison.

"How did he think he could do that without my memorized piece of the code?" Antonio wondered. "Well, wait a minute. He initiated a *test*. He just wanted to see if he *could* blow it up."

"He was a late comer to the mission team," Veronica pointed out. "Maybe the fact that you have a required part of the code just escaped him, and he thought he could do it all by himself."

"He's been logging in here and tampering quite a bit." Antonio said, as he viewed more logs. "What's this? He had Mr. Stokes engage a code 6 1 6? Why would he call Stokes right before dinner last night and order him to jettison Covenant's garbage, and then rescind the command before it was carried out?"

"We dumped the trash right before entering orbit. It's standard protocol," Veronica noted.

"Honey, what would Lamans gain by blowing up Covenant?" Jean asked.

"Good question, sweetheart. Our mission charter doesn't outline a protocol for what takes place if we are unable to return to Earth, but even if it did, who would feel compelled to follow it? Maybe Lamans has political aspirations and wants to make sure we don't take all of our technological expertise and machines back to Earth with us—technology that he could harness to take control of the planet.

"Anyway, what he's been doing here is a definite breach of protocol. These indiscretions may be grounds for me to relieve him of command, but I don't really want to attempt arresting him in the palace. Gosh! He must be losing it! He must have known I would discover this."

Just then Antonio's communicator beeped. It was the captain.

"Tony?"

"Yes, sir."

"Dr. Lansing doesn't answer her com. Is she with you?"

"Yes, sir. Her com is off." He then repeated to the captain the story Veronica had concocted.

"I'm afraid that I've upset her terribly," Lamans said, "but I guess my apology will need to wait till morning. Thanks, Tony."

"Good night, sir."

When Lamans was off of the communicator, Jean asked, "Tony, how about the other officers, the ones staying in the palace; are they safe?"

"You're asking me to think like Lamans. I don't think I can. We don't know what he's up to or what his motives are. However, I need to find Commander Oakley and convince her to take command," he said, standing to take his leave.

"You be careful!" Jean ordered.

≈

"I appreciate your candor, Father. Thanks for bringing your concerns to me," King Einniv told Bishop Scofield. "I believe that your captain thinks I'm a silly old fool. I've been suspect of his motives for quite some time. He's always seemed somewhat phony to me, so I've been watching him. He thinks he's been evading my guards, but they've seen his every move. He's been meeting with the Unifists and is probably the reason that they paid me a visit. I have undercover guards out guarding your shuttles right now."

"God bless you, Your Highness. It is sad that we have to seek protection from our own leader. We appreciate your kindness and understanding."

Chapter 17

Missionaries

Elon woke and slid out of his bunk. The shuttles were not large ships. The bunks folded out from the walls and were barely large enough to fit one person, much less a married couple—not the ideal lodging for newlyweds. He was the first to wake, and he knelt and watched his bride sleep, but found himself unable to keep from touching her hair. She awoke with a start, and he apologized with a kiss. They decided that, if they hurried, they could make it to Mass on time. Antonio awoke when he heard the opening whoosh of the shuttle door.

"Where do you two think you're going?" he asked.

"To Mass," Veronica answered.

"Not without us," Antonio insisted, and the four were soon on their way. When they were outside of the shuttle he turned to Veronica and said, "You see those guys picking up shells on the beach?"

"Yeah."

"Look familiar?" Antonio asked.

"Well…yeah I guess they do," Veronica answered.

"Those are our guards. Einniv has changed his strategy. They're undercover now," Antonio pointed out.

"Is that a good thing or a bad thing?" Jean asked.

Antonio just shrugged his shoulders and said, "Time will tell."

"Did you find Tessa last night?" Veronica asked.

"Yes. She is in Shuttle 1 but has refused to assume command. She wants to give the Captain opportunity to explain his actions."

By the time the four of them arrived at Immaculate Conception, they should have been ten minutes late for Mass, but it had not yet started. In a few minutes both of the bishops came out. Bishop Hadrian was vested for Mass, but not Bishop Scofield, who appeared sad and agitated as he walked slowly to the front of the sanctuary.

"We are gathered today on the saddest of occasions," he said. "Last night the king, a kind and just man, went to meet his God. We pray this Mass today for the repose of his soul."

When Mass was over, a tearful Veronica turned to her husband and said, "We need to go back to the shuttle and get my medical bag. I want to figure out what killed Einniv."

Antonio would not allow them to go to the palace without him, so the two couples went together. The king's personal physician was happy to see Dr. Lansing, as his own examination had revealed nothing. With a series of simple scans, she concluded that the king had died of a brain aneurysm.

While the king was mourned, his body examined and reexamined, the captain was busy. Senga Namreg, the Unifist minority leader of parliament, had sought him out and invited him to a meeting of the heads of parliament and the master judges.

"We are faced with a unique problem," stated Immit Grebblow, the majority leader. "The king has no heir; the royal line has completely vanished. There are no provisions in our constitution to deal with this scenario. In past years we have had discussions to address this concern, but nothing has been decided. I hope you do not mind that we have invited Captain Lamans, our friend from Earth, to take a consulting role in this meeting. The captain has a great deal of experience with various forms of government, and is likely the most disinterested man in this room."

The captain took the floor. "Before the rest of you arrived, I was telling Mr. Grebblow and Mr. Namreg that on Earth there are several governments that function just like yours, but with some minor differences. Some have an elected president who essentially does the same job as your king. Others maintain the vestige of a monarchy, but that monarch is essentially powerless, with most of the duties being taken up by a prime minister, who is none other than the majority leader of the parliament."

Senior Master Judge Elroc Namnoss had some thoughts. "Those are very interesting things for us to consider, Captain, and we appreciate your interest and candor. However, gentlemen, the immediate problem is the running of the government while parliament and the judiciary work these things out. There is no question that we can arrive at a suitable solution, but ours was no token monarchy. Someone needs to take up the monarchial duties while these things are decided."

"Your honor, I agree," said Mr. Grebblow. "Do you have a suggested methodology for selecting that person, or do you have a person in mind?"

"I do not have a particular person in mind, but I do have a method in mind. I think that all of the people required to make a recommendation are sitting in this room. I think we can choose an

interim leader and seek approval from the full parliament. That
approval would require a two thirds majority."

"I agree with His Honor's methodology," Mr. Namreg said, "*and* I
have a person in mind. I believe that the perfect person for the job is
Captain Lamans."

The room burst into a rumbling of discussion amidst which
Lamans put up his hands in pushback position and said, "I didn't come
in here to sign up for *that!*"

Mr. Grebblow stood and put up his hands to silence the group.
"Mr. Namreg, why do you think the captain is the right man for the
job?"

"It's really very simple. He is the captain of a starship that has
enough fire power to blow up this entire planet. If he wanted to rule
our world he could already be doing so. You've seen their shuttle craft.
Some of you have seen them fly. Their technology is a century and a
half ahead of ours. He didn't come to this meeting seeking power,
because it would already be his if he so chose."

"That is a very interesting point, Mr. Namreg," said Judge
Namnoss, "in light of which I would support your nomination."

"Gentlemen, wait a minute," Lamans protested, "nomination?!"

In a few minutes of discussion it was decided. Lamans forsook his
mock objections and put on his best humble face. By noon the full
parliament had voted and the judiciary had approved. Lamans was
interim leader.

Antonio had been lurking around the palace and parliament
picking up whatever information he could and had gathered enough to
know that the new man in charge was Lamans. As such involvement
represented a grievous breach of mission protocol, Antonio
immediately contacted Chief Oakley, who assumed command and
ordered the entire mission team to report to the shuttles.

Neither Bishop Scofield nor Hadrian was wearing his com. Tessa
finally found Bishop Scofield in the sacristy, but he resisted her order.
"Commander...I mean, *Captain* Oakley, with all due respect, we
priests cannot abandon our most important mission. I understand your
concern for our safety, but our lives are in God's hands now. We have
a church to serve."

Reluctantly Tessa agreed, but offered, "Let me give you armed
guards."

"No, dear lady," the bishop insisted. "Lamans has a whole army at
his disposal. Do not endanger anyone else." He saw the fear in her eyes.

"David will be alright, Tess," he assured her. "We pose no threat to Lamans."

"I hope you're right, Excellency," she said. "I pray you're right!"

Within the hour, the crew huddled inside of Shuttle 1.

"As you may have heard," Tessa told them, "a couple of hours ago I relieved Captain Lamans of his duties. I am now your acting captain. The mission charter is more than a little hazy about what happens to this team if the star cruiser becomes incapable of returning to Earth. One could conceivably judge Captain Lamans' political involvement in a favorable light if one conceded that this mission team—given that we do not in fact know whether another ship will venture our way any time soon, if ever—should be disbanded and integrated into the local society. Our clergy are not here with us because they have already made their decision.

"So I pose the question: Do any of you want to be relieved of your duties so that you are free to seek a position in local society?"

After an awkward silence, Veronica said, "I am married to a man from this world. Our work is here. Star cruiser or no star cruiser, I will never return to Earth. I had already made that decision, Tessa, when you made your initial observations about the damage to the ship. Nevertheless, I think we should continue to work as a science team. We owe Earth something for this huge investment. We can radio our findings back to them.

"But this job generates no income, and hiding out in a shuttle is no way to live. We need homes in which we can raise families. The shuttles can become our offices, and Star Covenant, our orbiting laboratory. Someone has to be in charge of these space vehicles and scientific gear, and that would be you, Tess. I suspect that most of us will be able to find work as teachers and researchers. We can do much to improve the lives of people here while making lives for ourselves, and do so without abandoning the spirit of the mission charter. However, I think that continuing as a military unit is rapidly outliving its usefulness."

"Wow! Thank you, Doctor. That was well put. Any other thoughts on the subject?" Tessa asked.

When no one responded, she said, "I propose this: The political situation in Ogeeremma is a bit tense right now. It may be in our best interest to maintain military discipline for another couple of weeks until things settle down. Thanks to our fuel conversion team we have an ongoing supply of shuttle fuel, allowing multiple trips back to

Covenant, and we will not starve in two weeks. If you want to seek employment, do so. If you want to seek a mate, do so. But I want everyone to wear their coms and to be ready for action should it become necessary.

"I do not want to malign the captain unnecessarily, but I think you should know that he has violated several security protocols in the last two days, including tampering to see if he could, by himself, enact the self-destruct sequence of Star Covenant. I believe that he is in a very dangerous state of mind, which places all of us in potential danger. Before calling this meeting we blocked all of his access and shut down his com connection, but he still knows way too much about us and our machines not to be considered a threat.

"Furthermore, up until now we have been guarded day and night by the king's guards. I'm sure that is about to come to an end. I think it advisable to ditch the uniforms. If you're going out and about, try and blend in. Put your com in your pocket. Don't go out alone. I would prefer to see teams of three or four. We have firearms that can be issued. You may want to consider carrying a handgun for self defense."

All were in agreement with Tessa's plan. In fact, there was an air of relief among the crew, as if they had wanted to move on with their lives and had just been given permission.

Lamans was like a kid in a candy store as he went through the king's files. "Einniv was never bright enough to use an advantage he'd been given," he mumbled to himself in reference to the king's reluctance to use military force. Soon he had fished out every list and every record and a chart detailing the chain of command. It was all too easy. "Like takin' candy from a baby," he mumbled.

In a short time, he had separated the military into two groups and drawn up two separate command structure charts, one for field commanders and one for home defense commanders. The selection process was a simple one: Unifists were all in the home defense structure and all others were in field command structures. "It's just too easy!" he cackled to himself when he had discovered that nearly all of the principal intelligence officers were Unifists. Several notable Unifists among them were already onboard with the recent world view Lamans had helped to form in the minds of Refficul and Slyved. He summoned them all to his office.

"The death of a monarch always presents interesting national security issues," Lamans told the room full of brass. "While we sort out the future of Ogeeremma's constitutional government, our enemies will be eyeing us up, assessing our vulnerability, and perhaps assuming our inadequacy. Do we see any increased activity on their part?"

Gen. Niknoss noted, "The Revotfellians, as you know, have had forces at our border forever, but those forces have recently swelled and there is a lot of activity in their camps. The same can be said for the Addanacians, though their government lacks the hawkish tendencies of the Revotfellians."

"And what do we have for forces at the borders that would prevent invasion?"

"Why, nearly nothing, Mr. Lamans. You've seen the troop dispersion data. Our pants are down!"

"Thank you, General. Our pants down indeed! We shall soon correct that," Lamans assured them. "Do we have any reason to believe that our enemies have operatives among us? Will they know what we're doing before we do it?"

"Though it could be said that King Einniv was guilty of letting our guard down, his policies did not harm our intelligence work," Gen. Niknoss informed him. "All of us in the room were in service before Einniv took the throne. The king has neither harmed nor helped our mission. His was an attitude of benign neglect. We have been able to perform our function without hindrance, and I believe it is safe to say that our ranks are clean. However, our borders have been ill protected. It's possible that there are operatives within our country; however, to our knowledge they've never had dual agents, so any operatives will be simple observers without access to meetings like this, unless, of course, our security has been so lax that this room has been bugged."

Lamans was now wishing that he had access to the shuttles. There he could use equipment that would scan the entire palace for bugs in a matter of minutes. Then he wondered if Tessa was taking advantage of that technology. She would be able to scan the palace, determine bug frequency, and receive signals if any were being generated. The thought made him uneasy.

After the meeting, Lamans met with Parliament to inform them that intelligence information indicated that national security was endangered, so he would be sending extra troops to the borders.

Days later, when every non-Unifist soldier in the kingdom had been sent out of the capital, Lamans called a meeting of the remaining generals. His followers had diligently endorsed him as the Chosen One among the ranks at every level.

"It is time," he told them, "to rise to our destiny. The days of fulfillment are upon us. Do not our hearts ache for the unity to which we are called? We must march upon the Garden and destroy the instrument of the Deceiver, the tree through which all evil has entered the world. I can see by the look in your eyes that you wonder how we shall pass by the angel without dying. I shall pass first. If I am truly the Chosen One, we shall not die."

Lamans strolled through the palace gardens. He looked in all of Oilenroc's favorite places. The old prophet was nowhere to be found, and no one from the Covenant mission team was anywhere near the palace. He came to the conclusion that Tessa must have them all secured in the shuttles. However, it occurred to him that Bishop Scofield would never leave his precious church.

An hour later, the palace guards apologized to the bishop profusely for interrupting him and for insisting that he come to the palace with them. Though the interim leader had just purged the command structure, the rank and file remained, and these new Christians were not keen on doing his bidding. But the bishop, gracious as ever, put them at ease as they made their way back to the palace.

"Bishop Scofield, thank you for joining me. How is the diocese coming?" Lamans asked.

"The diocese is coming along nicely, Cliff, growing by leaps and bounds."

"Are you being assisted by any of our friends from Earth, Father?"

"Only Bishop Hadrian and Fr. Schmidt."

"Where has the rest of the crew gone?"

Tessa had instructed the three priests to withhold no information from Lamans. "The rest of the crew is confined to the shuttles. Tessa does not want to become involved in any of the political fallout of a regime change. You are, no doubt, aware by now that you left her no choice but to declare herself captain on account of your political involvement."

"I surmised as much, Father," he said, smiling. "Step over here. I want you to see who my guests are." In the courtyard below, a courtyard enclosed completely by the palace, were the seventeen and all of the orphans. "Wasn't it nice of them to join me? They're getting a tour of the facility and some treats, things they don't normally get at the orphanage."

"What is it that you want, Lamans?" Bishop Scofield asked.

"What is it with you, man? Do you think that I only do nice things because I want something?" The bishop just gave him a blank look. "Okay, so I do want something. I want to see Veronica and Elon."

"What do the seventeen and the children have to do with that?" the bishop demanded.

"Must you be so melodramatic? Does it make you feel so righteous to force it from my lips? Okay then! They're not going anywhere," he said, pointing to those in the courtyard, "until Elon, Veronica, and Jasmine are in my meeting room! And I may not remain such an amiable host for long! I suggest that you go to the shuttle and convince those three to come and see me before I lose my patience."

"I will not attempt to bring Jasmine!" the bishop insisted.

"Weren't you listening, man?"

"She just had surgery! Leave her alone!"

"Surgery? Is she ill?" Lamans asked.

"She had fertility restoration surgery."

"What? Why? I thought she was starting a convent?"

"She wanted to..."

"Oh Jeez! Just never mind...I don't even want to know! Just bring mc the newly-weds!"

"Tony, Bishop Scofield is at the shuttle door," Veronica informed him,

"Is he alone, Mr. Stokes?" Antonio asked the pilot.

"Scanning indicates all clear, sir."

"Let him in."

In a moment the bishop was up the ramp, and the door whooshed shut behind him.

"Your Excellency, how are you?" Veronica asked.

"I am fine, my dear. How's Jasmine?"

"I'm really doing well, Father," a happy but subdued Jasmine chirped from a bunk nearby. The bishop smiled and held her hand while he gave her his blessing.

"Where's Elon?" he asked.

"Here I am, Father," Elon said as he came from the far end of the vessel where he had been doing a reading lesson. "Veronica's teaching me to read."

"That's wonderful, Elon, but I'm afraid I'll have to interrupt your lesson even further."

"What's happening, Bishop?" Antonio asked.

"As we speak, the seventeen and all of the orphans are touring the palace by invitation of His Benevolence, King Clifford. Lamans insinuated that his benevolence will soon wear thin unless Elon and Veronica accompany me back to the palace."

"We must go!" Veronica insisted.

Antonio frowned. "Let's see…how does this work? Lamans takes hostages, uses them to get more hostages…then what? How many times does he repeat this scenario until he has control of these ships, and therefore, the planet?"

"He doesn't want these ships, Tony," Veronica said. "He wants Elon. He thinks Elon can get him into the Garden."

"Then why does he want you?"

"If you wanted to motivate Elon, whom would you hold as hostage?" she asked.

"He wanted Jasmine too," Bishop Scofield said, "but I told him that simply was not possible, given her condition. He finally gave up on it."

"She would have been his expendable chip to motivate me!" Veronica said. "He's in a dangerous state of mind. We have to go for the sake of the seventeen and the children!"

"I can't let you go!" Antonio insisted.

"I'm sorry, Tony. This isn't your decision. Surely you can see that we must go?" she countered.

Antonio stood between Veronica and the shuttle door. "We can take him out, Ronnie. I can arrest him."

As they argued, Jean checked to be sure her automatic weapon was in her purse, and then climbed the narrow stairs that led to the cockpit. No one was there. She went to the back of the cockpit area and activated the top hatch. Once on top the craft, she followed emergency evacuation procedures, sliding down the blended wing and then climbing onto a tiny ladder beyond the ailerons. She climbed down carefully, and when her feet hit the sand, looked around to see if anyone was watching her. Through the open door on the other side of the craft, she could hear her husband and Veronica still arguing. *Time to straighten out a slime ball,* she thought as she trotted toward the city.

"We have friends among the palace guards, Ronnie," Antonio argued. "You don't need to put your life on the line."

"My life was on the line as soon as I boarded Covenant, Tony," Veronica insisted. "We're missionaries; read the charter! Besides, I would rather that *my* life was on the line than the lives of dozens of children. You have to stop feeling responsible for our security. We're here; your mission is accomplished. If you want to help, pray."

"Captain," Antonio said into his com, still blocking the exit.

"Yes, Commander?" Tessa answered.

"Can you come to Shuttle 2, Tess?" he asked. When he was off the com he said, "Sorry Ronnie. Whatever's good with the Captain is good with me."

Jean looked back and saw the door opening on Shuttle 1. She ducked behind a tree and watched as Captain Oakley came out and headed for Shuttle 2. In a minute Tessa was in Shuttle 2 and apprised of the situation. "We can take him out, Tess," Antonio repeated. "We have friends in the palace guards."

"I know we do, Tony," The captain said, "but I believe the situation is more complex than that. I had a long conversation with Einniv before his death. There were many Unifists in high places in the military before he took the throne. He was able to replace some of them through attrition, but he did not want to precipitate any sort of military coup, so many still remain. He was much more successful with the palace guards, where only three Unifists remain. Still, there are army troops crawling all over the palace grounds this morning, and I suspect that they are all Unifists whom he has gathered around himself. No doubt they are all eager to ingratiate themselves with their new leader. It's an explosive situation. I don't want to start an armed confrontation between the guards and the army. I don't like the alternative any more than you do, but I think Ronnie's right."

Within the hour, the bishop, Veronica, and Elon joined Lamans in the palace garden. "Welcome, my friends, welcome. Look about you. As beautiful as this is, its beauty is but a shadow of the Garden we shall soon visit."

"Sir, you cannot enter the Garden. The angel will destroy you!" Elon warned. "I have seen the bodies of Exiles who tried to enter. It cannot be done!"

"Elon, I'm counting on you to change all of that. You see, Veronica will be the first to enter. Will your angel strike *her* down?"

Bishop Scofield bristled. "What kind of a man would sacrifice an innocent woman to save his own hide?" he demanded. Lamans slapped the bishop's face so hard that he knocked him to the ground.

"I will go first!" Veronica said, glaring at Lamans. "I'm not afraid to die!"

"I don't think you need to fear," Lamans sneered. "Lover Boy will take care of the angel. Won't you, Elon?"

"Sir, I have no control over the angel," Elon insisted, "and the angel is not the only reason that you cannot enter the Garden."

"Silence!" Lamans growled. Struggling to regain his composure, he asserted, "What will be, will be! I have rooms arranged for you to stay the night. Your friends and their orphans will also be my guests. They will be well fed and entertained, as will be everyone in the kingdom once my work is done. Do not leave without my permission. Do not cross me and all will go well for your friends."

Veronica fidgeted a little as the buzzing of her com tickled her collar bone.

"Answer your com, Veronica," the keen-eared Lamans ordered.

"Ronnie, have you seen Jean anywhere," Antonio asked her over the com.

"Why, no, Tony," she answered, not wanting to say anymore and tip Lamans' hand.

"She's missing, Ronnie. I'm afraid she's decided to take matters into her own hands!"

"Don't move, Lamans!" a high-pitched, raspy voice came from the bushes behind him.

"Dr. Escobar!" Lamans greeted her without turning to look, recognizing immediately her signature voice. "To what do we owe the pleasure, my impetuous friend?"

"You're not my friend! And the pleasure," she informed him, "would be to put a bullet in your worthless, self-centered carcass!"

"Jean, must civility go out the window whenever there's a difference of opinion?" he asked.

"Shut up! Let the Gardeners and the children go!"

"Or?" he asked.

"Or you won't live long enough to wish you had!" Jean promised.

Lamans laughed. "It wouldn't be like you to shoot an unarmed man, Jean," he told her. "I know you too well. You like guns a lot, but you couldn't kill those murderous Moles, and you won't kill me."

Jean's jaw dropped. *How could he have known?* she wondered.

"I wanted you on this team, Jean," Lamans said. "Had I not, you and Tony wouldn't be here. I'm far better connected than people might expect for someone with my stick-in-the-mud personality. I'm a risk taker, but I don't like stupid risks. I wanted the best surgeon along on this voyage. I trusted you; now I'm asking you to trust me. Besides, no one's going to hurt the children or your friends. In the morning Veronica and Elon will accompany me to the Garden, and everything will be wonderful."

"Moles murdered my sister-in-law, and now you want to play games with Ronnie's life. I won't let that happen!" Jean declared.

"Nor will Elon!" Lamans insisted. "No one's going to die, Jean! I love Veronica. Trust me, she's in no danger. You have two choices: shoot me, or walk away. I'm not about to play rough with a pregnant woman, so what happens here is up to you. I'm taking our friends to their rooms, and you're going to put your weapon back into your purse and take yourself back to Tony. Veronica, Tony must be just sick with worry. Please give him a call and let him know that his wife and child are on the way home, and then give me your com."

As Lamans walked away with her friends, Jean dropped the gun back into her purse. *He's right; I am impetuous!* she thought, getting teary-eyed. She tried to turn her emotions off. *Use your brain woman! You have an opportunity here!*

After he had seen his guests to their rooms, Lamans called together his generals. "I want you to muster a force of one thousand of your best troops," he told them. "Have them at the strait by 10:00 A.M. The sea will be at low tide and we will be able to wade it without a problem. I do not expect to encounter resistance, lest it should be from my fellow Earthlings, but it would be against their mission charter to do so. Hence, on this side of the strait our troops will be flanked by armored vehicles, but the troops themselves, the ones to wade the strait, shall carry only swords and axes."

"But Mr. Lamans, most of our troops do not even have real swords," a general lamented, "only ceremonial ones."

"Ceremonial will do, General, but be sure they bring real axes. Our victory will be ceremonial in nature, a victory of superior intellect over ancient fears!"

Chapter 18

Power

Minding her healing incisions, Jasmine sat up with care and peered at the clock. It was 4:53 A.M. and the first rays of dawn were creeping into the horizon. The shuttle bunks were a far cry from hospital beds, but she seemed to be healing well. She had refused meds, and this was the third time that movement in her sleep had caused enough pain to awaken her. She carefully stood, and then knelt, remaining there in prayer for a quarter hour.

With her day's commitments given to prayer, she stood with resolve and opened the door to her tiny wardrobe. She smiled at herself as she looked at her garments. Though there was only room for half a dozen outfits, she had chosen to bring along her first Holy Communion dress. She pulled it out now and quietly began to put it on. Glancing down at herself, she almost laughed out loud, for she had sleepily slipped into the lace jacket without first putting on the satin dress. *Looks like a negligee!* she thought. *Perfect for going to see my Eternal Lover!*

Standing at the shuttle door, having thrown on her garments in the proper order, she worried that the door's opening whoosh might wake the others, but the only other way out was the top hatch, and she was in no condition for that. Once outside the shuttle, she hid behind a tree waiting to see if anyone would follow her out. When no one did, she hiked to the sea.

The sun peeped over the horizon and the view stole Jasmine's breath. *What a glorious day to die!* she thought. She had come dressed for the occasion. Bedecked as his bride, she was ready to meet her eternal groom. She knew that Lamans had chosen to use Veronica as a guinea pig for testing the relative safety of entering the Garden. She prayed that, if her own lifeless body was found lying upon the shore, Lamans would repent of what he was doing and give up the quest, and Ronnie would be safe.

She shivered as she waded into the cool water. Soon it was up to her chest. She had not given this venture much thought and realized now that the tide was too high to wade across the strait. She raised her right arm, intending to swim the American crawl, and pain shot through her abdomen. *It will do Ronnie no good for me to die at sea,* she thought. After treading water for a bit, she gingerly attempted a breast stroke and was soon into deep water. Every stroke and every kick tugged at her incisions, and the salt water began to burn. She aimed for the rising sun, grit her teeth, and prayed with each stroke. After what seemed an eternity, she was able to touch bottom. She waded the last hundred yards and knelt in six inches of water to say her final prayers. She was out of breath and in agony. Feebly stumbling to her feet, she struggled toward Eden, and as her second foot left the last of the sea and fell upon dry land, she collapsed into a motionless heap in the perfect white sand.

Veronica coaxed one eye open just wide enough to see her husband kneeling in prayer by the bed, and on hearing a little rustling sound, opened both eyes wide enough to see the bishop spreading a cloth over a night stand in an effort to set up a makeshift altar. She deduced that she must have already slept through a fair amount of noise and wondered futilely why she always had to be the last to awaken. When her eye caught the bishop's, he winked at her and stepped out of the room long enough for her to slip out of bed and dress. After dressing, she called to him as she knelt down beside her husband.

"The One has heard my plea!" Elon announced to her joyfully.

"What did you pray for, my love?" she asked.

"I prayed that the angel of the Lord would not harm you. Mary has secured this blessing for us!" Veronica gave him a squeeze and thanked him for his prayers.

Not knowing for sure how much time they had, the bishop moved Mass along as fast as he could without being irreverent, but did take time for a brief homily. "We have before us a huge task. We must show the nations that the path away from death is the path that leads to the New Tree of Life, not the old. Even though Mary did not live in the Garden and did not eat from the tree of life, death was unable to claim her, for she arrived in the world grafted to Life itself. Today, the Father will help us in this task. Jesus told Pilot: 'You would have no power over me if it had not been granted by my Father.' So it is also that God's mightiest general, the Immaculate One, will rule the day, while Mr. Lamans, pitiful, unsuspecting pawn that he is, will unwittingly play his part in salvation. We offer this Mass for him."

The door to the suite burst open, and Lamans entered accompanied by guards. "Pitiful, unsuspecting pawn, Father? Really…a king should get more respect from his faithful subjects," Lamans said. "The difference between Pilot and me is that Pilot was not a scientist. He had an opportunity to study the awesome power Jesus wielded, and he blew it. My dear Veronica, you look surprised. Does it surprise you that I believe Jesus had power? You should know by now that demonstrable power is *all* that I believe in. This morning you will witness an exercise in power: Elon's power with the keepers of the Garden to shut down the shields, my power of deduction and leadership to use whatever means available to unite this planet in a single cause, and the power of technology that the Garden possesses to restore this planet to glory. When that restoration is complete, you can witness forever the power and benevolence of my kingship!"

Veronica jeered, "I saw your power and benevolence when you slapped a holy priest last night!"

"That was indeed a bad moment," Lamans said, almost genuinely. "I apologize, Father. I don't know what came over me."

"That's funny, I do: greed and lust!" Veronica informed him.

"My dear, I hope that in time I can prove you wrong."

Veronica surprised her husband by leaving his side and walking over to Lamans. She stopped just inches from him and looked him in the eye, as best their difference in stature would allow. "Not long ago, you and I had dinner on the Covenant. We talked about power. Do you remember the conversation?" she asked him.

"I never forget a moment with you, my dear. You said something to the effect that one's greatest strength, and therefore, one's ultimate power, lies in knowing one's own weaknesses. Yes?"

"You remember it, but you don't believe it!" she observed.

"Quite to the contrary, Angel! You said that self-pity and denial of your true feelings were your own greatest weaknesses, and that at times you had allowed them to trap you in a nauseating swirl of indecision. But you forgot to mention one other weakness of yours: transparency. I can see the amazement in your eyes, woman. You're astonished that I remember the details of a conversation we had weeks ago." Veronica broke eye contact in an effort to derail what seemed to be an impending romantic overture. With a finger he gently lifted her chin, regained eye contact, and said, "But unlike you, I have only one weakness, and she will not be my undoing, will she!"

Stepping away, he turned and said, "It is early Father. I leave you to your Mass. The guards will come for you in half an hour to take you to breakfast. I do intend to be a good host. Then we shall go on our little excursion. It's a beautiful day, a perfect day in which to change the world!"

Within the hour they were at the beach. Lamans, dressed in the ivory linen suit and matching hat he had purchased for his first meeting with the Moles, led them to the front of a long column of men flanked by armored cars with machine guns. The shuttles were nowhere to be seen.

"I see that Tessa has wisely decided to avoid a possible confrontation," the bishop commented to Veronica.

"Not seeing them here makes me uneasy," she replied.

When Jasmine opened her eyes, a handsome face filled her view. *Were his lips just touching mine?* she wondered. As he moved away she felt something in her mouth, something delicious. She chewed the morsel, swallowed it, and felt power enter her limbs. She began to raise her head, and two stunning guys were there immediately to help her to sit up in the lush grass.

One of them asked, "How are you feeling, queen of my heart?" From her grassy throne, the dazed queen counted seven charming, naked courtiers at her service. She heard them murmuring things like "she is so beautiful!"

Did the angel with the revolving sword slay me? she wondered. *Is this heaven? Where's Jesus?* A huge tree towered before her, and hanging on that tree were...her clothes! *I'm naked!* "Wh...why did you undress me?" she stammered.

The one who had shared the morsel of fruit via a kiss answered, "Queen of my heart, your clothes were wet and dirty. We washed them for you."

Attempting to stand produced excruciating tummy pain. *Definitely not heaven!* she thought as she fell backwards into their loving arms. "You need more fruit," the kisser said, offering the rest of the fruit from which he had obtained her first nibble. As she ate she noticed them gazing at her tummy, and she glanced down in time to see the evidence of her incisions vanish from sight. She stood at last, in perfect health.

She searched the faces of her healers. They were seven of the most stunning creatures ever. Each loving gaze instantly communicated the qualities of a perfect mate, and a part of her heart screamed, *Where were you guys twenty years ago!* However, waking impressions of having passed into glory faded as the ancient puppeteer yanked at her strings, attempting to make her heart dance with lust, but the puppeteer wasted his time. Indeed, in their innocence, these men reminded her of the little boys she cared for at the hospital. How could she lust? It was indeed charming to have them call her "Queen of my heart," but she could not return the compliment, for her heart was given to *the* King.

They love me, but they do not need me, she thought. Her love for them was instant and deep—love at first sight—but here in Eden that love would never need to be bold or brave or sacrificial. She was in the midst of paradise, the object of real love and deep reverence, but she had come to learn that life and happiness were not about her. Bishop Scofield's words came to her: "True fulfillment is found in being gift to others." The Jesus she saw in these flawless men was not hungry, or dirty, or beaten. The orphans were on her mind. They needed her. They needed Jesus. She needed to meet Jesus in them and to be Jesus to them. Lust is hollow when you've known passion!

She praised God that she was alive, for it meant that Veronica would be safe. Contemplation of her King drove her to ecstasy, and she collapsed into her attendants' arms. An awed lover placed his hands upon her head and prayed. A moment later he smiled and said "She is on fire for the Lord! Let's take her home with us." He gathered her into his arms and said, "She will love the Lilac Valley."

Lamans, with microphone in hand, jumped up onto one of the armored vehicles that flanked his thousand swordsmen, and addressed them. "Today is a new beginning for every nation on our planet. It is the beginning of the return to unity and the end of the reign of death. Today we carry weapons, but we do not need them, for today we go on pilgrimage, not to battle. When we have eaten from the wellspring of life, that great tree which God intended for all, we shall be empowered for our holy mission. We shall destroy the tree of knowledge, which the Evil One has used to his advantage, and embark on our glorious, holy campaign to bring unity to this fragmented world! We march toward the Garden as the mortal children of Iddra and Lerrol, but we return, in naked glory, the invincible children of Ekim and Ateer!"

The troops cheered. At 10:00 A.M. sharp, the column moved into the water. The distance across the strait was about seven hundred meters, with the water level coming to the top of an average man's leg. Elon carried Veronica in his arms, all the while praising God through the intercession of the One. As the column approached shore, just before stepping onto dry land, he stopped to offer one last prayer of thanksgiving.

"Come on, get it over with!" Lamans barked. Suddenly the shallow water in front of them began to churn, increasing until it formed a veritable geyser. The column fell back and everyone stood in amazement.

"The angel is warning us!" Elon told them.

Lamans eyes were the size of golf balls. He had not expected such a display. However, when his adrenaline flow eased, he searched the skies. "There's your angel!" he shouted, pointing, "and there's another one...should be one more...oh, yeah, there we go; angels all over the blessed place!"

He grabbed Veronica's com from his pocket. "My compliments, Tessa; your timing is impeccable, but your little show's not going to make any difference. If these troops don't get the opportunity they were promised today, things could get ugly when they get back to Ogeeremma! Is that what you want, Tess? Hovering and gravishifter firepower eat up an awful lot of fuel. Can you afford that?"

"If Veronica dies today, so do you, Cliff!" Tess assured him.

"Whoa! You've been hanging around Dr. Jean too much! Relax, Tess, nobody's going to die today!" he insisted. The geyser subsided, and Lamans ordered, "Let's get this over with, Elon!"

Veronica was still in Elon's arms. Smiling with confidence, he carried her ashore and lowered her to the ground. As her feet touched the sand, a strange look came over her face. She lost all expression, her eyes fell lazily shut, and her limp body folded and slapped the wet sand.

"Veronica!" Elon yelled, crouching over her body and touching her face.

"What the hell have I done?" Lamans asked himself, falling to his knees in the shallow water.

His com buzzed. "What the hell have you done?" Tessa asked. "If she's dead, you're dead, Cliff!"

Lamans' universe had been gutted, but as he knelt in deep remorse, he heard a sneeze. It was a distinctly feminine sneeze. He looked up quickly. Veronica lay motionless in the sand, in exactly the same position as before. Cliff began to laugh.

"Dammit woman!" he shouted through laughter. "I used to think that *you* were the worst actor in the world, but that was before I met Elon! You should've seen the look on his face after you sneezed! You need to do a better job of casting!" Veronica was up on her elbows now looking at Lamans. She never quite knew what to expect from him. Just when she thought she knew what he was made of, all of the rules would change.

"Column forward!" Lamans commanded and marched toward dry land. He joined Elon and Veronica on the beach. "You are just full of surprises, aren't you, Ronnie!" he said, still smiling at her trick.

"Today is not a day for cowardice, but for glory!" he proclaimed to the troops, none of whom had obeyed his command. He turned and marched as he shouted "Column forward!" once again. After a moment of hesitation, the column moved forward.

As Lamans marched alongside Elon and Veronica, he turned and said, "Elon, I must admit that, at first, I had misjudged your level of knowledge about the workings of this place. It is clear now that you know far more than you are sharing. Soon you will have yet another opportunity to show your influence."

However, Elon insisted, "I am but a beggar before the Almighty. The decision, and the glory, are his."

"Right!" Lamans shot back, feigning agreement through an impish smirk.

The Garden contained every type of terrain that Earth has, except for desert. The beach under their feet was like any other, except that it was perfect: perfect water temperature, perfect sand, perfect sky above, perfect sea animals about, and perfectly beautiful human beings distancing themselves from the intruders. The sandy beach would soon give way to grassy prairie, and then to flowery meadow sprinkled with an occasional tree, which in turn would yield to gently rolling hills with more trees.

No sooner had they begun to cross the lush grass, than Veronica began to notice something bizarre. Her eyes sought Elon's with a questioning glance to see if he saw the same things. As they marched along, thistles grew up instantly, and perfectly healthy trees developed flawed bark, some yellowed leaves, or a dead branch here and there. The grass on which they tread was withered, while thirty feet away it remained perfectly green, all to turn brown shortly after they passed over it. So pronounced was the change that toward the rear of the column they were kicking up a dust cloud walking over what had been perfectly green grass but a few minutes past.

Lamans seemed oblivious to the changes and turned to Elon to ask, "Where is the tree?"

Elon pointed to the top of a huge tree that could be seen sticking out of a hollow which lay ahead and to their right.

"Excellent!" Lamans proclaimed as he led the way.

The column of men followed him over the hill and into the hollow. If one pictured the hollow as an amphitheater, the tree would be the stage. Here and there Gardeners could be seen leaving as the troops filed in and formed a semicircle around the tree. The entire troop stood awestruck. The magnificent tree of life, though not overly tall, was very broad with a massive trunk and huge strong limbs running long distances in all directions. It appeared easy to climb and was dripping with fruit.

Lamans had been busy watching the troops file in, and now turned and took his first good look at the tree. There were clothes hanging on it! He frowned, walked over to the garments, and read the military name tag on the collars. "J. Babasa," he read. After a moment he began to chuckle, and then to laugh uncontrollably. Bent over with his hands on his knees, he laughed on and on. When finally in control of himself he said, "Oh the irony, the absolute irony! I was concerned about getting in here safely. Elon says that one must be sinless to enter, and then we get here and a slut's using the tree of life for a friggin clothesline!" He began to laugh all over again.

Veronica went to slap his face, and he grabbed her arm before it struck. "What? Her negligee's hanging right here!" he said, touching the lace jacket with his free hand, "and she's gone! Okay, so I shouldn't have used the 's' word, but she couldn't keep her hands to herself on Earth, and now you think she's…what? Off playing bocce ball somewhere? Give me a break!

"But truthfully," he went on with a thoughtful smile, "I just gained a great deal of respect for Ensign Babasa. She beat me into paradise! She had you believing that she wanted to be a fertile nun," he paused to chuckle, "when in fact she hoped that she could come over here, enjoy wild, never-ending sex, and have babies painlessly. She loves babies. If you're going to have them, paradise is the place to do it! What the hell else is there to do here? It's what they do all day long! Do you see any tennis courts? Golf courses? Shuffleboards? Televisions? They do what we were designed to do!

"Elon, Elon, Elon," Lamans said, shaking his head and chuckling. "How did Jasmine get past the angel? It had to be through your influence. You have the most beautiful woman on Freqmod eating out of your ungrateful hand, and you're busy setting up a rendezvous in paradise with the local nymph. I'm impressed!"

"Sir, I didn't..." Elon began.

"Silence! Keep your traitorous mouth shut!" Lamans shouted.

Resuming his composure, he addressed the troops. "Paradise is ours!" he said as he picked a fruit and took a bite. "The events prophesied so long ago shall now become reality in your sight." As he took a second bite, a leaf fell from the tree, and some of the fruit began to shrivel. "You who have marched with me today shall be forever a privileged class!" Lamans declared between chomps. With his eyes fixed on his audience, he took two more bites. Now dozens of leaves began to fall, and the fruit was visibly shrinking. The troops were beginning to look worried, some of them angry. Two more bites, and the leaves and fruit veritably rained from the tree. Lamans noticed their expressions, and heard the thuds of fruit striking the ground. Turning, he made a sweeping gesture toward the tree and said, "Help yourself to the fruit of...damnation! What the hell's going on!"

He had turned just in time to see the last leaf fall, the trunk crack, and bark fall in patches from the limbs. In utter silence, a thousand men stood in shock. Lamans turned toward Elon and snarled, "What have you done?" He pulled a gravishifter from his pocket and pointed it at Elon's head.

Bishop Scofield stepped into the weapon's path. "He's done nothing!" he said. "Look about you, man! Look at the grass, the weeds, and the trees. Our very presence here is poisonous to the Garden. We are unfit for paradise!"

"Shut up, Scofield!" Lamans barked. "Enough of your moralizing! The man knows another explanation! Take me to those who control this! NOW!"

"I will speak to him, but he will not change the nature of things," Elon replied.

"Don't give me that! He let the shields down for you!" Lamans pointed out.

"He responded graciously to a just request, to spare the lives of the innocent. How is justice served if I request that the unjust be allowed to live forever?"

Lamans took offense and struck Elon with the gravishifter, knocking him to the ground with a bleeding gash in his head. He grabbed Veronica, held the grav to her head, and said to Elon, "That tree better start sproutin'!"

Before Elon could respond, Veronica grabbed Lamans' wrist and raised his arm. He fired into the air while she twisted her body and ploughed her knee into his abdomen. Elon was amazed. He had never seen fighting between men, much less seen this sort of ability in a woman. Veronica wrested the gun from the winded Lamans and stood back with it trained on him. He shouted to the troops, "Defend your king!"

"Your king is dead!" Veronica screamed, "And he was killed with this weapon!" She glared at Lamans. "I never figured it out till now, because gravs were not issued for this mission. *This* produced the strange noise on the recording! Set on the lowest setting they barely hum. *You* killed King Einniv *and* Captain Benson, you murdering scum!"

"She's insane!" Lamans insisted. "Will you let her treat the Chosen One this way?!"

As they spoke, seven of the Unifists who were loyal to Einniv came forward. The lead man drew a sword and ran it through Lamans. A look of alarm and then amazement came over Cliff's face as the sword was withdrawn. He stood undamaged! Enraged, the seven men took turns running their swords through him or trying to lop off his head, while he smiled and danced about to give them free access.

Bishop Scofield asked Elon, "How long does the effect of the fruit last under these conditions?"

"Not long at all," Elon assured. "We must warn him of the danger to his unrepentant soul."

The troops tired of their slashing, and as they backed away, Lamans grabbed the grav from Veronica's hand. "There, now that everyone's had their fun," he hissed. He aimed it at Veronica, and looking at Elon insisted, "You need to contact your friends."

Elon changed the subject. "Sir, I must warn you: When someone who eats of the tree is subjected to great violence, the protection that the fruit provides is quickly spent!"

"Now why would you tell me that, even if it was true? You've been out of the Garden so long you're starting to think like a devious Exile!"

"I tell you because I am concerned for your unrepentant soul!" Elon insisted.

"Now…isn't that Scofield's job? Don't worry Elon, not even I can kill me!" he said as he put the grav to his head and pulled the trigger. A thousand people winced in shock and disgust as the right side of Lamans' head was scattered about the landscape, but then stared intently to see if it would regenerate.

Veronica shuddered and looked away when a bloodied half of Lamans' hat landed near her feet, but something besides blood had caught her attention. Turning back to look at it, she realized that a com was pinned inside of it. She unpinned Jean's com and examined it. It was set to full-time *send.* "Tess?" she said into the instrument.

"Ronnie!" Tessa answered. "Is Lamans dead?"

"It would appear so, Tess," she said.

"We have you on screen. We're about a kilometer to the north of you, close enough to keep our shields focused and protect you guys from any grav fire. Unfortunately, we couldn't protect Cliff from himself. We have to put this shuttle down now, things are really starting to overheat from all of the hovering and shield use. See you on the other side of the strait, Ronnie."

"Thanks, Tessa!"

His heart burdened with the passing of a wasted life, Elon walked slowly to the captain's side and collapsed to his knees. However, as he knelt, eyes closed and deep in prayer for the departed soul, he heard gasps all around. He opened his eyes to see a one-eyed Cliff gazing up at him, a sinister half smile on the remaining half of his lips. Moments later, when his head had completely regenerated, Lamans grabbed the grav and aimed it at Elon.

"Don't pray for *me,* buddy," he said in a hushed taunt, "pray for yourself!"

Veronica turned away from him. "Tess! He's alive!" she whispered into Jean's com.

Lamans stood, strutted cockily before the troops, and said, "Why? Why did the tree dry up? Was it on my account? I say yes! But not due to any fault! It dried up because God wanted me and me alone to have the power! Why? Because I *am* the Chosen One! Think about it. If a throng of men had this power, who would lead? What would keep the unscrupulous from usurping the disadvantaged? God has given me and me alone the power to rule.

"Though gracious, wise, and kind, I must also be a just ruler. Justice must be served! There is one here who is my enemy; therefore, he is *your* enemy. Like a common spy, he stole his way onto our vessel. Though we treated him with kindness, he killed our captain! With sorcery he fooled our priest and illegally wed the woman I was courting! He murdered your king with the same voodoo that killed our captain! While feigning devotion to the love of my life, he set up for himself a mistress in paradise!" Standing before Elon he screamed, "Spy! Murderer! Thief! Adulterer! Traitor! You must die!" He turned to Refficul and Slyved and ordered, "Seize him!"

Veronica searched the skies. No shuttles in sight!

The two men grabbed Elon and held him. "Hang him on the tree of death!" Lamans commanded. After positioning their prisoner under a large limb, the two just stood there looking at their chosen one.

"What are you waiting for?" Lamans demanded.

Refficul shrugged and said, "Sire...we have no rope."

Lamans thrust his hands up as if to say, *Idiots!* "Use your belts!" he seethed.

Slyved removed his and synched it around Elon's neck. Refficul attached his to Slyved's and went to hitch it to the limb, but as he reached up, his pants went down. The troops began to cackle and Lamans lost all patience. "Get the hell out of the way!" he screamed.

There appeared in Lamans' countenance some semblance of melancholy mixed with his evil resolve as he aimed the grav at Elon's heart. However, all emotion went from his eyes as he steadied his aim and squeezed the trigger. As he did so, Veronica stepped in front of Elon. Lamans reacted in time to divert his aim, but the grav went off and cut a path of carnage through the Unifist troops.

"You can't kill me, can you?" Veronica asked a visibly shaken Lamans. "You really do see yourself as a benevolent king, don't you? Is your love stronger than your need for power?" she asked as she moved slowly toward him.

She wondered now if shooting himself in the head had been an act of desperation, an invitation to the fates to bless him with all or nothing. It seemed he had been blessed with the *all*, but was that *all* enough?

Lamans started to lift the grav in Veronica's direction, but stopped, for he knew that she knew—his self-worth was all bound up in acquiring her. His mind and emotions reeled. How had he allowed this to happen?! He dropped the grav and held his hands out to her, but Veronica stopped short of his reach. She saw agony in his eyes, perhaps his realization that, Elon or no Elon, he would never be the king of her heart, and his need could never really be filled. He wore a pained frown that screamed of the human condition: so little brain, so little time, and so much to consider—a frown as new to his face as his thoughts were to his heart.

She stepped back as he approached. Hands that had reached for her now clasped his head as he winced in pain, but she saw more than pain in his eyes; he was seized with panic. She wondered if he feared that the power of the tree had been insufficient for a complete recovery from his little demonstration, or if her demonstration of love for Elon—a love stronger than death—had allowed Lamans to glimpse the darkness in his own soul: darkness that lay outside the realm of the old tree's healing power, the darkness of self-betrayal.

He staggered now to that tree a few feet away. There was nothing on its branches. He fumbled through the dry leaves on the ground to find shriveled fruit. Propped against the trunk, he stuffed his mouth with the dry remains and began to chew, but as he prepared to swallow, his chewing turned to choking, and he spit the leathery fruit on the ground and gazed heavenward. He mouthed a dozen breathless words toward heaven, reached in Veronica's direction, and slumped over. Dr. Lansing checked his pulse as she gazed over at her praying husband, then sighed as she pushed Cliff's eyelids shut. Bishop Scofield came over to pray and anoint the body.

The stunned Unifist troops were now fully deflated. With their champion dead and their cause nullified, they began to make their way back out of the hollow. However, Lap Slyved picked up the bloodied grav and shouted to his companions, "Who could stop an army armed with these?"

Veronica quickly pointed out, "We have only one of them with us, brought here illegally by Lamans. Its power source will soon be depleted."

Slyved aimed it at Veronica. "Then you will recharge this one, and bring us more of them from Earth!" he said, ignoring the Gardener beside him. Elon knocked the weapon out of Slyved's hand and punched him in the face.

"No, she won't!" he said. All were amazed at this bold Gardener. Some of the Unifists even had fleeting mental images of a Gardener army led by Elon to unify the planet.

Elon picked up the grav, aimed it straight up, and fired repeatedly until it was empty. "Let's all go home before the tide comes up!" he said, extending a hand to the Vice Enabler who was still on the ground. Slyved refused his hand and haughtily jumped up on his own.

Elon turned to embrace his wife, but she had left his side. He found her at the tree touching Jasmine's garments, a thousand questions storming through her eyes. "I'm sure she's okay!" he assured her.

The army filed out of the hollow, but Elon and Veronica stayed by the tree. The bishop conscripted some of the Unifists to carry Lamans' body and the bodies of the dead troops back to the strait. "I must be getting back to my diocese," he said to the newlyweds. "I'm certain Jasmine is okay, but you need to find her. I suggest looking wherever you would expect to find the most children. I will be praying for you."

When everyone else had gone, the newlyweds turned to look at the tree and discovered that it was rapidly budding and blooming. Beautiful music filled the air as singing Gardeners entered the hollow from the other side. By the time their song was through, there was edible fruit on the tree. Veronica said to her groom, "You might as well eat as long as you are here."

"I eat from the New Tree of Life now," he replied. "We were created for God, not for the Garden. I do not want to prolong the journey. However, I do have a deep desire to see my beautiful wife, in the Garden, attired as God intended."

They moved among the trees and removed each other's clothing. Time stood still for the two of them, but especially for Veronica. She felt a freedom beyond anything she had ever imagined.

Elon took her on a tour of the Garden, at first avoiding people as much as possible. Then, as she became more comfortable, they made their way to The Lilac Valley. There they found a throng of children enamored with something in their midst. Elon called the names of some of the older ones whom he recognized. The children he had called came his way, and others were immediately drawn to them as well. In no time, they each had small ones clinging to their legs. As the original crowd of children dwindled, the reason for their gathering became clear when a tall woman at the center of the group stood to see who had arrived.

"Jasmine!" Veronica shouted, running to her.

The two friends went to embrace, but ended up clasping hands and just looking at each other for a moment, a little uneasy about their nudity. "Awe, come 'ere, you!" Jasmine said at last. "When in paradise…" she said, as they gave each other a squeeze. Veronica began to laugh. "What's so funny?" Jasmine asked.

"I just thought of Skink," Veronica explained.

"Skink?!"

"Yeah, can't you just see his headline?"

Jasmine got it. "Oh yeah…'Former FBI Captain Woos Lansing Heiress with Naked Embrace!'"

Veronica giggled, but then turned serious. "You came to the Garden to sacrifice yourself for me, didn't you, Jazz?!"

"I came here to sacrifice myself for Jesus," Jasmine corrected her.

"To save *my* life! Thank you!" Veronica said, squeezing her again.

"You are so welcome!" Jasmine said. She placed her hands on Veronica's shoulders and held her at arm's length. "Now…you need to give me your honest opinion, woman," she said. "I've decided on a name. What do you think of Sister Mary Veronica Aniram of the Sacred Image?" Veronica's teary smile provided the answer.

"Enough hugging; I'm hungry," Elon declared climbing upon the low limb of a nearby tree. "Catch," he called to Veronica and Jasmine as he tossed to each of them a piece of fruit unlike any Veronica had ever seen. Jasmine passed hers to a child and pressed her hand to her tummy indicating that she had already eaten plenty. A starving Veronica devoured hers. Its flavor was unbelievable, and when she had finished, she asked for another. "Oh no, you must try one of these," Elon insisted. Soon his bride had consumed a half dozen different incredible fruits and protested "No more!" when he offered yet another.

As they rested in the shade after their repast, the afternoon thanksgiving music began. It began with a low thumping and rapping of objects, followed by simple but harmonious humming. The young girls rose to dance to the slow but building beat, and were soon joined by the boys. Elon explained the liturgy as it progressed. "The virgin women are next," he said as the ladies began to grace the dancing space.

Veronica looked at Jasmine. "To Jesus, you're a virgin," she said.

"I know, Ronnie," Jasmine answered. "Soon I will vow to make of the rest of my life a dance for Him, but these are your people now, Ronnie, your family. This is your day."

When God's daughters had offered up their heavenly dance, they focused their love on the virgin men who swiftly synced to the prayerful prance. Questioning eyes fell upon Elon when he did not join their humble strut. Then married couples entered the liturgy. Veronica could not help but notice that the other dancers gave extra room to Elon when he contributed his reverent steps. She felt uneasy, and had not yet joined in the frolicking, when Elon began to motion to her. By that time the tune had become an inspiring pulse that praised God with every word and every beat. The dancers gave themselves to the Lord and basked in the glow of his loving gaze. The more Elon gestured his invitation, the more room his fellow dancers allowed the two, thus contributing to the summons. "Dance for the kings of your heart!" Jasmine persuaded her. Veronica could resist no more and ambled gracefully to Elon. All eyes were upon them.

She danced as she had never danced before. She danced for her husband, and she danced for her God. Hundreds of men watched her as she twirled and swayed her naked body in ways she would not have dreamed possible, but in those men's eyes she saw no lust, for in her they saw the Giver in the gift. She felt unbelievable joy and freedom. Never had her body and soul seemed such a single entity. On Earth, men had oft eyed her as a piece of meat, without regard to her soul, or holy men, like Bishop Scofield, had guarded their eyes so as to properly serve her soul. However, there in the Garden, in a way for the first time, she felt whole.

When the vivacious prayer had finally ceased, Veronica enjoyed many introductions to Elon's friends and received so many hugs and kisses that her husband could see that she was beginning to tire. So he did a summersault in her direction, coming out of it with his shoulder at her hips, and hoisted her upon one shoulder. "I must take my bride to meet her new family while there is still something left of her," he announced.

"Will you join us?" Veronica asked Jasmine.

"Thank you, but I'm wondering if Elon can recommend a quiet place to pray," she said.

"There are many such places in the Walnut Forest," Elon said. "We will take you there."

A quick detour past the tree of life allowed Jasmine to dress. Immersed in the sea of naked humanity that inhabited the Lilac Valley, it had been easy to forget about her own nudity, but now she prepared for a more intimate meeting with Elon's family, including his very handsome unmarried brothers. Along the way they came upon a man whom Elon knew quite well but had not seen for several years.

"Nevets. How are you, my friend?" Elon greeted him. "It has been many years!"

"Yes, Elon, too many!" he said, embracing his friend. He then turned immediately and bowed to Jasmine. "Queen of my heart!" he exclaimed. "I had heard that Exiles had entered the Garden, but never did I expect that one would be so breathtaking!"

"Thank you, sir," she said. "It is a pleasure to meet you!"

Elon introduced his friend to Veronica. "Elon married? My, my, what next?" Nevets asked. He took her hands, and stood back looking into her eyes. "Queen of my heart, you have such beautiful eyes; you must have a beautiful soul!" he said. "And what perfect breasts!" Veronica blushed and looked quite uncomfortable as he kissed her on each cheek. Being sensitive, as Gardeners are, Nevets sensed her discomfort and asked, "Did I say something wrong, my queen?" Elon opened his mouth to speak, but his friend continued. "Oh yes..." Veronica could see his nostrils flare slightly, "you also are mortal, and not accustomed to our ways. I hope that I did not offend you."

"I will be fine," she said. "Thank you for the nice compliments. It is really a pleasure meeting you."

As they continued on to meet his family, Veronica asked Elon quietly, "Do I stink?"

"You smell different than Gardeners. You smell...mortal."

"So...we stink to you!" she insisted.

Jasmine overheard their conversation and began to laugh. "Come on, Ronnie, give him a break. Neither of us has had a shower in a while."

"You do not stink to me!" Elon insisted. "Women of the Garden smell like spring blossoms. Women of Exile smell like...well...like autumn leaves. Your fragrance is wonderful to me. It reminds me of the eternity we will have together when death takes us from this world."

"But...you will not die; you are immortal. You will be assumed...won't you?"

"That is up to the Father. I now eat from the New Tree, and may pass as he passed."

"Just one thing puzzles me," Veronica said, still thinking about stinking. "How does a Gardener, who's never been to Exile, know how an Exile smells?"

"The only thing that is not perfect in the Garden," Elon explained, "is the scent of death on the wind as it comes across the strait from the direction of the Exile nations. Every Gardener is familiar with it and fears Exile on account of it."

"So, I smell like death!" Veronica surmised.

Elon sighed a tired sigh, and Jasmine said, "Give it a rest, Ronnie; he loves you just the way you are. What more do you want?"

"I'm sorry," Veronica said, putting an arm around her man.

At the feet of the mountains, the splendor of the Walnut Forest called them into its thick embrace. They soon found Elon's family enjoying an afternoon rest in one of their favorite places, a grassy clearing next to the small waterfall of a mountain stream.

The threesome caught his mother's eye as they climbed the hill at the edge of the clearing. She jumped up from her resting place on the gnarly roots of a great old tree, and stared as if she saw a ghost. At last she squealed "Elon!" as she ran to meet them. She threw her arms around him and held him for a moment and then pushed him to arms length to look at him before hugging him again, a process she repeated as she spoke.

"Where have you been, my beautiful son? We thought you had gone to glory! We had mourned your absence and celebrated your passing, but now you are here!" As she spoke, his six brothers and his father, who had all heard the fuss, gathered to greet him, and he was able to answer her questions within the hearing of all.

"I'm sorry," she said at last to Veronica and Jasmine, "I didn't mean to be rude," and then to Elon, "Who is this beautiful Exile?"

"This is our friend, Jasmine, who has come from another world to do missionary work."

"Another world?" his father asked.

"Yes, Father, it is a long story that I shall be glad to tell."

"And who is this angelic one?" Elon's mother asked, approaching Veronica. "Is…she…?"

"Yes, Mother, this is Veronica, my mate."

His Mother took Veronica's hands in hers and stepped back from her at arm's length to look at her. "Elon, she is the most beautiful thing

I have ever seen!" she said, and then proclaimed, "I have a daughter!" and gave Veronica a big hug. She held her hands as before and contemplated her new daughter. "Soon these most beautiful breasts will be feeding my grandchildren. Oh what glorious days lie ahead!" she said, hugging her again. But then, as she finished the embrace and stepped back, Veronica noticed a little flaring of her nostrils. "Oh my! Oh my dear sweet daughter! You also are...mortal!" Tears came to her eyes. "I have waited a century and a half for you. Am I to give you up so soon?"

Elon's father came forward, bowed reverently, and said, "My daughter!" And sitting on a rock, he beckoned her over to sit at his side. "I have foreseen your presence here among us. You are holy and pure, like the One. We are deeply honored to have you in our family and in the Garden! Your mother expresses concern for your passing, but we should not be here to see it! Immortals were not meant to inhabit this world longer than mortals. We are all created for God, and we should be gone into glory before your passing.

"Things in the Garden must change. Your mate, a man wiser than his father, has spoken of the things that must come to pass. Tomorrow we will go to tear down the walls around the tree of the forbidden fruit. The Exaggerator must know that we do not fear his lies, or death, or the loss of the Garden. We fear only the loss of the Lord!"

"Forgive me, Father," Elon said, "but tomorrow we must return to Exile. We have much work to do there."

"And we shall join you there when our work is done!" his father declared.

Suddenly Elon's mother, her eyes fixed on her long missing son, came to notice his bleeding hands. "What have they done to your hands, my son?" she asked, taking them in hers and kissing them.

"Mother, that is a story I shall reserve for when you come to visit us in Exile. It will be much simpler to explain then."

"Will this happen to all Gardeners who enter Exile?" she asked.

"Oh no," he insisted, "this is a special blessing from God." The look on her face told him that she had absolutely no clue what he meant.

Veronica noticed that Jasmine looked faded and distant. She went to her, put an arm around her waist, and turned her away from the others to talk. "You look tired, Jazz," she said simply.

"It's been a long day," Jasmine sighed with a tired smile. "I think I was up even before you!"

Veronica giggled at her little dig. "Everyone's up before me!"

"I need some prayer time, Ronnie," Jasmine said, looking still more vulnerable. "I missed the Eucharist this morning, and it's been such a busy day. I'm having trouble staying in the present. I'm not sinless; I don't belong here and the Devil knows it. He wants to convince me that I'm the product of my past—the product of my sins—but Jesus erased that past. I need to contemplate him to regain my strength."

Elon and Veronica excused themselves from the family and escorted Jasmine up to Elon's old prayer spot. "For me, this is a holy place," Elon explained. "It is where the One first revealed herself, and it was on just such a night that, in prayer, she took me to Star Covenant. This is her mountain, and if you invoke her, she will bring you to her Son. Everything that you may need is here. The trees are full of food, the mountain stream is glorious to drink, and the forest carpet makes a wonderful bed. We will be sleeping with my family just down the path, and will accompany you back to Ogeeremma in the morning."

"Are you sure you want to be up here all alone?" Veronica asked.

"I won't be alone, Ronnie, but thanks for your concern." As they started to walk away, she added, "However, I would love for you to say night prayers with me."

Veronica and Elon prayed with their friend until she fell deep into contemplation, and then returned to his family. As soon as they were within earshot, Elon's brother Enor eagerly inquired, "Where and when will you be making love next?" The blood went from Veronica's face.

Elon's father came to the rescue. "Forgive your brother's exuberance," he said to Veronica. "My sons have waited many years for a sister to serenade." Then, turning his attention to his sons, he added, "But my daughter has already suffered many a custom unusual to her. I do not expect that she desires a prayer audience during love making. We will allow them privacy."

Veronica sighed with relief. "Thank you, Father!" she said.

"Privacy? In the Garden?" Enor asked, and shrugging his shoulders, took a few steps and held back branches to provide a view. Veronica rose from her seat and came to the opening to take a look. Within view, next to the brook, next to the waterfall, behind the waterfall, and all around were couples making love. Near each couple a group of loved ones sang and played a prayerful serenade.

Veronica turned to her brother-in-law and asked, "Doesn't watching that make you...well...you know...hot?" She had already covered this whole subject with her husband, but the oddity of the situation just overtook her.

"Do you mean, longing for intercourse?" he asked.

"Yes! Exactly!"

"No," he insisted candidly. The rest of the family chuckled a little.

Veronica tried to think of an appropriate analogy. "When you see someone eating something and smell the delicious food, doesn't that make you hungry?"

"No, my daughter," her father-in-law answered, shaking his head. "Our passions are controlled by our wills, and our wills are in tune with God's will. The smell of good food being eaten by my neighbor may remind me of my own hunger, but it will not make me hungry if I am not already so. My sons are without mates. Seeing others making love may remind them of their longing for a mate, but it will not fill them with lust. Just as hunger is given that we may eat and not die, desire is given that we may complete each other, experience the joy of God in each other, and bring forth children.

"Elon has told us of the horrible things he has witnessed in Exile. Unlike Exiles, Gardeners are incapable of desiring only a person's body. When the Lord fills us with desire, it is for a person, not a body. Therefore, we are incapable of lust. We desire only our mates. If God has not given us a mate, we may long for one, but that longing is for a person, not for pleasure."

Veronica nodded understanding but grabbed Elon's hand and pulled him through the opening in the branches, which Enor still provided, and on toward the falls. His family gave one another a knowing smile, and his mother said musically, "Grandchildren!" Veronica led her husband to a secluded area by the falls. She remembered the telescopes of Ogeeremma as she selected a place to spend the night.

The next morning the two woke with their minds on things back at Ogeeremma. After bidding his family farewell, they dressed and sought out their companion. They found Jasmine rested, radiant, and ready. As they headed for the strait, Veronica was full of questions for her husband.

"Is it just me, or does everyone here have a fascination with breasts?" she asked him.

"The spirituality of the Garden is primarily one of thanksgiving," he told her. "We celebrate the abundance God gives and seek to praise him for it in all we do. As we are given no greater power or privilege than to cooperate in the creation of more human beings, breasts are both a symbol of that gift, and of the tremendous abundance God provides."

She smiled at her husband, who could seem almost pretentiously serious when he started teaching about spiritual things. "It just seems so…pagan, like some ancient fertility rite," she insisted, images of museum pieces flipping through her mind. But then she thought, *At least the ancients had fertility in mind. Modern Earthmen are the ones with the adolescent fascination for breasts as playthings.*

They were just about out of the trees, and though Jasmine had been following their conversation, she became distracted when the beach came into view. "Sea lions! There are sea lions on the beach!" She announced, quickening her pace.

"You go ahead, Jazz, we'll catch up in a bit," Veronica told her.

Elon resumed their conversation. "Our ways seem strange to you," he said, "because, by contrast, Christianity is an Exile religion, a religion of salvation. Gardeners do not require salvation from original disobedience. Our only fault is a lack of appreciation for God's gifts; therefore, thanksgiving for his abundance becomes the central religious theme of our lives."

"You've taught me so much, honey," Veronica told him. "You've helped me to make thanksgiving the central theme of my life. It seems to work for Exiles as well."

Elon stopped walking, turned, and smiled at his bride.

"What is it?" she quizzed, smiling back and searching his eyes.

"You're funny!" he said. "I know of no one who appreciates God's gifts more than you! We are not so different. In fact, among the Earth Scriptures there are many filled with prayers of thanksgiving, even thanksgiving for our bodies. Have you forgotten the scripture that says, 'Blessed the womb that bore you and the breasts that nursed you,' and another that says, 'I am fearfully and wonderfully made'?"

As she played with his top shirt button, she said, "Hmmm…thanks for jogging my memory, Mr. Perfect Recall," and then added, as she opened the button, "You *are* fearfully and wonderfully made! How could I forget *that* scripture?!"

"Tonight I will refresh your memory some more," he said.

"Great! But, why wait until tonight?" she said, opening another button.

"Because I don't have 'perfect recall' and I don't have a Bible with me," he said, pretending to ignore her advances. "Besides, we have a friend waiting for us on the beach. Tonight I will read for you the 'Song of Songs!'"

"Wow! What kind of a teacher rewards forgetfulness?" she asked.

"The kind who does not want his pupil to graduate!" Elon quipped.

When they arrived at the strait, they found Jasmine hugging a monstrous sea lion. "Do you think he'll give me a ride to the other side," she asked.

"He will if you ask him to," Elon explained. "Otherwise, we'll need to swim; the water's too deep to wade." As they stood ankle deep in the water discussing their circumstances, they saw a shadow and heard the rumbling of Shuttle 1. Tessa took the craft right down above the water and yelled, "Jump in!"

When all three were safely aboard, she began to apprise them of the things that had taken place since their departure the day before.

"We have heard about Lamans," she said. "Needless to say, there are many different volatile camps concerning our presence here. The same could be said about the attitude toward the Gardeners in Ogeeremma and the new Christian sect. So far there are only violent words. I hope they can be defused."

"Violent words are the stretching exercise for violent acts," Veronica assured her.

Despite a recent meeting of the mission team, in which it was decided that everyone would seek a new life, the crew had been called back together until the incident in the Garden had played itself out. With the return of Elon, Veronica, and Jasmine, all three shuttles headed for a rendezvous at Star Covenant. In a way, it was a routine trip. It was time to study all of the data that Covenant had been recording from space, to add to it the data that had been collected from the ground, and to make sure that all of it was being properly transmitted back to Earth.

"So am I the only one who was a little creeped out about crawling back into this old tin can again today?" Tessa asked the crew as they attempted some semblance of decorum in the ten percent gravity of the Covenant's chapel. "After this meeting, we all have plenty of duties aboard this craft, duties we would have been tending to under normal circumstances. But first I thought it would be good to talk about things that have been observed so far in our brief stay on the planet.

"We have been here long enough to see strange, incredible differences in weather patterns between the Garden and the exiled world. In accord with Captain Lamans' instructions, we have been testing for force fields or other phenomenon. We have detected no technological explanation for any of these weather differences. I will continue to encourage scientific study of the planet, if for no other reason than to add further data to the only conclusion I can come to so far: there is some sort of divine intervention at work here." She invited Veronica, Elon, and Jasmine to relate the fascinating events that had occurred in the Garden. When they had finished, she continued her thoughts.

"After we return to the ground, I will no longer act as your captain in any capacity. Veronica insists that these space vessels have been placed in my care. I will attempt to be of service to all. I am not sure that we can continue to keep the shuttles on the beach near Aseeremma. The political unrest may make that unwise.

"On a personal level, given the vast spiritual opportunities on Freqmod, I am daily becoming less and less the scientist and more and more the missionary. There are many Unifists in high places in Ogeeremma. Their recent trauma in the Garden may have backlash for Christians. Lamans erred grievously, not only in the murders he committed, but in his involvement in the politics of the planet. I do not know if we can reconcile the problems he has created and be allowed to continue our studies living among them. However, I believe that this mission is ordained by God. We have the opportunity to bring Christ to those who sorely need him, both in the Garden and in Exile, and I intend to facilitate that by any means possible.

"Continuing any of the studies you have begun is totally optional, as I am no longer your captain. But if you want to continue them, I will work with you, both on the studies, and on sponsorship so that we can all make a living. It is my hope that you will all use your gifts and abilities to make the planet a better place, without unduly padding your own pockets.

"I will return to Aseeremma to engage Parliament before I bring this entire crew down. I hope we can reestablish trust and help them to stabilize their country."

To the list of planned studies, Tessa added scanning the surface of the planet to check on military operations. All troop placement and movement was noted, and they listened to news broadcasts from both Ogeeremma and Revotfell.

Armed with new information, she took a select crew aboard Shuttle 1 and headed for Aseeremma. They would set down in the palace garden. Its high walls and huge trees would provide excellent cover. It was 5:07 A.M. in Aseeremma. The dark of night would allow them to slip in unnoticed.

On the way, she called Bishop Scofield on his com. "Sorry to wake you, Excellency, but I and a small crew are coming in on Shuttle 1 to see if we can begin to mend the mess Lamans has left. I'm looking for any new info you can give me."

"Well, Tess…where to start?" he yawned as he propped himself up on a pillow. "As you might expect, there is a great deal of unrest. Many of the Unifists are simply beside themselves over the event with Lamans. On the positive side, having given up their dreams of terrestrial immortality, some of them have embraced Christianity. Others seem to have cast off religion altogether, but I am told there remains a core group that is working hard to concoct a new line of reasoning to pursue the same old ends."

"Wow! That's scary!" Tessa said. "In the past they've shown themselves to be a little too creative in that regard. What do you think we can do to mend this breach?"

"Well, of course an apology for the actions of our captain is in order," Bishop Scofield told her. "We must somehow distance ourselves from the behavior Lamans exhibited. Along those lines, I think that diversion might be the best strategy. We have a lot to offer this planet. Get Drs. Ronnie and Jean into the hospitals. Hook our scientists up with the universities. I have parishioners in these fields; they will make excellent contacts. If we can beat the perception that we were Lamans' henchmen, we are probably in a better position than ever to help these people."

"Just one more question, Excellency. How are you and David doing?" she asked.

"We're doing just fine, Tess. We are extremely busy and will welcome all the help we can get once things settle down, but we're fine. As you know, the local Eknarfian population is mostly dark skinned, which may account for why they have adopted Bishop Hadrian as one of their own. David loves them so much! Unfortunately, we're both so busy that we don't get to talk much."

Segoots Eert peered down the barrel of his pistol into the twilight. "Who goes there?" he demanded. He had just relieved the night guard at the garden entrance of the palace. Before Lamans had taken the country's reins, Segoots had been the captain of the guard, a position he had lost just three days past when Lamans purged the command structure of all Christians.

"Segoots, don't shoot! It's Chief Oakley."

"Chief?" Segoots split the night with his flashlight, and found four faces coming in his direction.

"Captain Eert, please forgive us for being so early, and for coming from this side of the palace, but I thought it best to come quietly. Our craft is parked in the garden. We are here to speak with Parliament, if possible. Can you arrange that?" Tessa asked.

"I can't arrange much anymore," Segoots lamented, "I'm just a guard now. Your Captain Lamans put Trebbay Lecksiss in charge. I think he's already in his office. I'll take you to him."

Trebbay Lecksiss was a tall, gaunt man with liquid eyes, large lips, and a comb-over. Though fastidious about his appearance, he always looked as if he needed a shave. As Segoots brought the foursome into his office, Lecksiss peered at them over the top of reading glasses.

"Captain Lecksiss, you have visitors," Segoots announced.

"Yes, Chief Oakley, it's good to see you," he said as he stood to offer his hand. He was a guard with whom they were familiar, and Tessa reintroduced him to Elon, Veronica, and Antonio. "What can I do for you?" Captain Lecksiss asked.

"Our Captain Lamans was a murderer," Tessa proclaimed, "he murdered our Captain Benson and your king. He took power illegally and then usurped it. His ways are not our ways. We want to work toward healing the damage he has done."

Captain Lecksiss invited everyone to take a seat. He placed his glasses on his book and leaned on his elbows. "Many things are wrong in Ogeeremma," he said. "For instance, I am sitting where Segoots should be sitting. He was removed because he belonged to the wrong religion. Now, I am joining his religion. Isn't life funny?"

"Indeed it is," Tessa agreed. She told him about the things they had discovered with surface scans from the Covenant, of particular interest, the information about enemy troops, information that would be vital to the next leader of Ogeeremma.

"I received word late last night," Captain Lecksiss said, "that we have a new leader. Parliament decided to make their majority leader our prime minister until such time when the Constitutional Committee makes their recommendation. Immit Grebblow is our prime minister."

Mr. Grebblow was glad for the information the Earth people brought. He was a passionless man with small unreadable eyes and a long narrow nose. Leaning back in his chair, he looked down that nose at them and spoke. "I believe that our enemies are amassing at our borders, not because we were without a monarch, but because your Captain Lamans sent most of *our* army to the borders. Naturally, that prompted a reciprocal response on the part of our neighbors. I will be visiting those neighbors to let them know what has happened and to propose a schedule for the reduction of troops to end this insanity. In the mean time the immediate danger is that our capital city remains virtually unguarded."

The Prime Minister graciously accepted the apologies of the Earth people for the actions of Captain Lamans and assured them that life in Ogeeremma would be better than ever. He encouraged them to carry on with all their work and insisted that they were welcome at the palace any time. Though not the gregarious, transparent man that Einniv had been, Grebblow seemed genuine and earnest, and the four left his office with renewed optimism.

Chapter 19

The New Tree

Eramthgin Slyved was handsome beyond his years. At the tender age of nineteen, he turned heads of all ages, and at six foot six, he was hard to miss. His six-foot-tall girlfriend appreciated the fact that he was taller than she. He knelt now at Mass with her, in the last pew. Neither he nor she was yet officially received into the church, but their hearts were committed. Eram ached to be baptized and receive the Eucharist, but greatly feared his father, Lap Slyved. The Vice Enabler would kill him, he thought, if the old man found out that he had become a Christian. His father had seen him with Aillissek and had warned him not to see her again. "I will select for you a proper Unifist mate at the proper time!" he had shouted. "Do not let me see you hanging around with that Christian trash!" *What will he do when I become Christian trash?* Eramthgin wondered

Somehow it didn't matter. Eram had never experienced anything like the feeling that had rushed through his soul the first time he set eyes on Aillissek. *She's a sneak preview of God,* he thought, *and smells like spring blossoms from another world!* The most incredible thing about her was her eyes. It seemed to Eramthgin that she was looking directly into his soul. *I could just as well be naked,* he thought, *I can hide nothing from this woman!*

After Mass they shared sweet conversation as they strolled along the river through a nearby wooded park, a beautiful haven in that otherwise run-down part of town. He ran away from her in mock escape until he became winded and braced himself against the sloped trunk of a great tree, his long, wavy blond hair tousled across his face from the running. She caught up to him and embraced him. As he was taller than she and was leaning back against the tree, her face came to the level of his chest, and she took the opportunity to place her ear over his heart and enjoy for a moment the beauty of its rapid beating.

Suddenly she jerked into an upright position, moving so quickly that their bodies bumped painfully together. She turned around quickly to see a man running away from them.

"What is it Aillissek?" Eram asked, but he needn't have. When she turned back toward him his face was filled with horror, for his eyes had found the handle of a dagger protruding from her back.

"That man did something to me!" she said.

Eram struggled to speak. "There's...a knife in your back, honey! Can't you feel it?!"

"A little. Please remove it," she said.

He withdrew the shiny blade from her back, but to his amazement, there was no blood on it. It had entered her back at heart level. He quickly unbuttoned her dress to uncover the most beautiful back his eyes had ever seen, a back with no wounds anywhere! In amazement he ran the tips of his fingers up and down the gentle bumps of her lovely spine, while his eyes filled with joyful tears. "It's a miracle!" he proclaimed.

Eramthgin retrieved the shiny titanium blade from the grass where he had thrown it. On the handle was engraved *Commander Cliff J. Lamans, U.S.A.* He looked again in the direction of the man who had done the stabbing, and saw that he had stopped his retreat and was watching them from behind a tree. Eramthgin broke into a run to pursue the stabber. The criminal quickly disappeared among the foliage along the river and could not be found.

When Eram returned to her, Aillissek led him to a park bench, pushed him onto it, and curled up on his lap. "I have something to tell you," she said. "I suppose that my well-being *is* a miracle, but perhaps not in the same sense as you perceive it to be." As she spoke, she wondered how they had become so much in love while knowing so little about each other's pasts.

$$\approx$$

Loof Luffitip drew a pistol from his pocket and leveled it at Lap Slyved. "We had a deal! Now give me my money!"

"You slime bucket! We had a deal, and you didn't live up to it!" Lap insisted.

"How was I to know the vixen was immortal? I drove a dagger into her heart! What more would you have me do! Your son removed the knife and they went on their merry way. I sneaked up on them an hour later and she was still on his lap talking and laughing as though nothing had happened. Now give me my money!"

Not wanting to be shot, Slyved tossed a wad of bills in Luffitip's direction and gestured for the man to get out of his sight. Then he telephoned the Grand Enabler.

"Rev, we have a problem!" he announced over the phone, "We gotta talk!" They had never tried to have a Christian killed before, and indestructibility was a roadblock they'd not expected.

Within the hour, they rendezvoused on an empty nearby school playground, away from all ears. The Grand Enabler, seated on a merry-go-round, sat thinking silently.

"What the hell are we gonna do Rev?" Lap asked despondently.

"Are you sure this guy's legit?" Refficul asked.

"He's done work for us before and has always come through," Lap assured him. "He's major scum; will do anything for money. He wouldn't screw up a good thing."

Lap's response was met with another minute of silence. Finally Mr. Refficul crossed his legs and leaned back against the framework of the merry-go-round. "Well, if we can't beat 'em, maybe we'll join 'em," he declared.

"What the hell are you talking about, Rev?"

"The Christians. If we can't beat them maybe we'll..."

"What! You've been saying all along what a bunch of wimps they are, that they stand in the way of unification and salvation!"

"Don't be a damn fool, Lap! Learn to roll with the blows! When you get new information, you need to apply it. Would God make these people indestructible for no logical reason? Do we not need to respect the gifts the Almighty gives? Man! This is such a role reversal! Usually you would be the one saying these things to me. What's wrong with you!"

"I guess I'm just angry over this thing with my disobedient kid," Lap lamented. "Who the hell does he think he is choosing a partner without my approval?"

"You're living in the past, old buddy. Get over it," Refficul insisted. "Life as we knew it is over, and just maybe it's a sign of what we've been waiting for. You know what I think? I think I've been a stupid ass. Oilenroc's been reading the Earth scriptures and talking his fool head off about the New Tree of Life. Well, maybe the old fossil's not such a fool after all. Like idiots, we followed Lamans, an Earth man, but rejected Earth's scriptures. Maybe this New Tree of Life *is* the source of the power we seek. We won't be getting any from the old tree! What else is left? Perhaps all these Christians really need is leadership."

"It still just blows my mind that you're suggesting we become Christians!" Slyved said, shaking his head.

"Got a better idea?" Refficul asked him.

Eramthgin scoured the "Help Wanted" and "Rooms for Rent" sections of the paper, hoping to find full-time work and abandon his father's domain.

The phone rang, and his father picked up. "Telephone, Eram," he said. It was Aillissek.

"I can't believe your father let you take this call," she said.

"Nor can I, Ail," he agreed. They spoke at length uninterrupted. When they had finished, his father entered the room.

"Was that the lovely Christian girl you've been seeing," he asked.

Eram braced himself. "Yes."

"I'm sorry that I was angry at you and tried to control your life. I will do that no longer. You may see her as much as you please, with my blessing."

Eram was speechless. What had changed his father's heart? He called Aillissek back and explained the situation. "Do you want to meet my parents?" he asked.

The Slyved home was large and accommodating. Though expensive, it had a rustic look, a style an inveterate hunter would love. Eram welcomed his lovely friend into the great room. Aillissek was immediately fascinated by the animal skins gracing the walls and floor around the fireplace, and by a chair made completely of elephant tusks. As she and Eram conversed, she took pleasure in running her fingers through a fur draped over the back of that chair and then down the silky smoothness of its polished ivory arms. Eram's mom was in the kitchen cooking, and his dad had just started cleaning an elephant gun in a far corner of the large room.

As he eased the cleaning swab into the muzzle, Lap wondered if the gun was loaded, and was an instant embarrassment to himself for not having checked. Then he noticed that, in its position on the table top, it was aimed squarely at Aillissek. His mind raced. What if it *was* loaded? What if it was to fire…accidentally? Then he would know for sure! But…killing was against the commandments. But…she couldn't be killed, so how could he sin? Besides, he didn't know if it was loaded or not, so actually, it would be like an accident anyway… wouldn't it?

He closed his eyes and stopped breathing as his finger squeezed the trigger. The roar of the gun deafened everyone in the room. Mrs. Slyved came screaming from the kitchen. The force of the huge bullet had knocked Aillissek off of her feet. Lap's mind had been so busy with justification that he had not heard his son begin to introduce this lovely girl to him. She had turned to face him, and took the bullet directly in the chest. Now she lay on her back in the fireplace, motionless and covered with soot.

Lap had counted on acting out deep regret if the situation required it, but no acting was required, for he was seriously disgusted with himself. He had paid for death before, but its reality had never stared him down. He groveled now on his knees, repeating a lie: "I'm so sorry. I didn't know it was loaded..."

After a moment, Aillissek opened her eyes. Eram was hunched over her. He took her hand and helped her up. His mother came over to examine her. There was a hole in the front of her dress and a hole in the back, and a huge hole in the masonry of the chimney. Mrs. Slyved turned the poor thing away from the men folk and unbuttoned the front of the tattered dress. As she did so, even under the circumstances, she could not help but think, *What kind of a girl doesn't wear a bra?* Soon Aillissek's beautiful chest was fully exposed, and there was no wound to be found. Mrs. Slyved exclaimed, "It's a miracle!" and knelt in prayer. She had not noticed Lap making his way over, and her sudden change in posture had exposed the girl to his line of sight. He quickly looked away, as the view was more than he had anticipated.

"My deepest apologies, dear girl!" he said, still facing away. "But how is it that you have survived my foolish carelessness?"

"God our Father protects me from all harm!" she proclaimed.

"Praised be our God!" Lap added.

Mrs. Slyved took a soot-covered, ragged Aillissek upstairs to bathe and put on a clean dress.

Rev Refficul seated himself once again on the merry-go-round at the school playground. "This had better be good," he told his fellow Enabler. "This place is kinda creepy at night!"

"There's something you need to know," Slyved insisted. "The last time we met, you wondered if the guy I hired to eliminate the girl was legit. Well, you don't need to wonder anymore."

"Why?"

"Because I saw her take an elephant slug through the heart and get back on her feet moments later."

"Well, isn't that something," Refficul said jumping to his feet. "The only guy I know with an elephant gun is you! So...who fired this shot?"

Slyved knew he was in trouble. "I was cleaning the gun...I didn't know it was loaded..."

"So you pulled the trigger to see if it was, and it just happened to be aimed at this woman! What kind of a fool do you take me for, Lap? Dammit! We are the Enablers of the Chosen One for two reasons and two reasons only: we prepare the way for his coming, and we keep the ancient commandments! Are two rules too many for you to remember?! How the hell do you expect God to be on our side now?"

"God will be on our side, Rev, because there will be no one else. We will be the first Christian Unifists and we will lead the army of the Lord into battle. Who else is there to do his work?"

Nearly half an hour after morning Mass had ended, Bishop Scofield was still on the church steps visiting with morning worshipers. When the last of them had bid him farewell, he went to the tabernacle to spend a few minutes in prayer before leaving for the hospitals to do his rounds.

As he knelt in the front pew, he was distracted by a small group of men. Though their faces were familiar, he couldn't place them. The five of them made a grand but awkward display of bowing and genuflection before the tabernacle, and then interrupted the good bishop's prayers.

"Please Father," Rev Refficul said, "tell us about the New Tree of Life. We are familiar with the old tree of life, which we have heard has dried up. However, we are told that the New Tree of Life is available to Exiles."

The bishop remained in silence for a moment, finishing his prayers, and then rose to stand among them.

"The *New Tree of Life* is figurative speech for a person, the Word of God made flesh," he said. "God took on a human nature and lived among Exiles, teaching, healing, and serving others until he was murdered by them. He freely gave up his life to accomplish our salvation. We, who are baptized into his Mystical Body, share in his death and resurrection and are freed from the bondage of sin."

Slyved gestured toward the tabernacle. "And...his bones are here, in this little gold coffin-box thingy?"

Bishop Scofield noticed the Unifist pendant still hanging from the neck of one of them. He bowed his head for a moment to pray for patience.

"No. This box contains no dead bones," he answered at last. "It contains life: the body, blood, soul, and divinity of the living Son of God. Before he died, he blessed bread and wine and declared them to be his body and blood, so that when we eat these consecrated things, we might become partakers in his sacrifice, partakers in his divine life. His Apostles have handed on this power to the priests of the Lord, that his power and grace might be available to all who seek the Father."

"The power of which you speak...is this the power that Elon had over the demon at the cemetery?" Lap Slyved asked.

"It is."

"Give it to us, that we may be successful against our adversaries!" Refficul insisted.

Now the bishop became very wary of his visitors. "First you must profess your faith, and humble yourselves. You must allow your pride to be washed away in the waters of Baptism," he told them.

A look of alarm came over them, as though the sacrament was a completely unexpected road block. Refficul bowed low and said, "Excuse us a moment, Father," and led his little troop out a side door to converse. Once outside, he asked his companions, "What exactly does scripture say about all of this?"

"That 'the army of the Lord, which feasts upon the tree, shall make war on the dominion of death,' and when their champion returns, that is, he who is called the King of Kings, 'death will be destroyed forever,'" Lap informed him.

Because he questioned their motives, Bishop Scofield thought about escaping. However, they were back too soon.

"Who is the King of Kings?" Refficul asked.

"Jesus Christ, known in your scripture as 'the Word' or 'the New Tree of Life.' He is the son of the living God, made flesh," the bishop instructed them.

"And when shall he return?" Slyved asked.

"At the end of time, when the Gospel has been proclaimed to all nations."

"Father, how often must one eat of this bread, which is the New Tree?" Refficul asked.

"I eat of the sacred body every day," the bishop answered. "Holy Mother Church insists that the faithful partake at least once each year."

"And this food will give us eternal life?" Slyved asked.

"Yes, if you live in accord with..."

Refficul interrupted, "Thank you, Father, but we must be going...thank you!"

Bishop Scofield stood shaking his head looking after them. Why had he not trusted his instincts and slipped away from them? He feared now that it would only be a matter of time before he would see the results of their insincerity.

When they had adequately distanced themselves from the bishop's hearing, the Grand Enabler said, "Everyone in our band must become Christian! The power lasts up to a year! I see now how God's plan works. Do you remember what Oilenroc said? He said that Exiles will obtain higher places in the kingdom because, unlike Gardeners, we must constantly fight evil. Oilenroc, however, believes we are destined for some other place he calls heaven. Of course, we find nothing in scripture about coming into glory in some other kind of place. We know that glory will come to us here. What need is there for a king of kings in some far away fantasy world? Kings are for real people in a real world!"

Unifist Hall was filled to the brim. A newcomer would have thought such attendance to be the result of a growing movement, but in truth, every single last diehard Unifist had made a special effort to attend this meeting.

The Grand Enabler addressed them at length concerning recent developments. With impassioned tone he described his faith journey, the happenings in the Garden, and his newly held convictions about the New Tree of Life. However, as he had predicted to the Vice Enabler, his message proved to be too radical for some of the brethren. Therefore, when he made the pitch for becoming Christian, a third of their ranks walked out. With a scornful eye, he gazed upon those who remained...were they really with him? He challenged them, cursed them, and questioned them. Another two dozen left. Then one of the remaining men stepped forward with a question.

"If eating from the new tree makes a man indestructible, why did Lamans not survive blowing his own head off?" he asked. "I had seen him attending church with the Christians, and I was there when he died."

"Are you a Unifist or not?" Refficul demanded. "I say you are not, because if you were, you would know that God does not protect those who break the ancient commandments. Lamans was a murderer. It does a man no good to eat of the New Tree if he does not obey the commandments."

"What about the king?" the man demanded. "He was a Christian. Lamans was able to murder him. What was the king's sin?"

Refficul opened his mouth, but nothing came out. He had not anticipated this scenario. Slyved came to the rescue: "Einniv was ahead of his time. They say that he had no heirs? Perhaps he had none in Ogeeremma, but no doubt the Garden is running over with them! You see, he's been keeping company with beautiful Gardener women, who are not subject to the ancient law. I'm afraid His Highness got a little ahead of us. He broke the ancient commandment concerning sex by starting to celebrate the Unification before it occurred!"

A shadow of apprehension swept over Rev Refficul's face before he swallowed hard, set his jaw, and nodded his agreement. Then he steeled his gaze at the remaining men as he weaved through the crowd, eye to eye. At last he strutted to the front of the room, looked upon them and smiled. What remained was the hardest core, about two hundred men who would follow him into hell! Numbers were not important, he told them. Success was all about providence. They were the right people in the right place at the right time. Their steadfast attention to God had placed them in the eye of opportunity. They would eat from the New Tree. They would be invincible!

Prime Minister Grebblow's plan was ready for action. He had successfully negotiated the gradual removal of troops from Ogeeremma's borders, a plan which had taken a couple of weeks to put into place. Aseeremma still remained largely unprotected.

In those two weeks, the remnant of the Unifist cause had managed to partake of the New Tree. The eager group gathered on a farm outside the city. They came ready for battle, with machine guns, rifles, grenades, and every other type of armament they could get their hands on and fit into their vehicles.

The Grand Enabler was beside himself with rage. "Where have you been the last twenty years?" he screamed at them. "Did you bring your swords?" he screeched, as he walked among them. "Did you bring your axes? Where is your faith? Will you retain your invincibility by insulting God? We eat from the New Tree, but are we not still Unifists? We will march into battle naked, armed only with swords and God's truth, or we will not march at all!"

There was a great stir and debate in the camp, after which half of the men left.

"Either we are insane, or we are right!" he told the remaining hundred. If we are wrong, we will die discovering our error, but if we are right, we will unite the world and set in place a divinely ordained dynasty that will rule till the end of time! Are we ready?!" he shouted.

They responded, at the top of their lungs, "We are ready!"

"Humph! No you're not!" he said, curtly. "I see only one axe among a hundred men. Go home and get your axes, and meet me on the beach near the graveyard."

By prior arrangement, nine of the troop met them on the shore with boats, and the heavily laden craft were soon approaching the shores of paradise. "Are you sure we can land safely without Elon with us?" one of them asked.

"Of course I'm not sure!" Refficul responded. "It wouldn't be called *faith* if I was sure, would it?"

When they were a few feet from shore the Grand Enabler stood upon the prow and jumped onto land just as the boat beached. The troops joined him, marveling at their leader's bravery as their own feet hit the sand.

A short time later they stood at the opening in the walls surrounding the great tree. "Lap, the walls have been breached. Why? What is the significance?" Refficul asked.

"I know of none, other than that our job just got easier," Slyved replied.

Attracted by the arrhythmic pounding of axes, Gardeners watched from a distance as the ancient, majestic tree sprawled, with a thunderous cracking of limb and branch, into a disheveled heap. The Exile troops danced about with delight, and Refficul climbed onto the felled trunk to strike the stately pose of a conqueror. When they had sufficiently basked in the glory of the moment they started the walk back to the beach.

"Grand One, something just occurred to me," Slyved told Refficul. "I can't believe I never thought of this before! Lamans attempted to eat from the tree of life without first cutting down the tree of knowledge! That's why it dried up! He was punished for not fulfilling the prophecy properly! Perhaps now the tree lives again!"

Refficul stopped and stared at him thoughtfully, then asked, "If it lives, can we eat from both the old and the new tree? I mean, indestructible is indestructible. Can one be doubly indestructible?"

"Lamans was indestructible only for a time, Rev. The bishop said that the power of the New Tree lasts for up to a year. Between the two, perhaps the power becomes permanent," Slyved ventured. "Are there not Gardeners who eat from both trees?"

"Lap, you never cease to amaze me," Refficul told him as he led the troop toward the hollow that surrounded the great tree. As he came over the crest of the hill, the restored magnificence of the mighty tree stole his breath. He fell to his knees and said, "Thank you, Lord!" With tears in his eyes he turned to Slyved and said, "Thank you, Lap! We've done it! We've really done it! The world is ours!"

Remembering Lamans painful last moments, Refficul picked a fruit and ordered the rest of the men to pick one as well. "On my command, you will embrace your final destiny! Eat!" he shouted. As they all took a bite, the tree dried up in a flash, and the remainder of the fruit shriveled in their hands.

"Why did it shrivel?" he asked Slyved.

"So that it will not be available to Gardeners, Grand One," Slyved answered without a moment's hesitation.

"And why does the Almighty not want it available to Gardeners?"

"Because they are not Unifists!" Slyved declared triumphantly. "They have had thousands of years to cut down the tree of knowledge. They have not carried out the Lord's will. The Earthlings have a scripture that says 'the first shall be last and the last shall be first.' Our time has come! The tree will be nice and green when we need another bite."

"We must test its effect!" Refficul told Slyved. "Run me through!"

"Grand One, I cannot..."

"Run me through, dammit!" Refficul shouted. Slyved drew his sword and pointed it at his commander. "What are you waiting for?" Refficul shouted. "Where is your faith?" Finally the Grand Enabler pulled his own sword and fell on it. The troops winced in horror as the tip of the blade came through his back. Refficul rolled onto his back, his hands still on the handle. The men gathered around, and just when they were all bent over him, staring intently, his eyes popped open and he laughed uproariously. Then withdrawing the sword from his abdomen, he stood and addressed them.

"Who can stop us now! We have eaten from both trees! We are fulfilling every prophecy! Remove your clothing and claim your inheritance! We march on Revotfel!"

Having returned to Exile, the naked troops boarded vans and drove to an open area near the border of the rival kingdom, arriving there about noon.

Revotfell's Gen. Olletsoc Tobba gazed disdainfully at a message from the high command. "I've been in the military too long," he told his aid, "or we've outlived our purpose. All we do anymore is move troops around, like a glorified boy's camp that never ends." The general didn't long for war; he simply found his job pointless. He could at least be baby-sitting people who rightfully required it.

Gen. Tobba kicked back in his chair and looked around the room. He had been in the military all his life and had risen to the top of the pack, a position that allowed a certain amount of autonomy. His office décor was not standard military issue. Perusing his walls, he soothed his eyes and mind with the beautiful images he had assembled. Collecting art in a culture focused on function was difficult, and he had put a great deal of effort into acquiring the works that graced both home and office. It was not considered a manly endeavor in Revotfell, but no one dare say so to the general. His gaze became fixed, as it often did, upon his favorite work, a painting of life in the Garden. Though he had owned the painting for years, the scene seemed to beckon him now more than ever.

His phone lit up. "General, I have Col. Nomis on the line," his aid said.

"Elknufrag, what's happening?" Gen. Tobba greeted his friend.

"General, I just thought maybe you could use a good laugh. We've discovered about a hundred naked men carrying swords and marching toward our border here. They're still a few miles out. If you were to drive over here you might find it amusing."

"Elk, who are these people?"

"Don't know yet, sir. Maybe they've escaped from a loony bin."

Gen. Tobba was looking for an excuse to leave his desk, and the drive between his office and the colonel's outpost was a scenic one. In thirty-five minutes he was in Col. Nomis' office gazing at the intruders through a pair of field glasses. After studying the group for a moment, he lowered the binoculars and rubbed his long chin. "They're a bit too far away to recognize faces, but it almost has to be those fool Unifists," he said.

"You've had dealings with them, haven't you, Ollet?" Col. Nomis asked.

"Yes. Amicable dealings I might add. We purchased our daughter-in-law, Nevveh, from Slyved and Refficul. Best thing we ever did. Nevveh is the light of our lives. Slyved saved her from starvation in the streets of Aseeremma. She's the prettiest thing you'll ever see. Ogeeremman women are incredible beauties, next thing to Gardeners, they say, and you've seen our grandkids, all cuter than puppies."

Unbeknownst to the general, Slyved hadn't saved the child from the streets. In true Unifist logic, he saw orphanages as an offense against the ancient law, and he had kidnapped her from Airrellav's small orphanage. This child had introduced the general's entire household to the teachings of the Prophets of the One, teachings which all of them had accepted, that is, all but the general, who remained uncomfortably agnostic.

The general and the colonel were close friends. Some would argue that they were closer than men of unequal rank should be. While Gen. Tobba had not fully bought into the teachings of the Prophets, his friend and colleague had. Nomis would place gentle pressure upon the general to reconsider his beliefs when the opportunities arose.

Tobba raised his field glasses to take another look. The peculiar swashbucklers were now close enough to be recognizable. "Get me a sharpshooter over here on the double!" he told the colonel. The sharpshooter arrived and accompanied the general out to the guard tower.

"You see the tall one toward the middle? The tall gaunt fellow? He's second in command," the general told the rifleman.

The soldier looked through his scope. "Second in command, sir? How can you tell, sir? By the uniform or the medals?" The general gave him a stern enlisted-men-don't-waste-a-general's-time-that-way sort of look, and then broke into a laugh.

"I want you to wound him, soldier."

"Yes, sir."

The rifleman exhaled slowly and squeezed off a shot. Lap Slyved had been leaning into a double-time stride. When the bullet struck he bolted straight upright with his hands flung into the air. In a moment his knees gave out, and he crashed flat on his back.

"Sorry, sir," the sharpshooter apologized, "he side stepped just as I fired."

Through his binoculars, Gen. Tobba could see Refficul crouched over his friend, listening for a heartbeat.

"It's okay soldier. He's a casualty of war."

The Unifists just stood and stared at their leader. Their world had come to an end.

"What the hell are we gonna do now?" one of them asked Refficul. "We don't even have a damn pair of underwear to make a white flag!"

"Lap Slyved was carrying a huge sin," Refficul assured the troops. "He broke the ancient law by attempting to murder someone, and he never repented. Sin has ruined his immortality. It will not affect those of us without sin! Forward...march!" he commanded, lifting his sword into the air and charging forward.

Gen. Tobba could not believe his eyes. "The big guy's dead and they're still coming at us! What the hell's wrong with them? Soldier, pick out one of the guys toward either end. Just wound him, please."

"Yes, sir."

Another shot rang out and a naked warrior dropped his sword and grasped his right upper arm. As the blood oozed through his fingers, he fell to his knees.

"Alright, Rev, old buddy, what was *his* sin?!" one of the troops bellowed. "Looks like we're *all* sinners!"

The wounded swordsman was one whom Refficul knew quite well, a devout Unifist who followed every letter of the ancient law unfailingly. The Grand Enabler was lost for words. He had been unable to enable anyone or anything. He was a gross failure to everyone, including himself. His grand religion, once embraced by thousands of the masses and many in high places, had degenerated into a pitiful band of cultist freaks.

Refficul thought about falling on his own sword again to test the power of the tree—perhaps he was the only one without sin. But then he recalled Lamans' unfortunate little demonstration. What if this had nothing to do with sin? What if it was just some voodoo the Gardeners had played on Lamans, and now on him?

The history of his cult suddenly filled his head. One night thirty years past, in a drug enhanced drunken stupor, Unifism had sprouted in Refficul's abused brain. A part of him had known that there was more to life than addiction, and that sprout soon grew into a creed that gave purpose to his otherwise meaningless existence. His ensuing successful proselytizing had boosted his ego through the roof. However, what had loomed as an epiphany then, the turning point of his life, emerged now as little more than drunken stupidity and addiction to ego. Power had become his god, and that god had just died a humiliating death.

Standing naked at the border of Revotfel, all he knew for sure was that Revol Refficul was not ready to die. In all of his wheeling and dealing, death had never entered into his plans—it was what he had planned to avoid! He stuck the point of his sword into the hard soil, and purposely bent it until it broke in half. He held the broken halves up for his enemy to see, then, casting them down to the ground, went down on one knee in a humble bow of homage. The rest of the troop followed suit.

Gen. Tobba put down his binoculars. "They have surrendered," he told Nomis. "I'm glad they didn't put up a fight. It's a pity to kill good slaves. Bring their leader to me. Oh...and get some clothes on them. I've seen too much already!"

Col. Nomis frowned. "I'm happy for you, sir," he said, "I mean...you really have a marvelous daughter-in-law. But selling and buying human beings just doesn't seem right, Ollet. The Assembly is moving to outlaw it you know."

"Then I'd better make the sale quickly, Elk! I know a man who'll take all of these guys for breeding stock. I know you don't like the means, but you can't argue the results. You've seen my grandkids. We Revotfellians are bright—our technology is twenty years ahead of Ogeeremma's—but man are we ugly! Ogeeremmans, on the other hand, are a handsome but dull to average-witted race. Do you know what you get when you combine the two? You get pretty *and* smart! But try to get an Ogeeremman to marry a Revotfellian of their own free will? Good luck! They are quite aware of their own good looks, and they have a sharp eye for beauty."

"My friend, does any of that justify buying, selling, and breeding human beings like cattle?"

"I don't know, Elk. I can tell that my daughter-in-law loves my son, homely or not. As for these guys, you tell me: Would you rather go to prison or be rented out as a stud?"

"But, sir, most of these men already have wives and children. What about them?"

"Seems like something they should have considered before marching on Revotfell!" the general insisted, getting defensive with his friend. "Anyway, I'm eager to hear their story. While on the one hand,

I'm angry that someone with whom I've done business would attack me unprovoked, I am amused and intrigued that they came so boldly with so few to conquer so many and did so poorly."

As he knelt in the dirt waiting to be taken prisoner, Revol Refficul thought about how he had gotten into this predicament. His thoughts produced a moment of clarity: *The wench is a Gardener!* he thought. *Eram's girlfriend is a Gardener, not a Christian! That's why she didn't die. Damned meddling Gardeners!*

He wondered how long this immortality thing could go on. After all, he had twice seen the tree shrivel and die with his own eyes. Was it green again, now that no Exiles were near it? He decided that it didn't matter. The angel no longer kept Exiles out of the Garden, which meant that the tree would soon be permanently dried up. *The whole damned planet is destined for Exile!* he concluded. *The Gardeners have forsaken their destiny and condemned the entire planet to Exile! They lost their appreciation for the Garden. That is why the angel of the Lord no longer defends it for them!*

A hatred of Gardeners, which had been budding in his heart for some time, was now coming into full bloom. If this was the end of his glorious campaign, he would avail himself of one last pleasure before he was enslaved: vengeance.

He thought about how Slyved had told everyone that Einniv was able to be murdered because of his philandering with the women of the Garden. *What a damn fool I am,* he thought. *I believed the lying hyena because it was convenient and saved face. I deserve to die!*

The Unifist were herded into the confines of the compound, while their deflated leader was delivered to Col. Nomis' office.

"Revol Refficul. Is business getting this tough? Did I not pay my bill? To what do I owe the displeasure?" Gen. Tobba asked of the man who stood before him in chains. Refficul was silent. The general frowned. "You have nothing to say to me? You are about to be enslaved for the rest of your life, and you have nothing to say to me?"

Refficul bowed low. "Gen. Tobba, I do not deserve an audience with you. I am a fool, easily deceived by the wily Gardeners."

"What does marching on my borders have to do with the Garden?"

"Nothing to do with the Garden, sir. If Gardeners would stay in the Garden, I would have no problems at all, but they do not. They have overrun Ogeeremma."

"Really? Why would a Gardener go to a godforsaken place like Ogeeremma?" the general wondered.

"To care for the poor and the sick. Some of them have joined the religion brought by the Earth men."

The general sipped his tea thoughtfully. "And the Prophets...what do they think of this Earth religion?

"Many of them have also joined, General."

"What is the attraction, Refficul? Is it just a fascination with a religion from outer space? What do these people have that a Gardener, or an Ogeeremman for that matter, would want?"

"Actually, sir, their religion is a lot like that of the Prophets, with some new twists."

"How so?"

"Well, the Prophets believe that a king will come to forgive our transgressions and unite the world. The Earth people, Christians, as they are called, believe that this king has already come, but that he is not a king of this world, but rather of the next, and that he will come again and take the just to his kingdom."

"The next world?" the general asked.

"Yes, sir. They call it heaven."

"Do you believe in this heaven, Refficul?"

"I am no Christian!"

"Then what the hell are you?! Are you still a stinking Unifist? How far has that gotten you?" Tobba demanded, leaning forward in his chair and studying Refficul with an intimidating stare.

"The Gardeners have ruined everything," Refficul muttered at the floor.

"What's that?"

"The Gardeners, sir. Their actions do not conform to scripture, and they do not care."

"And why should they care about Exile scriptures? If the prophets are right about all of this, it's *our* ancestors who screwed up. Why should the word we write dictate what Gardeners do?"

"I don't know, sir. Everything used to be so simple, but they've messed it all up. Did you know that Gardeners are now marrying Exiles? Do you want a beauty from the Garden for your second son? He will be ready for a wife soon. Ooh...you should see them. They delight the eye beyond all telling! And smart? Smarter, I dare say, than Revotfellians! They stay young forever, and..."

"You're changing the subject, Refficul."

The Grand Enabler fell silent. He had been caught changing the subject, but he had managed to set the hook. Gen. Tobba stood, walked to a window, and peered out for a few moments. He looked over his shoulder at his prisoner.

"You belong to me. You realize that don't you?"

"Yes, sir."

Tobba stared at the horizon again, lost in thoughts about people from outer space and the technology they must have, and thoughts about a beautiful Gardener daughter-in-law and half-Gardener grandchildren. This fool of a captive named Refficul knew too much to be put out to pasture. What really irked Tobba was that he could see that Refficul knew that the hook had been successfully set—that the general had been drawn into the web of a self-declared fool!

The General came and stood face-to-face with that fool and said, "The Unifist sect was based entirely on the promise to turn this globe back into paradise: no sickness, no hunger, no war, no death, and no bad weather. Now you tell me that what you have been seeking, the Gardeners are abandoning…and you expect me to believe you!"

"I don't expect you to take my word for it, General. I can take you to them."

"What about this Earth religion? Can't their king be the Great Unifier you've been expecting?"

"I think not. Theirs is a strange faith, one enamored with death," Refficul insisted.

"And this is attractive to Gardeners, because…?"

"I'm afraid, sir, that you will need to ask that question of a Gardener."

"So…you no longer believe in a Great Unifier?"

"I don't know what I believe. Maybe the Chosen One is from Revotfell. Maybe I am speaking to him."

Gen. Tobba clicked his heals and puffed his chest, as though called to attention, and with mock solemnity declared, "Perhaps you are right!" He broke into a laugh, and continued to laugh as he turned and yelled to the guard, "Get 'im outa here!"

Ellehkim Tobba set down her tea and picked up the phone. It was her husband, the general.

"What do you know about Gardeners, my love?" he asked.

"Oh, just the standard stuff. Things we know from telescopic photos and sound recordings," she answered.

"Such as?"

"You know...that they're beautiful, musically talented, good dancers, and naked all the time. That they're immortal and have not a care in the world."

"Have you ever met one?"

"Now what kind of silly question is that, dear? Everyone knows they never leave the Garden, and that we can't enter the Garden."

"That's what I thought. Say, I'm way over in Otnorot. Mind if I go to dinner with Elk?"

"Of course not, dear. Give Elk my love. By the way, he probably knows more about Gardeners than I do."

Though Gen. Tobba was homely, like most Revotfellians, one could not but notice, Elk thought, a sort of nobleness in his features, despite their disproportion. The general sucked down half of his drink without a breath, and then snuggled back in the comfy booth of the little café and eyed his friend.

"Elle says to give you her love," the general said, "and to ask you about Gardeners. Why does she refer me to you?" he asked Col. Nomis.

"As you may recall, I'm not Revotfellian, I'm Ogeeremman," Nomis informed him. "We moved here because my dad was the ugliest cuss in Ogeeremma. After Mom died he couldn't find a wife there to save his life. When I was a child my family lived in Aseeremma, right on the strait across from the Garden. There used to be coin-operated telescopes there set up on the walking bridge over the river. I dropped a lot of change into those things so I could view the Garden, and one time some friends and I rowed out into the strait, and we got to see Gardeners playing with dolphins and whales."

"What did you think about what Refficul had to say today? Why would Gardeners come into Ogeeremma?"

Elk thought for a moment. "Why'd you become a soldier, Ollet?"

The general grinned at his friend, and cocked his head. "So...it's answer-a-question-with-a-question time, is it? Okay then...because I thought it would be exciting."

"Would you want to do it for another 300 years? 400 years?"

"Hmmm...so you think the Gardeners are just bored?"

"Maybe. Or unfulfilled. Can every day be a holiday and still feel like a holiday? Can you appreciate health if you've never been sick? Freedom, if you've never been incarcerated? Peace, if you've never seen war? Truth, if you've..."

"Elk! I get the picture, okay!"

"Well, that just addresses the boredom part, my friend. The need to give of oneself to others is the deepest need of all. I've seen how you give of yourself to your family, to your friends, to your troops."

"Yeah, yeah, I'm a regular prophet," the general chuckled.

"You get pleasure out of giving to others…"

"So?"

"So that's what this conversation is about!" Elk insisted.

The general grinned at his friend's exasperation. "So you think that Gardeners cross the strait because it makes them feel good to help others," he summarized.

"Maybe."

"Hmmm…so much for Unifism, huh?"

The general's mention of Unifism shifted Elk's mind to a different gear. "Ollet, what are we gonna do with the hundred clowns we've got locked up?" he pressed.

"I don't know, Elk, but I really want to go to Aseeremma and see what's going on. We need to know what Ogeeremma could do against us with Earth technology in their hands."

Elk leaned on his elbows to get closer to his friend. "We both know that's not the reason you want to go there. Your soul's searching for answers. I can see it in your eyes."

"Okay…I live with a house full of Prophets, and it seems likely to expect that some or all of them will join this new Christian religion thing. I need to understand these Earth people and this Garden connection."

"And you need another daughter-in-law."

The general smiled wryly. "Family's important, Elk."

Col. Nomis smiled back, and wearing that smile, leaned still closer. With his face propped up on his hands, he sat gazing at his friend. The general became a little uneasy with this loving but curious gaze. "What's up Elk? I feel as though you're looking through me!" he objected.

"Perhaps I am. I've known you for so long that I can probably tell you things about yourself that *you* don't even know."

The general laughed. "Probably!" he agreed. "I *have* made it a point to forget a few things!"

"Do you remember when we were seventeen, and your family had a big reunion?" Elk asked.

"Of course. I asked you to stay the night and attend the affair with me the next day, because I didn't have any male cousins in my own age group and didn't want to be the only guy stuck with a bunch of ineligible girls," the general reflected. "Of course, they weren't ineligible for you, Cousin-in-law!"

Col. Nomis smiled at the memory of Ollet introducing the beautiful girl who would become Mrs. Elknufrag Nomis. "There's something that I've never told you, Ollet. The night before, when I stayed over, you had gotten a phone call and I was left to kill some time in your room. I noticed the end of a poster board sticking out from behind your dresser. I sneaked a peek and discovered that it was a huge drawing you had done of Ellehkim. I was stunned. You'd never let on that you had any interest in her, and I had no idea that you could draw."

"She was like a little piece of the Garden right there in our school," the general smiled, remembering his wife at seventeen.

"She was gorgeous! Enough so, that I had already asked her to the school dance, and she had accepted," the colonel admitted. The general's eyes widened with Elk's revelation of forty-year-old information. "There I was all set up for a date with the girl my best friend was apparently wild about."

"Really? So...what'd you do?"

"Well, not only did I feel as though I was cutting into your territory, but in eight hours of family reunion I had become seriously connected to your cousin, Leah, and ended up inviting her to the same dance. So...I simply went to Elle and told her the truth, that I had met someone who had turned my world upside down and hoped she would forgive me if I broke our date for the school dance. She was deeply touched by my honesty and gave me a big thank-you kiss, but then wondered out loud where she would find a date with the dance so close."

Now the general's eyes really bulged, "So you told her about me, and that's why she asked me to the dance?"

"And all these years you thought it was just because you were so hot," Nomis teased him.

"I don't know if I should kiss you or slap you!" Gen. Tobba said gruffly to his friend.

"Please...I'll take the slap!" Col. Nomis insisted.

The two laughed heartily while the general extended his hand for a shake. "Thanks, Elk! But...why'd you keep that all secret for forty years?"

"Well, you were pretty puffed-up about being asked to a dance by the prettiest girl in school. Seriously, there was a huge change in your self-esteem. You became a leader. At a time when boys weren't encouraged to draw anything but machinery, you started bringing drawings of landscapes, still lifes, animals, and even of Elle to school to show your friends, and nobody laughed at you!"

"At least not to my face they didn't. It probably helped that I was three inches taller than anyone else in the school."

"Maybe. But I had seen you take plenty of grief before. The new you had a different aura, one that you've never lost. It's an aura that commands respect," Nomis insisted.

"Sounds like you're taking credit for *all* of my success, my friend," the general complained.

"Oh no...don't get that impression. I was merely a pawn, the right person in the right place at the right time. The rest was Providence. You are where God wants you to be in life."

"Really?" the general asked, leaning back and sipping his drink. Letting down his guard completely, he added, "Then why do I feel so...lost?"

"Because God's knocking at your door, Ollet, and you're taking your own sweet time to answer it," Elk insisted.

Ollet Tobba fidgeted into an upright position, chugged the rest of his drink, and asked, "Isn't it bad enough that I have to credit you with launching my life? Now you want to relaunch it."

"I'm just a pawn. Pawns obey their masters. I answered the door and found that it was for you. That's all that I can do."

Gen. Tobba folded his hands with his elbows on the table, propped his forehead on those folded hands, and sat in silent thought for a long moment. At last he spoke. "I have a crazy feeling that whatever my fate is, it is inextricably bound up with this strange bunch of naked scoundrels we dealt with today. Do you suppose my dear cousin Leahpar could live without your pretty face for another hour or so?"

"What do you have in mind, sir?"

"Before I go home, I need to see Refficul for a few minutes, but I need to think a little first. Can you have him at your office in say...half an hour?"

The two had driven separately, and when they had finished their meal, Elk left to fetch the Grand Enabler.

Ollet stepped out of the little café. As he looked around the small town the utilitarian nature of the architecture was suddenly offensive to him. He had managed to collect a few photos and paintings of the architecture in Aseeremma. Ogeeremmans, it was said, would rather have a beautiful building that functioned poorly, than an ugly one that functioned well.

Yet Ollet Tobba knew that it would take more than terrestrial beauty to fill the yearning in his soul. He watched two small boys kicking a ball back and forth to each other on the sidewalk, and tried to remember what it was like to be small, to have that innocence of mind and heart. As he watched, his eyes met the eyes of one of the boys, and it seemed for a moment that he was staring into his own soul from an earlier time. He wondered what the eight-year-old Ollet Tobba would think of Gen. Tobba, and doubted that he would be impressed with himself. The sun was setting over Main Street in Otnorot. It seemed to the general that the sun was setting on his life as well. *Life is always more questions than answers*, he thought, *but I need answers!*

Rev Refficul looked like a man who'd been running around naked in the sun all day and had missed a couple of meals. He dragged his chains and fatigues into the colonel's office where the general was waiting.

"Thanks, Elk. Take a seat Refficul; you look beat. Have you eaten?" the general inquired.

"Yes, thank you."

"Would you like a shot?" the general asked as he poured himself some whiskey.

"Please," Refficul responded, and when handed the small glass, cradled it in his hands and pressed it to his lips like a long overdue potion.

The general seated himself facing Refficul. "I have to know one thing," he declared, leaning forward with his elbows on his knees. "I have to know how the hell you thought a bunch of bare-assed guys with swords was going to dance in here and win a battle. Had you come to believe that *you* were the Great Unifier?"

Tobba could tell that his prisoner did not want to answer. At their first meeting, Refficul had managed to change the subject to avoid this question, but now the defeated Enabler knew that he had to come up with some sort of rationale.

After a bit of fidgeting, he answered, "I was led to believe, by a colleague, that partaking in the religion of the Earthlings would make one indestructible. I was a fool!"

"Were you, or did you perhaps not get something right? You said earlier that their religion was 'enamored with death.' How do you leap from that to believing that following it would make you immortal?"

"I don't know…I was in a hurry. I want you to know that we didn't come here to kill anybody. If we had, we wouldn't have come naked, carrying swords. The whole idea was for you to realize that we couldn't be killed, after which you would have surrendered, and we'd all be one big happy kingdom, and…."

"Dammit man! Forget that! Answer my question! Get 'im outta here, Elk! Lock him up and throw away the key!" the general shouted as he got up to leave.

"Wait, wait…I'm sorry!" Refficul begged, and he began to spill his guts. Starting with the escapades of Capt. Lamans, the trip into the Garden, the shriveling of the tree of life, the disillusionment of the cult, his own frustration with everything crashing down; he laid it all out. "Elon, the Gardener who is married to an Earthling, had been unable to cast out a demon until he had become a Christian. I wrongly assumed that this power was part of a larger package of powers that fulfilled the Unifist interpretation of scripture. I assumed that Christians were immortal, and that this Christ was the Great Unifier."

The general paced and thought out loud. "So…Exiles can enter the Garden, but after they do, it's not Garden anymore. Huh! Seems it's what we do best! Well, I think that you and some of your colleagues may have earned a trip back to Ogeeremma. Of course, you'll be wearing death collars and we'll be holding the switches, but it could still be fun. Sleep well, Grand Enabler. You may yet enable something!"

Revotfell's Minister of War, Nocknil Maharba, complained to his secretary as he pointed to the sign on his door: "When are they going to change my title? My wife just hates people calling me the Minister of War. She feels that people think I'm not doing my job unless the country's at war!" It had been more than ten years since Revotfell had been in any kind of a conflict, long enough to make hawks uneasy. It seemed that every exiled nation had a few citizens for whom any conflict was a good conflict.

"Mr. Maharba, I have Gen. Tobba on the phone for you," his secretary informed him.

"I'll take it in the library," he answered, and then nestled into one of the library's large leather chairs and closed the door of the nearly soundproof room. "Gen. Tobba, how are you?" he asked.

"I'm fine, Mr. Maharba. I thought the Minister of War should be informed about the shortest war ever to take place."

"Okay, Ollet, I know there's a joke here so let's get right to the punch line."

"I guess that did sound like a setup for one of my corny jokes, but I wouldn't call you, sir, just to tell a joke. No, we were actually attacked yesterday. Attacked by Ogeeremmans."

"Attacked by Ogeeremma?"

"No sir, not Ogeeremma, Ogeeremmans...about a hundred of 'em, all naked and carrying swords."

"Unifists?"

"Yup."

"Anybody get hurt?"

"One death, more or less accidental. While they were still at quite a distance, I wanted to wound one of their leaders so as to deflate their aggression and avert any serious bloodshed, but I'm afraid the attacker zigged when my rifleman zagged, and the poor chap didn't make it."

"What are we doing with the rest of them?"

"Incarcerated for now, sir."

"Is that the end of it, General?"

"I believe they were the last desperate remnant of a now dead religion. Some former adherents will no doubt try their hand at perverting some other faith, but I think the militants are gone forever."

"What makes you think so?"

"Ah, that is a little longer story; one I'd rather tell in person."

It was a short drive from the general's office to the Ministry Building, and the general was soon nestled into another leather chair facing the minister.

"Things are not the way they used to be, Ollet," Minister Maharba told him. "The king is very serious about taking any and all steps that will ensure lasting peace and an open relationship with Ogeeremma. This troop reduction thing was a simple first step, but any little thing that can be done to build trust will be done. We may want to send these invaders back to Ogeeremma to stand trial. Their attack violated

Ogeeremman law, and if they're going to sit in jail, we'll let Ogeeremma pay for it."

"Mr. Maharba, that brings up an important point. I've not heard any intelligence reports out of Ogeeremma in a long spell. Do we no longer have agents there?"

"Last year we pulled out our last two. We had hoped that we would be enjoying a little more free flow of information by now, but things are moving more slowly than we anticipated."

The general related to the minister all of Refficul's tales of people from Earth, Gardeners in Ogeeremma, and a desecrated Garden. The minister's eyes grew wide. He had, of course, heard about the people from Earth—things of that magnitude will drift across otherwise closed borders—but he had heard no details, and nothing about the Garden.

"I don't think we can afford not to go there, Mr. Maharba," the general declared.

"What are you proposing?"

"Sir, it would seem that the Garden is a nation with whom we need to establish relations. All of our past history with them is the same. Anyone who has ever tried to enter has died a mysterious, instant death at their border. We share no borders with them, and our nearest access is through Ogeeremma. We have been invaded by Unifist, so we have a right to investigate them. They are essentially a nation within a nation. We can only investigate them in Ogeeremma."

"Are you sure you're a general? You sound more like a politician to me!" Mr. Maharba joked.

"Certainly, sir, you would not argue against the notion that war and politics are nearly one and the same; both owe their ultimate success to the fine art of leveraging every advantage and exploiting every weakness."

The minister smiled. "So…give me the specifics of this 'investigation.'"

Chapter 20

Generals

Ellehkim Tobba kissed the back of her husband's neck as she pressed the warmth of her body up against his. He moaned with pleasure and grasped one of her groping hands. She broke the morning silence with "I think you just want to go to Ogeeremma to look at pretty girls."

"Can't buy if you don't shop," he answered. She drew away from him, and leaned up on an elbow.

"The world's just not like that anymore, sweetheart. Our second son will have to get a wife the hard way."

"I know, dear," he said, turning around to embrace her, "I will honor the new ways. And I would be lying to you if I told you that I will not enjoy looking at the women of Ogeeremma, but the most that any of them could ever hope to thrill me would be to remind me of you."

She crawled on top of him, kissed him and said, "You are an inveterate sweet talker."

"Obviously the result of pragmatism," he countered.

"So you think that I'm so easily satisfied?"

"Oh no. It takes more than talk," he said, turning her on her back.

An hour later she rapped on the shower door. "Your breakfast is almost ready, love. Didn't you have a meeting with Elk this morning?"

"Yes, but it got pushed back an hour for another meeting," he answered.

"Huh? What other meeting?"

"The one with you, darling."

The general smiled at himself in the mirror. He always loved the way his bride of thirty-five years made a fuss over him in his uniform. He stepped into the kitchen to receive his daily morale boost, but his wife was lost in prayer. Kneeling by the living room picture window, she praised God for the wonders of creation as she gazed out upon a scene glistening with morning dew. The general knelt down beside her. The new day was breathtaking. He wanted to believe. He wanted to have the faith that Elle and his friend Elk had. Why was it so hard for him? Elle had told him that faith was a gift, that is was impossible to believe without the help of God. Ollet had asked God for this gift. Why had he not received? Was he asking for the wrong reasons? Was he destined to face death as a miserable, stubborn old agnostic?

Ellehkim turned, gave him a peck on the cheek, and whispered, "I'll get your breakfast. You look fabulous this morning!"

Before the general sat down to eat, he gave Col. Nomis a quick call. "I'm running a little late, Elk."

"General, we have a problem," Nomis told him. "Col. Snatas turned up here this morning demanding to see the prisoners. Says that he will be part of the intelligence mission into Ogeeremma."

"I'll be there soon," Gen. Tobba said, hanging up and heading for the door.

"Stop right there, Ollet Tobba! Come back here and eat this breakfast!"

"Yes, dear," he said, smiling and seating himself obediently.

"What's Elk got going that's so important that you'd skip breakfast?"

"You remember that family military picnic a couple years back?"

"Of course."

"Remember the colonel who snubbed Nevveh when he was introduced?"

"The guy who you said hates anyone or anything beautiful?"

"He would be the one. Well, it seems that someone wants him to be part of this mission. He was in intelligence for many years, a spy in Ogeeremma back in the days when they were our mortal enemies. Well, he was at the compound this morning making demands."

Col. Nomis was in the exercise yard with the prisoners when the general arrived. "Looks like a formal affair out in the exercise yard, Elk. What's up?" the general asked.

"A little funeral service for Slyved, sir," Col. Nomis informed him.

"Where's Col. Noinim Snatas?"

"I kicked him out."

"What? Why?"

"Sir, we're holding these men until their fate is decided. This is not a torture facility. I couldn't see what purpose it served to let Snatas curse and swear at them and slap them around. You seem concerned that I put a stop to it…"

"Elk, I trust your judgment, but I would be a little leery of getting too far on the wrong side of this guy. He has deep connection to the monarchy. He was a close personal friend of the king's father."

"Those were different days, Ollet. Does this king know what a jerk he is?"

"Obviously not, if Snatas has managed to secure a position on this team. I'm calling the minister after our meeting."

Minister Maharba answered his own phone, "Good morning, Maharba here."

"Good morning, Minister, this is Gen. Tobba."

"Good morning, General."

"Is the budget so short that you've lost your secretary, sir?"

"No, no," he laughed, "I just let her go to lunch with her old friend, Gen. Snatas."

"*General* Snatas, sir? When did *that* happen?"

"The king promoted him just an hour ago. Snatas, because of his experience in Ogeeremman intelligence, shall be in charge of your little investigative foray."

Gen. Tobba was speechless. After a moment, the minister asked, "General, are you there?"

"Yes, sir."

"Is something wrong, sir?"

"Mr. Minister, Colonel, I mean, *General* Snatas has a deep hatred of Ogeeremmans, and…"

"Nonsense, Ollet. Snatas is Ogeeremman by birth. How did you get the impression that he hates his countrymen?"

"I've heard his rhetoric, sir. I've seen his attitude. He was incredibly rude to my Ogeeremman daughter-in-law for no other reason than her roots."

"Ollet, it's not like you to bring personal things into the professional realm."

"Sir, personal things aside, I want to go on record as having said that Snatas' involvement in this mission is all wrong for the tone of relationship that the king is trying to establish with Ogeeremma."

"Duly noted, General, and I appreciate your candor; however, I did not make this decision and I seriously doubt that I can effectively undermine Snatas' standing with the king. Eltsac Tollemac was just a small prince when he first came to know Snatas. The general is like family to him, with influence wide and deep." In spite of his forgone conclusions to the contrary, as the conversation came to a close, the minister had to ask, "Why would Snatas hate his own people, General?"

"I don't know the man well," Tobba responded, "but as I understand, he was tormented as a child because of his looks. As Ogeeremmans go, even froggy old Col. Nomis is more handsome. Snatas was marginalized by everyone, including his own parents, who had serious alcohol and drug problems. Eventually he was snatched from the gutter and sold into Revotfell, not as a future groom or adopted son, but as a slave laborer. Through Revotfell's slavery-reduction laws, he purchased his citizenship and moved up through society, but remains extremely bitter toward his roots. It is said that he has a special hatred for Gardeners, that he blames much of Ogeeremma's fixation with beauty on their fascination with the nearby Garden. He accuses them of 'Garden worship.'"

For the next couple of weeks, Gen. Tobba and Col. Nomis put in long hours discussing the impending mission. They wanted to be on the same page with each other before their first meeting with Gen. Snatas. However, after two full weeks neither Tobba nor Nomis had been contacted by the general. In a morning meeting, just after they had decided that they needed to inquire about the proposed schedule for this adventure, they received a call from Maharba.

"Good morning, Minister, we were just about to call you," Gen. Tobba answered.

"General, have you spoken to Gen. Snatas?"

"Why no, sir, that's why we were about to call you."

"Ollet, we have a serious problem on our hands! How soon can you be at the palace?"

"I'm leaving right now, sir."

Upon the general's arrival, the minister of war accompanied him out into the palace garden. "His highness is afraid to talk freely in the palace," Maharba told him, "Snatas is a master spy, and we don't know what could all be bugged around here!"

The young monarch greeted the two men with heartfelt gratitude, momentarily masking his alarm, but then got right to business. "These are dark days, gentlemen. It appears that I have been deceived. I was unwise to bend to old alliances. Noinim Snatas is more like family to me than anything. Apparently, he also considers himself royalty and has taken power into his own hands."

King Eltsac quit talking as an aid approached. "Excuse me Sire, sirs, but I was told that you would greatly appreciate this message from Col. Nomis," the aid said.

The message was addressed to Gen. Tobba, who read it aloud. "It says, 'General, I was informed just a few minutes ago that Revol Refficul is not among the prisoners. He was not missed until roll call. Apparently our night guard is also missing.'" Gen. Tobba put the note in his pocket and informed them that "Revol Refficul was the leader of the Ogeeremman Unifists we are detaining at Col. Nomis' outpost."

"Snatas!" the king proclaimed. "Gen. Snatas needed him. It's the only explanation. You see, he has gone off on his own without any further discussion of the purpose or permissible means of this mission, and he does not answer any radio calls. I conceived this as a mission with a couple dozen good men at most, each with very specific talents and tasks. But it appears that Snatas has wandered off with about two hundred troops. I greatly fear that he is about to plunge us into war!"

"Your Highness, have you considered contacting the Ogeeremmans?" Gen. Tobba asked.

"I fear that, should I do so, I might perhaps avert war at the expense of the lives of two hundred of Revotfell's finest," the king responded. "I am hoping, General, that you can give me another alternative."

"We can go after them, Sire. I can take a small band of men. I can relieve him of command."

King Eltsac thought for a moment. "I'm sure Snatas was not foolish enough to travel as a single band. I believe you will find yourself looking for any one of many small groups of men. Though Snatas was slated to lead this mission, you are still above him in the overall chain of command. Unless he has officers within these groups who bear some secret allegiance to a cause other than the greater good of Revotfell, you should be able to take command of a group and have them lead you to the rendezvous point.

"General, I was a fool," the young monarch admitted. "I was apprised of your concerns with Snatas and chose to ignore them. I ask your forgiveness and place the future of the kingdom in your hands. My trust is absolute. Do whatever you deem appropriate to right this situation."

The general gestured his acceptance with a quick formal bow, and declared, "We must lose no time!"

Within hours Gen. Tobba met with his new team, which consisted of Col. Nomis, two of the Unifist captives, and eleven members of the kings own elite force, the Vanguard Tollemac.

"Gentlemen, I am well aware of your skills," Tobba said, addressing the Vanguard. "No doubt you are already aware of the importance King Eltsac places upon this mission. The situation is serious; there is no room for error. We must leave immediately."

Fortunately, the Vanguard had always shared totally in all intelligence gathered by the kingdom, but now it seemed likely that Snatas had been keeping them out of the loop on some things. Still, though they had no agents within Ogeeremma, all of the old contacts remained in place. The same people who helped Snatas would perhaps cooperate with the Vanguard as well. They launched their excursion from Col. Nomis' headquarters. The small troop outpost, having practically no strategic significance, had no counterpart on Ogeeremma's side of the border. Instead, there were just miles and miles of rocky, rolling hills, and scraggly meadows barely suitable for pasture. The Ogeeremmans did daily air reconnaissance of the wilderness and the outpost, but the border was wide open at night.

They maneuvered through the dark in rough-terrain vehicles, night vision glasses allowing them to pass through without the use of headlights. Two hours of driving through wilderness took them to their first known contact. "Do they know we're coming?" Nomis asked the Vanguard's Major Cirederf.

"We radioed a coded message, but received no response."

They parked the vehicles a couple hundred meters beyond the outbuildings of the old farmstead, and three members of the Vanguard moved through the darkness and up to the house. In fifteen minutes they returned.

"Our friends are dead!" reported Maj. Cirederf, "apparently for about four hours now. Snatas has a good head start on us. Their military vehicles are hidden in the barn and in the trees."

"How many vehicles?" Gen. Tobba asked.

"Five, sir," Cirederf said. "Five ten-passenger vehicles. Apparently they have split the 200 troops into four groups of fifty."

"That murdering scum!" the general seethed. "There goes our opportunity for less conspicuous transportation. It is a good thing that most of Ogeeremma's military is still at our borders, and this route has already allowed us to slip past them. However, troop withdrawal is scheduled to start in two days. We must keep moving."

"Unfortunately, General, these people might also have been able to tell us where to rendezvous. Now we are aimless."

"Not entirely, Major. Can there be any doubt that the final destination is Aseeremma, or somewhere near?"

"Of course, sir, but Aseeremma is a very big town," Cirederf pointed out.

The general sighed. "I hope that our Unifist prisoners can provide something helpful."

Dr. Veronica Elon, as she now called herself, kissed her praying husband on the cheek as she left him to go to work. They had just attended Mass together, and he was staying to pray, but she was finding it very difficult to leave his side. Pain from the wounds in his hands had become so great that he was no longer of much assistance at the hospital or orphanage. In fact, the caress of those hands, for which she longed night and day, had become almost foreign to her because of the great pain that any contact caused him. She prayed now mostly for strength against self-pity, strength to offer up her suffering so that she would not feel cheated by a husband and a Creator whose relationship seemed, more and more, to be excluding her.

When she had gone, Elon went into full ecstasy. The only other person left in the church was Jasmine, who was also lost in communion with her Savior. With hands extended to God, Elon prayed, oblivious to his surroundings and to the fact that he and Jasmine were no longer the only ones in the church. A chain cuff was placed around his left wrist and his arm pulled behind his back. His right arm was also pulled back and chained, and still he remained lost in prayer.

"What's wrong with him?" Gen. Snatas sneered.

"He has mental problems," explained Revol Refficul. "He thinks about this Jesus guy from Earth who got nailed to a wooden beam and hung out to dry, and he gets so emotionally involved that his hands bleed: a perfectly psycho nutcase if you ever saw one!"

"And we want this nut why? For fun?"

"He is the one who started the movement of Gardeners into Ogeeremma. He is a leader. If you want to conquer the Garden and enslave the Gardeners, understanding this guy will go a long way toward understanding them," Refficul explained.

"I don't want to mess away a bunch of time waiting for you to even some score that doesn't matter to me! The purpose this circus serves had better become obvious to me or you'll not live to enter the Garden!" Snatas thundered.

A nervous Refficul managed a quiet, "Understood, sir."

Noticing that Jasmine was undisturbed by his shouting, Snatas asked, "What's up with the tall one? Is she a Garden psycho too?"

"No, she's a harmless Earth psycho," Refficul assured him.

Soon they had gathered the seventeen from the orphanages and taken them to the riverside park near the church. Revotfellian guards were placed at the orphanages to keep the children and others from seeking help. The seventeen were tied to a cluster of small willow trees near the river's bank. All but a few of the two hundred troops in Snatas' group had made it to this rendezvous location. Because of the insane scope of the mission, Snatas had chosen fine soldiers, but none above the level of Sergeant—he had no desire to be second guessed by mid-level officers.

"Is this all of the Gardeners in Ogeeremma?" the general inquired.

"Oh no, sir, but these were the first here, and are the primary leaders of the movement," Refficul explained.

"This had better be good, Refficul," the general insisted.

"My only purpose, sir, is to show you what fools they are. The better we understand them, the easier it will be to enslave them."

"What do you mean, 'we'? You are my slimy slave as well! Have you forgotten your place?"

Refficul trembled and managed to stutter, "I only hope to ingratiate myself by serving you well, my lord."

"Well, then get on with it, man!"

The old fool grabbed hold of his emotions. He envisioned himself once again as the Grand Enabler and managed to stand proud. With the cocky air of a criminal prosecutor, he approached Elon.

"Oh, Great Prophet Elon...you are a prophet, aren't you?" he asked.

"Some say that I am," Elon responded humbly.

"Tell me, how old are you?"

"I am 118 years old."

"And your parents?"

"My father is 153, and my mother is 147."

"Are Gardeners immortal?"

"They are, so long as they eat from the tree."

"And what tree is that?"

"The tree of life, in the Garden."

"Are Gardeners indestructible?"

"So long as they eat from the tree."

"So...are you indestructible, Elon?"

"No."

"Why not?"

"Because I have eaten from the New Tree of Life."

"So, the New Tree makes you weaker?"

"No. The old tree makes the body immortal. The New Tree, Jesus Christ, the Son of the Living God, invites us to make a sacrifice of our present lives, and draws us into a deep, everlasting life of love."

"Sacrifice? There is nothing in the scriptures about making of your life a sacrifice!" Refficul insisted.

"It is in the Earth scriptures."

"Are you from Earth, or here?"

"I am of God."

Refficul approached Gen. Snatas. "Sir, may I borrow your sword?"

"Don't try anything stupid!" the general hissed as he handed it over.

Refficul continued to address Elon. "So, man of God, what happens if I lop off your friend's head? Will he still live?"

"Does not the scripture forbid you to murder?"

"One cannot murder a Gardener. They are immortal!" Refficul insisted.

Tied to the nearest tree was one of the seventeen, named Cozzie. With one skillful swipe, Refficul whacked off Cozzie's head. The Gardener's body hung lifeless, his hands still tethered to the tree, while his head lay on the ground in a pool of red. Refficul stepped back and stared, shocked by his own act. Suddenly, in the sight of all, Cozzie's clothes fell empty to the ground.

In spite of the guards who had been placed at the orphanages, word of the abductions was out—two hundred armed soldiers are hard to miss—and courageous Christians had sneaked into the park out of concern for their friends. They had seen the beheading, but they had also seen Cozzie's smiling head rejoin his radiant body. His glow had increased until, in blinding light, he had faded from sight. But the faithless Refficul had seen nothing but the results: empty clothes.

"Where did he go?" Refficul demanded of Elon.

"He has gone to his glory!"

"Don't give me that damn glory nonsense! The only glory that there will be is in the one kingdom!" Refficul insisted.

"That's right!" Elon agreed.

"I mean here, not in some fantasy world!" Refficul screamed angrily, but then his frown faded and an evil smile began to twist his lips as he recognized an opportunity. "Where are your grandparents, Elon?" he asked coyly.

"In the Garden."

"And your great grandparents?"

"In the Garden."

"And your great, great, great grandparents? Ha! You look at the ground. You need not answer. All you know are *stories* of glory. Today we have seen what the New Tree really does. It turns people to nothing!" He grabbed Cozzie's clothes and shouted to all those around, "How shall this body be resurrected? How?! He is gone forever!"

"His body is already resurrected!" Elon informed him. "Did you not see his flesh become whole again? Did you not see his radiant smile and his eyes so full of life? Did you not see him glow until he became a blinding light?"

"All I saw was a dead body disappear! Do you take me for a fool?" Refficul glanced about and demanded, "Did anyone else see what the great Elon saw?"

Before anyone could answer his question, Gen. Snatas lost his patience. "Refficul, why the hell is it that you think I give a damn about any of this?"

Refficul was so full of himself that he could not abandon his cocky attitude to save his own life. He turned and walked away. When he heard the general's pistol being cocked, he turned around and beckoned, with a single pointer finger, for Snatas to come to where he stood, out of earshot from the rest of the group. Snatas, pistol still cocked and pointed at Refficul, walked over to him and said, "This had better be good, dirt bag; my patience is gone!"

"My lord, are you not the least bit curious to know if someone else saw what Elon claims to have seen?" Refficul whispered. "Will you miss an opportunity to make him look like the fool he is? Elon and his friends from Earth are heroes to most Ogeeremmans. It would serve you well to soil the legend before you wreak havoc on his people, lest Ogeeremma come to their aid. You have not the resources to fight Ogeeremma *and* Earth!"

Refficul was a fool, but Snatas was a maniac, one who did not like being instructed by a fool, especially when the fool was making sense. With a swift backhanded swing, he struck Refficul in the face with his pistol, knocking out two teeth in the process. As Rev lay moaning on the ground, the general gave an order. "All those who did not see that man smile and glow before he vanished, stand over here," he said, pointing to the area where most of the Revotfellian troops already stood. Pointing to the captive Gardeners, he added, "All who saw the light, stand over here."

Seven stalwart Christians, who had been hiding nearby, moved to this spot. Among them was Tessa Oakley. "Is this it?" Snatas bellowed at Elon. "Is this the extent of your influence?" The general had hated Ogeeremmans and Gardeners all of his life, and being in their presence had swelled his hatred beyond control. With the vilest look on his face, he barked another order. "Kill all those who have seen the light!"

Most Revotfellians held Gardeners in awe, and these troops were no exception. They had no desire to massacre unarmed men and women for no apparent reason, so the general's command prompted only bewildered stares and the stirring of feet.

Just as Snatas opened his mouth to scream at his troops, another person stepped into the clearing between the troops and the captive Gardeners: Gen. Olletsoc Tobba. The Vanguard and Col. Nomis suddenly appeared from behind trees and bushes, brandishing automatic weapons.

Snatas took on a look of alarm, but Gen. Tobba simply went and stood among those who had seen the light, and asked, "Is there no soldier here who can obey a simple command?"

Inspired by the beloved general's bold move, twelve of Snatas' troops and three of the Vanguard threw down their weapons and joined the seers. No one else moved a muscle. All were silent.

Col. Nomis finally managed hoarsely, "Ollet...what are you doing? Order Snatas to stand down. These are loyal troops!"

But the general ignored him. "Who is there among you who can obey a simple command?" he demanded again. "Gen. Snatas has given an order!"

Finally, Snatas came forward and declared, "I can!"

"Of course you can, General; you've been lusting after my command position for years," Gen. Tobba noted.

"Tobba, what is your game here?" Snatas demanded.

Gen. Tobba smiled the most peaceful smile as he explained, "You see these people here beside me? Many of them have lived in the Garden for hundreds of years, but they have found their happiness out here. I want what they have found. I saw their friend rise."

"You've lost your mind, Tobba, just like your buddy, Elon!" Snatas declared. "Refficul, you were right: Their psychosis is contagious!" he roared. He looked about and proclaimed, "I'm going to give those who *think* they saw the light a few seconds to clear their heads and get the hell out of the way!" Three of the Revotfellian troops ran back to their ranks.

Snatas aimed his pistol at Gen. Tobba's chest and shouted, "Am I the only good soldier here?! The general has given an order!" He stared Ollet Tobba in the eye for a second, and then, at point blank range, shot him through the heart. The general's face twisted in pain, but he did not fall. Instead, his grimace turned to the most beautiful smile. He glowed for a moment, and vanished.

Elon smiled upon the empty uniform that had fallen to the ground beside him. "Today is indeed the dawn of a new age," he proclaimed, "for a mortal has entered glory with soul *and* body!"

Gen. Snatas screamed, "Finish the general's command!" But though he scoured their ranks with a scornful gaze, not a single man made an effort to obey. When the general looked back upon the seers, he found a new face. Veronica stood in front of Elon. She had saved her husband's life once; God willing, she would do so again. In her hand she held the only weapon she had been issued, a titanium dagger.

Snatas began to laugh at her. "Ooh, I'm scared!" he said. Noting her startling beauty, he wrongly deduced that she was from the Garden. "Is this the way it works in the Garden? Are you the angel who guards the border? Ha! Is that your revolving sword?"

"I am a woman!" she shouted at him.

"I don't give a damn what you are!" he bellowed. "Let's see how good you are with that dandy little sword!" He aimed his pistol at her forehead and pulled the trigger. Veronica felt the wind of the bullet as it zipped past her ear. Snatas went to take another shot, but the gun jammed. Turning to the troops, he shouted, "Finish the general's command!" but they did not respond. While Snatas cursed at the soldiers, Veronica turned and cut the ropes that bound Elon.

The infuriated general finally grabbed a machine gun from a soldier, and began to mow down all of the seers. Elon grabbed Veronica in his arms and turned his back toward Snatas. All the seers vanished as they were shot, except for Elon, Veronica, and Tessa. Elon remained standing, hunched around his valiant wife, but Tessa lay bleeding on the ground. In rage and exasperation, the general emptied the gun on Elon, and Veronica felt her husband begin to collapse on top of her.

When Snatas had spent all of his bullets, the maniac rushed toward the couple to beat them with the emptied gun. Hearing his steps, Veronica surmised that he was out of bullets, and struggled to free herself from her fallen husband. As Snatas raised the gun in the air to strike them, she emerged from beneath Elon and thrust her dagger deep into the general's abdomen. The stupefied Snatas dropped the gun and stared at her in amazement. His knees gave out, and he fell backward clutching the handle of the dagger.

Time stood still and all else faded from existence as Veronica turned to gaze upon her fallen husband. Why had he not gone into glory like the rest? The holes in the back of his shirt wrenched her heart and took her breath. Dazed, she ran her fingers over his bullet riddled back. *If only he had eaten from the old tree one last time!* her heart screamed, but then she realized that he was not bleeding. She pulled him onto his side, and placed her ear over his heart. Its vigorous rhythm brought tears of joy. She looked up at him through those tears, and his grin invited an exuberant embrace.

As Elon stood, a dumbfounded Rev Refficul approached him Through the muffle of bleeding lips and missing teeth he asked, "How is this possible? Why did you not die? Have you forsaken the New Tree for the old?" The old Unifist's eyes probed Elon's for answers.

Elon smiled gently, and speaking loud enough to address the crowd that was gathering around him, proclaimed, "Who can fathom the ways of the Creator? While bullets ripped through my flesh, I stood in his presence. Careful was he not to reveal too much of his glory, for so great is his kindness that, had I asked to stay, he would not have forced me to come back here. The faintest glimpse of glory reveals all else, even the Garden, to be Exile! The true Garden, which lies within our hearts, has been restored, and all flesh redeemed. There is no real king but the King of Heaven whom my friends have gone to see. Their deaths are a sacrifice for your souls. Will you waste their sacrifice?"

As Elon finished speaking, Veronica was on her com. "Where are those ambulances?" she shouted into the communicator as she hunched over Snatas. "The conflict has ended and we have two people down!" Earlier that day a clever orphan had evaded the Revotfellian guards and found Veronica at the hospital. Veronica had ordered ambulances to stand by and had alerted the city police. The police had encircled the park, but slightly outnumbered, were hoping that armed engagement would not be necessary.

Veronica carefully extracted the dagger from the general's midsection while treating the wound with a Restowand. As the General's wound began to mend before her eyes, she recalled all the times she had attempted to heal Elon's hands to no avail.

"Let me die!" Snatas implored her. "Why are you helping me?"

"Well, first of all, General, I'm a woman—not an angel—just an ordinary Exile woman. Secondly, I'm a doctor, and helping people is what I do."

"Beautiful people only care about themselves!" he informed her.

"Don't talk, and lie still," she advised him as two men approached with a stretcher.

She winced at the piercing sound of a bullhorn as the shrill voice of the Aseeremma Police captain said, "Revotfellian troops! We have no desire to engage you." The speaker went on to suggest a meeting between himself and the leader of the invasion force. Col. Nomis went immediately to engage him in discussion.

Amidst the commotion, Tessa Oakley found herself in the arms of a strong man. He gently carried her away from the crowd.

"I can walk! You don't need to fuss," she insisted, but Bishop Hadrian would not put her down, and continued to smother her brow with tender kisses. He set her on a park bench to examine her wound. She lifted her skirt to reveal a gash high in her thigh where a bullet had grazed her.

As he fashioned a bandage from a clean handkerchief and his belt, the bishop asked, "Why didn't you flee when the general allowed the opportunity?"

"When he ordered everyone who had seen the light to stand in that place, I was hiding in some bushes. I had no need to go there. No one would have known the difference. I went because it seemed like an opportunity to witness to the Lord's work. Had I run away when he offered the opportunity it would have been like denying God, like saying that I hadn't seen Cozzie miraculously taken. Later on, I might have been singled out as a Christian and killed anyway, and my death would have been a pointless, wasted death rather than martyrdom."

"So…you think the rest all died a martyr's death? Even the general who encouraged his own death?"

"David, the Lord took him, soul *and* body! I know his theology was less than perfect, but his heart and his soul were yearning for his

Creator in such a powerful way. His trust in the Lord was invincible," she said, looking into the bishop's eyes. "Trust is the beginning and foundation of all love, and this man had incredible trust."

Her eyes went wide as David's lips touched hers for the first time. He stopped kissing her to ask, "Do you trust me?"

"With all my heart!" Tessa answered, "But...," he interrupted her with another kiss, but she squirmed free to finish. "What about your vow?"

"Celibacy?" he asked.

"Of course!" she shot back.

Her heart was reeling through a thousand miles of emotion and projecting it in her eyes, searching, it seemed, for the exact point in time when she had fallen in love with this man. Her reeling heart pulled up the scene of one of their first conversations. They were working together on the garden decks and he was giving her a wonderful explanation of consecrated celibacy. "I am a priest. I stand in the place of Christ," he had said. "As the Church is *his* bride, she is mine as well." He had hesitated for a moment, seemingly uncertain as to whether he should continue, but at last had added, "I don't know if I can adequately express this, but celibacy is, in a certain sense of the mystery, kind of the ultimate sexual expression. Our sexuality is both carnal and spiritual. I have consecrated my body and soul to God, and he is the only one who can really fulfill our entire being. Though I have chosen not to procreate, I can bring *spiritual* children to God."

Deep irony suddenly struck Tessa, like an unexpected plunge in a vat of icy holy water. She had begun to fall in love with David while she had listened to him wax poetically about the beauty of his celibacy!

David jolted her daydream with, "You know that I have the Holy Father's permission to..."

"To forsake your vow should procreation be required for *survival*," she finished for him.

"Yes, survival, but he left that decision to be made at my own discretion," the Bishop said, as he checked her bandage, tracing a cross of blessing on her beautiful thigh. "That day on the Covenant, after we had hit that piece of space junk and you had announced that the ship was unfit for a return voyage, my heart made a decision. It has been waiting for my mind to catch up. Today, you destroyed my indecision. This is now a matter of survival: For my heart to survive, it must have you!"

"Aren't you being a bit presumptuous?" she asked. "Who in their right mind would want to be married to a bishop? What kind of life would that be?"

"Is that what I see in your eyes?" Bishop Hadrian asked. "That you are not in your right mind? It is my stock and trade to peer into human hearts: the purer the heart, the more transparent. You can hide nothing from me. You're in love. Every fiber of your being shouts it! My heart's not strong enough to ignore that!"

"You told me once that you 'stand in the place of Christ,' that 'the Church is your bride.' If that's the case, what's left for me? To be your concubine?"

She was right. Her words seemed raw and harsh, as truth often does. Bishop Hadrian stood. With tense hands he smoothed the furrow in his brow as he turned to gaze at the church tower in the distance. Was one bride not enough? He loved his ministry and his church. He had never felt so torn. The pained look on his face was more than Tessa could take. She touched his leg gently and he looked down into her longing eyes. "I'm sorry, David!" she said sweetly. "I do trust you! Follow your heart, and I will follow you! I would be so honored to be at your side serving the Church!"

He went to one knee and kissed her lips. She reciprocated deeply, but then squirmed to terminate it so that she could ask, "Why now, man? What took you so long? Here we are in broad daylight, my skirt pulled up, a bullet hole in my thigh, and you're…"

He cut her tirade short with the best means available, another kiss, and then answered her question. "Why now? I don't know. Being a bishop and all, I guess I just have a thing for martyrs." He went to kiss her again, but she placed her fingertips over his lips. The look in her eyes told him that she needed to hear the real reason. He did not disappoint. "The thought of losing you nearly killed me!"

Meanwhile, upon Col. Nomis' return from his meeting with the Aseeremman police captain, he gathered the troops into a tight group and addressed them. "Gen. Tobba was dispatched by King Eltsac specifically to stop this illegal action led by Gen. Snatas. It is not in our interest or Revotfel's to engage the local police. To that end, you will leave all of your weapons on the ground where you stand, retreat to your vehicles, and return immediately to Revotfel. I have offered myself as hostage and will be staying until such time that Ogeeremma sees fit to allow my return."

In the commotion caused by the disbanding troops, Nomis called the remaining members of the Vanguard aside. "Snatas was filled with hatred for Ogeeremma and the Garden," he said. "But as you can see, neither Christians nor Gardeners present a threat to Revotfell. They possess no earthly power and have no ambitions. It is the Unifists who have great ambitions! It is they who have attacked our borders! Go to their halls and get lists of names, but be cautious. I don't want any more killing. Before Ogeeremma's armies return from other borders, act quickly to gather our intelligence!"

The colonel turned to Elon and said, "I am sorry for the loss of your friends."

"Do not be, for they are in a better place," Elon assured him. "I can see that you had a great love for your general. Be confident that he is in glory with the Father. His simple faith has assured his place, along with that of my friends."

Col. Nomis smiled through teary eyes. "If I am allowed to return to Revotfell, I will send you money. With it I humbly request that you place a statue on this spot, as is our custom, to honor the general."

"With respect, sir, I would rather place a statue to honor that greatest of all generals, the one whom he now serves!"

"Who might that be?" the colonel wondered.

"The One who stands before us!"

"I see no one!" Nomis said, turning about.

"Look again."

When Col. Nomis turned around again, the One began to appear as the Immaculate Conception. A brilliant white light emanated from her body, so that all who looked upon her were barely able to look long enough to see that she was a beautiful young woman. As all knelt in prayer, her image faded from view.

Caressing his face in her hands, Veronica interrupted her husband's meditation. Invaded by her tender touch, he grasped her waist and hoisted her toward heaven, spinning for joy before finally lowering her for a sweet kiss. She was delighted and puzzled. Something was different. As always, he was gentle, yet his hands were so strong and sure upon her waist. At last the difference came to her. She pulled away, grasped his hands, and turned his palms up.

"The wounds are gone! The wounds of the Savior are gone! What does this mean?" she asked, her face paling for fear that he was on the brink of glory.

The great prophet responded with the prophecy Veronica had longed to hear her entire life. "My brave, brave wife," he said. "I will take up a new sacrifice, the sacrifice of fatherhood. As your name indicates, you are a true image, and your womb shall become a wellspring of the image of God. Like the One, who is called the Queen of Prophets, you shall come to be revered as the mother of many prophets!"

Her husband's prophecy excited her entire being, and she gave him a long, deep kiss that told him she was way more than ready for the task. As they kissed, a breeze blew up from the river, and Veronica felt something soft and silky around her bare ankles. She looked down and saw that the breeze had blown Aniram's dress against her feet. She stooped and picked up the gown and buried her face in it. The lingering sweet scent of her adopted big sister brought her to tears. She wrapped the garment around her neck like a scarf, and said to Elon, "On Earth we have a custom. When very holy people die, people whose lives have been a great example to others, often times their clothing or other personal things are saved in remembrance of them. We call these things relics. They connect us in a special way to those who have gone into glory."

Elon removed his bullet riddled shirt to use it as a bag. Tears of thanksgiving welled in Veronica's eyes as she beheld his woundless back and caught daylight through the two dozen bullet holes in the back of the garment. He retrieved all of the clothing and items on the ground while she went to check on Tessa. She found her friend safely in Bishop Hadrian's arms as he carried her to Oilenroc's vehicle. "I'll come to the hospital with you," she told her.

"Ronnie, I don't need to go to the hospital. The bullet barely scratched me, but David won't quit babying me."

The Bishop just smiled and said, "I think she'll be fine, Doctor. I just want to make sure the wound is cleaned up and dressed properly."

"Then why won't you put me down?" Tessa complained.

"Because, for a very long time I've wanted to hold you, and now any excuse will do," he answered.

Veronica turned to Elon and said, "We have to go to the orphanage and break the news about the seventeen to the children. They'll be devastated."

As Veronica and Elon sprinted off in the direction of the orphanage, Bishop Hadrian helped Tessa into the backseat of Oilenroc's car.

"I saw her, David," she said. "I saw the Virgin Mary. All my life I've been told that the apparitions of saints were just silly Catholic imagination, that God doesn't need any help from humans to do his work."

"He doesn't," the bishop responded, and noting her puzzled look, contemplated an explanation. After a moment's thought, he said, "Do you remember meeting my nephew Joshua at the AGC mission crew picnic?"

Shortly before embarking on the long voyage, the crew members and their families had enjoyed a picnic sponsored by the AGC. The gathering was intended to help families let go slowly and find some consolation in knowing that their loved ones belonged to a crew which was becoming a family of its own. Bishop Hadrian's sister and family had flown in from South Africa to attend. The officers of the crew had donned aprons for the occasion and served up the goods as crew and family filed by with their plates, but little Joshua had refused to leave his uncle's side.

"How could I forget Joshua?" Tessa answered. "He's the sweetest little thing. Five is such a cute age to start with, but he's extra cute, like his uncle! I can still see him in that adult-sized apron trying to help you dish up the hotdogs."

"Do you think he was much help?"

"That's an odd question. No, but he sure enjoyed it. I think I retrieved half a dozen hotdogs from the ground before he got the hang of it."

"So...why'd we let him help? He just created more work for us."

"Hmmm...so, what are you saying? That the saints are God's five-year-olds?"

The bishop ignored her question and asked another, "Do you remember our little discussion in the park when I was preparing my homily last week?"

"The one about 2 Peter? The part about becoming 'partakers in the divine nature?'"

"Yeah...that one. You see, we *are* God's five-year-olds. It brings us, and the saints in heaven, incredible joy to be able to help, and..."

"I know what you're going to say next," Tessa interrupted, "that, just as it was a ball for you to watch little Joshua do his best, even though his *help* wasn't really needed, it's a great joy for God to watch his unselfish saints in action."

"No, smarty-pants, I wasn't going to say that, but that's very good! I was about to say something about 2 Peter, that's why I brought it up."

There was a moment of silence as they accelerated through a busy intersection. Tessa looked at David with *Well, what were you gonna say?* written in her comically wide open eyes and cocked head.

He brushed the tip of her nose with his and locked eyeballs with her, "You finished my thought once...figured maybe you wanted a second shot at it."

"Okay," she accepted the challenge. "2 Peter..." She paused for a minute to collect her thoughts, and speaking slowly while she thought, said, "You were going to say that, by helping God, we share in his life: He's everywhere; we're there with him. He is all love; we love with his love. He knows all things; we share in that knowledge. He's all powerful; through him we can accomplish all things."

"Wow! Did you hear that Oilenroc? That's my girlfriend who said that! I was also going to say," he continued, while turning to face Tessa, "that the saints are more than just pampered children, they are trusted friends, generals in the army of God, troops armed only with his invincible divine love."

"Hmmm...Jesus is our King, and Mary is generalissimo," she reasoned.

"Bingo, señorita!"

"By the way," she added, "I don't want to be your 'girlfriend.'"

"Oh?" he asked.

Oilenroc parked at the emergency entrance of the hospital. The bishop swung open the huge door on the curb side, got out, and helped Tessa to her feet. He lifted her onto the curb, and when she was standing with her face level to his, he could see in her expression that she was not amused by the fact that he was ignoring the bait.

"Was I supposed to call you my fiancée? Did you think that what I said in the park amounted to a proposal? Is that why the ambiance made you so upset?"

"We established that you were willing to have a wife and that I was willing to be that wife."

"And?"

"And I don't believe in Limbo, David, and I don't want to live there!"

"I don't believe in Limbo either. It's poor theology, you know," the bishop assured her.

She rolled her eyes heavenward, and when her gaze returned to the man of her dreams, she found him on one knee in the gutter. He took her hands in his and asked, "Is this really the time and place, my love?"

Tessa smiled with delight, and running her fingers into his thick hair, stooped, pressed her lips to his, and after a quick kiss said, "No! And my leg is killing me! Could you please carry me in?"

When she was in his arms, he asked, "What happened to little Miss I-can-take-care-of-myself?"

She grinned back at him with peaceful resolve, and said drolly, "She was martyred."

David carried her into the hospital, smiling to himself and asking God why both his bride and his bride-to-be had to be so high-maintenance. As he was about to put her down, a nurse called, "Excellency!" When he looked in her direction, she continued, "Father, a man on third floor is begging for a priest. We believe that he is near death!"

Tessa kissed his cheek and ordered, "Go quickly, David!" As she watched her man run away, she advised herself, *"It's a good thing he looks good from behind, because it's a view that you had better get used to, girl!"*

On their way to the orphanage, Veronica and Elon stopped at the church. In preparation for her pending religious vows, Jasmine had been spending long hours in prayer before the Blessed Sacrament. She was already wearing the habit that the bishop had approved, a simple white cotton dress. Her glorious long hair was tied in a tail and would only come down when she prayed in private, dancing before her Spouse and King. Veronica smiled warmly at the sight of her friend and gently touched her arm. "Sister, a terrible thing has happened," she told her.

Veronica and Elon told her of the day's events as the three walked to the orphanage. On their arrival the children ran out to meet them. It seemed that these little ones already knew something was wrong, for some of the youngest hugged them and wouldn't let go. Once inside, Elon laid out the clothing of the seventeen on a table and explained to the children that their friends had gone into glory. Many of them began to cry, as did Elon and Veronica. A still shirtless Elon touched the red satin garment that was around Veronica's neck. Seeing his pain, she took it from her own neck and placed it around his. The feel of the satin reminded him of the touch of Aniram's embrace, which, coupled with her lingering fragrance, brought him even more to tears.

"There was a time when Aniram wore many different dresses," Elon noted, "but since my return, she has seldom worn anything but this."

"That is an Ogeeremman wedding gown," Veronica explained as she dabbed a tear from her husband's cheek. "Red is the traditional Ogeeremman color for the occasion. When she learned that she would never be *your* bride—and was taught that Christ spoke of himself as the bride-groom and of the Church as his bride—Aniram decided she would dress as His bride every day for the rest of her life."

As Elon absorbed this new information, Veronica excused herself with, "I'll be right back." He watched as she went up the open staircase to their room, and sat staring blankly after her, too emotionally spent for any new business to cross his mind. In a few minutes she emerged from the room. She took four steps down the stairs and stopped. It is hard to say which Veronica liked better, getting surprised or giving surprises, for indeed, she loved both. Her eyes met the teary eyes of her husband, who stood to drink in the sight of her. She wore the little white satin evening gown she had worn the night of their wedding, an occasion as of yet not properly celebrated with the rest of the community. He just stood there with his mouth agape, basking in the radiance of her smile. At last he removed Aniram's garment from around his neck, kissed it, placed it on the table in front of him, and turned and left the building.

Veronica's smile faded away, and she began to admonish herself. How could she have been so insensitive? Elon had just lost a friend of seventy years, a friend whom he had, for many years, longed to marry, and here was silly Veronica, within hours of that friend's passing, trying to cheer her husband with happy memories of their wedding.

The large mess hall of the orphanage had filled with a host of mutual friends. All of Elon's family was there, and most of the crew of Star Covenant. After a quick trip to the hospital, Tessa Oakley and Bishop Hadrian were there, as were Bishop Scofield and Fr. Schmidt. In the midst of all the bustle, two orphan girls noticed a crestfallen Veronica seated on the stairs in her lovely gown, and went to surround her with affection. Good intentions not withstanding, their questions about the dress and her tears made the moment still more difficult. She gathered the little ones onto her lap and held them tight while she prayed, soothed by the occasional innocent kisses they laid on her cheeks.

Veronica decided that she must find and console her husband, but first she would remove the offending garment. As she stood and turned to go to her bedroom, she received a serious tug on the hem of her skirt. She turned to see an urchin's smiling face. "What do you want, honey?" she asked the little girl. The child merely pointed toward the front door. What Veronica saw nearly took her breath away, for there stood her husband wearing a big smile and a military dress uniform, the one he had worn for their wedding.

The little girls who had come to her aid now each took Veronica by a hand and led her down the stairs. When they reached the bottom step, Antonio and Jean entered the room dressed as they had been the night of Elon and Veronica's wedding. An elated Veronica now ran to her husband. He placed his hands on her tiny waist and hoisted her into the air, slowly lowering her until her lips met his.

When they had finished kissing, she asked, "Do you like my dress?"

"I love your dress! Do you like my suit?"

"I guess," she said with a wink. "You make the suit look very nice. It's just that, well…you know, I really don't like clothing."

"I'll see what I can do about that!" he declared, squeezing her.

They hugged Antonio and Jean, thanking them for their part in the impromptu surprise. Bishop Scofield raised his hands in the air in an effort to quiet the group. When at last the room settled, he addressed them.

"Dear friends. We have gathered together this evening to console one another over the loss of our friends. But in here," he said, placing his hand over his heart, "we know that they have not gone. Glory is a state of being, not a place. Our friends have gone nowhere. They are right here with us. Yes, we will miss the sound of their voices, their fragrance, the touch of their hands, and their smiling eyes, but our faith tells us that they are here among us, and that they are immeasurably happier than we can imagine. Tomorrow morning I will celebrate a Requiem Mass for them, but tonight, let us soothe our grief by celebrating their happiness, and let us invite them to celebrate our happiness. I see before me a bride and her groom who have had no opportunity to celebrate, with their community, the covenant relationship they have entered. Please celebrate with us as they renew their vows."

Veronica could hardly believe what was happening. Why was she so impulsive? She had only meant to cheer up her husband, and now, on the eve of the passing of so many dear friends, the Bishop was inviting the mourners to join in a wedding celebration. She certainly would not blame people if they were offended. However, the room fell hushed, and she momentarily forgot her remorse when she gazed into Elon's eyes. They repeated their vows for all to hear, the Bishop prayed a blessing, and his introduction of the couple brought the assembly to applause.

With this applause, even as she kissed her husband, Veronica once again felt the awkwardness of the situation. She was uncomfortable being the center of so much attention, a mere distraction from the momentous events of the day. As the applause subsided, she began to hear people singing an old Ogeeremman folk song, a very danceable old jig. As she looked about to see from where the voices were coming, the garments of the seventeen suddenly disappeared from the table where Elon had placed them, and in another moment, eight couples appeared out of nowhere dancing in an open area between the tables. Cries of joy rang from everywhere in the room as they all recognized the faces of the dancers. After doing the math, Veronica turned to Elon and said, "Someone's missing."

The song came to an end, the dancing stopped, and out of the midst of the dancers stepped a small child. She was about nine years old, with beautiful golden hair cascading down past her hips. Veronica leaned in her direction and said, "Aniram?"

Seeing the child, who so many years ago had rode all around the Garden on his back, Elon looked to heaven and said, "Thank you, Lord, for this beautiful vision."

But the sweet child said, "Vision?" and grasped Elon by the hand. The warmth of her touch made him tremble. She grasped Veronica with her other hand and tugged the two into the midst of the dancers. As the couple knelt to embrace her, she said, "I have a song for you, and it would make me very happy if you would dance to it." She began to sing and was soon joined by the sixteen dancers. They sang the lovely, haunting melody of the old Ogeeremman seven-step Wedding Waltz.

When at last the bride and groom were able to take their eyes off of Aniram, they stood, embraced, and with eyes closed, began to sway slowly to the music. As they did so, the seventeen broke into harmony. Toward the end of the second verse, Elon realized that he could no longer hear a nine-year-old voice among them. He opened his eyes and beheld the mature bride of the Lamb in her red satin wedding gown, blessing them with her approving smile.

Sunil and her brothers began to accompany the singers, and everyone in the hall now sang along. Sunil's band had taken to practicing at the orphanage and giving lessons to the orphans, and they were well versed in the old Ogeeremman folk tunes. When at last Veronica opened her eyes, she was facing the table where Elon had placed the garments of the seventeen. All of the clothing was once again neatly placed on the table, and though the dancers were nowhere in sight, she could still hear the voices of their glorified friends. At peace at last, she smiled serenely at her husband and laid her head once again on his shoulder.

The next tune was a rousing jig, and everyone joined in the dancing. Wine was poured and shared, and food was brought from many homes in Aseeremma until all had enjoyed a veritable feast. They danced on and on into the night.

At midnight, between songs, Bishop Scofield held a glass of wine high for all to see, while Bishop Hadrian and Tessa began to tap their glasses with the tableware. When he had everyone's attention, he said, "Through the evening I have given some thought to what I might say by way of a little send-off speech. However, I have decided that there is nothing I can say about these two that this crowd does not already know, so I will speak directly to the bride and groom.

"Veronica and Elon, I love you. The love you have for each other feeds my heart. St. Paul was of the opinion that the unmarried state of consecrated life was the surest, most undistracted road to the heart of the Almighty. Perhaps he was right, but if holy spouses—like the two of you—are distractions, they are glorious ones! I have no doubt that you will lead each other and many others to eternal life. And speaking of others, it takes more than dancing to beget children!" He raised his glass high in the air, waited a moment for others to raise theirs, and said, "To the honeymoon!" The room burst into applause as the newly-weds kissed.

The long, obnoxious honking of a car's horn interrupted their kiss, and the couple stepped out to see Oilenroc's old jalopy. It was all done up by the Covenant crew in mid-twentieth-century Earth regalia for the event: tin cans, toilet paper, and tooth paste.

Veronica turned to Bishop Scofield and said, "But...we have to pack before we leave."

The Bishop laughed melodiously and said, "I've been to the place where you're going. Trust me, you don't need to pack!" While Oilenroc whisked the couple toward his car, the bride kept glancing back at the Bishop with a puzzled look. What he meant finally sank in, and she flashed him a huge grin just before stepping into the vehicle.

As Oilenroc began to drive, Veronica asked, "Who will care for the orphans? The seventeen are gone, and now we're leaving too."

"The children will be well cared for, my dear," Oilenroc answered. "The family of God will see to their needs."

Elon knew that his excited and nervous bride could not go long without asking another question, and he began to chuckle when she said, "I thought we were heading for the beach." The ever calm Oilenroc just smiled back at her in the rear view mirror and continued to drive. Suddenly realizing that Antonio and Jean had not been among the well wishers who had sent them off, she said, "We must go back. It's bad manners to leave a wedding party without thanking your attendants." But Oilenroc just kept driving. In a few minutes, he drove into a large parking lot and stopped alongside Shuttle 1. The shuttle door whooshed open and Antonio and Jean came down the ramp.

"Welcome to Paradise Airlines," Antonio said.

Veronica laughed, but shivered in the night air. The chivalrous groom removed his jacket and placed it over her bare shoulders. "How do we know that we can take a shuttle into the Garden?" she asked Antonio. "Perhaps Elon's prayers only covered a single event."

"Unknown to most, Bishop Hadrian has been visiting the Garden regularly to seek more help for the Church," Antonio answered. "We will be safe."

Minutes later, the shuttle's feet clattered against the hard surface of the Plateau. The newlyweds walked out into the night air and Veronica said, "I guess I won't be needing this," as she removed her husband's jacket.

Jean brought out a water-proof container and said, "There is a compartment in here for the clothes you're wearing, and another one containing clean clothes for your return trip and for attending Mass."

"Attending Mass?" Veronica asked.

"Yes. The Garden is now officially a parish. Bishop Hadrian will be offering Mass every day at 10:00 AM by the tree of life."

Handing a com to Veronica, Antonio said, "Call us when you're ready...but if it's less than two weeks from now, I won't come anyway."

The honeymooners embraced their best man and maid of honor in a foursome hug and sent them on their way. Alpha Centari B was nearly directly overhead and bathed the landscape and the lovers in its warm orange glow. When they had undressed each other, Veronica suddenly leaned against her husband saying, "I don't feel so well," and proceeded to faint in his arms. The long day had taken an immense emotional and physical toll on the poor woman. Elon gathered her into his arms and carried her to a grassy hollow that lay a short distance from the Plateau. Seated against the trunk of a great tree, he held his wife while she slept with her head resting on his chest. Noticing that one of the tree's succulent fruits hung within his grasp, he picked it, took a bite, and via a kiss, placed it in his wife's gaping mouth. In a moment her body detected the great medicine, and she opened her eyes. Elon fed her another morsel. Her eyes grew when she realized what she was eating. "Honey, the tree will dry up again!" she warned.

"It is medicine," he insisted. "Eat and enjoy."

She finished the fruit and stood to stretch, mesmerizing Elon with her beauty as she swayed in the midnight glow. And then, to his amazement and amusement, she picked him up and began to carry him away.

"Where are you taking me, my love?" he asked

"To the mountain top, where I will fulfill your every desire," she said with sultry tone.

"If you would fulfill my every desire, do not waste all the power of the fruit on carrying me up the mountain!" he insisted.

They ascended Ekim in a series of sweet lovers' chases; now he captured and carried her; then she captured and carried him. They laughed until they could laugh no more. Unseen to Veronica were the Gardeners whom they had awakened by their antics along the way. However, the groom had caught the eye of his friends and had given them a wink, so the word was out that the great prophet Elon and his beautiful Exile bride were on the mountain. A crowd began to follow them with great stealth. Always eager for an opportunity to serenade, the throng of lovers was intrigued by this lively lovers' chase.

At last the newlyweds found themselves near the summit of Mount Ekim. Enthroned upon Elon's lap, his queen surveyed the awesome, orange-lit landscape for a long moment and said, "This is the end of paradise, isn't it, my love?"

"It is the beginning of the Lord's Kingdom," he answered. "Paradise was a springboard to a fuller life, but it will always be with us."

He came to her, and as her flesh became his, he whispered, "The two worlds have now become one."

With his soul engulfed in hers, she exclaimed, "Paradise just became heaven! You will always be my garden!"

There was a groaning like quiet thunder in the distance, but Veronica could see that Elon's face was framed by cloudless night sky. The rumble grew until it became clear that it was the drone of baritones chanting, their voices drawing nearer. Then ever so softly, altos and sopranos took up a melody and harmony, until a thousand voices rang through the night air. Owls and crickets joined the strain, and the lovers could hear the angels singing...and the seventeen.

"I so love a serenade!" the bride cooed into the groom's ear.

In a month they would call Antonio on the com, don clean clothing, and return to work...but the honeymoon would never end.

Chapter 21

The Best Possible World

Rosalie leaned up against a statue to eat her little bag lunch. "I made my lunch all by myself," she told her aunt Mary Jo. "The sandwiches have my favorite cheese, and I've got an oatmeal cookie with raisins, and I've got fresh apricots. Now I'm gonna eat my favorite lunch sitting by my favorite statue," she said as she leaned up against the likeness of Gen. Olletsoc Tobba.

Mary Jo looked up from her book and pushed her long, black curly hair aside to smile at her niece. With robin's-egg-blue eyes, fair skin, and just the right amount of freckles, she was the very image of her mother. The nineteen-year-old was commander in chief of seven nieces and nephews who had decided to spend the day in the park. Mary Jo had envisioned a peaceful afternoon reading a book in the sun-dappled shade, while her nieces and nephews wore out the playground equipment.

She had brought along her mother's copy of Emmanuel Voronin's *Two's Company, Three's Liturgy*. Bishop Ian Scofield had read from that very pamphlet at her mother's first wedding, and Veronica had loaned the precious keepsake to Mary Jo with stern orders to "Guard it with your life!" The sight of their pretty little aunt reading had engendered questions about the pamphlet, and as one thing led to another, the entire morning had become an Earth/Freqmod history lesson. Mary Jo smiled at the sight of Rosalie leaning up against the statue of Gen. Tobba, and thought that this had turned out to be the perfect place to finish their impromptu lesson.

"Why is that your favorite statue?" she asked her niece.

"Because he has a funny face!" Rosalie giggled with brutal honesty.

"Do you like the other statues?"

"Yeah, they're nice. 'Specially this one," she said pointing to the icon of the Blessed Mother.

"Do you know who that is?"

"Yeah, that's Mary."

"You mean…that's a statue of *her*?" four year old Airrellav asked, pointing to Mary Jo.

"No, it's not a statue of Mary *Jo*, it's Mary, the mother of Jesus," Rosalie explained to her cousin. "Are you gonna finish your story while we eat?" she asked her aunt.

"I suppose I can," Mary Jo answered.

Before she could start, a little blond six-year-old man needed clarification. "So then Grandpa didn't go into glory very soon, or dad wouldn't have four brothers and four sisters, right?" he asked.

"You're right, Elon. He didn't go into glory until two years after you were born. Your Grandma misses him very much, but sometimes she speaks with him on her walks in the Garden."

"Can we go to the Garden?" Elon asked.

"I'm sure you've been there many times and didn't even know it," Mary Jo assured him

"Can we eat from the tree of life and become invisible?"

"You mean invincible?"

"That's what I said!"

"No. After it was discovered that the angel no longer guarded the way, everyone started to go there, and the tree dried up. But there is still wonderful fruit to eat on the other trees, and it is still a very beautiful place."

"Are all the animals still tame? Will they do work for people?"

"My, you are just full of questions, Elon! The animals are tame for some of the holiest Gardeners, like those in the Lilac Valley, but are afraid of Exiles, except for your Grandma Veronica. They just love her.

"Many of the Gardeners became Christian and left the Garden. They still live among us and are known for their great purity. They are no longer immortal, but when they get old and die, their bodies go immediately into glory."

"I don't understand." Elon insisted.

"I'm sorry...too many big words?"

"Yeah. What's immor..."

"Immortal?"

"Yeah."

"Having a body that is immortal means being able to live forever on this world."

"Instead of going to heaven?"

"Well, yes, I guess so."

"I wouldn't want that. I wanna be with Grandpa and Jesus someday."

"I do too, honey."

"Now that Grandpa's gone," Rosalie said, "I bet Grandma's sure glad that her friend Melanie came to live here."

"She's very glad, Rosalie. They spend a lot of time together since Melanie's husband died. It's kinda like old times when they were young single girls."

"'Cept they got a whole big buncha grandkids now!" Elon pointed out.

"Speaking of Grandma, why don't you guys ask *her* all of these questions instead of me," she said nodding at an approaching cyclist. Veronica's long, snow-white hair billowed in the wind as she pedaled toward them. Dressed in pink petal pushers and a white cotton blouse, she was as pretty a sixty-eight-year-old as one could imagine. Melanie came pedaling a hundred or so feet behind her.

"Grandma!" the kids yelled.

"Hi Mom, hi Melanie," Mary Jo called to them.

"Well, hi, honey," Veronica managed. Winded from racing Melanie, she let her lungs catch up for a bit, then added, "Looks like you have quite a crew,"

"They're wearing me out with their questions. I told them that it was time for you to take over," Mary Jo informed her.

"Questions? About what?" Veronica asked, looking at the kids.

"About you and Dad, and the history of Freqmod," Mary Jo told her.

"Well, let's hear 'em," Veronica invited.

"Did the Revotfellians keep all the Unifists as slaves?" ten-year-old Cozzie asked.

"Slavery became illegal in Revotfell," Veronica answered, "and eventually the Unifist invaders were released, but their religion is mostly gone now. Col. Nomis became Christian along with the rest of his family. King Eltsac, the king of Revotfell, became Christian, as did many other Revotfellians."

"What happened to the Unifist leader guy after he got his teeth knocked out?" Rosalie asked.

"Rev Refficul? You see him all the time," Veronica answered.

"What? Where?" Cozzie asked.

"You know Brother Thomas, the really old monk who cleans the grounds and cares for the flowers around the church and the cemetery?" Mary Jo asked.

"You mean the raggedy old guy who's always smiling and has teeth missing?" Rosalie asked.

"Yes. Brother Thomas is Revol Refficul," Veronica explained.

Cozzie thought out loud. "Then…it's kinda like he got his wish. Like he's helpin' to make the whole world back into the Garden," he noted. Veronica just smiled and nodded her head in agreement with his observation.

"What about the tree of the forbidden fruit?" Cozzie asked. "Did the Gardeners tear down the walls? Can we go see it?"

"Well, if you want to know about the Garden, it's better to show than to tell," Veronica said. "Does everybody have a bicycle, or a place to ride on one?" With assurances that they did, she said, "Well then, let's go. There's no better place to learn about the Garden than *in* the Garden!"

Within a few minutes they were all pedaling across the Saints Airrellav and Oilenroc Bridge, which had been built over the Elon strait. Veronica stopped mid-bridge to teach a little lesson.

"Only taxis, delivery trucks, bicycles, and pedestrians are allowed to cross this bridge. The Garden is a very special and protected place, and we all want to keep it that way, so don't be messy when we get there."

Soon they were in the Garden and dismounted on the beach to take a breather.

"I've been to this beach before," Cozzie said. "I didn't even know I was in the Garden though."

"Your grandfather and I used to come here and play with the seals and sea lions quite often when we were first married," Veronica told them. "Oh, there are some seals right now!" she said, running to greet three of them as they waddled up onto the land. The children laughed as the threesome played catch with one of Veronica's flip-flops, but the creatures made a beeline back to the water when the grandkids came too near.

"Well, Cozzie," Veronica said, "let's go answer your question about the tree of knowledge." After pedaling for some time, they turned their bikes onto a narrow road, which wound though a series of small wooded hills, and continued on until they came to a large, flat open area. The road ran through an opening in an imposing stone wall, and a hundred yards farther, through an opening in another tall stone wall. Towering above that second stone wall could be seen a number of large, beautiful stone buildings. As they passed through the second wall, the children began to see a courtyard in the midst of the buildings. The courtyard held a wondrous flower garden. The setting was so peaceful that no one spoke as they followed their grandma to the center of the space. As Veronica deployed the kickstand on her bike she nodded at something on the ground and said, "Here it is, Cozzie."

"The tree of knowledge?" he asked. Veronica nodded. "That's all that's left?"

The children went to touch the massive trunk, and as they contemplated its history, Veronica said, "This is not the first time that you've seen the tree of knowledge. The cross portion of the crucifix in the basilica is made of wood from the tree of knowledge, and the corpus portion, that is, the part carved to look like the body of Jesus, is made of wood from the tree of life."

"Did the Gardeners cut down the tree of knowledge?" Cozzie asked.

"No, the Gardeners made the openings in the walls that we just came through, but it was the Unifists who cut the tree down," Mary Jo answered.

"Why is the Jesus on that cross bare-naked?" Elon asked.

Oh boy! How to explain to a six-year-old? Mary Jo thought. "You want to answer that one, Mom?"

Veronica smiled at her. "When Earth people first came here, Elon, all of the people in the Garden were naked. They were sinless and innocent, and their bodies were not a temptation to each other. Jesus was also sinless. When we see the image of his naked body, it reminds us that he died to take away our sins so that we can go to heaven where no one sins."

"If Jesus took away our sins," Cozzie asked, "why can't we just go naked now?"

"We can! Go ahead!" Veronica told him and stood there watching. Cozzie smiled and glanced around at his cousins. "I'm waiting," she said amidst their snickers. "Just doesn't feel right does it?" she asked him. As he shook his head *No!* she said, "Jesus forgives our sins, but we are not innocent in the same sense that Adam and Eve were in the beginning. We know that our bodies are a temptation to one another, even though our sins are all forgiven."

Behind her, she heard Mary Jo fussing with a nephew and turned around to see that Elon had taken the cue and quickly stripped down to his under shorts. "Sometimes Mama lets Jimmy run around the house with no clothes on!" Elon informed her.

"Jimmy is only three, Elon. The older we get, the more responsible we must be about our bodies," she told him.

As he slid one leg back into the trousers Mary Jo held for him, he asked, "What does responsible mean?"

"It means being very careful to do the best thing for others and to use what God has given us wisely, Elon—we have to use our smarts," she said, tapping her noggin with her pointer finger. "You will understand when you get a little older. Many things change as we get older, but don't ever lose that beautiful innocence you have."

"Do any of you know what these buildings are?" Mary Jo asked.

"Is this the college?" thirteen-year-old Xavier asked.

"Yes it is," Mary Jo answered. "In fact, this is the college where Bishop Hadrian teaches."

"Why does Bishop Hadrian teach college?" Xavier asked. "Why doesn't he just do bishop stuff?"

"Because being a bishop was much too hard on his marriage," Veronica explained, "and he asked to have his duties reduced so that he had more time for his family."

"Isn't being a bishop more important than being married?" Xavier pressed.

"Archbishop Scofield can change the things that a priest or other bishop has to do," his grandma informed him, "but he can't change the stuff that a husband and father has to do. Kids need their daddies, and mommies need their husbands. That was God's plan from the beginning and no one can change it, not even the Holy Father."

"Now that Bishop Hadrian's wife is dead, is he gonna go back to doing bishop stuff?" Xavier asked.

"No. He's past retirement age," Veronica explained.

"Are you gonna marry him, Grandma?" Elon asked.

"Why do you ask, honey?" Veronica asked, grinning.

"Cause I saw you kiss him after church last Sunday," he informed her.

"Oh. Well then, that makes it official!" she kidded. "I do like being married, but he hasn't asked me," she added with a smile.

The things you learn when you hang out with a six-year-old! Mary Jo thought.

"What happened to Jazz?" Rosalie asked, quite enamored with the name.

"Oh, my good friend, Jasmine," Veronica said. "I'm so glad you asked! Let's go see."

Their Grandmother mounted her bike and led her entourage out of the courtyard. After they had pedaled for quite some time, Mary Jo hollered, "Mom, you gotta slow down, we're getting too spread out!"

Veronica, Xavier, and Cozzie were out in front of the pack, but Mary Jo and Melanie rode side-by-side having a good chat. Veronica glanced back and said, "Sorry. We're almost there." In the distance, behind a hill, a steeple reached toward heaven. The road was a deep trough carved through the side of a large hollow, and at the center of that hollow stood the Basilica of the King of Kings.

They parked their bikes at a fountain in front of the church. "Does anyone know what used to be where this fountain is now?" Veronica asked.

"The tree of life?" Cozzie guessed.

"Very good!" his grandma complimented. Then placing a finger to her lips, she quieted their chatter as they climbed the steps of the basilica. Once inside, they all genuflected and made their way toward the main altar. On the way they passed a pair of stained glass windows that caught everyone's attention.

"Grandma, I know that the space ship in the picture is the one you came on from Earth, but what's with the old car?" Cozzie asked.

"That's a good question, Cozzie. Does anyone know the answer?" Veronica asked.

"That's St. Oilenroc's car," Xavier informed them. "He was always giving people rides, and now he's the patron saint of taxi cab drivers."

"Very good, Xavier," his grandmother praised him.

"That car is so cool!" Xavier added.

"And that's the oola lana," Rosalie said, giggling and pointing to the large orange star in the upper corner of the left window.

"You like that name, don't you," her grandma observed.

"Is that supposed to be you and Grandpa in the Garden?" Cozzie asked, referring to a naked couple depicted in the window.

Before Veronica could answer, a giggling Elon noted, "You used to have black hair...and no clothes! How come you didn't have no clothes on?"

"Everybody in the Garden was naked then," she explained, "and I was the only Exile married to a Gardener, so I was treated like family.

"Is there anything special about the stars in the windows?" she asked them. When no one answered she said, "Count them."

"They represent the seventeen!" the quick counting Cozzie proclaimed.

"Very good," his grandmother told him.

Then, putting a finger to her lips to quiet them, she went into the sacristy and turned on some lights. Under the main altar, behind glass, lay the body of a beautiful woman.

"This is the body of a very dear friend of mine. Her name was Jasmine," she told them. "She became Sister Mary Veronica Aniram of the Sacred Image, but she only lived for seven years after taking her vows. She was doing missionary work in Eknarf, and was ordered by a judge not to preach the word anymore. When she appealed to a higher court and won, the first judge secretly sent a thug to threaten her. She continued to preach, and three of that evil judge's henchmen beat her unconscious and left her for dead. Two years later, she died from her injuries.

"Eighty-seven women joined her order while she was living. After she died, a lot of miracles took place through her intercession, and she was named a saint. When her body was exhumed during the canonization process she was found to be incorrupt."

"What does that mean?" Elon asked.

"It means that her body never decayed. It's still just the same as the day she died," Mary Jo explained.

"That's kinda creepy," Cozzie commented.

"And weird!" Elon insisted.

"I don't think it's creepy, Cozzie. I think it's beautiful!" his grandma declared. "But I guess it is a little weird, Elon."

Mary Jo reflected on just how weird it was. St. Veronica's own memoirs described her lustful youth. According to Archbishop Scofield, gifting a reformed life with the sign of incorruptibility heralded an unprecedented level of Divine love and mercy.

"Why's she wearing a wedding dress?" Elon asked.

"That's her first Holy Communion dress," Veronica answered.

"She musta been a real big kid!" Elon declared.

His grandmother giggled, and said, "No, honey, she was an adult before she made her first Holy Communion. This was also the dress she wore when she took her vows to be a sister. As she was dying, she asked that she be buried in this dress because she was on her way to see her husband. That's also why her hair is laid out so beautifully rather than being in a tail the way she always wore it."

"On her way to see her husband?" Rosalie asked. "I thought she was a sister!"

"She was a sister, Rosalie, but in a way, through Jesus, we are all married to God," Veronica explained.

"That's weird," Cozzie insisted. Veronica just smiled and said, "Hopefully, someday it won't seem quite so weird to you."

"I don't see him here today," Xavier said, "but whenever I've been here with Mom during her afternoon prayer hour, there's this real old guy praying by the altar."

"Oh, that's Mr. Alvin Dobbs," Melanie told them. "He's an Earth man who was Jasmine's partner and friend when she was a police woman. He came here on the starship with me. He was in love with Jasmine and wanted to see her again. By the time we arrived, she had become Reverend Mother Mary Veronica Aniram, and had already been assaulted by those evil men. Even though she was really sick, she was overjoyed to see Mr. Dobbs. He loved her very much and took care of her the last two years of her life. On her request, he took her by wheel chair to the prison so she could forgive the men who had beaten her. Since her death Mr. Dobbs has dedicated his life to prayer."

"Are those men still in jail?" Cozzie asked.

"Those men were scheduled to be executed, but St. Veronica begged that they be spared, and then spent time visiting them. They became Christians. One died, and the other two are still in prison."

When the questions subsided, the history lesson moved back outdoors.

"What is that big wall down there?" Rosalie asked.

"That is the wall around the Lilac Valley," Veronica informed her. "Only full-blooded Gardeners live there, and no Exiles are allowed to go in. It is the only place in the Garden where people still live without clothing. The Gardeners there dedicate their lives to prayer, worship, and great learning. The greatest teachers in most of the Universities on Freqmod have come from the Lilac Valley. These Gardeners usually live for about a hundred and twenty years, show little sign of aging, and often go directly into glory without dying."

"Are they invisible?" Elon asked.

"You mean invincible," Mary Jo coached.

"Yeah. Can they be killed?" he asked his grandma.

"I'm afraid I can't answer your question, Elon. I know that they are very strong, but I don't know if anyone's ever tried to kill one of them," she informed him.

The adults became engaged in conversation while the children waded in the fountain pool. Unseen to the adults, Bishop Hadrian approached the fountain. "How's the water?" he asked the children.

"It's cold!" Rosalie told him.

"You kids rode your bikes all the way out here to wade in cold water?" he asked them.

"No, Aunt Mary Jo and Grandma have been giving us a history lesson," Cozzie told him.

"History lesson, huh? Okay, let's see if you learned anything. Who's the Prime Minister of Ogeeremma?" the bishop asked.

"Juanita Escobar," Xavier answered.

"Very good! Who was the first Earthling born on Freqmod?"

"Juanita Escobar," Xavier answered again.

"No she wasn't!" Cozzie insisted. "It was her twin brother, Antonio."

"Very good, Cozzie," Bishop Hadrian told him. "Antonio was born ten minutes before Juanita. Who can tell me who Antonio and Juanita's parents are?"

"Grandma's friends!" Elon shouted.

"What are their names?" Cozzie asked him.

"Umm...Tony and Jean!" Elon answered.

"Wow, you guys are a walking encyclopedia," the bishop said with a chuckle.

"I got a question for you," Elon said to the bishop.

"Okay. Is it a history question?"

Ignoring his question, Elon asked, "Are you gonna marry Grandma?"

The bishop chuckled a bit and said, "*Future* history! I can't answer future history questions." Elon just stood and looked at him, apparently waiting for a satisfactory answer. "Do you think I should?" the bishop asked at last.

Elon nodded an energetic *yes*.

"Okay. Go say to your grandma: Bishop David Hadrian wants to know if you'll marry him so he can be my grandpa. Can you say that, just like that?"

Elon nodded yes and dutifully approached his grandmother and posed the question. Veronica giggled and turned toward Bishop David to flash a smile of appreciation for the novel, oddly romantic means of proposal, and Elon dutifully returned to him with an answer: "She said to tell you, 'Of course, I thought you'd never ask!'"

The bishop made his way over to Veronica and chuckled as he placed his arms around her and kissed her forehead to seal the deal. As they embraced, he felt someone tug on his coat tail and turned to see his little emissary. "What is it, Grand-son-to-be?" he asked.

"What am I?" Elon asked.

"What do you mean, son?" Bishop Hadrian asked.

"Before you got here we was talkin' 'bout Gardeners and Exiles; am I a Gardener kid or an Exile kid?"

"Oh...why do you ask?"

Cozzie joined in: "'Cause we wanna know if we can sin or not."

"I see. Well, first of all, anyone with free will can sin," the bishop assured them. "When a Gardener and an Exile marry, each of their children will have unique gifts and unique trials. Some are able to hear God's voice from a very early age, while others really struggle with controlling themselves. God gives us gifts and he allows our trials. Both are given for our benefit, so we must never take pride or discouragement at having either of them. Both gifts and trials are given for the glory of God and for our glorification in him. The thing to keep in mind is that God has given us the best possible world in which to grow and become more and more like him.

"Are you making of your lives a sacrifice?" the bishop asked them.

"I'm trying, but I'm not so sure I know 'xactly what it means yet," Elon admitted.

"That's okay. I'm almost seventy and I'm still not doing it perfectly," Veronica assured her grandson, and added, "It's a good thing that God is in control, not us!"

"Yeah, that's a good thing!" Elon agreed.

It is indeed a good thing…

to give control to God!

TWO'S COMPANY; THREE'S LITURGY

By

Emmanuel James Voronin

Author's Prayer

Lord, if these pages contain anything that is true or uplifting,
May the glory be yours!
If they contain anything which is mine alone,
Or contrary to the Catholic faith,
Have mercy on your ignorant servant.
May your wisdom be recognized and embraced,
And my ignorant utterances forgiven and forgotten.

Introduction

Some time ago a friend said to me, "You're fond of saying that life is a liturgy and that marriage has a liturgical aspect about it, but I'm not exactly sure what you mean." This pamphlet is my attempt to articulate that analogy.

My dictionary defines liturgy generally as "an established form of public worship," and more specifically as "the Eucharistic celebration." So how can all of life be liturgical in nature?

Life becomes what we make of it. If we see it as chaotic and meaningless it can never be liturgical, but if we see it as symphonic, we may find ourselves eager to play our part.

But liturgy is boring, isn't it? It's like hearing the same old tune over and over. One could conclude that if life is liturgical, life must be boring. However, if we see liturgy as boring, it is perhaps because we don't know our part. No wonder it's the same old tune. How can it be symphonic if we don't know the score, haven't learned our part, and are paying no attention at all to the director?

Fulfillment in life is dependent upon full participation. If we are to experience life as liturgy, we must know our part and play it well. If we do not, we condemn ourselves to a life of experimentation, disappointment, frustration, and boredom. Nowhere is this more evident than in marriage. Regarding marriage, human history records entire eras in which it seems that no one knew the score, had learned his part, or paid any attention to the conductor.

By now you may be tiring of my inability to stick with a metaphor. Is the subject liturgy or symphony? Metaphorically, there's really not much difference. In a manner of speaking, intentionally or unintentionally, a symphony always gives praise to God, in the very least, by drawing attention to the wonder of his creation and the yearnings of the human soul. Liturgy is a divine symphony. Life is meant to be liturgy. Are you familiar with the score? Do you know your part? Is your rapt attention given to the conductor? Do you love the orchestra? Are you an example or a distraction for your fellow members? If you like doing your own thing, remember that improvisation is only useful if it complements the score—you are the instrument, not the composer.

Your life, no matter how brief or brash, like a lone cymbal crash, is still part of the symphony: that eternal liturgy which is our destiny.

My Dear Mrs. Lansing,

I am so pleased that you inquired about this pamphlet, and as this is the very copy from which I read at your wedding, I trust it will become a precious keepsake. Your love shall be my keepsake. You and your spouse shall always remain in my heart and in my prayers. May the Father grant you the gift of seeing his Son in each other. May the grace of your holy marriage spill forth into every life that touches yours, and may God bless you abundantly with the fondest desire of your heart, to bring children as precious gifts back to him.

In Christ,
Fr. Ian

He must increase, I must decrease.

These words of John the Baptist echo down through the centuries, resonating with our lives in so many ways. But let us consider just one of those ways. Let us consider St. John's attitude and the effect of attitude upon the sacred covenant relationship we call marriage.

Attitude? Yes attitude! No, this is not a motivational brochure, no self-help guru here. The only spiritual help that any of us can provide for ourselves is to learn to say yes to our Creator. The presence of the Almighty within the soul cannot increase if the ego does not decrease. John's attitude was the antithesis of Lucifer's, who demanded that God must decrease so that he himself might increase. The first step toward reducing the ego is to trust God, and the power to trust can only be found through his grace. Therefore, the ever important first step toward real happiness in this realm and salvation in the next is an attitude of openness to grace, to the power God gives us. Somehow, amidst all of the doubt and pain, we must accept the grace to say yes to the Lord, to entrust our lives ever more to his loving plan.

It has been said that most of what we need to know in life to succeed we learned in the first grade. If our simple secular wisdom recognizes the importance of laying a foundation for our own children, can we not expect that the first lesson in God's lesson plan for us will also beautifully meet our needs? Those who would marginalize the book of Genesis have either not understood it, or have been threatened by the naked truths it reveals.

...in the beginning it was not so.

Matthew 19:8

In the above comment concerning divorce, our Redeemer invited his listeners to reconsider their perception of the Law of Moses. He indicated that what Moses had allowed, in order to placate the masses in the desert, should not have become the standard by which to judge God's intentions. Moses had the unhappy task of leading hundreds of thousands of whining humans into a wilderness. They impetuously dragged every measly little disagreement before him and demanded that he render judgment. Eventually, his father-in-law would convince him to delegate this power, and for future reference, Moses would write down the results of judgments he had rendered. These legal precedents would come to be known as the Law of Moses.

In regards to divorce, Jesus indicated that Moses had caved in to pressure:

Because of your hardness of heart he wrote you this commandment.

Mark 10:5

Many in modern times have been of the opinion that Holy Mother Church should cave in to pressure, that she should placate the masses by relaxing her views on divorce, pre-marital sex, contraception, homosexual acts, abortion, and so forth. However, the Church's focus has happily remained where Christ directed it: in the beginning, in Genesis. In the words of the Creator we find our roots, not in the hardness of our hearts.

At the beginning of his pontificate, John Paul the Great gave the world a gift, a series of talks which have come to be known as *The Theology of the Body*. This wonderful work prompts us to consider our bodies, to consider how, not only in our souls, but in our very flesh we mirror the image of our God. We are not ghosts in machines, as some have suggested; rather, we are composite beings. Our souls will always yearn to occupy our bodies, and we are male or female to our very core.

You surely will not die! For God knows that when you eat of it your eyes will be opened, and you will be like God, knowing good and evil.

Genesis 3:4,5

The first and most profound human defect, which exists even in the innocent, is a lack of appreciation for the gifts that the Almighty gives. Relative freedom from this most basic defect is the mark of spiritual prodigy. This lack of appreciation was scarcely evident in the young Doctor, St. Therese of Lisieux, or a twelve-year-old St. Imelda of Bologna, and was completely absent in Mary the mother of Jesus.

However, it was the defect of our first parents even before the fall. Indeed, it was the defect of the pre-fallen angels. I say defect, because it was not a sin. They had not yet made the decision to disobey, but they had also not made any commitment to serve, or to love, and had not nurtured an appreciation for the incredible gifts freely given by the Almighty. They were not "full of grace."

We bear this most basic defect from birth and will likely struggle with it all of our lives. It is the operative defect among those of us who have fallen away from, or refused attraction to, the practice of the faith. I say operative, because I do not suggest that we possess the innocence of our pre-fallen first parents—we have likely yielded to disordered passions as well—but operative because this is the fault by which we all maintain our resistance to personal change.

"I believe in God, but..." You can fill in the rest. Most of us have heard this prelude to an excuse repeatedly, a prelude to excuses for the lack of a spiritual dimension to our lives, or for that spiritual dimension's diminutive size. The insinuation of this innocent sounding little prelude is always the same, that belief in God is enough. Unfortunately, it may be just enough to condemn us.

You see, even Satan believes in God. He knows that God is omniscient, almighty, omnipresent, eternal, and all loving, but he does not love God in return. To admit to God's existence, and yet maintain no demonstrable relationship with him, is to blatantly take him for granted. Taking Providence for granted will cast an ominous shadow over our relationships with others, especially our relationships with our spouses. It is not enough to believe that our spouses exist. We must love them with a godly love.

Nobody ever uses, as a prelude to an excuse, the phrase "I love God, but...." For example, nobody ever says, "I love Jesus Christ, but I just don't feel the need to go to church." Those who actually cultivate a relationship with the Almighty are drawn to worship, both private and public. After all, who among us is madly in love with his bride, but never mentions her in conversation with his friends? Never sings her praises? Never spends time with her? Never takes her out of the house for fear of being seen with her? If we really love the Father, Son, and Holy Spirit, if we experience them as persons, we won't be afraid of being associated with them, and will spend time singing their praises.

He himself bore our sins in his body on the tree, so that we might die to sin and live for righteousness; by his wounds you have been healed.

1 Peter 2:24

St. Peter says of Christ, "he himself bore our sins...so that we might die to sin." We are frail and sinful. Embrace our frailty, and we are empowered by Christ to die to sin. Strive for personal power, and we embrace sin. Nowhere is this truth more evident than in the marriage covenant.

So...if Christ bore our sins, and we are expected to be Christ-like, must we bear each others sins? Consider the following:

When choosing a marriage partner, it often seems that we are attracted to people very different than ourselves; as the saying goes, opposites attract. Have you ever wondered why? It seems to me that, through God's design, we simply are not destined to marry someone who has the same faults that we have. We get a whole new batch when we marry: a whole new set of nasty habits! My bride's perfection was seriously compromised when she and I became one flesh, but with Jesus' help, she struggles to see beyond my weaknesses and imperfections, to see me with His eyes. Having assimilated each other's faults through marriage, we are less likely to hold in contempt others who display the same defects. As each of our spiritual boundaries widens, and our spiritual family grows, if we are Christ-like, we assimilate more and more faults, and our love and tolerance grows—not love and tolerance for sin, but love and tolerance for sinners. Scripture teaches that Christ "bore our sins in his body." Although I believed this teaching to be true, it did not become concrete for me until I saw it in this light. Now at last I see the beauty of Christ's metaphor, how completely we are "his bride."

...the wedding day of the Lamb has come, his bride has made herself ready.

Revelation 19

...the one who does not love his brother whom he has seen, cannot love God whom he has not seen.

1 John 4:20

Love of God and love of neighbor are inseparable. Honoring Christ above selfish desires and honoring one's spouse above selfish desires are inseparable themes. Therefore, to adequately understand our role within the marriage covenant, we must understand our basic existence, our relationship to our Creator.

In him we live and move and exist.

Acts 17:28

In the above quote, St. Luke proclaims that we exist within God. As God's essence is intellect and will, if we exist within him, we are a product of his imagination and his love, for his infinite goodness allows him to will only love, never evil. The dictionary tells us that imagination is "The mental power of forming images of unreal or absent objects." God's infinite imagination exceeds this definition, for the images he forms within his intellect constitute the sum total of reality, both spiritual and physical. The instant the Almighty should fail to hold us in his thoughts and his heart, we would fail to exist. That realization is at once humbling and glorifying.

All things created are held in existence by his love. God does not will the evil choices we make, but he wills our ability to make them.

Lucifer was like God in all things but love, and like all other creatures, lacked the power to create. In his jealousy he chose to create the only thing any of us can create: evil. All of the creative things we do are done with and through the creative power of God. Even evil is made possible through the use of the most precious gift God has given, our free will, the gift which allows us to be truly like him.

God is incapable of evil. In fact, the creation of evil is not creation at all. If I walked into your home on a cold winter's day and opened all of the windows, you could say that I had created a cold house, but to refer to such an act as creation would actually be a misuse of the word. Evil is always subtractive. By diminishing a good, in this case, by releasing the heat, I would have produced a cold environment, an act which can hardly be considered creation.

In the beginning was the Word, and the Word was with God, and the Word was God.

John 1:1

God is the simplest of all beings. That is, he exists for a single purpose, to love. Because of this simplicity, and because of his perfection, and because he exists outside of time and knows all things, St. Augustine reasons that God thinks only a single thought. St. John describes that thought to us as "the Word." The second person of the Trinity is the Word, the thought of God, a thought that contains all truth, truth which attains the status of personhood.

So we must ask: What constitutes a person? Self-knowledge and free choice are hallmarks of personhood; however, if the Second Person of the Trinity, God the Son, is the perfect thought of the Father, complete and all encompassing, what free choices remain for him? In our own life experience we find that decisions and choices fall on the heels of new information, but no new information can come to the Word, for he is the totality of wisdom and knowledge personified. So then, what decision was/is there to herald the personhood of the one who is all encompassing?

God the Son's defining choice is none other than to choose our salvation. He freely chose to take on a human nature and suffer an excruciating death for our sake. This choice has been a defining trait of his existence for all eternity. It was, perhaps, the 'stumbling block' of the fallen angels. St. Augustine conjectures that Lucifer refused to serve a God who would lower himself to take on the nature of a human being, a creature so far beneath an angel in the natural order of things.

God the Father and God the Son make one other eternal choice: they choose to love each other and us. The eternal, unfathomable love that the Father and Son share is personified in the Holy Spirit.

What choice was/is there to herald the personhood of the Spirit? His choices are infinite! He said yes to the mission of salvation, to the espousal of the Blessed Virgin, to infusing the love of Christ into his church: to empowering the salvation of the universe. He is the personification of love, the personification of an infinity of good choices. Without his infinite power to love, without his infinite choice, we cannot choose love.

Before I formed you in the womb I knew you, before you were born I set you apart.

Jeremiah 1:5

So what about the nature of *our* existence? Well, as you can see, it is no small thing to be a product of God's imagination, as all realities take form within his intellect. Our unchanging God lives within the eternal moment; therefore, the fact that we are here indicates that he has conceived of our existence for all eternity. By our very nature we are destined for incorporation into the Godhead, and enter existence grafted to the Word. Scripture says, "I have carved you on the palm of my hand." What could be more intimate than that?

Spiritual things are not more real than physical things, but they are of a higher order of existence. The Bible that you hold in your hand is a clump of biomass. When you read the words, that thought/prayer passing though your mind and soul is of a higher order than the paper from which it was read. So man, a composite being, has a physical reality and a spiritual reality, a lower and higher order of existence. Our first parents had balance; the senses of their spiritual being were as keen as their physical senses. Besides having the physical senses of sight, hearing, smell, taste, and touch, they had the spiritual senses that allowed them to perceive the omniscience, benevolence, and omnipresence of their creator.

Most of us have had some experience with an individual who is blind or deaf. We know that the reduction or elimination of one of the physical senses results in a sharpening of the remaining ones. Thus, blind people develop very sensitive hearing. After our first parents sinned, it became necessary for them to attempt to hide from God. Their keen natural spiritual sense of the Almighty was too much to endure when in the state of sin. They attempted to camouflage themselves with leaves. However, before long, those physical senses that had been so dominated by their spiritual senses came to dominate their perception of all things.

Behold, the man has become like one of Us, knowing good and evil.
Genesis 3:22

It is interesting to note that, while Satan clearly lied when he told Eve that she would not die from eating the fruit, he did not lie when he said that partaking of the fruit would open her eyes and she would be like God, knowing good and evil. The Exaggerator always tells just enough truth to bait the hook. Of course, he conveniently withheld the knowledge that, had she rejected his temptation, she would also have known good from evil. Even more interesting is God's reaction to the fall. His words are so matter-of-fact, proclaimed in a seemingly positive light. Our parents had sinned, paradise had been defiled, and yet our heavenly Father was, from all eternity, prepared to bring about our salvation.

Scripture goes on to say that Adam and Eve begot children in their own image (like begets like). So it is that we are born with the same impediments; our spiritual senses are retarded, and our physical senses so easily rule the day. Our perception of our existence is skewed. We perceive the physical world as the "real world" and often pass off our perception of the spiritual as our own imaginings.

A savior would be born of woman. If like begets like, would not his nature be partially fallen? Could the fallen rescue the fallen? No, the Savior would issue from a body and soul imbued with grace, a body and soul without defect. Because the defining decision of the Word is the essence of his salvific sacrifice, and because his decision occurred within eternity (and the mind of God is immutable), this incredible grace could be made available to Mary. The Son of Man would issue forth from nothing less than The Immaculate.

Like begets like. Yet, it is argued that if God could break that cycle at the conception of Mary, he could just as easily have done so at the conception of Christ. Of course, he could have. However, in so doing, though Christ would have become the new Adam, we would be deprived of the new Eve. Some insist that the Immaculate Conception was not necessary for our salvation. They are right, but fortunately for us, our Father showers us with gifts well beyond our needs. If, in John Paul's parlance, woman is the archetype of humanity—the *embodiment* of receptivity—it follows that the new Eve is the archetype of redeemed humanity: the *perfection* of receptivity! Could the Father have created a more perfect vessel to deliver the ultimate gift of his own Son? Could the Father have conceived a more perfect birthday gift for that Son? Could the Creator have conceived a more perfect spiritual mother for his Mystical Body?

Like our first parents before the fall, Mary would live her life seeing a balance between the eternal and the temporal, and by special grace, she would do so with a profound appreciation for God's gifts. The new Eve would be conceived with both the gift that the first Eve had discarded *and* the one she had demanded. That is to say, our first parents had traded original justice for an opportunity to become "like God"; therefore, the new woman would inherit the gift of conscience passed on by her natural parents; however, unlike our anemic consciences, Mary's imbued knowledge of good and evil would be perfected by the gift of original justice. She would know perfect balance between her spiritual and physical gifts.

Thus Mary's state, from conception on, was what Eve's state would have been had she conquered temptation. This special grace empowered Mary's response to God. Her yes, spoken in response to Gabriel's message, was certainly not her first yes to the Father. This fourteen-year-old woman would respond, to her Cousin Elizabeth's praise, with a lengthy prayer of praise for the Almighty, a prayer which drew deeply from the ancient testament and brought new life to phrases borrowed from the prophets and psalmists. Mary lived a life immersed in prayers of praise. She lived her life in the moment, in the presence of the Eternal One, a continual yes!

However, we live out our days very firmly rooted in the temporal. Our lives are played out, bit by bit, in what often seems inescapable drudgery. Our pleasures slip by quickly, and our work drags on. We ruin the present by worrying about the future. The great Christian apologist, C. S. Lewis, says that the past is frozen and the future does not yet exist, but that the present touches eternity. Therein lies the secret to happiness in our current realm. The present does in fact touch eternity, and eternity exists outside of time. Therefore, the defining decision of God the Son is at once ancient and ever-present.

At the Consecration of the Mass we view the Son of God in that defining moment, not an eternity ago, but now. Christ's death on Calvary is a specific historic event: the temporal affirmation, by his sacred humanity, of his eternal, ever-present decision to sacrifice himself for our salvation. It is this decision that we witness at the Consecration, his commitment to sacrifice revealed again and again in the mystery of his body and blood, in the mystery which engulfs our lives.

Existence could, therefore, be considered essentially liturgical in nature. In Revelations, St. John describes to us a scene from heaven. In this scene, all of creation, celestial and terrestrial in origin, are seen worshiping the Lamb. Why the Lamb? Why not some other symbolic representation of the Savior?

The symbolic representation of Jesus as the Lamb of God is very specific: he is the sacrifice to appease for our sins. In the symbol of the lamb, we see that infinite decision of the Son, that defining moment of his personhood. It is in the face of this decision that the Cherubim lie prostrate, the Seraphim hide their faces with their wings, and all of heaven cries out "worthy is the Lamb." In fact, it is this eternal decision that defines the very nature of heaven!

Heaven is shown to us in Revelations as an eternal liturgy, a celebration which encompasses all of our existence. In the celebration of the Mass, we immerse our past in God's forgiveness, heap our present cares as gifts upon the altar, and relinquish our future to his mercy, all while the present touches eternity and we witness the Lamb's eternal sacrifice. To further link the physical and temporal to the spiritual and eternal, Jesus gives us his body and blood. In the Eucharist, the physical and temporal take on a singularity with the spiritual and eternal, a singularity which will not be enjoyed in fullness until we come into glory. The Eucharist, that foretaste of heaven, will pass away when we pass into eternity and praise the Lamb in the glory he has reserved for us, that eternal liturgy.

For if you are living according to the flesh, you must die; but if by the Spirit you are putting to death the deeds of the body, you will live.

Romans 8:13

The above quotation from Romans is one of several of the Apostle Paul's writings that have often been so misunderstood and misused through the years. On a secular level, our culture has accepted the notion that sexual desire and pleasure are the Devil's arena, while in fact, nothing could be further from the truth.

The reality is that the Devil hates sex; he absolutely loathes it! Our sexuality is what makes us the most like God. We cannot create, only God can, but we can do the next best thing: co-create, or if you will, procreate. Even though Satan puts forth a huge effort to separate sex from procreation in our culture, and achieves a fair amount of success at it, he hates the outcome. Though he hates procreation most of all, sexual pleasure and intimacy also nauseate him. And if a married couple should pledge an embrace that is open to life and invite their Creator into that embrace? Well, the ancient serpent just has nothing to offer. When we turn all of life's pleasures and trials into prayer, and humbly point to the Lord as our source of pleasure and strength, we have left the Devil very little with which to work.

Just as the sacrifice of the Mass touches eternity and we transgress time and witness the eternal decision of the Savior, so the sacramental act of marital intimacy, for those who would invite the Creator to the celebration, has the ability to transgress time, to take the participants to a time when the passions were not at war with the will, a time when God was in control. Poets throughout the ages have made note of the lover's gaze in which time stands still. While participation in marital intimacy presents a great deal of opportunity for self-sacrifice, it falls by nature into the realm of the Garden; it is distinctly a celebration of the bounty of the Creator!

Adam and Eve were created for love. Adam clearly expressed his immediate infatuation: "This one, at last, is bone of my bones and flesh of my flesh." But when God asks Adam if he has eaten from the tree, Adam responds, "The woman whom you gave to be with me, she gave me from the tree, and I ate." Wow! Way to cover for the team there, big guy! He gets caught with his pants up and immediately passes the blame!

Adam's and Eve's immediate fascination for each other had cost them nothing. It required no commitment, no decision; it was not love. The mistrust they had for their Creator, displayed by their disregard for his loving warning about the dangers of the tree, is a clear indication that they did not love him and were therefore incapable of truly loving each other. When they sinned, God withdrew his loving control. He allowed them the decision making power to which they had laid claim, and their eyes were opened. They then looked upon each other with lust and mistrust, for God was no longer in control of their passions.

This is about the saddest, most unromantic tale ever told. Two people had the opportunity to form a threesome with the God of Passion for a perpetual love-fest, and they forsook it for a fruit snack! However, fortunately, in Christ we find the grace to do otherwise. There are only two things for which Holy Mother Church retains the words *foretaste of heaven*: the Eucharist and the marital embrace.

> **I call heaven and earth to witness against you today, that I have set before you life and death, the blessing and the curse. So choose life in order that you may live...**
>
> Deuteronomy 30:19

In the above passage, Moses addresses his fellow wilderness sojourners and expounds upon the ancient law. He explains how the law offered to the hearer both blessing and curse, a decision for life or death. Christ is the perfection of the law; therefore, in the Eucharist, he is also a blessing or a curse. Adam and Eve were created to live in paradise. They lived each day walking and talking with the Lord, enjoying a communion which is hard for most of us to imagine. Lucifer was God's greatest creation. He was the most beautiful, powerful, and talented of the angels. Like Adam and Eve, he lived in communion with God. However, communion is only salvific if we choose it.

Lucifer did not choose communion with the Omnipotent, he was created enjoying it, as were Adam and Eve. Choosing to consume the body and blood of Christ should not be confused with choosing to commune with God. For example, Holy Mother Church has called sexual intercourse, in the context of the marital embrace, a foretaste of heaven. Conjugal love is a holy and beautiful communion when it is the celebration of a decision and a commitment to love. Fornication and adultery can never be considered communion. Similarly, taking part in the Eucharist is salvific only when it is the culmination of a decision and a commitment to love.

When I was a youngster, I was shown a metaphorical film in Catechism class. In this film soldiers were sitting around a fire discussing the impending mission, one which was to be extremely dangerous. No man was expected to partake except of his own choosing. A cup was passed from man to man, and those who drank from the cup symbolically committed themselves to the battle. This symbol comes to mind for me often as I take the cup of Jesus' blood. This Communion must become for us a literal surrender of all earthly security, a commitment to battle against the Liar and against our own unbridled passions.

The night before his death, in contemplating his imminent passion, Jesus prayed to his father saying, "If it be your will, let this cup pass from me, yet not my will but your will be done." His life is the template for our lives, and his prayer a guide for our approach to our own suffering and death. Every day lived as one of his disciples offers unique opportunities for a sort of dry martyrdom, a dying to our selfish desires by serving others.

Can you drink the cup that I drink or be baptized with the baptism with which I am baptized?

Mark 10:38

Above are Christ's words given in response to a dispute his disciples were holding as to whom among them was the greatest. The Lord's challenge to them—a challenge to die the kind of death he died: a challenge to martyrdom—remains as a challenge to all disciples for all time. We must pay heed to the bloodless martyrdom that drinking from the cup of Christ demands of us, or we invite a curse by our participation.

...whoever eats the bread or drinks the cup of the Lord unworthily sins against the body and blood of the Lord. A man should examine

himself first; only then should he eat of the bread and drink of the cup. He who eats and drinks without recognizing the body eats and drinks a judgment on himself. That is why so many among you are sick and infirm, and why so many are dying.

1 Corinthians 11:27-30

Certainly not everyone can be expected to be at the same level of understanding concerning the sacrament, and God is gracious and condescending in his love of the innocent, the young, and those new to the faith. But there is a danger for those of us who would, year after year, consume the flesh of the God-man as food for the journey without keeping our minds and hearts set on the fulfillment of that journey. Those who drink from the cup, but don't go to battle, follow the way of Judas, who was blinded by his own sin and ambition. His spiritual senses were completely dulled. He ate, walked, and talked with the Son of God but remained evil. Through the blinding action of sin, Satan was able to convince him that what he was doing was good. He partook of the body and blood of Christ, but he did not commune with the Savior. He ran from love and commitment.

What about our love and commitment to spouse? We drank from the wedding cup; we are committed to the battle. No, not battle against our spouses, battle against the Evil One, with our spouses at our sides! How many of us are running from real love and commitment? How many of us are traitors, like Judas, fighting on the side of the Devil against our spouses?

The one who sat on the throne said, "Behold, I make all things new."

Revelation 21:5

There is a marital phenomenon that secular society refers to as "the seven-year itch." In this scenario, by the time the seventh or so year of marriage rolls around, the honeymoon is over, and things are looking pretty dull. Truly, there is often a point in the marital journey where there seems to be a fork in the road. A couple may travel along ever so nicely enjoying the rich pleasures of their bodily union and the effervescence of their infatuation, but there comes a time when those blessings are no firm wheelbase for the increased load, a point in time when, if God is not at the center of their union, fueling their voyage, the road is likely to get too rocky for them to navigate on their own. However, our God says, "Behold, I make all things new," and the marriage covenant is his domain. How can I be bored with my spouse when I see in her the reflection of Infinite Love, love which eclipses all imperfection? She was still exciting after seven years, and will be exciting after seventy-seven years.

The successful marital embrace brings three distinct pleasures. The first is like unto that received from a hug and a kiss on the cheek given by a small child. This is the pleasure of tender touch and nearness, and of the love given by an innocent soul. This kind of pleasure is part of the thrill of a first kiss between an innocent man and woman, and remains part of the marital embrace for those who allow their personal and marital innocence to be constantly renewed by their Redeemer. Jesus said, "Behold, I make all things new." A sense of innocence can be regained; even the deeply sinful can be reconciled.

The second pleasure is completely spiritual. It is the pleasure of soul experienced in Holy Communion. Many a saint has gone into ecstasy after Communion, sometimes to the extreme of physically levitating, but even those of us who are less blessed experience the peaceful excitement of being one body with our Creator. Another spiritual exercise of the saints is that of spiritual communion, a devotion practiced by holy people when they are physically unable to receive the actual Eucharist. In the marital embrace, there is the pleasure of soul within soul as bodies intertwine, a pleasure greatly enhanced by awareness of God's Holy Spirit within one's mate. Marital intimacy is an opportunity for a dimension in spiritual communion that has escaped many of the faithful.

The third pleasure is carnal delight. While physical existence is of a lower order than spiritual existence, it is still an essential good. Our bodies are grand manifestations of God's love for us, and the delight of physical intimacy should be considered a great gift and celebrated with great joy. However, this pleasure by itself will not lead to fulfillment; it is an earthly pleasure, and Earth is not our final destination. We are made for the heart of God and can only be made whole in him.

A wife does not have authority over her own body, but rather her husband, and similarly a husband does not have authority over his own body, but rather his wife. Do not deprive each other, except perhaps by mutual consent for a time, to be free for prayer, but then

return to one another, so that Satan may not tempt you through your lack of self-control.

1 Corinthians 7:4-5

A person involved in a relationship built mostly on carnal delight lacks the comforts of innocence and communion of soul during days of abstinence. Many in the early twenty-first century laughed at those who chose natural family planning over contraception and sterilization, which were rampant in that age. However, two millennia ago, as revealed in the above scripture, the great apostle Paul saw the merit of occasional, purposeful abstinence. There is deep irony in the oft observed correlation between contraceptive use and sexless marriage. When self-control is relinquished, God's help is not sought, and spousal intimacy is taken for granted. Everyone loses.

For centuries the great Judeo/Christian teachers have warned of the dangers of pleasure and the flesh. How is it that an essential good presents such great danger to the soul? By nature, if we could choose everything that would enter our lives, we would choose only pleasure, never pain. Pleasure is dangerous only because it is more difficult to give to God than pain; more difficult because it is always our natural choice, and we tend toward self-worship; that is, we choose the gift over the Giver, worshipping the ability to choose rather than the Creator of that ability. Through our natural inheritance, we tend to see pleasures as conquests, not gifts; as acquisitions, not intimacies. All creation is sacred; therefore, all legitimate pleasures are intimacies with our Creator if we but choose to make them so. True appreciation for that which pleases was the key to happiness in Eden. Appreciation for *everything* that God sends our way is the key to the Kingdom.

David, the shepherd, was favored by God, an upright youth who loved the Lord. However, as king, he went on to commit serious sins of lust. Why was it that this otherwise godly man lost control of his passions? He had multiple wives and endless opportunities for passionate embrace. Why did he steal another man's wife at the expense of that man's life? Is it because absolute power corrupts absolutely? Did his ability to choose become a god in itself? Indeed, is that not the very definition of the concept of corruption by absolute power? Could David have committed such an offense had he habitually offered all of his pleasures to the Lord? Had he been born under the New Covenant, would this same man have avoided such an offense by living a life of grace in a Eucharistic, monogamous relationship? We who enjoy the abundant graces of the Savior must never point an accusing finger at David.

What absolute powers do *we* wield? Do contraceptives not give us absolute veto power over our reproductive gifts? How many of us have come to worship our right to choose, even to the point, like King David, where we are willing to shed innocent blood for that right?

But whoever is joined to the Lord becomes one spirit with him. Avoid immorality. Every other sin a person commits is outside the body, but the immoral person sins against his own body. Do you not know that your body is a temple of the Holy Spirit within you, whom you have from God, and that you are not your own? For you have been purchased at a price. Therefore, glorify God in your body.
1 Corinthians 6:17-20

In the final analysis, life is all about choices. Once clearly understood, these choices are simple—not easy, but simple. We get to choose between the security of this world, that thin veil of the physical which our dull souls perceive as reality, and the security of the Infinite, that incomprehensible love which envelops all of our existence. With heartfelt gratitude we celebrate the pleasures of soul and body, or we choose to take those pleasures for granted. We can make a sacrifice of our suffering or hate our very existence on account of it. We choose between commodity and intimacy, death and life. I pray that we will choose wisely. Let us not be distracted by a fruit snack.